W.H. Pinnock

The Laws and Usages of the Church and the Clergy

SALZWASSER VERLAG

W.H. Pinnock

The Laws and Usages of the Church and the Clergy

Reprint of the original, first published in 1863.

1st Edition 2022 | ISBN: 978-3-37500-231-2

Verlag (Publisher): Salzwasser Verlag GmbH, Zeilweg 44, 60439 Frankfurt, Deutschland
Vertretungsberechtigt (Authorized to represent): E. Roepke, Zeilweg 44, 60439 Frankfurt, Deutschland
Druck (Print): Books on Demand GmbH, In de Tarpen 42, 22848 Norderstedt, Deutschland

THE LAWS AND USAGES

OF THE

Church and the Clergy.

THE CONDUCT, ORDER, AND RITUAL OF PUBLIC WORSHIP.

Evening Prayer—Litany—Holy Communion.

[Vol. I.]

BY THE REV. W. H. PINNOCK, LL.D.

1863.

PREFACE.

We have in this, and the preceding Volume, gone through the several Rubrics of the Book of Common Prayer affecting the rites, ceremonies, and order, of *Public Worship;* and have endeavoured, as will be seen, to elucidate them with the most rigid impartiality—not leaning, designedly, to any section in the Church, but dealing out those conclusions which the preponderance of Law and Usage compelled us to arrive at. The task has, indeed, been a difficult one; because, in writing for the Church at large, truth and justice have forced us into the citation of every authority, whether they opposed, or favoured, one's own personal opinion, or predilection. It is, however, a matter of considerable satisfaction to know that the views we have advanced, are those entertained by the generality of our Bishops. The result of our labour and research we now commit to the kind patronage of our Clerical brethren, with the fervent desire that it may be found acceptable and useful. Should their encouragement of this Volume call for a like treatment of the Rubrics in the "Occasional Services," we trust we may be able at some future time to devote to this end what little leisure we can command from the claims of an important Parish, the requirements of theological study, and from more exclusively spiritual engagements.

THE AUTHOR.

Somersham Rectory.
Huntingdonshire, 1863.

The Order and Ritual

OF

PUBLIC WORSHIP.

(*continued.*)

Evening Prayer.

273.—THE preliminary observations we thought it desirable to address to the OFFICIATING MINISTER when about to commence the MORNING PRAYER may possibly be useful to him in the present instance also, when about to begin the EVENING PRAYER. To avoid repetition, however, we will merely bring forward the leading points, referring him for more detailed information to the earlier pages of the preceding volume, where the subjects are treated *in extenso*.

¶. 'THE ORDER FOR

'EVENING PRAYER

'DAILY THROUGHOUT THE YEAR.'

274.—The ORDER FOR EVENING PRAYER, or 'EVENSONG,' as it is called in the Liturgy of 1549, is an abridgment of the ancient Offices of Vespers and Compline. It may be used at any time after 12 *o'clock* at noon: and should there be two such Services after mid-day, *i. e.* one in the *Afternoon*, and one in the *Evening*, the customary Service may be used in both instances; or, to avoid iteration, the *Litany*, or *Ante-*

Communion Office, may be employed in either case, provided, however, the sanction of the Bishop has been first obtained. (See 'DIVISION OF THE SERVICES.' *Vol.* **B**).

L'ESTRANGE, after commenting upon the *catechizing* of the youth of the Parish (see *postea*) says:—'The Office *Catechistical* 'being past, EVENING PRAYER is to begin. But why not *Afternoon*, 'rather than *Evening* Prayer? I answer, because then the sun 'and consequently the light begins to decline. It seems the Greek 'Church had *two Services in the Afternoon*, one at our *three*, their '*nine;* and another at the close of the *Evening*, as appeareth by 'the Council of Laodicea, *Can.* 18. decreeing, περὶ τοῦν, κ. τ. λ. "That the same service of Prayers ought to be made use of both at "the ninth hour and at Evening." This *at Evening* was at candle-'lighting, whence the Prayers appropriated to it, were λυχνικαὶ 'ἐυχαὶ, as the Psalms λυχνικοὶ ψαλμοὶ, or ὕμνοι, &c. "candle-light 'Hymns:" the reason is, because when the candles were first 'lighted their mode was to glorifie God with an hymn, one form 'whereof is still extant in these words, φῶς ἱλαρον, κ. τ. λ. "Blessed Jesus Christ, thou cheerful brightness of the holy "immortal glory of the heavenly and holy Father, when the Sun is "set, no sooner do we behold the *Evening light* to shine, than we "glorifie the Father, Son, and Holy Ghost." &c. (*p.* 98).—*Alliance of Divine Offices.*

The Rev. J. JEBB, animadverting on the preference shewn for the EVENING SERVICE, makes these very just remarks:—'In *country Parishes*, this has been connived at to a great extent: 'and, in order to meet the degenerate notions of the people, the 'MORNING SERVICE has actually been curtailed, by the omission of 'the *Sermon;* and this, with every Office that can be transferred, 'is thrown into the *Evening*, or as it is vulgarly called, the '*Afternoon Service.* The habits of society, both among rich and 'poor, have much to do with this; but the habits of the rich 'ought to be rebuked and withstood by the Clergy; and as to the 'poor, the rich are to be blamed for that iniquitous overtasking 'of their bodies, which often renders a total rest, even from 'Church-going, on Sunday mornings, a matter not of choice, but of 'necessity. For these and other offences against our poorer 'brethren, God will call the wealthy of this nation to judgment.' (*p.* 402).—*Choral Service.*

275.—Adherence to the Rubrical direction, '*Daily throughout the year*,' with regard to the EVENING SERVICE, will not in every case be acceptable, or practicable; where it may be so, let it by all means be adopted; and should the usage already exist, it ought not to be suffered to fall into desuetude. But to attempt the practice where no Congregation will be found to respond to the effort, is a questionable propriety. (See *Vol.* **B**).

276.—*Punctuality* must be one of the first considerations in the mind of the young Clergyman. He should be in the Church sufficiently early before the commencement of Divine Service to see that every thing is in order, and in readiness, and to ascertain what *Baptisms*, *Churchings*, *Catechizings*, *Publishing of Banns*, or other duty, he may be required to engage in during the time of Service. Many Congregations have a great objection to the introduction of any *Occasional Service* during the MORNING, or EVENING, PRAYER; care should be taken, therefore, that the Officiating Minister confines himself to the directions of the Rubrics in this matter.

The Rev. R. SIMPSON says:—'In some Churches, *Marriages* are 'solemnized in the middle of the Service, and *Thanksgiving of 'Women after Child-birth*, these things are highly indecorous. 'Nothing but a *Baptism* is directed to be performed during the 'regular Morning and Evening Service, and the reasons for this are 'stated in the Rubric ordering the same.' (*p.* 169).—*Clergyman's Manual.*

Exactitude of attendance is more particularly necessary when officiating in a *strange Church*, as it will be essential for the Minister to learn whether any peculiar usages prevail there with which he may not be acquainted, or which may be different from his ordinary practice.

277.—*Bowing on entering, and leaving, Church*, or on *going to, and receding from, the Altar*, is not defensible by any legal authority now in force. The ceremony is certainly harmless in itself; but if it cause a weak brother to offend, or prove obnoxious to the Congregation at large, it would be unwise, to say the least, to set the feelings of one's People at nought. (See *Paragraph* 7, *supra*).

278.—The *Robing* should be accomplished with care, and the *Vestments* be clean, and in good order. The Officiating Minister should indulge in no fantastic changes, but keep to what the Congregation have been accustomed to see, unless, however, a fresh Academical degree gives sanction to an alteration of the *Hood*. (See *Paragraph* 8, *supra*).

279.—While proceeding to the *Reading-Desk* an *organ symphony* is admissible, but it should not be too noisy. This the Clergyman can legally control. (See *Paragraph* 12, *supra*).

Where there are *Choristers*, and a regular staff of Clergy, it is customary to enter and retire in procession; the Choristers first, followed by the Deacons, then the Priests, and lastly by the Rector or Vicar. The Deacon or Priest of junior degree precedes the one of senior degree.

Neither of the *Chairs* at the north and south sides of the Altar, and which, by the way, are unecclesiastical positions for them, nor the *Sedilia*, should, strictly speaking, be occupied by a Clergyman during the Morning, or Evening, Prayers. *Stalls*, or *Benches*, are more correct. The *Sedilia* may be used at Sermon time.

280.—Should any '*Churching of Women*' be required before beginning the Service, the Minister must proceed to the *Altar*, if such be the usage, and at the conclusion, pass to the *Reading-Desk*. In some Churches, the *organ* at this point fills up the hiatus by a *Sanctus*, or short *symphony*. But this must depend on the custom of the place. No capricious novelties should be introduced. (See *Paragraph* 13, and *postea*).

281.—*Singing* before the commencement of Divine Service, common as it may be in some localities, particularly before EVENING PRAYER, is contrary to the strict letter of the Rubric, and should not, therefore, be fancifully introduced, nor without due consideration, and proper sanction. (See *Paragraph* 16, *supra*).

[CATECHIZING.]

282. It was formerly the practice, in accordance with the injunctions of the 59th *Canon* (of 1603), to publicly *catechize* the youth of the Parish for *half-an-hour before* the beginning of EVENING PRAYER; thus—

'Every Parson, Vicar, or Curate, upon every Sunday and 'Holy-day, *before* EVENING PRAYER, shall, *for half an hour* or 'more, examine and instruct the youth and ignorant persons in his 'parish, in the *Ten Commandments*, the *Articles of* the *Belief*, and in 'the *Lord's Prayer;* and shall diligently hear, instruct, and teach 'them the *Catechism* set forth in the Book of Common Prayer. 'And all Fathers, Mothers,' &c.—CANON 59.

Although the *Canons* of 1603, generally, are binding on the Clergy at the present day, yet a later rule than the 59th *Canon* above quoted; viz. the *Rubric* following the CATECHISM in our authorized Book of Common Prayer, and which was introduced at the last Review (1662), supersedes the authority of this Canon; and enjoins that this *Catechizing* of the youth of the Parish shall take place immediately *after the Second Lesson* at EVENING PRAYER: thus,—

(*a*) ¶. '*The* CURATE *of every Parish shall diligently upon Sundays 'and Holy-days, after the Second Lesson at* EVENING 'PRAYER *openly in the Church instruct and examine so 'many Children of his Parish sent unto him as he shall think 'it convenient, in some part of this Catechism.*' (1662)—Present Book of Common Prayer.

In the previous Liturgies (of 1549, 1552, 1559, 1604), this *Rubric* was similar in its directions to the 59th *Canon*, requiring the *Catechizing* to be performed *before* the Evening Service. It stood at the end of the Office for Confirmation in those Prayer Books. The Rubric may be said, indeed, to have originated this particular Canon; it thus read,—

(*b*) '*The Curate of every Parish*, (*once in six weeks at the least, 'upon warning by him given, shall upon some Sunday or Holy 'Day.* 1549) *or some other at his appointment, shall diligently 'upon Sundays and Holy days half an hour before* EVENSONG '(EVENING PRAYER, 1559), *openly in the Church instruct and 'examine so many Children of his Parish sent unto him as the time 'will serve, and as he shall think convenient, in some part of this 'Catechism.*' (1549, 1552, 1559, 1604).—KEELING 284, 285.

But this earlier *Rubric* (*b*), not possessing any authority amongst us now, can in no way effect the question under consideration. The 59th *Canon*, likewise, being superseded by the *Rubric* (*a*) of the present Book of Common Prayer, the *catechizing* of the children, therefore, publicly before the Congregation must not be attempted previous to the reading of the

Second Lesson, as that Rubric prescribes. (see *postea*). This discrepancy in the two authorities has been well elucidated by ARCHDEACON SHARP, as follows:—

'There is a Rubric in the Liturgy at the end of the *Catechism* 'for the direction of Ministers in this matter; which is indeed 'properly the direction of the Canon new modified with respect to 'the Clergy, though the injunctions on Parents, Masters, and 'Mistresses, stand verbatim the same in both......The *Canon* enjoins 'that it be done "*before* EVENING PRAYER;" but the *Rubric* says, "*after the Second Lesson* at EVENING PRAYER." The *Canon* 'requires it should be continued for "half an hour or more:" the '*Rubric* leaves the time for the performance indefinite. Upon these 'accounts Mr. Wheatly is at a loss how to reconcile the *Canon* with 'the *Rubric*. And so must every body be who compares them together. 'But the comfort is, there is no need of reconciliation, when there is 'no need that both should stand. The latter directions, supposing 'their authority only equal, would supersede the former. The '*Rubrics*, in all the old Prayer Books till the *last Review* in 1662, 'did agree with the *Canon* in this matter. But as the alterations 'upon the revisal then made of the Liturgy are more authentic, and 'more binding upon us than the *Canons* are, we can be under no 'difficulty in determining by which of them to square our conduct 'in this business. Whether indeed these changes made in the '*Rubric* have really been for the better, may be much doubted. 'But that we are to abide by them, and not by the *Canon*, in this 'case, will, I suppose, admit of no doubt.' (In a *Note* is added,— 'The reason of the alteration was, that the *Catechism* being 'performed in the midst of Divine Service, the elder persons as well 'as the younger might receive benefit by the Minister's expositions, '&c. But the worthy persons who made all this alteration have 'been miserably disappointed in their good intentions, for this very 'thing has drove *Catechism* almost out of the Church.') However, 'let it be observed, that all that part of this *Canon* that relates to 'the power of the Ordinary in censuring neglect of duty herein, 'whether it be in Ministers, or in Parents, Masters, and Mistresses,* 'remains yet in its full force. With this only difference, that 'the neglect of Ministers, to be censured by him, is not to be 'measured any longer by the rules laid down in the *Canon*, but by 'those which were since enjoined by the *Rubric*.' (*p.* 210).—*On the Rubrics and Canons.* Charge. A. D. 1747.

283.—Seeing then that the *Catechizing* of the youth of the Parish is to be deferred till the conclusion of the *Second Lesson*, the Officiating Minister will at

---

* The censures of the Ordinary might reach the consciences of Parents, Masters, and Mistresses, in the days of Archdeacon Sharp, and in the antecedent period; but the Laity of the present age have completely out-grown the leading strings of Bishops, and the terror of Ecclesiastical censures. No *Canons* of the Church are binding upon the Laity unless enforced by the Imperial Parliament.

once prepare to commence the **Evening Service.** Being in the *Reading-Desk*, his *private prayer* accomplished, and the proper places in the Bible, and Prayer-Book, made readily accessible by the insertion of the *book-markers*, he will proceed as follows, and not otherwise.

I. THE INTRODUCTION.

The Sentences.

¶. '*At the beginning of* Evening Prayer *the Minister shall read 'with a loud voice some one or more of these Sentences of the 'Scriptures that follow.*' &c. (1662).

(Minister turning to the People—Minister and People standing.)

284.—The introductory, and concluding, portions of the Evening Service are almost identical with those of the Morning. This Rubric, and the parts introduced into the Morning Service at the Revision of the Prayer Book in 1552, *viz.* the *Sentences*, *Exhortation*, *Confession*, and *Absolution*, were not placed at the commencement of the Evening Prayer before the Review in 1662, although the Rubric of 1552, heading the Morning Prayer, included also the Evening Prayer in its injunctions, ordering, '*at the beginning both of* 'Morning Prayer, *and likewise of* Evening Prayer, '*the Minister shall,*' &c. Notwithstanding, however, that this was retained at the Revision in 1559, and at that of 1604, yet during these periods (from 1552 to 1662) the Evening Service more frequently began with the *Lord's Prayer*, as it previously had done, and as had been directed in the Liturgy of 1549.

Bp. Overall (*cir.* 1614—19) thus remarks on this neglect:—'Not that the Priest should *begin* Even-song with the Lord's 'Prayer, before he has read the *Sentences*, *Confession* and *Abso-'lution*, as at Morning Prayer, as he is by the Rubrick here 'enjoyned; but that after those *Sentences*, &c. as a preparation, 'both to Morning and Evening Prayer, he should begin and say, '*Our Father*,' &c. And therefore, because many neglecting that 'preceding Rubrick, which rules this, do begin the Even-song 'here, it gave occasion to the Puritans, in their survey, to ask, "Whether Ministers were not as punishable for that neglect, as for 'not wearing of a Surplice"? And truly I think they are. It is the '14th *Canon* that forbids Ministers to diminish any part of *Divine* '*Service*, as it is appointed in regard of Preaching, or any other 'respect, which they that curtail Service are wont to alledge.' (*p.* 23).—*Additional Notes to* NICHOLLS' *Book of Com. Prayer*.

The omission of this introductory matter from the EVENING PRAYER in the Liturgies of those days has been attributed to the deficiency of the instructions given to the Printer, but which was at last rectified in the *Revision* of 1662, when the Rubrics we now have, and the portions we are speaking of, were inserted in both of the Services.*

285.—*Posture.*—The attitude universally adopted by Minister and People during the reading of the SENTENCES is that of *standing;* the Minister facing the Congregation. (See *paragraph* 17, *supra*).

286.—*Reading*, not *Intoning*, nor *Chanting*, is the *prescribed* method of uttering the SENTENCES; any deviation from this rule is the dictum of fancy, or of *choice*, and strictly requires the sanction of authority. There are some Clergymen who look upon these SENTENCES as *Antiphons* rather than Exhortations; and therefore explain the rubrical direction, "*read with a loud voice*," as denoting '*musical notation*,' and not "*reading*" in the common acceptation of the term. Any *doubt* the ordinary is to determine. (See *paragraphs* 18, 19, 20, *supra*).

287.—One or more of these SENTENCES may be read, according to the discretion of the *Officiating Minister;* who will also select such as may seem more suitable to the circumstances of the day. (See *paragraph* 21, *supra*).

Many adopt this arrangement following:—

For *Advent.*—"Repent ye," "O Lord correct," "Enter not," &c.
For *Evens.*—"Hide thy Face," &c.

---

* In the AMERICAN LITURGY, the *Rubric* is simply this:—'*The* '*Minister shall begin the* Evening Prayer, *by reading one or* '*more of the following Sentences of Scripture.*'

For *Week Days.*—"When the wicked man," "I will arise," "If we say," &c.
For *Lent*, and *Fridays.*—"The Sacrifices," "Rend your heart," &c.
For *Sundays*, and *Festivals.*—"To the Lord our God," &c.
For *Vigils*, and *Wednesdays.*—"I acknowledge," &c.

THE EXHORTATION.

¶......'*And then he shall say that which is written after the said 'Sentences.'* (1662).

(Minister turning to the People—all continue standing.)

288.—At the conclusion of the SENTENCES, the Minister will proceed to read the EXHORTATION or ADDRESS, as directed in the Rubric; he and the Congregation continuing in the same posture. (See *paragraphs* 23, 24, 25, *supra*).

THE CONFESSION.

¶. '*A General Confession to be said of the whole Congregation 'after the Minister, all Kneeling.*' (1662).

(Minister and People kneeling.)

289.—This *Confession* should be deliberately enunciated by the Minister, and as he concludes each sentence, indicated by a *capital letter*, the Congregation should take it up, and repeat it aloud; not '*with*,' but '*after*' the Minister. The *posture* of all is to be that of '*kneeling*.' (See *paragraphs* 26 to 30, *supra*).

290.—The '*Amen*,' being in the *same* type as the text, is to be repeated by both Minister and People. (See *paragraph* 31, *supra*).

291.—In addition to what has been already observed on the subject of the *Confession*, we may draw attention here to '*the Exceptions to the Book of Common Prayer*' taken at the Savoy Conference (A. D.

1661) against this Confession being *too general;* more especially as the fear of the present age is that 'Confession' may become *too particular:* thus—

'That whereas the public Liturgy of a Church should in reason 'comprehend the sum of all such sins as are ordinarily to be 'confessed in prayer by the Church, and of such petitions and 'thanksgivings as are ordinarily by the Church to be put up to 'God, &c.—the present Liturgy as to all these seems very defective. 'Particularly......The *Confession* is very defective, not clearly 'expressing original sin, nor sufficiently enumerating actual sins, 'with their aggravations, but consisting only of *generals;* whereas '*Confession* being the exercise of repentance, ought to be *more* '*particular.*' (*p.* 309).—CARDWELL'S *Hist. of the Conferences.*

To which the Bishops reply:—'This which they call a defect, 'others think they have reason to account the perfection of the 'Liturgy, the Offices for which being intended for common and 'general Services, would cease to be such by descending to 'particulars, as in *confession of sin;* while it is *general*, all persons 'may and must join in it, since in many things we offend all. But 'if there be a *particular enumeration* of sins, it cannot be so *general* 'a Confession, because it may happen that some or other may by 'God's grace have been preserved from some of those sins 'enumerated, and therefore should by confessing themselves guilty, 'tell God a lie; which needs a new confession.' (*p.* 344).—(*ibid.*)

THE ABSOLUTION.

¶. '*The Absolution or Remission of sins to be pronounced* '*by the Priest alone, standing; the People still kneeling.*' (1662)

(The Priest standing—the People still kneeling).

292.—No *Deacon* is permitted to pronounce this ABSOLUTION, nor are the People to repeat it after the Minister. It is to be uttered by a '*Priest alone.*' If a Deacon should be officiating, he must omit this ABSOLUTION, and pass on to the Lord's Prayer. No Collect or Prayer should be introduced by way of substitute for the ABSOLUTION. (See *paragraphs* 32—39, *supra*).

The Rev. R. SIMPSON says:—'In the performance of Divine 'Worship *no Deacon* should read the '*Absolution,*' but pass on to the 'Lord's Prayer;' there is no authority, for the substitution of any 'Collect in the place of the 'Absolution,' it having never been 'contemplated by the Compilers of the Liturgy that any Church 'should be left under the care of a Deacon alone. It is a monstrous 'abuse.' (*p.* 169).—*The Clergyman's Manual.*

293.—*Posture.*—The Priest is to ***stand*** while pronouncing the ABSOLUTION, and with his face toward the People;* the People are to continue *kneeling.* A *Deacon* officiating will also retain the attitude of *kneeling.*

294.—The '*Amen,*' being in a different type from the context, is to be uttered by the Congregation only. (See *paragraph* 40, *supra*).

THE LORD'S PRAYER.

¶. '*Then the Minister shall kneel and say the Lord's Prayer; 'the People also kneeling, and repeating it with him.*' (1662).

(Minister and People Kneeling).

295.—In the earlier Liturgies, as has been before observed, the EVENING SERVICE commenced at this point with the '*Lord's Prayer.*' A little difference will be observed in the wording of this Rubric here, and in its parallel position in the MORNING PRAYER. In the present instance there is an omission of the words, '*with an audible voice,*' and of the concluding sentence, '*both here, and wheresoever else it is used in Divine Service.*' The reason doubtlessly was that the repetition of such instructions would be unnecessary and superfluous in the EVENING PRAYER, when the MORNING SERVICE must have taught the Officiating Minister, and he have practised, the prescribed usage.

296.—The Minister and People are to be *kneeling;* and care must be taken that the People repeat the Lord's Prayer '*with,*' not 'after' the Minister; and that the '*Amen*' be uttered by both Minister and

---

* The Reader is particularly requested to correct an error in *paragraph* 38 of Vol. ɵ., treating on this attitude of the Priest. In the last line for, 'he turns *from* the People,' read 'he turns *to* the People.'

People. (See *paragraphs* 45 to 60, *supra*). Dr. Corrie, in his edition of Wheatly, makes the following comment upon the expression '*with the Minister,*' which it would be well to compare with our remarks at *paragraphs* 29, and 49.

'In many parts of England it is the practice for the Congregation 'to repeat each petition in the LORD'S PRAYER simultaneously "*with the Minister*," but in the CONFESSION to repeat each clause, 'not "*with*," but "*after*" him. This practice, however, is by no 'means uniform. It may, moreover, be doubted whether the 'framers of the Rubric in 1661 intended the Congregation to 'observe any distinction between the manner of repeating the 'CONFESSION and the LORD'S PRAYER; for whilst they direct the 'same rule ("repeating *with*" the Minister) to be observed "wheresoever else" the Lord's Prayer "is used in Divine Service," 'the Rubric in the Communion Service, which directs every petition 'in that prayer to be repeated "*after*" the Minister, was left 'unaltered.' (*p.* 113. *Note*).—WHEATLY'S *Ill. of Book of Common Prayer*. Dr. Corrie's edition.

II. THE PSALMODY, AND READING.

THE VERSICLES.

¶. '*Then likewise he shall say.*' (1662).

(All still kneeling.)

297.—The four Versicles occurring here are identical with those in the MORNING PRAYER: The two former were not originally used at EVENING PRAYER. The ancient Service Books, and the Liturgy of 1549, omit them; but the desire of our Reformers to assimilate the two Services led to their introduction here in 1552. These Versicles are to be repeated *alternately* by the Minister and People, as directed by the initial words '*Priest,*' and '*Answer;*' and all are to continue *kneeling*. (See *Paragraphs* 61—65. *supra*). Here also the introduction of the same two Versicles as had been suggested for the Morning Service was recommended by the Royal Commissioners of 1689; but without effect. (See *paragraph* 64, *supra*).

The Gloria Patri, or Doxology.

¶. '*Here all standing up, the Priest shall say.*' (1662).

298.—This Doxology is similar to that in the Morning Prayer: the word '*Priest*' indicates the part to be uttered by the Minister; and the word '*Answer*,' that by the People. All are to be *standing;** and the term '*say*' forbids this Doxology to be *chanted.*

The *obeisance* practised in a few ancient village Churches by the aged at the word '*Son*,' in deference to old custom, is a usage that need not be interfered with; yet no authority can be found permitting it to be enforced. (See *paragraphs* 67 to 70, *supra*). In some Churches, however, it is laid down as a Rule, 'to *bow* at the names of the several Persons of 'the Holy Trinity in the Doxology': (*Churchman's Diary*, p. 8.): at the same time turning to the Altar. This is derived from the Sarum Breviary, and an ancient Canon, which thus reads:—

"Quotiesque dicitur Gloria Patri et Filio et Spiritui Sancto, ad "eadem verba, Deo humiliter se inclinent."—Wilkin's *Concil.* iii. 20.

The Alleluia Versicles.

(The Minister facing the People, and all still standing.)

299.—These two Versicles, like those in the Morning Prayer, are to be alternately repeated by '*Priest*' and '*People*,' as the Liturgy enjoins. In those Churches where the *Alleluia* (or *Hallelujah*) is chanted from Easter to Trinity Sunday in the Morning Service, so also it is done at Evening Prayer, by the same rule of 1549. (See *paragraphs* 71, 72, *supra*).

---

* In the *Scotch Liturgy* the Rubric relative to posture annexed to this Doxology, thus reads:—'*All standing up, as often as it is 'repeated.*'

The Psalms.

¶. '*Then shall be said or sung the Psalms in order as they be* '*appointed.*' (1662).

(The Minister and People still standing.)

300. There is no Psalm, or Canticle, in the Evening Prayer answering to the '*Venite*' of the Morning Prayer; so that at the close of the Alleluia Versicles the Minister proceeds at once with the Psalms appointed for the day. (See *paragraphs* 85—89, *supra*). The Rubric permits them to be '*said or sung*,' he will therefore follow the custom of the place (see *pars.* 90 — 95, *supra*). All musical accompaniment is at his discretion, and under his control.

The method of announcing the prescribed Psalms, whether thus —'*The sixth Evening of the month, the 32nd Psalm*'; or thus, '*Day six, Evening Prayer. Psalm* 32'; or otherwise; will be according to his usual habit. Some Clergymen omit the announcement altogether, holding it to be a corruption of modern times, and without rubrical authority, or canonical sanction. (See *pars.* 97, 98, *supra*).

The *Officiating Minister*, where '*saying*' is practised, ought to begin each Psalm, and read the alternate verses; and in every instance take the first versicle of the '*Gloria Patri;* which is to be repeated after every Psalm, and after each division of the 119*th Psalm:* when, however, the doxology is *chanted*, as is now very generally done, Minister and People will chant together. Where the Psalms are *chanted*, they are chanted antiphonally, *i.e.* from opposite sides of the Choir or Church. *Saying* the Psalms in *monotone* is indefensible. (See *pars.* 99, 100, *supra*).

Standing is the proper posture for both Minister and People. (See *pars.* 101, 102, *supra*).

301.—The *Rubrics* of the older Liturgies differed but little from that in our present Book of Common Prayer, and require no illustration beyond what the paragraphs just referred to supply. They read thus:—

'Then the Psalms in order as they be appointed in the Table for 'Psalms, except there be proper Psalms appointed for that day. (1549, 1552, 1559. 1604.)

THE VOLUNTARY.

(Minister and People sitting.)

302.—This musical interlude, like as in the MORNING PRAYER, is at the discretion of the Officiating Minister. It is a remnant of old custom, and generally a mere exhibition of the skill of the organist, and may well be dispensed with. Where it prevails, *sitting* is the posture adopted. (See *pars.* 108—110, *supra*).

THE LESSONS.

¶. *'Then a Lesson of the Old Testament as is appointed.'* (1662).

(The Minister standing—the People sitting.)

303.—As early as the times of Benedict (A. D. 530), and Amalarius (A.D. 820), a short Lesson followed the Psalms at Vespers. The Sarum Breviary adopted the rule of the ancient Egyptian church, which limited the Lesson to the Old Testament; and this has been followed by the Church of England. The portions of Scripture appointed to be read will be found in the *Calendar*, or in the *Table of Proper Lessons*, at the beginning of the Prayer Book; and the rule, which guides the choice of the *Lessons* for MORNING PRAYER, will apply also in the selection of those for EVENING PRAYER, whether for Sundays, ordinary days, Saints' days, or Holy-days. (See *pars.* 111—124. *supra*).

304.—The choice to be made, when Sundays and Saints' days, or two Holy-days, *coincide*, follows the general rule we have already given, viz :—

GENERAL RULE:—*An ordinary Sunday* (i. e. a Sunday not peculiarly connected with our Lord's life, or ministry) *yields to a Saint's-Day; and a Lesser Festival gives way to a greater.*

Except:—When any of the Lessons of the superior day are appointed in the *Apocrypha*, the *Canonical Scriptures* directed for the inferior day are to be preferred.

This subject is largely discussed in the previous Volume, to which we must refer our Readers who wish for full information. (See *pars.* 125—127, *supra*).

305.—The LESSONS should be *read* very distinctly, and due regard had to the *quantities* of the *Proper Names*. (See *pars.* 128—132, *supra*). The *expurgations* also that are desirable should be previously noted, as has been already advised. (See *pars.* 133—135, *supra*).

306.—The *Reader* of the LESSONS is permitted by the Rubric in the MORNING PRAYER to be a *Layman*; and by consequence this is thought to be equally allowed in the EVENING PRAYER, though such is not implied in the Rubric of the EVENING SERVICE. When a *Layman* so officiates, he should be a good reader, and of unimpeachable character. He should also wear a *Surplice*. A *Layman*, however, seldom performs this office, except the Lessons are read from a *Lectern*, as we have before explained. (See *pars.* 136—139, *supra*).

307.—The Reader is to *stand*, and so '*turning 'himself as he may best be heard of all such as are 'present*'; whence is inferred a permission to use a *Lectern*. (See *pars.* 139—144, *supra*). In some places, when not from the *Reading-Desk*, or *Lectern*, the LESSONS are read from the Lector's Stall in the Choir.

308.—The *announcement* of the LESSONS is to be simply, '*Here beginneth such a Chapter, or such a verse of such a Chapter, of such a Book;*' and strictly speaking, the announcement should be made by the *Officiating Minister*; and not by the *Lay-Reader*, if such is employed. And similarly, at the termination of the LESSONS, the conclusion is to be announced only by the *Officiating Minister*, and in these brief words, '*Here endeth the First Lesson*,' or '*Second Lesson*,' as the case may be. (See *pars*. 145—147. *supra*.) Where a *Lectern* is used, the Reader at the close of each Lesson retires to his place: in some Churches he turns round and faces the Altar during the chanting of the Canticle following the *First* Lesson.

309.—The *Rubrics* on the Lessons in the previous Liturgies were a little fuller than the one in our present Prayer Book; but the matter omitted will be found to be embodied in '*The Order how the rest of Holy Scripture is appointed to be read*,' in the prefatory portion preceding the Calendar. The old Rubric was as follows:—

> '*Then a Lesson of the Old Testament as* (*it* 1549) *is appointed* '*likewise in the Kalendar, except there be proper Lessons* '*appointed for that day*.' (1549, 1552, 1559, 1604.)

THE MAGNIFICAT. *Luke* i. 46.

¶. '*And after that*, Magnificat, (*or the Song of the Blessed Virgin* 'Mary) *in English, as followeth*.'—(1662)

(The Minister and People standing.)

310.—This hymn, the *Magnificat*, so called from its first word in the Latin version, occupies the same place in our Liturgy as it did in the ancient Service Books: it followed the '*Little Chapter*' at Vespers in the Salisbury, York, and Hereford Uses, and was thus known to Amalarius (A. D. 820), and some think, to Benedict (A. D. 530) also. Bingham, in his Christian Antiquities, tells us that the *Magnificat* was sung in the Morning Service of the French Church so early as A. D. 506. This Canticle is well adapted to follow the Lesson from the Old Testament in our Services, from providing us with an inspired expression of joy at the fulfilment of God's gracious promises—a joy equal to the interest the holy Virgin had in the mysterious birth and blessing she anticipated. This Hymn is prescribed in the Liturgy of 1549, and in the subsequent Revisions; and we find it to have been employed, likewise, in all the Offices of the reformed Churches abroad. The Royal Commissioners of 1689, in their '*Alterations and Amendments*,' proposed substituting *Psalm* viii. for the *Magnificat*; but their suggestions were not approved.* The *Magnificat*, and *Nunc Dimittis*, are usually preferred to the *Psalms* set down as their alternatives.

Dean Comber beautifully justifies the use of this admirable Hymn in these words:—'As soon as the blessed Virgin was filled 'with the Holy Ghost she uttered this divine Canticle, which is the 'very first Hymn recorded in the New Testament, and may be 'reckoned the first fruits of the Spirit; and therefore it hath been 'anciently used among the Christians, and is received at this day 'into the Service of all the reformed Churches of Holland and 'Germany, as well as retained in ours, where it is placed very 'fitly after the *first Lesson* at Evening Prayer, in which are 'usually set forth those acts of God's gracious providence over the 'pious, and those prophecies and promises of a Saviour to come, 'for which this Hymn doth praise the Lord: the blessed Virgin 'then experienced God's goodness to his servants, and saw the 'accomplishment of all His promises, and in this form she expressed 'her joy and gratitude; and when we hear in the *Lesson* like 'examples of His mercy, and are told of those prophecies and 'promises which are now fulfilled in Christ's birth, we may be 'expected to rejoice with her in the same words.'—(quoted in Mant's *Book of Com. Prayer*, in loco).

Dr. Bennett remarks:—'By the use of this *Hymn*, though 'composed by the Blessed Virgin upon so particular an occasion, 'we do extol and magnify God for those great mercies which she 'had at that time so deep a sense of. And we use this Hymn im-'mediately after the *First Lesson*, wherein those mercies are so 'frequently and fully promised and declared; and immediately 'before the *Second Lesson*, wherein we find that they were so 'exactly and plentifully fulfilled and enjoyed.' (*p.* 77).—*Paraphrase on Book of Com. Prayer*, in loco. A. D. 1708.

311.—The *Magnificat* in those Churches which can boast of a Choir of the least efficiency is usually

---

* In the *American Liturgy*, this Hymn is omitted from the Evening Prayer.

chanted: where, however, such practice does not prevail, Minister and People read it alternatim. The *posture* to be assumed by all is that of *standing*.

Cantate Domino.

¶. '*Or else this Psalm; except it be on the Nineteenth Day of the 'Month, when it is read in the ordinary course of the Psalms.*' (1662).

Cantate Domino. Psalm xcviii.

312.—This Psalm was introduced into Edward's Second Liturgy, the *Revision* of 1552; by way of variety, as well as to meet the scruples of those who questioned the propriety of the *Magnificat*. The 98*th Psalm* is well adapted to express the thanksgivings of God's adopted children for deliverance from their spiritual enemies, or for any great and temporal blessing. David designed it to celebrate the gratitude of Israel for the victories God's mercy had vouchsafed them; and we can with greater reason sing forth our praises, and rejoice in our hearts, that "The Lord hath declared His salvation."*

313.—On the *Nineteenth Day of the Month* this Psalm, *the* 98*th*, occurs in the ordinary course of Psalms, and therefore should not here be used in the place of the '*Magnificat.*' When employed it may be either *chanted*, or said *alternatively* by Minister and People, according to the usage of the Church. The *posture* adopted is that of *standing*.

Wheatly says:—'When the *First Lesson* treats of some great 'and temporal deliverance granted to the peculiar people of God, 'we have the 98*th Psalm* for variety; which, though made on 'occasion of some of David's victories, may yet be very properly 'applied to ourselves, who, being God's adopted children, are a 'spritual Israel; and therefore have all imaginable reason to bless 'God for the same, and to call upon the whole creation to join with 'us in thanksgiving.' (*p.* 139)—*Rat. Ill. of Book of Common Pruyer.* Corrie's Ed.

---

* In the American Liturgy, another Psalm follows the *Cantate* to be used as a substitute headed with the Rubric—'*Or this. Bonum est confiteri.* Psalm xcii.'

The Rev. J. Jebb remarks:—'The *Cantate*, and *Deus misereatur*, 'might perhaps be reserved for occasions of great national rejoicing, 'and for the evening of Easter Day; when the 98*th Psalm* comes 'in with magnificent effect, as a triumphal song, after the 14*th* '*chapter of Exodus*, commemorating the overthrow of Pharaoh and 'his host, the whole being typical of Christ's benefits; who, by His 'Resurrection has at the same time made the waters of Baptism 'available to us, and has overcome for us our strongest enemies.' (*p.* 410).—*Choral Service.*

The Rev. W. Palmer observes:—'The Psalm, *Cantate Domino*, 'when used here, is to be considered as a responsory Psalm since it 'immediately follows a Lesson; and this is in accordance with the 'seventeenth Canon of the Council of Laodicea, which appointed 'Lessons and Psalms to be read alternately.' (*p.* 285).—*Lit. Orig.* Vol. I.

THE SECOND LESSON.

¶. '*Then a Lesson of the New Testament, as it is appointed.*'—(1662)

(The Reader standing, and turning to the People—the People sitting.)

314.—At the conclusion of the *Magnificat*, or *Cantate Domino*, the Second Lesson is to be read precisely after the same manner as the First Lesson. The use of two Lessons in the Evening Service is of very great antiquity, and appears to be derived from the practice of the Egyptian Church at the beginning of the 5th century: we find, likewise, that the *Second Lesson* was always taken from the New Testament. (*Cassian.* l. ii. Inst. Cœnob. c. 4.)

315.—The Lessons are appointed in the *Calendar*, and in the *Table of Proper Lessons* preceding it, at the beginning of the Book of Common Prayer: and it should be remembered that when there is a concurrence of Saint's-Days with Holy-Days, the choice of Lessons and of Collect should coincide. Many Clergymen, however, set aside the Lessons from the Apocrypha when they have the choice of Canonical Scripture. (See *par.* 123—5, *supra*, and First Collect, *postea.*)

316.—The Reader of the *Second Lesson* in Churches where two or more Clergymen officiate, is usually the Incumbent, or superior Minister, on account of the pre-eminence attached to the New Testament over the Old Testament Scriptures. The *manner* of announcing, reading, and concluding, these Lessons, and the *posture* of the Reader, while thus officiating, are similar to those employed in the First Lesson.

317.—At the termination of the *Second Lesson* the order of EVENING PRAYER is liable to interruption by the demands of the Statute Law, and of certain Rubrics of the Prayer Book, with regard to the three points following, and which we place in the order usually assigned to their performance—

(a.) *Publication of Banns of Marriage.*

(b.) *Catechizing the Children.*

(c.) *Baptisms.*

(*a*) PUBLICATION OF BANNS OF MARRIAGE.

318.—When the EVENING PRAYER should happen to be the first Service of the Sunday, as it may be in certain remote Village Churches; or when the *Publication of Banns* may have been omitted in the previous Service of the Sunday, the Marriage Act, 4 *Geo.* IV. *c.* 76. *s.* 2. requires that *Banns of Matrimony* shall be published in the EVENING SERVICE "*immediately after the Second Lesson:*" thus—

'All *Banns of Matrimony* shall be published in an audible 'manner in the Parish Church or in some public Chapel in which 'Banns of Matrimony may now or hereafter be lawfully published, 'of or belonging to the Parish or Chapelry wherein the persons to 'be married dwell according to the *form* of words *prescribed by the* '*Rubric prefixed to the Office of Matrimony in the* BOOK *of* COMMON 'PRAYER, upon *three Sundays* preceding the solemnization of the 'Marriage during the time of MORNING SERVICE, or of EVENING 'SERVICE (if there be *no Morning Service* in such Church or 'Chapel upon the Sunday upon which such Banns shall be so 'published) *immediately after the Second Lesson*;' &c.—4 *Geo.* IV. *c.* 76. *s.* 2.

319.—Although there is some difference of opinion, as we have already fully shown (in *pars.* 170—173, *supra*), respecting the conflicting directions of the above *Statute*, and the Rubrics of the Prayer Book, yet we need not repeat our arguments here; nor attempt again to reconcile the variance of the Law and Rubric; all we would now say is, that the Clergy are bound to follow the rule imposed by the *Act of Parliament* above cited: and, therefore, *immediately after* the conclusion of the Second Lesson, the Officiating Minister should here *publish the Banns of Matrimony*, if any; provided the publication has not previously been made on that Sunday.

It would be as well, perhaps, to annex these two opinions below which were accidentally omitted from the authorities quoted under *par*. 173.

WHEATLY states:—'Before any can be lawfully married together, the *Banns* are directed to be published in the Church, 'i. e. public proclamation (for so the word signifies) must be made 'to the Congregation, concerning the design of the parties that 'intend to come together. This care of the Church to prevent 'clandestine Marriage is, as far as we can find, as old as Christianity 'itself. For Tertullian tells us, that in his time all Marriages were 'accounted clandestine that were not published beforehand in the 'Church, and were in danger of being judged adultery and fornica-'tion. And by several ancient Constitutions of our own Church, it 'was ordered, that none should be married before notice should be 'given of it in the public Congregation on *three several Sundays* 'or *Holy-days*. And so it was also ordered by the Rubric prefixed 'to the form of Solemnization of Matrimony in the Book of Common 'Prayer, viz. that *the Banns of all that are to be married together be 'published in the Church three several Sundays or Holy-days, in time of 'Divine Service;* unto which was added at the last Review, *imme-'diately before the sentences for the Offertory;* but it is ordered 'by a late Act of Parliament, that *all Banns of Matrimony shall be 'published upon three Sundays preceding the solemnization of 'Marriage, immediately after the second Lesson.*' In a Note is 'added as follows—['It is almost superfluous to remind the reader 'that recent Acts of the Legislature have gone far to render 'nugatory these and other provisions of this Church for preventing 'clandestine Marriages.'] (*p.* 475).—*Rat. Ill. of Book of Common Prayer.* Dr. Corrie's Edition.

The REV. J. PURCHAS observes:—'In the "sealed books," after 'the word Communion is this clause, "*and the Banns of Matrimony 'published;*" these words have been omitted in later editions of the 'Prayer Book,—the Queen's Printer, the delegates at Oxford, and 'the Syndics at Cambridge, having not only committed a breach 'of the Act of Uniformity, but having assumed to themselves the 'province of Convocation. The Marriage Act, 26 *Geo.* II., *c.* 33, 'on which this unauthorized omission is based by a wrong interpre-

'tation thereof, would seem to provide for the publication of Banns 'of Matrimony after the Second Lesson at Evening Prayer in 'churches where *there is no Morning Service;* and after the Second 'Lesson at Morning Prayer *as well as after the Nicene Creed* when 'the services are divided; *but when they are combined, not after the* '*second Lesson*, but after the Creed, as the unmutilated rubric 'directs. For the words of the Act are not, during Morning Prayer 'or Matins, but "during the time of Morning Service," i. e. such 'divine offices as take place before noon. Such is the course for 'those who regard Parliament as having authority to alter or in-'terpolate rubrics......The rubrical direction of the "sealed books," 'the only authorized standard of our present Prayer Book, must be 'observed, and such observance is moreover in accordance with the 'right interpretation of the Marriage Act.' (*p.* 38).—*Directorium Anglicanum.*

320.—The *Publication of the Banns* must be from the Banns' Book, and not from loose papers; and any person, '*forbidding the Banns*,' should be desired in as brief terms as possible to attend in the Vestry after Service, and state his objections; which should be taken down in writing, and his signature attached. (See *par.* 185. *supra.*)

(*b*) CATECHIZING THE CHILDREN.

¶. '*The* CURATE *of every Parish shall diligently upon Sundays* '*and Holy-days after the Second Lesson at* EVENING 'PRAYER, *openly in the Church instruct and examine so many* '*Children of his Parish sent unto him as he shall think it* '*convenient in some part of this Catechism.*' Rubric after THE CATECHISM.—(Present BOOK OF COMMON PRAYER).

321.—Immediately after the reading of the Second Lesson, and the Publication of the Banns of Marriage, if any, then the Officiating Minister, or assistant Clergyman if present, should proceed to examine and instruct the Children of the Parish in the *Church Catechism*, according to the direction of the *Rubric* above cited. The discrepancy between the injunction of the 59*th Canon*, and the *Rubric*, with regard to the fittest time for the performance of this duty has been already elucidated (*par.* 282. *supra.*), still, this discrepancy has given rise to a difference of usage. Some Clergymen prefer the *half hour before* the EVENING SERVICE, as enjoined in *Canon* 59., others think, the better time to be *after the* SECOND LESSON, as laid down in the *Rubric;* while the majority are led to dispense with public Catechizing altogether, from the objections raised against it by the more educated of their Congregations: this is particularly the case in those localities where custom or fashion has made the 'EVENING SERVICE' the chief Service of the day. These last mentioned Clergymen confine their catechetical instruction to the School Room.

322.—The *Rubric* of the First Liturgy of Edward VI. (A. D. 1549), found at the end of the CONFIRMATION OFFICE, required this *Catechizing* to be, '*once in six weeks at the least, upon some Sunday or* '*Holy Day, half an hour before Evensong.*' The subsequent Liturgies of 1552, 1559, and 1604 omit the words, '*once in six weeks at the least,*' and direct simply that the Children shall be diligently catechized '*upon Sundays and Holy Days, half an hour before* '*Evening Prayer,*' (*Evensong.* 1552). At the *Revision* of the Prayer Book in 1662, the Rubrics affecting the public *catechizing* of Children were transferred from the "CONFIRMATION OFFICE" to the end of 'THE CATECHISM;' and that change made in the wording which appoints the performance of this duty to be '*after the Second Lesson,*' instead of '*before Evening Prayer.*'

The origin of these rubrical directions may be traced, probably, to the Injunctions of CROMWELL (*temp.* Henry VIII.) in 1536, and 1538, which thus read:—

Item; That ye shall *every Sunday and Holy-day* through the 'year, openly and plainly recite to your Parishioners, twice or 'thrice together, or oftener, if need require, one particle or sen- 'tence of the *Pater Noster,* or *Creed,* in English, to the intent they 'may learn the same by heart; and so from day to day, to give them 'one little lesson or sentence of the same, till they have learned the 'whole *Pater Noster* and *Creed,* in English, by rote. And as they 'be taught every sentence of the same by rote, ye shall expound 'and declare the understanding of the same unto them, exhorting 'all Parents and Householders to teach their Children and Servants 'the same as they are bound in conscience to do. And that done, 'ye shall declare unto them the *Ten Commandments,* one by one '*every Sunday and Holy-day,* till they be likewise perfect in the 'same.—*Item;* That ye shall in Confessions every Lent, examine 'every person that cometh to Confession unto you, whether they 'can recite the *Articles* of our Faith, and the *Pater Noster* in 'English, and hear them say the same particularly; wherein if they 'be not perfect, ye shall declare to the same, That every Christian 'person ought to know the same before they should receive the 'blessed Sacrament of the Altar,' &c.—*Burnet's Hist. of the Reformation* (Nares' ed.) Vol. IV. *p.* 101.

At the beginning of the reign of Edward VI. (1547), we have this Injunction:—

'Whether they have not diligently taught upon the Sundays 'and holy-days their Parishioners, and specially the youth, their '*Pater Noster*, the *Articles of our Faith*, and the *Ten Commandments* in English; and whether they have expounded and declared 'the understanding of the same.'—CARDWELL'S *Doc. Ann.* I. 7. 25.

The *Reformatio Legum* prescribes one o'clock in the Afternoon as the most suitable hour for *Catechizing*: thus—'Pomeridiani 'temporis horam primam Minister explicando *Catechismo* tribuat, et 'in ea re vel integram horam ponat, vel aliquid eo amplius, si 'videbitur, modo concioni non sit impedimento, quam in Ecclesia 'Cathedrali populus expectabit; omnino enim illam præteriri non 'placet aut destitui *Catechismum* pertractet vel ipse Parochus, 'vel ejus Vicarius, et magnam in eo diligentiam adhibeat; summam 'enim utilitatem et præstantem usum habet in Ecclesia Dei fre'quens inculcatio *Catechismi*, quem non solum a pueris edisci, sed 'etiam ab adolescentibus attendi volumus, ut in summa religionis 'erudiantur, et puerorum piam assiduitatem sua præsentia co'honestent.'—*De Divin. Off.* c. 9. (*Cardwell's* ed. *p.* 92).

In the *Injunctions* of Elizabeth (1559) *Catechising* was enjoined every Holy-day, and every second Sunday, half an hour before EVENING SERVICE: thus—

'Every Parson, Vicar, and Curate shall, upon *every Holy-day* 'and *every second Sunday* in the year, hear and instruct the youth 'of the Parish for *half-an-hour at the least before Evening Prayer*, 'in the Ten Commandments, the Articles of the Belief, and the 'Lord's Prayer, and diligently examine them, and teach the *Cate-chism* set forth in the Book of Common Prayer.'—CARDWELL'S *Doc. Ann.* I. 195.

The *Canons* of 1571 imposed upon the Clergy the necessity of *Catechizing* the Children *every Sunday and Holy-day*:— 'Omnibus Dominicis et festes diebus statum a meridie præsto erunt 'in templis, ubique minimum ad duas horas legent et docebunt '*Catechismum*.'—CARDWELL'S *Synodalia*, p. 121.

After this came the *Canons* of 1603, the 59th of which also enjoined that the *Catechizing* should be performed *half-an-hour before* EVENING PRAYER; (see *supra*, par. 282.); this, however, has been *superseded* by the Rubric of our present Book of Common Prayer, the Revision of 1662, as we have already explained. The change thus imposed did not seem to answer the expectations of the Clergy generally, nor did it meet with the approbation of the people, as the opinions cited below clearly prove. We find that the Royal Commissioners, in their proposed '*Alterations*' in the Liturgy (A. D. 1689), endeavoured to reconcile the difference of opinion entertained with regard to the time of Catechising, by suggesting the introduction into the Rubric of the words—'*either before Evening Prayer or*'—immediately after the word '*Holy-days*,' so that the Rubric would read:—'*The Curate of every Parish shall diligently upon Sundays and Holy-days* either before Evening Prayer 'or *after the Second Lesson*,' &c.* but this was never carried out.

323.—That *public Catechizing* is a very valuable and important means of instructing the Children and the more unlettered of our Congregations in the doctrines of the Church is scarcely disputed: the time *when* public Catechizing can be more effectively performed is a question demanding the greatest judgment and discretion on the part of the Officiating Minister. In some Churches, *Catechizing* supplies the place of the Evening, or Afternoon, *Sermon;* particularly when it is practised immediately after the Second Lesson: in other Churches where the *Litany* only is used in the Afternoon, or Evening, *Catechizing* is often substituted for the *Lecture*, yet not systematically.

324.—The *proper place* of the Officiating Minister when *publicly Catechizing*, or examining the Children, is the *Reading-Desk*, or his *Stall in the Chancel*, the Children *standing* in rows, the Boys on one side, the Girls on the other, or in a semicircle, as near to the Officiating Minister as practicable. If *lecturing on the Catechism* is preferred, the proper place for the Clergyman is then thought to be the *Pulpit*, he *standing*, the Children, the while, *sitting*. The particular portion of the Catechism to be the subject of examination is usually prepared beforehand.

---

* In the AMERICAN LITURGY the Rubric is:—'*The Minister of every Parish shall diligently upon Sundays, and Holy-days, or on some other convenient occasions, openly in the Church, instruct or examine so many Children of his Parish sent unto him, as he shall think convenient, in some part of this Catechism.*'

The Rev. R. Simpson says:—'It will be well for the Minister, 'when he gives notice of his intention to *Catechize*, to state the '*portion* on which he purposes to question the children, and to 'request them in the mean time, to look out as many *passages of* '*Scripture* as they can find, which may serve to illustrate and con-'firm it. The Minister will find it of infinite service to provide 'himself with *facts* and *anecdotes* explanatory of his subject.' (*p.* 126).—*Clergyman's Manual.*

We will now annex a few opinions on the general subject of Catechizing *openly in the Church.*

Bp. Cosins (*ob.* 1671) remarks:—'It is not said here, That he 'shall do it upon *every Sunday*, and *every Holiday;* and therefore 'the words are to be understood, *as often as need requires*, according 'to the largeness or number of children in his Parish. In the 'second of K. *Edward* he was limited to do it *once in six weeks, at* '*least;* against which words (as being too large a time, and the 'Ministers in *Germany* doing it otherwhiles *three times in a week*) 'Bucer took exception; whereupon it was thus ordered in the 'fifth of K. *Edward*, and set down in terms indefinite, though he 'urged to have it *singulis Festis.*'—*Add. Notes to* Nicholl's *Book of Com. Prayer*. p. 58.

Dr. Nicholl's (*ob.* 1712), commenting on the alteration made in the Rubric in 1662, observes:—'The reason of the alteration, I 'presume, was, that *Catechism* being performed in the midst of 'Divine Service, the elder persons, as well as the younger, might 'receive benefit by the Minister's expositions, and that the presence 'of Masters and Parents, might be an encouragement to their 'Servants and Children, to a diligent performance of their duty 'therein. But the worthy persons who made this alteration, have 'been miserably disappointed in their good intentions; for this very 'thing has drove *Catechism* almost out of the Church: For now if 'Ministers Catechize in Prayer-time, they will drive away their 'Congregations, in most places. So that there being no other 'time appointed by the Rubrick, the exercise thereof is most 'shamefully neglected; and the Nation feels the dismal effects 'thereof, by the loose principles of some persons, and the ignorance 'of others. Happy would it be were the Rubrick altered to what it 'was before, and the custom which obtained before the wars 'revived; which was, That the children were *Catechized* on *Saturday* 'in the afternoon (when there was always publick Prayers) and 'the Servants and Apprentices *after Evening-Prayer* on *Sundays.* 'For if there were a separate time allotted for *Catechism*, as 'formerly, the elder people would not be tired as they pretend 'to be, with this exercise; and younger people being only among 'themselves, and the Minister, would not be under that great 'concern, as we frequently observe them to be in the midst of a full 'congregation.'—*Book of Com Prayer* in loco.

Wheatly states:—'The times now appointed for *catechizing* 'of children, are *Sundays and Holy-Days.* Though Bishop Cosin 'observes, this is no injunction for doing it *every* Sunday and 'Holy-day, but only *as often as need requires*, according to the 'largeness or number of children in the Parish. And it is true, 'that by the *first Book* of King Edward VI. it was not required 'to be done above *once in six weeks*. But BUCER, observing that 'this was too seldom, and that in several Churches in Germany 'there was catechizing *three times a week*, urged, in his censure 'upon this Rubric, that the Minister should be required to *catechize* '*on every Holy-day*. Upon this exception indeed the Rubric was 'altered, but expressed notwithstanding in indefinite terms. So 'that *Bishop Cosin* was of the opinion, that no obligation could 'be urged from hence, that the Minister should perform it on *all* 'Sundays and Holy-days. And indeed by the Injunctions of Queen 'Elizabeth, it was only required *upon every Holy-day, and every* '*second Sunday* (*i. e.* I suppose *every other Sunday*) in the year: 'though it is plainly the design of the present Rubric, that it should 'be done *as often as occasion requires*, *i. e.* so long as there are any 'in the Parish who are capable of instruction, and yet have not 'learned their *Catechism*. And therefore, in many large Parishes, 'where the inhabitants are numerous, the Minister thinks himself 'obliged to *Catechize every Sunday;* whilst in Parishes less 'populous, a *few Sundays* in the year are sufficient to the purpose; 'and therefore in such places the duty of *Catechizing* is reserved 'till *Lent*, in imitation of an old custom in the primitive Church, 'which had their more solemn *Catechisms* during that season. But 'now how to reconcile the *59th Canon* to this exposition of the '*Rubric*, I own I am at a loss: for that requires every Parson, 'Vicar, or Curate, *upon every Sunday and Holy-Day*, to teach and 'instruct the youth and ignorant persons of his Parish, in the '*Catechism* set forth in the Book of Common Prayer; and this too 'upon pain of a *sharp reproof* upon the first complaint, of *suspension* 'upon the second, and of *excommunication* till he be reformed, upon 'the third. (*p.* 447.)—*Rat. Ill. of Book of Com. Prayer*. Dr. Corrie's edition.

SHEPHERD says:—'In the early ages of Christianity, *catechizing* 'was never performed in the Church; neither did it in England, till 'after the Restoration, interfere with the Public Worship. Were a 'separate time allotted for *catechising*, as was formerly done, the 'youth would be freed from the embarrassment, which they 'experience, when called upon by the Minister to answer 'interrogatories in the midst of a numerous Congregation: And it 'is perhaps desirable, that the practice of *catechizing* children and 'servants early in the *Afternoon*, or *before the Evening Service*, 'should be again revived. After all, I conceive, that what we have 'to complain of, is not so much the awkwardness of the time in 'some particular places, as the too general neglect of the duty. 'The early Fathers insist much upon the importance and necessity 'of *catechizing*. The extreme care that was taken in the primitive 'Church to instruct the Catechumens in the principles of 'Christianity is generally known, and its beneficial effects were 'as generally experienced......Nothing indeed contributed more to 'the enlargement of the Protestant Faith, than the diligent 'catechising, practised by the reformed Divines. To the truth of 'this the Romanists themselves bear witness. In their preface 'to the Catechism set forth by order of the *Council of Trent*, they 'complain, that, "the age is sadly sensible what mischief they "(the Protestants) have done the Church (of Rome) not only by "their tongues, but especially by those writings, called Catechisms." (*p.* 280).—*Elucidation of Book of Com. Prayer*. Vol. II.

Bp. Mant says:—'The frequency and length of publickly 'catechizing at Evening Prayer in the time of Divine Service in the 'Church are left to the Clergyman's Judgment: but the total 'neglect of it is the breach of an order, as wise and salutary, as 'it is direct and plain: and the benefits of it are poorly supplied by 'a second Sermon, and by School instruction.' (*p.* 46). In another work this Bishop remarks:—'The duty of giving religious instruction 'to the young people of his Cure, is solemnly enjoined on the 'parochial Clergyman; and it is enjoined with circumstances of 'time and place, which appear designed to impress the Catechumens 'with a sense of the seriousness of the employment, to engage them 'at the same time in the devotions of the Congregation, and thus to 'associate in their minds the ideas of growing in religious knowledge, 'and of partaking with others in Divine Worship. For an omission 'or neglect of this duty, unless it be *really impracticable*, it would 'be difficult to assign a satisfactory reason. If there existed 'sufficient causes in the nature of the thing itself, or in the religious 'condition of the people, for instituting the practice, these causes 'may well operate with undiminished force for upholding it, 'circumstanced as we at present are. Would we wish our members 'to proceed generally in a course of religious duty, when they are 'old? we must train them up during childhood in the way wherein 'they should go. But with respect to this and to the other instances 'now specified, and to any others which may possibly be conceived, 'in which the plea of *impracticability* is set up for the non-observance 'of a clear and positive law; the reader may be reminded that 'although the plea, if correct, is unanswerable (for according to the 'old maxim, "nemo tenetur ad impossibile"), yet it behoves us to 'take especial care to guard ourselves against all delusion, and to be 'assured that the plea is indeed correct, and is not devised or 'admitted by us as a specious pretext to cover our own real 'indifference to the obligation of the law, or our own actual 'indolence in the execution of it.' (*p.* 70).—*Clergyman's Obligations.*

The Bp. of St. David's (*Dr. Thirlwall*) observes:—'It is 'probably never more likely to answer these ends [of benefiting 'the young], and at the same time to strengthen the attachment of 'those of riper years to the Church, than where such instruction is 'given, according to the intention of the Church, *in the presence of* '*the Congregation.* I am convinced that many of our Churches 'would be much better attended, if this practice were revived.— *Charge.* 1842.

The Rev. J. Jebb says:—'The Catechism, or rather the '*Catechetical Institution*, hortatory and explanatory, prescribed to 'be used *after the Second Lesson of* Evening Prayer, is never 'used in Cathedrals. But though these Churches are not Parochial, 'it ought not to be forgotten, that the Chapters have cure of souls 'over the Boys of the Choir: and it is but fitting, that occasionally 'at least, these should have the same advantages of public instruction 'afforded to the children of inferior Churches. The observance of 'the Rubric in this respect, now largely revived in Parishes, is of equal obligation in Choirs.' (*p.* 556).—*Choral Service.*

The Rev. E. Monro speaking of *Catechizing in public*, says:—'It 'clearly is the essentially Catholic mode of instruction, and while 'its benefits to the child instructed are great and manifest, the use 'to all who are present at Church is equally important; while the 'children are catechised the adults present are led, perhaps for the 'first time in their lives, to question themselves, and to reason as 'to the great truths of religion, and it becomes one of the most 'important opportunities of shedding light on the darkness which 'broods over the minds of men and women among us. In *catechising 'in Church* during the EVENING or AFTERNOON SERVICE prominence 'can be given to those points, so essential to be believed and yet so 'imperfectly known, the doctrine of the ever-blessed *Trinity*, the '*Incarnation* and the *Atonement;* it will become an opportunity of 'explaining the nature and offices of the Ecclesiastical Seasons of 'the year; and, if it immediately succeeds a Baptism, of explaining 'to sponsors the nature of the duties they have just entered upon.' (*p.* 148).—*Parochial Work.*

The REV. J. C. ROBERTSON says:—'Doubtless, if we could now 'establish such a system of *catechizing* as our Church contemplates, 'we might hope to do vast good; influencing our Parishioners in 'their early years, and using the young as instruments for the 'instruction of others. And if it be argued that by such *public 'catechizing* we may drive people away from our Churches, let it be 'considered whether we may not lose at least as many, whether 'to the sects or to utter ungodliness, by the neglect of it. There 'can be no doubt that if we could get over the first difficulties, the 'gain would after a few years greatly preponderate. (*p.* 243)......... 'It does not appear that *catechetical instruction* must necessarily be 'uninteresting to the hearers, or a severe tax on their patience 'and charity. *Rubrics*, *Canons*, and other documents throughout 'suppose something different from a mere asking of questions and 'receiving the prescribed answers. Much of an interesting kind 'may surely be drawn out and communicated in the course of the 'examination.' (*p.* 246).—*How shall we conform, &c.*

MR. J. A. STEPHENS (*Barrister-at-law*) remarks on this *Rubric:*— 'This language is imperative upon the Curate to *catechize upon 'every Sunday and Holy-day, after the Second Lesson at* EVENING 'PRAYER; the only discretionary power vested in the Curate is, the 'number of children to be *catechized.* Some Clergymen imagine 'that because the word "*all*" has not been inserted before "Sundays 'and Holy-days" the Rubric is satisfied if the catechizing takes 'place occasionally; but there are no grounds for such a 'construction. It is plainly the design of the Rubric that the 'Minister should *catechize* his parishioners on *every Sunday and 'Holy-day;* i. e. so long as there are any in the Parish who are 'capable of instruction, and yet have not learned their Catechism.' (*p.* 1474).—*Book of Common Prayer.* E. H. S. Vol. iii.

(c) I. BAPTISMS, (*Infant.*)

(a) ¶. '*The People are to be admonished, that it is most convenient 'that* BAPTISM *should not be administered but upon 'Sundays, and other Holy-days, when the most number 'of People come together; as well for that the Congregation 'there present may testify the receiving of them that be 'newly Baptized into the number of Christ's Church; as 'also because in the Baptism of Infants every Man 'present may be put in remembrance of his own profession 'made to God in his* BAPTISM. *For which cause also it 'is expedient that* BAPTISM *be ministered in the Vulgar 'tongue. Nevertheless, (if necessity so require), Children 'may be baptised upon any other day.*'

(b) ¶. '*And note, that there shall be for every Male-child to be 'baptized two Godfathers, and one Godmother; and for 'every Female, one Godfather and two Godmothers.*'

(c) ¶. '*When there are Children to be baptized, the Parents shall 'give knowledge thereof over night, or in the morning 'before the beginning of* MORNING PRAYER, *to the Curate. 'And then the Godfathers and Godmothers, and the People 'with the Children, must be ready at the Font, either 'immediately after the last Lesson at* MORNING 'PRAYER, *or else immediately after the last Lesson 'at* EVENING PRAYER, *as the Curate by his discretion shall 'appoint. And the Priest coming to the Font, which is then 'to be filled with pure Water, (and standing there, shall 'say,*'—PUBLIC BAPTISM OF INFANTS. Present Book of Common Prayer (1662).

(d) ¶. '*And if they* (Persons as are of Riper years) *shall be found 'fit, then the Godfathers and Godmothers (the People being 'assembled upon the Sunday or Holy-Day appointed) shall 'be ready to present them at the Font immediately after 'the Second Lesson, either at* MORNING, *or* EVENING, 'PRAYER, *as the Curate in his discretion shall determine.*'—BAPTISM TO SUCH AS ARE OF RIPER YEARS. Present Book of Common Prayer (1662).

325.—*Banns of Marriage* having been published, if necessary; and the *Catechizing of the Children* openly in the Church having been accomplished where such is the custom; the Officiating Minister will then, in accordance with the Rubrics of the Baptismal Offices (*c. d.* above), proceed to baptize such Children as he may have been apprized of '*over-night, or in the Morning before the beginning of Morning Prayer,*' and of those Adults who shall have given the required notice, and been duly examined. We shall not here enter into any of the controverted questions affecting the Sacrament itself, but merely endeavour to elucidate the *Order* and *Ritual* of the *Ministration*, leaving the doctrinal points to a future opportunity.

326.—In the Rubrics of the Baptismal Services, the first feature which presents itself to our notice is the epithet '*Public;*' the earlier Office is entitled "THE MINISTRATION OF PUBLIC BAPTISM OF INFANTS *to be used in the Church.*" The meaning to be assigned to the word '*Public*' the Rubric explains to be "*upon Sundays and other Holy days, when the most number of people come together;*" and the reason given is—"*as well for that the Congregation "there present may testify the receiving of them that "be newly baptized into the number of Christ's Church, "as also because in the Baptism of Infants, every man "present may be put in remembrance of his own "profession made to God in his Baptism:*" these explanations, combined with the last words of the title of the Office, viz.—"*to be used in the Church,*" sufficiently lay down the rule—that (a) the PUBLIC BAPTISM OF INFANTS is to be administered *in the Church:*—(b) that it is to be administered only on *Sundays and Holy-Days*—(c) that it is to be administered in the presence of the *Congregation;* and, according to another Rubric, (d) that it is to be administered "*immediately after the* SECOND LESSON *of* MORNING, *or* EVENING, PRAYER;" and further, (e) that *previous Notice* is to be given; and (f) certain *God-Parents* to be provided. Any deviation from these injunctions *unless*, as the Rubric permits, '*necessity so require,*' when "*Children may be baptized upon any other day,*" is, strictly speaking, contrary to the law and discipline of the Church of England; and any *refusal* by the Officiating Minister to administer PUBLIC BAPTISM when thus called upon, is visitable with suspension for the space of three months,' as laid down in CANON 68. thus:—

'No Minister shall *refuse* or *delay* to *Christen* any Child 'according to the Form of the Book of Common Prayer that is 'brought to the Church to him upon *Sundays* or *Holy-days* to be 'Christened......*convenient warning* being given him thereof 'before, in such manner and form as is prescribed in the said 'Book of Common Prayer. And if he shall *refuse* to Christen 'the (Child)......he shall be *suspended* by the Bishop of the Diocese 'from his Ministry by the space of *three months*.'—CANON 68.

327.—The phrase '*to Christen*' in this Canon implies '*the making of a Christian*,' and is identical with '*to Baptize*.' The poor often confound the two expressions; and some even think that '*Christening*' and '*naming the Child*' before the Registrar of Births, &c., mean the same thing. Care should be taken clearly to disabuse their minds of so preposterous and unsanctifying an idea.

328.—The *exceptional cases*, when "*Children may be baptized upon any other day*," are those of Children who are too weak to be brought to Church, or too sickly, and in danger of death. For these a special Service is provided in, "THE MINISTRATION OF PRIVATE BAPTISM OF CHILDREN IN HOUSES; the first Rubric of which declares that it must be "*a great and reasonable cause*," which can sanction such a departure from the rules of the Church; and that this 'cause' is "*to be approved by the Curate*." It is an excellent practice for the Officiating Minister to require a '*certificate*' from the Medical attendant, declarative of sufficient "*cause and necessity*," before consenting to a *private ministration* of Baptism. There are other instances, however, where *custom*,—originating, it may be, from the *inconvenient position* of the Font, too remote perhaps from the Congregation, or in too cramped a situation; or from the difficulty of procuring *God-parents* on the Sunday; or from long established usage—has sanctioned the administration of Baptism *not during Service time*, but at some hour before, or after, MORNING, or EVENING, PRAYER; and in some cases not even on the *Sunday*. Before attempting to alter this variance from the direction of the Rubric, it would be well previously to obtain the advice and countenance of the Diocesan, the proper authority in all cases of doubt and difficulty that may interpose between the Minister and his people. Besides which, it may be stated, in any interference with ancient usage that may not meet with the general approval of the Congregation, the latter will probably appeal to the Bishop against what they would call an innovation; the Ordinary, therefore, if forewarned will be forearmed.

329.—The Office of Public Baptism of Infants in our Prayer Book is derived chiefly from the Baptismal Service in Hermann's '*Consultation*,' and appears to embrace the three Offices in the Old Service Books designated the "*Ordo ad Faciendum Catechumenum*," "*Benedictio Fontis*," and the "*Ritus Baptizandi*." (Sar. Brev.) It is not our design to discuss here the various Rubrics of the Baptismal Offices, but only so much of them as bears upon the introduction of the *ministration of Baptism* into the Morning, or Evening, Prayer, on Sundays, and Holy-days, leaving other questions till we arrive at the Offices themselves. Previous to the Reformation the usual seasons of Baptizing were *Easter*, and *Whitsuntide;* the former, commemorative of Christ's Resurrection, of which Baptism is a figure; and the latter, of the out-pouring of the Spirit on the day of Pentecost, when 3,000 were baptized by St Peter. The Eastern Church adopted the period of the *Epiphany* also in remembrance of Christ's baptism; and later, about the *8th, or 9th, century*, the Latin Church broke through these limitations, and baptized at all times of the year.

330.—With regard to our own Church, we find a Constitution of *Otho*, A. D. 1237, enjoining the Feasts of *Easter* and *Whitsuntide* to be the solemn times of public baptizing: and a subsequent Constitution of *Othobon* A. D. 1268, admitted '*exceptions* in cases of necessity.' *Abp. Peckham* A. D. 1281. permitted children born at other times than eight days before Easter, or Whitsuntide, to be baptized '*prout placuerit ipsis parentibus*,' when it pleased their parents: and such usage continued down to the time of the Reformation. About A. D. 1543—7. appeared the "*Consultation*" of HERMANN, Abp. of Cologne, drawn up by Bucer and Melanchthon, in which was this direction:—

'We will that *Baptism* be ministered *only upon the Sundays and* '*Holy-Days when the whole Congregation is wont to come together*, if 'the weakness of the Infants let not the same, so that it is to 'be feared that they will not live till the next Holy-Day.' (*p.* 164.).—

From this work, as has been already observed, was derived much of the Baptismal Service in our own Prayer Book. The first Rubric of the Office in the earlier Liturgy of Edward VI. (A. D. 1549.) is very explanatory of the ancient usage, and of the change which the Reformation effected: it read thus:—

(*e*) ¶. '*It appeareth by ancient writers, that the Sacrament of* '*Baptism in the old time, was not commonly ministered but* '*at two times in the year, at Easter and Whitsuntide;* '*at which time it was openly ministered in the presence of all* '*the Congregation: which custom (now being grown out of* '*use,) although it cannot for many considerations be well* '*restored again, yet it is thought good to follow the same as* '*near as conveniently may be. Wherefore the people are to* '*be admonished, that it is most convenient that Baptism* '*should not be ministered, but upon Sundays, and other* '*Holy-days, when the most number of people may come* '*together: as well for that the Congregation there present* '*may testify the receiving of them that be newly Baptized* '*into the number of Christ's Church, as also because in the* '*Baptism of Infants, every man present may be put in* '*remembrance of his own profession made to God in his* '*Baptism. For which cause also, it is expedient that* '*Baptism be ministered in the English tongue. Nevertheless* '*(if necessity so require) children ought at all times to be* '*Baptized, either at the Church or else at home.*'—KEELING, 235.

Evidences of the old usage which limited Baptisms to *Easter*, and *Whitsuntide*, we have in the authorities following:—

BP. OVERALL (*cir.* 1614—19) writes:—'Tempus Baptismi 'Congruum est Sabbatum Sanctum Paschæ, et vigilia Pentecostes. 'De Conj. Dist.'—*Additional Notes* to NICHOLL'S Book of Common Prayer, *p.* 55.

L'ESTRANGE states:—'At *Easter*, because it was the monument 'of Christ's Resurrection, to which Baptism did refer. (*Rom.* vi.) 'For this cause, saith St Basil, no time more proper to receive,

'*Gratiam Resurrectionis*, the benefit of our Resurrection than *in die* '*Resurrectionis*, on the day of the Resurrection, the Paschal day. 'At *Whitsunday*, in memory of the three thousand persons baptized 'that day, (*Acts* ii.) And for children, all such as were born after '*Easter*, were kept until *Whitsunday*, and all born after *Whitsunday* 'were reserved until next *Easter*; unless some imminent danger of 'death created a necessity of accelerating Baptism; but this custome 'of baptizing, onely at *Easter* and *Whitsunday* must onely be 'understood in reference to the Western Church; for without 'controversie it is, that they of the East assigned also the Feast of '*Epiphany* for this Sacrament, and this was done in memory of our 'Saviour's being, as it is supposed, baptized on that day, upon which 'there is extant an excellent oration of Gregory Nazianzen.' (*p.* 231.).—*Alliance of Divine Offices.*

Dr. Nicholl's writes:—'There was a custom which obtained in 'the Ancient Church taking its rise from an extraordinary respect 'which was thereby thought to be paid to the day of our Saviour's 'Resurrection, *viz.* that no Baptisms were to be performed, unless in 'case of absolute necessity, but only at *Easter*. And this not upon 'the Feast day itself, but upon the Eve or Vigil thereof......But in 'the African Church Baptisms were celebrated twice in a year, at '*Easter* and *Whitsuntide*......These two solemn seasons of Baptizing 'were used in St. Ambrose's time......and also in the time of 'St. Austin......In the time of Pope Leo, who lived in 440, there 'was a custom in Sicily to have a solemn Baptism upon the Feast 'of *Epiphany*......But before his time the Baptisms were performed, 'not only at the Epiphany, but upon *Christmas-day* likewise, and 'other Festivals.........But though the Latin Churches, especially 'those in Italy, kept to the two great solemnities of *Easter* and '*Whitsuntide*, for celebrating the Baptisms; yet the Greek Church, 'and several other Churches baptized on other days......The French 'Church likewise celebrated a solemn Baptism upon Christmas-day... 'which custom, Menardus in his Notes upon Gregory's Sacramentary, 'proves, did obtain in that country, down from Constantius's time. 'The same custom obtained in England in Gregory the Great's time, 'as appears by one of his letters (*Lib.* vii. *Ep.* 30.).—About the 8*th* 'or 9*th century* the time for solemn Baptism was enlarged, even in 'the Latin Church who seemed all along to have bound it up into 'the narrowest compass especially in Italy and the adjacent 'provinces. For by order of Pope Victor, Baptism was enjoined to 'be celebrated all the Easter week......Agreeable to this was that 'Canon of the Council of Tribur held A. D. 895......But Gregory, 'Turanensis says, that this was an usage long before his time in the 'French Church, when he writes that in the 4th century "more "than a thousand persons were baptized within those seven days." 'The same person likewise writes, that Baptism was celebrated in 'France upon St. John Baptist's day. But after all this, in the 9*th* 'century the Italic usage of baptizing only at *Easter* and *Whitsuntide* 'was supported by the authority of Charles the Great (*cap. Car.* 'l. v.); and by the 4th Canon of the Council of Mentz; yet I cannot 'find that these Injunctions were much observed, for the restriction 'of the Council of Tribon took away the force of them......But 'before the 12*th century* without any Council or Decree, the Paschal 'and Pentecostal Baptisms vanished, all Churches, moved by the 'reason of the thing, going into frequent Baptisms at other times.... 'After this time particular Churches made what orders they thought 'fit to settle the times of baptizing. Indeed here in *England*, 'Othobon in his Constitutions, made 1236, orders that Baptisms 'should be performed after the Roman method, "upon the Saturday 'before Easter and the Saturday before Whitsunday." But the 'Synod under *Abp. Peckham* takes notice of this order "that from 'the time of its making to that time, *viz.* A. D. 1281. it was 'neglected;" and for the future enjoins, "that, according to the 'ancient custom here in *England*, the Parents should be at liberty 'to have their children baptized as soon as they were born, or 'afterwards (*i. e.* the next Easter) as they should think fit." This 'was a home-stroke at the Roman Court, to dispense with one of 'their Decretal Laws, and which was so lately inforced by a 'Constitution of one of their Legates.'—*Book of Common Prayer* in loco.

331.—The Rubric of 1549 [(e) *supra*] was but slightly altered at the *Revision* in 1552. In the last clause, instead of '*Children ought*,' &c., the new reading was '*Children may*,' &c., and the subsequent words '*either at the Church or else*,' were omitted. Thus the Rubric continued until the final Review in 1662, when the first section, beginning with '*It appeareth*,' and ending with '*conveniently may be*,' and the next word '*wherefore*,' were left out; '*may*' before '*come together*' was also omitted; and the conclusion, '*Children may at all times be baptized at home*' was changed to '*Children may be baptized upon any other day*.' (See Rubric (a) *supra*.)

The *Second* Rubric [(b) *supra*] was altogether an introduction of the last Review in 1662.

The *Third* Rubric [(c) *supra*] was originally in the first Liturgy of Edward VI. A. D. 1549, as follows; where will be seen also the changes introduced in 1552, and retained in the subsequent Revisions of 1559, and 1604.—

(*f*) ¶. '*When there are Children to be Baptized upon the Sunday, 'or Holy-day, the Parents shall give knowledge over-night or 'in the Morning afore the beginning of Mattins*, (*Morning 'Prayer*, 1552, 1559, 1604) *to the Curate. And then the 'Godfathers, Godmothers, and people with the Children, 'must be ready at the Church door* (*Font*, 1552, 1559, 1604), '*either immediately afore the last Canticle at Mattins* (*after 'the last Lesson at Morning Prayer*, 1552, 1559, 1604), *or 'else immediately afore the last Canticle at Evensong* (*after 'the last Lesson at Evening Prayer*, 1552, 1559, 1604), *as the 'Curate by his discretion shall appoint. And then standing 'there, the Priest shall ask whether the Children be baptized 'or no. If they answer no: then shall the Priest say thus.*— (KEELING 236, 237.).

The *Fourth* Rubric [(d) *supra*], indeed the whole Office for *Adult Baptism*, was introduced only in 1662.

332.—The earlier Rubrics we find were confirmed by the *Canons* of 1603-4, as may be seen in *Canon* 68 quoted above, and which are still binding upon the Clergy; so that the practice of the Church of England with regard to the precise *time when* public Baptism of *Infants*, or of *Adults*, should be administered is clear and indisputable, and strictly in accordance with the rule laid down in *par* 326 *supra*. The *only discretionary power* vested in the Officiating Minister by the Rubrics is the choice of, *either* after the Second Lesson *at Morning Prayer*, *or* after the Second Lesson *at Evening Prayer*. In support of these views we will annex the opinions following:—

Bp. Cosins (*ob.* 1672); commenting upon the Rubrical direction, '*When the most number of People may come together*,' adds:—'And 'therefore, it is presently afterwards ordered, That it shall be done 'in *Service-time* after the *Second Lesson at Morning or Evening* '*Prayer:* but because people used not so diligently to come to 'Service, *Bucer* in his censure said, It would be better to do *it* '*immediately after the Sermon*, (for there were most people at *that*) 'wherein nevertheless he prevailed not; for these Rubricks we see 'continue still. The ancient Church was wont to administer this 'Sacrament of Baptism, *immediately before the Sacrament of the* '*Lord's Supper;* for that they were *Gemina Ecclesiæ Sacramenta*, 'the *Twin-Sacraments*, and therefore to go together. It is the 'custom of divers Churches to do so still. They both make a 'Communion among Christians.' (*p.* 55).—*Add. Notes to* Nicholl's *Book of Common Prayer*.

Dr. Nicholls says:—'The wise Reformers of our Liturgy 'thought it too great a liberty to be left to the Parents to keep 'their Children from Baptism, from the time of their birth to the 'following *Easter*, (which was indulged by the Provincial Council, 'only a little to comply with the See of Rome, who tenaciously 'adhered to an old custom the reason of which was vanished) and 'therefore very prudently order that the people should be 'admonished, to bring their Children to Church for Baptism upon '*Sundays* only and *Holy-days*, and that in any time of the year, not 'with any particular regard to those Sundays or Holy-days, but 'because the largest Congregations then meet, at Church, who may 'be witnesses of their reception into the Church, and may thereby 'receive benefit, by refreshing their memories with a recital of those 'sacred engagements, which they themselves formerly made.'—*Book of Com. Prayer* in loco.

Wheatly speaking of the appointment after the Second Lesson observes:—'The reason of which I take to be, because by that time 'the *whole congregation* is supposed to be assembled; which shews 'the irregularity, which prevails much in some Churches, of 'putting off *Christenings* till the whole Service is over, and so 'reducing them, by the departing of the congregation, to almost 'private Baptisms.' (*p.* 398).—*Rat. Ill. of Book of Common Prayer.* Dr. Corrie's ed.

ARCHDEACON SHARP, commenting on the injunction requiring 'Baptisms to be "*administered only on Sundays and Holy-days,*" with the allowance, "*if necessity so require, that Children may be* "*baptized on any other day,*"—says:—'The reason of the former 'part of this *Rubric* is plain enough: that this Office, which is 'designed to be a *Public* one, shall not be used on such days, or at 'such hours of the day, when there is *no public Service* performed, 'or *Congregation* attending; and when consequently the adminis-'tration of BAPTISM would only be *private* in effect, though executed 'within the walls of the Church, and with the Public Form. But 'how the allowance is to be interpreted depends upon the meaning 'of the word "*necessity;*" which can hardly be conceived to take 'place here in any such strict sense as it is used in the Rubric 'before the Office of PRIVATE BAPTISM. For what necessity can 'there be to prefer any other day for Public Baptism before a '*Sunday* or *Holy-day*, which would not equally warrant a Private 'Baptism; that is to say, supposing the expression "*if necessity so* '*require*" be tantamount to that other in the following Office, "*if* '*need shall compel.*" If there were room to believe that both these 'expressions related to the same cases, or "*urgent causes,*" then the 'allowance to Baptize "*on any other day*" must be understood only 'of Private Baptisms. But as I fear it can hardly be so construed, 'especially as provision is made for such cases in the Private 'Office, so neither am I able to assign the instances of which it may 'be properly understood. Should it be alleged that no more might 'be intended by the expression than to except some cases of "*great* '*inconvenience,*" as it seems to be opposed to the words foregoing "*most convenient,*" this meaning might well enough be approved, if 'such construction might be allowed. Under such uncertainty, the 'point that I chiefly rest upon is this: that it doth not appear that 'we of the Clergy have any power lodged with us to judge and 'determine what are these cases of necessity or inconvenience 'which deserve a dispensation, or *exception* from the general rule. 'It is said that "*the people shall be admonished*" to bring their 'Children to be Baptized "*only on Sundays or Holy-days.*" Which, 'I suppose, with regard to us is no more than a general direction to 'discourage their neglect of this Rubric, as we have opportunity, 'and to put them in mind (as often as there shall be occasion 'to remind them) to bring their Children when there is a '*Congregation* to witness their Baptism. "At least on such days, "and at such hours, as there is Public Service usually performed." 'And if they comply with the Rubric thus far, as to bring their 'children to Church on any day when there is stated Service, 'taking upon themselves to answer for the necessity of the case, 'and withal give notice to the Curate of their intention "*either the* "*night before,*" or "*in the Morning before Prayers begin,*" as a 'following Rubric directs, I do not see that the Baptism of their 'children can be refused or postponed. But then, on the other 'hand, how far a Curate, though he take not upon himself to judge 'of the *necessity* &c., may take upon himself to Baptize on any day, 'or hour of the day, "*when there is no Public Service*," is another 'question. This, I think, is clear, that he may justify himself in '*refusing* to do so, both by the Office, one part of which is the 'Public "*reception of the Baptized Infant into the Congregation of " Christ's flock*," and by the Rubric which enjoins that the Baptism 'shall be administered "*immediately after the Second Lesson either " of Morning or Evening Prayer;*" which of the two is left to the 'Curate's discretion, but *his discretionary power goes no further*. 'You will observe that, for the same reason Baptism ought never to 'be *deferred* till the stated Service is over, where it can be 'performed in time of Service; which proviso I put in on account of 'those places, as *Cathedral* and *Collegiate Churches* for instance, 'where the usual situation of the *Font* is at so great a distance from 'the Choir, or place of Divine Service, as to render the compliance 'with this injunction impracticable.' (*p.* 18—20).—*On Rubric and Canons.* Charge A. D. 1733.

Bp. Mant states:—'The rule of the Church concerning the 'time and place of Public Baptism, either at Morning or Evening 'Prayer, is plainly laid down in her Rubricks before "*the Ministra- 'tion*," and ought to be observed. Where "*a great cause and 'necessity*" exists, Baptism may be ministered "*in houses:*" but, 'for this ministration of Private Baptism, a special office is pro- 'vided; and the Public Office ought not to be used except in a 'Church......The ministration of Baptism is part of the Book of 'Common Prayer, which the Church has prescribed, and which her 'Ministers have voluntarily and solemnly undertaken, for the guide 'of their ministrations: the same, without adding to or diminishing; 'that, and no other. (*p.* 45).—*Hor. Lit.*

Dr. Goodwin (*Dean of Ely*), remarking upon the introduction of the Baptismal Service immediately after the Second Lesson, says:— 'You will find that this place is marked out, not as the best place, 'but as the only place, for the introduction of the *Baptismal Service;* 'no *discretion* therefore is left to the Clergyman, and though in 'some Churches a different practice is adopted, you will see that 'such practice has no sanction in the Prayer-Book. I do not 'mention this for the sake of throwing blame on any one, but 'because unfortunately the regulations of the Prayer-Book have in 'some parts been so long neglected, that a Clergyman who Baptizes 'Infants *after the Second Lesson* is sometimes looked upon as 'making an innovation, whereas in fact he has no option left to 'him, but is plainly ordered to Baptize then, and in general at 'no other time......The *Publick Baptism* of Infants is not a Service 'at which the Congregation merely happen to be present,—not one 'to which they are to listen impatiently as though it were an 'interruption of that in which they are engaged,—but that it is 'a Service in which they are all to join,—no interruption of the 'general worship but a part of it,—a Service, in which charity 'for the helpless Infant, and gratitude for their own adoption in 'Jesus Christ, alike demand that they should join with all their 'hearts.........Look upon *Baptism* as the orthodox process for giving 'the Child a name, and the Service is a tiresome addition to the 'Morning or Evening Prayers; look upon *Baptism* as the actual 'bringing of little children to Christ, and as the memorial of having 'been once brought to Him yourself, and then the Service is one 'which will call forth the warmest prayers, and give rise to the 'most useful self-questionings.' (*p.* 95).—*Guide to the Parish Church.*

The Rev. J. Jebb observes upon the injunctions to baptize immediately after the Second Lesson:—'The compliance with this 'rule is, impossible in most Cathedrals, from the great distance 'of the Font from the Choir. The Rubric, it is to be observed, 'is *not so stringent* upon this point as some suppose. Though it 'implies its performance *after the Second Lesson* as a thing 'desirable, it does not positively enjoin it. The people are *to be* '*ready at the Font*, after the last Lesson; but it does not say 'explicitly that the Service shall then begin.' (*p.* 525).—*Choral Service.*

The Rev. J. C. Robertson says:—'It is proper, *generally*, that 'the Office should be introduced into the Public Service, *after the* '*Second Lesson*, as the Rubric appoints. In populous town-parishes, 'the Ordinary is the best judge of the matter; but in answer to 'a common objection it may be observed, that unless the questions 'be put separately for each child, the difference of time occupied 'will be trifling, unless the number of receivers be immoderately 'great (*p.* 235)......The first Rubric before the Office for *Private* '*Baptism* is probably little observed. It certainly cannot plead 'Catholic sanction, as in ancient times Baptism was ordinarily 'administered only at a particular season in the year. (See the 'Rubric before the Office until 1662.) Distance from the Church, 'coldness or wetness of weather, and many family circumstances '(besides the natural desire of the Mother to witness the admission 'of her child "*into the congregation of Christ's flock*,") may surely 'be "*approved by the Curate*" without express application, as 'reasons for dispensing with the very early administration of this 'Sacrament which is here prescribed. (*p.* 240).—*How shall we Conform*, &c.

Mr. W. Cripp's (*Barrister-at-law*), says:—'The *discretion* of 'the Curate mentioned in both places (the Rubrics of the Offices 'for the Public Baptism of Infants, and for the Baptism of such as 'are of Riper years) evidently extend only as to whether the 'Baptism should be after the last Lesson *at Morning* or *at Evening* '*Prayer*. The above direction is positive; so that it appears that a 'Curate who administers Public Baptism, whether of Infants or of 'Adults, *at any other time than that above directed*, is acting in 'defiance of the laws of the realm, and renders himself liable to be 'proceeded against in the Ecclesiastical Courts; but *custom* appears 'to have sanctioned a very frequent departure from the strict 'Rubrical directions in this respect.' (*p.* 648).—*Treatise on the Laws relating to the Church and the Clergy.* 3rd Edition.

Mr. A. J. Stephens, (*Barrister-at-law*), writes:—'The ancient 'church administered the Sacrament of Baptism immediately before 'the Sacrament of the Lord's Supper; because they were *gemina* '*Ecclesiæ Sacramenta.* The period of time at which the ceremony 'of Baptism ought to be performed, viz., "immediately after the 'last Lesson," seems to be absolutely fixed by the Rubric, and if the

'Clergyman act in opposition thereto, he is guilty of a breach of 'the Laws Ecclesiastical.'—*Book of Common Prayer*. E. H. S. (*p*. 1170). In another work this author observes in almost similar words:—'Thus the *period of time* at which the ceremony of 'Baptism ought to be performed seems to be absolutely fixed, 'and if the Clergyman act *in opposition to such injunctions*, he is 'punishable in the Ecclesiastical Court.' (*p*. 96).—*Laws Relating to the Clergy*.

333.—At the appointed time, therefore, the Officiating Minister, or the *Assistant Clergyman*, if such help is prepared, will proceed to the '*Font*,' and administer the necessary *Baptisms*, care being taken that every preliminary arrangement has been attended to, so as to secure order, quiet, and reverence. The details of the *ritual* of the Administration will be given in the proper place hereafter: it will be sufficient, perhaps, to observe here, that during the function the Officiating Minister will *stand*, except at the Lord's Prayer, and Collect annexed to it, following the Collect of 'Reception;' but even on this point there is a difference of opinion. Some Clergymen hold that the word '*all*,' in the Rubric—'*Then shall be said, all kneeling*'—does not include the Officiating Minister: thus—

The Rev. J. Purchas lays down this injunction:—'With regard 'to posture, the Priest should *stand* in every part, without 'exception.' (*p*. 126). Further on, the same writer states:—'The 'Priest during the entire Service will *stand* on the platform of the 'Font, in order not only to perform the function conveniently, but 'to be seen of the People in the action of pouring the water. 'Immediately after the Child is baptized, and without descending 'from the stone platform of the Font, the Priest will proceed with 'the Collect of Reception,—he will thus be seen by the faithful 'when he makes the sign of the Cross on the Child's forehead. 'The prayer should be said without the use of the Office Book. 'After the prayer he will (without leaving the platform) deliver 'the Child to the person in charge of it.' (*p*. 131).—*Directorium Anglicanum*.

It will be better that the Collect of 'Reception' should be learned by heart, as it will be very inconvenient to have to read it from the Office Book while the attention is engaged in making the sign of the Cross upon the forehead of the Child.

334.—Should the *Font* be situated in a remote part of the Church, or in some obscure corner, or, possibly, in a *Baptistery* adjoining, or parted off within the Church, the Baptism must not be administered in the *Reading Desk*, at the *Communion Table*, or in some other open place of the Chancel, as is sometimes done, and, as a necessary consequence, with water in an *ordinary Basin*. This is a most irreverent and indecorous practice, and totally at variance with the Rubrical directions, and the designs of the Church. This may be elucidated by a few authorities :—

Bp. Overall (*cir.* 1614—19) observes:—'The Rites of Baptism 'in the primitive times were performed in rivers and fountains, 'where the persons to be Baptized stood up and received the Sacra- 'ment; which manner of Baptizing the ancient Church received 'from the example of our Saviour, who was so Baptized by *John* in '*Jordan*. And sure this was convenient for that time, when their 'converts were many, and men of years. A reason also may well 'be, for that those ages were otherwise unprovided of *Fonts*, and 'such conveniences, which are now in use, which was the cause 'why this manner of Baptizing was used also in after-times, in such 'places, where no *Fonts* were.' (*p.* 55).—*Add. Notes to* Nicholls' *Book of Common Prayer*.

L'Estrange (*cir.* 1659—90) says:—'When Christianity first 'entered the world, she did not find all utensils fitted to her hand, 'but was constrained to take what occasion did supply: whence it 'is, that as at first *houses* were her *Churches*, so *rivers* were her '*Fonts*. No other *Baptisteries* had she for two hundred years; this 'is evident from *Justin Martyr* and *Tertullian;* the first treating of 'persons fitted for the sacred seal, saith, ἔπειτα ἄγονται κ. τ. λ., "*then* (that is, after we had prayed together *for* and *with* them as "in the foregoing words) *they are led by us to some place where* "*there is water.*" Now, lest it should be conceived that this ex- 'pression may admit of a *Font* within the Church, (as we use to 'carry children according to the rites of our Church) in the pursuit 'of this narrative he goes on thus, "Ἡμεῖς κ. τ. λ. "*Then we, after* "*the believer is thus washed, return with him to the place where the* "*brethren are assembled for Common Prayer*. The second "*Aquam* "*adituri ibidem*," &c. *Being ready to step into the water there also,* "*as we had done a little before in the Church, the Priest holding us* "*up by the head, we make abrenunciation of the Devil*," &c. Clear 'proofs that the places where they Baptized were distant from the 'Churches. Probably their practice was counter to ours, for as we 'bring water to our Churches, so in all likelihood they carried their 'Churches to the water, that is, they had their places of religious 'assemblies near unto rivers, (not unlike the *Proseucha* mentioned '*Acts* xvi. 17.) for the better accommodation of this Sacrament. 'After the second century Baptisteries were erected, but not con- 'tiguous, or annext to Churches, but a little separated from them; 'and not everywhere neither, but only nigh unto Cathedrals, called 'therefore *Ecclesiæ Baptismales*, Baptismal Churches; not long 'after, they were brought into the Churches, and there disposed 'near the door, at the lower end, denoting thereby, that persons

'Baptized did in that Sacrament make their first ingress into 'Christianity, who were therefore situated, by *Nazianzen's* descrip-'tion, ἐν προθύροις κ. τ. λ., *in the entry to godliness.*' (*p.* 232.).—*Alliance of Divine Offices.*

Dr. Nicholls remarks:—'In the very early times of Christ-'ianity, whilst the faithful were under a state of persecution, there 'was no settled place of administering the rite of Baptism. The 'Apostles Baptized in ponds and rivers; and in any other place, 'where there was convenience of water. Thus Philip Baptized the 'eunuch in a watery place, which they met with accidentally in the 'road, (*Acts* viii. 38.). But the Apostles likewise began a custom 'in their time, of Baptizing in houses: and so it should seem that 'St Paul was Baptized, (*Acts* ix. 17, 18); there being no mention of 'any river: probably the water which was about the house, serving 'for that occasion. The same seems to be the case with the jailor, 'who was converted by St Paul, and was "*Baptized, he, and all his, 'straightway,*" (*Acts* xvi. 33.). This custom of Baptizing in houses, 'where the congregations of the faithful met, continued for the first 'ages, when the persecution obliged them to perform all religious 'acts with as much privacy as might be. After the empire became 'Christian, and temples were everywhere erected, a *Baptistery* or 'room to Baptize persons in, was joined to the Church; where the 'persons, who were Baptized, had the prayers of the congregation 'for God's blessing upon them. This being neglected by some 'persons, who performed the Baptismal rites in private houses and 'oratories, they thereby seeming to slight the publick Baptisteries, 'occasioned the 59*th Canon* of the *Constantinopolitan Council* under 'Justinianus the younger: "Let not Baptism be celebrated in any "oratory within a private house: but they that would partake of "an undefiled Baptism, let them go to the publick Churches, and "there let them enjoy this gift. But, if it shall be proved against "any one, that he has transgressed against this ordinance, if he be "a *Clergyman*, let him be deposed; and if he be a *layman*, let him "be excommunicated." Our Church has not been so severe, as to 'have recourse to excommunications and depositions, upon the 'breaking in upon this duty: but she orders, that "the Baptism be 'administered in the Church," in the *public congregation:* "that "the congregation there present may testify the receiving of them "that be newly Baptized into the number of Christ's Church." 'And it is a pity that so wholesome a constitution should be 'trampled under foot by the vanity of some, and the compliance of 'others, though there be not so great a penalty annexed to it, as 'formerly was.'—*Book of Com. Prayer,* in loco.

Archdeacon Sharp remarks:—'Wherever the *Font* is, there, 'and there only, can this Office be regularly performed; which we 'of the Clergy should take the more notice of, because it is the 'only point in these previous Rubrics, placed at the head of the 'Office, which is expressly charged upon the Minister: "*the Priest "coming to the Font and standing there shall say.*" There is an 'obvious remark to be made upon this restriction as to place; viz. 'that no Minister ought to use this Public Form in a private house, 'or indeed *in any place* except at the Font itself, to which the use of 'it is restrained.' (*p.* 20).—*On Rubric and Canons.* Charge A. D. 1733.

335.—The case may possibly arise that a Clergyman may have to consider the propriety of administering in the Church the Baptismal rite to *his own Child.* It would be better, perhaps, that he should procure the services of some friend who shall be a Priest or Deacon of the Church of England: if such assistance fail him, then he has no alternative; lay assistance, would be out of the question. The ancient usage coincided with this view; thus:—

'Pater vel Mater non debet proprium filium de sacro fonte levare 'nec baptizare, nisi in extremæ necessitatis articulo, tunc enim 'bene possunt sive præjudicio copulæ conjugalis ipsum baptizare, 'nisi fient aliquis alius præsens qui hoc facere sciret et vellet.'—*Ritus Baptizandi.* MASKELL's Mon. Rit. i. *p.* 30.

The only modern opinion we find expressed on the subject is that by *Mr. Purchas,* whom, as the exponent of the extreme Ritualists, we may here quote: he says:—

'It of course is quite irregular for a Priest to baptize his own 'child in the Church. If there be a Deacon he may, in such a case, 'administer the Sacrament, although in the presence of the Priest.' In a *Note* is added—'In most Parishes it will be easy to obtain the 'aid of a brother Priest (or Deacon). But the Priest must not 'baptize his own Child *in Church under any circumstances.* He 'may at home, if there be immediate danger.' (*p.* 132).—*Directorium Anglicanum.*

336.—At the conclusion of all Public Baptisms the Officiating Minister should see personally to the *removal of the Water* left in the Font. If a facility is afforded in the Font itself, this might be employed before the Minister returns to his place, as it would be but a momentary act. If, however, there is no such provision at hand, the *water* may remain till *after* EVENING PRAYER is finished.

RECEIVING INTO THE CONGREGATION.

¶....'*If the Child, which is after this sort Baptized* (Private 'Baptism), *do afterward live, it is expedient that it be brought 'into the Church,* &c.—(1662). Present Book of Com. Prayer. PRIVATE BAPTISM.

337.—The *Receiving of a Child,* which has been *privately baptized,* into the Congregation, usually takes place, like as Public Baptism, *immediately after the*

Second Lesson, although no such direction is laid down in the Rubric. It is customary also to perform this portion of the baptismal ceremony at the Font. It will occasionally arise that Children will be brought to be *baptized*, at the same time as others are brought for *reception into the Church*. This would be better avoided, as there is a little difficulty in combining the two Services. Some Clergymen accomplish it after a fashion; although such a proceeding is not sanctioned by the Rubric, or other authority. In large and populous Parishes the blending of the two Offices may be necessary, from the pressure of much occasional duty. In these cases, it is usual to adopt the method suggested by *Archdeacon Sharp*, which is to place the two classes apart round the Font, and proceed with the Office for the "PUBLIC BAPTISM OF INFANTS" till after the *Sanctification of the Water*, taking care to caution the Sponsors of the Children 'to be received' not to answer the *third* demand, viz. "*Wilt thou be baptized in this Faith*:" then, before baptizing those who have never submitted to the Rite, the Officiating Minister will repeat the *Collect of 'Reception,'* &c., over the Children brought to be admitted into the Congregation; and after baptizing the others, he will continue with the Service for both parties unto the end. It is found preferable, however, to make the two Services distinct, and perform them at separate times. The '*Certification*' required by the Rubric is made before commencing the ordinary Office.

ARCHDEACON SHARP says:—'We want some direction likewise 'in what manner we are to use this Office, when there is one or 'more children to be Baptized, as well as one or more children 'to be *received* by it into the Congregation. The greatest part 'of each Office, being word for word the same, may reasonably and 'consistently be applied to both cases, and be used in common; 'provided those parts of each Office which are particular and 'appropriate to the different cases be also used separately. And 'this I take to be the usual practice. Nor doth it seem liable 'to censure, though it is *not authorized* by any Rubric. And all the 'ends and uses of both Offices are as completely answered this way, 'as if they were to be performed distinctly. But this indeed is said 'upon a supposition that the questions to be put to the Sponsors 'are, as was above observed they ought to be, put on behalf of *each* '*child*. For the *third question* in the first Office cannot possibly 'be made an interrogatory in the second. And I may here further 'remark, that we are to observe the same rule in certifying 'the Private Baptisms of those with whom the second Office is 'to be used. That is to say, when there are more than one to 'be *received* into the Congregation, we must *certify the Baptism* 'of each of them distinctly, whether Baptized by ourselves or by 'others: as appears from the manner in which those certificates are 'printed, if compared with the rest of the Office.' (*p.* 29).—*On Rubric and Canons.* Charge A. D. 1733.

The Rev. J. C. ROBERTSON remarks:—'Attempts are often 'made to *combine the Service for Public Baptism* with that for '*receiving into the Congregation* Infants which have been privately 'Baptized. *No combination* can be made, however, without 'destroying the significant differences of the two Offices, in which 'the Church's view of the Sacrament is remarkably shown. Nor, 'again, is it desirable that each should be gone through at full 'length in the same Service. Perhaps, therefore, the best way 'of managing the matter may be by arranging that Children in the 'two states shall be brought at different times; which may easily 'be done if previous notice be required, as the Rubric directs.' (*p.* 241).)—*How shall we Conform*, &c.

ADULT BAPTISMS.

338.—The Baptism of *Adult Persons* is also enjoined to be '*immediately after the Second Lesson* [see Rubric (d) *supra*]; but it cannot possibly be combined with the *Baptism of Infants.* This Service should therefore be distinct: and the Officiating Minister, who must in this case be in *Priests' Orders*, will proceed after the same manner and order as enjoined for the Baptism of Infants, in accordance with the Office especially appointed for the "Baptism of such as are of Riper Years."

The necessary instructions laid down in the several Rubrics of the different Baptismal Services will be elucidated in their proper places. (See *postea.*)

339.—The *Baptisms*, and *Receptions*, being concluded, the Officiating Minister should return to the place whence he came before he proceeded to the Font. It is very irregular, if not irreverent, for him to retire to the Vestry-Room to *disrobe* himself, and thence pass to a private seat. Immediately the Officiating Minister is in his place, then will follow the usual *Canticle* of the Evening Prayer.

NUNC DIMITTIS. *St Luke* ii. 29.

¶. '*And after that*' (the Second Lesson) '*Nunc Dimittis*, (or the 'Song of Simeon) *in English, as followeth.*'

(The Minister and People standing.)

340.—The *Song of Simeon*, designated the '*Nunc Dimittis*' from the two leading words of the Latin version, is of very ancient use in the Church. It is mentioned in the Apostolical Constitutions (*lib.* vii. *c.* 48.) as being employed at Vespers, or Evening Prayer; Amalarius also speaks of it being used at Compline in his day, A. D. 820. This Song is beautifully adapted to follow the reading of a Lesson from the Epistles; and well portrays our joy at seeing with the eyes of faith the Salvation of God.

341.—In the *first Liturgy* of Edward VI. A. D. 1549, this Canticle occurs alone without an alternative; the 67*th Psalm* having been introduced at the *Revision* in 1552. The parenthetical clause '(*or the Song of Simeon*)' found no place in the Rubric before the last Review in 1662. In the '*Alterations*' proposed by the Royal Commissioners in 1689, the '*Nunc Dimittis*' was struck out, and '*Psalm cxxxiv.*' substituted in the Rubric. But these suggestions were never accepted.*

342.—The *posture* to be assumed by Minister and People is that of *standing*, as in the other Canticles: and where any thing approaching to a Choir exists, the '*Nunc Dimittis*' is usually *chanted*.

DEAN COMBER writes:—'After the *Second Evening Lesson* out 'of the Epistles of the holy Apostles, *this Hymn* is most commonly 'used; the author of it is supposed to be that holy doctor whom the 'Jews call *Simeon the Just*, son of the famous Rabbi Hillel, a man of 'eminent integrity, and one who opposed the then common opinion

* In the AMERICAN LITURGY, 'the *Nunc Dimittis*' has no place, in its stead are 'Psalm lxvii:' '*or this.* Psalm ciii.'

'of the Messiah's temporal kingdom. The occasion of composing it 'was his meeting Christ in the Temple when He came to be offered 'there, wherein God fulfilled His promise to him that he should not 'die till he had seen the Messiah; taking Jesus therefore in his 'arms, inspired with joy and the Holy Ghost, he sang this "*Nunc* '*dimittis*:" and though we cannot see our Saviour with our bodily 'eyes as he did, yet He is by the writings of the Apostles daily 'presented *to the eyes of our faith*; and if we were as much 'concerned for Heaven, and as loose from the love of this world as 'old *Simeon* was, and as we ought to be, we might upon the view of 'Christ in His Holy Word by faith, be daily ready to sing this '*Hymn*; which was indited by the Spirit, recorded in Holy Writ, 'and is adopted into the Public Service of all Christian Churches, 'Greek and Latin, Reformed and Roman, and used to be sung 'in extraordinary by divers Saints and Martyrs a little before their 'death.'—(quoted in MANT's *Book of Com. Prayer* in loco; and appropriated by WHEATLY in his *Rat. Ill. of Book of Com. Prayer p.* 140. *Dr. Corrie's* ed.)

DR. BENNET, observes:—'This Hymn comes very properly '*after the Second Lesson*, which is always taken out of the *New* '*Testament*, wherein is contain'd and deliver'd to us that Gospel, 'the enjoyment and participation of which is the ground and 'foundation of the whole Hymn. I must add, that this Hymn is 'address'd to God, and since it may be us'd as the personal prayer 'of every devout Christian, therefore let none repeat it after 'a careless manner; but consider to whom they speak it, and 'utter the whole with a suitable devotion.' (*p.* 82).—*Paraphrase on the Book of Com. Prayer.*

DEUS MISEREATUR.

¶. '*Or else this Psalm; except it be on the Twelfth Day of the* '*Month.*'

'*Deus Misereatur.* Psalm lxvii.'

(Minister and People standing.)

343.—This *Psalm* (the *lxvii*th), distinguished by the first two words of the Latin version, '*Deus Misereatur*,' was introduced into the *Second* Liturgy of Edward VI. A. D. 1552, as an occasional substitute for the "*Nunc Dimittis.*" It may be looked upon as a responsory Psalm, and can be used at any opportunity; '*except*,' as was inserted in the Rubric at the *last Review*, 1662, '*on the* 12*th day of the Month*,' when it occurs in the ordinary Psalms of that day. The Rubric of 1552 was simply—'*Or else this Psalm, Deus Misereatur.* Psalm lxvii.' The Rubric of 1559 was—'*Or this Psalm* (Deus misereatur nostri) *in English.*' In the *Revision* of 1604, the original Rubric of 1552 was adopted: while at the last *Review* in 1662, the Rubric assumed the form quoted at the head of this section.*

344.—The *posture* to be assumed by Minister and People is that of *standing*, as at the other Psalms. And where there is a competent Choir, the '*Deus Misereatur*' is usually *chanted*. When this Psalm is *read* by Minister and People *alternatim*, the first versicle of the *Doxology* must fall to the Minister to repeat.

Dean Comber writes of this Psalm:—'The parallel to the 'former Evangelical Hymn is this Psalm of David, who prayed 'for that "*saving health*," which old Simeon rejoiced to see: '(*Ps.* lxvii. 2; *Luke* ii. 30;) and both of them praised God upon the 'foresight they had, that it would be made "known" to us, and 'to all people, as it is this day by the voices of the Apostles. 'Since David indited this Psalm for a form of Prayer, for the 'sending of this salvation, and of praises to God, to be used by 'those who should see it accomplished, it cannot but be very 'suitable for our use, after we have heard out of the Epistles, how 'this salvation appeared to us, and to all men.'—(quoted in Mant's *Book of Com. Prayer* in loco).

Dr. Bennet observes:—'This *Psalm* is so call'd, because in the 'Latin Version it begins with these words. And it is very properly 'us'd *after the Second Lesson*, which is always taken out of the 'New Testament; because therein we may conveniently express 'our desires of the further propagation of the Gospel. This Psalm 'is also a Prayer to God, and therefore it must be not barely 'repeated, but addressed to our Maker in the most solemn manner.' (*p.* 83).—*Paraphrase upon the Book of Com. Prayer.*

Wheatly writes:—'Instead of it (*Nunc dimittis*) sometimes the '*lxvii. Psalm* is used, (being one of those that was introduced in 'King Edward's second Liturgy,) which, being a Prayer of David 'for the coming of the Gospel, is a proper form wherein to express 'our desires for the further propagation of it.—N. B. It ought to be 'noted, that both the 67*th* and 100*th Psalms*, being inserted in the 'Common Prayer-books in the ordinary Version ought so to be 'used, and not to be sung in *Sternhold* and *Hopkins*, or *any other* '*metre;* as is now the custom in too many Churches, to the 'jostling out of the Psalms themselves, expressly contrary to the

* In the American Liturgy the Psalms prescribed to follow the reading of the Second Lesson are *Psalm* lxvii, and *Psalm* ciii.

'design of the Rubric: which, if not prevented, may in time make 'way for farther innovations and gross irregularities.' (*p.* 141).—*Rat. Ill. of Book of Com. Prayer.* Dr. Corrie's Ed.

The Apostles' Creed.

¶. '*Then shall be said or sung the Apostles' Creed by the Minister 'and the People, standing.*' (1662).—Present Book of Com. Prayer.

345.—The *Creed* will be found among the prayers of Compline in the Anglo Saxon, and early English, Offices; and was placed here with the Suffrages, Lord's Prayer, and Supplications, with the view of preserving uniformity with the Office of Morning Prayer, and only after the *last Review* in 1662; although in the *Revision* of 1552 a Rubric was introduced requiring the use of the Creed in this place.

In the Prayer Book of 1549, after the "*Nunc Dimittis*," the Rubric was:—

> '*Then the Suffrages before assigned at Matins, the Clerks 'kneeling likewise, with three Collects. First of the day;*' &c. (1549).

But in 1552, the "*Deus misereatur*" was introduced; after which came this Rubric:—

> '*Then shall follow the Creed with other Prayers as is before 'appointed at Morning Prayer, after* Benedictus. *And with 'three* (*the*, 1559) *Collects; First of the day;*' &c.—(1552, 1559, 1604).

This Rubric continued, (with the exception of '*three*' changed to '*the*' in 1559), till the *Revision* of 1662, when the present Rubric was framed. Among the '*Alterations*' of 1689 it was proposed that the words "*or sung*," and "*Apostles*," be struck out; and after "*Creed*," the following words inserted, "*commonly called the Apostles' Creed*;" but these changes were never effected.*

* In the American Liturgy, the same Rubric and arrangement occur, as in the Morning Prayer of that book; where also the *Nicene Creed* is permitted to be substituted, at the discretion of the Officiating Minister. (See *supra*: par. 213.)

Bp. Cosins remarks:—'In the Second of *Edw.* VI. the Minister 'is appointed to say the *Creed* and the *Paternoster* alone, and the 'Choir to answer, "*But deliver us from evil. Amen.*" And the '*Kyrie Eleison* is ordered to be said before the Creed: but no '*Dominus vobiscum*, with the Answer ordered to be said, till after 'the Versicles, immediately before the Collects.'—*Add. Notes to* Nicholl's *Com. Prayer*. p. 22.

346.—The *Athanasian Creed* is not to supply the place of the Apostles' Creed in Evening Prayer, as is prescribed on certain occasions in the Morning Prayer.

347.—The history of the *Apostles' Creed* has been briefly narrated in the Morning Office (*pars.* 211—213, *supra*); so that it need not be repeated here; where also have been explained '*the manner of saying*' the Creed (*pars.* 214, 215); the *posture* of '*Standing*,' as prescribed in the Rubric (*par.* 216); the *turning to the East* (*pars.* 217—221); and the *bowing at the name of Jesus*, (par. 222).

348.—The "*Amen*" being of the same type as the text is to be said by Minister and People.

III. The COLLECTS, and PRAYERS.

The Preces.—The *Salutation*.

¶. '*And after that, these Prayers following......the Minister first 'pronouncing with a loud voice*,'—Present Book of Com. Prayer.

(Minister and People standing.)

349.—The Salutation, "*The Lord be with you,*" and its response; together with the Exhortation, "*Let us pray,*" the Lesser Litany, Lord's Prayer, and Versicles following, were introduced into the Evening Office at the same time as the Apostles' Creed, viz: after the Revision of 1662. This was done with the view of meeting the injunction imposed in the Rubric placed before the Creed in the *Second Liturgy* of Edw. VI. (1552.), but which had been neglected by the Officiating Minister because they had not been put here in print. The remarks, therefore, which these portions drew from us in their place in the Morning Prayer will serve equally in this.

350.—The *posture* of Minister and People during the repetition of the *Salutation*, and the *Exhortation*, is that of *standing*. The Minister, the while, turning to the People.

THE LESSER LITANY.

'Lord have mercy upon us.'

&c. &c.

(Minister and People kneeling.)

351.—Here, as in the Morning Prayer, this Litany is to be repeated *alternatim* by Minister and People. The *Posture* of *kneeling* is enjoined in the Rubric introduced here from the Morning Office, and which reads as follows :—

¶. '*And after that, these Prayers following, all devoutly 'kneeling, the Minister first pronouncing,*' &c.

These brief supplications may certainly be considered in the light of Prayers; and in the previous Liturgies we find the directions *to kneel* refer particularly to them: thus—the Rubric of the Liturgy of 1549, immediately preceding the *Lesser Litany* in the Morning Prayer, prescribes :—

'*Then shall be said daily through the year, the prayers following, 'as well at Evensong as at Matins, all devoutly kneeling.*'—(KEELING. 23.).

A slight deviation was made in the wording of this Rubric at the next *Revision* (of 1552); as well indeed as an addition to it; thus

'*And after that, these prayers following, as well at* EVENING '*PRAYER as at* MORNING PRAYER, *all devoutly 'kneeling, the Minister first pronouncing with a loud voice.*' (1552, 1559, 1604).—KEELING. 22. 23.

At the *last Review* (in 1662) the reference to the EVENING PRAYER was omitted; while the added words (of 1552), which we have just spoken of, refer to the Salutation, and the Exhortation, then introduced.

352.—We may add, that the *Lesser Litany*, the *Lord's Prayer*, and the *Supplications* following, have been appended to the Evening Service from time immemorial. Mr. Palmer in his *Origines Liturgicæ*, (Vol. i. p. 287.), speaks of their having been adopted in the ancient Uses of Salisbury, York, Hereford, &c., as well as in those of the Anglo-Saxon period. Benedict (A. D. 530.) mentions the *Lesser Litany*, and the *Lord's Prayer*, as being used in his time at the close of Evening Prayer.

The Lord's Prayer, (the second time).

¶. '*Then the Minister, Clerks, and People, shall say the Lord's* '*Prayer with a loud voice.*'—Present Book of Com. Prayer.

(Minister and People kneeling.)

353.—The repetition of the Lord's Prayer towards the conclusion of the Evening Service is a very ancient usage. Benedict, as we have just observed, speaks of it as practised in his day (A. D. 530.): and prior to this, we find the Council of Girone (A. D. 517.) directing that the *Lord's Prayer* should be said by the Priest every day after Vespers.

354.—The *Lord's Prayer* was enjoined to be used here by the Rubric of King Edward's *Second Liturgy* (1552), as we have remarked above (*par.* 349.); but it was not *printed* in the text of the Evening Prayer till after the *last Review* in 1662; at which time it appeared with the Rubric preceding it, exactly as in the Morning Office. The *Doxology* was in like manner omitted from it; whence we find in the "*Alterations*" of 1689, that it was suggested to insert before the "*Amen*,"—"*For* "*thine is the* "*kingdom, the power and the glory, for ever and ever.*" But this was never carried out.

355.—For the elucidation of the *Rubric*, we must refer our Readers, with the view of avoiding repetition, to the place in the MORNING PRAYER (*pars*. 234—237, *supra*.), whence this Rubric is borrowed. The Minister and People together are to say the *Lord's Prayer* 'with a loud voice,' all *kneeling*.

The SUPPLICATIONS.

¶. '*Then the Priest standing up shall say*.'

(The People kneeling.)

356.—These *Versicles* were introduced from the Morning Office after the *last Review* in 1662, with the Apostles' Creed, and all that follows up to this point, in order to enable the Officiating Minister to comply more readily with the practice enjoined in the Rubric of the Liturgy of 1552, as we have just explained, (*pars*. 345—349, *supra*). It will be only necessary, therefore, to direct the attention of our Readers to what has been said respecting these *Versicles* at the place where they occur in the MORNING PRAYER. (See *pars*. 238—240, *supra*.)

357.—We referred there also to certain changes in these Versicles proposed among the "*Alterations*" put forward by the Royal Commissioners in 1689, but we omitted to state these following :—

At MORNING PRAYER.—In the Rubric, the word "*Minister*" was inserted in the place of "*Priest*."

Among the Versicles which follow; the first, second and third times, the word "*Priest*" is unaltered: the fourth and fifth times altered to "*Minister*."

The Versicle.—"*Because there is none other that fighteth for us*, "*but only thou, O God*." Altered to, "*That we may serve Thee* "*without fear all the daies of our Lives*." (p. 11.)

At EVENING PRAYER.—In the *Rubric* and among the Versicles, the word "*Priest*" altered to "*Minister*" in the first, second, and third instances; but not in the fourth, fifth, and sixth instances. (*p*. 13.).

The Versicle,—"*Because there is none other*," &c. is likewise altered, as above.

.. The COLLECTS (Orationes).

(*a*). ¶. '*Then shall follow three* COLLECTS; *the first of the Day;* '*the second for Peace; the third for Aid against all* '*Perils, as hereafter followeth; which two last Collects* '*shall be daily said at* EVENING PRAYER *without* '*alteration.*'—Present Book of Common Prayer.

(Minister and People kneeling).

358.—The characteristic features of what are called *Collects* (orationes), the origin of the term, and their early introduction at the close of MORNING, and EVENING, PRAYER, have been already discussed in the preceding Volume (*Vol.* e. *par.* 241.). Where also, has been explained what is meant by the '*Collect of the Day,*' spoken of in the Rubric; and direction given as to the choice of *Collect* when there is a *concurrence* of a HOLY-DAY and SAINT'S-DAY. (See *pars.* 242—246, *supra*). The question, however, will now arise, as to what Collect is to be used in the EVENING PRAYER of a *Sunday*, of a *Week-day*, and of a *Holy-day?* And to arrive at this decision with respect to '*Eves* and *Vigils*' it will be necessary to learn, at what time EVENING PRAYER, properly so called, used to begin.

The Collect for the Evening of Sundays, and Week-days.

359.—On SUNDAYS the Collect, or Collects, used in the MORNING PRAYER are to be repeated in the EVENING PRAYER; some authorities, however, advance exceptions, as will presently be seen. And, according to the Rubric in the prefatory part of the Prayer Book, under the heading, '*The Order how the Rest of Holy Scripture is appointed to be Read,*' the Sunday Collect is to be employed during the *entire week*, thus:—

(*b*). ¶. 'The *Collect, Epistle,* and *Gospel,* appointed for the '*Sunday* shall serve *all the week after,* when it is not 'in this Book otherwise ordered.' (1662).*— Present Book of Com. Prayer.

The expression '*otherwise ordered*,' in the above Rubric, refers, in the *first* place, to the *Collect*, &c., that may be prescribed for some *Holy-Day*, or *Saint's-Day*, when the ordinary Collect of the Sunday before will be superseded: in the *second* place it refers to the *Vigils* or *Eves* of *Sundays*, and such *Holy-Days*, &c., as require their Collects to be used in the EVENING SERVICE *next before*, as laid down in the *Rubric* preceding THE COLLECTS; thus—

(c). ¶. '*Note, that the Collect appointed for every Sunday, 'or for any Holy-Day that hath a Vigil or Eve, 'shall be said at the* EVENING SERVICE *next before.*' (1662).—Present Book of Common Prayer.

This Rubric was only introduced at the last Review in 1662; and we must now ascertain what Holy-Days have *Vigils* or *Eves*.

The Collect for Vigils or Eves.

360.—What HOLY-DAYS have *Vigils* or *Eves*, for that some *Holy-Days* have not *Vigils*, nor *Eves*, the wording of the *Rubric* just cited would lead us to infer, we shall learn in the TABLE *of Vigils, Fasts*, &c., introduced into the Prayer Book, immediately following the Calendar, at the Revision of 1662; as well as in the Act, 5 & 6 *Edw*. VI. *c*. 3.

Thus, in the TABLE *of Vigils*, &c., these *Eves* or *Vigils* following, which we have arranged according to the date of their occurrence, are to be observed in

---

* The earlier directions of the Liturgies of 1549, 1552, 1559, and 1604, were as follows:—

'Ye must note also that the Collect, Epistle and Gospel, 'appointed for the Sunday, shall serve *all the week after;* 'except there fall some Feast that hath his proper.'—(KEELING, *p*. xxv.).

In the SCOTCH LITURGY (1637) the following words are added to this Rubric:—'his proper *Collect, Epistle and Gospel, as it is 'on Ash-Wednesday, and on every day in the holy week next before 'Pasch or Easter.*'—(KEELING, *p*. xxiv.).

the Church of England, and the *Collects* to be used are those of the *Holy-Day* following: thus—

The *Evens*, or *Vigils*, before.

CHRISTMAS-DAY	Dec. 25.	*S. Peter*	June 29.
Purification of V. Mary...	Feb. 2.	*S. James*	July 25.
S. Matthias	Feb. 24.	*S. Bartholomew*	Aug. 24.
Annun. of V. Mary	Mar. 25.	*S. Matthew*	Sep. 21.
EASTER-DAY	(*moveable*).	*S. Simon, and S. Jude*	Oct. 28.
ASCENSION-DAY	(*moveable*).	*All Saints*	Nov. 1.
WHITSUNDAY	(*moveable*).	*S. Andrew*	Nov. 30.
S. John, Baptist	June 24.	S. Thomas	Dec. 21.

By the Statute law it is enacted

'That every EVEN or DAY *next going before* any of the 'aforesaid Days of the Feasts of the *Nativity of our Lord*, &c.... '(see *supra*)......other than of *St John the Evangelist*, and *Philip* '*and James*, shall be *fasted*, and commanded to be kept and 'observed; and *none other* EVEN or DAY shall be commanded to 'be *fasted*.'—5 & 6 *Edw.* VI. *c.* 3. *s.* 2. A. D. 1552.

*** This enactment was repealed by 1 *Mary Sess* II. *c.* 2, but re-enacted by 1 *Jas.* i. *c.* 25., and has since been confirmed by the *Rubrical* TABLE in the Liturgy, which has been amended and enforced by the Statute, 24 *Geo.* II. *c.* 23. (For the correction of the Calendar).

The *Canons* of 1603, which are still binding on the Clergy, enforce the keeping of the *Eves* of Holy-Days; but the term *Vigil* is not employed.

In the 14*th Canon* (of 1603), entitled '*The Prescript Form of Divine Service to be used on Sundays and Holy-Days*,' we find the observance of the *Eves* of Holy-Days enjoined: thus—

'The COMMON PRAYER shall be said or sung distinctly, and 'reverently upon such Days as are appointed to be kept holy 'by the Book of Common Prayer, and their *Eves*,' &c.—CANON 14.

The 17*th Canon* (of 1603), directing "*Students in Colleges to wear Surplices in time of Divine Service*," prescribes the *Surplice* to be worn on the *Eves* of these Holy-Days: thus—

'All Masters and Fellows of Colleges or Halls, and all the 'Scholars and Students in either of the Universities, shall in 'their Churches and Chapels, upon all Sundays, Holy-Days, and 'their *Eves*, at the time of Divine Service, wear *Surplices* 'according to the order of the Church of England: and such 'as are Graduates shall agreeably wear with their Surplices such '*Hoods* as do severally appertain unto their degrees.'—CANON 17.

361.—There are certain HOLY-DAYS, however, which have no *Vigils* assigned to them, such are those *Feast-Days*, which fall during seasons of rejoicing, and which on that account admit no *Vigil* of fasting. (*Ascension-Day* is excepted, as its Eve is one of the *Rogation-Days*): thus—

Between *Christmas-Day* (Dec. 25), and the *Purification of V. Mary* (Feb. 2), we have the EVES omitted of

S. Stephen	Dec. 26.
S. John, the Evangelist	Dec. 27.
Holy Innocents	Dec. 28.
Circumcision of our Lord	Jan. 1.
S. Paul's Conversion	Jan. 25.

Between *Easter* and *Whitsuntide* we have the EVES omitted of

S. Mark	April 25.
S. Philip, and S. James	May 1.
S. Barnabas	June 11.

S. Michael and All Angels (Sep. 29.) has *no Vigil* prescribed, from this Feast-Day commemorating those created beings who passed through no previous life of suffering. (*Wheatly* 201. Dr. Corrie's Ed.)

S. Luke's Day (Oct. 18.) has also *no Vigil*, from having been formerly preceded by a Feast-Day, *S. Etheldred's*, now removed.

362.—As the ten Holy-Days above mentioned have no *Vigils* appointed, either by the Rubric, or by Statute law, custom has not sanctioned the use of the *Collects* peculiar to those Days in the EVENING SERVICE immediately preceding them. The Collect of the *Sunday before* is the one generally employed in these cases.

363.—With regard to *New Year's Eve* (Dec. 31.), or, as some term it, the *Eve* of the *Circumcision*,—although, *Rubrically*, the *Circumcision* has no appointed *Vigil*,—there is some difference of opinion as to what *Collect* ought to be employed. The *Rubric* after the Collect for *St Stephen's Day*, (Dec. 26.), directs:—

¶. '*Then shall follow the Collect of the Nativity, which shall be 'said continually unto New Year's Eve.*' (1662).—Present Book of Common Prayer.

*** In the three previous Liturgies of 1604, 1559, and 1552, instead of '*New Year's Eve*,' the expression was '*New Year's Day;*' and in that of 1549, the Rubric was simply '*Then shall follow a Collect of the Nativity*.'*

The change of '*Day*' into '*Eve*' would imply that some alteration in the *Collect* was designed in the EVENING SERVICE immediately preceding the *Circumcision-Day;* but as this day has no acknowledged *Vigil*, the change is thought to have been an inadvertence, and therefore *the Collect of the Nativity* is to be employed.

WHEATLY says:—'It is a mistake in those who use the Collects 'of all Holy-days whatsoever upon the Evening before. I know, 'indeed, it may be urged against this last observation, that the '*Collect of the Nativity* is directed by another Rubric to *be said* '*continually from Christmas-Day unto New Year's* Eve; and what 'makes this objection the stronger is, that before the last Review of 'the Liturgy, the Christmas Collect was to be said unto *New-Year's* '*Day*. The changing *Day* therefore for *Eve* looks something 'remarkable; and as if they purposely designed that the *Collect* '*of the Circumcision* should be used on the Evening before, and that 'the *Collect of the Nativity* should be then left off: the Church 'always speaking exclusive of the time or place it mentions in any 'such directions. What answer to make to this, I own I am at 'a loss. The best I can think of is, that *New-Year's Eve* being the 'common name given to the last day of the year, the person that 'altered the Rubric might imagine, that the *Feast of the* '*Circumcision* had really an *Eve* belonging to it. But whatever 'might be the occasion of the alteration, I think it can be urged no 'otherwise against what I have said, than as a single exception 'from a general rule.' (*p.* 204).—*Rat. Ill. of Book of Com. Prayer.* Corrie's Ed.

364.—As to the *Purification-Day* (Feb. 2.), which has a *Vigil* appointed in the Liturgy, some question the propriety of employing the Collect at the EVENING SERVICE next before, because of the expression in the Collect, "*Thy only begotten Son was* THIS DAY *presented in the Temple.*" Can the phrase "*this day*" be used on the *Eve* preceding? An

---

* In the SCOTCH LITURGY of 1637, the Rubric was:—'*Then* '*shall follow the Collect of the Nativity, which shall be said every day* '*in the week unto New Year's Day: but instead of the words* [and 'this day to be born] *the Presbyter shall say* [at this time to be 'born].'

The AMERICAN LITURGY follows our Rubric of 1662, using, however, '*until*' in the place of '*unto*.'

answer will be found more fully in our remarks presently on the *hour* of EVENING SERVICE with respect to *Eves;* in the mean time, we may observe, that Rubricians generally interpret the words "*this day*," to mean '*this time*,' so that the Collect is admissible on the *Eve* before, as well as on the *Purification-Day*. (See JOHNSON's, and WHEATLY's, opinions, *supra;* and BP. WARBURTON's observation *postea*.)

365.—Again, with relation to *St John the Baptist's Day*, a question arose respecting its *Vigil*, when that should fall on *Corpus Christi Day*. Although this latter day is not admitted in the Church of England as a Holy-Day, yet the elucidation of the question we are considering may be assisted by the quotation of Pope Leo's injunction respecting *Corpus Christi Day*, which will shew also how the *Eves* and *Holy-Days* were formerly accommodated when they happened to concur. *Pope* LEO's rescript to *Archbp. Warham*. (A. D. 1519.), was as follows:—

'To our Venerable brother *William*, Archbishop of Canterbury, 'Legate, born to us and to the Apostolical See, *Pope Leo the Tenth*. 'Venerable brother, health and Apostolical benediction. Your care 'has prompted you to ask of us on what day you ought to enjoin a '*Fast* to your people, since on this year the *Vigil of the Nativity of* '*the blessed John Baptist* falls on the *Feast of the most holy Body* '*of Christ:* having therefore taken mature deliberation with our 'brethren on this point, we think fit thus to answer you, viz., that 'we ordain by this constitution for ever to endure, that the *Vigil of* 'the *Nativity of the blessed John* aforesaid, when it falls on the [*ut* '*supra*] feast of the *Body of Christ* (in which the remembrance 'of our Saviour, on whom our salvation depends, is called to mind), 'in regard to so great a festival solemnity, the *Wednesday* ought to 'be fasted, and is to be fasted as that *Vigil:* and we command, 'that for the future it be so observed by all, when the said *Vigil* 'falls on the feast of the *Body of Christ:* therefore you our brother 'shall command the people committed to you throughout the 'province of Canterbury, and your suffragans, that on the present, 'as well as all future years, in which the *Vigil* of the said *John* '*Baptist* shall fall on the feast of the *Body of Christ*, they fast 'on the foregoing day, that is, *Wednesday*, and observe that as the '*Vigil* in veneration and devotion to the said Nativity. Dated 'at St Peter's, Rome, under the seal of the fisher, on the nineteenth 'day of February, 1519, in the sixth year of our Pontificate.'—(JOHNSON's *Canons* Vol. II. *p.* 530.). To this, JOHNSON adds the following *Note:*—'The feast of *Corpus Christi* was always on the '*Thursday* in the week next after *Whitsun-week*. If this feast had 'a *Vigil* assigned to it, there might have been a question raised 'whether the two *Vigils* could have been kept on the same day; 'but *Midsummer-day* having a *Vigil* and *Corpus Christi* none, I 'cannot see any grounds that our Archbishop had to doubt, but 'that the *Vigil of Midsummer* was to be anticipated, the other feast 'intervening, according to the old rule, that if a *Vigil* fall on a '*Sunday* it is to be kept on the foregoing *Saturday*: for by parity of 'reason if a *Vigil* fall on a *Holy-day*, it is to be kept on the day '*foregoing that Holy-day*. See *Decretal.*, lib. iii. *tit.* 46. *c.* I.'—(*ibid. p.* 531.).

366.—*Eves* and *Vigils* originated, probably, in the necessity which was imposed on the early Christians of holding their assemblies at night from fear of persecution: subsequently, when this danger was removed, they would devote the *Evenings* previous to the *Sunday*, or to a *Holy-Day*, to fasting and to prayer, to prepare their minds for the solemnities and worship of the day succeeding, hence '*Vigiliæ*,' watchings. Others trace the origin of *Eves* and *Vigils* to the old Jewish computation of days—from *Evening to Evening*, or *sunset to sunset*—when the *Holy-Day* would commence at about 6 *o'clock* on the Evening before; and the *Collect*, &c., be, therefore, a legitimate portion of the *Holy-Day* Service. (See BINGHAM's *Eccl. Antiq.* bk. xiii. c. x. s. 11. &c.). But much of the difficulty involved in this consideration hangs upon the difference between the terms *Eve*, and *Vigil*. Many consider them *synonymous* expressions; while others maintain that *Eve* implies simply the Evening before *every* Holy-Day; and *Vigil*, the Evening *fast* before *certain* Holy-Days, those enumerated in the TABLE *of Vigils*, &c., annexed to the Calendar in the Book of Common Prayer. (See *supra*).

Wheatly, and the generality of Ecclesiastical writers, do not admit this distinction, nor that *every Holy-Day* has its *Eve* (see par. 360, *supra*); while certain Rubricians of the present day rigidly insist upon it; in proof of which we will quote a passage from *Mr. Purchas's* "Directorium Anglicanum," which is considered to be an exponent of the views of the more extreme section of the Church of England; thus—

'Not that a Vigil or Eve is implied to be one and the self-same 'thing, but that the Collect for Fast days which have of course 'neither Vigil nor Eve, must not be said at Evening Service next 'before. It is convenient to remember that Fast days have *no* 'Evens, and that Festivals *have* always; the Collect for a Festival 'is *always* said at the Evening Service next before. The day before 'a Festival, if fasted is called its Vigil, if unfasted its Eve. If a 'Festival which has a Vigil fall on Monday, Saturday is the Vigil, 'Sunday the Eve. The Church never fasts on the Lord's Day. 'An Eve is not a Fast. It is to be noted in the above case that the 'Collect for the Festival will not be said at all on the Vigil, but 'on the Eve at the Evening Service next before. That is, not 'at Evensong on Saturday, but on Sunday. The Collect for a 'Saint's day, and that alone, save in certain exceptional cases, is to 'be said on its Eve at first Evensong, or on its Vigil except the 'Feast fall on a Monday, in which case Saturday is the Vigil and 'Sunday the Eve......The Collect for the Festival and that alone, is 'to be said at the Evening Service next before, whether it be 'that of Vigil or Eve.'—In a *Note* is added:—'The distinction 'between Vigils and Eves will be manifest from a consideration 'of the Rubric for S. Stephen's Day. "Then shall follow the "Collect of the Nativity which shall be said continually until New "Year's Eve. Thus, though the Circumcision has no Vigil, its Eve 'is recognized by the Book of Common Prayer in accordance with 'Catholic usage, and its Collect, and that alone, is to be said on 'that Eve. Again, Christmas Day has a Vigil, but if it falls on 'a Monday, the Rubric upon Vigils commands the Vigil to be kept 'on the Saturday preceding. In which case, if Vigil and Eve be 'the same thing, the Collect for the Fourth Sunday in Advent must 'be said at the Evening Service on Saturday without the First, 'thus violating the Rubric which orders "this Collect is to be 'repeated every day with the other Collects in Advent until Christmas 'Eve." If however we take Christmas Eve to be the first Evensong 'of the Nativity, that is, the Evening Service next before, the 'matter is quite plain, the order of Collects varies as follows: Vigil 'of Christmas.—At Evensong, Saturday Service, Coll. (1) 4th 'Sund. in Advent (2) Advent. Eve of Christmas.—At Evensong, 'Sunday Service, Collect for Christmas.' (*p.* 79).—*Directorium Anglicanum.*

On the other hand, we may give DR. HOOK's opinion, which seems to consider *Eve* and *Vigil* as synonymous. He writes in his *Church Dictionary* under the word '*Evens*' thus:—

'EVENS, or VIGILS. The nights or Evenings before certain 'Holy-days of the Church,' (here follows a passage on the origin of Vigils in the words of PALMER—*Origines Liturgicæ*, Vol. i. *p.* 202.). Again, under the word VIGIL, we have this:—'VIGIL. 'The night or Evening before certain Holy-days of the Church,' (here comes a quotation from Wheatly.).—*Church Dict.*, 6th edit.

But some elucidation of the nature of these fasting-days or *Vigils*, will, perhaps, explain better what the Church of England designs by the appointment of such Holy-days. We will therefore cite a few authorities on the subject.

L'ESTRANGE, (*ob.* cir. 1659—60) writes:—'As for the *Fasts* 'intended in the Kalendar by our Church as antecedent to their 'respective *Holy-days*, I find no direct nor express example of them 'in the Primitive Church. But very obvious, nothing more, is 'the devout practice of those early Christians, imploying the nights 'preceding their great Festivals in humicubations, *lying on the floor*, 'watchings, tears, and such outward acts of inward humiliation. 'But in tract of time abuses stealing in, and defiling those sacred 'exercises, the Church, say learned men, changed those *Night-vigils* 'and Watchings into *Diurnal Fasts*. But it will be here demanded, '*Why are Fasts prefixed to some Holy-days, and not to all?* My 'answer is, proceeding in due order. The first of *Jan.* being the '*Circumcision* is but of late known by that name, and anciently 'called the *Octave of Christ's nativity*, and *Octaves* never were 'assigned their *Vigils* in the primitive Church. The *Epiphany* 'is no Saint's-day. Again, if *Theophilus Alexandrinus*, as he is 'cited by *Riccardus* upon *Proclus*, deceive me not, it was a fast-day 'itself ἐν ῇ μίχρις κ. τ. λ. *in which we were wont to fast till night.* 'Now a Fast-day could not have a fasted Vigil. As for *S. Mark*, 'and *Philip* and *Jacob*, they fall within the fifty days after *Easter*, 'which priviledged them from having fasts. Amongst all the rest 'only *St Michael*, and *St Luke* have no fasts. Not *St Michael*, 'because Ritualists observe, the Angels did not enter into their joys 'through sufferings. Not *St Luke*, because another day formerly of 'great esteem in our Church falleth upon the Eve thereof.'—*Alliance of Divine Offices*, p. 58.

DR. BENNET (*ob.* 1708) says:—''Tis well known, that the 'primitive Christians did frequently spend the *Night* in Watching, 'Fasting and Prayer. Such Nights are called *Vigils*, that is, 'Watchings. An *Eve*, properly speaking, is the Evening before 'an Holy-Day; but now 'tis commonly used for the *whole* Day 'before an Holy-Day; and it was anciently spent in Fasting and 'Prayer, the better to prepare people for the next day's solemnity. 'These holy exercises our Church was very desirous to continue; 'but our devotion is at so low an ebb, that they are generally 'neglected, and we have little more than the names left. Now 'for special reasons, too long to be inserted, some Holy-Daies 'have no *Vigils* or *Eves*; that is, the Evenings, Days, or nights 'preceding them, are not ordered to be spent in Fasting and 'Prayer, as those before the generality of Holy-Days are.' (*p.* 125).—*Paraphrase on Book of Com. Prayer.*

JOHNSON (*ob.* 1725) remarks in his *Vade-Mecum*:—'This first 'part of the Festivals was, very early among the primitive 'Christians, spent in Hymns and other devotions; (see the '*Martyrdom* of St *Ignat.*) which were oft-times continued till late 'in the night, and were from thence called *Vigils*; which *Vigils* 'were by degrees enlarged, till at last the *whole preceding day* 'was call'd by that name: nor only so, but latterward they were 'so loath to part with their religious Feasts, that they did not 'think them ended at the beginning of the next Evening, but 'lengthen'd out the Solemnity so long as the twilight continued. 'And what *Lyndwood* says of our *Lady-day*, may, I suppose, be 'applied to all other Feasts of the Church; *viz.* "*Quoad festivitatem, 'sive celebrationem Divini Officii, incipit Annunciatio, in primis 'Vesperis, finitur post secundas.* L. I. T. 3. c. *Nullus*, verb. *Ante Annunciationem.*"—Vade-Mecum. *Vol.* i. *p.* 176.

WHEATLY says:—'In the primitive times it was the custom 'to pass great part of the *night* that preceded certain Holy-days in 'religious exercises and devotion; and this *even* in those places 'which were set apart for the public worship of God. And these 'exercises, from their being performed *in the night-time*, came to 'be called *vigiliæ*, *Vigils* or *watchings*. As to the original of this 'practice, some are inclined to found it upon the several texts 'of Scripture literally understood, where *watching* is enjoined as 'well as *prayer;* particularly upon the conclusion our Saviour 'draws from the parable of the Ten Virgins: "*Watch, therefore, "for ye know neither the day nor the hour wherein the Son of "man cometh.*" But others, with greater probability, have imputed 'the rise of these *night-watches* to the necessity which Christians 'were under of meeting in the *night, and before day*, for the exercise 'of their public devotions, by reason of the malice and persecution 'of their enemies; who endeavoured the destruction of all that 'appeared to be Christians. And when this first occasion ceased, 'by the Christians having liberty given them to perform their 'devotions in a more public manner, they still continue these '*night-watches* before certain Festivals, in order to prepare their 'minds for a due observation of the ensuing solemnity. But 'afterwards, when these *night-meetings* came to be so far abused 'that no care could prevent several disorders and irregularities, the 'Church thought fit to abolish them: so that the *nightly watchings* 'were laid aside, and the *Fasts* only retained, but still keeping 'the former name of *Vigils*.' (*p.* 199).—*Rat. Ill. of Book of Com. Prayer.* (DR. CORRIE'S Ed.)

Time of Evening Prayer.

366.—The time of EVENING PRAYER may be any hour *after* 12 *o'clock, mid-day:* but, in the matter of *Eves* and *Vigils*, the hour must not be anterior to 6 *o'clock* P.M. It is at this Service that the *Collect* of the *Holy-day* following, if it has an Eve or Vigil duly appointed, is to be used; and, according to the opinion of some Rubricians, because the *Holy-Day* begins at 6 *o'clock on the Evening before.* It is the more general practice, certainly in civil matters, to reckon our days *from midnight to midnight;* whence it is that many Clergymen completely set aside the *Rubric*, standing at the head of the Collects, conceiving it to belong to an age, or to a system, which computed the days *from sunset to sunset.* These likewise dispense with all consideration of *Eves* and *Vigils*, holding them also to have fallen into desuetude. Consequently they use the *Collect of the Sunday* every day of the week following, except on the occurrence of a Holy-day, on which day only they use the especial Collect of the *Holy-day.* We must, however, urge our Readers in all instances to adhere, as nearly as may be, to the directions of the *Rubrics;* especially when it is by no means impracticable, and where it has been the custom of the place.

The following opinions will throw some additional light on this subject:

JOHNSON remarks:—'*Scriptural days* begin at *six in the Evening*, 'and end at *six the next Evening;* according to those Texts in the 'first of *Genesis*, "*the Evening and the Morning were the first,*" "*second,*" &c. "*day.*" Now if the *Paschal* Full Moon happen *after* '6 *a clock* at Night of the *Civil Sunday*, then it is on Monday 'according to the *Scripture account*, and so *Easter Day* ought by no 'means to be observed on that day, nor before the following 'Sunday. For tho' the Church does not affect to keep *Easter* 'on the same day with the *Jews*, yet she has divided her Nights 'and Days according to the *Scriptural* and *Civil Account.* And 'tho' our *Civil Day* begins from *Midnight*, yet our *Ecclesiastical* '*Day* begins at *six in the Evening:* And therefore the *Collect for* '*the Sunday* is to be read on what in our *Civil Account, is called* '*Saturday Evening*, and *the Collect for every greater Festival at* 'EVENING PRAYER *next before.* The proper time for *Vespers*, or 'EVENSONG, is *six a Clock*, and from that time the Religious Day 'begins; therefore where EVENING PRAYER is read at its proper 'Season, the Collect for *the Purification* may well be used, as 'the Rubric directs, on what we call the *foregoing Evening;* 'notwithstanding those words, "*thy only Son was this day* "*presented in the Temple.*"......But observe that tho' the Church 'day *begins at six in the Evening*, yet in our Liturgy the Rubrics 'are to be understood according to the *Civil Account, ad captum* '*vulgi*......As therefore, the Church complies with the State in 'reckoning *January* the First Month of the year, and in calling the 'last of *December New-Year's-Eve*, (Rubric *after the Collect for* 'St Stephen's-day), in condescension to the capacities of the people, 'and to avoid confusion; and yet expressly says, that the '*Ecclesiastic* year begins not till *Lady-day*, so she does the same 'thing in calling the beginning of the greater Festivals, the *Evening* '*next before*, namely, because according to the State Account, the 'foregoing day is not ended till *Twelve at Night:* Tho' I think 'all Divines, Rationalists, and Canonists, are agreed, that the Sacred 'Day begins at *six in the Evening*, and which yet once at least, 'viz. in the Collect on *Purification-day*, the Church mentions as 'part of the Feast.'—*Vade-Mecum.* Vol. i. *p.* 198 (174.)

WHEATLY, after quoting the earlier portion of the preceding paragraph from JOHNSON'S *Vade-Mecum* with regard to the *Collect* for the '*Purification*' being read on the Evening before, adds:—'But 'against this supposition lie two objections: the one is, that there 'are very few Churches which begin Prayers *after six in the* '*Evening*, which Mr. Johnson affirms to be the proper time for 'Vespers or Even-song: though if they did, the same difficulty 'would occur what *Collect* we must use at Evening Prayer upon 'the Festival itself, for then, according to Mr. Johnson, another day 'begins. But farther, if the day begins *at six o'clock on the Evening* '*before*, then the Collect of every Festival ought to be used on 'the foregoing Evening; whereas the *Rubric* only orders, that the '*Collects* for *Sundays*, and such *Holy-days* as have *Vigils* and *Eves*, 'be said at the preceding Evening Service, and consequently 'supposes that the Collects of such Festivals as have no Vigils 'are only to be used upon the Festivals themselves.' In a *Note* WHEATLY further remarks:—'Mr. Johnson has been pleased to 'reply to this, that "it is so certain that *six is the hour of* "*Even-song*, that no man will dispute it who is not a perfect "stranger to things of this nature." That it was so formerly, 'whilst the old canonical hours of prayer were strictly observed, 'I readily allow. But that it is so still, I was not aware: for I own 'myself to be so much a stranger to things of this nature, as to 'have been hitherto of the opinion (though I shall be glad to alter 'it, when I shall be better informed) that, upon reducing the seven 'Offices into two, viz. MATINS and EVEN-SONG, or Morning and 'Evening Prayer, as we now generally call them, there were no 'hours fixed for the saying of either. The same learned gentlemen 'says farther in the same place, that "they who terminate the "Feasts within certain minutes, and because *six is the hour of* "*Vespers* will allow no latitude, have never considered that in "the Scripture language (which is the best guide in this matter) "what is expressed by the *Evening and going down of Sun*, in "one text (*Deut.* xvi. 6.), is called the time *between the two* "*Evenings* in another (*Exod.* xii. 6.). And the time of the "Evening Sacrifice is expressed by this last phrase (*Numb.* "xxviii. 4.). And it is notorious that this was any time between "the *ninth* and *twelfth* according to them, the *third* and *sixth* with "us." These texts of Scripture I have seen before; and have since 'considered how far they help Mr. Johnson's argument. But I 'cannot see yet that they prove any more than that they who 'began the day punctually at *six* one evening, ended it as 'punctually at *six* the next. But that the Church of England 'divides her nights and days according to the scriptural, and not 'the civil account, is his assertion, and not mine. To him it is 'clear, but not to me, that Feasts are to be kept from *Even-song* 'to *Even-song* inclusively. That the Festival day is not past till '*Even-song* is ended, I willingly grant: but that the Festival begins 'at *Even-song before*, wants, I think, a better proof. That the '*Collect* for a Holy-day that hath a Vigil or Eve, is to be said at the '*Evening Service next before*, the Rubric appoints: but that the 'Evening before is therefore part of the Festival, I know not how 'to reconcile with another Rubric that calls the *Eve* or *Vigil* a 'Fast. I rather take it, that the *Evenings before* such Festivals 'as have *Vigils* are designed by the Church to be preparations 'to the Festivals, rather than parts of them: and therefore I know 'not what Mr. Johnson means when he tells us, "that *Holy-days* "which begin not till Morning Prayer are not perfect Feasts, but "were deemed to be of inferior rank by them that had the ordering "of these matters." When he gives us his authority for what he 'asserts, I shall readily submit: but till then I shall be of the 'opinion, that some Festivals which have not Vigils are as perfect 'Feasts as some others which have: and that their not having 'Vigils assigned them, was not because they are of inferior rank, 'but for the other reasons that I have given above.' (*p.* 208).—*Rat. Ill. of Book of Com. Prayer.* (Dr. Corrie's Ed.).

In Abp. Islep's *Constitutions*, A. D. 1362, we read:—'In the first 'place the holy *Lord's day*, beginning at *Vespers* on *the Sabbath-day*, '*not before*, lest we should seem professed Jews: and let this be 'observed in Feasts that have their *Vigils*,' &c.—Johnson's *Canons*, Vol. II. *p.* 426.

Bp. Warburton, in his Notes on Wheatly's Illustration of the Book of Common Prayer, writes:—'Suppose it true that the 'Ecclesiastical day begins at *six in the Evening;* yet how does it 'appear that *Vespers* and *six o'clock* are the same? *Six o'clock* 'is rather the time for *Compline*, being the twelfth hour.—See 'the *Missale Gallicanum Vetus*, where the *Vespera* is distinct from, 'and prior to, the *duodecima* [*De Liturgia Gallica*, *p.* 356.] And 'yet *duodecima* is the *initium noctis* not the *Vespera*. (See 'Mabillon's Note). Many like instances might be given from old 'Missals. See the *Missal Goth.* p. 240, where the *Vespera* is plainly 'distinct from *initium noctis*. *Vespers* have been very differently 'reckoned at different times, and in different places. The *Hora* '*Lucernaris* was towards the close of the day, sometimes at 3 *o'clock* 'or *Nones*, sometimes at 6 *o'clock*, or 12*th hour*, and sometimes 'at 5 *o'clock*, or 11*th hour*. *Six o'clock* seems to have been 'calculated only for the old division of the day by four canonical 'hours at the end of every quarter of the day, or at every three 'hours. *Tertia*, 3 in the morning; *Sexta*, 12 o'clock; *Nona*, 3 in 'the afternoon; *Vespera*, 6 o'clock. But this order was altered 'after the *Prima* and *Compline* were introduced: one at *seven* in the 'Morning, the other at *six* in the Evening. Then *Vespers* were 'at *five* in the Evening. For thus were the hours reckoned here in 'Wickliff's time: 1. *Prima*, 7 o'clock; 2. *Undern*, 9 o'clock; '3. *Mid-day*, 12 o'clock; 4. *None*, 3 o'clock; 5. *Evensong;* 6. *Compline*, '6 o'clock. (See Mabillon, *de Liturg. Gallican.* p. 55.). May not 'the Festival as well be supposed to begin at 3 *o'clock in the* '*Afternoon* before? This was the rule for *Sunday's Festival* by 'the laws of *Edgar* and *Knute*......I do not, however, think that the 'Ecclesiastical division of the days (whatever it be) is concerned in 'the matter. The reason rather for the rule of *Collects* before and 'after the precise days is to be fetched from the law of the Festival, 'which may be a *whole week* in some case or longer: and so long 'the *same Collect* is proper. Proper for the time that we are 'ordered to meditate particularly on that Festival to the time that 'it ceases, or is succeeded by something else. As to the words "this day," used in the *foregoing Evening* to the *Purification*, they 'mean only '*this time:*' or possibly the compilers of the Collect 'might not consider that it was to be used otherwise than upon the 'very day.—*Vigils* in old Calendars are never reckoned *to the day* 'of the Festivals, but always to the day preceding. (See Vigil of 'John Baptist, June 23rd in Bede, and June 28th.).'—DR. CORRIE'S Edition, *p.* 202.

Rev. W. PLUMMER says:—'It is worthy of consideration, 'whether the *Psalms* and *Lessons* ought not to follow the same 'rule; that is, whether precisely the same service ought not to 'be said on St Bartholomew's Eve at *six o'clock in the Evening*, as is 'said on St Bartholomew's Day at *three o'clock in the afternoon;* 'and so on throughout the year. Mariners always consider the day 'to *begin at six o'clock in the evening*, and it appears to me that 'the Church does the same. If this rule were followed, the mixing 'of the *Collect* for one Festival with the *Lessons* and *Psalms* of 'another, would be avoided: and the Service for each day would be 'kept distinct.' (*p.* 92).—*Observations on Book of Com. Prayer.*

A Sunday no Eve.

367.—When a Feast-day falls on a *Monday*, the Eve, if it has one, is not to be kept on the *Sunday Evening* before, but on the *Saturday Evening* previous, as is enjoined, not only in a Rubric of the Book of Common Prayer, but in the Statute law. The *Rubric* thus reads:—

(*d*). ¶. '*Note, that if any of these Feast-days fall upon a 'Monday, then the Vigil or Fast-day shall be kept 'upon the Saturday, and not upon the Sunday next 'before it.*' (1662).—Present Book of Common Prayer.

By Act of Parliament, it is directed:—

'When any of the said Feasts (the Evens whereof be by this 'Statute 5 & 6 *Edw.* VI., commanded to be observed and kept 'Fasting-days) do fall upon the *Monday*, then the *Saturday* next 'before, and *not the Sunday*, shall be commanded to be fasted for 'the EVEN of any such Feast, or Holy-day.'—5 & 6 *Edw.* VI. *c.* 3. *s.* 5.

368.—In such cases, therefore, the *Collect* to be used on the *Saturday* EVENING SERVICE, if such Service is at 6 *o'clock*, or later, must be that of the Monday's Festival, and the Collect of the Sunday which would have otherwise been employed, must be omitted.

We will quote the opinions of *Wheatly*, and of *Archdeacon Sharp.*—

WHEATLY observes:—'All *Sundays* in the year being appointed 'by the Church to be observed as Festivals, no *Vigil* is allowed 'to be kept upon any of those days: there being a particular Rubric 'to order, *that if any of the Feast-days that have a Vigil fall upon a 'Monday, then the Vigil or Fast-day shall be kept upon the 'Saturday, not upon the Sunday next before it.* But from hence a 'query ariseth, viz., on which EVENING SERVICE the *Collect for the 'Festival* is to be used: the Rubric indeed relating to this matter 'seems to be worded very plain, viz., *That the Collect appointed for 'every Sunday, or for any Holy-day that hath a Vigil or Eve, shall 'be said at the Evening Service next before;* but then this Rubric 'seems to suppose that the day before is the *Vigil* or *Eve;* and 'makes no provision in case the Festival falls upon the *Monday*, 'when we are directed by the Rubric above cited to keep the *Vigil* 'or Fast upon the *Saturday*. Here then we are left at an 'uncertainty, nor can we get any light by comparing our present 'Liturgy with any former Common Prayer Book, because both 'these Rubrics, together with the table of *Vigils* or *Eves*, were first 'added at the last Review. According to MR. JOHNSON, indeed, 'who imagines that the Collect for the Festival is appointed to 'be used upon the Evening before, because then the Holy-day 'properly begins, we ought to read the Collect upon the *Sunday 'evening*, though the *Vigil* be kept upon the *Saturday*. For he 'observes, that "the Church of England has divided her *nights* and "*days* according to the Scriptural, not the Civil account:" and "that "though our civil day begins from *Midnight* yet our ecclesiastical "day begins at *six in the evening*. And therefore the Collect for "the Sunday is to be read on what in our civil account is called "*Saturday Evening*, and the Collect for every greater Festival at "EVENING PRAYER next before." (*p.* 201).—*Rat. Ill. Book of Com. Prayer.*

ARCHDEACON SHARPE writes:—'It is uncertain, as the directions 'now stand, whether the *Collect for a Holy-day* that hath a *Vigil* '(supposing the Lord's day to intervene between the Vigil and 'the Festival) shall be read *"on the Eve"* on which the *Vigil* is 'ordered to be observed, or "in the *Evening immediately before*" '*the Festival* according to another Rubric. They whose rule it is to 'act closely up to the letter of Rubric, must *separate the Collect 'from the Vigil.* But they who plead the supposed intention and 'reason of both the Rubrics, think they may dispense with the 'letter of that Rubric which orders the Collect to be read on the 'Evening before the Holy-day, and use the *Collect on the Vigil* 'in compliance with the supposed design of the other Rubric. In 'either case conformity to Rubric is aimed at, though diversity 'of practice necessarily prevents uniformity.' (*p.* 61).—*On Rubric and Canons.* Charge, A. D. 1735.

369.—It must also be borne in mind that on all those occasions in which the *Collect of the Holy-day* is used at any EVENING SERVICE, the *Collect of the Sunday*, directed to be used on all ordinary days during the week, must be *omitted;* for the using of *two Collects*, except especially ordered, is not sanctioned by the Book of Common Prayer.

WHEATLY observes:—'Whenever the *Collect of a Sunday* or 'Holy-day is read at the EVENING SERVICE *before*, the *weekly* '*Collect* that had been in course must be omitted and give place. 'And the same rule, as I take it, should be observed upon the '*Holy-day itself*, upon which *no other Collect* ought to be used, 'but the proper one for the day. For the Rubric, at the end of "*The order how the rest of Holy Scripture is appointed to be read*," 'directs, that *the Collect*, &c. *for the Sunday shall serve all the week* '*after, where it is not otherwise ordered*; which supposes, that in 'some places it is otherwise ordered, which must be (as it was 'worded in all the old Common Prayer Books) when *there falls* '*some feast that hath his proper*, i.e. when any day falls that hath a 'proper or peculiar *Collect*, &c. to itself: upon which occasions 'the *Rubric* plainly supposes, that the *Collect for the Sunday* shall 'be left out and omitted: the Church never designing to use '*two Collects* at once, except within the octaves of *Christmas*, and 'during *Advent* and *Lent*; when, for the greater solemnity of those 'solemn seasons, she particularly orders the *Collects* of the principal 'days to be used continually after the ordinary Collects.' (*p.* 205).—*Rat. Ill. of Book of Com. Prayer.* Dr. Corrie's Ed.

With some Ritualists, however, there is a difference of opinion.

The Rev. J. PURCHAS writes:—'When the second Evensong 'of a Festival concurs with the first Evensong of a commencing 'Festival, the proper use of Collects on such Evensong will be '(1) Coll. for the Office of the morrow, (2) Coll. for the day.' (*p.* 80).—*Directorium Anglicanum.*

370.—From what has been now advanced respecting the *first Collect* of the EVENING SERVICE, it may be laid down as the customary usage:—

I. *That* the *Collect of the Sunday* is to be used at the EVENING SERVICE *next before*, i.e. on *Saturday Evening;* provided the SERVICE is not earlier than 6 *o'clock*, P.M.—(*Rubric* before the Collects.)

II. *That* when a *Holy-Day* occurs, and that Holy-Day has a *Vigil* or *Eve* prescribed in the Book of Common Prayer, the *Collect of that Holy-Day* must be used on the *Vigil* or *Eve* going before; if, that is to say, the SERVICE of the *Vigil* or *Eve* is not earlier than 6 *o'clock*, P.M.—(*Rubric* before the Collects.)

III. *That* when the *Holy-Day* having an appointed *Vigil* or *Eve* falls on a MONDAY, the *Vigil* or *Eve* is to be kept on the *Saturday* before, and not on the Sunday.—(*Rubric* in the TABLE *of the Vigils*, &c.)

*** *Note.*—Those who hold that *all Holy-Days* have *Eves* require the *Collect of the Holy-day* to be employed in the EVENING SERVICE just before, even if it be a Sunday. (See *supra*, par. 366.)

IV. *That* the *Collect of the Sunday* is to serve all the week after, except when otherwise ordered by the Rubric.—(*Note* in the Preface, in "*The Order How the Rest of Holy Scripture is appointed to be read.*").

ANNOUNCING THE COLLECT.

371.—*Announcing the Collect* to the Congregation is a usage not imposed by the Rubric, and, therefore, as has been observed in the MORNING PRAYER, should not be adopted. (See *par.* 248, *supra.*)

THE POSTURE.

372.—The *posture* to be assumed by Minister and People during the repetition of this, and the following Collects, is not imposed in the Rubric here; but in the parallel Rubric in the MORNING PRAYER "*all kneeling*" is enjoined; which, therefore, may well be admitted as the proper attitude in this place for Minister as well as People. The Rubric of the *First* Liturgy of *Edw.* VI. (1549), directed the Priest to "*stand;*" thus—

'*The Priest standing up and saying,*
'Let us pray.
'*Then the Collect of the Day.*' (KEELING, *p.* 25.).

But this injunction was omitted from the subsequent Liturgies, and in the *Revision* of 1662, the present Liturgy, the order, '*all kneeling*,' was introduced; and this is the general practice; although in some few Churches, particularly where undue preference is given to the Rubrics of the Liturgy of 1549, as following the more ancient usages imposed in the old Service Books, '*standing*' is observed.

'*The Second Collect at Evening Prayer.*'

The Collect for Peace.

(The Minister and People still kneeling).

373.—The *Collect for Peace* has occupied a place in the Offices of the English Church for upwards of 1200 years, and has been found as early as A. D. 494, in the Sacramentary of Gelasius. It differs in language from its twin Collect in the MORNING PRAYER, yet the subject is the same, viz., supplication for peace; but rather *inward* peace, as the more essential requisite for the repose of night.

The *Posture* for Minister and People is that of *kneeling*.

DEAN COMBER (*ob.* 1699) writes:—'*Peace* is so desirable a 'blessing, we cannot ask it too often; and since there are two kinds 'of peace, *external* and *internal* peace, we by outward peace in the 'Morning to secure us against the troubles of the world, in which 'the business of the day engageth us; and *inward* peace in the 'EVENING to comfort and quiet our minds when we are to take our 'rest.'—(quoted in MANT's *Book of Com. Prayer*, in loco.).

WHEATLY says:—'But in that for the EVENING we ask for '*inward* tranquillity, requesting *for that peace which the world* '*cannot give;* as springing only from the testimony of a good 'conscience; that so each of us may with David be enabled to 'say, "*I will lay me down in peace, and take my rest,*" (Ps. iii. 8.); 'having our hearts as easy as our heads, and our sleep sweet 'and quiet.' (*p.* 155).—*Rat. Ill. of Book of Com. Prayer.*

'*The Third Collect for Aid against all Perils.*'

(The Minister and People still kneeling.)

374.—This Collect is peculiar to EVENING PRAYER, and has been so employed for nearly 1400 years. It is found also in the Sacramentaries of

Gregory, A. D. 590, and Gelasius, A. D. 494. Prior to the *last Review* of the Prayer Book in 1662, this Collect concluded the printed Office; yet it was customary to employ the Prayers which follow, with the exception of that of *St Chrysostom*, then annexed to the LITANY.

In the *First* Liturgy of *Edw.* VI. (1549), the closing words of this Collect were '*Jesu Christ,*' not 'Jesus Christ,' which latter was an amendment of the *Second* Liturgy (of 1552).

In the '*Alterations*' suggested by the Royal Commissioners in 1689, it was proposed to erase, "*Lighten our darkness we beseech thee, O Lord, and,*" and to substitute in their place, "*Almighty God who hast hitherto preserv'd us in safety this day, by thy &c.*"*

BISHOP PATRICK also desired to insert after the word '*night,*' as follows:—

'Pardon whatsoever we have done amiss and settle our holy 'purposes to do better for the time to come: That, laying ourselves 'down to sleep with these godly Resolutions in our hearts, They 'may awaken with us in the Morning, and we may daily grow more 'watchful in all our waies, for the love of thy only Son our Saviour 'Jesus Christ. Amen.' (*p.* 14).—*Alterations in the Book of Com. Prayer*, &c.; printed by *order of House of Commons*, June, 1854.

But these suggestions were never effected.

The *posture*, like as in the other Collects, is to be that of *kneeling* for both Minister and People.

DEAN COMBER observes:—' This is peculiar to and proper for the 'Evening. We are always indeed environed with danger; but none 'are more dismal, sudden and unavoidable, than those of the night, 'when darkness adds to the terror, and sleep deprives us of all 'possibility of foresight or defence; so that he must be an atheist, 'and worse than heathen, who doth not then by a special prayer 'commit himself to God's providence, the knowledge of which doth

* In the AMERICAN LITURGY a similar alteration has been made. In the place of "*Lighten our darkness, we beseech thee, O Lord; and,*" we find these words—"*O Lord our heavenly Father, by whose Almighty power we have been preserved this day;* By thy great mercy," &c.

'enlighten our minds, and makes us full of inward peace and 'comfort when we are in the darkest shades of night: therefore 'we pray with David, "*Lighten our darkness we beseech Thee, 'O Lord,*" (Ps. xviii. 28.) Light signifies, in Scripture, knowledge 'and comfort, and under this metaphor we pray for both, namely, 'that our understandings may be enlightened with the knowledge 'of His providence, and our hearts cheered with the assurance of 'His protection.'—(quoted in MANT'S *Book of Com. Prayer*, in loco.)

THE ANTHEM.

¶. '*In Quires and Places where they sing, here followeth the 'Anthem.*' (1662).—Present Book of Com. Prayer.

(The Minister and People standing).

375.—The singing of an *Anthem* here, and in the parallel place in the MORNING PRAYER, was not enjoined before the last *Revision* in 1662, when the above Rubric was introduced in each Office. The origin of the term, and the nature of the *Anthem*, have been already touched upon (*pars.* 254, 255, *supra*); therefore, we need merely observe here, that it is more usual to sing a *Hymn* or *Anthem* at this place in the EVENING SERVICE than in the MORNING SERVICE, on account of the Office in the former case being briefer. Where an *Anthem* would prove too elaborate, a *Hymn* is generally introduced, especially in Village Churches. Whatever is to be sung, however, should be given out by the Minister, or one of the Officiating Clergymen, if more are present, rather than by the *Lay-Clerk*. Nor is it *essential*, although, indeed, it has become very customary, to introduce by way of preface to what is to be sung, these words—"*Let us sing to the praise and glory of " God.*" That the singing is to the praise and glory of God is a matter of course, and known to all.

The *posture* at singing, and at all offering of praise, is universally, in the Church of England, that of '*standing*.'

[A SERMON.]

376.—The original intention of the *Sermon* was to illustrate and explain the portion of Scripture appointed for the Gospel, whence the ancient name given to it of *Postil*, i. e. *post illa* (sc. Evangelica), the exposition of the Preacher. And on which account also we find the *Sermon* following, as directed in the Rubric, as closely as possible the reading of the Gospel in the Ante-Communion Office of the MORNING SERVICE; a circumstance which gave rise to the assertion—during the controversy upon the Preaching Dress, whether, that is to say, it should be Surplice or Gown,—that the *Sermon* is a *part of* the Communion Office. But in the EVENING SERVICE there is no portion of the Communion Office introduced, and, consequently, no reading of Scripture except what is appointed for *the Lessons*, and none requiring elucidation but these *Lessons*; hence the introduction, occasionally, of a *Sermon* at this particular place, although no mention is made of an *Evening Sermon* in the Book of Common Prayer. Ever since the Reformation the EVENING SERVICE on the Sunday in some Cathedrals, and other Churches, has been constantly accompanied by a *Sermon*. Still, for the most part, the *catechizing of the Children* before the commencement of EVENING PRAYER, or *after the Second Lesson*, had been allowed for a long period to answer the purpose. In more modern days, however, a *Sermon* has been deemed requisite; and it is usually delivered at the close of EVENING PRAYER; but in some few instances it has been introduced in this place, *immediately after the Anthem*, as in Westminster Abbey, &c., and in some London, and other city Churches.

377.—In those Cathedrals and Churches where the *Sermon* is delivered *immediately after the Anthem*, it is the usual practice for the Preacher to pass from the *Reading-Desk*, or his *Stall* in the Chancel, to the Pulpit, habited in the Surplice; and at the termination of his discourse to return to the place whence he moved, and there remain till the conclusion of EVENING PRAYER. As this usage, with regard to the time of delivering the *Sermon*, prevails only in Cathedrals, and with the stricter Rubricians, the preaching in a Gown at this part of the Service is very rarely seen. After the *Sermon*, where such is here preached, the Officiating Minister proceeds with

THE FIVE PRAYERS.

378.—The *five Prayers*, which now follow, are identical with those employed in the like place in the MORNING PRAYER, and as we have already discussed their characteristic features when going through the Rubrics of the MORNING OFFICE (see *pars.* 257—270, *supra*), we shall have but little to say respecting them here.

'*A Prayer for the Queen's Majesty.*'

(Minister and People still kneeling).

379.—This Prayer, and those for the Royal Family, for the Clergy and People, and that of St Chrysostom, are generally regarded as *Memoriæ*, or Commemorations. In the previous Liturgies, they stood at the end of the Litany, and were only introduced into the MORNING and EVENING OFFICES at the *last Review* in 1662.

Among the '*Alterations*,' &c., suggested by the Royal Commissioners in 1689, it was proposed with regard to the Prayer for the reigning Monarch to strike out the words '*most gracious*' before '*Sovereign Lord and Lady*.' Likewise, after "*heavenly gifts*," it was recommended to insert "*direct all their counsels to thy Honour and Glory, bless all their righteous undertakings*." And again, "*strengthen them that they may vanquish and overcome all*," were struck through for omission. Further, the words "*and finally*" were amended to "*and that*." (Printed by *order of the House of Commons*, June, 1854.) But none of these changes were carried into effect. (See also *pars*. 257, 258, supra).

'A Prayer for the Royal Family.'

(Minister and People still kneeling).

380.—What alterations may be imposed by the Privy Council under the authority of the Statute, 13 & 14 *Car*. II. *c*. 4. *s*. 25, by reason of any removal by death of the ruling Monarch, or change in the title of a Member of the Royal Family, should be carefully noted by the Officiating Minister in the margin of the Prayer Book. For further remarks, see *pars*. 258, 259, *supra*.

'A Prayer for the Clergy and People.'

(Minister and People still kneeling).

381.—This Prayer is of very great antiquity, as has been already observed; nor have we any thing to add beyond what we have already advanced. (See *pars*. 260—262. *supra*).

[THE OCCASIONAL PRAYERS.]

¶. 'PRAYERS AND THANKSGIVINGS UPON SEVERAL OCCASIONS '*To be used before the two final Prayers of the Litany, or of 'Morning and Evening Prayer*.'—Present Book of Common Prayer.

382.—The above *Rubric*, which stands at the head of the PRAYERS and THANKSGIVINGS following the LITANY, directs that here, before the *two final Prayers*, are to be introduced such of the OCCASIONAL PRAYERS and THANKSGIVINGS as occasion may require. Some of them are but rarely called for. Those of constant occurrence, and used in the EVENING SERVICE are—

1. The *Prayer in the Ember Weeks* for those about to be 'ordained.' (See *supra*. Vol. B.)

2. The *Prayer for the Parliament* during the Session.

3. The *Prayer for All Conditions of Men*. (It must not be forgotten to give public notice of such '*sick persons*' as desire the Prayers of the Church in their behalf *before commencing* this Collect. It is usual, though not strictly Rubrical, to proclaim,—'*The Prayers of the Congregation* (or *Church*) *are desired for A. B.—C. D.—&c.*' The names, however, need only be mentioned the first time, if they are numerous; and in such cases say, '*for many sick Persons.*' At the marginal intimations in the Prayer, immediately following 'body, or estate,' say, as the Rubric directs, '*especially those* (or *him*, or *her*) *for whom our Prayers* '*are desired*,' and make some *slight pause*, so as to give opportunity to any of the Congregation to add some inward supplication.). See *postea*.

Archdeacon Sharp writes:—'The Rubrics are deficient in 'their direction, whether, before "the *General Intercession*" or "the *General Thanksgiving*" in the daily Service, the names of 'those persons who "*desire the prayers of the Congregation*," or "*desire to return thanks*," shall be publicly recited or no. Some 'suppose, both from the reason of the thing, and from the wording 'of the interpolations to be used on those occasions, that it is 'implied, the names of the persons, on whose account the additions 'are to be inserted in the prayers, should be particularly recited, 'and notified to the congregation. But others, who suppose this 'will fall under the notion of "*publications in time of Divine* "*Service*," which by another Rubric is limited to the injunctions of 'the Ordinary, will for that reason be of another opinion.' (*p.* 62).—*On the Rubric and Canons*. Charge, A. D. 1735.

4. The *General Thanksgiving*. (Before commencing this *Thanksgiving*, the Churching of Women must take place, where such is the custom. (See Churching of Women, *postea*). The *names* also of those who wish to offer thanks to Almighty God for any special mercies must here be proclaimed; and care taken to introduce in its proper place the marginal Rubric, viz.:—"*particularly to those* (or *him*, or *her*) "*who desire* (or *desires*) *now to offer up their* (or *his*, " or *her*) *praises and thanksgivings for Thy late mercies* "*vouchsafed unto them*," (or *him*, or *her*). The *Woman* who may have just been '*Churched*,' which service is her especial thanksgiving, must have no distinct participation in this "*General Thanksgiving*.") See *postea*.

Bp. Mant remarks:—'The "*Churching of Women*" seems to me 'to take its place most suitably with the other "Thanksgivings "upon several occasions," or before "the *General Thanksgiving*," 'but is *not to be alluded to therein.* The Minister should continue 'in his Reading Pew, the woman "kneeling down in some "convenient place," such "as hath been accustomed," or "as the "ordinary," if there be cause for consulting him, "shall direct." (*p.* 51).—*Horæ Liturgicæ.*

The three *Prayers* above enumerated, and the *General Thanksgiving,* having been said, *all still kneeling,* the Officiating Minister will then pass to

'*The Prayer of S. Chrysostom.*'

(The Minister and People still kneeling.)

383.—This Prayer has been fully elucidated in its place in the MORNING OFFICE, to which we will refer our Readers for any information respecting it they may desire. (See *pars.* 264, 265, *supra*).

The Benedictory Prayer.
'2 *Cor.* xiii.'

(Minister and People still kneeling).

384.—The closing of the EVENING OFFICE with a '*Benedictory*' *Prayer* has been in use both in the Greek and Latin Churches from about the 4th century: and we find the practice existed also in the Anglo-Saxon period of our own Church. But this Prayer was not introduced into our Liturgy till *the Revision* of 1559, when it was placed at the end of the *Litany.* In the *last Review,* 1662, it was also made the termination of the MORNING, and EVENING, OFFICES.

385.—The words in the Prayer Book slightly differ from those used by S. Paul. The change from the second person to the first, from "*you*" to "*us,*" naturally imparts to the passage the character of a *prayer* rather than of a *benediction,* as the original was designed to be. The consequence is, that, like as with prayers, the *posture* of both Minister and People should be that of *kneeling*. Were it purely a *benediction*, then the Minister might *stand*, as is usually done at the Benediction closing the Communion Office. (See *pars*. 266—268, *supra*). The value of the Priest's benediction in that place is thus beautifully expressed by Bp. Sparrow:—

Bp. Sparrow (*ob.* 1685) says:—'This Blessing of the Bishop or 'Priest was so highly esteem'd in the primitive times, that none 'durst go out of Church till they had receiv'd it, according to 'the Council of *Agatha*, Can. 31. in the year 472. And the third of '*Orleans*, Can. 22. And when they received it, they did it *kneeling*, '*or bowing down their head*. And the Deacon, to prepare them 'to it, was wont to call out immediately before the time of the 'Blessing, in such words as these; "*Bow down yourselves to the* "*Blessing*," Chrys. Liturg. The *Jews* received it after the same 'manner, *Ecclus*. c. 1. v. 19, 20, 21......And the same promise of 'God's assistance, and ratifying the Priest's Blessing, we have in the Gospel, St *Matt*. x. 13. St *Luke* x. 5., where our Saviour charges 'his Apostles and Disciples, that into whatsoever House they enter, 'they should *say* not *pray*; *Say* with authority, "*Peace be to this* "*house*," and (not if your prayers be fervent, or if they in the 'house join in prayer with you, but) "*if the Son of Peace be there*"; 'that is, if he that dwells in the house hinders not, nor resists your 'Blessing, if he be a person capable of so much good as your 'Blessing, (for this is signified by this Hebrew Phrase, *Son of* '*Peace*) "*your Peace shall rest upon him*": But if he be not such a 'Son of Peace, "*your Blessing shall return to you again*"; which it 'could not be said to do, unless Virtue, together with the Blessing, 'had gone out from them.' (*p.* 57).—*Rationale*.

[The Psalmody.]

386.—The *Benedictory Prayer* being concluded, the Congregation, if there be *no Sermon*, disperse; if otherwise, a *Psalm* or *Hymn*, in some few Churches a *Sanctus*, is here introduced, and the Preacher meanwhile ascends the Pulpit. It is the duty of the *Officiating Minister* to 'give out' the Psalmody, and *not the Parish-Clerk*, or other *Lay-functionary*.

Bp. Mant observes:—'It is the order of the Church, that "*nothing shall be proclaimed or published in the Church*," during the 'time of Divine Service, *but by the Minister*. Therefore the 'singing of a *Psalm* should be proclaimed, not by the *Parish Clerk*, 'or any other person, but the *Clergyman*. There is a decency and 'propriety in calling upon the Congregation to "*sing to the praise* '*and glory of God*:" and it is well to remind them of the fit 'posture for that act of devotion. I know of no more suitable 'form of announcement than this: "*Let us stand up and sing to the* '*praise and glory of God such a Psalm, such and such verses*." (*p.* 52).—*Hor. Lit.*

There has been, however, a difference of opinion expressed on this matter, which, to be just, we must also quote.

The Rev. E. Scobell, referring to the Rubrics of the *first* Liturgy of Edw. VI. when speaking of the Vestments, quotes the following:—"Then shall the *Clearkes* sing in English for the Office "or Introit, as they call it, a Psalme appointed for that day." To this he adds:—'And it was the duty of one of these *Lay-Clearkes*, 'who "form a part of the foundation of Cathedrals and whose "special duty it is to perform the Service to Music," to *give out* 'or name the Psalm or Hymn to be sung: a duty still performed in 'Cathedrals, and in Parish Churches also, where the *Parish Clerk* 'is the Precentor or Leader of Singing upon the same principle.' (*p.* 36).—*Thoughts on Church Matters.*

The Quarterly Review remarks:—'It has been usual, as 'we all know, for the Parish Clerk to '*give out*,' as it is called the 'metrical Psalm, in this formula—'*Let us sing to the praise and* '*glory of God*'— so and so—and after quoting the Rubric following 'the Nicene Creed, which says that "nothing shall be proclaimed "and published in the Church during Divine Service but by the "Minister," which, the Reviewer adds, some ultra-Rubricians 'consider forbids the *Clerk* to give out the Psalm! We really 'cannot conceive any grounds for this opinion......who......can 'doubt that the prohibition as to *proclamations* and *publications* has 'relation only to extraneous or secular matters, and not to such 'a point of ritual routine as the giving out the Psalm, which 'cannot in common sense be called either *proclaiming* or '*publishing?* Then see the practical consequences; the *Minister* 'assumes the duty hitherto performed by the *Clerk*, which *Clerk* 'the Canon directs to be chosen '*for his competent skill in* '*singing*'—so that when the *Minister* shall say 'Let *us* sing, &c.,' 'it might be expected that he would indeed sing out the Psalm 'as the Clerk used to do. But no such thing......the *Minister* says "*Let us sing*," but never attempts to sing, he *reads* out the 1*st verse*, 'and leaves the *Clerk* and the *Congregation* to do the rest. Now if 'it be proper that the Minister shall *proclaim* or *publish* the 1*st* 'verse of the Psalm before the Congregation shall presume to sing 'it—why not the 2*nd*, why not the 3*rd* verses?—with which, 'however, we have never heard him meddle; for alas! after having 'exclaimed from the Altar '*Let us sing*,' and given out the 1*st* verse, 'he forthwith retires into the Vestry to put on his Gown for the 'Sermon, and does not re-appear until the *Psalm* is nearly done, 'in which, even then he does not pretend to join, but kneels down 'in the Pulpit in private prayer. Here is a tissue of contradictions, 'whereas in the Old practice there was consistency, and, what is 'still better, good sense......It may be said that this *rationale* of 'ours only applies to the Psalm in this one part of the Service— 'just so; but, according to the new practice, this is the only place 'where a Psalm *can* be properly sung, because as, *ex hypothesi*, 'the giving out the Psalm is a *proclamation* or *publication*, and 'as there is no other place appointed for proclamation or publication 'than between the Nicene Creed and the Sermon, no Psalm ought 'to be given out except in that interval; and lo! in that interval 'there is no *Rubrical* authority for *singing* at all! Nor indeed is 'there any authority for any extraneous singing, except as to the '*Anthem* in places where *they* sing; i.e. not the *Minister* nor even 'the Congregation, but *Choristers* and persons appointed to sing. 'But that is not all. If the Minister is bound to give out the '*Psalm*, and repeat the 1*st verse*, why is he not equally bound 'to give out and repeat the *Anthem?* This would be—if the point 'be worth reasoning—much more necessary, because the *Psalm* is an 'authorized form of words—the *Anthem* is any thing that the chief 'of the Choir chooses to sing:—to be sure he acts under orders—'but so does the Clerk; but if the one may not give out the *Psalm*, 'how can the other give utterance to the *Anthem?*..... By this 'over-strict interpretation of the Rubric they are establishing, in 'this trifle, a serious departure from the Rubric. Can they shew 'us by what *Rubric* the *Metrical* Psalms are sung in Churches at 'all; by what *Rubrical* authority the *Minister* can announce 'them?......The *Metrical* PSALMS are not recognized by any Rubric, 'unless introduced in Quires and 'places where they sing' as an '*Anthem*, and therefore the wise and prudent usage has been—'not that the Minister shall make the *metrical version* part of 'the Liturgy, but that, at certain intervals of the Minister's duty, 'the *Clerk* should invite the rest of the Congregation to sing to the 'praise and glory of God one of the Metrical Psalms, which 'although no part of the Liturgical Office, and therefore *not to* '*be given out by the Minister*, are allowed by Royal authority, and 'may be voluntarily sung in the intervals we have stated by the 'Congregation, of whom the *Clerk* is the Coryphæus......we have 'confident hopes that this practice...will be on better consideration 'abandoned — that the Minister may be relieved from an 'embarrassing and almost ridiculous position, and that the *Metrical* '*Psalms* may not be treated as if they formed (which they do not) 'an integral part of the Liturgy.' (*pp*. 282—4).—In a *Note*—'Those hypercritics who fancy they can find in the Rubric a 'prohibition to the *Clerk's* giving out the Psalm would find it much 'more difficult to find any Rubrical authority for having a *Clerk* 'at all. *Clerks* are only authorized by custom, and by the Canon.' (*p*. 284).—No. cxliii. *May*, 1843.

387.—When in the Pulpit, the Preacher *either* kneels down on entering to offer up a private supplication for the assistance of the Holy Spirit on what he is about to say, *or* he awaits, *standing*, the conclusion of the singing or introit. No *sitting* is sanctioned in the Pulpit. (See *pars*. 270—272, *supra*).

388.—Occasionally there may be one or more Clergymen *assisting* the Officiating Minister; in such instances the division of the 'duty' varies according to the number there may be engaged. The more usual partition is for the *chief Minister* to take the portions especially belonging to the priestly function, and for the *assistant Cleric* to read the Psalms, Lessons, and more secondary parts. The SERVICE may also be distributed into—(*a*) the *Introduction* to the end of the Lord's Prayer; (*b*) the *Psalmody and Reading* to the end of the Apostles' Creed: (*c*) the *Collects and Prayers* to the close of the Office. (See page 1105). Or another may minister at *Baptisms*, or at *Churchings*, or at the *Litany*. With regard to the COMMUNION OFFICE see *postea*.

[THE SERMON.]

389.—At the termination of the *Psalmody*, or '*Sanctus*,' the Preacher will either proceed to call on the Congregation to join him in prayer, using the 'Bidding Prayer,' or other prescribed formularies, concluding with the 'Lord's Prayer;' or he will simply proclaim—'*In the name of the Father, and of the Son, and of the Holy Ghost. Amen;*' and then proceed to give out his text. The former method is the more usual, the latter is the exception, and practised only by extreme Ritualists. Extemporaneous prayer is inadmissible. Some, however, as soon as the Psalmody is over, give out their text without any prayer or introductory matter. At the *close of the Sermon* it is customary to offer the general ascription of glory and praise to the Holy Trinity, thus:—"*And* "*now, to God the Father, God the Son, and God the* "*Holy Ghost, be ascribed, as is most justly due, all* "*honour, power, might, majesty, and dominion, henceforth* "*and for ever, Amen;*" and conclude with one of the *Collects*, and the *Benediction*, from the end of the Communion Office; the former beginning with—"*Grant, we beseech Thee Almighty God, that the words* "*which we have heard,*" &c., the latter, with—"*The* "*Peace of God which passeth All understanding,*" &c. In the Churches of the more extreme section the *Collect*, and *Benediction* are generally omitted. Upon the Prayer *before the Sermon*, see *postea*, and ARCHDEACON SHARPE's strictures on *Canon* 55. in his Work on '*The Rubric and Canons*,' p. 169. During the repetition of the '*Bidding Prayer*' the Preacher and the People should *stand*.

Bp. Mant remarks:—'*Extemporaneous prayer* in Public Worship 'is altogether repudiated by the Church, and she allows no prayers 'but those of her own Liturgy. If therefore any Prayer be used '*before the Sermon*, it should be taken from the Book of Common 'Prayer. But I can find no authority for any prayer there, and 'it is my belief that not any is intended by the Church. Her 'silence indeed seems to be conclusive. The *55th Canon* in the 'English Code, which is the nearest approach to an authority, 'contains a *form*, which is however not precatory, but injunctive or 'monitory: "*Ye shall pray for Christ's Holy Catholick Church*, &c.": 'so that this form, whatever may have been, and may be, its 'authority for the purpose to which it was directed, is in fact *no* '*authority for a Prayer*. If, however, the popular prepossession 'should be in favour of a *Prayer before the Sermon*, and the Minister 'should think it desirable to indulge such a prepossession, he might 'perhaps, I will not say justify, but excuse his indulgence on the 'plea of *long-continued usage*, in a case which he may deem not 'clearly defined, and where the negative is not secured by an 'express prohibition. Still, I cannot but retain my opinion, that 'the silence of the Church is very expressive: (for surely, had she 'intended any prayer to be here introduced, she would have 'declared her intention, not merely by a general order, but would 'have moreover ordered what the prayer should be:) and that 'therefore for the Sermon to follow immediately, without the 'intervention of a prayer, is the course agreeable to her mind 'and rule. For the Evening, if a *Sermon* be needed, the same 'course might be taken as in the Morning: the *Sermon* being '*followed by the Blessing*.' (*p.* 57).—*Hor. Lit.*

¶. '*Here endeth the Order of* Evening Prayer *throughout the* '*Year*.'

THE ATHANASIAN CREED.

¶. '*Upon these Feasts;* Christmas-Day, *the* Epiphany, *Saint* 'Matthias, Easter-Day, Ascension-Day, Whitsunday, *Saint* John 'Baptist, *Saint* James, *Saint* Bartholomew, *Saint* Matthew, '*Saint* Simon, *and Saint* Jude, *Saint* Andrew, *and upon* Trinity 'Sunday, *shall be sung or said at* Morning Prayer, *instead of* '*the* Apostle's Creed, *this Confession of our Christian Faith*, '*commonly called* The Creed of Saint Athanasius, *by the* '*Minister and People standing*.'— Present Book of Common Prayer.

(Minister and People standing).

390.—The Creed, bearing the name of *S. Athanasius* from embodying the doctrines of the Holy Trinity and Incarnation as taught and defended by that great and persecuted man, has been attributed to various divines, yet to no one of them can the honour of the production be assigned with any degree of certainty. There is, however, indisputable evidence, both internal and external, that it was not from the pen of Athanasius. *Athanasius* was Bishop of Alexandria in the 4th century, the place of his birth, of which the date is not precisely known, and there he died, A. D. 375.; but this formulary of faith has not been traced earlier than the 5th century, nor is any mention made of it, under the designation by which it is now known, before the 7th century. The writings of Athanasius, moreover, are all in the Greek tongue, whereas the original of this Creed is in the Latin language.

The history of the *Athanasian Creed* has been most critically handled by *Dr. Waterland*, to whose admirable and learned Treatise we must refer such of our Readers as wish for full information. According to this writer the Creed is of Gallican origin; was first admitted into the Gallican Psalter, which conveyed it to those countries where that Psalter was received; was first noticed by Gallican Councils and Bishops; and commented upon by Gallican writers. *Dr. Waterland* believes it to have been composed by HILARY, *Bishop of Arles*, about A. D. 429; and to have been recognized as a rule of faith in A. D. 550; and admitted into the Offices of the Gallican Church not later than A. D. 670, when the powerful name of *Athanasius* was affixed to it "to recommend, and adorn it." But it was not till about A. D. 800, that this Creed was received in England. The Church of Rome did not acknowledge it before the 10th century; while the Greek Church, after altering it so as to accord with their peculiar dogma respecting the procession of the Holy Spirit, admitted it in the 7th century. *Dr. Waterland's* view, however, regarding the authorship of this Creed has been controverted by *Mr. Harvey* in his "History and Theology of the Three Creeds;" the latter fixing its date at A. D. 401. The *Rubric* of our Liturgy is careful not to commit itself on this disputed point, and therefore designates it as "*commonly called the* "*Athanasian Creed.*" Be the truth as it may, it is universally admitted that this Creed is not the work of *Athanasius;* that it was not known for the first 400 years of the Christian era; that the Author of the Creed has yet to be discovered; and that there is strong evidence to prove its Gallican extraction, and that the original was written in the Latin tongue. The translation, however, in our Prayer Book is, according to *Bp. Short,* taken by mistake from the Greek. (*Hist. of English Church,* p. 589. *Note*).

DR. NICHOLLS says:—'This Creed has, by many, been attributed 'to St *Athanasius,* because *Marcellus* and he are said to have left 'Confessions of their faith with *Julius,* Bishop of *Rome;* and that '*Athanasius* gave in this Creed as his Confession. But 'tis plain, 'that *Athanasius* was not the author of it; because it does not 'appear to have been known to any till the sixth Century. 'Besides, this Creed opposes the *Nestorians, Eutychians* and '*Monotholites,* all which Hereticks sprang up after *Athanasius's* 'time. But however 'tis very ancient; for some passages out of it 'are quoted in the Council of *Toledo,* held A. D. 683. And, 'tis cited 'by Radulphus, and other authors, who wrote about the same time. 'It is an excellent epitome of the doctrine establish'd by the four 'first general Councils concerning the Holy Trinity.' *Book of Com. Prayer,* in loco.

DR. WATERLAND (*ob.* 1740) writes:—'Upon the revival of the '*Arian* controversy in Gaul, under the influence of the Burgundian 'Kings, it was obvious to call one side *Athanasians,* and the other 'side *Arians;* and so also to name the orthodox faith the '*Athanasian* Faith, and the other *Arian.* This Creed therefore, 'being a summary of the orthodox and Catholic faith, might in 'process of time acquire the name of the *Athanasian Faith,* or '*Fides Athanasii,* in opposition to the contrary scheme, which 'might as justly be called *Fides Arii,* or the *Arian Faith.* The 'equivocalness of the title gave a handle to those that came after to 'understand it of a form of faith composed by *Athanasius;* just 'as the equivocal title of *Apostolical* given to the Roman Creed 'occasioned the mistake about its being made by the *Apostles*...... '*Hilary* once Abbot of Lerins, and next *Bishop of Arles,* about 'the year 430 composed the exposition of faith which now bears 'the name of the *Athanasian Creed.* It was drawn up for the use 'of the Gallican Clergy, and especially for the diocess or province 'of *Arles.* It was esteemed by as many as were acquainted with it, 'as a valuable summary of the Christian faith. It seems to have 'been in the hands of *Vincentius,* Monk of Lerins, before 434, by 'what he has borrowed from it; and to have been cited in part 'by *Avitus* of Vienne about the year 500, and by *Cæsarius* of Arles 'before the year 543. About the year 570, it became famous 'enough to be commented upon like the Lord's Prayer, and

'Apostles' Creed, and together with them. All this while, and 'perhaps for several years lower, it had not yet acquired the name 'of the *Athanasian Faith*, but was simply styled the *Catholic Faith*. 'But before 670, Athanasius's admired name, came in to recommend 'and adorn it. *History of the Athanasian Creed*, chap. viii.

Dr. Hook says:—'The learned, at this day, however they may 'differ in their opinions about the age, or author, make no question 'but that the composition was originally in Latin. The style and 'phraseology—its early acceptance with the Latins, while unknown 'to the Greeks—the antiquity and number of the Latin MSS. and 'their general agreement with each other, compared with the 'lateness, the scarceness, and the disagreement of the Greek 'copies—all seem to demonstrate this.'—*Church Dict.*, 6th edit. *in voce.*

When to be used.

391.—The *Rubric* in our present Prayer Book directs that the *Athanasian Creed* shall be said on certain Holy-days, the thirteen therein specified; the design being that it should be repeated once a month, as near as may be. In the earlier Liturgies this Creed will be found inserted before the conclusion of the Evening Prayer; where the *Rubric* thus reads:—

'*In the feasts of* Christmas, the Epiphany, Easter, the 'Ascension, Pentecost, *and upon* Trinity *Sunday, shall be sung or* '*said immediately after* Benedictus, *this Confession of our* '*Christian Faith.*'

'*Quicunque Vult, &c.*'—(1549). Keeling, 37.

In the Liturgies of 1552, 1559, and 1604, other Holy-days were added, and the Rubric was changed to the following:—

'*In the feasts of Christmas, the Epiphany, Saint Matthias,* '*Easter, the Ascension, Pentecost, Saint John Baptist, Saint James,* '*Saint Bartholomew, Saint Matthew, Saint Simon and Jude, Saint* '*Andrew, and Trinity Sunday, shall be sung or said,* immediately 'after Benedictus, *this Confession of our Christian Faith.*'*—(1552, 1559, 1604).—Keeling, 36, 37.

---

* There was no heading to this Creed in 1549; but from 1552 to 1662 it was, occasionally, "*Evening Prayer*," and sometimes '*Quicunque Vult.*'

In the old Service Books of Sarum, York, and Hereford, the *Athanasian Creed*, termed "Psalmus *Quicunque Vult*," was usually sung on Sundays after the appointed Psalms in the Office of Prime: and *only* on Sundays. It was not till the period of the Reformation that it was employed on Holy-days: the Apostles' Creed was also at that date directed to supply its place on other days than Sundays and the appointed Holy-days, after the example of the *revised* Roman Breviary of Cardinal Quignon A. D. 1536. (See *par*. 211, *supra*).

392.—The title of '*Quicunque Vult*' was given to this Creed by Honorius of France, A. D. 1130.; and it was so designated in England in the 13th century. In the old Breviaries it was called the 'Psalm *Quicunque*.' The first Liturgy of *Edw*. VI. (1549), called it '*Quicunque Vult, &c.*'; this title was omitted in the two following *Revisions* of the Prayer Book (of 1552 and 1559), but was restored to it in the *Revision* of 1604.

Why *certain Holy-days* were selected on which the repetition of the *Athanasian Creed* seemed more especially fitting, Bp. Sparrow informs us; his opinion too is the basis of *Wheatly's* remarks on this subject.

Bp. Sparrow (*ob*. 1685) says:—'This Creed is appointed to be 'said upon the days named in the *Rubric*, for these reasons; partly, 'because those days, many of them, are most proper for this 'confession of the Faith, which of all others is the most express 'concerning the Trinity, because the matter of them much concerns 'the Manifestation of the Trinity, as *Christmas*, *Epiphany*, '*Easter-Day*, *Ascension-Day*, *Whitsun-Day*, *Trinity-Sunday*, *and* 'St *John Baptist Day* at the highest of whose Acts, the Baptizing 'of our Lord, was made a kind of sensible Manifestation of the 'Trinity, partly, that so it might be said once a month at least, and 'therefore on St *James*, and St *Bartholomew's* Days; and withal at 'convenient distance from each time, and therefore on St *Matthew*, '*Matthias*, *Simon* and *Jude*, and St *Andrew's*.' (*p*. 41).—*Rationale*.

In the Scotch Liturgy of 1635, these words following were annexed to the Rubric, "*the Presbyter and all the People standing*."—(Keeling, 36.)

The *Athanasian Creed* is altogether omitted from the American Liturgy.

393.—Many objections have been made from time to time against the use of the *Athanasian Creed* in Divine Worship, on the ground that certain of its denunciations are couched in language so violent and condemnatory, as to give offence to the consciences of those who otherwise would be ready to accept the main principles taught in this Creed. The Royal Commissioners of 1689, endeavoured in their *Revision of the Liturgy* to meet these scruples by proposing a reduction of the *number* of the Holy-days on which this Creed should be used, and adding to the Rubric a passage explanatory of the "damnatory Clauses." The Rubric as suggested thus read:—

'*Upon these Feasts; Christmas-day*, —, —, *Easter-day*, '*Ascension-day*, *Whitsunday*, —, —, —, —, —, —, —, *Trinity-* '*Sunday*, and upon All Saints, *shall be* —, —, *said at Morning* '*Prayer* by the Minister and People standing, *instead of* the 'Creed commonly call'd *the Apostles' Creed, this confession of* '*our Christian Faith, commonly called the Creed of Saint* '*Athanasius*. The Articles of which ought to be receiv'd and 'believ'd as being agreeable to the Holy Scriptures. And the 'CONDEMNING CLAUSES are to be understood as relating only 'to those who obstinately deny the substance of the Christian 'Faith' ('according to the 18th Article of this Church.'*)—(*From the Copy, printed by* order of the House of Commons, *June*, 1854).

394.—But these alterations were never carried out, and the opposition has survived to the present day; many Clergymen, indeed, may now be found, who will not introduce the *Athanasian Creed* as directed by the Rubric. They object, as well to some of the doctrines it contains, as to the condemnation pronounced against those who disbelieve them. But in reply to such objectors may it not be argued that the doctrines advanced are not at variance with what are promulgated in the Articles of our Church, nor are they opposed to what are set forth at the beginning of the Litany, nor repugnant to the language of the two other Creeds, of the Doxology, of

---

* These last words were afterwards struck through: the *hyphens* indicate the omissions, and the roman type marks the additional matter.

the Form of Baptism, nor substantially different from the concluding sentences of many of our Collects; nor indeed antagonistic to numerous passages of the New Testament. These important principles of the Holy *Trinity* are certainly laid down in the *Athanasian Creed* with brief and stringent precision; and so it was necessary to do at the times when they were originally penned; nor did the Nonconformists at the Reformation, although rejecting the Liturgy at large, refuse to subscribe this Creed, as may be seen among our citations below. There is no doubt that this Creed contains much that is beyond the comprehension of man, and so does Scripture. The phraseology also may occasionally appear obscure and open to exception; but a candid examination, and fair interpretation, will remove from the unprejudiced mind much that may have raised objection, or given cause of offence. The two or three "*damnatory clauses*," moreover, are not levelled at those who cannot understand, or cannot approve every expression in the Creed, but at such only as deny that "*the* "*Three Persons are one God;*" or reject, what the Creed calls, "*the Trinity in Unity.*" This alone is implied to be '*the Catholic Faith.*' (See *Abp. Secker's* remarks, *postea*.).

With regard to the changes proposed in 1689 to meet the dissentient opinions then rife touching the *Athanasian Creed*, we may cite one or two authorities to show that the question was actually discussed among the Royal Commissioners whether this Creed should be retained or not.

We will first quote the ARTICLE of our Church on "*The Three Creeds*":—

'The three Creeds, *Nicene* Creed, *Athanasius's* Creed, and 'that which is commonly called the *Apostles'* Creed, ought 'thoroughly to be received and believed: for they may be proved 'by most certain warrants of holy Scriptures.'—ARTICLE VIII.

We will now cite the opinions of certain well known Nonconformists:—

RICHARD BAXTER (*ob.* 1691) writes:—'For my own part, as I 'unfeignedly account the doctrine of the Trinity the very sum 'and kernel of the Christian Religion, (as expressed in our 'Baptism), and *Athanasius's Creed* the best explication of it that 'ever I read, so I think it very unmeet in these tremendous 'mysteries, to go further than we have God's own light to guide 'us.'—*Works by* Orme. Vol. XXI. *p.* 313.

DR. CALAMY too, another Nonconformist, states in his *Life of Baxter* (Vol. I. *p.* 455), that it was concluded 'that lest the wholly 'rejecting it (the *Athanasian Creed*) should by unreasonable 'persons be imputed to them as Socinianism, a *Rubric** should 'be made, setting forth or declaring the curses denounced therein 'not to be restrained to every particular Article but intended 'against those that denied the substance of the Christian religion 'in general.' (See these words also in CARDWELL's *Hist. of the Conferences*, p. 432.)

To this, DR. WATERLAND says, 'it was therefore unanimously 'agreed still to retain and impose this Creed;......and indeed it 'must have appeared very astonishing in the eyes of all the 'Reformed Churches, Lutheran and Calvinist, (who have the 'greatest veneration for this Creed) to have seen it wholly rejected 'by the English Clergy, when there had been no precedent before 'of any one Church in Christendom that had done the like. All 'that ever received it, have constantly retained it, and still retain 'it.'—WATERLAND on *the Athanasian Creed*, ch. xi. p. 281. *Postscript*, Second Edition. (See also BP. SHORT's *History of the Church of England*, p. 589.)

Passing to the divines of our own Church, we may give a few of the more weighty opinions.

HOOKER (*ob.* 1600) says:—'The *Creed of Athanasius*...... 'concerning that truth which Arianism so mightily did impugn, 'was, both in the East and the West Churches, accepted as a 'treasure of inestimable price, by as many as had not given up 'even the very ghost of belief......These Catholic declarations of 'our belief, delivered by them, which were so much nearer than we 'are unto the first publication thereof, and continuing needful 'for all men at all times to know, these confessions, as testimonies 'of our continuance in the same faith to this present day, we 'rather use than any other gloss or paraphrase devised by 'ourselves, which though it were to the same effect notwithstanding, 'could not be of the like authority and credit.' *Eccl. Polity.* Bk. V. c. 42. p. 551.

DEAN COMBER (*ob.* 1699) writes respecting this Creed:—'None 'can deny it to be pure and orthodox; for it contradicts expressly 'all those *heresies* which the Catholic Church condemned in the 'primitive Councils: as to the TRINITY teaching us, That we must 'not confound the Persons (with *Sabellius*); for there is one Person

---

* The *Rubric* referred to by *Calamy*, was drawn up by the Royal Commissioners of 1689, and is cited above.

'of the Father, another of the Son, and another of the Holy Ghost, '&c. Nor yet may we divide the substance (with *Arius*, and '*Ennomius*), for the Godhead of the Father, of the Son, and of the 'Holy Ghost, is all one, &c. Not only the Father is God, but 'the Son is God (which *Arius* denied), and the Holy Ghost is God '(which *Macedonius* would not grant); and yet it doth not follow '(as the *Arians* pretended), that there are three Gods. Again, as 'to the INCARNATION of our Saviour, it declares that he is very 'God of the substance of his Father (against *Arius*, *Samosatenus*, 'and *Photinus*), and very man of the substance of his Mother '(which *Apollinaris* denied), of a reasonable soul (which the same 'heretic disowned), and human flesh (which the *Valentinians* 'allowed not); and yet he is not two (as *Nestorius* dreamed), but 'one Christ. One, not by confusion of substance (as *Entyches* 'held), but by unity of person. These are the chief heresies, and if 'they were wrong, and the Catholic Church (which condemned 'them) in the right, then this *Creed* is orthodox, and the very 'quintescence of the ancient divinity.'—*Companion of the Temple*, I. p. 361.

DR. WATERLAND (*ob.* 1740) writes:—'That this *Creed* is not '*Athanasius's* is certainly true: but our Church receives it not 'upon the authority of its compiler, nor determines any thing about 'its age or author: but we receive it, because the truth of the 'doctrines contained in it "may be proved by most certain "warrants of Holy Scripture," as is expressly said in our *eighth* '*Article*. I may add, that the early and general reception of this '*Creed* by Greeks and Latins, by all the Western Churches, not 'only before but since the Reformation, must needs give it a much 'greater authority and weight, than the name of Athanasius could 'do, were it ever so justly to be set to it. *Athanasius* has left some 'Creeds and Confessions, undoubtedly his, which yet never have 'obtained the esteem and reputation, that this has done: because 'none of them are really of the same intrinsick value, nor capable 'of doing the like service in the Christian Churches. The *use of it* 'is, to be a standing fence and preservative against the wiles 'and equivocations of most kinds of hereticks. This was well 'understood by *Luther*, when he called it, "a bulwark to the "Apostles' Creed;" and it was this and the like considerations that 'have all along made it to be of such high esteem among all the 'Reformed Churches, from the days of their great leader. (*p.* 50.)... 'To conclude; so long as there shall be any men left to oppose the 'doctrines which this Creed contains, so long will it be expedient, 'and even necessary, to continue the use of it, in order to preserve 'the rest; and, I suppose, when we have none remaining to find 'fault with the doctrines, there will be none to object against the 'use of the Creed, or so much as wish to have it laid aside.' (*p.* 59).—(quoted in MANT's *Book of Com. Prayer*, in loco.)

WHEATLY observes:—'Whether this Creed was composed by '*Athanasius* or not, is matter of dispute. In the Rubric before it, 'as enlarged at the [*last*] *Review*, it is only said to be *commonly* '*called the Creed of St Athanasius*: but we are certain that it 'has been received as a treasure of inestimable price both by the 'Greek and Latin Churches for almost a thousand years. As to 'the matter of it, it condemns all ancient and modern heresies, and 'is the sum of all orthodox divinity. And therefore if any scruple 'at the denying salvation to such as do not believe these articles; 'let them remember, that such as hold any of these fundamental 'heresies are condemned in Scripture: from whence it was a 'primitive custom, after a confession of the orthodox faith, to pass 'an anathema against all that denied it. But, however, for the ease 'and satisfaction of some people who have a notion that this Creed 'requires every person to assent to, or believe, *every verse* in it 'on pain of *damnation;* and who therefore (because there are 'several things in it which they cannot comprehend) scruple to 'repeat it for fear they should anathematize or condemn themselves; 'I desire to offer what follows to their consideration, *viz.* That 'howsoever plain and agreeable to reason every verse in this Creed 'may be; yet we are not required, by the words of the Creed, to 'believe *the whole* on pain of damnation. For all that is required of 'us as *necessary to salvation*, is, that *before all things we hold the* '*Catholic Faith: and the Catholic Faith is* by the 3rd *and* 4*th verses* 'explained to be this "*that we worship one God in Trinity, and* "*Trinity in Unity: neither confounding the Persons, nor dividing the* "*substance.*" This therefore is declared necessary to be believed: 'but all that follows from hence to the 27*th verse*, is only brought 'as a proof and illustration of it; and therefore requires our assent 'no more than a Sermon does, which is made to prove or illustrate 'a Text. The text, we know, is the word of God, and therefore 'necessary to be believed: but no person is, for that reason, bound 'to believe every particular of the Sermon deduced from it, upon 'pain of damnation, though every tittle of it may be true. The 'same I take it to be in this Creed: the belief of the *Catholic Faith* 'before mentioned, the Scripture makes necessary to salvation, and 'therefore we must believe it: but there is no such necessity laid 'upon us to believe the *illustration* that is there given of it, nor 'does the Creed itself require it: for it goes on in the 27*th* and 28*th* '*verses* in these words, "*So that in all things as is aforesaid, the* "*Unity in Trinity, and the Trinity in Unity, is to be worshipped.* "*He therefore that will be saved, must thus think of the Trinity.*" 'Where it plainly passes off from that illustration, and returns back 'to the 3rd and 4*th verses;* requiring only our belief of the *Catholic* '*Faith*, as there expressed, as necessary to Salvation, *viz.* that "*One God," or* "*Unity in Trinity and Trinity in Unity, is to be* "*worshipped.*" All the rest of the Creed, from the 29*th verse* to the 'end, relates to our Saviour's *Incarnation;* which indeed is another 'essential part of our faith, and as necessary to be believed as 'the former: but that being expressed in such plain terms as none, 'I suppose, scruple, I need not enlarge any farther.' (*p.* 145).—*Rat. Ill. of Book of Com. Prayer.* Dr. Corrie's Ed.

Abp. Secker (*ob.* 1768) writes:—'Our *dissenting brethren*, after 'they had long objected to other parts of our Liturgy, consented 'readily to subscribe this *Creed:* the articles of which are the 'common faith of the Catholic Church, or by immediate consequence 'deducible from it; and little or nothing more. There are indeed 'several things in them, beyond our comprehension as to the 'manner: but the Scripture hath the same......The *condemnation* 'contained in two or three clauses of this Creed, belongs, (as the most 'zealous defenders of our faith in the holy Trinity, agree, and as 'every one, who reads it considerately, will soon perceive,) not to 'all, who cannot understand, or cannot approve, every expression 'in it; but only to such as deny in general the "*Trinity in Unity*," 'or three Persons who are one God. *This* alone is said to be the "*Catholic Faith*." The words, that follow after, "*for there is one* "*person of the Father*," and so on, are designed only to set this 'forth more particularly. And the conclusion from the whole is, 'not that "*in all things*" which are "*aforesaid*," by the use of 'every term above-mentioned, but "*in all things*, AS IS *aforesaid*, "*the Unity in Trinity is to be worshipped*."—*Works*. Vol. iii. *Sermon* xxvii. *p*. 434, 435.

SHEPHERD (*ob.* 1805), who derives much of his view from *Horbery's* 18th Sermon, thus observes:—'The objections made to 'this Creed by those who believe the Scripture to be the word 'of God, and that this Creed, in general, contains nothing that is 'contrary to that word, are, that it is *unintelligible* and *uncharitable*. 'To the former of these objections it has been replied, there is a 'great difference between understanding the meaning of the Creed, 'or the doctrine which it sets forth, and comprehending the thing 'itself, or the mystery to which this doctrine relates. It is easy 'enough to understand the Catholic or orthodox doctrine, concerning 'the *Trinity*, which the Scripture teaches, and the Church has 'always received; but to comprehend the *mystery of the Trinity* 'itself, is impossible. For we cannot conceive the *manner*, how 'Three Persons are one God, nor how the One God subsists in 'Three Persons. By not attending to this necessary distinction, 'a man may suppose he does not understand the *doctrine of the* '*Creed*, merely because he cannot comprehend the *mystery of the* '*Trinity*.—This latter is above his understanding. But is that the 'fault of this *Creed?*—Supposing the *Creed* expunged from the 'Liturgy, would he have clearer conceptions of this mysterious 'truth? Or will any other Creed, or exposition of the faith, that 'human ingenuity can devise, enable a *finite* capacity to comprehend 'an *infinite* object?—......As to its *uncharitableness*, the condemning 'or *damnatory clauses*, as they have been called, do not extend to 'each of the particular explications here given, but are intended 'only to secure the general doctrine......In the English translation 'there is the appearance of a harsh expression not warranted by 'the original, "*He that will be saved must thus think of the Trinity*." 'This passage might perhaps be more faithfully rendered, '*Let him* '*who desires to be saved, thus think of the Trinity*.' (Qui vult 'servari, ita de Trinitate sentiat.) These words, which have been 'strangely styled a *damnatory clause*, do not imply even so much as 'a censure. They are an application of the introduction, which 'simply states, what no Christian will deny, that whoever is 'desirous of salvation, and expects it upon the terms of the Gospel, 'must first of all believe the doctrines of the Gospel......... 'Notwithstanding the excellence of this Creed, the expediency of 'using it in a public Liturgy has been questioned by Divines, who 'both steadfastly believed the doctrines it contains, and approved of 'the expositions of them it delivers. I think it probable that they 'argued upon this principle.—Our Congregations being infected with 'no erroneous opinions in matters of faith, being in general happily 'unacquainted, not only with the nature but even with the very 'names of the various corruptions against which this Creed 'explicitly guards, there is less occasion in our Public Worship 'for the recital of so minute an explication of points which are 'confessedly abstruse.' (*p.* 239).—*Eluc. of Book of Com. Prayer.* Vol. I.

Bp. Cleaver observes:—'A Creed of this kind may be 'considered as a preservative against heresy, applicable as occasion 'shall require; and useful just so far as the danger of error shall 'occur. If this Creed therefore be not in daily use, it will be 'desirable to remind the unlearned of such a preservative, by the 'repetition of it *at stated times*, and upon those occasions especially, 'when the great and leading objects of our faith are made the 'subjects of our meditation......To the *Sceptic*, the *Arian*, and the '*Socinian*, we do not expect to find such a Creed acceptable, 'because it was designed to restrain the fantastick and pernicious 'opinions started on their part upon the subjects contained in it.'—(quoted in Mant's *Book of Com. Prayer*, in loco. p. 58.)

Waldo states:—'With respect to the public reading of this 'Creed, which it is become the practice *to omit* in some places, it is 'desirable for the Clergy to consider, how offensive this omission 'must be to the orthodox part of their Congregation, who are 'thereby deprived of an opportunity of professing their faith 'publickly in the manner which the Church has directed. And 'they may be asked, whether is it more reasonable to offend those 'by an irregular omission; or to disgust the heterodox by reading 'what they are commanded?'—(quoted in Mant's *Book of Com. Prayer*, in loco. p. 58.)

Bp. Mant says:—'The use of "the Creed of St Athanasius" on 'the appointed days is imperative on the Church's Ministers and 'People. "*Upon these Feasts*," she says, naming them, "*shall be* "*sung or said at Morning Prayer*," instead of the Apostles' Creed, 'this Confession of our Christian Faith.' (*p.* 48).—*Hor. Lit.*

The Rev. W. G. Humphry remarks:—'We may observe that 'this Creed consists, in a great measure, of *negations*. It was 'manifestly drawn up for the purpose of contradicting and 'excluding certain heretical opinions, which were at the time in 'circulation, respecting the doctrine of the Trinity, and the union 'of the divine and human natures in our blessed Lord. At the 'present day, therefore, it may well be found obscure by the 'unlearned, who are without any knowledge of those heresies. By 'some persons it is thought not only obscure, but presumptuous; 'because, as they say, it attempts to penetrate inscrutable 'mysteries: whereas it is itself a protest against the presumptuous 'definitions which had been already hazarded; and it is only for the 'purpose of rebutting them that it has recourse to any positive 'statements of doctrine. No one is qualified to understand, and 'much less to criticise the terms of this Creed, till he has informed 'himself of the religious controversies which were rife at the time 'when it was composed. It has been said, that we do not wisely, 'to retain in our public Services a formulary, which to a great 'portion of our people, is unintelligible. But to this it may be 'replied, that we cannot safely lay aside a bulwark which has been 'instrumental in protecting the Church against a set of opinions at 'one time very prevalent, and even now by no means extinct.' (*p.* 157).—*Treatise on Book of Com. Prayer.*

395.—These quotations will be a sufficient answer, we trust, to those Clergymen who refuse to conform to the injunctions of the *Rubrics* requiring the use of the *Athanasian Creed;* and whose refusal is more on account of the *phraseology* in which the great principles of the Trinity, and of the Incarnation are expressed than from any opposition to the doctrines themselves. We cannot therefore imagine that the impossibility of enunciating clearly to the satisfaction of all thinkers, by reason of the imperfection of human language, these important mysteries of our faith is ground enough for the *Officiating Minister* to infringe the order and discipline of our church in this matter.

Two *Rubrics* of our present Book of Common Prayer—one before the *Apostles' Creed* in the MORNING OFFICE, and one before the '*Quicunque Vult*' itself—require the Athanasian Creed to be employed in the MORNING SERVICE on certain Holy-days, and the Officiating Minister is bound to obey. The *Holy-days* specified in the Rubric are as follow:—

CHRISTMAS-DAY	Dec. 25.	*S. John, Baptist*	June 24.
The *Epiphany*	Jan. 6.	*S. James*	July 25.
S. Matthias	Feb. 24.	*S. Bartholomew*	Aug. 24.
EASTER-DAY	(*moveable*).	*S. Matthew*	Sep. 21.
ASCENSION-DAY	(*moveable*).	*S. Simon, and S. Jude*	Oct. 28.
WHITSUNDAY	(*moveable*).	*S. Andrew*	Nov. 30.
TRINITY SUNDAY	(*moveable*).		

MANNER OF UTTERANCE.

'*To be sung or said......by the Minister and People standing.*'

396.—The *Athanasian Creed* used to be looked upon in the old English Offices in the light of a Psalm, and was in fact entitled "the Psalm, *Quicunque Vult.*" This will account for the custom generally prevailing of repeating, or singing antiphonally, this Creed in the same manner as the Psalms. To this end, we find it divided into *verses*, and pointed with the *colon* for chanting. In Parish Churches it is usually repeated by Minister and People *alternately*, but where an efficient choir exists it is often chanted *antiphonally*.

In some Churches it is read through by the Officiating Minister alone, for the reason that the alternate verses are not in *italics* to mark the responses of the People, as is the case in the Litany, and other parts of the Service. This is not correct, for if this argument were sound, it would apply equally to the Psalms of the day. Many, however, prefer, that this CREED should be '*said*' by the People *with* the Minister, as in the other Creeds, and in the Lord's Prayer. (See *pars.* 49. 214.)

The *Rubric* leaves the matter discretionary, merely requiring that it shall be '*sung or said.*'

BP. MANT writes:—'This duty is injoined upon "the Minister 'and people *standing*." The *mode* is not specified: but the division 'of the Creed *into verses*, after the manner of the Psalms and 'Hymns, seems to indicate the like mode of delivery, which is in 'my opinion preferable to the mode used in the Apostles' Creed, 'which is a more continuous composition. The *singing* of the 'Athanasian Creed, as well as of the Apostles', though permitted 'by the Church, is less suited to a common parochial congregation, 'than the *saying* of it.' (*p.* 48).—*Hor. Lit.*

The REV. J. JEBB observes:—The *Athanasian Creed* 'retains 'with us, in the mode of its performance, the character of a *Hymn*; 'being divided into *verses*, with the mark of the Choral pause, 'the *colon :* and, like the *Psalm*, is repeated in Parish Churches '*alternately* by Minister and people; in Choirs, is sung alternately 'to a Chant. The structure of the Hymn is most artificial, and 'in strict accordance with the rules of Hebrew composition, so as 'to present a poetical character, fit for choral recitation......In some 'Choirs, where the Responses are not sung, as at Trinity College, 'Dublin, the *Athanasian Creed* is parochially read: but this is most 'anomalous, and arises from the false notion that Creeds are not 'Hymns, contrary to the universal acceptation of the Church.' (*p.* 355).—CHORAL SERVICE.

The REV. W. PALMER states:—'The *Athanasian Creed* was 'sung like the Psalms in the English Offices, and it was even 'designated by the title of the Psalm *Quicunque.* These circum- 'stances account for the custom of repeating and singing this 'Creed in the same manner as the Psalms, which still prevails 'in the Christian Churches of England.' (*p.* 268). *Orig. Lit.* Vol. 1.

POSTURE.

397.—With regard to *posture*, this is sufficiently defined in the Rubric, which directs that the Minister and People shall be '*standing.*'

THE LITANY.

¶. '*Here followeth the* LITANY, *or General Supplication, to be 'sung or said after* MORNING PRAYER *upon* Sundays, Wed-'nesdays, *and* Fridays, *and at other times when it shall be 'commanded by the Ordinary.*' (1662).—Present Book of 'Common Prayer.

[Give notice of the Sick to be prayed for.]

(Minister and People kneeling.)

398.—The LITANY, or *General Supplication*, as the Rubric explains it, is a Service highly important from engaging the hearts and voices of both Minister and People in common intercession. The term *Litany* (Litaneia, λιτανεία), is derived from the Greek λιτανεύω, (λίτομαι, λιτή), *to pray earnestly* or *intently;* and was originally applied to any prayer or supplication, public or private. Eusebius thus employs the word, when speaking of the Emperor Constantine's habit of retiring for prayer (λιτή, λιτανεία) before a battle, and on other occasions. (*Vit. Const.* ii. 14. iv. 61.) Subsequently, and which is the sense entertained at the present day, the word *Litany* more particularly denoted that form of prayer where the Minister utters a short request, to which the People add a brief supplication in the way of response. Such was the usage in the time of Tertullian in the Communion Office, and other Services of the Church. (*Clem. Const.* viii. 5, 6. 10.). On the cessation of persecution in the 4th century, Basil of Neocæsarea (A. D. 370), tells us that the term *Litany* acquired a more extended signification, implying the religious penitential Services performed in the *Public Processions* of the Clergy and People. These *Processions*, styled also "Processional Supplications," arose in the time of Chrysostom of Constantinople (A. D. 398). It would seem that the *Arians* being forbidden to hold public worship within the city, used to assemble about the porticos at night, and at day-break on Saturday and Sunday Morning march through the streets of Constantinople, singing heretical Hymns and Anthems antiphonally, as they proceeded to their Churches outside the walls. *Chrysostom*, therefore, to prevent the orthodox believers from being enticed away by these attractive gatherings, instituted similar nocturnal processions, which, by the liberality of the Empress Eudoxia, were of far more gorgeous and splendid a character than those of the heterodox Arians. (*Socrat.* Hist. Eccl. vi. 8; *Sozom.* viii. 8.). Subsequently, we find, that *Litanies*, accompanied by fastings and prayer, were commonly prescribed on occasions of public calamity, or national benefit.

From the Eastern Church, Processional Supplications passed in the 5th century to the Western Church, (Palmer's *Orig. Lit.*), where they were at first called *Rogations*, or *Supplications*, and eventually, *Litanies*. MAMERTUS, bishop of Vienne in Gaul, appears to have instituted the more solemn and regular *Litanies* or *Rogations* in the Western Church. About A. D. 450, on account of many severe visitations of Providence in the form of droughts, pestilences, &c. this Bishop directed *Litanies*, or *Rogations*, to be celebrated on the three days preceding the Feast of the Ascension. These were continued annually throughout Gaul, and from being the only days in the year devoted to such Processional Supplications, they acquired the name of "The Rogation Days." (see *Vol.* **B.**) Shortly after this, they were introduced into the Anglo-Saxon Church, and the only remnant of these Processional Rogations which has survived to us is the "*Perambulation of Parishes.*" These have been already fully explained. (see *par.* 161. *Vol.* **B.**). *Litanies*, however, were not confined to these three specific days, but were celebrated whenever circumstances arose calling for such Service; as at periods of humiliation, particularly during *Lent*, and weekly on *Wednesdays* and *Fridays*, the two ancient fasting days.

Gregory the Great at Rome composed, about A. D. 590, a very elaborate Litany, known as the

Litania Major, and likewise the *Litania Septiformis*, or *Septena*, from the company being arranged into seven classes: he also applied the term Litany to the persons officiating, as well as to the Service: while others have limited the meaning to only a portion of the Service; either to the *Kyrie eleison*, or to the *Invocation of the Saints*, or to the prayers following the *Kyrie eleison*. There is much confusion of opinion relative to the exact application of the word, and therefore it is difficult at the present time to determine the question with precision. There is no doubt that the *Litany*, as a *General* or *Processional Supplication*, became a distinct Office about the time of Theodosius in the East, and Mamertus in the West, A. D. 460: at one period it was made up entirely of *Psalmody;* at another, it consisted of *Kyrie eleison*, *Christe eleison*, *Kyrie eleison*, repeated each a hundred times: at a later period, about the 8th century, it comprised the Invocation of the Trinity, and of the Saints, and the singing of Anthems. The Invocation of Saints in Litanies is peculiar to the Western Church, and cannot be traced higher than the 8th or 9th century. At the Reformation, the Church of England rejected this feature; and the uttering of *Litanies*, is now confined to within the Church, the Processions out of doors having occasioned such scandal as to call for their suppression.

399.—Our *English Litany* seems in great part, to be derived from the *Litania Major* of Gregory the Great: still, it is indebted for many of its excellencies to the ancient Liturgies of the Eastern and African Churches. At the same time, we may observe, that our Rogation or Litany days come to us more immediately through the Gallican Church. Prior to the Reformation, there was some slight difference in the language and arrangements of the Litany in the different dioceses, like as there existed in the various Uses; and the Litany was in the Latin tongue: but towards the close of the reign of Henry VIII., it was put into English by Cranmer,

A. D. 1544; and this translation was ordered by royal authority to be used in Churches on certain fasts and festival days, and in processions. In 1545, another Prymer, in addition to those of 1535, and 1539, was put forth, which contained this English version of the Litany; and the same version was inserted in the *first Liturgy* of Edward VI., A. D. 1549. The modern interpolations of the Romish Church, viz. the invocations of the Virgin Mary and of Angels, Patriarchs, Prophets, and of Saints, and a few Collects, (see *Maskell's* Mon. Rit. ii. 95; *Palmer's* Orig. Lit. i. 314.), were, however, then omitted. At the period of the Reformation, also (in the time of Edward VI.), the processional accompaniment of the Litany was discontinued; but the 'Perambulation of Parishes' on the Rogation days has survived to the present time, as we have already observed.

400.—The LITANY comprises six distinct portions, which have been designated the (a) *Invocations*, (b) *Deprecations*, (c) *Obsecrations*, (d) *Intercessions*, (e) *Supplications* or *Suffrages*, and (f) the *Prayers*.

(*a*) The INVOCATIONS. (four clauses.)

401.—The *Invocations*, at the opening of the Litany, are addressed to the *three Persons* of the blessed Trinity in succession, and then conjointly. They number four clauses, and are answered by the Congregation in the same words. *The People should begin to follow the Minister immediately he has uttered the first two words*, "O GOD," &c. In some places, the Congregation do not take up the several clauses till the Minister has finished uttering them. The first method is the more usual; care should be taken to pause at the *comma* after "*Father*," so as not to connect it too closely with the words following. Many Clergymen forget this, and read, "*O God, the Father of heaven*," &c. instead of, "*O God, the Father......of heaven*," &c. (Pater de cœlis Deus, &c.)

WHEATLY says:—'The design of the people's repeating these 'whole verses after the Minister is, that every one may first crave 'to be heard in his own words; which when they have obtained, 'they may leave it to the Priest to set forth all their needs to 'Almighty God, provided that they declare their assent to every 'petition as he delivers it.' (p. 169).—*Ill. of Book of Com. Pr.* Dr. Corrie's Ed.

402.—The earlier Litanies usually commenced with, "*Kyrie eleison*, (Κύριε ἐλέησον), *Christe eleison, Christe audi nos*;" and then followed, "*Pater de cœlis Deus, Miserere nobis*," &c. The *Kyrie eleison* clause was omitted by Cranmer in his translation in 1544. He added, however, the words, '*miserable sinners*' to each invocation; and likewise, to the invocation of the third Person, the passage, '*proceeding from the Father and the Son*.' In the *Revision* of 1689, it was proposed to alter the *first* clause into, '*O God the Father, Creator of heaven and earth, have mercy*,' &c.: and the *third* clause into, '*O God the Holy Ghost, our Sanctifier and Comforter, have mercy*,' &c.; but these changes were never adopted. Next to the invocations of the Trinity, the Litanies of the Western Church, not Eastern, introduced the invocations of the Virgin Mary, and of the Saints, which were so numerous, the Roman Breviary, indeed, numbering more than sixty, and so variable likewise, that *Cranmer* omitted the greater part of them from his translation in 1544, retaining only the three following, and their concluding clause, '*orate pro nobis*:' thus—

'Saint Mary, mother of God, our Saviour Jesus Christ, *pray 'for us*.'

'All holy Angels and Archangels, and all holy orders of blessed 'Spirits, *pray for us*.'

'All holy Patriarchs, and Prophets, Apostles, Martyrs, Confessors, 'and Virgins, and all the blessed company of heaven, *pray 'for us*.'

but these also were wholly omitted from the Litanies of Edward VI.

(*b*) The DEPRECATIONS. (six clauses.)

(Commencing with—'*Remember not, Lord*,' &c.)

403.—The portion of the Litany next following, called the *Deprecations*, is prefaced by a kind of prayer deprecating our Lord's forbearance. It is a translation of the antiphon or anthem which stood after the penitential Psalms preceding the Litany, in the old Breviaries; and began, '*Ne reminiscaris Domine delicta nostra*,' &c.—'Remember not, Lord, our offences,' &c. It was introduced here by Cranmer, in his translation of 1544, in the place of the brief clause, '*Propitius esto: parce nobis Domine;*' and it has the response annexed to it, '*Spare us good Lord,*' but which is not, like the responses that follow, essential to complete the sense of the clause preceding.

404.—The five next sentences, with their responses, are a paraphrase of the petition in the Lord's Prayer, '*Deliver us from evil.*' They commence with the word '*From,*' and were grouped together by Cranmer in 1544. Previously, each separate clause was responded to by '*Libera nos Domine.*' In the *two Liturgies* of Edward VI., (of 1549, and 1552), the last of these Deprecations thus read:—

> 'From all sedition and privy conspiracy; *from the tyranny of 'the Bishop of Rome, and all his detestable enormities;* from 'all false doctrine and heresy, from hardness of heart, &c.'—KEELING. p. 43.

The portion in *italics* was struck out in Elizabeth's Liturgy of 1559; and at the last Revision in 1662, on the restoration of Charles II., the words '*rebellion,*' and '*schism,*' were introduced, in order to deprecate the troubles of Church and State, from which the nation, had so lately recovered.

405.—In the *proposed Revision* of 1689, various alterations were suggested in these Deprecations, which it will be as well to noticè, as there is a call for Revision at the present time. The *sixth clause,* commencing, 'From all evil and mischief,' &c., was changed thus:—

> 'Good Lord, preserve and deliver us from all evil and mischief, 'from sin, from all the deceits (and temptations?) of the 'world, the flesh, and the devil, and from thy wrath,' &c.—(*Printed by order of H. of Commons*, June, 1854.)

And after the response, '*Good Lord deliver us,*' this was added:—

> 'From all infidelity and error, from all impiety and profaneness, 'from all superstition and idolatry.—*Good Lord deliver us.*'—(ibid.)

In the *seventh clause,* 'From all blindness of heart,' was struck out; and instead of 'malice and all uncharitableness,' was introduced, 'revenge, from all rash censure, contention and uncharitableness.'—(ibid). The *eighth clause** was expunged, and the two following inserted in its place:—

---

* In the AMERICAN LITURGY, the commencement of this clause is thus altered:—'*From fornication and all other deadly sin,*' &c., to '*From all inordinate and sinful affections,*' &c.

'From drunkenness and gluttony; from sloth and mis-spending
'of our time; from fornication, adultery, and all uncleanness,
'*Good Lord deliver us.*'
'From lying and slandering, from vain swearing, cursing, and
'perjury, from covetousness, oppression, and all injustice,
'*Good Lord deliver us.*' (ibid.)

In the *ninth clause*, 'sudden death' was altered to '*dying suddenly and unprepared.*' (ibid.)

It should be impressed upon the People, that the responses are not the only portions which appertain to their need and condition: the preceding clauses enunciated aloud by the Minister, should be uttered *mentally* by them, and the response be made aloud to mark their participation in the petitions offered up to the throne of grace. Nor is it to be supposed that the reiterated use of '*Good Lord deliver us,*' and of "*We beseech thee,*" &c. is a mere vain repetition. The following remarks of an old writer are confirmatory of this view:—

DR. BENNETT says:—'These words, '*Good Lord deliver us,*' are 'put in the last place, that the people might not seem to beg 'deliverance from they knew not what; but after they had *mentally* 'utter'd the several particulars together with the Minister, they 'might in this summary manner vocally beg deliverance from them 'all. And certainly, since their joining *vocally* in Prayer is so very 'allowable, as I have already shewn; no words cou'd more properly 'be vocally utter'd by them, than those which are but few, and 'those the principal ones, which include the substance of the whole 'Prayer. I must add, that the frequent use of, "*Good Lord, deliver* '*us,*" cannot be charged upon us as a tautology or vain repetition. 'For if you take notice, 'tis every time applied to distinct matter, 'and consequently makes a distinct Prayer. So that 'tis no 'more a tautology, or vain repetition, than if a man should, as he 'certainly must, frequently say in any other Prayer, such words 'as these, '*Grant O Lord,*' &c., '*We beseech thee,*' &c. What has 'been said of these words, "*Good Lord deliver us,*" may easily be 'apply'd to the following form, "*We beseech thee to hear us, Good* '*Lord,*" which has alwaies a respect to the words going before, 'and every time 'tis us'd makes a distinct Prayer. I have already 'said, that when a Prayer is us'd by way of Responses, &c., both 'Minister and People are to join, at least mentally, in the 'whole; tho' they vocally pronounce only their respective parts.' (*p.* 99).—*Paraphrase of Book of Com. Prayer.* A. D. 1708.

(*c*) The OBSECRATIONS. (three clauses.)
(Commencing with—'*By the mystery of,*' &c.)

406.—Having called upon our Lord in the Deprecations to deliver us from so many and great evils, the Church now *beseeches* our Redeemer to do so by the consideration of His former great mercies. These petitions, collected into three clauses with their responses, were called by the Latins, '*Obsecrations.*' The first two specify the *means* by which this delivery can be accomplished; viz. by the merits of Christ's passion: the third indicates the *time* when we wish to be delivered. The *Obsecrations* are derived from the earlier English Litanies, and those of Hermann, and of Quignon; but in these originals the responses were annexed to each separate petition.

407.—An *alteration* was suggested in the *twelfth clause* by the *Revisers* of 1689, who recommended, instead of the phrase, "*by thy Cross and Passion,*" that these words should be used, "*By thy Passion on the Cross.*" Likewise, in the place of, '*and by the coming of the Holy Ghost,*' they proposed should be used, '*by thy sending of 'the Holy Ghost, and by thy continual Intercession at the Right 'Hand of God.*' But these suggestions were never adopted.*

(*d*) The INTERCESSIONS. (twenty-eight clauses.)

(Commencing with—'*We sinners do beseech thee,*' &c.—and ending with the *Kyrie eleison.*)

408.—The *Intercessions* which follow are derived from the best and most ancient Litanies extant; and in tone and structure they form a characteristic feature of every known Liturgy. The Apostolic injunction that '*intercession be made for all men,*' (1 *Tim.* ii. 1.), is clearly illustrated in the order and arrangement of these Intercessions, which give to all estates of men and to their temporal and spiritual wants, due rank and importance. Supplication is made (1) for the universal Church—(2) then for the Queen and Royal Family—(3) for the Clergy—(4) for the Nobility—(5) Magistrates, and all in authority —(6) for the People—(7) nations at large—(8) for spiritual blessings for the Soul—(9) help and comfort for the afflicted, distressed, and absent—(10) for all men—(11) for our enemies—(12) for bodily support—(13) and lastly for amendment of life. We then call

* In the AMERICAN LITURGY, the thirteenth clause has an alteration in one of the petitions; reading, '*in all time of our prosperity,* instead of, '*in all time of our wealth.*'

upon the Saviour '*to hear us*' by reason of His divinity as '*the Son of God:*' to *grant us peace* and *mercy* by His humanity as *the Lamb of God;* and we again implore him *to hear us* in his mediatorial office of '*the Christ.*' It will have been remarked, doubtlessly, that from the beginning of the Deprecations to the close of the Intercessions, the second Person of the Trinity is alone addressed, in dependence on the promise that 'whatsoever we ask of the Father in His name, He will give unto us;' and, like as this portion of the Litany commences with an invocation of the Three Persons of the Godhead, so it concludes with the *Kyrie eleison,* a shorter invocation, and which is generally known as the *Lesser Litany.*

409.—But few changes have been made in the language of the *Intercessions* since Cranmer's translation of the Litany introduced into the *Prymer* of 1544: those which have been accomplished, are the following:—

The 14*th clause* of the *Litany*, the (first of the Intercessions) in the Liturgies of 1549, 1552, 1559, 1604, read '*thy holy Church universally*;' the last word was changed into '*universal*' in the Scotch Liturgy, and in the Revision of 1662. In the *alterations,* suggested in 1689, the addition of the following sentence to the end of the petition was proposed, '*and this in particular of which we are Members :*' but it was never effected.

The 15*th clause* in the Liturgy of 1549 was, '*That it may please Thee to keep Edward VI. thy Servant, our King and Governor.*' In Elizabeth's Liturgy of 1559, the clause was altered to what we now have in our present Book of Common Prayer, except that the name of '*Victoria*' supplies the place of that of '*Elizabeth.*' Similar alterations have taken place when there has been a change in the reigning monarch. At the time of the *last Review* in 1662, power was given by the *Act of Uniformity* to the Privy Council to make these necessary alterations in the Prayers, Litanies, and Collects of the Liturgy, (see *par.* 258. *Vol.* II.), thus:—

'Be it further enacted by the authority aforesaid, that in all 'those Prayers, Litanies, and Collects, which do any way relate 'to the King, Queen, or Royal progeny, the *names be altered* and 'changed from time to time, and fitted to the present occasion 'according to the direction of *lawful authority.*'—(13 & 14 *Car.* II. c. 4. s. 25.)

In the proposed Revision of 1689, it was suggested to alter the word '*keep*' to '*guide*,' and to omit the epithet '*most gracious*.'*

The 16*th clause* of 1549, had the reading, '*may always have affiance in thee*,' which was changed in 1559 to '*may evermore have affiance*,' &c., and this was maintained in the subsequent Liturgies. The pronouns '*his*,' and '*he*' were, as the occasion required, altered to '*her*,' and '*she* :' a similar change occurs in the next clause.

The 17*th clause* had no other alteration than that of the pronouns, as we have just mentioned: it was suggested, however, by the *Reviewers* of 1689, to read '*giving them a prosperous and happy reign over us*,' instead of '*giving them the victory over all their enemies*.'

The 18*th clause* was first introduced into the Liturgy in that of 1604, where it reads:—'*That it may please thee to bless and* '*preserve our gracious Queen Anne, Prince Henry, and the rest* '*of the King and Queen's Royal issue* :' this was altered in the Prayer Book of 1662, to '*That it may please thee to bless and* '*preserve our gracious Queen Catharine, Mary the Queen-Mother,* '*James Duke of York, and all the Royal Family*.'† A clause for the Parliament was suggested by the *Reviewers* in 1689, to follow this petition: it thus read:—'*That it may please Thee to direct* '*and prosper the High Court of Parliament, in all their consultations,* '*to the advancement of thy glory, the good of thy Church, the safety,* '*honour, and welfare of their Majesties and their kingdoms*.' To which was annexed the usual response '*We beseech thee*,' &c.

The 21*st clause* in behalf of Magistrates, &c. had the following addition suggested by the *Reviewers* of 1689, '*That it may please* '*Thee to take their Majesties forces by sea and land into thy most* '*gracious protection and to make them victorious over all our* '*enemies*.'

The 24*th clause* also was subject to amendment by the *Reviewers* of 1689: '*to love and dread Thee*,' was altered thus—'*to love Thee* '*above all things, to dread to offend Thee, and diligently*,' &c.: to

---

* In the AMERICAN LITURGY greater alterations have been made in this point by reason of the difference in the Government of that country. Clauses 15, 16, 17, 18, 20, 21 of the English Litany have been merged into this one clause, '*That it may please* '*Thee to bless and preserve all Christian Rulers and Magistrates,* '*giving them grace to execute justice, and to maintain truth*.'

† Similarly in the SCOTCH LITURGY of 1637: '*That it may*, &c. '*gracious Queen Mary, Prince Charles, and the rest of the Royal* '*issue*.'——KEELING. *p.* 44.

which was annexed this clause following, '*That it may please Thee* '*to incline and enable us to pray alway with fervent affection, in* '*every thing to give thanks, to depend upon Thee and trust in Thee* '*to delight ourselves in Thee, and cheerfully to resign ourselves to* '*thy holy will and pleasure.*'

The 25*th clause* was followed by the *Reviewers* of 1689, with one running in these words, '*That it may please Thee to endue us* '*with the graces of humility and meekness, of contentedness and* '*patience, of true justice, of temperance and purity, of peaceableness* '*and charity.*' 'We beseech Thee,' &c.—but this was never sanctioned.

The 29*th clause* was recommended by these same *Reviewers* of 1689, to be expanded into two clauses, each with the usual response, the first to be:—'*That it may please Thee to preserve* '*such as travel by land or by water, all women labouring of child,* '*young children, all sick and dying persons.*'—'We beseech Thee,' &c. The second clause was to be:—'*That it may please Thee to shew* '*thy pity upon all prisoners and captives; upon all that are* '*persecuted for truth and righteousness sake; upon all that are in* '*affliction,*' ["especially those for whom our prayers are desired."] 'We beseech Thee,' &c.—these suggestions, however, were never assented to.

410.—The *Intercessions* conclude with the Lesser Litany, or *Kyrie Eleison*, in order that we may terminate as we began by addressing the ever blessed Trinity; and the three clauses, it will be remarked, are each repeated by Minister and People in immediate succession, not *alternatim*, as in the Morning and Evening Prayer.*

(*e*) THE SUPPLICATIONS, OR SUFFRAGES.

(Commencing with the *Lord's Prayer*, and continuing to the *Prayers*).

411.—This concluding section of the Litany, which seems to have been put together about A. D. 600, begins with the *Lord's Prayer*, headed by this Rubric, introduced only at the last Review (1662):—

* In the AMERICAN LITURGY, there is the following Rubric standing before the Lesser Litany:—"*The Minister may at his dis-* "*cretion omit all that follows, to the Prayer,* We humbly beseech "Thee, O Father, &c."

¶ '*Then shall the Priest, and People with him, say the Lord's Prayer.*' (1662).

An attempt was made to alter the word '*Priest*' to '*Minister*' in this Rubric by the *Reviewers* of 1689, but it failed: they also suggested the introduction of the Doxology,—'*For thine is the kingdom,*' &c.—but with equal unsuccess. A marginal note was likewise annexed, to this effect:—'*Q. Whether when there is 'a Communion, the Lord's Prayer is not to be here 'omitted.*' (See Alterations of 1689, in Book of Common Prayer, printed by order of the House of Commons, 1854). The *Lord's Prayer* found a place in the Litany through the piety of our ancestors, who deemed it right that so valuable and incomparable a model of prayer should be in every Office.

412.—A *Versicle* and *Response* follow, adapted from *Psalm* ciii. 10, in which we supplicate our Heavenly Father mercifully to temper His chastisements. The old expression '*after,*' found in these passages must not be exchanged by the Officiating Minister, or People, for the explanatory clause '*according to,*' as is used in the *American Liturgy*, and as some Clergymen among us have been known to do. (See *par*. 22.). The headings of these two versicles are in our present Book of Common Prayer, '*Priest,*' and '*Answer,*' (1662) which clearly point out by whom they are to be employed: in the previous versions the headings were, '*The Versicle,*' and '*Answer.*' (1604), ('*The Answer.*' 1549, 1552, 1549.)

'Let us pray.'

[Prayer against Persecution.]

413.—The *Prayer* against persecution, or as the old Salisbury Missal has it, "*For Tribulation of Heart,*" now occurs; headed by the words, "*Let us pray;*" a Rubric designed to intimate to the Congregation that their duty is not over with the uttering of responses, but that they should repeat with the Priest, yet *inaudibly*, the Prayers which follow: and this direction should not be omitted, nor carelessly enunciated. The

Reviewers of 1689 wished to expunge this Rubric; but its usefulness is well explained by Sparrow in his Rationale; or as Dr. Corrie, in his edition of Wheatly on the Common Prayer, says:—

'In ancient Liturgies these words, (*Let us pray*), often served 'as a mark of transition from one sort of prayer to another, 'viz. from what the Latins call *Preces* to what they term '*Orationes;* the *Preces* were those alternate petitions which 'passed conjointly between the Priest and People; the *Orationes* 'were those that were said by the Priest alone, the People only 'answering Amen.' (*p.* 179.)

Bp. Mant observes:—'The short exhortation to prayer, oc-'casionally occurring in the Litany and elsewhere, should by no 'means be omitted or slurred over as of no account, but should 'be enunciated with deliberate seriousness.' (*p.* 51.)—*Hor. Lit.*

In the *Churchman's Diary* we read:—'In the Litany, "*Let us 'pray,*" is not addressed to the people, as it is after the Creed. It is 'the sign that the Priest is about to gather together the suffrages 'which have been offered before in common with the people, and to 'present them to God.'—Pub. by *Masters.*

The subject of this prayer being continued in another form, to be used by the people, as the Italic print indicates, the usual "*Amen*" is not annexed.

[Versicles, and Doxology.]

The *Versicle* is derived from *Psalms* xliv. 26; lxxix. 9., and is followed by a passage from *Psalm* xliv. 1. employed by the Minister to stimulate the faith of the People, who respond in another *Versicle*, and then Minister and People testify their praise in the *Doxology*. The *first* clause of this Doxology, when '*said*,' always falls to the Minister to repeat; the *second*, consequently, to the People. In the last *Revision* (1662), the second clause was headed with the word '*Answer*' to point out by whom it was to be employed: the omission of '*Priest*,' or '*Minister*,' as a heading to the first clause may have been accidental. In the *Alterations* suggested by the Reviewers in 1689, the Doxology here is struck out, probably as not being thought admissible in a Litany. The *Doxology* is not to be repeated in a *standing* posture as in other cases, either because of its close connexion with the Supplications and Suffrages preceding and following; or, it may be, from no exceptional rule being required when Litanies were used in Processions, and because when these Processions ceased, no direction was introduced. In the time of *Bishop Sparrow* (*ob.* 1685), this Doxology was chanted, as in the Psalms; he says:—

'Here in the Litany, it is said in a way somewhat different; for 'after that the Priest and People have in the Supplications afore-'going, besought God, that He would arise, help and deliver them, 'as He did their forefathers of old, for His Name's Sake and 'Honour, the Priest does Collect-wise sum up this; praying, that 'by such deliverances, all glory may redound to God the Father 'Son, and Holy Ghost, as it was in the beginning, is now, and ever 'shall be, &c., the People answering only *Amen*, as it were after a '*Collect*,* and continuing *kneeling*, because both this, as it is here 'used, and other parts of the Litany before and after, are matters 'of humble supplication, and so most fit to be tendred to God, in 'that posture.'—(*Rationale*. p. 62.) * In a *note* is added:—'In the 'present Office the People answer, '*As it was in the beginning*,' '&c., as in other places.'

414.—The *Suffrages* and *Responses* following the doxology, are addressed exclusively to Christ, the *Son;* the portion to be said by the *People* being distinguished only by Italic type: they close with a passage from the Psalms, *Ps.* xxxiii. 22., separated into a part for the '*Priest*,' and a part for the '*People*,' as indicated by the Rubric at the beginning of each of the clauses.

(*f*.) The PRAYERS.

¶. '*Let us pray*.'

415.—The Minister next addresses *God the Father* in behalf of the people, for the sanctification of every trouble; using, with slight alteration, the form employed by Gregory, eleven hundred years ago. In the *Revision* of 1689 it was proposed to omit the Rubric, '*Let us pray*,' preceding this prayer; and, in the text, to substitute '*justly*' for '*righteously*.' The *Reviewers* also suggested the introduction at the end of the Prayer of the following Rubrics:—

'*Then the Minister continuing in his place shall use this 'Collect:*'

'Almighty God to whom all hearts, &c............Amen.'

'*Then shall the Minister rehearse distinctly the Tenn Com- 'mandments, and the People, still kneeling, shall after every Com- 'mandment ask God mercy for their transgression thereof for the 'time past, and grace to keep the same, for the time to come, as 'followeth*.'

'God spake these words, &c. (As in the Communion Office).

'*Or sometimes the eight Beatitudes, especially on Communion days*. (See the Communion Service.)

'*Then shall follow the Collect for the Day*.

'*Then the Epistle and Gospell*.

'*Then* (if there be no Communion) *the Nicene Creed*.

'*Then the General Thanksgiving, &c*.

'*The Prayer commonly called S. Chrysostom's*.'

'*The Grace, &c*.' '2 Cor..xiii. 14.'

'*Then the Minister shall declare unto the people what Holy- 'daies or Fasting-daies, are, in the week following to be observed; 'and then also, if occasion be, shall notice be given of the Com-*

'*munion, and the Banns of Matrimony published, and Breifs*
'*Citations, and Excommunications read; and nothing shall be*
'*proclaimed or published in the Church during the time of Divine*
'*Service but by the Minister, nor by him anything but what is*
'*prescribed in the rules of this Book or enjoined by the King,*
'*or by the Ordinary of the place, not being contrary to the Laws*
'*of this Realm.*

[Note in the margin.] 'This Rubric was occasioned by 'K. James's enjoining his Declaration, (which was against Law), '*to be read in Churches.*'

'*The Singing Psalm.*

'*Q.* of what Translation.

'*QQ.* whether the Minister may not here be directed to use in 'the Pulpit before Sermon, "*the Prayer for the whole state of* '*Christ's Church,*" &c. accommodated to the purpose; or some such 'other Prayer?

'*Note that when there is no Communion at all this shall be* '*read in the same place with the rest of the Service.*'

The Occasional Prayers.

(The Minister and People still kneeling.)

416.—According to the Rubric preceding the general "Prayers and Thanksgivings," standing in our Liturgy immediately after the *Litany*, the Officiating Minister is directed to introduce one or more of them, as occasion may require, *here*, before the '*Prayer of St Chrysostom.*' The Rubrick is:—

¶. '*To be used before the two final Prayers of the Litany, or of* '*Morning and Evening Prayer.*'

The Minister will, therefore, employ such of them, when the occasion or season shall arise, as explained in our elucidation of the Morning Prayer, or of the Evening Prayer (*Par.* 263. *Vol.* **E.**; and particularly *par.* 382. *Vol.* **F.**), to which we refer our Readers, in order to avoid repetition. The more usual Prayers introduced into the Litany are:—

1. The *Prayer in the Ember Weeks* for those about to be ordained. (See *Vol.* **B.**)
2. The *Prayer for the Parliament* during the Session.
3. The *General Thanksgiving*. (See *par.* 382. supra.)

'*A Prayer of St Chrysostom.*'

(Minister and People still kneeling.)

417.—At the close of the *General Thanksgiving,* the Officiating Minister will go back to the '*Prayer of St Chrysostom,*' (see *pars.* 264, 265. supra), which he will follow with the *Benediction,* 2 *Cor.* xiii. In the Liturgies of 1559, the *Prayer of St Chrysostom* at the end of the Litany was preceded by the '*Prayer for the Queen's Majesty,*' and a *Prayer for the Clergy* and *People.* In the Liturgy of 1604, between the *Prayer for the King's Majesty* and the *Prayer for the Clergy and People,** was introduced '*A Prayer for the Queen and Prince, and other the King and Queen's Children;*' and after that '*For the Clergy and People*' was introduced the '*Prayer to be said in the Ember Weeks.*' In 1549, and at the last *Review,* 1662, no printed matter interposed in the Litany between the Prayer, "We humbly beseech Thee O Father," &c., and the *Prayer of St Chrysostom;* but in the last Revision (1662,) the *Rubric* following the Litany, and the "PRAYERS and THANKSGIVINGS" annexed to it were introduced, as we have just shewn† (*par.* 415.).

The BENEDICTORY PRAYER.

2 *Cor.* xiii.

418.—This *Benediction* was added to the Litany in the Prayer Book of Elizabeth, (1559.)—(See *pars.*

---

* In the SCOTCH LITURGY this was entitled '*A Prayer for the Queen, Prince Charles, and the rest of the Royal Progeny:*' and thus began,—"Almighty God the fountain of all goodness, we "humbly beseech Thee to bless our gracious Queen *Mary,* Prince "*Charles,* with the rest of the Royal Progeny; endue, &c." so with the prayer for the Clergy, which was in the Scotch Liturgy, entitled '*A Prayer for the holy Clergy,*' and thus read:—"Almighty "and everlasting God, who only workest great and marvellous "things, send down upon our Bishops, Presbyters, and Curates, "and all Congregations," &c. (KEELING, 50, 51.)

† In the AMERICAN LITURGY, we find only the '*General Thanksgiving*' placed between the Prayer, "We humbly beseech Thee, O Father," &c., and the "*Prayer of St Chrysostom.*"

384, 385,)—and, with the '*Prayer of St Chrysostom*,' belonged especially to this Service. The *Litany*, however was then a distinct Office by itself; but it is now used generally with the MORNING PRAYER, and the closing prayers peculiar to the *Litany* mentioned in the preceding paragraph, were at the last *Revision* (1662), appended also to the *Morning Office*. (See KEELING, 24. 48—52.)

When the LITANY *is to be used.*

419.—The commencing words of the Rubric, "*Here followeth the Litany*," &c. has no reference to its position in Public Worship; but merely implies *here* below is the Litany. According however to this *Rubric* placed at the head of the Litany in our present Book of Common Prayer, the Office is directed to be used "*after* MORNING PRAYER on *Sundays*, *Wednesdays*, and *Fridays*, and *whenever* commanded by the Ordinary;" consequently, on the remaining days of the week, unless otherwise appointed by the Ordinary, the Officiating Minister has not authority, *suo motu*, to use the Litany. The *Rubric* referred to thus reads :—

(*a*) ¶. '*Here followeth the* LITANY, *or General Supplication*, '*to be sung or said after Morning Prayer upon* 'Sundays, Wednesdays, *and* Fridays, *and at other times*, '*when it shall be commanded by the Ordinary*.' (1662).—Present Book of Common Prayer.

420.—There are *three* questions involved in this Rubric, demanding our careful consideration, viz.
(I.) The *days* on which the LITANY is to be used.
(II.) The *time* or *place* in MORNING PRAYER when it is to be introduced.
(III.) Its use as a *distinct Service*, inferred by the phrase "*after* MORNING PRAYER."

I. Of the DAYS.—With regard to the *Days* on which the *Litany* is to be used, we find it laid down in the Rubric with sufficient clearness; and therefore the question needs but little comment. *Sundays*, *Wednesdays*, and *Fridays*, are the only specified days;

the exceptional occasions are when the Ordinary may prescribe the use of the LITANY on one or other of the four remaining days of the week. In the first Liturgy of Edw. VI., that of 1549, the LITANY stood between the *Communion Service*, and the Baptismal Office, with the simple title of "THE LITANY AND SUFFRAGES;" and a Rubric directing its use was placed immediately after the Communion Service, and thus read:—

(b) '*Upon* WEDNESDAYS *and* FRIDAYS *the English Litany shall 'be said or sung in all places, after such form as is ap'pointed by the King's Majesty's Injunctions. Or as is or 'shall be otherwise appointed by his highness. And though 'there be none to communicate with the Priest yet these days '(after the* LITANY *ended), the Priest shall put upon him,'* &c. (1549).—KEELING. 41. 229.

421.—Here we find the LITANY prescribed for *Wednesdays* and *Fridays* only. In addition to this we discover among the *Notes of Explication* at the end of this Liturgy, not only a permission to use portions of Scripture on certain days *instead of* the LITANY; among which days are mentioned *Whitsunday* and *Trinity-Sunday*, whence we may naturally infer that the LITANY was tacitly used on *Sundays* generally; but likewise we observe that a very important privilege is allowed to the Officiating Minister of *omitting* the LITANY whenever he might think fit. This discretionary power is laid down in the last two Rubrics, thus:—

(c) '*Also upon* Christmas day, Easter day, *the* Ascension day, ' Whit-Sunday, *and the* Feast of the Trinity, *may be used any 'part of Holy Scripture hereafter to be certainly limited and 'appointed in the stead of the Litany.*

(d) '*If there be a* Sermon, *or for other great cause, the Curate 'by his discretion may leave out the* Litany, *Gloria in 'Excelsis, the Creed, the Homily, and the Exhortation to the 'Communion.'* (1549.)—KEELING. 357.

There are some Clergymen of extreme views who omit the LITANY on *Fridays*, should a '*Feast*' happen to fall on that day; how far they may be legally correct we are not able to decide. We quote what is considered an authority:—

The Rev. JOHN PURCHAS writes:—'*The* LITANY *ought not to be* '*said* on Fridays, if a Festival come on that day; because, of course, 'the Office of the *Feast* takes the place of the Office of the *Feria*. 'This does not apply to Sunday, because it is the *one* Feast on 'which the Rubric before the Litany orders it to be used.' (*p.* 122.)—*Directorium Anglicanum.*

422.—At a later period, we have the *Canons* of 1603-4, enjoining the use of the LITANY on *Wednesdays*, and *Fridays*, (no mention being made of Sundays,) and, it would seem, as a *distinct Service;* thus:—

(e) 'The LITANY shall be said or sung, when and as it is set down 'in the Book of Common Prayer, by the Parsons, Vicars, '&c.......Upon *Wednesdays* and *Fridays* weekly, though they 'be not Holy-days,' &c.—CANON. 15.

The question of the LITANY being used as a *distinct Service* will occur presently; in the mean time we may observe that the reason why *Wednesdays*, and *Fridays* are alone appointed for the Litany was because they were the prescribed fasting days of the early Church — *Wednesday*, on account of being the day of Christ's betrayal, and *Friday*, the day of His crucifixion.—So says L'Estrange, and other writers.

BP. SPARROW (*ob.* 1685.) observes:—'The *Litany* is appointed 'in the *Rubrics* to be read on *Wednesdays* and *Fridays*, the days 'kept in the *Greek* Church for more solemn Fasts, because the '*Bridegroom* was then taken from us, being sold by *Judas* on '*Wednesday*, and murthered on *Friday*, (*Epiphan. adv. Aërium*). 'And tho' our Church, in imitation of the Western, hath chang'd 'the *Wednesday* Fast to *Saturday*, yet in memory of the *Eastern* 'custom, she still appoints the LITANY to be used upon *Wednesday*. '*Friday* was, both in the *Greek* Church and *Latin*, a Litany or 'Humiliation-Day, and so is kept in ours. And whosoever loves 'to feast on that day rather than another, in that holds not com'munion with the antient Catholick *Church*, but with the *Turks*, 'who, in contumely of Christ crucified, feast that day.' (*p.* 65.)—*Rationale.*

423.—We may add here, perhaps, that it was once the practice of the English Church to repeat the Litany *after* MORNING PRAYER, and as a *distinct Service* during the greatest part of Lent; as we may gather from the *Salisbury Breviary*. Upon this usage Mr. Palmer makes these remarks:—

'The *Litany* was said with the gradual Psalms, after the Office 'for the third hour, from Monday in the first week of Lent, to

'Wednesday before Easter, whenever there was no proper Service 'of Sundays, or Holy-days.'—*Orig. Lit.* note, *Vol.* i. p. 316.

424.—Thus far we have the use of the LITANY authoritatively ordered on *Wednesdays* and *Fridays;* and by inference only on Sundays. The next public order enforces its use on *Sundays* particularly; and on any other day the Ordinary may appoint. This direction occurs in the *second* Liturgy of Edw. VI, that of 1552, wherein the LITANY is transferred to the place it now occupies in our present Book of Common Prayer, and the Rubric heading it altered to admit the use of the Litany on *Sundays* also; and to give authority to the *Ordinary* to prescribe its use at *other times*. It thus reads:—

(f) '*Here followeth the* LITANY, *to be used upon Sundays,* '*Wednesdays, and Fridays, and at other times, when it* '*shall be commanded by the Ordinary.*' (1552, 1559, 1604). —KEELING. 40, 41.

The Rubrics of 1549, referred to above (b. c. d.), were omitted in the *Revision* of 1552; and the new Rubric, and transposition of the Litany, then adopted, continued in the later *Reviews* of 1559, and 1604; and *Sundays*, *Wednesdays*, and *Fridays*, have been the prescribed days for the Litany down to our own time. Why *Sunday* was added, Bp. Cosins thus tells us:—

BP. COSINS (*ob.* 1672.) says:—'These *Litanies* were wont to be 'said at the celebration of the Eucharist, as in the ancient Church, 'so in this also, 2 *Edw.* VI. when the Communion was administered '(as it still ought to be in Catholic Churches) every *Sunday* at the 'least. Now although the condition of the Church be not for the 'present capable of so excellent a custom, yet was there good 'reason, that the *Litanies* should be prescribed upon those days 'howsoever, as being the next solemnity to the Eucharist in the 'Publick Service of God, observed from the beginning of the 'Church: and because they contain matter of supplication, for 'the diverting of God's judgments, and obtaining His Blessings, 'nothing could be more suitable than to add them to the Daily 'Morning Service, upon *Wednesdays* and *Fridays*, as the exercise 'of that continual humiliation before God, to which the observation 'of those days was intended, to the unspeakable benefit of the 'Church, and the continual discharge of those most excellent 'Offices of Fasting, Prayer, and Alms, among Christians.'—*Add. Notes to* NICHOLLS' COMMON PRAYER. *p.* 23.

425.—II. The next question is that of the *time and place* in MORNING PRAYER when the *Litany* is to be introduced. Our present Rubric at the beginning of the Litany is that of the Liturgies of 1552, 1559, and 1604, enlarged; having at its commencement the additional words following in *italics*:—

(g) 'Here followeth the Litany, *or General Supplication, to be* '*sung or said* ('used' 1552, 1559. 1604.) *after Morning* '*Prayer* upon Sundays, Wednesdays, and Fridays,' &c. (1662).

426.—Now, the office of MORNING PRAYER in all our Liturgies previous to the last *Review* in 1662, terminated with the *Third Collect, for Grace;* and we may infer from the annexed Rubric of the SCOTCH LITURGY, A. D. 1637, immediately following this Collect, thus:—

(h) '*After this Collect ended, followeth the Litany; and if the* '*Litany be not appointed to be said or sung that Morning,* '*then shall next be said the prayer for the King's Majesty,* '*with the rest of the prayers following at the end of the* '*Litany, and the Benediction.*' (1637.) KEELING. 24.

as well as from this Rubric *heading* the LITANY in this same Scotch Liturgy.

(i) '*Here followeth the Litany, to be used after the third* '*Collect at Morning Prayer, called the Collect for Grace,* '*upon Sundays, Wednesdays, and Fridays, and at other* '*times when it shall be commanded by the Ordinary, and* '*without omission of any part of the other daily Service of* '*the Church on those days.*' (1637.)—KEELING. 40.

And likewise from the Rubric in the last *Review* (1662) above cited (g), coupled with the Rubrics placed after the said '*Third Collect, for Grace*' in that same *Revision* of 1662, which is the Prayer Book used at the present day, and which we here annex:—

(k) ¶. '*In Quires and Places where they sing, here followeth* '*the Anthem.*'

'*Then these five Prayers following are to be read here,* '*except when the Litany is read; and then only the* '*two last are to be read, as they are there placed.*' (1662.)

It may be inferred we say, from the above Rubrics, independent of other evidence, that the LITANY, long before the last *Revision* of the Prayer Book in 1662, was generally, by tacit consent, *annexed to* the MORNING PRAYER, and brought in immediately after the '*Third Collect, for Grace:*' an '*Anthem*' being employed in Cathedrals, and the more fashionable Churches, and populous places, '*where they sing*,' to relieve the Congregation, and facilitate its introduction. We are said to be indebted to Bp. Cosins for the alterations made in the *Rubrics* affecting the Litany in the last Review (1662), from the following suggestion of his at the Savoy Conference in 1661:—

Bp. Cosin says:—'There is no appointment at what time of 'the day, or after what part of the Service it (the *Litany*) ought to 'be said; so that a contentious man may take his liberty to say it 'after 'Evening Prayer,' or at any time of the day upon *Sundays*, '*Wednesdays*, and *Fridays*, &c. at his own choice, unless an order 'be here added; to confine him.'—*Add. Notes* to Nicholls' *C. Pr. p.* 68.

427.—From the above remarks it is evident that the *time* and *place* indicated by the Rubrics for introducing the Litany in Morning Prayer on *Sundays*, *Wednesdays*, and *Fridays*, is between the '*Third Collect, for Grace*,' and '*The Prayer of St Chrysostom*:' although the *Rubric* at the head of the *Litany* implies that it may be used '*after the Morning Prayer*' as a *distinct Service*, which brings us to the next enquiry.

428.—III. *Of the use of the Litany as a distinct Service?*—It is to be regretted with regard to this point that the *Canons* (of 1603) and the *Rubrics* of our Liturgy are not in harmony. The 15th *Canon* requires the Litany to be used *alone* on *Wednesdays*, and *Fridays*: it makes no mention of the Sunday, nor any allusion to Morning Prayer. On the other hand, the *Rubric* directs the Litany to be *preceded* by Morning Prayer, and adds *Sundays* to the *Wednesdays* and *Fridays* on which it shall be used; at the same time it omits to state whether the Litany shall follow Morning Prayer *immediately*, or at an *interval of time*. There are, therefore, as might be supposed, differences of opinion and diversities of practice. As we have already said so much on this question in our strictures on the "Division of the Services" in *Vol.* B. *pars.* 172—180, it will be sufficient here, we hope, to refer our Readers to those pages rather than weary them with a repetition of arguments and opinions, or burthen our space unnecessarily with reiteration. It would be right, however, that we express our own decided opinion on this point; which is, that we think it would be desirable that the Officiating Minister should be invested with a discretionary power to *detach* the LITANY from the MORNING PRAYER whenever he may think it expedient to do so.

429.—As a *distinct* and *independent Service*, however, we find that the ORDINARY is permitted by the following portion of the Rubric already quoted, to direct the use of the LITANY, when he may think it desirable. Thus:—

¶. '......*at other times when it shall be commanded by the 'Ordinary.'* (1662.)—Present Book of Common Prayer.

The *Ordinary*, consequently, who is usually the *Bishop of the Diocese*, can at his discretion sanction the use of the LITANY as a *distinct Service;* and whenever the Officiating Minister may think this expedient, an application to his Diocesan will generally obtain the required concession.

DR. BURN explains the term ORDINARY, *ordinarius* '(which is a 'word we have received from the Civil Law), is he who hath the 'proper and regular jurisdiction, as of course and of common right, 'in opposition to persons who are *extraordinarily* appointed. In 'some Acts of Parliament we find the *Bishop* to be called Ordinary, 'and so he is taken at the Common Law, as having *ordinary* 'jurisdiction in Causes Ecclesiastical; albeit in a more general 'acceptation, the word *ordinary* signifieth any Judge authorized to 'take cognizance of Causes in his own proper right, as he is a 'Magistrate, and not by way of deputation or delegation.'—*Eccl. Law.* Phillimore's Ed. *Vol.* iii. *p.* 39.

'The *Ordinary*,' says MR. STEPHENS, 'according to the acceptation of common law, is usually taken for him that hath *ordinary* 'jurisdiction in Causes Ecclesiastical, immediate to the King. He 'is, in common understanding, the *Bishop of the Diocese*, who is the 'Superior, and, for the most part, Visitor of all his Churches within 'his Diocese; and hath *ordinary jurisdiction* in all the causes aforesaid for the doing of justice within his Diocese, *in jure proprio et 'non per deputationem.*' *Laws Relating to the Clergy.* Vol. i. *p.* 158.

Many Bishops prefer the LITANY ON occasions of large *Confirmations;* and in other cases where the MORNING and EVENING PRAYER would be too lengthy for the particular duty to be performed by them.

430.—The LITANY was originally looked upon as a *separate* and *distinct service:* we find it so in the time of Henry VIII.; his successor, however, Edward VI. in his "Injunctions" (1547), ordered it to be used immediately before high mass. (CARDWELL'S *Doc. Ann.* II. §. 23.). The Rubric also of the *first Liturgy* of Edward (1549), directed it to be said on Wednesdays and Fridays, *just before* the Ante-Communion Office, to which, indeed, it was then generally considered a preparation. (See *Rubric* (b) *supra*). In the COMMINATION SERVICE, we find the Rubric of this *first* Liturgy implied an interval between the *Litany* and MORNING PRAYER, and allowed time enough for the Congregation to go home and return to Church again before the Litany was begun;

'*After* MATTINS *ended,** *the People being called together by the* '*ringing of a bell, and assembled in the Church: the English* 'LITANY *shall be said after the accustomed manner; which ended,* '*the Priest shall go into the Pulpit and say thus:* (1549).—KEELING. 347.

431.—In the Liturgy of 1552, the Rubric at the Litany ordered its use on *Sundays* as well as on Wednesdays and Fridays, "and whenever the *Ordinary* should appoint." (See Rubric (f) supra); this sanctioned the use of the LITANY as a distinct service at *Confirmations*, as is now frequently done, and on certain days at the Universities of Oxford and Cambridge. But in 1559, *Elizabeth*, as Edward before her, ordered, by her Injunctions, 'that the *Litany* should be said 'immediately before the time of Communion of the 'Sacrament;' and 'that weekly upon *Wednesdays* and '*Fridays* not being Holy-days, the Curate at the 'accustomed hours of Service shall resort to Church,

* In the subsequent Liturgies of 1552, 1559, and 1604, the words, '*after Matins ended,*' were altered to, '*after* MORNING PRAYER.'

'and cause warning to be given to the People by 'knolling of a bell, and say the *Litany* and *Prayers*:' Here a separation would be implied. In 1571, it was ordered by the "Injunctions" of Abp. Grindal, that 'the Minister was not to pause or stay between the '*Morning Prayer*, *Litany*, and *Communion*......to the 'intent the People might continue together in prayer, 'and hearing the word of God, and not depart out of 'the Church during all the time of the whole Divine 'Service.'—CARDWELL'S *Doc. Ann.* lxxvii. Here was a union of the Services. The usage, therefore, seems then to have been variable; and the Rubric at the *last Review* in 1662, was even incompetent to point out the correct hour at which the LITANY should be said when it employed the indefinite language of '*after* MORNING PRAYER.' Nor did the alteration in the Rubric at the *Commination Office* in 1662 throw any additional light on the subject; for it merely says:—

¶. '*After Morning Prayer, the Litany ended according to 'the accustomed manner, the Priest shall in the Reading-Pew, or Pulpit say.*' (1662).

The Rev. J. C. ROBERTSON, when remarking that, '*Daily Service* 'was never general in Parish Churches, either before or since the 'Reformation; that on *Wednesdays* and *Fridays*, the LITANY was 'commonly read in the times which we have been reviewing, (for 'the most part apparently without the Morning Prayers)' &c., to which the Author adds this note:—Mr. Lathbury is of opinion that 'because the rubric of 1662 describes the Litany as "to be "sung or said *after Morning Prayer*," we are not now at liberty to 'use it alone on Wednesdays and Fridays. (*Hist. Convoc.* 195). The 'only one of the extracts in this section which clearly requires a 'previous reading of the Morning Prayer is that from Gunning's 'Articles,* of a date later than the alteration of the rubric. If, as 'is most likely, the words were introduced in consequence of 'Cosins' suggestion, which is given by Nicholls, (see *par.* 425, *supra*) 'we may be justified in supposing them to mean only that this 'Office shall not be read at a wrong time of the day. In any case,

---

* Bp. *Gunning's* Visitation Article, to which reference is made, is:—'Whether every Minister celebrate Divine Service upon all 'Sundays and Holy-days, not omitting also other days appointed 'by the Book of Common Prayer, as Wednesdays and Fridays, '(with the Litanies added), and the Eves of every Sunday and 'Holy-day, with Ember and Rogation days?'—(*ib.* p. 52.)

'they cannot bind us to use the Litany *immediately* after Morning 'Prayer, so as to combine the two in one Service. Cosin himself, 'while he desires the insertion of an order that the Litany be said 'after Morning Prayer, argues for a disjunction of the Offices, and 'we know that he incurred persecution by practising it.' (*p.* 54. *note*).—*How shall we Conform to the Liturgy.*

We have, however, said enough on this subject, seeing we have fully elucidated the point in a previous Volume (*Vol.* **B**); and we must therefore, now proceed to the next enquiry.

¶. '*To be sung or said.*'

[SINGING.]

432. *Litanies* having been originally employed in Processions; we can well imagine that they were usually '*sung*,' and that it was not till the Litany became a part of Divine Worship in our Parish Churches at the time of the Reformation that '*saying*' the Litany was put in practice. In the Preface of the *Prymer* of Henry VIII, set forth in English by Whitchurch, we have the following clause (the *Italics* are ours):—

'And suche among the people as haue bokes and can reade, 'may *reade* them, quietly and softly to themselfe: and suche as 'can not reade, let them quietly and attentively geue audience in 'time of the sayde prayers, hauying theyr myndes erect to Al-'mighty God, and deuoutly praying in theyr heartes, the same 'petitions whiche do entre in at theyr eares, so that with on sound 'of the heart and one accorde, God may be glorified in his churche.

'And it is to be remembered, that that whiche is printed in 'the *great letters*, is to be *sayd* or *song* of the priest with an audible 'voyce, that is to saye, so loude and so playne, that it may wel be 'vnderstand of the hearers. And that which is in the *litle letter*, is 'to be answered of the quier, soberly and deuoutly.'—See MASKELL'S *Mon. Ritualia.* Vol. II. *p.* 97. *note.*

In addition to this we have the Rubric of the *Salisbury Breviary* giving this direction:—

'Quicquid sacerdos dicit de Litania, chorus idem repetat plenè 'et integrè usque ad prolationem *ut pacem nobis dones* Tunc 'respondeat chorus *Te rogamus audi nos* tantum: et sic de singulis 'usque ad *Kyrie Eleyson, Christe Eleyson, Kyrie Eleyson.*'—(See PALMER'S *Orig. Lit.* Vol. I. p. 330.

At the Reformation, in the *Injunctions* of EDWARD VI. (A. D. 1547.) 'the Priests with others' are 'to *sing* or *say* plainly and distinctly the Litany.' (CARDWELL's *Doc. Ann.* I. 14.)

433.—In the *first Liturgy* of EDWARD VI. (A. D. 1549.) the Rubric requires that '*the English Litany shall be said or sung*' &c. At the COMMINATION SERVICE of this same Liturgy, the heading Rubric requires that '*the English Litany shall be said after* '*the accustomed manner*' &c. (1549; so in 1552, 1559, 1604). But the Rubric at the beginning of the Litany in the subsequent *Liturgies* of 1552, 1559, 1604, and in the *Scotch Liturgy* of 1637, seems to compromise the question by ordering the Litany, instead of '*to be said or sung*,' to be '*used*,' &c.

The 15th *Canon* of 1603 orders that, 'The LITANY 'shall be *said* or *sung*, and as it is set down in the 'Book of Common Prayer &c.........upon *Wednesdays* 'and *Fridays* weekly, though they be not Holy-days, 'the Minister at the accustomed hours of Service, 'shall resort to the Church or Chapel, and warning 'being given by tolling of a Bell, shall *say* the LITANY 'prescribed in the Book of Common Prayer, &c.'

At the *last Review* in 1662, which forms our present Book of Common Prayer, the Rubric at the head of the LITANY was altered, directing '*the* LITANY, *or* '*General Supplication, to be sung or said*, &c.' While at the COMMINATION SERVICE, in this Liturgy of 1662 the Rubric was altered to '*the* LITANY *ended* '*according to the accustomed manner*,' &c.

Again, we find in the '*Alterations*' suggested by the Royal Commissioners in 1689, in a *note* against the Rubric at the head of the LITANY, the remark, '*the Litany never to be sung*'; and the words '*sung or*,' in the Rubric, directed to be omitted.

434.—From these evidences we are led to the conclusion that since the Reformation the LITANY has been '*sung*,' or chanted, in Cathedrals, and where the Services were conducted chorally; but in Parish Churches generally, it was '*said*,' i. e. *read* responsorily by Minister and People, audibly and distinctly. We may set it down as a general rule that wherever in the Book of Common Prayer the Rubric uses the expression, '*sung or said*,' it implies that the Service is to be performed *chorally*, or *Parochially*, as the circumstances demand. Our views will be confirmed by the citations following:—

COLLIS, in his '*Rubrick of the Church of England examined*' writes:—'The words "*sung or said*," every where signify the same 'as "*Minister* and *People*." The word, "*sung*," relates to a hymn 'in parts; as in *Choir Service*, one side "*singing*," one verse, and 'the other another: and the word, "*said*," relates only to the '*Parochial Service*.'—*Quoted in* MANT's Book of Com. Prayer, *p.* 17.

WALDO, in his "*Commentary on the Liturgy*," says:—'To answer 'the pious design of the Church, and that these incentives to 'devotion may have their full effect, it is necessary that the 'Minister, who officiates, should *read* every sentence with great 'energy and deliberation; making a proper pause after each, that 'the People may have time to answer.'—*Quoted in* MANT's *Book of Com. Prayer*, p. 67.

The REV. J. JEBB, observes:—'The Rubric places "*sung*" before '"*said*;" hereby, as Dr. Bisse remarks, giving a preference to '*singing* over *saying*. As will be presently shewn, the Litany is 'expressly adapted for *singing*: and therefore it is most absurd to 'discontinue its musical performance in Choirs, where the responses 'to Morning and Evening Prayer are *sung*, as at York. It was '*sung* when first used in the Reformed Church of England. "On 'the 18th day of September, 1547," *Heylin* relates, "the Litany was '*sung* in the English tongue in St Paul's, between the Quire and 'the High Altar, the singers kneeling half on the one side, and half 'on the other." (*Hist. Ref.* p. 42.). It was more frequently *sung* 'in ancient times than now. Thus, at the Consecration of Archbishop Parker, "the elect of Chichester having exhorted the people 'to prayer, betook himself to *sing* the Litany, the Choir answering." '(*Life of Parker*. Bk. ii. ch. 1.) In the same Archbishop's regulations for Eastbridge Hospital, it is directed that the Children there 'educated, should in the Hospital Chapel three days in the week, '*sing* with a loud voice the Litany. (*ib.* App. Bk. iii. No. 58.) At 'the Convocations in old times it was *sung*, whereas it is *now simply* '*read*. And at the Coronations of our Sovereigns, as at that of 'King George III., it was *sung* by two Bishops, the Choir making 'the Responses to the Organ. This practice was discontinued at 'the last three Coronations, and the ancient Church of Westminster, 'at the celebration of the greatest national solemnity, was disgraced 'by the adoption, in this respect and in others, of the *modern* '*Parochial mode*.' (*p.* 431.)—'The *Music* to which the Litany is 'usually sung is a very ancient *Chant*,......as ancient as any *Chant* 'possessed by the Western Church.' (*p.* 440).—'The structure of 'the Litany, as shown in the preceding Section, is fully carried out 'by the *choral* performance. Thus, the Invocation, and Kyrie 'Eleison, which is parallel to it, as also the clause, "O Christ, hear 'us," are successively *sung*, in the *same notes*, by both Ministers and 'Choir.' (*p.* 441).—'The Minister's part, throughout the Litany, 'after the Invocation, is uniformly *chanted in all Choirs* which 'follow the ancient form, with a cadence more varied than that 'used in the first part of the Chant.' (*p.* 443).—In York Cathedral 'an admirable Litany, attributed to a composer of the name of 'Wanless, was in use till within the last half-century......The 'Litany in that Church is at present *read as in Parish Churches.*' (*p.* 445.)—*On the Choral Service.*

[SAYING.]

435.—MANNER OF SAYING. There is a difference of practice in Parish Churches with regard to the uttering of the responses at the beginning of the Litany, in what is called the 'Invocations,' from the Rubric giving no direction. The first four clauses will be seen to be printed first in *Roman* type, and again *verbatim* in *Italic.* In some Churches the Congregation will wait for the Officiating Minister to have *finished* the entire sentence before they follow, like as they do in the remaining parts of the Litany; while in other Churches, the Congregation repeat each clause *with* the Minister, beginning immediately after he has pronounced the first word, as is done at the Lord's Prayer, and Creeds. The more correct method, and certainly the more devotional method, for 'Parochial' use is for the Congregation to repeat these responses '*with*' the Minister, as is the practise in the Lord's Prayer, and in the Creeds; and '*not after*' the Minister, as in the Psalms, and in the other parts of the Litany. The expression, '*have mercy upon us,*' cannot be appropriate in a part belonging exclusively to the Minister: the plural pronoun '*us*' naturally implies that he and the People should utter the invocations *jointly* and *together.* It has been objected to this, that the printing of the *response* in a different type points out, as in other parts of the Liturgy, the distinctive portions for Minister and People, and that such are to be said *separately*, and *alternatim;* but this we must deny, as in the *Lesser Litany*, the practice we advocate is universally adopted. *Chorally*, however, and where intoning is practised by the Minister, the *antiphonal* method is thought to be the more correct; and may be generally preferred. But we will give a few opinions.

BISHOP MANT says:—'For the *Invocations* at the beginning of 'the Litany *no rule is prescribed.* Possibly however the repetition 'of each sentence *severally* may give countenance to the supposition 'that each should be recited severally, first by the Minister and 'then by the people. And yet in *Parochial use*, whatever may be 'thought of the Choral Service, I am of opinion, that, as in the case 'of the "General Confession" the putting up of these addresses by 'the Congregation *together with* the Minister, rather than *independently* of him, falls in better with the Church's spirit of combined adoration.' (*p.* 50.)—*Hor. Lit.*

The REV. J. JEBB writes:—'Here it is in place to remark upon 'an abuse tolerated in some Churches; the *simultaneous recitation* 'of these parts by Priest and people, like the Confession, Creed, and 'Lord's Prayer. This practice impairs the whole rationale of the 'Service, and the express letter of the Prayer Book, in which, the 'same words are *repeated in a different type*, to show as distinctly 'as possible that the People or Choir are *not to begin* their part till 'the Minister *has finished* his. It would be quite as correct to 'repeat the words, "Good Lord, deliver us," while he is reading the 'suffrage which precedes them.' (*p.* 441.)—*On the Choral Service.*

The REV. SAMUEL ROWE remarks:—'As the response in the four 'first sentences of the Litany is an exact repetition of the invocation of the Persons of the holy, blessed, and glorious Trinity, it 'would appear more consistent with the general tenor of the 'Liturgy, for the People *to follow* the Minister, *than to wait until* '*his sentence is finished* before they begin the response. The same 'remarks will apply to the concluding responses, "Lord have 'mercy," &c., and the effect will be found, in practice, no less 'animating than it is in other parts of the Service, or even more so 'when we are led to a climax of devotion ending in the Lord's 'Prayer." (*p.* 138.)—*An Appeal to the Rubric.*

436.—The Minister and People must be careful in the saying of the first sentence of the Litany to adhere rigidly to the punctuation, *pausing slightly* after the word '*Father;*' thus,—'O God, the Father,...... of heaven,' &c.; and not, as many do, completely ignore the *comma*, and destroy the sense, by proclaiming in one breath God to be 'the *Father of heaven*' merely. With regard to those portions of the Litany coming between the Invocations and the Lesser Litany, where there is the portion in Roman type to be said aloud by the Minister, and that in Italic forming the response of the People, care should be taken that the Minister and People do not disturb each other by beginning their respective parts too quickly in succession. The Minister should be allowed to finish completely his portion before the People utter a syllable of theirs; and the People, likewise, be suffered to close their sentence before the Minister proceeds with what he has to follow. At the same time, it must not be forgotten, that although separate parts are assigned to Minister and People for vocal utterance, yet each should mentally enter into what is spoken by the other, so as to form one joint petition; for, it must be evident, that the sense of one part is not complete without the words of the other. This should be carefully urged upon the People.

[ANNOUNCING THE PRAYING FOR THE SICK.]

437.—*Before commencing* the LITANY, it is customary in some Churches for the Officiating Minister to proclaim: — "*The Prayers of the Congregation* (or *Church*) *are desired for A. B.* * * *, *C. D.* * * *, &c.; or, if there are many, "*for several sick persons;*" and on arriving at the Intercession, beginning with, 'That it may please Thee to preserve all that travel 'by land or by water; all women, labouring with child, '*all sick persons*, and young children,' &c. to introduce after 'all sick persons' the Rubrical expression found in the "*Prayer for all conditions of Men*," thus — "*especially* him (her *or* them) *for whom our Prayers are desired.*" Other Clergymen will only make the announcement *before beginning* the Litany; leaving the 'Intercession' unaltered.

There is no Rubrical authority to defend this *announcement*, or this *interpolation;* yet, where it has been the custom, no hasty suspension of the usage can be recommended; while, if Diocesan, Minister, and People, are agreed as to the propriety of maintaining the custom, the Rubrical strictness of to-day cannot suddenly, nor satisfactorily, supersede the laxity of the past. To introduce the practise, however, where it has never prevailed would be unwise as well as incorrect, (see *par.* 382.): for although the *marginal*

Rubric in the "*Prayer for all conditions of Men,*" &c. has been advanced in defence of the usage, from the fact of that Prayer being a *substitute for the Litany*, and directed '*to be used at such times when the Litany is not appointed to be said;*' still there is no Rubric attached to the Litany itself authorizing such extra '*publications in time of Divine Service.*' There are some Clergymen who, instead of any announcement or interpolation, merely make a *pause of a few seconds* after the expression '*Sick Persons*' in the 'Intercession,' so as to give opportunity to the People to offer up mentally any private supplication for a friend or relation. The few opinions following may be acceptable.

Bp. Mant says:—'The omission of all allusion to the individuals, for whom prayers are desired, in the supplication for "*all sick persons,*" seems an indication that no special commemoration should be made of them in the Litany.' (*p.* 51.)—*Hor. Lit.*

The Rev. Wm. Bates observes:—'There is no authority for 'mentioning the names of the *sick persons* for whom we pray.' (*p.* 357.)—*College Lectures on Christ. Antiq.*

The Rev. John Purchas writes:—'When persons in *sickness* 'desire the prayers of the Church, *notice should always be given* '(though *not by name* after the first time) at the commencement of 'the Litany in these words, "*The Prayers of the Church are desired* '*for A. B.*"......(here follows the Intercession)......'After the words '"*sick persons*"' (in the Intercession quoted) a *pause* should be 'made for the offering up of special prayer; but *no clause* should be 'inserted such as "*especially for those,*" &c.' (*p.* 121.)—*Directorium Anglicanum.*

The Rev. Samuel Rowe remarks:—'There is no authority for 'inserting in the Litany, after the petition for "all sick persons," 'the sentence, "*especially those for whom our prayers are desired;*" 'although it is a custom which very extensively prevails, and the 'words, with their accompanying Rubric from the "Prayer for All 'Sorts and Conditions of Men," have crept into some editions of the 'Common Prayer Book. (Those by the late John Reeves, King's 'Printer, temp. Geo. iii.).' (*p.* 139.)—*An Appeal to the Rubric.*

The Place where the Litany is to be said.

438.—It can hardly be a question at the present day *where* in our Parish Churches the Litany is to be said. Universal custom assigns it to the ordinary

Reading Desk. There is a Rubric, however, at the head of the COMMINATION OFFICE, directing the Officiating Minister to say the introductory portion of that Service '*in the Reading-Pew, or Pulpit;*' and another Rubric before Psalm 71 in that Office, requiring the after part of the Service to be said '*in the place where they are accustomed to say the Litany;*' thus referring to an especial locality where it was usual to repeat the Litany Service. This can mean no other than the ancient *Fald-stool*, or *Litany-stool*, standing sometimes in the Chancel, sometimes in the Nave in front of the Rood-Screen, and facing the East, at which it was formerly the practise, and now also in some Cathedrals, to '*say* or *sing*' the LITANY; but which in respect of Parish Churches is a usage completely obsolete. Should the Litany be again employed as a separate and distinct Service, it is possible that the use of the *Litany-Stool* may be revived; yet this cannot legally be done without the sanction of the Ordinary, as *Canon* 15 enjoins.

We have said so much in illustration of this subject in a preceding Volume (*Vol.* **C.**), under the head *Litany-stool*, that we may be excused, perhaps, from giving more here than a kind of summary of what we have before stated, with a few other confirmatory opinions.

Beginning at the period of the Reformation we have in

1547.—An *Injunction* of Edward VI. directing, 'the Priests with 'other of the Quire to kneel in *the midst of the Church* and sing or 'say plainly and distinctly the Litany......and in Cathedral or 'Collegiate Churches, the same shall be done *in such places* as our 'Commissaries in our Visitation shall appoint.'—CARDWELL'S *Doc. Ann.* i. 15.

ABP. CRANMER in his *Articles* of the same year, asks 'whether 'they......have said or sung the said Litany in any other place but 'upon their knees *in the midst of their Church.*' (*ib.* i. 46.)

1549.—In the first *Liturgy of* Edw. VI. (1549), the Rubrics in the COMMINATION OFFICE, as we have before observed, order '*the Litany to be said after the accustomed manner,*' and refers also to the '*place where they are accustomed to say the Litany.*'

1559.—In this year *Elizabeth* re-issues the Injunctions of Edward VI. on this point; and there are several authors of repute who quote this Injunction with the addition following (in Italics).—'The Priests with other of the Quire shall kneel in the midst of the 'Church *at a low Desk before the Chancel-door anciently called the* '*Fald-stool*, and sing or say,' &c. *Bp. Andrewes* cites these words; and after him *Wheatly*, and many modern writers, quote them.

1603-4.—CANON 15. directs that, 'The Litany shall be said or 'sung.,.....*in some convenient place* according to the discretion of the 'Bishop of the Diocese, or Ecclesiastical Ordinary of the place.'

1641.—At this period it was a charge against the Laudian Bishops, that they introduced 'reading the Litany in the midst of 'the body of the Church in many of the Parochial Churches...... 'pretending for their innovations the Injunctions and Advertise-'ments of Queen Elizabeth, which are not in force, but by way 'of commentary and imposition,' (i. e. exposition.)—CARDWELL'S *Conferences*. 273.

1662.—In this year was accomplished the *last Revision* of the Liturgy; and the only difference made in the Rubrics from those of the preceding Liturgies, with regard to *the place* for *saying* the Litany, is the addition to the Rubric of the COMMINATION OFFICE preceding *Psalm* 71. of the words '*in the place*,' before the direction —'*where they are accustomed to say the Litany.*'

In 1637, the Royal Commissioners suggested nothing among the proposed '*Alterations in the Book of Common Prayer*,' affecting the subject now under discussion.

439.—The conclusion we must arrive at from these varied evidences is that the LITANY at the present day is to be '*said*' in Parish Churches in the *Reading-Desk;* and that in Cathedrals it is to be '*sung or said*' according to the custom which has prevailed; i. e. either at the *Litany-stool*, or *Fald-stool*, in the midst of the Choir,—or by the Priest and Choir alternately, or Choir alone antiphonally,—the Priest and Choir keeping their usual places.*

---

* The AMERICAN LITURGY affords us no help in this matter; for the *Commination Service* is omitted from that Book, and in the stead the last three prayers *preceding* the Benediction in our own Office are annexed to the Collect for *Ash-Wednesday*, with this Rubric:—'*At Morning Prayer, the Litany being ended, shall be said* '*the following Prayers immediately before the General Thanksgiving.*'

We may here quote an opinion, which appears to reflect Cathedral practise, and not Parochial usage; and follow it with a citation showing the result of an attempt to introduce the *Litany-stool* into Parish Churches.

The Rev. John Puchas writes:—'The low *Desk* for the Litany 'should be placed as the Sarum Processional directs *in the midst of* '*the Choir*, viz., between the Choir and the Altar, that is, at the 'eastern end of the Stalls, at the commencement of the Sacrarium. 'Some ritualists hold that the Desk should be placed in *front of the* '*gates of the Rood-Screen*, or in the *midst of the Nave;* the ancient 'English use seems preferable.' (*p.* 121.)—*Directorium Anglicanum.*

The Rev. J. H. Pollen, in his '*Narrative of Five Years at St Saviour's, Leeds*,' where the practise of very extreme views in Ritual and Doctrine brought down upon the Officiating Clergy grave Episcopal censures, thus remarks:—'The Bishop (of Ripon) 'was very angry. The Vicar in his distress offered to make any 'concessions of any matters that offended the Bishop, and to put 'himself in his hands; *e.g.* the Clergy and Choir used to say the 'Services in the Chancel. When they said the *Litany*, all came out 'into the *Nave and knelt in a half circle round a Fald-stool and sung* '*it so.* The Bishop disapproved of this, and ordered the Choir to 'leave the Chancel and sing the Services in the Nave. This was 'done, and the space under the centre tower was fitted for a *chorus* '*cantorum*, &c., &c.' (*p.* 55.)

The Posture at the Litany.

440.—The only authority directing what posture is to be assumed at the Litany Service is that of the 18th Canon, (of 1603-4), which enjoins '*Kneeling*' for Minister and People, thus:—

'In the time of Divine Service, and of every part thereof, all due 'reverence is to be used......All manner of persons then present 'shall reverently *kneel upon their knees*, when the General Con-'fession, Litany, and other Prayers are read;' &c.—Canon 18.

This order is doubtlessly derived from the Injunctions of Edward VI. (1547) which read:—

'Immediately before High Mass, the Priest with others of the 'Quire, shall *kneel* in the midst of the Church, and sing or say 'plainly the Litany,' &c.—Cardwell's *Doc. Ann.*

This Injunction was re-issued by Elizabeth in 1559; and the practise has continued to the present day.

441.—There is, however, no *Rubric* in the LITANY Office directing the *posture* to be adopted during its recital. Those Clergymen who hold the Canons of 1603 to be of secondary authority compared with the *Rubrics* of the LITURGY, infer, from the *Litany* being introduced in the MORNING PRAYER after the *third Collect*, that it must follow the rule laid down in the Rubric, last going before that Collect, which is the one preceding the '*Collect for Peace*,' where it is directed

¶. '*Then shall follow three Collects......all kneeling.*' (1662.)—Present Book of Com. Prayer.

Others, like Mr. Jebb (see *postea*), derive the usage of *kneeling* at the Litany from a passage in the *prophecy* of *Joel* (ii. 17.), thus—'*Let the Priests, the 'Ministers of the Lord, weep between the porch and the 'altar, and let them say, Spare thy people, O Lord,*' &c.; a conclusion, however, drawn by inference only, and not from *positive* statement.

442.—There is a third party who tell us, that '*standing*' is the proper posture for the Minister, and '*kneeling*,' that for the People, from the Rubric antecedent to the one before the '*Collect for Peace*,' cited above, and which immediately precedes the Suffrages, directing an alteration in the attitude of the Minister, but not of the People; thus—

¶. '*Then the Priest standing up shall say.*' (1662.)—Present Book of Com. Prayer.

The advocates of this usage consider that these Suffrages are analagous to the Litany, and that if '*standing*' is the proper posture for the Minister in the one case, it must be so in the other. This argument, however, is not tenable; for in such a case the Minister must continue standing throughout all the Prayers, &c., which close the Litany, for no subsequent Rubrical direction occurs to change this posture to the more consistent one of *kneeling* when repeating those Prayers, which, on non-Litany days, are uttered by the Minister *kneeling* in accordance

with the Rubric before the '*Collect for Peace.*' Many who employ the LITANY as a separate Office adopt this usage of '*standing.*'

L'ESTRANGE writes:—'The accustomed posture was ***kneeling***, 'for so was it appointed in the Queen's Injunctions, (*Injunc.* 18), 'and in those of Edward VI. (*Injunc.* 23.) "The Priests shall "***kneel*** in the midst of the Church, and sing or say plainly and "distinctly the Litany." Indeed, what fitter posture can there be 'than ***kneeling?*** Excellently saith St Chrysostom, (Ἵκετου σχῆμα 'καὶ γνώμην καὶ φρόνημα τὸν εὐχόμενον ἔχειν δεῖ,) "It is fit that he "who applies himself to prayer should put on the outward garb and "deportment, as well as the inward mind of a supplicant." Hom. 'in *Ps.* 4. What scheme suits a supplicant better than ***lowly kneel-'ing***, and can we ***kneel*** too low at such supplications as these? 'The motions of the body ought to keep pace with the affections of 'the soul; when this is most transported with zeal, the members of 'the body must move at the same rate; the higher the spirit soars 'in prayer, the lower falls the body. When our Saviour prayed in 'the garden his first posture was (θεὶς τὰ γόνατα, "***falling upon his 'knees***," Luke xxii. 41.); but (γενόμενος ἐν ἀγωνίᾳ, "being brought 'to his agony," and to pray (ἐκτενέστερον,) 'more ardently,' '(ἔπεσεν ἐπὶ πρόσωπον αὐτοῦ,) 'He cast himself prostrate upon '*his face,*' Matt. xxvi. 39.) Now if the LITANY be, as certainly it 'is, our most fervent resort to God, fit it is it should be made in the 'most significant, that is, in the lowest posture of supplication.' (*p.* 102.)—***Alliance.***

WHEATLY says:—'The posture, which the Minister is to use 'in saying the Litany, is not prescribed in any present ***Rubric*** 'except that, as it is now a part of the Morning Service for the days 'above mentioned, it is included in the Rubric at the end of the 'Suffrages after the second Lord's Prayer, which orders ***all to kneel*** 'in that place, after which there is no direction for ***standing.*** And 'the Injunctions of King Edward and Queen Elizabeth both appoint, 'that the "Priests, with others of the Choir, shall ***kneel*** in the 'midst of the Church," &c. As to the posture of the ***People***, nothing 'need to be said in relation to that, because whenever the Priest '***kneels***, they are always to do the same.' (*p.* 167).—***Rat. Ill. of Bk. of Com. Prayer.*** Dr. Corrie's Edit.

The REV. J. JEBB, says:—'Our Ritualists agree that this pos-'ture (***kneeling***) of saying the Litany is adopted from the passage 'in Joel, (ii. 17.) which speaks of the Priests, the Ministers of the 'Lord, when making their special Litanies for the sins of the People, 'weeping between the Porch and the Altar.' (*p.* 436.)—***On the Choral Service.***

The REV. THOMAS LATHBURY remarks:—'Some singular cus-'toms prevailed even in Parliament in connection with the Book of 'Common Prayer. In the House of Commons, 1558–9, February '11th, The ***Litany*** was said by the Clerk ***kneeling***, and answered 'by the whole house on their ***knees***, with divers prayers.' (*p.* 114.) —***Hist. of Book of Common Prayer.***

The following writer defends the usage of the Minister *standing*, and the People *kneeling*.

The Rev. Samuel Rowe observes:—'Some have thought, that 'as there is no specific direction in this *Rubric* for the posture in 'which the Litany should be said, we should consider it as included 'under the Rubric which follows the Apostle's Creed, which directs 'that the "prayers following" should be said by "*all devoutly kneeling*." This, however, will scarcely be deemed probable, when it is 'considered that the Litany was, as above stated, originally intended for a distinct Service. But if this Rubric be allowed to 'extend so far as to the Litany, it can only apply to the *Congregation*, and *not to the Minister*, because, after the aforesaid direction has been given as to *kneeling at the Prayers*, the Priest 'is expressly ordered to *stand*, when he says the interlocutory 'sentences before the three Collects, whilst the People *kneel* according to the former Rubric, the latter making no alteration in their 'position. And this, as it appears to me, affords a convincing argument from analogy, as to the posture in which the Litany should 'be sung or said, because these suffrages form a kind of little 'Litany, and therefore, in the absence of any express Rubric, the 'order for them may be taken as no unsafe indication of the proper 'course to be observed on a kindred occasion; which, from the 'above considerations, would appear to be, that the Minister 'should *stand* and the People *kneel*, on the same principle that 'the Lord's Prayer is so said in the Communion Service.' (*p.* 137.) —*An Appeal to the Rubric.*

By whom the Litany may be said.

443.—There is no *Canon* or *Rubric* directing by whom the Litany is to be said. In Parish Churches it has long been the custom for the *Officiating Minister* and the *Congregation* to take alternate parts, as indicated by the distinction of type. In Cathedrals, and Colleges, we sometimes find the Litany performed by *Laymen* only; to this there are grave objections, although it is not forbidden by the Rubric in the Prayer Book. *Bp. Sparrow* admits that a Priest, Deacon, or '*other*,' may take the earlier portion as far as the Lord's Prayer, but the remaining part must be taken by a Priest. In the Library of Brazenose College, Oxford, there is said to be a copy of the original version of the Litany in black and red letter set to music; with this preliminary instruction:—

'Ande it is to be remembred, that that whiche is printed in 'blacke letter, is to be sayde or songe of the *Priests* in an audible 'voice......and that whiche is in the redde, is to be answered of the '*quiere* soberly and devoutly.'

If we add to this the instructions given in the *Injunctions* of Edward VI, and Elizabeth, enjoining that 'the *Priests* with *others of the Quire* shall kneel in the 'midst of the Church and sing or say plainly and 'distinctly the LITANY,' &c., we may conclude that this was the prevailing practice; although occasionally, and here and there, from the paucity of Clerics in full orders, it was permitted to the *Deacon* to say the Litany; and where these were wanting, a *lay Reader* would be allowed to officiate in this service. At the present day, however, the employing of Laymen in such office in Parish Churches would excite great scandal, and draw down such strong reprobation, as to cause the attempt never to repeated.

We annex a few opinions, among which will be found some very severe strictures on what these authors term an illegal and unjustifiable practice.

BP. SPARROW says:—'In the *former part* of the LITANY, the '*Priest* hath not a part so proper, but that it may be said by a '*Deacon*, or *other*, and it useth to be sung by such in Cathedral 'and Collegiate-Churches and Chapels; and both it, and all other 'our alternate Supplications, which are as it were the lesser 'Litanies, do much resemble the antient Prayers indicted by the 'Deacons, as we have said; but in the latter part of the Litany, '*from the Lord's Prayer to the end*, the *Priest* hath a part more 'peculiar, by reason of the eminency of that Prayer, and that 'other Collects follow wherein the *Priest* doth recommend again 'the petitions of the People to God (as in that Prayer, '*We humbly* '*beseech Thee, O Lord*,' &c.) and solemnly offers them up to God in 'the behalf of the People, to which the People answer *Amen*.' (*p.* 62.)—*Rationale.*

DR. BENNET writes:—'I think myself oblig'd to take notice of 'a most scandalous practice, which prevails in many such Congre- 'gations, as ought to be fit precedents for the whole Kingdom to 'follow. 'Tis this; that *Laymen*, and very often *young boys* of 'eighteen or nineteen years of age, are not only permitted, but 'oblig'd, publicly to perform this Office, which is one of the most 'solemn parts of our Divine Service, even tho' many *Priests* and '*Deacons* are at the same time present. Those persons upon whom 'it must be charg'd, and in whose power it is to rectifie it, can't but 'know, that this practice is illegal, as well as abominable in itself, 'and a flat contradiction to all primitive order. And one would 'think, when the Nation swarms with such, as ridicule, oppose, 'and deny the distinction of Clergy and Laiety; those who possess 'some of the largest and most honorable preferments in the Church, 'should be asham'd to betray her into the hands of her profess'd 'enemies, and to put arguments into their mouths, and declare by 'their actions, that they think any Layman whatsoever as truly 'authoriz'd to Minister in Holy Things, as those who are regularly 'ordain'd. Besides, with what face can those persons blame the 'Dissenting Teachers, for officiating without Episcopal Ordination, 'when they themselves do not only allow of, but require the same 'thing? (*p.* 94. *note*).—*Paraphrase of Book of Com. Prayer.*

Dr. BISSE observes:—'Now though this practice may seem 'to have a wrong appearance, when *Priests* are present, and for 'that reason hath been abridged in these later days; yet in vindi-'cation of the Church, which admits of no irregularity, it is proper 'to show this offence to be grounded on a mistake. For in the 'present case, the voice of the singer, whether *ecclesiastic* or *laic*, 'is to be considered not as of a *Priest*, but *Precentor*, *vos præ-'currens*, going before, and leading on the Congregation; which in 'general Confessions, as well as Supplications or Litanies, has 'been allowed.'—(Quoted in JEBB's *Choral Service.* p. 437. *note.*)

WHEATLY remarks:—'The singing of this Office by *laymen*, as 'practised in several *Cathedrals* and *Colleges*, is certainly very un-'justifiable, and deservedly gives offence to all such as are zealous 'for regularity and decency in Divine Worship. And therefore '(since it is plainly a practice against the express rules of our 'Church, crept in partly through the indevout laziness of Minor 'Canons and others, whose duty it is to perform that solemn Office; 'and partly through the shameful negligence of those who can and 'ought to correct whatever they see amiss in such matters) it can-'not surely be thought impertinent, if I take hold of this oppor-'tunity to express my concern at so irreligious a custom.' (*p.* 167.) —*Rat. Ill. of Book of Com. Prayer.*

The REV. J. JEBB, speaking of the *Ministers* by whom the LITANY is to be performed, writes:—'The regular Choral use 'assigns this to *two of the inferior Clergy*. Bishop Sparrow says, 'that the Litany used to be sung by *Deacons*, in Collegiate Churches 'and Chapels. Playford and Low both mention *two of the Choir* '......The former Litany is regularly sung at St Paul's *by two Minor 'Canons*, and at New College *by two Chaplains*. But at Lichfield 'and Exeter an apparently anomalous custom prevails, of assigning 'it to a *Priest* and a *Lay Vicar*, and at Lincoln to *two Lay Vicars*. 'This latter custom seems to have been more prevalent formerly 'than now. In the Cathedral of Lincoln, *two Laymen* still chant 'this part of the Litany; at Lichfield and Exeter, a *Priest* and *Lay 'Vicar* are associated in this duty: a *Priest* in all instances per-'forming the *latter part*, which begins at the Lord's Prayer. This 'anomalous custom is apparently justified by ancient formularies. 'In the Sarum Processional, the Ministers of this Service are usually 'called *Clerks of the second form:* and the Septiform Litany, used 'on Easter Even, is appointed to be sung *by boys:* so that it was 'clearly not restricted to the Clergy. (*p.* 436.)......But none of 'these directions imply a restriction to, or a preference of *Laymen*. 'Under the term *Clerks of the second form*, were included *Deacons*. '......Against the singing *by Laymen* most of our Ritualists have 'strongly declaimed: and though Dr. Bisse shows that it is not 'irregular, (being, indeed, *contrary to no Rubric*), yet his argument 'is rather an apology, than an approval. (See above.) The allo- 'cation of the Litany to *Deacons* is plainly the most primitive 'custom: the analagous Service in the old Liturgies being assigned 'to that order. (*p.* 437.)......The whole analogy of our Service, and 'all our notions of propriety are repugnant to the practice of giving 'the lead in any act of prayer to *Laymen*, and actually assigning a 'subordinate place to the *Clergy*, who then merely respond with 'the Congregation. But when the solemn nature of the supplica- 'tion is considered, as comprising the most awful invocations of 'her God which the Church has framed, and Prayers of the deepest 'urgency, and most comprehensive fulness, it seems a most lament- 'able perversion to continue a custom, which is after all founded upon 'ambiguous usages and directions, and which the religious feelings 'of the sober-minded must naturally resent. (*p.* 438.)......If the '*Deacons* are permitted to perform this part of the Service, the 'permission is to them a privilege, of which they ought not to 'be deprived. But even were the license to *Laymen* to perform 'it clearly recognised by the Church at large, still nothing would 'prevent those in Orders from undertaking this subordinate duty, 'and thus removing the scandal which certainly has ever attached 'to this strange practice. The *Priest-Vicars* and *Minor Canons*, as 'before observed, represent the *Deacons* of the primitive Church. 'And thus at St Paul's the former Litany is properly sung by *two* '*Minor Canons*; at Christ Church, in Dublin, *by the Junior Vicar*: 'the *Senior Vicar* in the latter place performing the concluding 'part.' (*p.* 438.).—*On Choral Service*. In another work this Author makes these additional observations:—The LITANY 'when 'said is repeated alternately, as *verse* and *response*, by the *Minister* 'and *People*. But the regular Choral usage is, not that *the Minister*, 'or a *Priest*, but *two Chanters* (not necessarily Clergymen) should 'sing together those parts which the Minister reads in a Parish 'Church, and which in old choral books are here called *versicles*; 'as far as the Lord's Prayer exclusive......Now if in a Choir, the '*Minister* were to read, or simply *intone* the versicles of the first 'part of the Litany, that Service would then not be *sung* but *said*, 'according to the meaning of the Rubric, even though the Responses 'were sung; the word *singing* including the *whole* portion of the 'Service then specified, not a part only.' (*p.* 545.)—STEPHENS' *Book of Common Prayer*, E. H. S.

The REV. J. C. ROBERTSON observes:—'Burnet (*Own Time*, ii. '636.), and Wheatly complain of a practice of allowing the Litany 'to be said in Cathedrals by *Laymen*.........Unseemly as the very 'notion of such a practice appears, however, it is not, as to the 'earlier part, forbidden by the PRAYER BOOK. There is no limita- 'tion in the Rubric; and *Bishop Sparrow*,—himself one of the 'Commissioners who revised the *Liturgy* in 1662,—writes (*Rationale*, '78): "In the *former part* of the Litany, the *Priest* hath not a part "so proper but that it may be said by a *Deacon, or other*, and it "useth to be sung by such in Cathedral and Collegiate Churches "or Chapels." It would appear from *Sparrow's* words that the '*latter part* of the Litany was in his day said by the *Priest* only. 'In the early years of the Reformation, when *Deacons* were the 'only resident Clergymen in many Parishes, and indeed the person 'licensed to officiate was often only a *Lay Reader*, it is evident that 'no such rule could be observed. The Rubric of 1662, expressly 'names the *Priest* as the Minister in this part of the Office; custom, 'admits *Deacons* also to read it.' (*p.* 148.)—*How shall we conform to the Liturgy.*

¶. '*Here endeth the Litany.*'

444.—In the *first Liturgy* of Edward VI. (*i. e.* of 1549), the Litany concluded with the *Prayer of St Chrysostom;* at the head of which in the *next Review* (in 1552), was introduced the Rubric following:—

'*And the Litany shall ever end with this Collect following.*'

At the same time all the "OCCASIONAL PRAYERS,"—for '*Rain,*' '*Fair Weather,*' and others—then existing, were interposed between the prayer, 'We humbly beseech Thee, O Father, &c. and '*the Prayer of St Chrysostom.*' In the *Revision of* 1559, these 'OCCASIONAL PRAYERS' were removed and placed after the 'Benediction' (2 *Cor.* xiii.); and the LITANY made to conclude with the prayer, "O God whose nature and property," &c. (KEELING. 59.). In the *last Revision,* that of 1662, the 'Occasional Prayers' were altogether separated from the Litany, and the conclusion of the Office by the Benediction indicated by the short Rubric at the head of this section—'*Here endeth the Litany.*' Certain of the '*Prayers and Thanksgivings,*' however, as occasion required, were appointed to be used before the two final Prayers, either of the *Litany,* or of the *Morning,* and *Evening, Service;* as we shall presently notice.

[PSALMODY.]

445.—At the end of the LITANY, either as a separate Office, or when connected with MORNING PRAYER, or the COMMUNION SERVICE, *Psalmody* of some kind is generally introduced. In many Churches the *Version of Psalms* by Brady and Tate at the end of the Prayer Book is employed; in others, a 'Collection of Psalms and Hymns,' is made use of. In this matter, the Incumbent has the privilege of exercising his own judgment; from the fact of there being no authorized *metrical* Version of the Psalms, nor any 'Collection of Psalms and Hymns,' emanating from authority which he is bound to prefer. Whatever selection may be adopted, the Psalm or Hymn should be announced by the *Officiating Minister*, and never by the Parish Clerk, or other person. The *Rubric* in the Communion Office thus directs:—

¶. '*Nothing shall be proclaimed or published in the Church, 'during the time of Divine Service but by the Minister.*' (1662).

The usual method of accomplishing this, is to say as has been before observed—"*Let us sing to the* "*praise and glory of God, the*——*Psalm* (or *Hymn*), "*page*——;" or simply to announce the Psalm or Hymn. (See *pars*. 271, 272. 386. *antea*).

PRAYERS AND THANKSGIVINGS.

(The Minister and People kneeling.)

446.—It might have been supposed that our admirable LITANY was sufficiently full and expressive to meet all the exigencies of our dependent condition on the mercy and goodness of an All-wise Providence; but there are certain occasions of temporal suffering, when the judgments of the Almighty are in the earth, in order, 'that the inhabitants of the world may learn righteousness' (*Isai.* xxvi. 9.), against which it becomes us of necessity to pray; and, there are likewise, certain classes of men and individuals, in whose behalf we ought at particular times and under special circumstances to intercede—and for which the Litany, as a *General Supplication*, does not expressly provide. To meet these peculiar evils, and conditions, and to express also the thankfulness due to Almighty God from a grateful heart for the removal of the one, and for the mercies conveyed in answer to the other, the Church has appointed the PRAYERS and THANKSGIVINGS, we are now about to consider, with the view of suiting the emergency to which they are individually appropriate. They comprise a prayer—

(1.) *For Rain*; (in time of great drought).
(2.) *For Fair Weather*; (in time of excessive Rain).
(3.) *In time of Dearth and Famine*; (for cheapness and plenty).
(4.) Ditto.
(5.) *In time of War and Tumults*; (for preservation and deliverance).
(6.) *In time of any common Plague or Sickness*; (for the visitation to be withdrawn, and the judgment to be averted).

These are called *Deprecations*; after which follow, a Prayer—

(a.) *In the Ember Weeks, to be said every day, for those that are to be admitted into Holy Orders.*
(b.) Ditto.
(c.) *A Prayer that may be said after any of the former.*
(d.) *A Prayer for the High Court of Parliament.*
(e.) *A Collect or Prayer for all Conditions of Men.*

These, with the exception of the 'Prayer to be said after any of the Former,' are called "*Intercessions*;" and we find that it was customary to append such special prayers to the ancient Litanies.

WHEATLY remarks:—'The usual calamities which afflict the 'world are so exactly enumerated in the preceding Litany, and 'the common necessities of mankind so orderly set down there; 'that there seems to be no need of any additional prayers to 'complete so perfect an office. But yet because the variety of the 'particulars allows them but a bare mention in that comprehensive 'form; the Church hath thought good to enlarge our petitions in 'some instances, because there are some evils so universal and 'grievous, that it is necessary they should be deprecated with a 'peculiar importunity; and some mercies so exceeding needful at 'some times that it is not satisfactory enough to include our desires 'of them among our general requests; but very requisite that we 'should more solemnly petition for them in forms proper to the 'several occasions......In the Western Missals there is a *Collect*, 'and an *Epistle* and *Gospel*, with some Responses upon every one 'of these subjects, seldom indeed agreeing with any of our forms; 'which are the shortest of all, being not designed for a complete 'Office, but appointed to be joined to the *Litany*, or *Morning* and '*Evening Prayer*, every day while the occasion requires it; that so, 'according to the laws of Charles the Great, "in times of *famine*, '*plague*, and *war*, the mercy of God may be immediately implored, 'without staying for the King's Edict.' (*p.* 183).—Rat Ill. of Book of Com. Prayer.

COLLIS observes:—'These *Occasional Prayers* and *Thanksgivings* 'are only to be made use of when we are generally distressed 'upon emergencies; not as some persons have desired, when they 'thought them requisite, but when there is a grievous necessity.' (*p.* 78).—*On the Rubric.*

SHEPHERD says:—'There are seasons, when either some 'calamity is so predominant, or some *blessing* so necessary, that 'it may become proper to deprecate the one, or to supplicate the 'other, with extraordinary importunity......But so much have we 'of these Realms been indebted to the mercy of his Providence, 'that within the remembrance of more than the present generation, 'some of these forms have not been found necessary. The forms 'themselves, however, for the credit of the Compilers of our 'Liturgy, are so plain and perspicuous, that no particular elucida-'tion of them can be required. It may, therefore, be enough to 'observe, that similar Prayers occur in ancient Liturgies, from 'which some of these appear to be chiefly taken: and that each 'is well suited to the emergency to which it is appropriated by our 'Church.' (*p.* 284.)—*Elucidation of Book of Com. Prayer*, Vol. I.

447.—These PRAYERS and THANKSGIVINGS, for the several occasions to which they refer, are appointed by the *Rubric* at the head of the collection, and which was prefixed at the *last Revision* of 1662,—

¶. '*To be used before the two final Prayers of the Litany, or* '*of Morning and Evening Prayer.*' (1662.)

that is to say, before the '*Prayer of St Chrysostom.*' The necessity calling for their introduction, is, for the most part, left to the discretion of the Officiating Minister: the exceptions are the Collects for the *Ember-Weeks*, the 'Prayer for the Parliament,' which a specific Rubric directs '*to be read during their Session*;' and the 'Prayer for All Conditions of Men,' which, according to another Rubric, is only '*to be used at such times when the* LITANY *is not appointed to be said.*'

448.—POSTURE.—The Minister and People during the repetition of these PRAYERS and THANKSGIVINGS are to continue *kneeling*. (See *par.* 440. *supra*).

THE PRAYERS.

(1.) '*For Rain.*'

449.—The Prayers (1.) '*For Rain,*' and (2.) '*For Fair Weather,*' are found in the *first Liturgy* of Edward VI. (1549); and in that Book stood after the six Collects at the end of the Communion Office; in the *second Liturgy* of Edward (1552), they both, with the prayers following—for (3. 4.) '*the time of Dearth and Famine;*' (5.) '*the time of War and Tumults;* '(6.) '*the time of any Common Plague or Sickness;*'—were inserted between the prayer, 'We humbly beseech Thee, &c. and 'the Prayer of St Chrysostom;' which, as BP. COSINS says, 'is a direction to us where to read them when need is.' (NICHOLLS', *Add. Notes*, p. 25.): and it was in the *Revision of* 1662, that they were put into the place they now occupy: their respective *Thanksgivings*, however, were not annexed till the time of James I. (1604). The title of the prayer, we are now discussing, was, in the Liturgies of 1552, 1559, and 1604, '*For Rain, if the time require.*' In 1662, the original and more simple title, '*For Rain,*' was restored. The prayer seems to be derived from a similar one in the Sacramentary of Gregory, long used by our remote ancestors when the occasion required.*

(2.) '*For Fair Weather.*'

450.—This prayer '*For Fair Weather*' has followed the fortunes of its companion '*For Rain,*' as shown above; and is taken in some measure from the Sacramentary of Gregory. The *Royal Commissioners*, in their attempted *Revision* of the Liturgy in 1689, proposed an enlargement of the title to, '*A General Collect for Fair Weather;* but their suggestions were not adopted, as we have had occasion repeatedly to remark.

(3.), (4.) '*In Time of Dearth, and Famine.*'

451.—These two prayers for '*the time of Dearth and Famine,*' were introduced into the Liturgy of

---

* In the SCOTCH LITURGY (1637), the first clause of this prayer '*For Rain*' is appropriated from the Prayer '*in the time of Dearth and Famine;* thus:—'O God, heavenly Father, whose gift it is that 'the Rain doth fall, the Earth is fruitful, Beasts increase, and Fishes 'do multiply; Send us,' &c. (KEELING. 52).

In the AMERICAN LITURGY the prayer '*For Rain*' is the second in this Collection, following '*A Prayer for Congress. To be used during their Session.*'

1552; and they were continued in the earlier editions of Elizabeth's Prayer Book (1559); but the later impressions printed by Grafton omitted the second prayer, which, however, was restored in 1662, with some slight alterations; we also find that the prayer, 'O God, whose nature and property,' &c., and the 'Benediction,' were now first inserted (1559).* The brief Rubric, '*Or this*,' before the second Collect implies that the Officiating Minister can make use of *either* at his discretion.

(5.) '*In the time of War and Tumult.*'

452.—This prayer is similar to what is found in the earlier English Offices, and in the Sacramentary of Gregory. It was first inserted in the Liturgy of 1552, with the title of '*In the time of War;*' in the *Revision* of 1662, the words '*and Tumult*' were annexed to it. Among the '*Alterations*' suggested in 1689, the term '*confound*' in the Prayer was changed to 'disappoint.'

(6.) '*In the time of any Common Plague or Sickness.*'

453.—This prayer, which is the last of those called the *Deprecations*, was also introduced in Edward VIth's. *second Liturgy* (1552); and it has continued in the subsequent Prayer Books down to the present time. In the suggested *Revision* of 1689, the Italic clauses in the following sentence at the close of this prayer were proposed to be inserted,—' withdraw from us,' "*who humbly acknowledge our sins, and truly*

---

* In the SCOTCH LITURGY (1637), the leading clause of the first of these prayers for the '*time of Dearth and Famine*' was transferred to the prayer '*For Rain*,' as we have shown above; and in the place of it the following words were introduced, 'O God, 'Heavenly Father, which by thy Son Jesus Christ has promised to 'all them that seek thy Kingdom and thy righteousness all things 'necessary to their bodily sustenance: Behold,' &c. (KEELING. 54).

In the AMERICAN LITURGY, the *second* of the above prayers is not introduced.

repent us of them," this plague and grievous sickness, "*that being delivered we may glorify thy name.*"*

The Royal Commissioners also proposed the introduction of "*a Preparatory Prayer for the receiving of the Communion, to be read on the Lord's day, or some week day or days before.*" Likewise, '*A Prayer to be said in any time of Calamity :*" to which was added, "Qy. *of Prayers for the Army and Navy.*" (See copy of "The ALTERATIONS," &c. *pub. by Order of H. of Commons*, 1854.)

(a.), (b.) '*In the Ember Weeks,*' &c.

454.—The *Ember-Days* were originally certain days set apart by prayer and fasting, and acts of humiliation, such as the sprinkling of ashes on the head, &c., for consecrating to God the *four Seasons of the Year*, viz.: — Spring, Summer, Autumn, and Winter. Whence they were called the "Fasts of the Four Seasons," (*Jejunia quatuor temporum*), or the *Ember-Weeks;* and were not, as some suppose, originally designed for *Ordination.* (See Bingham's Antiquities, xxi. 2. §. 1.) They derive the name of '*Ember,*' possibly, from an old Saxon word, *umbryne*, or *ymbren*, meaning *circuit* or *course*,—the fasts returning at stated periods every year: or, probably, the term may come from the German word '*quatember,*' the 'quater-fastings' ('*quatuor tempora*'), whence by abbreviation *ember*: others again trace its origin up to our old word, implying '*abstinence*' or '*ashes:*' but the etymology of the term is very doubtful, as will be seen in the citations *postea.*

---

* In the AMERICAN LITURGY, the above Prayer is omitted; but after the Prayer for those to be admitted to Holy Orders, there follow three Collects, entitled, (1) "*In time of great Sickness and Mortality,*" made up of our Prayer for times of '*Plague and Sickness;*' another (2) "*For a Sick Person;*" and (the 3rd) "*For a Sick Child;*" both of which latter are derived from our Office for "The Visitation of the Sick." To these are annexed three others; one "*For a Person or Persons going to Sea;*" another, "*For a Person under Affliction;* and a third, "*For Malefactors after Condemnation.*"

455.—These *Ember-Days* of public prayer and fasting occurring at such regular periods, and in such opportune succession, were thought by the Ecclesiastical authorities of the fourth and fifth centuries to be very suitable times for the admission of Clerks into Holy Orders. Pope *Gelasius* (A. D. 498) is considered to be the first who selected these Seasons for *Ordination;* while some writers assign the concurrence of the *Ordination fasts* with those of the '*Four Seasons*' to Gregory VII. about A. D. 1080. Be this as it may, we find the usage not only exercised in the Church of England at an early period, but strongly advocated by many of her best Divines, and enforced also by more recent *Canons*, (those of 1603-4), which are still binding upon the Clergy of the realm. The 31st of these *Canons* thus reads:—

'*Four Solemn Times appointed for the making of Ministers.*'

'Forasmuch as the ancient Fathers of the Church, led by 'example of the Apostles, appointed *prayers* and *fasts* to be used 'at the solemn Ordering of Ministers; and to that purpose allotted 'certain times, in which only Sacred Orders might be given or 'conferred: we, following their holy and religious example, do 'constitute and decree, that no *Deacons* or *Ministers* be made and 'ordained, but *only upon the Sundays* immediately following *Jejunia* '*quatuor temporum*, commonly called *Ember-Weeks*, appointed in 'ancient time for prayer and fasting, (purposely for this cause at 'their first institution), and so continued at this day in the Church 'of England,' &c.—CANON 31.

456.—The particular days on which the four *Ember Fasts* were held, varied originally in different Churches, till it was ultimately decreed by the 14th Canon of the *Council of Placentia*, A. D. 1095, that they should be as follows:—

WEDNESDAY FRIDAY SATURDAY	following	*1st Sunday in Lent.* *Whitsunday.* *September 14th.* *December 13th.*

These are adopted as the '*Ember-Days*' in the '*Table*' of Fasts introduced into our Prayer Book at the *last Revision* in 1662; and their observance is consequently enjoined upon every Member of our Church. These Seasons, moreover, are imposed as the proper times for *Ordination*, by the 31*st Canon*, as just shewn; and this is confirmed by the preface of the '*Ordinal*,' which states:—

'And the Bishop knowing, &c......may *at the time appointed in* '*the Canon*, or else, on urgent occasion, upon some other Sunday or 'Holy-Day, in the face of the Church, admit him a Deacon,' &c.— (Ordination Services in present Book of Com. Prayer.)

457.—In addition to this, there is the *Rubric* at the head of two Collects standing among the 'OCCASIONAL PRAYERS,' which was inserted likewise at the *last Revision* of the Liturgy (1662); and from this Rubric the inference cannot but be drawn, that the *Ember* Season is the most fit and proper time for admitting men to *Ordination*. The Rubric directs that these *Collects* are to be said '*in the Ember Weeks for those that are to be admitted into Holy Orders*.' The *Ember-Weeks* here spoken of are the weeks in which the *Ember-Days* occur.*

We may conclude these remarks, which are intended to prove that the *Ember Season* is the proper time for *Ordination*, by quoting a few authorities; and then proceed to discuss the *saying of the Collects*, as directed by the Rubric.

HOOKER (*ob.* 1600.) 'never failed the Sunday before every '*Ember-Week* to give notice of it to his Parishioners; persuading 'them both to fast, and to double their devotions for a learned 'and pious Clergy; and to which he persuaded others, he added his 'own example of fasting and prayer; and did usually every *Ember* '*Week* take from the Parish-Clerk the key of the Church door, into 'which place he retired every day, and locked himself up for many 'hours.'—(WORDSWORTH's *Eccl. Biog.* iii. 518.)

GEO. HERBERT (*ob.* 1632), declaiming against the want of piety and the contempt shewn to the Clergy, used to say;—'One cure 'for these distempers would be, for the Clergy themselves to 'keep the *Ember-Weeks* strictly, and beg of their Parishioners to 'join with them in fasting and prayers for a more religious Clergy.' —(WORDSWORTH's *Eccl. Biog.* iv. 39.)

---

* The AMERICAN LITURGY, in adopting these two Collects, rejects the appellation of '*Ember*,' and prefixes this Rubric:—

'For *those who are to be admitted into Holy-Orders. To be used* '*in the weeks preceding the stated times of Ordination*.'

Bp. Sparrow (*ob.* 1685), says:—'The days of Fasting and 'Prayers in these weeks, are, *Wednesday, Friday, Saturday. Wednesday*, because then our Lord Christ was betrayed by Judas: '*Friday*, because then he was crucified: *Saturday*, because then 'we represent the Apostles' sorrow for the loss of their Lord 'lying in the grave. The causes of such religious Fastings and 'Prayers upon *these weeks* were formerly many......But the principal 'cause was for preparation to the solemn *Ordination of Ministers*; 'holy Church imitating the Apostles practice, who when they were 'to set apart men to the Ministry, prayed and fasted, before they 'laid on their hands (*Acts* xiii. 3.) And in after-times, at these 'solemnities, these *Ember-Fasts*, special regard was had to the 'Ordination of Priests and Deacons......And the second Council of 'Milan decreed herein to good purpose, (*Tit.* 1. *Decr.* 22.) "That 'upon the Sundays *before these Fasts*, the Priests should not only 'in their Parishes bid the solemn Fast, but every one in his several 'Parish should piously and religiously say the Prayers, and Litanies, '&c. that God's assistance being implored, both the *Bishop* may be 'guided by the Holy Spirit, in the choice of those whom he shall 'ordain, and also that *they that are ordained*, may grow in learning 'and holiness of life......By opinion of much people, these days have 'been called *Ember-Days*, because that our Fathers would on these 'days eat no bread, but cakes made under *embers*, so that by eating 'of them they reduced into their minds, that they were but Ashes, 'and so should turn again, and wist not how soon.' (*p.* 95.)—*Rationale.*

Gibson, explaining '*The times appointed in the Canon*' as directed in the '*Ordinal*,' says they are:—'The *jejunia quatuor temporum*, 'or *Ember-Weeks*; which became the settled times of *Ordination* 'about the fourth or fifth century; and. being gradually received 'by several Churches, as appears by the many Canons and Con-'stitutions to that effect,) we find them the Rule of the *Church of* '*England*, in the body of Canons drawn by *Egbert* Archbishop of '*York*, about the year 750. *Presbyterorum verò et Diaconorum* '*Ordinationes fieri oportet in quatuor temporum Sabbatis.* And so 'the practice continued to be, both here and elsewhere; and, in the 'Convocation, 1662, we find a special order of the President, by way 'of enforcement of the ancient Law; *quòd nullæ Ordinationes Cleri-* '*corum per aliquos Episcopos fierent, nisi intra* quatuor tempora *pro* '*Ordinationibus assignata*.' And with regard to the exception 'upon urgent occasion, on some other Sunday or Holy-Day,' this same author observes:—'This may *not be done at the discretion of the* '*Bishop*, but must have the Archbishop's Dispensation or Licence, 'as the practice hath been; and as it was understood to be a special 'prerogative of the *See of Rome*, in the times of Popery. Witness 'the Resolution of the Upper House of Convocation, in Queen '*Mary's* reign, that in order to make the number of Clergy suffi-'cient to supply the Cures, *the Bishops might be* authorized by the '*Pope*, to give Orders *extra tempora præscripta*.' (*p.* 160.)—*Codex.*

Johnson remarks:—'The Bishop, if he think fit may ordain on 'any *Sunday* or *Holy-Day*; but the times mentioned in the Canon, 'and referr'd to in the Rubrick, are the *Sundays* next after the '*Ember-Days*; which, in the Laws of King Alfred, (*c.* 39.) are 'call'd, *ymbryne dagas*, and in those of Canute, (*c.* 16.) *ymbren* '*fæsden*, i. e. the *Circular days*, or *Fasts*. The first of these weeks 'is in Spring or Lent, when corn and other seeds are sown; the 'second at *Whitsuntide*, when they are growing: the third in '*September*, when they are gathered and imbarn'd; the fourth in '*December*, when they are marketed, and used; on which four 'Seasons the *circle of the year* turns. Mr. *Somner* therefore thinks 'that these *Fasts* were first instituted, to beg God's blessing on the 'fruits of the earth, and ourselves in the use of them, and not only 'on account of *Ordination*. The Canonists call these *Ember-Weeks* 'as we corruptly write them) *quatuor anni tempora*, by which very 'words they denote likewise the four quarters of the year. See '*Lyndwood*, in Gloss. L. I. T. II. Quatuor in Anno' (*p.* 47.)—*Vade Mecum.*

ABP. SANCROFT, (*ob.* 1688), as we learn from *Cardwell*, agreed with his Suffragan Bishop in 1685, 'that they will ordain no man 'but upon the Lord's Days immediately following the *Jejunia* '*quatuor temporum*, except he have a faculty to be ordained *extra* '*tempora*; and such a faculty the Archbishop declares he will not 'grant but upon very urgent occasion.' (*p.* 305.)—(*Doc. Ann.* ii.)

WHEATLY, remarking upon the *Ember-Days* says, that they 'are certain days set apart for the consecrating to God the *four* '*seasons of the year*, and for the imploring His blessing by fasting 'and prayer, upon the *Ordinations* performed in the Church at 'those times; in conformity to the practice of the Apostles, who, 'when they separated persons for the work of the Ministry, prayed 'and fasted, before they laid on their hands. It is true, at the 'first planting of the Gospel, *Orders* were conferred at any time, as 'there was occasion: but as soon as the Church was settled, the '*Ordination of Ministers* was affixed to certain set times; which 'was the first original of these four weeks of fasting (*p.* 219.)...... 'The reasons why the *Ordination of Ministers* is fixed to these set 'times of fasting are these: first, that as all men's souls are con'cerned in the *Ordaining* a fit Clergy, so all may join in fasting 'and prayer for a blessing upon it: secondly, that both *Bishops* and '*Candidates*, knowing the time, may prepare themselves for this 'great work: thirdly, that no vacancy may remain long unsupplied: 'lastly, that the people, knowing the times, may, if they please 'be present, either to approve the choice made by the Bishop, or 'to object against those whom they know to be unworthy; which 'primitive privilege is still reserved to the people in this well con'stituted Church.' (*p.* 220.)—*Rat. Illus. of Book of Com. Prayer.*

DR. BENNET writes on this point:—'The Establish'd Church 'has appointed *four daies* in the year for the *Ordination* of Priests 'and Deacons, and *three daies* in the week going before the Ordina'tion to be observ'd as *daies of Fasting* and *Prayer* in the behalf of 'those who are to be ordain'd. These daies of Fasting and Prayers 'are call'd *Ember-Daies*......And the weeks in which those daies 'fall, are call'd *Ember-Weeks*.' (*p.* 118).—*Paraphrase upon the Book of Com. Prayer.*

SHEPHERD observes on the word *Ember*:—'Some suppose it 'signifies *ashes*, and some *abstinence*. Abstinence, or fasting, it is 'commonly known, was anciently accompanied with the act of 'sitting upon ashes or of sprinkling ashes upon the head. In the 'Western Church, the *Ember-Weeks* were styled *Jejunia quatuor 'temporum*, the 'fasts of the four seasons.' This title, as well as the 'usage mentioned above, appears to favour the derivation already 'given. But others derive Ember from a Saxon word, signifying '*course* or *circumvolution*, for the *Ember-Weeks* return at fixed and 'certain periods, and are fasts *in course*.' (*p.* 286.)—*Eluc. of Book of Com. Prayer.*

The REV. W. BATES says:—'The word *Ember* is derived by 'some from ἡμέρας, i. e. *dies*; days, by way of emphasis, the grand 'days of fasting; others conceive that they are called the days of '*Ashes* from an ancient custom of eating on those days nothing but 'cakes baked under *Embers* or *Ashes*, called *panem subcineritium*, or 'Ember bread; or from the religious custom of wearing *hair-cloth* 'and using *ashes* in times of public penance. Sir H. Spelman says, 'that the true and genuine word is *Imber*, from the Saxon *Imbrem*, 'i. e. a circle; because the *Ember-Days* move round the year, as it 'were, in a circle.' (*p.* 360.)—*Lectures on Christian Antiquities.*

The REV. C. J. ROBERTSON observes:—'The notices of *Ordina'tions* which appear in our Newspapers and Magazines will not 'allow us to doubt that some of the Bishops of this day prefer '*irregular times* to those appointed by the Prayer-Book for confer'ring *Holy Orders*. Surely there is much authority against this; 'nor can we suppose that such a practice does not cause something 'to be lost, by depriving the ordaining *Bishops* and their *Clergy* of 'those intercessions which the Church desires her children to offer 'up, with fasting, in their behalf, at the stated seasons of *Ordina'tion*.' (*p.* 268.—*How shall we conform to the Liturgy.*)

[The Prayers for Ember-Weeks.]

458.—The *two Prayers* for the Ember-Weeks, and the *Rubric* which accompanies them, were introduced into our Liturgy at the *Revision* in 1662; and, as Mr. Palmer says, they are quite peculiar to the English Ritual (*Orig. Lit.* I. 335.). The Rubric directs the Officiating Minister as to the using of these Prayers, stating:—

¶. '*In the Ember-Weeks to be said every day, for those that 'are to be admitted into Holy Orders*.' (1662.)

And before the second Prayer this brief Rubric, '*Or this*,' gives the privilege of selection to the Officiating Minister. Some light is thrown on this order by the Rubric in the SCOTCH LITURGY of 1637, whence the second Prayer is derived, thus:—

'*A Prayer to be said in the Ember-Weeks for those which 'are then to be admitted into Holy Orders; and is to be read 'every day of the week, beginning on the Sunday before the day 'of Ordination*.'—KEELING. 52. 58.

We thus learn, that one or other of these Collects is to be said *every day* of the *Ember-Week*, not on the *Ember-Days* alone, but on *every day of the week* preceding the day of *Ordination*. Where there is no *Daily Service*, the repetition of the Collect must be confined to the *Wednesday*, and *Friday*, preceding; and where even these days are without any public Service in the Church, then *one of the Collects* must be read on the *Sunday* previous to the day of Ordination. Of the two Collects, the *former* is to be used in the earlier part of the week, and the *latter*, on the days closing the week. It is important and desirable, that the Officiating Minister should carry out the injunctions of the Rubric here, although the Bishop of the Diocese in which he is 'serving' may from 'urgent cause,' as permitted by the '*Ordinal*,' depart from the season for Ordination prescribed by the *Canon*. But in this case, the Rubric is not sufficiently elastic to be strained so far as to sanction the use of these Collects to meet such exceptional practise.

To strengthen the design of these Collects, we find in the '*Alterations*' suggested by the Royal Commissioners in 1689, the following *Rubric*, which was proposed to be read immediately after the 'Apostles' Creed' on the Lord's Day next before any of the *Ember-Weeks*:—

'Whereas the Apostles did use prayer and fasting before they '*ordained*, and that it has been the practice of the Church to enjoin 'Fasts in the four weeks of the year commonly call'd *Ember-Weeks* 'before the Lord's-days appointed for *Ordination* to implore the 'blessing of God upon them that are *to ordain*, and upon those that 'are *to be ordained*; it is therefore earnestly recommended to all 'persons to spend some part of those days in prayer to God for his 'blessing on the Church, and on all that are to be sent out to 'officiate in it. And it is most solemnly charged on all that are 'concerned in *Ordinations*, chiefly on the persons that are *to be* '*ordained*, to spend those days in fervent prayer and fasting, for the 'due preparing of themselves to be initiated into Holy Orders.'—ALTERATIONS *in the Book of Com. Prayer prepared by the Royal Commissioners*. (1689.)

459.—With regard to the distinctive use of these Collects, we may be allowed to support our views, we trust, by annexing the following opinions:—

WHEATLY says:—'Since the whole nation is obliged, at these 'times, to extraordinary prayer and fasting, the Church hath provided '*two forms* upon the occasion, of which the *first* is most proper to be 'used before the Candidates have passed their examination, and 'the *other* afterwards. They were both added to our Common 'Prayer Book at the last Review; though the *second* occurs in the '*Scotch Liturgy*, just before the prayer of St Chrysostom, at the end 'of the Litany.......It is a mistake in those who imagine that these 'prayers are only to be used upon the *three Ember-days*, i. e. upon 'the *Wednesday*, *Friday*, and *Saturday* in every Ember-week; the 'Rubric expressing as plain as words can do, that one of them is 'to be said *every day* in the Ember-Weeks, i. e. *beginning* (as it is 'expressed in the Scotch Liturgy), *on the Sunday before the day of* '*Ordination*.' (*p.* 185.)—*Rat. Ill. of Book of Com. Prayer.*

COLLIS remarks:—'The *former* of these two prayers is thought 'to be most properly used in the *early part of the week*, as it is 'for the *Ordainers* and the *Ordained;* to guide the minds of the 'Bishops and their assisting Pastors, that they may, with wisdom 'and fidelity, make choice of persons, well qualified by their learn-'ing and piety, to be admitted into the Offices of the Ministry. The 'other is proper to be used toward the *latter end of the week*, to 'beseech God to afford the grace of His Holy Spirit to all those, 'who have been made choice of, and who are to be admitted to the 'Office of a Priest, or the administration of a Deacon.' (*p.* 79.)—*On the Rubric.*

SHEPHERD observes:—'The intention of the forms (the two 'prayers) is sufficiently obvious: and as the *Ordination* of Ministers 'is a subject of primary importance, it is to be regretted that one or 'other of the forms is not more generally read on the *Wednesday* 'and *Friday* in the *Ember-week*, in such of our Parish Churches as 'have Service on these days. Whether they were intended to be 'read *every day* in the Ember-weeks, or only on *every Ember-day* 'in the week, is a question that has not universally been answered 'in the same way. The words of the Rubric appear to countenance 'the former practice.' (*p.* 287.)—*Eluc. of Book of Common Prayer.*

Among more modern authorities we have the following:—

DR. BLOMFIELD (late *Bishop of London*) urges that:—'The 'Prayer for the *Ember-Weeks* should always be used as appointed.' (*p.* 65.)—*Charge.* 1842.

DR. MANT (late *Bishop of Down and Connor*, &c.) states:—So 'also should *one* of the prayers "in the *Ember-Weeks*" be devoutly 'said: and, in my opinion, "*on every day*" in the week: beginning 'with the Sunday before the first Ember-day, but not continued on 'the Ordination Sunday.' (*p.* 51.)—*Hor. Lit.*

The REV. SAMUEL ROWE remarks:—'It is deeply to be regretted 'that these timely and beautiful prayers should ever be omitted, 'as they too frequently are. This is a point surely, in which 'uniformity should be observed for every reason. As *Ordinations* 'do not always now take place at the *Ember-Seasons*, it has been 'thought expedient by some Clergymen to use the prayers on the '*day of Ordination in the Diocese where their Church is situated*, but 'though something may be alleged in favour of this practice, there 'appear more reasons for strict conformity to the *Rubric* than for 'departure from it in this case, as in most others.' (*p.* 144. *note.*)—*An Appeal to the Rubric.*

(c.) ¶. '*A Prayer that may be said after any of the former.*'

460.—This admirable Prayer is derived from the Sacramentary of Gregory, and it will be found also in the Prymers of Henry VIII. It was not introduced into our Liturgy till the reign of Elizabeth, where it appears in the Prayer Book of 1559, at the end of the Litany; and without any Rubric before it. In the *Revision* of 1604, and in that of 1662, it stood in the place it now occupies with the heading as given above; although, in some editions,—through the carelessness, or, rather, the ignorance of the Printer, who thought the words of the Rubric, '*after any of the former*,' implied that it should be the last of these Prayers,—we find it placed between that for '*All Conditions of Men*,' and the '*General Thanksgiving*.'

461. It is to be regretted that so excellent a Prayer is not oftener made use of than it is; at the same time, it must be impressed upon the Officiating Minister, that a *Deacon* cannot legally employ it in the place of the '*Absolution*' in MORNING, or EVENING PRAYER, as is too frequently done. (See *Vol.* **A.**). This prayer is not found in the American Liturgy.

DEAN COMBER says:—'This short devout Collect is joined to 'the ancient Litanies of the Western Church, and since sin is the 'cause of all the foregoing judgments, this may be added to any of 'the former, as a prayer for pardon of sin; for which reason also it 'is used by some devout men (when they use the Church Prayers 'in private,) instead of the Absolution.'—Quoted in MANT'S *Book of Common Prayer.*

(d.) ¶. '*A Prayer for the High Court of Parliament, to be 'read during the Session.*'

462.—It was a very ancient usage for Gentiles to offer sacrifices in behalf of their public Councils (*Aul. Gell.* xiv. c. 7.); and we find that the early Christians also were accustomed to pray for the

Roman Senate (*Tertul.* Apol. *Cap.* 32. Opp. *p.* 27.). In accordance with this practice, and the apostolic precept of praying 'for Kings and for all that are in authority,' we have the '*Prayer for the High Court of Parliament*,' which was introduced into the Liturgy at the *Revision of* 1662.

463.—This Prayer has undergone various fortunes and as various changes: it first appeared in front of the Preface of the "*Order for Fasting*," in the first year of CHARLES I. A.D. 1625, with a permissory clause attached, allowing its use 'after the *Letanie*' at the discretion of the Minister. *Bp. Laud* was held to be the author of it: and it comprised the first two sentences and the last of our present Collect. It subsequently lost its independence as a separate prayer, and became incorporated time after time into the Prayers and Thanksgivings offered up on particular occasions of public calamity, and on these occasions only; it was ultimately 'recast,' says CARDWELL (*Conf.* p. 234. *Note.*) 'for a special service, in the year 1661, and was thence transferred by the Convocation of the same period to the Book of Common Prayer.' The especial Service just alluded to was for a '*General Fast-Day*' on June 12th, 1661, on account of the 'Immoderate Waters,' and for the consequent '*Thanksgiving-Day*' on the 19th of the same month, when the trouble was alleviated, 'for the Blessed Change of Weather;' and here also was introduced the Prayer 'For a Blessing upon the High Court of Parliament now assembled.' (See CLAY'S *Book of Com. Prayer Illustrated*, p. XXV.: LATHBURY'S *Hist of Convoc.* p. 302.)

DR. BISSE speaks of this prayer as being 'of the like publick 'importance to the State as the former, viz. for the *Ember-Weeks*, 'is to the Church; and so both jointly to our Constitution; in 'which the Church and State are so united and linked together by 'the fundamental laws of this realm, that they cannot be divided 'without being destroyed: a maxim fully proved by the consul- 'tations of that memorable Parliament, which overturned both, and 'which gave occasion to have this very prayer added here to our 'public intercessions after the Restoration.'—(Quoted in MANT'S *Book of Common Prayer*, p. 73.)

464.—There is one clause in this Prayer which has wonderfully offended the scruples of our Nonconformist brethren from the very day that it was first promulgated, viz. '*Under our most religious and gracious King*' (Queen). This is nothing more than one of those titles of respect and veneration which the primitive Church gave to the Christian Emperors and Kings, as we find in the Liturgy of Basil, (GOAR *Rituale. Græc.* p. 171.). There is no foundation for the assertion that this clause was meant only as a compliment to Charles I., or to Charles II. However, the objections against it were so strong that in the "*Alterations*" proposed by the Royal Commissioners in 1689, it was suggested to change the expression '*our most religious and gracious King*' (Queen), to "*our sovereign Lord* (and *Lady*):" likewise, after the word '*King*,' it was proposed to add '*William;*' and after '*Queen*,' the name '*Mary*.'

The REV. M. PLUMMER says:—'*Most religious*, means most 'worshipful—applied to the Queen, means that she should be 'highly reverenced and respected. The Queen and Royal Family 'should be prayed for, even though they be heathens. (See *Ezra* vi. 10; *Baruch* i. 11.12; 1 *Tim.* ii. 2—4.).' This author then cites, '—"Let us pray for the safety of the most religious Augustus "Constantius;" and all the people immediately cried out with one 'voice, "Christ, help Constantius!" *Athan. Apol. ad Constant.*' (*p.* 88.)—*Observations on the Book of Com. Prayer.*

465.—WHEN TO BE USED.—According to the Rubric this Prayer is '*to be read during the Session*' of Parliament; and the Officiating Minister must understand by this, that it is *not* to be omitted on occasions of *adjournment* or *recess*, for the 'Session' is then still continuing; and terminates only with the *Prorogation.*

COLLIS says:—'If the Houses *adjourn* themselves for a fortnight 'or a longer time, it is still the same *Session:* but, if they are '*prorogued* for a shorter time, it is not reckoned a part of it, they 'not being then impowered to do business, as upon adjournments 'they are.'—(Quoted in MANT's *Book of Com. Prayer. p.* 74.)

DR. MANT, (late *Bishop of Down and Connor*, &c.) states.—'Notwithstanding a recess or adjournment of Parliament, the '*Session* is continued; so that the Prayer should be read until the '*Prorogation*, whereby it is terminated.' (*p.* 51.)—*Hor. Lit.*

466.—Among the '*Alterations*' of 1689, it was suggested to change the phrase '*Session*' in the Rubric, to '*Sitting;*' and to annex the words '*When 'the Litany is not appointed to be read.*' Later, we find in the body of the Prayer the word 'Dominions' substituted for 'Kingdoms,' which originated in an order of the Privy Council, dated 1st of January 1801, when our Monarchs discontinued styling themselves Kings of France; but whether this alteration is sanctioned by the Act of Uniformity is a debateable point.* The same change was made at that time in the first of the "Prayers to be used at Sea." (See STEPHEN'S *Book of Com. Prayer.* E. H. S. (*p.* clxxxix.)

(e.) ¶. '*A Collect or Prayer for All Conditions of Men, to be 'read at such times when the Litany is not appointed 'to be said.*' (1662.)

(Mention to be made of such as desire the Prayers of the Church.)

467.—This Collect was designed to answer the purpose of the Litany, as a general intercession 'for All Conditions of Men,' on those days when '*the Litany was not to be said,*' whence its appellation of the "*Lesser Litany.*" In accordance with this intent, it embraced in its original form many of the intercessions included in the other Collects for the King, Royal Family, Clergy, &c.; but the greater part of these intercessions were struck out at the Savoy Conference, and the abbreviated form

---

* The AMERICAN LITURGY in the place of this Prayer has a '*Prayer to be used at the Meetings of Convention,*' and at the end the following Rubric:—*During the period of the Session of any General or Diocesan Convention the above Prayer may be used by all Congregations of the Church, or of the Diocese concerned; the clause "here assembled in thy Name and Presence," being changed to* "now *assembled in thy Name and Presence;" and the clause "govern* us *in* our *present work*" to "*govern* them *in* their *present work.* '*A Prayer for Congress to be used during their Session,*' stands at the head of these "OCCASIONAL PRAYERS.

made to conclude with the same clause which terminated the longer original, and which would therefore naturally begin with the word "*Finally.*" Thus mutilated, it was put into the place it now occupies in the Book of Common Prayer of 1662. Dr. Bisse tells us that Bishop Gunning, once Master of St John's College, and not Bishop Sanderson, was the author of this Collect; and that he would not allow it to be used at the Evening Services of the College Chapel, because he had intended it solely as a substitute for the Litany in MORNING PRAYER on those days of the week when it was not prescribed. In our times, the custom has been, in deference to the Rubric at the head of these "*Occasional Prayers,*" taken conjointly with that belonging to the Collect itself, to use it "*before the two final Prayers of the Litany, or of Morning and Evening Prayer.*"

DEAN COMBER writes:—'We are expressly commanded to pray 'for all men, (1 *Tim.* ii. 1.); and though we do so in the *Litany* and '*Communion Office*, yet, that it might not be omitted any day, this '*Collect* is added to supply the place of the Litany, and, when that 'is not used, this is: hence some call it "*the lesser Litany,*" and it 'teaches us to express a hearty charity to all, especially to the '*afflicted*, and to those that are *sick*, who are usually prayed for in 'this form.'—(Quoted in MANT's *Book of Com. Prayer*, *p.* 74.)

SHEPHERD says:—'St Paul exhorts us to make Prayers and 'Supplications for all men; and the duty enjoined by the Apostle 'was practised by the ancient Christians in their daily devotions. 'In our Church however, till the *last Review* of the Book of 'Common Prayer, we had no particular form of *General Intercession*, 'excepting when the *Litany*, or the *Prayer for the Church militant*, 'was said. The want of such a form being thought a defect, the '*Prayer before us* was composed, and appointed to be used when-'ever the Litany was not.' (*p.* 290.)—*Eluc. of Book of Com. Prayer*, Vol. I.

The REV. J. PURCHAS states:—'The particular Rubric before 'the Prayer was evidently prepared to point out that though all 'the other prayers *might* be used, this *must*, when the Litany was 'not said; if it had been said, there was, of course, no use for it; 'but at all such times as the Litany was not appointed to be 'said there *was*. And it should be observed, that though the *fixed* 'time for the Litany is after Matins, it may on occasion be said '"at other times, when commanded by the Ordinary," e. g. in the 'Evening. And the title of the Prayer says, in that case, the '"Prayer for All Conditions of Men" is to be dropped. There 'certainly was a Prayer for the Church at Evensong, as well as 'at Matins, in the old Offices. (*p.* 123.)—*Directorium Anglicanum.*

[Marginal Rubric.]

'*When any desire the Prayers of the Congregation.*'

468.—There is an important passage in this Collect in which the Church commends to God's mercy and protection 'all who are any ways afflicted, or distressed in mind, body, or estate,' and an interpolation, at this point, of the words, '*especially those for whom our Prayers are desired.*' The Marginal Rubric:—

> '*This is to be said when any desire the prayers of the* '*Congregation.*'

together with the text, naturally implies that any member of the Church may be publicly prayed for who desires it, and has given due intimation to the Officiating Minister before the commencement of Divine Service. It is however much to be regretted that very few avail themselves of this excellent provision of our Church: the Poor, generally speaking, rejoice in the privilege, and to them, it seems, that this great boon is peculiarly confined. But, none are exempt from the sicknesses of our frail nature, nor from the casualties that are continually happening under the varied circumstances and conditions of mortal life: neither the possession of wealth, nor the enjoyment of prosperity, can release us from the necessity, nor should deprive us of the privilege, of praying for protection, or of praising for deliverance; yet how rarely do we hear of the rich and noble desiring the prayers of the assembled Church for help or for recovery. Let the Minister of the Parish exhort his flock to believe in the Apostolic injunction of St James, that 'the effectual fervent prayer of a righteous man availeth much' (*Jas.* v. 16.); and whether they are suffering from *sickness*, or from *poverty*, or *misfortune*, 'the prayer of faith shall save,' and deliver them.

469.—*Before beginning* this Collect, the *names* of those who desire the prayers of the Church in their behalf should be publicly proclaimed; and mention also may be made of the *affliction* under which they are suffering. It is usual, although, not strictly Rubrical, to say *aloud*—" *The Prayers of the* (*Church*, or) *Congregation are desired for A. B.* * * *, *and C. D.* * * *." Where many are to be prayed for, their names need only be mentioned the *first time;* on subsequent occasions, it is customary to repeat—" *The Prayers of the Congregation are desired for many sick persons.*" At the marginal notice, the interpolation, following the words '*body or estate*,' must be adapted to the circumstances of each case, as directed by the Rubric; and the Officiating Minister is then to say—'*especially those* (or *him*, or *her*,) *for whom our Prayers are desired;*' some *slight pause* may be made after this sentence has been uttered in order to afford an opportunity to members of the Congregation of adding *privately* the name of any relation or friend who may need this Christian sympathy.

470.—In some Churches, it is the custom to omit before the Collect all mention of any one desiring the prayers of the Congregation; and to make no allusion in the body of the Prayer to any especial case where the marginal Rubric suggests the interruption, but simply to *pause a few seconds* for private supplication. This usage is adopted by those especially, who imagine that the public utterance of *the names of the Sick* before the Collect is a breach of the Rubric following the *Nicene Creed* in the COMMUNION OFFICE, which says, that, '*nothing shall be* '*proclaimed or published, during the time of Divine* '*Service, &c......, but what is prescribed in the Rules* '*of this Book, or enjoined by the King, or by the* '*Ordinary of the place;*' but surely, the *marginal Notice*, and the *parenthetic Rubric*, point to some announcement to be made of such as desire the prayers of the Church, and come within the range of the permission, as being "*prescribed in the Rules of this Book.*" See this question further discussed *par*. 382. By no means must a Prayer be transferred to this place from the Office of the "VISITATION FOR THE SICK;" nor, indeed, any *Collect* substituted for the one here set down, nor uttered by way of addition to it.

DR. BISSE remarks:—'In this intercession for all mankind, for 'all Christians in all wants, there is provided a clause whereby any 'person may be prayed for in particular, if visited *with any kind of* '*affliction*, especially if with *bodily sickness*, which is chiefly in- 'tended in this place.' (*p.* 117.)—*The Beauty of Holiness in the Common Prayer.*

WHEATLY says:—'There being a particular clause provided in 'this prayer, '*to be said when any desire the prayers of the Congre-* '*gation*,' it is needless as well as irregular to use any Collects *out of* '*the Visitation Office* upon these occasions; as some are accustomed 'to do, without observing the impropriety they are guilty of in 'using those forms in the public Congregations, which are drawn 'up to be used in private, and run in terms that suppose the sick 'person to be present.' (*p.* 188.)—*Rat. Ill. of Book of Com. Prayer.*

ABP. SECKER, speaking of the '*Prayer for All Conditions of Men*,' and of the '*General Thanksgiving*' following, writes:—'Neither 'of these forms is taken from any other Liturgy: both are excel- 'lent: and every one, who desires it, may, by signifying that desire, 'have a separate share in either. This provision is a very useful 'and comfortable one: and we exhort you, on all fit occasions, to 'take the advantage of it. Only we must beg, that they, *who have* '*received benefit* by being prayed for, will not forget *to return thanks;* 'but conscientiously avoid our Saviour's reproof: *were there not ten* '*cleansed? But where are the nine?*' Luke xvii. 17. (*p.* 444.)—*Works*, Vol. 3.

SHEPHERD observes:—'We farther intercede for all that are 'afflicted, whether by *sorrow*, *sickness*, or *penury:* and more es- 'pecially for those that particularly desire our public intercession 'at the throne of grace. All these we commend to the fatherly 'goodness of God, beseeching him *to comfort and relieve them ac-* '*cording to their several necessities:* that is, to mitigate their *sorrow* '*of mind*, and assuage their *bodily pain*, and to relieve their *dis-* '*tressed estate*, as may be most expedient for them. In particular 'we pray that, during their *sufferings*, He will enable them to bear 'this visitation patiently: trusting that if they are restored to '*health* and *prosperity*, they will lead the rest of their lives to His 'glory: and assured, that if their sufferings terminate in death, to 'which, as to the only complete deliverance from the pressure of 'human woe, the good man must, in the gloom of *adversity*, look 'forward with secret delight; the issue will, to him at least, be 'equally fortunate and happy. Both here, and in the GENERAL 'THANKSGIVING, the *Rubric* appears to be somewhat defective. It 'is not expressly stated whether the *names* of those who *desire the* '*prayers of the Congregation*, and of those who *desire to return* '*praise*, should be *publicly announced by the Minister*. Both the 'reason of the thing, and the mode of expression adopted in the 'clauses inserted between brackets, seem to require that the Minister 'should notify to the Congregation the *names* of those, on whose 'account the additions are made. I am aware of the objection to 'this practice that may be drawn from the words of another Rubric, 'prohibiting all publications *in the time of Divine Service, except 'those that are prescribed by the rules of the Book or enjoined by the 'Ordinary of the place.* But in these two instances, the intention 'of the Church appears so evident, that by complying with it, we 'can scarcely be said to transgress any rule. And is not the 'general acquiescence of our Ordinaries nearly equivalent to an 'injunction?' (*p.* 291.)—*Eluc. of Book of Com. Prayer*, Vol. I.

Among more modern writers we have the following:—

The REV. W. BATES states:—'Some *officiating Ministers* insert 'the *names* of those who 'desire the *prayers* of the Congregation,' 'and of those who 'desire to *return praise*,' but there is a *Rubric* 'which prohibits all publications in the time of Divine Service, ex- 'cept those that are prescribed by the rules of the Book, or enjoined 'by the Ordinary of the place,' so that, unless a direct or tacit '*consent of the Ordinary* can be alleged, it is clearly *improper to do* 'so.' (*p.* 362.)—*College Lectures on Christian Antiquities.*

The REV. SAMUEL ROWE says:—'But it is much to be feared 'that there are few who rightly understand the privileges which 'belong to the *communion of saints*, or duly appreciate the im- 'portance of those claims which every individual member has upon 'the united supplications of the whole body of the Church. A 'general persuasion of the reality of those privileges would unques- 'tionably lead many to desire the *prayers of the Congregation*, who 'never think of it now; nor should those who have partaken in the 'benefit of those prayers ever omit the corresponding duty of *public 'thanksgiving*, though we are all more ready to cry like the nine 'Jews for deliverance from our maladies, than to return to thank 'the merciful Giver, like the grateful Samaritan. (*p.* 145.)—*An Appeal to the Rubric.*

At the *Conference of Australian Bishops* held at Sydney from October 1st to November 1st, A. D. 1850, it was thus decreed:—'It 'is convenient that the *names of the persons* for whom the Prayers 'of the Congregation are desired should be mentioned either before 'the Litany or before the Prayer for All Conditions of Men, as the 'case may be. The words "especially those for whom our Prayers 'are desired" may be inserted in the *Litany* in their appropriate 'place.'—*Eccl. Gazette*, June, 1851.

In the Introduction of the "*Churchman's Diary*," we read:— 'When persons in *sickness* desire the *prayers of the Church*, *notice* 'should *always be given* (though not by name after the first time) 'at the commencement of the *Litany* in these words, "The Prayers 'of the Church are desired for A. B." It is *not necessary to give 'notice before the Prayer for all Estates of Men*, as the Congregation 'are advertised of the fact in the Prayer itself.'—*Pub. by Masters.*

MR. A. J. STEPHENS, *Barrister-at-law*, observes:—'The *Rubrics* 'are deficient in their direction, whether, before "the *general* '*intercession*" or "*General Thanksgiving*" in the daily Service, the '*names* of those persons who "desire the prayers of the Congre-'gation," or "desire to return thanks," *shall be publicly recited* or '*no.* Some suppose, both from the reason of the thing, and from 'the wording of the interpolations to be used on those occasions, 'that it implied, the names of the persons, on whose account the 'additions are to be inserted in the prayers, should be particularly 'recited, and *notified to the Congregation:* but others, who suppose 'this will fall under the notion of "publications in time of divine 'Service," which by another Rubric is limited to the injunctions of 'the Queen or the Ordinary, will, for that reason be of another 'opinion.' (*p.* 593.)—*Book of Com. Prayer.* E. H. S.

[The Churching of Women.]

471.—It is customary *here*, in many places, to introduce the '*Churching of Women;*' intimation, of course, having been given previous to the commencement of Divine Service. The Officiating Minister continues in the Reading-Desk, and *standing up*, proceeds at once to read the Office for "The Thanksgiving of Women after Child-birth." Many Clergymen, in order to prompt the Congregation to join in the Service, announce—'*A woman* '(or, *Elizabeth F***) *desires to return thanks to* '*Almighty God for her safe deliverance from the perils* '*of Child-birth.*' This is by no means Rubrical, and where it is not the usage, it should not be introduced. We shall have more to say on the general subject, when we arrive at the Office for "The Churching of Women" by and by; in the mean time, our remarks must be considered as limited to the particular question of place under discussion. (See *par.* 382. *supra*, and *Vol.* E. *pars.* 13. and 204.)

472.—The *woman* is directed by the Rubric at the beginning of the Office to '*kneel down in some con-*'*venient place, as hath been accustomed, or as the* '*Ordinary shall direct;*' this '*convenient place*' is generally styled '*the Churching Pew;*' a Pew usually set apart for this especial purpose. Frequently, however, female modesty tempts the woman to occupy her customary seat, a practice which in the 16th and 17th centuries was considered *puritanical;* but now seems to be tacitly sanctioned by Clergymen at large; although the original design of the 'convenient and accustomed place' was—as the Bishops reply to the Exceptions taken by the Presbyterian Ministers at the Savoy Conference,—'that the Woman might be 'perspicuous to the whole Congregation, and also 'near to the Holy Table in regard of the Offering 'she is there to make.' (CARDWELL'S *Conf.* 362.) At the conclusion of the MORNING or EVENING SERVICE, as the case may be, the woman is to present her "*Offering*" to the Minister; unless the *Communion Office* is about to follow, when she would take advantage of the Offertory.

The special Service for the "*Thanksgiving of Women after Child-birth*" having been thus introduced, and being so complete in itself, no allusion should be made to the woman's case in the "*General Thanksgiving*" which follows.* See *Bishop Mant's* opinion, *par.* 382. *supra.*)

THANKSGIVINGS.

473.—The forms of Thanksgiving, which we are now about to consider, were not introduced into the Liturgy until the *Revision* of James I. in 1604. The divines, at the Hampton Court Conference of that date, imagining that there existed great deficiency of praise for special mercies and deliverances, drew up the Collects following to correspond with the several Prayers immediately preceding, and to supply

* In the AMERICAN LITURGY, the '*Prayer for All Conditions of Men*,' and '*the General Thanksgiving*,' are introduced before the two final Collects of Morning and Evening Prayer; and '*The General Thanksgiving*,' but not the former Prayer, occupies the like place in the Litany. Here is inserted the last Collect of our Office for "The Churching of Women" instead of the Office itself; with the title, "THE THANKSGIVING OF WOMEN AFTER CHILD-BIRTH," with this Rubric:—"*To be said when any Woman, being "present in Church, shall have desired to return thanks to Almighty "God for her safe deliverance.*"

to each of them an appropriate thanksgiving 'for the benefits received at God's hands.' The *General Thanksgiving* is of later date than the others.

'*A General Thanksgiving.*'

(Mention to be made of such as desire the thanksgivings of the Church.)

474.—This formulary was introduced into the Prayer Book at the *last Review* in 1662, and its composition has been ascribed to the pen of Bishop Sanderson; but LATHBURY tells us that its preparation seems rather to be due to Reynolds, Bishop of Norwich. (*Hist. Convoc.* p. 289.). It is an admirable summary of the continued and daily blessings which call for a public expression of our gratitude to Almighty God; and should never be omitted from the Morning, or Evening, Service; or from the Litany; as some Clergymen are occasionally disposed to do in violence of the direction of the Rubric annexed to the leading title, " Prayers and Thanksgivings upon several Occasions."

[MARGINAL RUBRIC.]

'*When any that have been prayed for desire to return praise.*'

475.—It is the usual practice before beginning this *Thanksgiving*, for the Officiating Minister, as at the '*Prayer for All Conditions of Men,*' to announce the *names* of those who desire to return thanks to God for the mercies they may have received. The words employed are generally "*A* * * * *B* * * * "*desires to return thanks to Almighty God for*———" (here the specific mercy should be mentioned); and on arriving at the place in the Thanksgiving where the interpolation occurs, the Minister must add—'*particularly to those,* (or *him*, or *her*) *who desire now* '*to offer up their praises and thanksgivings for Thy late* '*mercies vouchsafed unto them* (or *him*, or *her*.') The Marginal Rubric directs—'This to be said when *any* '*that have been prayed for* desire to return praise;' therefore, if any call upon the Minister to publicly *return thanks* for a mercy received, and which previously had *not been publicly prayed for* in the Church; the desire of such an one cannot *legally* be acceded to. There are cases, however, such as preservation from fire, or other sudden accident, when this rule at the wish of a faithful member of the Church may be relaxed; but this must be dependent on the general power or permission conceded by the Ordinary to the judgment of the Minister of the Parish. The remarks, bearing on the parallel case of announcing names at the '*Prayer for All Conditions of Men*,' will apply here, and to them we would refer our Readers; but we may add a few opinions.

Wheatly says:—'Considering how many blessings we daily 'receive from God, and that He expects nothing else from us in 'return but the easy tribute of love and gratitude, (a duty that no 'one can want leisure or ability to perform,) it is certain no excuse 'can be made for the *omission of it*......And to give more satisfaction 'still, by removing all shadows of defect from our Liturgy, there 'was one *General Thanksgiving* added to the *last Review* for daily 'use, drawn up (as it is said) by Bishop Sanderson, and so admirably 'composed, that it is fit to be said by all men who would give God 'thanks for common blessings, and yet peculiarly provided with 'a proper clause for those who, having received some eminent '*personal mercy*, desire to offer up their public praise: a duty 'which none, *that have had the prayers of the Church*, should ever 'omit after their recovery, lest they incur the reprehension given 'by our Saviour to the ungrateful lepers recorded in the Gospel, '*Were there not ten cleansed? but where are the nine?*' (*p.* 189.)—*Rat. Ill. of Book of Common Prayer*.

Abp. Secker writes:—'It is a more methodical summary of the 'several mercies of God *to us and to all men*, than we had before: it 'furnishes an opportunity of thanking Him more expressly for the 'late instances of His *loving kindness* to the *members of our own* '*Congregation:* and besides, as we cannot be too thankful to God; 'the acknowledgments, which we offered up in the beginning of the 'Service, are very properly repeated in the end. For surely we 'ought to ask nothing of God, without remembering, what we have 'received from Him.' (*p.* 444.)—*Works*, Vol. 3.

Shepherd remarks:—'A *General Thanksgiving* which is ap'pointed to be used in the Morning and Evening Service of *every* '*day* immediately before the two concluding Prayers......When any 'desire to return praise for especial mercies, there is a clause for the 'purpose, and the nature of the blessing is commonly *specified by the* '*Minister before he begins the Thanksgiving*.' (*p.* 293.)—*Eluc. of Book of Com. Prayer*, Vol. I.

The Rev. W. G. Humphry observes:—'Though placed among 'occasional thanksgivings, it has deservedly been received into the 'regular Service of the Church. It certainly gives to our devotions 'a more Eucharistical and cheerful tone. Nor is it out of place 'at the close of an Office of humiliation like the Litany. For after 'such an Office we need something to raise us as it were, and 'refresh us; and nothing is more suitable for this purpose, nothing 'is more apt to give us confidence for the future, than the recol- 'lection of God's mercies, vouchsafed to us in past times.' (*p.* 182.) —Treatise on Book of Common Prayer.

The REV. J. PURCHAS says:—'It is customary to introduce the 'General Thanksgiving *daily* in this place; but there is no Rubrical 'authority for its continual use, which rests on purely voluntary 'grounds. Some ritualists hold that its interpolation interrupts the 'Service. Others, with greater reason, that it perfects the Euchar- 'istic analogy of the Office, holding as it does a parallel position to 'the "Gloria in Excelsis" in the Liturgy. It would therefore 'perhaps be well, at any rate, to *omit it in the Litany* when followed 'by a Celebration of the Holy Eucharist, and from that Service and 'also from the Divine Office during Advent, Lent, and on Ferial 'days.' (*p.* 115.)—*Directorium Anglicanum.*

At the *Conference of Australian Bishops* held at Sydney from October 1st to November 1st, A. D. 1850, it was thus decreed:—'It 'is convenient that the *names of the persons* who desire to return 'thanks should be mentioned before the "*General Thanksgiving.*" 'The words, "particularly to those who desire now,' &c.," may be 'used for persons who have *not been specially prayed for.*'—*Eccl. Gazette*, June, 1851.

476.—The remaining *Thanksgivings* are for various specific occasions, and were incorporated into the Litany at the *Revision* in 1604, except the thanksgiving "*For restoring Public Peace at Home*," which was added at the *last Review* in 1662. At this latter date also, we find that they were all transposed from the Litany to the place they now occupy. They are seven in number, viz:—

(1.) *For Rain.* (1604.)
(2.) *For Fair Weather.* (1604.)
(3.) *For Plenty.* (1604.)
(4.) *For Peace and Deliverance from our Enemies.* (1604.)
(5.) *For restoring Public Peace at Home.* (1662.)
(6.) *For Deliverance from the Plague, or other Common Sickness.* (1604.)
(7.) Ditto.* (1604.)

---

* In the AMERICAN LITURGY the first five of these especial Thanksgivings occur, and the sixth also, but with the Title, '*For Deliverance from great Sickness and Mortality;*' the seventh is omitted; but in its place are added two other Thanksgivings, one '*For a Recovery from Sickness,*' the other, '*For a safe Return from Sea.*'

The forms, which were introduced in the Liturgy of 1604, had their titles beginning with the words—'*A Thanksgiving*' for &c., this was struck out at *the Revision* in 1662. We find, moreover, subsequently, that in the Collect '*For Plenty*,' it was suggested in the '*Alterations*' of 1689, to add after the expression 'fruits of increase,' the words 'and that we may use them.' No other changes were then, nor have been subsequently, proposed; and we may, therefore, conclude the consideration of these Thanksgivings with a quotation from Shepherd, who says:—

'When the petitions, which we may have offered up in any of the 'preceding Occasional Prayers, have been granted, and our desires 'fulfilled; when either a calamity has been removed or a blessing 'vouchsafed, it is evidently the intention of the Church, that praise, 'should be given to God, in the words of the *appropriate Thanksgiving* here prescribed: that is, in all cases where the ordinary 'form is not superseded by one that is special, and enjoined by 'authority.' (*p.* 295.)—*Eluc. of Book of Common Prayer*, Vol. I.

The Collects, Epistles, and Gospels,

To be used throughout the Year.

477.—The Collects, Epistles, and Gospels, which now come under our review, will not occupy us with the details of their history or characteristic features, as these questions fall not within the scope of our design, except in so far as they may help to elucidate the *Laws and Usages of the Church* involved in the Canonical and Rubrical points connected with them. First, then, with regard to the *Title*.

478.—In the *earlier Liturgy* of Edward VI. A. D. 1549, the title prefixed to this portion of the Liturgy was:—

'The Introits, Collects, Epistles, and Gospels,

'*To be used at the celebration of the Lord's Supper and Holy 'Communion, through the year: with Proper Psalms and 'Lessons for divers Feasts and Days.*'—(Clay's Book of Common Prayer Illustrated, *in loco*).

[Introits.]

479.—Among the early Christians the Communion Service began with the reading of Scripture (*Apos. Const.* ii. c. 57.); but about the 4th century, *Psalms* or *Anthems* were prefixed; and in the following century Pope Cœlestine appointed the Psalms of David to be sung before the Scripture Lessons; this Gregory the Great improved upon by substituting Anthems selected from the Psalms; and they acquired a particular appellation from the position they occupied in the Service; the *Anthem* was designated *Introitus* in the Roman Liturgy, *Ingressa* in the Ambrosian, or that of Milan, and in the English Church it was known under the name of *Officium*, or *Introit*. (Palmer's *Orig. Lit.* ii. 19.)

480.—These Psalms or *Anthems* were placed before every Collect, Epistle, and Gospel, and were appointed to their respective positions according to the illustration they severally afforded to the Epistle and Gospel of the day. And it was because they were sung or said while the Priest was entering within the Communion rails; or, as then termed, the Septum of the Altar, that the name of *Introitus*, or *Introit*, was applied to them. In Edward's *first Liturgy* these *Introits* were printed at full length; and annexed to them was the Doxology with a Rubric following, directing '*and so must every Introit be ended.*' We do not, however, find any allusion to these *Introits* in the *second* Liturgy of Edward VI. (A. D. 1552), nor is any reason assigned for their rejection; but the Proper Psalms and Lessons were then transposed in a tabular form to the beginning of the Prayer Book before the Calendar. Lists of these *Introits* may be seen in Wheatly's *Rational Illustration of the Bk. of Com. Pr.;* Shepherd's *Elucidation of the Book of Com. Pr.*; and in Stephens's *Book of Com. Pr.*; published by the Eccl. Hist. Society.

481. The modern substitute for the *Introit*, while the Minister is passing from the Reading-desk to the

Communion Table, is the ordinary *Psalmody* in Parish Churches, and the *Sanctus* or *Tersanctus* in Cathedrals; and in Edward's *First Liturgy* (1549), we find at the Communion Office, two Rubrics, which though conflicting in their directions, may be considered as the parent of the usage of connecting the Morning Prayer, or the Litany, with the Communion Office by the singing of Psalms in metre. One Rubric before the Lord's Prayer and Collect for purity of heart reads:—

> '*Then shall the Clerks sing in English for the Office, or 'Introit (as they call it), a Psalm appointed for that day.*' (1549.)—Keeling, 167.

Here the Clerks are ordered to sing the '*Introit;*' but in the Rubric following the above mentioned Collect, the Priest is directed to '*say*' this '*Introit;*' thus:—

> '*Then shall he* (the Priest) *say a Psalm appointed for the 'Introit: which Psalm ended, the Priest shall say, or else 'the Clerks shall sing,*' (Here follows the Lesser Litany.)—(1549.)—Keeling, 169.

Upon these opposing instructions Wheatly gives the opinion we annex:—

> 'For it is very certain, that the use of *Introits* to begin the 'Communion Office was not only unexceptionable, but of great 'antiquity in the Church: Durand proving that they were taken 'into divine Service before the time of St Jerom. And it is plain 'that they would still have been very useful, since the want of 'them is forced to be supplied by the *singing of Anthems* in 'Cathedrals, and *part of a Psalm* in metre in Parish-Churches. 'And therefore I cannot but think, it would have been much 'more decent for us to have been guided by the Church what 'Psalms to have used in that intermediate time, than to stand 'to the direction of every illiterate Parish-Clerk, who too often 'has neither judgment to choose a *Psalm* proper to the occasion, 'nor skill to sing it so as to assist devotion.' (*p.* 216.)—*Rational Illustration of Book of Com. Prayer.*

The Rev. J. Jebb thus comments on *Wheatly's* remark:—'*Wheatly* has remarked upon an ambiguity in the old Rubrics 'as to the use of the *Introit*. One Rubric directs the *Clerks* to *sing* 'it before the Lord's Prayer: another directs the *Priest* to *say* it 'after the Collect for Purity following the Lord's Prayer. It 'may have been intended that in Choirs the former method, in 'other places the latter should be observed (*p.* 460.).........In 'Clifford's book, published shortly after the Restoration, it appears 'that a *Voluntary* preceded the Communion Service at St Paul's. 'Shortly after this time, the custom arose, now universal in *Choirs*, 'of singing a *Sanctus* in this place: St Paul's, Westminster, and 'Canterbury, were the first to adopt it. To this there can be no 'objection, the *Sanctus* here having a peculiarly solemn effect, and 'its use being contrary neither to the Rubric, to the rationale of the 'Service, nor to primitive and Catholic custom (*p.* 461.)......In '*Parish Churches*, a *Metrical Psalm* is usually sung in this place, 'and very properly. It is suggested, that as a Psalm of a more 'penitential character is best suited for performance before the 'Litany, so before the Communion, ought it to be in a more 'Eucharistic strain, with special reference to the Festival. The 'words ought not to be varied too frequently, but such a limited 'selection made as may be readily familiarized to a plain or 'unlettered Congregation. This consideration is the chief obstacle 'to a practice, in itself commendable, which some Clergymen are 'disposed to adopt, that of selecting such a part of the *metrical* '*version* as may correspond to the ancient *Introit* for the day. 'It is possible indeed, that the desuetude of the *Introit* may be 'assignable to this cause. A practice has of late been adopted 'in a London Church, which to the Author has appeared very 'affecting and appropriate, as marking in a most significant manner 'the distinction between the Services, and the unity of the Com-'munion Office. A *total silence* is observed for some minutes at 'the conclusion of the Litany, and the precursory *Sanctus* does 'not begin till the Officiating Clergyman has gone within the 'Communion rails. This is certainly in strictest accordance with 'the ancient usage, which prescribed the *singing of the Introit* to 'begin when the Clergy had entered the Septum, or enclosure 'of the Holy Table. It is to be wished that some such practice 'were adopted in our Choirs; or that at least a low symphony 'were played till the Clergy had approached the Altar rail, when 'the *Sanctus* might begin. No regulation or prescriptive usage of 'the Anglican Church opposes such a practice; and in all such 'matters, indifferent in themselves, it never can be wrong to adopt 'those methods which tend best to edification.' (*p.* 462.)—*On Choral Service.*

THE COLLECTS.

482.—The term *Collect*, as we have already shewn, has had various interpretations assigned to it; some think it implies, that the prayer is *collected* out of the Epistle and Gospel;—others, that the alternate supplications of Minister and People otherwise expressed in Versicles and Responsals are here *collected* into one connected prayer;—while some think, that it is so named because such a compendious summary is offered up by a *collected* assembly of People (see *Vol.* II. *par.* 241.). Be this as it may, these Collects are of very early origin: some, indeed, can be traced as far back as the Sacramentary of Leo, A. D. 483;

others are to be met with in that of Gelasius, A. D. 494; and many are to be found in the Sacramentary of Gregory the Great, A. D. 590. They come to us, for the most part, through the ancient Missals of Salisbury, York, Hereford, &c. (PALMER's *Orig. Lit.* Vol. I. p. 343: NICHOLLS' *Book of Com. Prayer* in loco.), and, with the Epistles, and Gospels, always appertain to the Communion Service, as they anciently did to the Service of the Mass.

WHEATLY says:—'It is certain that Gelasius, who was Bishop 'of Rome, A. D. 492, ranged the *Collects*, which were then used, into 'order, and added some new ones of his own: which Office was 'again corrected by Pope Gregory the Great in the year 600, whose 'Sacramentary contains most of the *Collects* we now use. But 'our Reformers observing that some of these *Collects* were after-'wards corrupted by superstitious alterations and additions, and 'that others were quite left out of the Roman Missals, and entire 'new ones, relating to their present innovations, added in their 'room; they therefore examined every *Collect* strictly, and where 'they found any of them corrupted, there they corrected them; 'where any new ones had been inserted, they restored the old ones; 'and lastly, at the Restoration, every *Collect* was again reviewed, 'when whatsoever was deficient was supplied, and all that was but 'improperly expressed, rectified.' (*p.* 210.)—*Rat. Ill. of Book of Com. Prayer*.

483.—*Tables* of these Collects, illustrating their antiquity, the alterations made in them; and particularizing those which have been more recently composed, are to be found in the works of various writers.* The original *Tables* were constructed by Bishop Cosins, and published in Dean Comber's Companion to the Temple (p. 1. §. xx.); since which they have been corrected by modern scholars, whose emendations we shall avail ourselves of as we proceed. A careful perusal of the *Collects* will shew us that, generally speaking, they are founded on the *Epistle* and *Gospel*

---

* These TABLES may be seen not only in Dean COMBER's *Companion to the Temple*, but likewise in SHEPHERD's *Elucidation of the Book of Common Prayer*, Vol. II. p. 20; Bishop MANT's *Book of Common Prayer*, in loco; HUMPHRY's *Treatise on the Book of Common Prayer*, p. 185; PROCTER's *History of the Book of Common Prayer*, p. 245; STEPHENS' *Book of Common Prayer*, E. H. S. *Vol.* II. *p.* 607.

connected with them; or refer to the subject commemorated by the Holy-day Service.

THE EPISTLES AND GOSPELS.

484.—These *Epistles* and *Gospels* seem to be of like antiquity with the *Collects;* and have held the same relationship the one to the other for some centuries; if not in the time of the early Fathers, (as *Riddle* shews in his Christian Antiquities, *p.* 445.); yet certainly from the time of Augustine's mission into this Country, A. D. 595. antecedent to the Norman Conquest. The influence of Augustine's successors is visible in the appellation given to these portions of Scripture; for in the Eastern Church the Epistle is called '*the Apostle*' to this day; while in the Western Church it is known as '*the Epistle:*' occasionally, the Church of England has introduced for the Epistle a portion of the *Acts of the Apostles*, or of the Prophets, as being more appropriate to the day or season. Here we may remark, with Bp. Mant, that the terms "*Epistle*" and "*Gospel*" have two different senses, one, the technical expression for this portion of the Service; the other, the title of a book of Holy Scripture; this distinction is essential to the right interpretation of the Rubrics.

485.—These Epistles and Gospels may be divided into two great sections, the one *doctrinal*, the other *practical;* the former from *Advent* to *Trinity* developes the life of our Redeemer; viz. His *incarnation, nativity, circumcision, manifestation to the Gentiles, baptism, fasting, temptation, agony, cross, death, burial, resurrection*, and *ascension;* and the *descent of the Holy Ghost;* closing with praise and glory to the *Holy Trinity;* during all which we commemorate the unspeakable benefits that accrue to us from the love of God the Father, by the mediation and atonement of God the Son, and through the ministration of God the Holy Ghost. The latter section, from *Trinity* to *Advent*, teaches us 'the way in which we

should go,' during our pilgimage on earth, and how to live after Christ's example.

BISHOP OVERALL remarks:—'The Church has not appointed 'these following *Gospels* and *Epistles*, but upon special relation to 'the *time* wherein they are read. And it is admirable to see, 'with what order and wisdom all things are disposed and brought 'in *tempore suo*, that they might be the more kindly for the 'putting us in mind of what we are about, or what we have 'to do. The whole year is distinguished into two parts: the 'time of Christ's living among us here on Earth, which is the 'First: and our time of living here after his example, which 'is the Second: for the First are all the Sundays appointed from '*Advent* to *Trinity Sunday*, for the rest are all the Sundays after '*Trinity* to *Advent* again. (*Veteres distinxerunt hæc duo tempora 'in tempus Dominicæ Dispensationes, et tempus nostræ peregrina-'tionis.*) And because the first part is conversant about the Life 'of Christ, and the Mysteries of his Divine Dispensation, therefore 'beginning at *Advent* is the memory of his Incarnation celebrated, 'and after that his Nativity, then his Circumcision, his Manifes-'tation to the *Gentiles*, his nonage, his doctrine, his miracles, his 'passion, his Burial, his Resurrection, his Ascension, his sending 'of the Holy Ghost, all in a most absolute order. In all which, 'we see the whole story and course of our Saviour, in manifesting 'himself, and his divine mysteries to the world. So that the 'Gospels read through all this part of the year, have their chief 'end and purpose, to make us know and remember orderly with 'grateful hearts, what excellent benefits God the Father hath 'communicated unto us, first by His Son, then by His Holy 'Spirit, making us the Heirs of Heaven, that before were the 'Sons of Hell; for which unspeakable goodness we do most fitly 'end this part of the year, with giving praise and glory to the 'whole blessed Trinity. The Second part which contains all the 'Sundays after that, being for our guidance in the peregrination 'that we have living in this world, hath for it such *Gospels* in order 'appointed, as may most easily and plainly instruct and lead us 'in the true paths of Christianity; that those which are regenerated 'by Christ, and initiated in his faith, may know what virtues 'to follow, and what vices to eschew. Thus in the first part, we 'are to learn the mysteries of the Christian Religion; in the second, 'we are to practise that which is agreeable to the same. For it 'behoves us, not only to know that we have no other foundation 'of our Religion but Christ Jesus, born and crucified, and risen 'for us; but further also, to build upon this foundation such a 'life as he requires of us. And because the first part ends with '*Pentecost*, the giving us a new law in our hearts; therefore 'the second is to begin with the practice of that law. That 'as the Children of *Israel* did pass the Desert by the direction 'of *Moses*, so we may pass through this world by the guidance 'of our Saviour, and overcoming at last our spiritual enemies, 'we may come to our heavenly dwelling-place, and there remain 'with Him for ever.' (*p.* 25.)—Add. Notes to NICHOLLS' *Book of Com. Prayer*.

WHEATLY adopts the above opinions of Bishop Overall, but puts it into more modern language. (See his *Rat. Ill. of Book of Com. Prayer*, p. 211.).

SHEPHERD says:—'Long before the division of the sacred 'Books into *chapters* and *verses*, (which is a modern invention, 'and unknown to antiquity), it was customary both in the Greek 'and Latin Churches, to read, at the celebration of the Eucharist, 'some of the plainest and most instructive portions of the New 'Testament. With respect to the different portions which we 'read, they are so judiciously selected, that it would be difficult 'to find other passages more interesting, and more pertinent to 'the occasion and the season. The *Epistles* either enforce the 'practice of Christian virtue, or contain manifestations of divine 'mercy, and assurances of pardon and forgiveness. The *Holy* '*Gospel* relates either some remarkable narrative of the life or 'death of Christ; some eminent miracle, important parable, or, 'some striking part of his divine discourses. The *Epistles* convey 'instruction in the mysteries of our salvation; but the *Gospels* 'present us with the example of Jesus, to the imitation of which 'all other knowledge is but subservient.' (*p.* 29.)—*Eluc. of Book of Com. Prayer*. Vol. II.

[The RUBRIC.]

486.—We must now pass to the *Rubrical* directions affecting the COLLECTS at large.

¶. '*Note, that the* COLLECT *appointed for every Sunday, or for* '*any Holy-day that hath a Vigil or Eve, shall be said at* '*the Evening Service next before.*'*

This Rubric was introduced at the *last Review* in 1662, and directs

I. *That* the Collect of the SUNDAY is to be used at the Evening Service going before, i. e. on the *Saturday* preceding; but the term Evening must be limited to 6 *o'clock P. M.*, and after. (See this question fully discussed in *pars.* 359—370. *supra*, where many authorities are annexed.)

II. *That* the Collect of a HOLY-DAY, when that HOLY-DAY has a prescribed '*Vigil or Eve*,' is to be used in the *Evening-Service* going before, if at 6 *o'clock P. M.* or later. (See *ibid*, supra.)

III. *That* if such *Holy-day* falls on a MONDAY, the Collect must be used, *not* at the *Sunday Evening* Service going before, but on the SATURDAY Evening Service preceding. (See *ibid*, supra.)

The HOLY-DAYS with *Vigils or Eves* are enumerated in *par* 360. *supra* and will be distinguished as we proceed. The course to be adopted when there is a *concurrence of* HOLY-DAYS has also been ex-

* This Rubric is omitted from the AMERICAN LITURGY.

plained. (See *pars.* 166—168. *Vol.* **B.**; and *pars.* 245, 246. *Vol.* **E.**): the rule is briefly this:—

An ordinary SUNDAY (i. e. one not peculiarly connected with our Lord's Ministry) *yields* to a SAINT'S-DAY; and a *lesser Festival* gives way to a *greater.*

The great advantage arising from the observance of *Vigils* or *Eves* is the preparation it affords for the peculiar Services of the Festival of the morrow. The evening before the Sabbath is especially deserving of serious attention, and every effort should be made by the Clergy to induce their people to withdraw themselves for a short time from worldly occupations, and from vain, and too often unholy pleasures. What can be more unsatisfactory than to see the mass of the people devoting the closing hours of the week to late marketing, and shop-keeping; and the higher grades in too many instances trenching upon the Sunday itself in the feverish excitement of balls, and parties, and theatrical entertainments?

[The COLLECT, EPISTLE, and GOSPEL, to serve the Week.]

487.—The Collect, Epistle, and Gospel, which are employed on the SUNDAY, are to be used *throughout the week*, unless some *Holy-day* intervene, which has a Collect, Epistle, and Gospel, of its own. The Rubric directing this is to be found in the Introduction to the Prayer Book under the title, "THE ORDER HOW THE REST OF HOLY SCRIPTURE IS APPOINTED TO BE READ," and is as follows:—

'*Note* also, that the *Collect, Epistle,* and *Gospel,* appointed for 'SUNDAY shall serve *all the week after,* where it is not in this 'Book otherwise ordered.' (1662.)—*Present Book of Common Prayer.*

This order evidently implies more than a *Wednesday* or *Friday* Service; in fact, *Daily Prayer;* and where such may be the usage, the above injunction will be attended to. Every HOLY-DAY appointed to be observed in the Church of England will be found to have its peculiar Collect, Epistle, and Gospel, and when the *Holy-day* occurs in the week these will *supersede* the Collect, &c. of the Sunday. The Rubric of the preceding Liturgies, and that of the Scotch Liturgy, elucidate the subject further; thus:—

'Ye must note also that the *Collect, Epistle*, and *Gospel*, ap-'pointed for the SUNDAY, shall serve all the week after, except 'there fall some *Feast* that hath his proper.' (1549. 1552, 1559, 1604.)—KEELING. xxv.

In the SCOTCH LITURGY (1637), we find the same words, with this addition in Italics:—

'......his proper *Collect, Epistle, and Gospel, as it is on Ash-'Wednesday, and on every day in the holy-week next before 'Pasch or Easter. But on all those Days the Psalms and 'Lessons shall be the same which fall in course as they are 'in the Kalendar.*'—KEELING. xxiv.

It is not, however, customary to continue the Holy-day Collect, &c. beyond the day to which it belongs, unless especially appointed by the Rubric. *Wheatly* differs, as will be seen below.

BP. OVERALL says:—'The Epistle and Gospel are to be read 'every day of the week, as *every day* there should be a *Communion*. 'If people be *married* on a week-day, at that time by this Book 'they are injoined to receive: and so when women after childbirth 'are *Churched;* or when men in Cathedral Churches, where they are 'injoined it every Sunday at least, shall desire to have the *Communion* '*on the week day;* that then the *Collect, Epistle*, and *Gospel* shall be 'used, which was appointed for the Sunday.'—Quoted in MANT'S *Book of Com. Prayer*, p. xxxv.

WHEATLY observes;—'The direction above mentioned is still of 'use to us, if either at a *Marriage*, or at the *Churching of a woman*, '(at both which times a *Communion* is prescribed by the Rubric as 'convenient,) or upon any other such like occasion, the Sacrament 'be administered; at which times we are ordered by the Rubric 'I am speaking of, to use the *same Collect, Epistle*, and *Gospel* as 'were used the SUNDAY before, *where it is not otherwise ordered in* '*this Book*. Before the last Review it was said, '*except there fall* '*some Feast that hath his proper*.' (After referring to the Scotch Liturgy he adds,) 'In which case the Sunday Collect, Epistle, and 'Gospel are to *give place* to the proper Collect, Epistle, and Gospel 'for that day. And this, to be sure, is part of what is intended by 'the Rubric, as it stands now. Though the design, I suppose of 'altering the last words into, "*where it is not in this Book otherwise* '*ordered*," was for a direction also at such times as a new season 'begins between one Sunday and another, as it happens upon *Ash-'Wednesday* and *Ascension-day*. In which case the services of 'those days being placed between the services for the Sundays 'immediately before and after; I take that to be an order that 'the Collect, &c. for the *foregoing Sunday* shall be then left off, 'and the Collect, &c. for the Holy-day shall succeed as the Service '*for the remaining part of the week*.' (*p.* 213.)—Rat. Ill. of Book of Common Prayer.

When *two* HOLY-DAYS concur, the *less* gives way to the *greater*, as we have already explained; (see *pars.* 166—168. *Vol.* B.; 242—246. *Vol.* E.; and *pars.* 369. 482. *supra*): and it must be remembered that but *one* Collect is to be employed, except when Rubrically ordered; and that the choice of the *Epistle* and *Gospel* follows that of the Collect. (MANT. *Hor. Lit.*)

[When *two* or *more* COLLECTS are to be used.]

488.—At the two great seasons of *Advent*, and *Lent*, and during the *Octave of Christmas*, the Church appoints by a specific Rubric that the Collect of the *Season* should be used with the Collect of the *Day*: and on no other occasion, (with the exception of GOOD FRIDAY, when *three Collects* are appointed to be employed), is the Officiating Minister at liberty to repeat a second Collect; this is often improperly done at the *Eves* of Holy-days, and when a Sunday or a Holy-day, or two Holy-days, concur. (See *par.* 246. *supra.*)

489.—It must also be understood that the Collect is appointed for the Communion Service; and that the same, and both if two, must be used at MORNING and EVENING PRAYER. Hence we have these two Rules:—

I. Only *one* COLLECT (*the* COLLECT *of the day selected*) is to be read in Divine Service (except in those especial instances where *two* or *more* are appointed by the Rubric.)

II. The *same* COLLECT (*or* COLLECTS) is to be read at the COMMUNION SERVICE, as is used at the MORNING PRAYER, or LITANY, going before.

WHEATLY, remarking upon the week-day Collects not to be used on Holy-days or their Eves, says:—'Upon which occasions the Rubric 'plainly supposes, that the Collect for the Sunday shall be *left out* 'and *omitted*: the Church never designing to use *two Collects* at 'once, except within the octaves of *Christmas*, and during *Advent* 'and *Lent*; when, for the greater solemnity of those solemn sea-'sons, she particularly orders the Collects of the principal days to 'be used continually after the ordinary Collects.' (*p.* 205.)—*Rat. Ill. of Book of Com. Prayer*.

The REV. J. PURCHAS gives us a different view, as follows:—'It would be proper to say the Collects of "commemorated" Feasts 'at both the Communion and the ordinary Office; but the *head* 'Collects of Seasons, viz. Advent and Lent, at Holy Communion 'only.' (*p.* 36.).—Subsequently he says:—'When two *Holy-days* '"occur," the only notice commonly taken of the inferior in the 'English Church is by the use of its *Collect* as a memorial after that 'of the day; the translation of Festivals not being general amongst 'us. And this *memorial* is to be used at Matins and Evensong, 'as well as in the Communion Office. The head Collects of Sea- 'sons, viz. *Advent* and *Lent*, are only used as "memorials" in the 'Eucharistic, *not* in the ordinary Office.' (*p.* 83.)—*Directorium Anglicanum.*

[ANNOUNCING THE COLLECT.]

490.—Proclaiming aloud to the Congregation the *Collect of the Day* is contrary to the Rubric, and therefore *illegal.* Moreover, if necessary in ordinary cases, it must be especially so when the *Collect of the Season* is to be added to that of the *Day*, as in *Advent* and *Lent;* here the *second Collect* is never announced. This unauthorized usage should be avoided; the educated know the appointed Sunday and where to find the *Collect;* the unlettered need not the information for they have not Prayer Books, nor could they read them if they had them. (See *par.* 248. *supra.*)

[POSTURE.]

491.—The Officiating Minister, and People, '*all kneel*' during the repetition of these Collects of the day in MORNING and EVENING PRAYER, and in the LITANY, in accordance with the Rubric which indicates the introduction of the Collect, as well as with the 18*th Canon.* (See *par.* 30. 240. *supra.*)

Many Clergymen are guided by the Rubric preceding the *Versicles* going before the Collect, which directs the Priest to '*be standing up;*' and this diversity of usage they defend by what they consider an analagous case in the COMMUNION SERVICE where the Priest is instructed by the Rubric before the Collects for the Queen, '*to stand.*' But the latter being a eucharistic or thanksgiving Office cannot well be considered analogous to the supplicatory service of the former instance. Anciently, however, the usage was '*to stand;*' now, it is customary for '*all*,' i.e. Minister and People, '*to kneel*' during the repetition of the Collects in MORNING and EVENING PRAYER, and in the LITANY: but in the COMMUNION SERVICE for the Minister to *stand*, and the People to *kneel*.

The Rev. J. PURCHAS says:—'It may, however, be reasonably 'doubted whether, "*all kneeling*" in the Rubric before *the Orationes* 'of Matins applies to the *Priest* at all. For according to the 'ancient rule the Collects were invariably said *standing*.* And 'here is no direction for the Priest to *kneel*. There is for the 'People.' This is added by way of note:*—'Both Sarum, Roman, 'and Greek Offices order *the Collect* to be said *standing*, i.e. the 'Collect properly so called.'—(*p.* 117.)—*Directorium Anglicanum*.

The *Rubrics* affecting the EPISTLES and GOSPELS.

492.—There are several *Rubrical* questions involved in the delivery of the EPISTLES and GOSPELS, which, it will be better, perhaps, to elucidate here rather than defer their consideration until we arrive at the *Communion Office*. We may first premise that the *Epistle* has always taken local precedence of the *Gospel*, as being the harbinger or forerunner of the 'good tidings' of the Messiah's coming, and as being the words of the servant, which, therefore, must give the more honourable place to the words of the Master: this will explain the preference given to the Reader of the Gospel over that of the Epistle, as we shall presently see. Opinions, however, vary with regard to the origin of this precedence: we will cite two:—

WHEATLY says:—'As our Saviour's disciples *went before His* '*face to every city and place, whither He Himself would come* (Luke 'x. 1.); so here the Epistle, as the word of the servant, is read first, 'that it may be as a harbinger to the Gospel, to which the last 'place and greatest honour is reserved, as being the word of their great Master.' (*p.* 307).—*Rat. Ill. of Bk. of Com. Pr.*

SHHPHERD remarks:—'It is remarkable that the reading of the 'Epistle, should have always *preceded* the reading of the Gospel.

'The Epistle appears to have been regarded as a kind of harbinger 'or messenger to the Gospel. It was considered as the words of 'the *servant*, and the Gospel as the words of the *Master*, for whom 'the last or most honorable place was reserved. Some of the old 'Ritualists say, "The Epistle denotes the Office performed by the "Baptist, who was sent before the face of Christ to prepare his "way." Others are of opinion, that "it indicates the first mission "of the Apostles, when Christ sent them before his face to every "city whither he himself would come." Others assign very different 'reasons for this practice, but all agree that it is intended to shew 'peculiar reverence for the Gospel.' (*p.* 177.)—*Eluc. of Bk. of Com. Pr.* Vol. II.

ANNOUNCING and CONCLUDING the *Epistle*, and *Gospel*.

The EPISTLE.

493.—ANNOUNCEMENT.—In very early times we find that it was usual for the Reader to announce the title of the Book of Scripture from which he was about to read; the Deacon having first enjoined upon the People silence and attention. (PALMER *Orig. Lit.* ii. 45.). From this usage may probably be derived the practise of our own day, as directed in the *Rubric* in the COMMUNION OFFICE, which thus reads:—

(a) ¶. '......*And immediately after the Collect, the Priest shall 'read the Epistle, saying,* The Epistle [*or* The portion of 'Scripture appointed for the Epistle] is written in 'the——Chapter of——beginning at the ——Verse. *And 'the Epistle ended, he shall say,* Here endeth the 'Epistle......'—(1662.)—Present Book of Com. Prayer.

In the *first Liturgy* of Edward VI. (1549), the Rubric did not confine this office to a *Priest,* and it pointed, moreover, to a *special place* for reading the Epistle, thus:—

(b) '*The Collectes ended, the Priest, or he that is appointed, shall 'reade the Epistle in a place assigned for the purpose, saying,* 'The Epistle of Sainct Paule written in the——Chapiter of '——to the——*The Minister then shall reade the Epistle......*' (1549.)—CLAY p. 103; KEELING 175.

In the *second Liturgy* of Edward VI. (1552), we have an approximation to our own Rubric; and which, with but slight variation, was continued in the

Revisions of 1559, 1604, and in the *Scotch Liturgy* of 1637,* thus:—

(c) '*Immediately after the Collectes the Priest* (1589 *Minister*; '1622 *Priest*) *shal reade the Epistle, begynnyng thus.* The 'Epistle written in the——Chapter of——*And the Epistle* '*ended, he shal saye the Gospel, &c.......*' 1552, 1559, 1604.— (CLAY. B. of C. P. Illus. 103: KEELING. 174, 175.)

At the *last Review* in 1662, the Rubric acquired the form we now have (*see* (a) *above*); the words between brackets—*viz.* "[*or* The portion of Scripture appointed for the Epistle]"—'having been then added 'to satisfy some persons who charged the Minister 'with telling a lie, when he said the usual words 'before the portion of Scripture taken not out of 'an Epistle.' (Dr. BISSE: Dr. NICHOLLS.)

494.—The formulary most commonly used at the present day is that which adheres most closely to the language of the Rubric, and adopts the authorized titles of the Books of Scripture; thus, at the 1*st Sunday in Advent*:—

(a) '*The Epistle is written in the* xiiith *Chapter of* the Epistle 'of St. Paul the Apostle to the Romans, *beginning at the* 8th *verse*.'

or, when a portion of the Old Testament, of the Acts of the Apostles, or of the Revelation, is appointed in the place of a passage from an Apostolic Epistle, then is used, as at the 25*th Sunday after Trinity*, this formulary:—

(b) '*The portion of Scripture appointed for the Epistle is* '*written in the* xxiiird *Chapter of* the Book of the Prophet Jeremiah, '*beginning at the* 5th *Verse*.'

There is great difference of phraseology used in proclaiming the *Books* and *Chapters*, whence the Epistles are taken: some Officiating Ministers say (taking the above examples):—

---

* In the SCOTCH LITURGY (1637), this Rubric ran as follows:— '*Immediately after the Collects, the Presbyter shall read the* '*Epistle, saying thus:*—The Epistle written in the—— 'Chapter of——at the——Verse. *And when he hath done,* '*he shall say,* Here endeth the Epistle.' (KEELING. 176.)

(c) '*The Epistle is written in the* xiiith *Chapter of* the Romans, '*beginning*,' &c.

others say :—

(d) '*The Epistle is written in the* xiiith *Chapter of* St Paul's 'Epistle to the Romans, *beginning*,' &c.

others say :—

(e) '*The Epistle is written in the* xiiith *Chapter of* that to the 'Romans, *beginning*,' &c.

again, in the other formulary, (b), many will say :—

(f) '*The portion of Scripture appointed for the Epistle is written* '*in the* xxiiird *Chapter of* the Prophecy of Jeremiah, *beginning*,' &c.

or briefly :—

(g) '*The portion of Scripture appointed for the Epistle is written* '*ten in the* xxiiird *Chapter of* Jeremiah, *beginning*,' &c.

The formulary (e) using the pronoun '*that*' is decidedly incorrect, and originates in a misconception of the technical use of the terms '*Epistle*,' and '*Gospel*,' as applied to these portions of the Prayer Book (see *par.* 481. *supra*). With respect to the other formularies, they all, with the exception of the *first two* (a), (b), are sanctioned by no authority, and, therefore, those who use them can only advance the plea of custom in their defence. Again, it is by no means allowable to interchange at pleasure the introductory words '*The Epistle*,' and '*The portion of Scripture*,' &c., applying them indiscriminately in any, or in every case, as some Clergymen do.

Bp. Mant remarks:—'The phrase, "*the Epistle*," should be 'used, when the Epistle technically so called, is taken from an 'Apostolical Epistle: when the extract is made from some other 'book of holy writ, and only then, should be used the phrase, "*the* '*portion of Scripture appointed for the Epistle*." The word '"*Epistle*" in this Rubrick, and so likewise the word "*Gospel*," are 'each used in two different senses: the one being the *technical* '*phrase* for that particular portion of the Service, the other denoting 'a *book of holy Scripture*. In the latter case the use of the pronoun '"*that*" is a confounding of the two senses.' (*p.* 54.)—*Hor. Lit.*

The Rev. H. R. Moody says:—'In giving out the Epistle, 'the words, "*the portion of Scripture appointed for the Epistle*," 'should only be used when it is *not* taken from the Epistles, but 'from some other part of the Scripture; as on Whit-Sunday, and 'the 25th Sunday after Trinity.' (*p.* 34.)—*Hints to young Clergymen*

The Rev. J. Purchas states:—'In announcing the Epistle and 'Gospel the wording of the directions in the Rubric should be strictly 'followed, thereby avoiding such errors, as "the portion of Scrip-'ture appointed for the Epistle "*is taken out of*," &c. The words '"portion of," &c., obviously apply to those instances where "the 'Epistle" is taken from other parts of Scripture than the Epistles.' (*p.* 37.)—*Directorium Anglicanum.*

495.—Conclusion.—At the close of the *Epistle*, the Rubric directs the Officiating Minister to say, '*Here endeth the Epistle*,' any other expression is incorrect and illegal. Some Clergymen say, '*Thus ends the Epistle;*' others proclaim '*So ends the Epistle.*' Why this deviation from the prescribed form should be made, it is not easy to determine. Further, when the appointed Scripture is not taken from the Apostolic Epistles even then it is unnecessary to say, '*Here endeth the portion of Scripture appointed for the Epistle;*' because the term "Epistle" is here a *technical* phrase, as we have before observed, and of wider signification than it ordinarily enjoys when applied to the Apostolic Epistles. Still, the adoption of this formulary is more excusable, than the substitution of 'Thus,' and 'So,' for '*Here*,' which can advance no reason for the change. The longer formulary is, however, defended by *Archdeacon Sharp*, who, interpreting this Rubric, says:—

'There were orders given at the *last Revisal*, of which perhaps 'the reasons are not quite so discoverable, or at least not so satis-'factory. As, for instance, in this same Office for Communion 'there was a new direction given, that at the *end* of *the Epistle* the 'Minister should say, "*Here endeth the Epistle, or the portion of* "*Scripture appointed for the Epistle.*" (*p.* 78.)—*On the Rubrics and Canons.*

But whence *Archdeacon Sharp* derived this addition to the Rubric, we are at a loss to discover.

The Gospel.

496.—Announcement.—The Reader of the *Gospel* is required by the Rubric of our present Book of Common Prayer to proceed with its delivery immediately after the reading of the Epistle, thus:—

(a) ¶. '*Then shall be read the Gospel* (*the People all standing up*) '*saying*, The holy Gospel is written in the——Chapter 'of——beginning at the——Verse......'

In Edward VIth's *first Liturgy* (1549), this Rubric was somewhat fuller, thus:—

(b) '*Immediately after the Epistle ended, the Priest, or one*
'*appointed to reade the Gospel, shall saye*
'The holy Gospell written in the——Chapiter of——
'*The Clearkes and People shal answere*
'Glory be to thee, O Lorde.
'*The Priest or Deacon then shal reade the Gospel.*'
(1549)—CLAY's *Bk. of C. Pr. Ill.* 103: KEELING. 177.

In the *second Liturgy* of Edward VI. (1552) and two following *Revisions* of 1559, and 1604, the Rubric ran thus:—*

(c) '*And the Epistle ended, he shal saye the Gospel, begin*-
'*ninge thus*
'The Gospell, wrytten in the——Chapter of——
(1552. 1559. 1604.)—CLAY. 103: KEELING. 176. 177.

497.—At the *last Review* of the Liturgy (1662), the Rubric we now have was introduced, and its simplicity has left little room for diversity of practice. We have, however, some variation in the manner of announcing the Book of Scripture from which the Gospel is taken; the more correct method is to adopt the authorized title found in the Bible, thus (in the example of the *First Sunday in Advent*):—

(a) '*The holy Gospel is written in the* xxist *Chapter of* the
'Gospel according to St Matthew, *beginning at* the 1st *Verse.*'

some will say:—

---

* In the SCOTCH LITURGY (of 1637) the Rubric in the Communion Office was as follows:—

'*And the Epistle ended, the Gospel shall be read, the Presbyter*
'*saying:*—'The holy Gospel is written in the——Chapter
'of——at the——Verse. *And then the People all standing up*
'*shall say:* Glory be to thee, O Lord. *At the end of the Gospel,*
'*the Presbyter shall say:* So endeth the holy Gospel. *And the*
'*People shall answer:* Thanks be to thee, O Lord.'—KEELING.
176, 177.

But, immediately before the Gospel for the *First Sunday in Advent*, there stood this Rubric:—

'*When the Presbyter or Minister readeth the Gospel, the*
'*People shall stand up: And the Presbyter before he begin*-
'*neth to read the Gospel shall say thus:* The Gospel of our
'Lord and Saviour Jesus Christ, written in such a Chapter of
'such an Evangelist, beginning at such a verse. *And the*
'*People shall answer:* Glory be to God.'—KEELING. 68.

The AMERICAN LITURGY adopts our Rubric, but adds:—"*Here the People shall say*, Glory be to thee O Lord."

(b) '*The holy Gospel is written in the* xxist *Chapter of* St Mat-'thew's Gospel, *beginning*, &c.

others will say:—

(c) '*The Holy Gospel is written in the* xxist *Chapter of* that of 'St Matthew, *beginning*,' &c.

The employment of the pronoun '*that*,' in this last example (c), in order to avoid the repetition of the word '*Gospel*,' is open to the same objection as was advanced against the like usage in announcing the Epistle (see *par.* 494. *supra*).

The Rev. J. Purchas writes:—'The Gospel should be given out 'as "*according to*" ("secundum") each Evangelist. The Catholic 'theory being that there is and can be but one Gospel, though 'expressed "*according to*" the four writers.' (*p.* 37.)—*Directorium Anglicanum.*

This claim of attention in the Rubric we are considering is no modern notion, since we find an analagous practice adopted among the earliest Christians, as we may learn from Bp. Sparrow, and others.

Bp. Sparrow says:—'Let St *Augustine* testify for the *Latin* 'Church, in his preface to his Comment upon the Epistle of St *John*, 'and in his *Serm.* 10, *de Verb. Apost.* "We heard first, says he, "the Apostolical Lesson, then we sang a Psalm, after that the Gospel "was read:" Now let St *Chrysostom* testify for the *Greek*, *Hom.* 19. '*cap.* ix. *Act.* "The Minister stands up, and with a loud voice calls, "*Let us attend*: then the Lessons are begun:" Which Lessons are 'the *Epistles* and *Gospels*, as appears in his Liturgy, which follow im-'mediately after the Minister hath so call'd for attention.' (*p.* 69.) —*Rationale.*

498.—Conclusion.—At the termination of the Gospel there is no direction in the Rubric as in the case of the Epistle, for the Officiating Minister to say '*Here endeth the Gospel*,' he will, therefore, at once pass on to the *Nicene Creed.* Many, however, introduce this intimation of the close of the Gospel though irregular and illegal. Why it was omitted here, and why it was inserted after the Epistle, is not explained. Some imagined that the Creed was a continuation of the Gospel, and, therefore, such announcement would be out of place; but we will annex one or two opinions. The interruption by the People, both here, and before the Gospel, of the *Doxology*, will be explained presently.

Archdeacon Sharp says:—'There were orders given at the 'last *Revisal*, of which perhaps the reasons are not quite so dis-'coverable, or at least not so satisfactory. As, for instance, in this 'same Office for Communion there was a new direction given, that 'at the *end of the Epistle* the Minister should say, "*Here endeth the* "*Epistle, or the portion of Scripture appointed for the Epistle.*" But 'at the *ending of the Gopsel* he is left without direction, and so must 'proceed on to the *Nicene Creed.* They who undertake to account 'for every thing tell us, that the reason of this is, that the Gospel is 'supposed to be continued in the Creed, and endeth not properly 'till we conclude with "*life of the world to come. Amen.*" But, 'whether this be thought a satisfactory reason or no, yet the silence 'of the Rubric is a sufficient argument that we ought *not to put in* '*any words of our own at the end of the Gospel:* the want of an 'order in this case amounting to a prohibition.' (*p.* 78.)—*On the Rubrics and Canons.*

Shepherd in his *Elucidation of the Book of Common Prayer* (Vol. ii. *p.* 179.) uses the same argument as Archdeacon Sharp.

The Rev. J. Purchas writes:—'The *Gospeller* is not directed 'to say, "*Here endeth the holy Gospel,*" inasmuch as ancient Ritual-'ists teach us that the Gospel being everlasting has no end; or 'because, as some of them hold, that the Gospel finds its proper end 'in the Creed.' (*p.* 34. note.)—*Directorium Anglicanum.*

The Rev. S. Rowe observes:—'The Rubric before the *Nicene* '*Creed* expressly prescribes the terms in which the *Epistle* and '*Gospel* shall be announced by the Minister. Why the exact words 'should be ever departed from, when so explicitly appointed, one is 'utterly at a loss to conceive,—why we should say, "*so*, or *thus* ends 'the Epistle," instead of "*Here* endeth the Epistle,"—and why we 'should merely say "the Gospel" instead of "the *holy* Gospel," 'seems difficult to explain. If it be alleged that such innovations 'are, after all, mere trifles, it is evident that the Fathers of our 'Church did not think them too unimportant to be worthy of 'consideration; and the less important such things are, the more 'incumbent it is upon us to submit our notions to the authority 'of our venerable Liturgists.' (*p.* 148. *note.*)—*An Appeal to the Rubric.*

Mr. A. J. Stephens, *Barrister-at-law*, states:—'The Priest has 'no right to say any other form of words when he gives out the 'Gospel than that which has been ordered by the Rubric.' (*p.* 1136.) —*Book of Com Prayer.* E. H. S. *Vol.* II.

The Doxology.

"*Glory be to Thee, O Lord.*"

499.—It was a very ancient custom to give great prominence to the public reading of the Gospel. St Chrysostom tells us that 'the Deacon first stood up, and proclaimed with a loud voice, '*πρόσχωμεν*', (*let us attend*), which was several times repeated; and before beginning to read he cried out, '*τάδε λέγει Κύριος*' (*thus saith the Lord*). Hom. XIX. *on Act. Apos.* In the 6*th century* also, we learn, that the Congregation, at the enunciation of the title of the Gospel, and before the Reader began, stood up *en masse*, and aloud gave glory to God for His holy Gospel. Subsequently, in the Rubrics of the Roman Missal, we find, that it was customary to say at the end of the Epistle '*Deo Gratias*,' which was followed by the *graduale* or *alleluia*; and before the Gospel was read, the Reader used to proclaim '*Dominus Vobiscum*,' to which the people responded, '*Et cum spiritu tuo*:' then, after the announcement of the Gospel, they cried '*Gloria tibi Domine*;' and, at its close, '*Laus tibi Christe*' (*Rubr. gen Miss.* tit. x. 6.): while in the Mozarabic Missal, there was said here simply '*Amen*.' (See BONA *Rev. Lit.* II. vii. 4. and MASKELL's *Ancient Liturgies*). Whence the practise has been retained in the Church of England, and, at the Reformation, was incorporated into the *first Liturgy* of Edward VI. (1549); where the Rubric, after directing the announcement of the Gospel, thus enjoins:—

> '*The Clearkes and People shal answere*,
> 'Glory be to thee, O Lorde.' (1549).
> (CLAY. 103: KEELING. 177.)

Although this *Doxology* has been omitted from all subsequent *Revisions* of the Prayer Book, yet the practice has continued almost universally down to the present time. Its omission from the *last Review* in 1662 is the more remarkable, from the fact of the Rubric being retained in the *Scotch Liturgy** of 1637, which had great weight with the Hampton Court

---

* The Rubric in the SCOTCH LITURGY on this point when the Presbyter has announced the Gospel thus reads:—

'*And then the People all standing up shall say*, Glory be 'to thee, O Lord; *At the end of the Gospel, the Presbyter*

Conference, and was much consulted by them. The *Doxology*, therefore, is considered by very many Ritualists to have been left out accidentally by the Reviewers of 1662.

500.—At the *Conclusion*, likewise, of the Gospel, it was not unusual in earlier times to sing an *Alleluia*, or *Anthem*. A custom which tradition has in a measure retained in many of our English Churches to this day; where, the Gospel being ended, the Congregation exclaim "*Thanks be to thee, O Lord;*" or "*Thanks be to thee, O Lord, for thy Holy Gospel.*" This usage is not prescribed in any of the Liturgies of the Church of England; but it is found, like the preceding Doxology, in the *Scotch Liturgy* of 1637.

501.—As, however, there is no rubrical authority in our present Prayer Book for the *Doxology*, or the *Thanksgiving*, the only defence that can be set up for the usage is immemorial custom. We find, therefore, in most Churches, in fact, almost universally, that the Doxology

"*Glory be to thee, O Lord.*"

is *chanted*, or *said* by the Congregation, before the Gospel; and after the Gospel, though less frequently, the following '*Thanksgiving*' is *chanted* or *said*—

"*Thanks be to thee, O Lord.*"

The opinions following will be found, for the most part, to advocate and confirm the usage; and the absence of the Doxology from the present Liturgy is generally ascribed to inadvertence.

Bishop Overall observes upon the *Doxology*:—'Which was 'appointed in King *Edward's* Service Book, and is still used, how- 'ever it came to be be left out here. I think it was by the Printer's 'neligence, for the Statute at the beginning of this Book, says

---

'*shall say;* So endeth the Gospel: *And the People shall* '*answer;* Thanks be to thee, O Lord.'—Keeling. *p.* 176. 177.

In the American Liturgy, the Rubric directs, after the announcing of the Gospel:—"*Here the People shall say,* "Glory be to thee, O Lord."—

'nothing shall be altered but a few words in the Litany, and a 'clause at the delivery of the Sacrament: so that if it had pleased 'the Printer, this might have stood still.' (*p.* 39). — Additional Notes to NICHOLLS' *Book of Com. Prayer.*

BP. SPARROW writes: — 'As first, when the Gospel is named, 'the Clergy and the People present, say or sing, *Glory be to thee,* '*O Lord:* So it is in St *Chrysostom's* Liturgy, "*Glorifying God* '*that hath sent to them also the Word of Salvation:*" As it is in the '*Acts of the Apostles*, Ch. xi. 18. "*When they heard,*" &c. (*p.* 158.) '......After the Gospel is ended, the use was to praise God, saying, '*Thanks be to God for this Gospel.* So was it of old ordained (*Tolet.* '*Conc.* 4. Can. 11.) that the Lauds or Praises should be said, not 'after the Epistle, but immediately after the Gospel, for the Glory 'of Christ, which is preached in the Gospel. In some places the 'fashion was then to kiss the Book.' (*p.* 159.)—*Rationale.*

DR. BISSE says: — 'The other honour paid to the Gospel, was, 'that after the naming of it all the people *standing up* said, "*Glory* '*be to thee O Lord.*" This usage, borrowed from ancient Liturgies, 'our Reformers continued in ours; and, though afterwards discon- 'tinued in the Rubrick, yet *custom still continues* the use of it in 'most Cathedral and in many Parochial Churches: and the *voice of* '*custom* is in many cases the *voice of law.*'—quoted in MANT'S *B. of Com. Prayer* in loco.

WHEATLY writes:—'The custom of saying, "*Glory be to thee,* '*O Lord,*" when the Minister was about to read the holy Gospel, 'and of singing "*Hallelujah,*" or saying, "*Thanks be to God for his* '*holy Gospel,*" when he had concluded it, is as old as St Chrysos- 'tom; but we have no authority for it in our present Liturgy. 'The first indeed was enjoined by King Edward's first Common 'Prayer Book, and so the custom has continued ever since; and 'I do not find how it came to be left out of the Rubric afterwards. 'It certainly could have nothing objected against it, and therefore 'it is restored in the SCOTCH LITURGY; which also ordered, that, 'when the Presbyter shall say, "*So endeth the holy Gospel,*" the 'People shall answer, "*Thanks be to thee, O Lord.*" In our own 'COMMON PRAYER BOOK the Priest has no direction to say, "*The* '*Gospel is ended;*" the reason of which some imagine to be, because 'it is still continued in the *Creed* that followeth.' (*p.* 308.—*Rat. Ill. of Bk. of Com. Prayer.*

SHEPHERD observes: — 'In ancient Liturgies, and in our first 'Book of Common Prayer, when the passage to be read out of the 'Gospel was announced by the Minister, the people, to evince the 'joy with which they received it, were directed to say, "*Glory be to* '*thee, O Lord,*" though, in all the subsequent editions of our book, 'this direction has been omitted, yet the practice is very generally '*retained.* It was likewise customary in the ancient Church, after 'the *ending of the Gospel*, to say, "*Thanks be to God for his Holy* '*Gospel,*" a practice in some places still continued." (*p.* 178.)— *Elucidation of Bk. of Com Prayer.* Vol. II.

Of modern authorities we may quote those annexed: they merely advocate the introduction of the '*Doxology*' before the reading of the Gospel.

Bp. Mant remarks:—'At the reading of the Gospel it is ordered, 'that "*the people shall be all standing up.*" But for the acclamation 'of *Glory to God*, however in itself unexceptionable and becoming, 'there is no actual authority, it having been omitted, probably by 'an oversight......There is no provision for notifying the end of the 'Gospel, as there is of the Epistle.' (*p.* 54.)—*Hor. Lit.*

The Rev. J. W. K. Clay, speaking of the variations between impressions of the Prayer Book of the same year, says:—'That we 'may be indebted for many of them to the Printer himself and to 'the want of all proper supervision, rather than to deliberate design 'on the part of a competent Ecclesiastical power.' And with regard to the question we are now considering, the *omission of the Doxology* before the Gospel, he adds:—'It is only on the former supposition, 'that we can account, in any reasonable manner, for the absence 'from every edition of our Prayer Book but the first of a passage 'belonging to the Communion Service, ("*The Clearkes and People* '*shal annswere,* "*Glory be to thee, O Lorde*") which passage 'notwithstanding such absence, has met with due attention in our 'Churches down to this day.' (*p.* xxi. *preface*).—*Bk. of Com. Prayer Illustrated.*

The Rev. J. Jebb remarks:—'The *Glory* before the Gospel is 'a short Anthem, customarily kept up in all Churches, and forming 'part of the Choral system universally, though enjoined by *no* '*present Rubric.* It is to be found, however, in all the editions 'of the Prayer Book before the last Review, and is supposed to 'have been omitted through inadvertence. No direction exists for 'announcing the *termination of the Gospel*, which may be accounted 'for by the ancient custom, enjoined in the Scotch Prayer Book, 'and prevalent in many country Churches in England, though 'sanctioned by no Rubric, of saying or singing "*Thanks be to thee,* '*O Lord,*" when the appointed portion has been read.' (*p.* 481.)—*On the Choral Service.* (Mr. Jebb is in error in stating that this '*Doxology*' is found in all the editions of the Prayer Book before the *last Review.* See our observations above.)

The Rev. H. R. Moody writes:—'The "*Glory be to thee, O Lord,* 'before the Gospel, though not authorized by our present Rubric, is 'retained in most Cathedral and other Churches, having been 'ordered in the first book of Edward VI. and also used in the 'Ancient Church.' (*p.* 34.)—*Hints to young Clergymen.*

The Rev. W. Palmer says:—'When the Deacon had ascended 'the pulpit, or ambon, and announced the title of the Gospel, the 'people with one voice exclaimed, "*Glory be to thee, O Lord!*" 'This custom of giving glory to God for his holy Gospel appears to' 'have prevailed from remote antiquity in all the Churches of the 'east and west; and the Church of England has not ceased for 'many centuries to follow so pious and laudable an example.' (*p.* 51.)......'When the Gospel was *ended*, the Churches of Spain 'and Gaul anciently sung an *alleluia*, or anthem. A custom like 'this prevails in many Churches in England, where, the *Gospel* '*being ended,* the people say, "*Thanks be to thee, O Lord, for thy* '*holy Gospel,*" or, "*Thanks be to thee, O Lord.*" (*p.* 52.)—*Origines Liturgicæ.* Vol. II.

The Rev. J. Purchas notes:—'The Choir, after the announcement of the Gospel, turning eastward, sings "*Glory be to Thee. O Lord.*" And after the Gospel is sung "*Praise to Thee, O Christ.*" (*p.* 36.)—*Directorium Anglicanum.*

The Rev. J. C. Robertson remarks:—'The use of this Doxology would seem to have been customary in Hooker's time (v. 30. 3.) ......No Rubric on the subject was introduced at the last Revision, although Sancroft's book suggests an adoption of the Scotch order; the *Doxology*, however, has been very generally *retained* in practice, and may surely be so without blame.' (*p.* 215.)—*How shall we conform to the Lit.*

Mr. A. J. Stephens (*Barrister-at-law*) says:—'It must be remarked that neither the Minister nor the laity have a legal right, during Divine Service, publicly to say between the "Epistle" and "Gospel," "*Glory be to thee, O Lord,*" because it is not authorised by the Book of Common Prayer.' (*p.* 637. 1137.)......'At St Paul's Cathedral it has been customary to sing "*Thanks be to God*" at the end of the Gospel:—and in many Churches the Ministers say at the termination of the Gospel "*Here ends the holy Gospel,*" but this practice is *illegal*, because it is not sanctioned by the Book of Common Prayer.' (*p.* 639.)—*Book of Common Prayer.* E. H. S.

Posture *at the reading of the Epistle and Gospel.*

502.—It was the ancient usage at the reading of these Lessons, (the Epistle and Gospel), for Minister and People to *stand*, in order to mark their reverence for God's holy word (*Apos. Const.* l. ii. c. 57); but this posture becoming wearisome for the aged, infirm, and delicate, among the Congregation, these were permitted to *sit* a portion of the time; yet, at the *reading of the Gospel*, which contained the very words of Christ, and a record of His doings and sufferings, it was required that all should *stand;* and thus it has grown into general use for the People to *sit* at the reading of the Epistle: but by *Rubrical order* they are to *stand* at the reading of the Gospel. This Rubric was introduced at the last Revision in 1662, and seems to have been borrowed from the *Scotch Liturgy* of 1637, (see *par.* 499. supra); it thus reads:—

¶. '*Then shall be read the Gospel,* (*the People all standing up*) '*saying,*' &c. (1662)—present Bk. of Com. Prayer.

There is *no direction* given for the *laity* with respect to the Epistle: the Minister is guided by the previous Rubric before the Collects for the Queen, where it is directed, '*the Priest standing as before;*' and as no change of posture is ordered between these Collects and the reading of the Epistle and Gospel, he remains in that attitude. Some say that the People ought by the same reason to *kneel* during the reading of the Epistle, because there is no Rubric releasing them from this posture subsequent to the one at the head of the TEN COMMANDMENTS imposing it upon them. *Custom*, however, has settled the controversy. A few opinions confirmatory of the view we have taken may be desirable.

Bp. SPARROW says:—'While the Gospel is reading, all that are 'present *stand*. (Gratian, *de Consecr*. Dist. 1. *C*. 68.). And *Sozomen* 'in his History, (*l*. 7. *c*. 19.) tells us, it was a new fashion in Alex-'andria, that the Bishop *did not rise up*, when the Gospel was read; '*Quod apud*, &c. The reason was this; antiently, whensoever the 'holy Lessons were read, the people *stood* to express their reverence 'to the holy Word; (AUG. *Hom*. 50. *Nehem*. viii. 5.). But because 'this was counted too great a *burthen*, it was thought fit to shew 'our reverence especially at the reading of the Gospel, which 'historically declares somewhat which our Saviour spake, did, or 'suffered, in his own person; by this gesture, shewing a reverend 'regard to the Son of God above other messengers, altho' speak-'ing as from God.' (*p*. 158.)—*Rationale*.

NICHOLLS quotes the following remark touching the Epistle in these words:—'Anciently, the Congregation *sat* to repose them-'selves during the reading of the *Epistle;* but when the Epistle was 'read out of St Paul, the *soldiers*, in honour of him, whom, by 'reason of his being pictured with a sword, they adopted to be their 'Saint, *stood up*. DUR. *de Offic. divin*. lib. iv. cap. 16.'—*Common Prayer in loco.*

WHEATLY remarks:—'In St Augustine's time the people always '*stood* when the Lessons were read, to shew their reverence to 'God's holy word: but afterwards, when this was thought too great 'a burden, they were allowed to *sit down* at the Lessons, and were 'only obliged *to stand* (as our present order, which was first inserted 'in the Scotch Common Prayer Book, now enjoins us) at the *read-'ing of the Gospel*, which always contains something that our Lord 'did speak, or suffered in his own person.' (*p*. 308.)—*Rat. Ill. of Bk. of Com. Prayer.*

SHEPHERD observes:—'During the reading of the *Epistle*, the 'people are *tacitly enjoined to sit:* but when the *Gospel* is read we 'are required to *stand up*, to express our veneration for the words 'of our Lord, to shew our readiness to execute his commands, and 'to denote our determination to follow whithersoever he may call.' (*p*. 177.)—*Eluc. of Bk. of Com. Prayer*. Vol. II.

Among modern authors we may quote the following:—

The REV. W. PALMER writes:—'It was also usual for all persons 'to *arise* before the Gospel, and *stand* while it was recited. "*When* '*the Gospel is read*," says the ancient author of the Apostolical Con- 'stitutions, "*Let all the Presbyters and Deacons, and all the people,* "*stand in great silence.*" It was considered a peculiar custom of 'the Church of Alexandria in the fifth century, that the Pope or 'Patriarch of Alexandria continued *sitting* during the reading of 'the Gospel. In the Church of Constantinople the custom is pre- 'served still. The Priest exclaims, "Σοφία (Wisdom—*Stand up*— 'Let us hear the holy Gospel." In the west it has always been 'usual to *stand* when the Gospel is read; and the Church of Eng- 'land has for many ages adopted the custom.' (*p.* 51.)—*Orig. Lit.* Vol. II.

The REV. M. PLUMMER writes:—'The People *sit* during the 'reading of the Epistle, and *stand up* while the Gospel is read. (*p.* 101.)—*Observations on Bk. of Com. Prayer.*

MR. A. J. STEPHENS, *Barrister-at-law*, urges *kneeling* as the pro- 'per attitude for the *Epistle;* thus—'It is now the custom in the 'United Church of England and Ireland for the Laity to *sit* during 'the reading of the Epistle—but for this there is no Rubrical order. '*Kneeling* was the posture at the Collect, and there is no Rubrical 'direction to alter this position before the giving out of the Gospel.' (*p.* 620.)—*Book of Com. Prayer.* E. H. S.

The READER of the *Epistle and Gospel.*

503.—It is disputed amongst Clergymen, and needlessly, we think, whether in the Church of England a *Deacon* is privileged to read the *Epistle* and *Gospel.* Certainly the Rubric in the COMMUNION OFFICE of our present Book of Common Prayer narrows the liberty conferred by the original Rubric of 1549; and limits this function to a *Priest;* it enjoins:—

'*Immediately after the Collect the Priest shall read the* '*Epistle, saying, &c*......*The Epistle ended he shall say, &c.*' '......*Then shall he read the Gospel, &c*......' (1552. 1559. 1604. 1662.)

But in the Ordination Office of the *Deacon* we find the Bishop expressly empowering him to read the Gospel, and then and there directing him to perform the duty:—thus

'*Then shall the Bishop deliver to every one of them the New* '*Testament, saying:*'—

'Take thou authority to read the Gospel in the Church of God, 'and to preach the same,' &c.

'*Then one of them appointed by the Bishop,* (*putting on a* '*tunicle*, 1549) *shall read the Gospel*,' (*of that day*, 1552).—(1662.)—KEELING. 375.

It is evident, therefore, that the limitation of the Rubric of the Communion Office is superseded by the authority conferred by the Bishop in the Ordinal, and that a *Deacon*, as well as *Priest*, may read the Epistle and Gospel.

504.—According to the earlier Rubric of the Liturgy of 1549, it would seem that *Laymen* even read the Epistle and Gospel; for it directs:—

'*The Collectes ended, the Priest, or he that is appointed, shall* '*reade the Epistle*,' &c......(1549.)

But this is instantly corrected by the closing injunction, thus:—

'*The Minister then shall reade thepistle. Immediately after* '*the Epistle ended, the Priest, or one appointed to reade the* '*Gospel, shall saye*,' &c.

Then follows:

'*The Priest or Deacon then shall reade the Gospel.*'

In the next *Revision*, that of 1552, we have the rule, (which the Printer thought fit to correct in the edition of 1589):—

'*Immediately after the Collectes; the Priest* (1589. *Minister:* '1622. *Priest*) *shal reade the Epistle*,' &c.

while in the after clauses, the indefinite '*he*' occurs: so that it is clear, that the earlier Liturgies sanctioned the reading of the Epistle and Gospel by either a Priest or a Deacon; and the usage has since continued uninterrupted. We find too, from the Advertisements of Queen Elizabeth, (CARDWELL's *Doc. Ann.* i. 291.), which on this point have been incorporated into the *24th Canon* (of 1603-4) that:—

'In all Cathedral and Collegiate Churches the holy Com'munion shall be administered, &c......the principal Minister 'using a decent Cope and being assisted with the *Gospeller* 'and *Epistler* agreeably, according to the Advertisements pub'lished,' *Anno.* 7 *Eliz*......CANON 24.

and this *Gospeller* and *Epistler* were laymen;—like as were employed in the same capacity in the early Church, and known as the '*Lector*' or '*Reader:*' but the Church of Rome, about the 8th or 9th century, set this usage aside, and appointed the *Sub-Deacon* to the Epistle, and the *Deacon* to the Gospel; and from that Church the custom has come to us for ordained Ministers only to read these especial portions of Scripture. Enough has been said on this subject—a subject of very little moment at the present day and under the existing regime—so that, after citing a few opinions, we may pass on to one more feature connected with the reading of the Epistle and Gospel.

BISHOP ANDREWES says, with regard to the reading of the *Epistle* and *Gospel*:—'Here the other Priest, or if there be none, '*he that executeth*, descendeth to the door, adoreth, and then turning, 'readeth the *Epistle* and *Gospel*. In Cathedral Churches the *Epistler* 'is seldom a Priest; and therefore, as this Rubrick was ordained 'generally for all *England*, most places having but one Priest to 'serve it; so for Cathedral Churches it was ordained, by the 'Advertisement in Queen *Elizabeth's* time (that authority being 'reserved, notwithstanding this Book, by an Act of Parliament) 'that there should be an *Epistler* and a *Gospeller* besides the 'Priest, for the more solemn performance of the Divine Service.' (*p.* 38).—*Add. Notes to* NICHOLLS' *Com. Prayer.*

WHEATLY explains the Canon (24th) to mean:—'One Minister 'to read the Epistle, and another to read the Gospel, as is still 'generally the custom in Cathedral Churches; which was also 'provided for by the Rubrics in King Edward's first book, which 'orders that *the Priest*, or he that is appointed, *shall read the 'Epistle in a place assigned for the purpose*, (which from the modern 'practice I take to be on the *south side* of the Table;) and that '*immediately after the Epistle ended, the Priest, or one appointed*, '(which, as appears from the next Rubric, might be a Deacon) *shall 'read the Gospel*.' (*p.* 308.)—*Rat. Ill. of Bk. of Com. Prayer.*

The REV. J. JEBB states:—'The Rubric mentions the *Priest* as 'the Minister for the *Epistle* and *Gospel*. But by our Ordination 'Service, the reading of the Gospel is expressly assigned to *Deacons* 'as their proper Office. By Archbishop Grindal's injunctions, in '1571, it was required that the *Parish Clerks* should be able to read 'the First Lesson and Epistle. But the Rubric, which before the 'last Review designated the reader as the Minister, is now so altered, 'as to deprive the *laity* of this privilege, which in the unreformed 'Church belonged to the *Subdeacon*. The old Rubric assigned the 'Gospel to the *Priest* or *Deacon*, in accordance with the universal 'custom of the Eastern and Western Churches; in both of which, 'however, the superior Clergy used frequently to take this sub-'ordinate Office upon themselves.' (*p.* 480.)—*On Choral Service.*

The REV. J. PURCHAS remarks:—'At solemn Service the Epistle 'and Gospel should be read by an *Epistoler* and *Gospeller*. The 'usage of the universal Church is for these Ministers to *stand* during 'the greater part of the Communion Service as well as the Priest. '......The *Gospeller's* Office is to assist the Priest; the *Epistoler* to 'assist the Gospeller: or rather the *Gospeller* is to assist at the 'Holy Eucharist, directly and principally; the *Epistoler* to assist in 'it indirectly and subordinately. When there are none to assist 'who are Deacons, it is customary for Priests to act as Gospeller 'and Epistoler at solemn Service, *i. e.* to discharge for the time 'being, the Office not of their actual, but of their inferior and 'implical Order.........According to an injunction of Archbishop 'Grindal, a *layman* in surplice and cassock might read the Epistle.' (*p.* 34.)—*Directorium Anglicanum.*

The Rev. M. Plummer says:—'If a Priest and Deacon are 'present, the *Priest* reads the Gospel, the *Deacon* the Epistle.' (*p.* 101.)—*Observ. on Bk. of Com. Prayer.*

With regard to the *Epistle* itself we have the following:—

Shepherd writes:—'Dr. Nicholls has here remarked, "that the 'Church of Rome permits the reading of the Epistle to any eccle-'siastical person as low as a *Sub-deacon;* but that our Church in 'this Rubric does not allow it to be read, but only by a *Priest.*" 'The remark, however, was inadvertently made; for in our form 'and manner of *ordering Deacons,* "the Bishop delivers to every 'one of them the New Testament," saying, "Take thou authority 'to read the Gospel in the Church of God," that is, the books of the 'New Testament; and to read the *Epistle* in this Office, is one 'peculiar province of the *Deacon* or *Priest*, that assists the Bishop, 'Curate, or principal Minister.' (*p.* 178.)—*Eluc. of Book of Com. Prayer.*

The Rev. W. Palmer says:—'During the early ages of the 'Church, the apostle or prophet,' (i. e. *the Epistle*) 'was generally 'read by a *special reader* from the Ambon, or Pulpit, which stood 'in the middle of the Church amongst the faithful. The Church of 'Constantinople and the other Eastern Churches still retain the 'ancient custom of employing a *reader* for this Office. The Church 'of Rome abandoned it about the eighth or ninth century, when it 'became the office of the *Sub-deacon* to read the Epistle. We are 'blamed by Schultingius for permitting it to be read by the *Priest*, 'but it is only read by the *Officiating Minister* when no assistant is 'present: and we might with as much reason blame the Church of 'Rome for permitting the *Sub-deacon* to read the Epistle, of which 'there is no trace in primitive times: but it is in truth a matter of 'little importance. It was the ancient custom of the Church of 'England to read this Lesson from the *Pulpit.* When no other 'Clergyman was present who could read the Epistle, the *Priest* 'himself read it at the *right* or *south* corner of the holy Table, 'which thence obtained the appellation of *cornu epistolæ.*' (*p.* 48.) —*Orig. Lit.* Vol. II.

Mr. A. J. Stephens, (*Barrister-at-law*) states:—'The Church 'of Rome permits the reading of the Epistle to any ecclesiastical 'person, as low as a *Sub-deacon*, but if our Rubric be strictly 'construed, *no person but a Priest* can read the *Epistle* at the 'Communion Service,' (*p.* 1133.)—*Book of Com. Prayer*, E. H. S.

With regard to the Gospel we may cite the following authors :—

NICHOLLS' says:—'That the Gospel was allowed to be read by 'the *Deacon*, is plain from that of St Jerom, in his Epistle to 'Sabinianus: *Evangelium Christi*, &c. "You did read the Gospel 'which does belong to you as a Deacon." And from that of Gregory '(*l.* iv. *Epist.* 44.), *Astante cuncto Clero*, &c., "All the Clergy 'standing about, he chooses out the Deacons to read the Gospel, 'in the solemnity of the Communion Service." Which ancient 'custom our Church has regard to when in the Ordination of a 'Deacon, the Bishop says to the ordained person, "Take thou 'authority," &c.'—*Common Prayer in loco.*

The REV. W. PALMER writes on this head:—'It was generally 'the office of the *Deacon* to read the Gospel in the primitive ages. 'Thus we find it to have been in the patriarchate of Antioch, in the 'time of Jerome; and the same custom prevailed in the Churches 'of Gaul and Spain at an early period. In the patriarchate of 'Alexandria it was read by the *Archdeacon*, or chief of the Deacons; 'but in some Churches it was read by the *Priest* only, and on the 'Lord's day by the *Bishop*. In the Church of Constantinople it has 'always been read by a *Deacon*, except on some particular feasts, 'when the *Bishop* reads. The Church of England permits it to be 'read *either by a Deacon* or *a Priest.* In the fourth century the 'Deacon was preceded by *lighted wax tapers* to the Pulpit, in the 'eastern Churches, as a sign of rejoicing for the Advent of Him who 'was the light of men. The *bells also were rung* in some Churches '*before the Gospel*, and in Æthiopia, this ceremony has continued to 'the present day.' (*p.* 50.)—*Orig. Lit.* Vol. II.

The PLACE FOR THE READER of the *Epistle and Gospel.*

505.—There is no distinctive *place* appointed by the Rubrics of the Liturgy for the reading of the Epistle and Gospel; the only allusion made to this question is in the *first Liturgy* of Edw. VI. (1549), where the Rubric which we have lately frequently quoted, says, '*the Priest shall read the Epistle in a place assigned for the purpose.*' (KEELING. 175.). The custom now prevailing, and which is derived from ancient usage is, when two, or more, Clergymen are officiating in the Communion Office, for the *Epistle* to be read on the *south* side of "The Table," and the *Gospel* on the *north* side. When but *one Minister* officiates he reads them both from the north side: to pass from one side to the other is to affect Romish usage.

506.—In the early ages the Epistle and Gospel were read from a *Pulpit or Ambon* in the middle of the Church or Choir; in some Churches there were two *Pulpits* for this purpose, one on either side; that on the *south* side for the Epistle, and that on the *north* for the Gospel. In other places they were 'read, especially on ordinary days, from the steps of the Altar' *ante sacram mensam*, or *ad gradum chori;* but on Sundays and Holy-days from the Pulpit—often from the Rood-loft; later, these Scriptures were read from the *Priest's stall* in the Chancel; eventually from the '*Decent low Pulpit*,' i. e. the Reading-Desk; and now, from the COMMUNION TABLE, as we have shewn above. (See DURANDUS. i. 02. iv. 15. 24: GAVANTI *Thesaur*. i. 202-4: MASKELL'S *Antient Liturgies*, p. 34, 35, *notes: Sarum Missal*, fol. ii. iii: SCHMID. *Liturgik*. ii. 134: CARDWELL'S *Doc. Ann.* i. 63—81. ii. 201.)

The REV. J. JEBB remarks:—'The *place* for reading the Epistle 'and Gospel is undetermined by the Rubric. Ancient custom as- 'signs to the Gospeller a place near the principal Minister at the '*north side*, and to the Epistoler the *south side* of the Altar. In 'many of our Choirs, however, both these assistant Ministers *stand* '*at the south side*, for which no authority but local prescription 'exists. In some foreign Churches they read these Lessons at an '*Ambo*, or *Eagle*. In ancient times they were read from the Ambos 'on each side of the Choir.' (*p.* 480.)—*On Choral Service*.

The Rev. M. PLUMMER, observes:—'The *Epistle* is read from 'the south side of the Altar, the Gospel, from the north side.' (*p.* 101.)—*Obs. on Bk. of Com. Prayer*.

The REV. J. C. ROBERTSON says:—'When the Epistle and Gospel 'are read at or near the Altar by two Clergymen, it is customary 'that the *Epistler* should stand on the *south*, and the *Gospeller* on 'the *north*. It has, however, been said of late that "even where 'there is but one Clergyman officiating, before commencing the 'Epistle he should *cross to the Epistle side*, and *recross* before begin- 'ning the Gospel." (*English Churchman*, Vol. I. p. 246.). This 'practice is forbidden in Edward's injunctions of 1549, and in 'those of Bishop Ridley, where it is directed "that no Minister do 'counterfeit the popish mass in shifting the book from one place to 'another." (*Doc. Ann.* i. 63—81.). It has no kind of sanction 'from the Reformed Church......To revive it at this day—as is 'done, according to the writer whom I have quoted, "in at least 'one Church in London,"—is nothing better than a ridiculous and 'offensive playing at Popery.' (*p.* 214.)—*How shall we conform to the Liturgy*.

Mr. A. J. STEPHENS (*Barrister-at-law*) observes:—'In such of 'our Churches where the custom has been kept up of having *two* '*assistant readers* for the Epistle and Gospel, *both* were read at the '*south side:* but of late years, the more general and more regular 'custom has been to have the Gospel read, from the *north*, and the 'Epistle from the *south* side. (*p.* 649.)—*Bk. of Com. Pr.* E. H. S.

The REV. J. PURCHAS gives us the extreme view of this subject, thus:—

'Clergy acting as Gospeller and Epistoler, whether Priests or 'Deacons, should *stand* below the foot pace facing eastward. The 'parts which should be said by them are the Gospel and Epistle, 'the Exhortations, and the Confession. Where there is only one 'assistant, he should read the Epistle and Gospel on the proper 'sides. When the Priest (being without Epistoler or Gospeller) 'reads them, he *ought to go off the foot-pace.*' In a *note* he adds: 'The *Canon* (XXIV. of 1603), allows of two assistants—*Deacon* and '*Sub-deacon* in old times, now simply *Gospeller* and *Epistoler*. 'Ancient custom assigns to the former a place on the south side '(*ad latus Epistolæ*) on the step next to the platform, to the latter 'a place on his own step behind the Gospeller, a little towards the 'right. Both stand facing the east.' (*p.* 2.)—*Directorium Anglicanum*. See also *Clergyman's Diary* (*p.* 3.) Pub. by *Masters*.

THE FIRST SUNDAY IN ADVENT.

[On *Nov.* 30. if a Sunday; if not, on the nearest Sunday to *Nov.* 30.]
MORN. *First* Lesson...*Isai.* i. EVEN. *First* Lesson...*Isai.* ii.
(For the *Second* Lessons, see the date in the Calendar.)

THE COLLECT.

The EPISTLE.	The GOSPEL.
Rom. xiii. 8—14. *inclusive.*	*St Matt.* xxi. 1—13. *inclusive.*

¶. '*This Collect is to be repeated every day, with the other* '*Collects in Advent, until Christmas-eve.*'*

507.—The Season of *Advent* preparatory to the commemoration of Christ's NATIVITY has been set apart, like the Season of *Lent* preparatory to EASTER, from time immemorial. Some authorities assign its institution to St Peter himself (*Durand's* Rational, l. vi. c. 2. §. 2.); it probably existed before the time of Maximus Taurinensis, A. D. 450. It is certainly to be met with in the Gallican Sacramentary of the 6th or 7th century. The First *Sunday in Advent* falls on the 30th *of November*, (the *Feast of St*

* In the AMERICAN LITURGY this Rubric concludes:—"*until Christmas day.*"

Andrew), if a Sunday; if this be *not* a Sunday, it then falls on the *nearest Sunday* before, or after, the 30th of November. It is on this Sunday likewise, that the Church commences her Ecclesiastical cycle of Services, or the *Christian Year.* The Advent Season extends to four Sundays, computing backward from *Christmas-day;* and the Collect for the First Sunday in Advent is the *Collect for the Season.*

[The *Collect* to be repeated.]

508.—This Collect was originally introduced into the *first Liturgy* of Edward VI. (1549), for which book it was expressly composed; but the Rubric, directing it '*to be repeated every day with the other Collects in Advent, until Christmas-eve,*' was not appended until the *last Revision* in 1662. The Rubric is not sufficiently explicit as to the order to be adopted in using the two Collects; but, judging from the analogous Rubric for St Stephen's day, and that for Ash-Wednesday, it may be concluded that the *Collect for the Day* should first be read, and then the *Collect for the Season:* and such is the general practice.

509.—The phrase in the Rubric, '*until Christmas-eve,*' must not be considered as inclusive. At the EVENING SERVICE preceding CHRISTMAS-DAY, the Collect for the '*Nativity*' should be employed, and not the Advent Collect. (See *par.* 487. *supra*). This is confirmed by the opinions following:

The REV. SAMUEL ROWE remarks:—'The Collect for *Christmas-'day* should unquestionably supersede the *Advent* Collect on the '*Vigil* of that Festival.' (*p.* 153.)—*An Appeal to the Rubric.*

Mr. A. J. STEPHENS, (*Barrister-at-law*) writes:—'Whether the 'words "until Christmas-Eve" include that day or not, it may be 'observed, that the Collect for *Christmas-day* supersedes the *Advent* 'Collect on the vigil of that festival.' (*p.* 661.)—Book of Common Prayer. E. H. S.

THE SECOND SUNDAY IN ADVENT.

MORN. *First* Lesson...*Isa.* v. EVEN. *First.* Lesson...*Isa.* xxiv.

(For the *Second* Lessons, see the date in the Calendar.)

THE COLLECT.

[Followed by the *Collect for the Season.*—See *par.* 508.]

The EPISTLE. *Rom.* xv. 4.—13. *incl.*

The GOSPEL. *St Luke* xxi. 25—33. *incl.*

THE THIRD SUNDAY IN ADVENT.

MORN. *First* Lesson...*Isa.* xxv. EVEN. *First* Lesson...*Isa.* xxvi.
(For the *Second* Lessons, see the date in the Calendar.

THE COLLECT.

[Followed by the *Collect for the Season.*—See *par.* 508.]

The EPISTLE.	The GOSPEL.
I *Cor.* iv. 1—5. *incl.*	*St Matt.* xi. 2—10. *incl.*

THE FOURTH SUNDAY IN ADVENT.

MORN. *First* Lesson...*Isa.* xxx. EVEN. *First* Lesson...*Isa.* xxxii.
(For the *Second* Lessons, see the date in the Calendar.)
(The first *Ember Collect* to be used.)

THE COLLECT.

[Followed by the *Collect for the Season.*—See *par.* 508.]

The EPISTLE.	The GOSPEL.
Phil. iv. 4—7. *incl.*	*St John* i. 19—28. *incl.*

510.—The *Fourth Sunday in Advent* is, generally speaking, one of the Sundays in the "Ember Week," following the 14*th day of December*: the Collects for the *Ember-days* must, therefore, not be forgotten to be introduced before the '*Prayer of St Chrysostom*' in the MORNING PRAYER, LITANY, and EVENING PRAYER. The *first* of the two Ember Collects should be preferred on the Sunday before the Ordination day. (See *par.* 458. *supra*)

The Nativity of our Lord, or the Birth-day of CHRIST, *commonly called* CHRISTMAS DAY.

(Falls on *December* 25*th*, and has an appointed *Eve* preceding it.)

PROPER PSALMS.

MORN. *Ps.* xix. xlv. lxxxv.——EVEN. *Ps.* lxxxix. cx. cxxxii.

MORNING.	EVENING.
1*st* Lesson, *Isa.* ix. to *v.* 7. *incl.*	1*st* Lesson, *Isa.* vii. 10—16. *incl.*
2*nd* Lesson, *Luke* ii. to *v.* 14. *incl.*	2*nd* Lesson. *Tit.* iii. 4—8. *incl.*

(The *Athanasian Creed* to be used.)

THE COLLECT.

The EPISTLE.	The GOSPEL.
Heb. i. 1—12. *incl.*	*St John* i. 1—14. *incl.*

(And a '*Proper Preface*' in the COMMUNION OFFICE).

¶. '*The Collect of the Nativity, is to be said continually* (after 'the Collect of the day) *until New-Year's-Eve.*'—(See *Rubric* after the Collect for *St Stephen's Day.*)

511.—The Feast of the *Nativity of our Lord* may be traced up to the very earliest antiquity, although we have no certain evidence of the exact time of its first observance: doubtlessly it was celebrated in the time of the Emperor Maximin; for he is related to have burnt a Church in Nicomedia when full of Christians commemorating this festival (*Niceph.* Hist. l. vii.): it is, indeed, but rarely hinted at prior to the 4th century. In the *Eastern Church* up to this date it seems to have been celebrated on the *6th of January.* The Western Church however always kept the *Nativity* on the *25th of December*, relying upon tradition that this was the actual birth-day of our Lord. Many suppose that the Roman Church substituted the feast of the Nativity for the ancient *Saturnalian* revels which usually at this time concluded the year; and they did so in order that the new religion should not interfere with customary usages. To this date the Eastern Church also subsequently conformed.

The affix '*mas*' is of Saxon origin, and implies a *festival*, and was of common occurrence in the mediæval Church, as may be seen in the words Candle*mas*, Martin*mas*, Michael*mas*, Lam*mas*, &c. In the *first Liturgy* of Edward VI. (1549), occurs for the first time the *Collect* we now have; and there also we find that two Communions were appointed; but these were not enjoined in the subsequent Liturgies. CHRISTMAS-DAY, however, is observed as a day of *Public Worship*, and cessation of labour, throughout England, and the observance of it as such is enforced by *Statute Law*, as we have already shewn. (See *Vol.* **B.**)

Dr. WATERLAND remarks:—'The *Nativity of our Saviour* was 'celebrated by all Christians from the very beginning, but not 'upon the same day. It is generally agreed that our Saviour 'Christ was born in the year of the world 3760. The very day 'of our Saviour's birth was not agreed by those that lived in 'his time: within the compass of 200 years after His birth, there 'were three opinions concerning the day of His birth, for which 'there are reasons assigned. Some would have Him born on the '3rd; others on the 14th *of May.* Afterwards the *5th of January* 'was thought to have been the day of His birth: afterwards the '10*th of March*. By others His birth is placed in *Autumn*, not 'assigning the very day. But 'tis generally agreed that He was 'born on the 25*th of December*, though that be the day on which 'we celebrate our Saviour's nativity in all the Western Churches 'for some ages last past. The reason that is given why we 'celebrate it now rather than on any other time of the year 'is to imitate a famous Festival celebrated yearly about this 'time by the ancient Romans in memory of *Saturn*, an ancient 'King in Italy that first taught husbandry. And indeed they do 'find a likeness in the Ceremonies observed in the celebrating 'the Nativity of our Saviour and the more ancient heathen Festival 'called *Saturnalia*. In both they do feast all their relations, 'acquaintances, and neighbours; they did anciently in both Festi- 'vals bedeck their houses and their door-posts with greens and 'flowers; indulge themselves in dancing, seeing plays, and gam- 'bolls; divert themselves with some sports with their servants '"hail fellow well met:" they did also at both send presents to 'one another, &c. On the *Eve* before Christmas, the Pope gives 'a great entertainment, in the publick hall of his Palace at Rome; 'where the whole night is spent in eating and drinking. A de- 'scription of which we have in the Ceremoniale, *lib.* 2.'—WHEATLY'S *Rat. Ill. of Bk. of Com. Prayer*. Dr. Corrie's *Ed. p.* 221. *note*.

DR. BENNETT says:—'Tho' there are very different times assigned 'by learned men for the birth of our Savior, some placing it in 'one month, and some in another; yet the patrons of these several 'opinions may notwithstanding safely join in this Collect. Because 'the words, *as at this time*, need not be so rigidly interpreted, as 'if the precise time were fixed by the Church, and made a term 'of Communion. They are capable of being understood in a due 'latitude; and do necessarily imply no more, than that we do then 'commemorate the blessing of our Savior's Nativity, in which sense 'it may well be said, that He was *as at this time* born. And surely 'those who differ about the precise time of our Savior's birth, may 'notwithstanding join at once in the Office of a solemn Festival set 'apart in remembrance of it.' (*p.* 127.)—*Paraphrase on Bk of Com. Prayer*.

WHEATLY observes:—'Though the learned in most ages have 'differed concerning the day and month of our Saviour's nativity, 'yet we are certain that the Festival was very early observed in 'the primitive Church. And if the day was mistaken, yet the 'matter of the mistake being of no greater moment than the false 'calculation of a day; it will certainly be very pardonable in those 'who perform the business of the Festival with as much piety and 'devotion as they could do, if they certainly knew the time.' (*p.* 220.)—*Rat. Ill. of Bk. of Com. Prayer*.

ST STEPHEN'S DAY.*

(Falls on *December* 26th.)

MORNING.	EVENING.
1*st* Less. *Prov.* xxviii.	1*st* Less. *Eccl.* iv.
2*nd* Less. *Acts* vi. *v.* 8. to vii. *v.* 29. *incl.*	2*nd* Less. *Acts.* vii. 30–54. *incl.*

THE COLLECT.

The EPISTLE.	The GOSPEL.
Acts vii. 55—60.	*Matt.* xxiii. 34—39.

¶. '*Then shall follow the Collect of the Nativity which shall be 'said continually unto New-Year's Eve.*'—Present Book of Com. Prayer.

512.—The commemorations of the martyrdoms of *St Stephen*, *St John*, and of the *Innocents*, were considered very appropriate attendants on the festival of the *Nativity* of our Lord, and therefore were assigned the place we find them to occupy in the *first Liturgy* of Edward VI. (1549), and subsequent Liturgies. The Collects for *St Stephen's Day*, and for *Innocents' Day*, were remodelled at the *last Revision* in 1662: but the Collect for *St John's Day* comes to us from the Sacramentary of St Gregory.

BP. SPARROW writes:—'Immediately after *Christmas* follow, as 'attendants upon this high Festival, St *Stephen*, St *John*, and *Inno-'cents;* not because this was the very time of their suffering, but 'because none are thought fitter attendants on Christ's Nativity, 'than the blessed Martyrs, who have laid down their lives for him, 'from whose birth they received spiritual life. And there being 'three kinds of martyrdom; 1. *In will and deed*, which is the 'highest. 2. *In will* but *not in deed.* 3. *Indeed*, but *not in will.* 'In this order they attend *St Stephen* first, who suffered both in 'will and deed. Next *St John*, who suffered martyrdom in will, 'but not in deed, being miraculously deliver'd out of the boiling 'Caldron, into which he was put before *Post-Latin* in *Rome.* 'Lastly, the holy *Innocents*, who suffered in deed, but not in will; 'yet are reckoned amongst the Martyrs, because they suffer'd for 'Christ. Whose praise these His witnesses confess'd, and *shewed 'forth not in speaking, but in dying.*' (*p.* 78.)—*Rationale.*

Repetition of the Collect of the Nativity.

513.—Immediately after the Collect for *St Stephen's Day*, and others, coming within the Octave of the

---

* In the AMERICAN LITURGY, the Collects, Epistles, and Gospels, for *St Stephen's Day* with the Rubric annexed, for St John's and for Innocents' Day are placed after the Trinity Collects.

Nativity, the *Collect for Christmas-day* is appointed by the Rubric above quoted to be used. In the *first Liturgy* of Edward VI. (1549), the Rubric uniting this repetition to *St Stephen's Day*, simply enjoined:—

'*Then shall follow a Collect of the Nativity.*' (1549).—KEELING. 79.

At the next *Revision* (in 1552), this Rubric was expanded to what we now possess; but at the *last Review* in 1662 the concluding word was altered from 'New Year's Day' to '*New Year's Eve*,'* in order to mark that, as *New Year's Day*, which is the feast of the *Circumcision*, has no Eve or Vigil Rubrically appointed, *its Collect* is not to be used on the Eve before, but only the *Collect of the Nativity*.

The REV. SAMUEL ROWE speaking of the repetition of the *Collect of the Nativity* says:—'It would rather appear, by the some-'what different terms employed, that it was intended to be said '*on New Year's Eve*, as well as on all the days previously......The 'word "*unto*," instead of "*until*," in the preceding Rubric, implies 'a difference of direction, which is confirmed by the fact that the 'feast of the *Circumcision* (*New Year's Day*) has no *vigil*, and 'therefore no Collect proper for *New Year's Eve*, to supersede the 'ordinary Collects for the day.' (*p.* 153.)—*Appeal to the Rubric.*' (Cited also in A. J. STEPHENS' *Book of Com. Prayer*. E. H. S.)

ST JOHN THE EVANGELIST'S DAY.

(Falls on *December 27th.*)

MORNING.	EVENING.
First Lesson. *Eccl.* v.	*First* Lesson. *Eccl.* vi.
Second Lesson. *Rev.* i.	*Second* Lesson. *Rev.* xxii.

THE COLLECT.

(Followed by the *Collect of the Nativity.*)

The EPISTLE.	The GOSPEL.
I St John i. 1—10.	*St John* xxi. 19—25.

---

* In the SCOTCH LITURGY of 1637 the Rubric ran thus:—

'*Then shall follow the Collect of the Nativity, which shall 'be said every day in the week unto New Year's day: but 'instead of the words* [and this day to be born] *the Presbyter 'shall say* [at this time to be born].'—KEELING. 78.

THE INNOCENTS' DAY.

(Anciently '*Childermas*,' falls on *December 28th*.)

MORNING.	EVENING.
First Lesson. *Jer.* xxxi. to *v.* 17. *incl.*	*First* Lesson. *Wisd.* i.
Second Lesson *Acts* xxv.	*Second* Lesson. I *St John* v.

THE COLLECT.

(Followed by the *Collect of the Nativity*.)

The EPISTLE.	The GOSPEL.
Rev. xiv. 1—5.	*St Matt.* ii. 13—18.

THE SUNDAY AFTER CHRISTMAS DAY.

MORN. *First* Lesson. *Isa.* xxxvii. EVEN. *First* Lesson. *Isa.* xxxviii.

THE COLLECT.

(The same as that *of the Nativity*.)

The EPISTLE. *Gal.* iv. 1—7. The GOSPEL. *St Matt.* i. 18 25.

514.—This Sunday falling within the Octave it was customary formerly, and so now, to repeat on all the eight days some portion of the Service of the Feast-day itself; hence on this day is used the same Collect as that of the *Nativity*.

BP. SPARROW says:—'This Sunday hath the *same Collect* with '*Christmas-day*; and the Epistle and Gospel treat about the same 'business, the birth of Christ: for we have not yet done with the 'solemnity of Christmas. Thus great solemnities have some days 'after them, to continue, the memory of them, (*in prorogationem* '*festi*.' (*p.* 81.)—*Rationale*.

WHEATLY writes:—'It was a custom among the primitive Chris'tians to observe the *Octave*, or eighth day after their principal 'feasts, with great solemnity......And upon every day between the 'feast and the Octave, as also upon the *Octave* itself, they used to 'repeat some part of that service which was performed upon the 'feast itself. In imitation of which religious custom, this day 'generally falling within the *Octave of Christmas-day*, the *Collect* 'then used is repeated now; and the Epistle and Gospel still set 'forth the mysteries of our redemption by the birth of Christ.' (*p.* 226.)—*Rat. Ill. of Book of Com. Prayer*.

THE CIRCUMCISION OF CHRIST.

(Falls on New Year's Day, *January 1st*.)

MORNING.	EVENING.
First Lesson. *Gen.* xvii.	*First* Lesson. *Deut.* x. *ver.* 12.
Second Lesson. *Rom.* ii.	*Second* Lesson. *Col.* ii.

THE COLLECT.

The EPISTLE. *Rom.* iv. 8—14. The GOSPEL. *St Luke* ii. 15—21.

¶. '*The same Collect, Epistle, and Gospel shall serve for every* '*day after unto the Epiphany*.'

515.—The commemoration of the *circumcision of our Lord* on this day is of some antiquity, being mentioned by Ivo Carnotensis, *circ.* 1090: still, there has been no little controversy as to the exact period of its origin: anteriorly, in the 6th century, this day was observed as the *Octave of the Nativity* with more than usual solemnity, and this eventually being combined with the celebration of the Circumcision, led in a great degree to a confusion in the title and in the date of its institution. In the Roman and Gallican Missals it was designated as "*the Circumcision of our Lord, and the Octave of the Nativity:* in that of Sarum it was simply '*the Circumcision of our Lord,*' while in the Sacramentary of Gregory it was distinguished as, '*the Octave of our Lord.*' In all these, the Office of the day was pretty much the same, commemorating as well the *Circumcision*, as the *Nativity*. In the *first Liturgy* of Edward VI. (1549) it acquired the appellation we now find in our Prayer Book, viz. "the *Circumcision of Christ;*" and it was then that the Lessons, Collect, and Epistle and Gospel we now have were introduced. The *Collect* is derived from Gregory's Sacramentary: and the whole office, in putting before us the active obedience of Christ in fulfilment of a perfect righteousness, is well calculated to stimulate us to the imitation of our Lord's example. As to the commemoration of *New Year's Day* by Vigil Services the Eve before; this is a modern innovation, and a departure from Rubrical and Statute law, as shewn in Vol. **B**. *pars.* 144—147.

516.—*Repetition of the Collect.*—Should a Sunday, or other day, occur between the feast of the Circumcision and the Epiphany, this Collect, Epistle, and Gospel, are directed by the Rubric following the Gospel to be then used. This Rubric was introduced into the *second* Liturgy of Edward VI. (1552), and thus read:—

> '*If there be a* (*any* 1625) *Sondaie betwene the Epiphanie and* '*the Circumcision then shalbe used the same Collecte, Epistle* '*and Gospell at the Communion, which was used upon the* '*daie* (*used the day,* 1625) *of Circumcision.*'* 1552.—CLAY. in loco; KEELING. 82, 83.

This Rubric was continued in the *Revisions* of 1559, and 1604; and it was at the *last Review* in 1662, that it assumed the abbreviated form it now has.

BISHOP COSINS says:—'This was added in the fifth of King *Edw.* 'being *Casus omissus* before; for between the second and fifth year 'of that King, there happened a *Sunday* after *Circumcision*, and 'before the *Epiphany;* and they were at a loss, not knowing what 'to do with it; for in the old Missals it was cast upon the Octaves, 'whereof we had none left.'—Add. Notes to NICHOLLS' *Book of Com. Prayer*. p. 26.

The Rev. S. ROWE remarks:—The word "*unto*" is, as in the 'preceding Rubric, again used, and the Collect is to be continued on 'the evening of the day preceding the Epiphany, a feast which has 'no vigil.' (*p.* 154).—*An Appeal to the Rubric:* (cited also by Mr. A. J. STEPHENS' in his *Book of Com. Prayer*. E. H. S.)

THE SECOND SUNDAY AFTER CHRISTMAS DAY.

MORN. *First* Lesson. *Isa.* xli. EVEN. *First* Lesson. *Isa.* xliii.

(For the *second* Lessons see the date in the Calendar.

THE COLLECT.

The EPISTLE, and the GOSPEL.

(The same as for *the Circumcision of Christ*. See *par.* 516.)

THE EPIPHANY.

(Falls on *January* 6th.)

MORNING.	EVENING.
1*st* Lesson. *Isa.* lx.	1*st* Lesson. *Isa.* xlix.
2*nd* Less. *St Luke* iii. to *v.* 22. *incl.*	2*nd* Less. *St John* ii. to 11. *incl.*

(The *Athanasian Creed* to be used.)

THE COLLECT.

The EPISTLE. *Eph.* iii. 1—12. The GOSPEL. *St Matt.* ii. 1—12.

517.—On this day are commemorated three manifestations of the Redeemer: first, that of the birth of Christ to the Gentiles in the persons of the *Magi*, as exhibited in the Collect and the Gospel, and which was the especial object of the Western Church—then,

---

* In the SCOTCH LITURGY (1637) the Rubric of 1552 occurs with this addition:—

'......*upon the day of* Circumcision; *and so likewise upon* '*every other day from the time of the* Circumcision *to the* 'Epiphany.'—KEELING. 83.

that of the Trinity at the Baptism of Christ, as exhibited in the second Morning Lesson, and which was the chief object of the Eastern Church — then, that of Christ's glory and divinity, by His miracle of turning water into wine, as exhibited in the second Evening Lesson. Originally, the word '*Epiphany*,' or '*Manifestation*,' was applied to the day of the *Nativity* or Christ's manifestation in the flesh; and to this day, as Christ's manifestation to the Gentiles. From Christmas to the Epiphany the object seems to be to set forth Christ's humanity; and from the Epiphany to Septuagesima, His divinity by the record of His miracles. The Collect we have is derived from the Sacramentary of Gregory.

SHEPHERD says:—'The greater part of the Eastern Church, for 'the first three or four centuries, kept the feast of the *Nativity*, on 'the day which we call the *Epiphany*; that is, on the *sixth of* '*January*. The word *Epiphany* has been employed to denote 'Christ's Manifestation in four respects; 1. His Nativity, or Mani-'festation in the Flesh; 2. The appearance of the Star to the 'Eastern Magi, or his Manifestation to the Gentiles; 3. The Mani-'festation at his Baptism, when the heavens were opened, and 4. 'The Manifestation of his Divinity, by the first miracle which he 'wrought at the Marriage of Cana in Galilee; all of which were 'commemorated on this day, by the Churches of Jerusalem, Antioch, 'Egypt, and others of the East. But in the Western Provinces, the '*Nativity* and *Epiphany*, were celebrated on two distinct days. On 'the *Epiphany*, considered as a festival separate from the Nativity 'were commemorated......The Manifestation to the *Magi* in the Col-'lect and Gospel; the Manifestation at his Baptism in the second 'Morning Lesson; and his Manifestation by the Miracle of Cana, in 'the second Evening Lesson, which for this purpose is, contrary to 'common usage, taken from an evangelical and not from an episto-'lary writing.' (*p.* 59.)—*Eluc. of Book of Com. Prayer.* Vol. II.

THE FIRST SUNDAY AFTER THE EPIPHANY.

MORN. *First* Lesson. *Isa.* xliv. EVEN. *First* Lesson. *Isa.* xlvi.
(For the *second* Lessons see the date in the Calendar.)

THE COLLECT.

The EPISTLE. *Rom.* xii. 1—5. The GOSPEL. *St Luke* ii. 41—52.

THE SECOND SUNDAY AFTER THE EPIPHANY.

MORN. *First* Lesson. *Isa.* li. EVEN. *First* Lesson. *Isa.* liii.
(For the *second* Lessons see the date in the Calendar.)

THE COLLECT.

The EPISTLE. *Rom.* xii. 6—16. The GOSPEL. *St John* ii. 1—11.

THE THIRD SUNDAY AFTER THE EPIPHANY.

MORN. *First* Lesson. *Isa.* lv. EVEN. *First* Lesson. *Isa.* lvi.
(For the *second* Lessons see the date in the Calendar.)

THE COLLECT.

The EPISTLE. *Rom.* xii. 16—21. The GOSPEL. *St Matt.* viii. 1—13.

THE FOURTH SUNDAY AFTER THE EPIPHANY.

MORN. *First* Lesson. *Isa.* lvii. EVEN. *First* Lesson. *Isa.* lviii.
(For the *second* Lessons see the date in the Calendar.)

THE COLLECT.

The EPISTLE. *Rom.* xiii. 1—7. The GOSPEL. *St Matt.* viii. 23—34.

THE FIFTH SUNDAY AFTER THE EPIPHANY.

MORN. *First* Lesson. *Isa.* lix. EVEN. *First* Lesson. *Isa.* lxiv.
(For the *second* Lessons see the date in the Calendar.)

THE COLLECT.

The EPISTLE. *Col.* iii. 12—17. The GOSPEL. *St Matt.* xiii. 24—30.
[Often redundant, and used to supply a deficiency in the Trinity Collects, &c. when two are wanting.]

THE SIXTH SUNDAY AFTER THE EPIPHANY.

MORN. *First* Lesson *Isa.* lxv. EVEN. *First.* Lesson. *Isa.* lxvi.
(For the *second* Lessons see the date in the Calendar.)

THE COLLECT.

The EPISTLE. I *St John* iii. 1—8. The GOSPEL. *St Matt.* xxiv. 23—31.
[Often redundant, and used to supply a deficiency in the Trinity Collects, &c. when one is wanting.]

518.—It is not always that there are six Sundays after the Epiphany calling for these six Collects, Epistles, and Gospels; when there is an overplus here there is usually a deficiency of Collects, &c. for the Sundays after Trinity; this deficiency in the Trinity Collects is supplied by the redundancy here in the Epiphany Collects, as directed in the *Rubric* following the Gospel for the *Twenty-Fifth Sunday after Trinity*, thus:—

'......*the Service of some of those Sundays that were omitted after* '*the Epiphany shall be taken in to supply so many as are here* '*wanting*......'—Present Bk. of Com. Prayer.

It is usual to take the Service of the *6th Sunday after the Epiphany*, if only one Collect, &c. after Trinity be wanting, and the *5th*, and *6th Sundays after the Epiphany*, if two or three be wanting, and so on; taking the later Collects, as less likely to be soon repeated. (See the Rubric, *postea*.)

519.—It may also be remarked, that the Collect, Epistle, and Gospel, for the *Sixth Sunday after the Epiphany* were only added at the *last Review* in 1662. Prior to this, it was customary when a sixth Sunday should arise to repeat the Collect, Epistle, and Gospel of the *Fifth Sunday after the Epiphany*; as the following Rubric in the four preceding Liturgies directs; thus:—

> '*The vi. Sonday (if there be so many) shall have the same*
> '*Psalme, Collecte (the same Collecte.* 1552.) *Epistle, and Gospell,*
> '*that was upon the v. (Sondaie.* 1552).'—(1549. 1552. 1559. 1604.)—CLAY. in loco: KEELING. 88, 89.

In the Sarum Missal, says Wheatly, the Services of the *third Sunday after the Epiphany* supplied the omission; but this is incorrect, as the Sixth Sunday was there duly provided for.

THE SUNDAY CALLED SEPTUAGESIMA,

OR THE THIRD SUNDAY BEFORE LENT.

MORN. *First* Lesson. *Gen.* i. EVEN. *First* Lesson. *Gen.* ii.

(For the *second* Lessons see the date in the Calendar.)

THE COLLECT.

The EPISTLE. I *Cor.* ix. 24—27. The GOSPEL. *St Matt.* xx. 1—16.

520.—The three weeks preceding *Lent*, the *Quadragesimal*, or forty-days fast, are intended by the Church to prepare her people to devote the coming Season to self-examination, to the practice of religious abstinence, and to acts of more than ordinary humiliation and prayer. The names appropriated to these three Sundays, viz. *Septuagēsima*, (70th), *Sexagēsima*, (60th), and *Quinquagēsima*, (50th), are derived from the usual method then adopted of counting by *decades*, and are the Sundays which fall within the respective ten-day periods, computing backwards from Easter. *Wheatly* thus explains their nomenclature, and the method of computation :—

'Among the several reasons given for the names of these Sun-'days, the most probable seems to be this: the first Sunday in Lent, 'being *forty days* before Easter, was for that reason called *Quadra-'gesima Sunday*, which in Latin signifies *forty ;* and *fifty* being the 'next round number above forty, as *sixty* is to fifty, and *seventy* to 'sixty ; therefore the Sunday immediately preceding *Quadragesima 'Sunday*, being farther from Easter than that was, was called *Quin-'quagesima* (or fifty) *Sunday*, which is also fifty days inclusive 'before Easter: and the two foregoing Sundays, being still farther 'distant, were for the same reason called *Sexagesima* and *Septua-'gesima* (sixty and seventy) *Sundays*. The observation of these 'days and the weeks following appear to be as ancient as the times 'of Gregory the Great. The design of them is to call us back from 'our Christmas feasting and joy, in order to prepare ourselves for 'fasting and humiliation in the approaching time of Lent. . . . Some 'of the more devout Christians observed the whole time from the 'first of these Sundays to Easter, as a season of humiliation and 'fasting; though the generality of the people did not begin their 'fasts till *Ash-Wednesday*.' (*p.* 232.)—*Rat. Ill. of Book of Com. Prayer.*

THE SUNDAY CALLED SEXAGESIMA,

or the second Sunday before Lent.

MORN. *First* Lesson. *Gen.* iii. EVEN. *First* Lesson. *Gen.* vi.
(For the *second* Lessons see the date in the Calendar.)

THE COLLECT.

The EPISTLE. II *Cor.* xi. 19—31. The GOSPEL. *St Luke* viii. 4—15.

THE SUNDAY CALLED QUINQUAGESIMA,

or the next Sunday before Lent.

MORN. *First* Less. *Gen.* ix. *to ver.* 20. *incl.* EVEN. *First* Less. *Gen.* xii.
(For the *second* Lessons see the date in the Calendar.)

THE COLLECT.

The EPISTLE. I *Cor.* xiii. 1—13. The GOSPEL. *St Luke* xviii. 31—43.

521.—It may be remarked here, that the *Tuesday* following *Quinquagēsima Sunday* was in mediæval times the day on which the People were accustomed to confess to the Priest their sins to fit them for the better observance of the coming season of Lent, and for due preparation for the receiving of the holy Sacrament at Easter. It was generally known as

Shrove Tuesday, or *Shrove-tide*, from the old Saxon word *Shrive* to confess, (perfect, *Shrove*). The Reformation dispensed with the practice of the confessional; and the day survives only in the recollection of the People from the annual recurrence of certain festivities; of which they are reminded in some localities by the tolling of the Church bell—a time-worn usage, incomprehensible to some, and ridiculously interpreted by many.

WHEATLY says:—'The *Tuesday* after *Quinquagesima-Sunday* is 'generally called *Shrove-Tuesday;* a name given it from the old 'Saxon words *shrive, shrift* or *shrove*, which in that language 'signifies to *confess;* it being a constant custom amongst the '*Roman Catholics* to confess their sins on that day, in order to 'receive the blessed Sacrament, and thereby qualify themselves 'for a more religious observation of the holy time of *Lent* imme-'diately ensuing. But this in process of time was turned into a 'custom of invitations, and their taking their leave of flesh and 'other dainties; and afterwards, by degrees, into sports and merri-'ments, which still in that Church make up the whole business 'of the Carnival.' (*p.* 243.)—*Rat. Ill. of Book of Com. Prayer.*

SHEPHERD remarks:—'The *Tuesday* after Quinquagesima is 'called *Shrove Tuesday*, or *Shrovetide*, from shrove, the preterite of 'shrive, an antiquated word which signifies *to hear* or *to make con-'fession.* On this day it is usual for the people to confess their sins, 'that they might be better prepared for the observation of the 'ensuing season of penitence, and for receiving the Sacrament at 'Easter. It was afterwards perverted into a day of idle sports and 'amusements; and till within a few years, in many parts of Eng-'land, its anniversary was distinguished by riot and drunkenness, 'by bull-baiting, cock-fighting, and such other diversions, as were 'calculated to promote cruelty, inhumanity, and everything the 'most opposite to the virtues, which it was the intention of the 'Church to teach and encourage.' (*p.* 74.)—*Eluc. of Book of Com. Prayer*, Vol. II.

THE FIRST DAY OF LENT, COMMONLY CALLED ASH WEDNESDAY.

PROPER PSALMS.

MORN. *Ps.* vi. xxxii. xxxviii. EVEN. *Ps.* cii. cxxx. cxliii.

(*No* LESSONS *appointed:* therefore see *date* in the Calendar.)

THE COLLECT.

For the EPISTLE. *Joel* ii. 12—17. *incl.*

The GOSPEL. *St. Matt.* vi. 16—21. *incl.*

¶. '*This Collect is to be read every day in Lent after the Collect 'appointed for the Day.*'

(The COMMINATION SERVICE to be used.)

522.—From this season of abstinence and self-denial, exercised by the early Christians preparatory to the great festival of Easter, taking place in the *Spring* time of the year, it has acquired from the Anglo-Saxon word *lencten*, Spring, or lengthening of days, the name of *Lent*. As a fast it cannot be pronounced an Apostolical institution; nor as an early Christian usage can it claim to be of forty days duration. Originally it extended to but forty hours—from the hour of the Crucifixion to that of the Resurrection. Eventually other days and even weeks were added, until about the fifth century, in the time of Gregory the Great, the *Lenten fast* extended to six and thirty days, (i. e. *six weeks* exclusive of the *Sundays*, which were always considered feast days). In the 12th century, about A. D. 1190, Gregory II. prefixed *four days* more, beginning with *Ash-Wednesday*, in order to supply the deficiency of the Sundays, and to make the Fast comprise *forty days*, after the example of our blessed Lord, of Moses, and of Elijah, and in conformity with the Jewish preparation for their great annual expiatory sacrifice of forty days of solemn humiliation, (See EUSEBIUS. *Eccl. Hist.* v. c. 23, 24. *Const. Apos.* v. c. 12.). It is not for us to enter here on the various degrees and methods of fasting, for this would fill a volume: it will be sufficient therefore to quote merely the additions to the Rubric explanatory of this Season, and which were suggested by the *Reviewers* of the Liturgy in 1689. Annexed to the Title—"*The First Day of Lent, commonly called Ash-Wednesday*," they proposed to add as follows:—

'*See the Commination.*
'*A Sermon or Homily then to be used.*
'Whereas the observation of the Fast of Lent is an antient and 'usefull custom, designed for the bringing of all Christians to a 'serious examination of their lives past; to repent of their sins, 'and to fitt themselves for the worthy receiving of the Com-'munion at Easter. It is most earnestly recommended to all 'persons, but more particularly to all Churchmen, to observe 'that time religiously, not placing Fasting or devotion in any 'distinction of meats, but spending larger portions of their time 'in prayer, meditation, and true abstinence, and in works of 'charity, forbearing feasting and entertainments.
'*This is to be read the Lord's day before Ash-Wednesday.*'
—(Printed by order of House of Commons. *June.* 1854.)

523.—We may remark, that the *Fast-Days* of the Church of England enumerated at the beginning of the Prayer Book are enforced by the *72nd Canon* (of 1603–4), and by Statute Law, 5 & 6 *Edw.* VI. *c.* 3: 24 *Geo.* II. *c.* 23; and the Act of Uniformity, 13 & 14 *Car.* II. *c.* 4., as we have fully shewn in our discussion on the "*Fast-Days*," &c. *pars.* 144—159. Vol. B.

524.—The *First Day of Lent* formerly had the title of *Caput Jejunii* 'the Head of the Fast;' and from the practice of sprinkling ashes on the heads of the penitents on that day it was also called *Dies Cinerum*, the day of Ashes, or '*Ash-Wednesday*.' (GRATIAN. 1 *Part. Decr. Dist.* 50. *c.* 64.) This second title was introduced in the *first Liturgy* of Edward VI. A. D. 1549; but struck out at the *Revisions* in 1552. 1559. and 1604; it was however restored at the *last Review* in 1662.

525.—The PSALMS preferred for MORNING AND EVENING PRAYER are six of the *penitential Psalms* of David, as we have pointed out, and not those of the ordinary course. The seventh penitential Psalm being appointed for the COMMINATION OFFICE. These were all composed by the royal Psalmist in times of affliction, and are well calculated for seasons of humiliation and repentance.

526.—*Proper Lessons* are not appointed for this day, which is considered an accidental omission: possibly they may have been thought unnecessary from the extensive quotations from holy Scripture introduced into the Office itself.

SHEPHERD observes:—'It is remarkable that no selection of '*proper Lessons* has been made for *Ash-Wednesday* in any of our 'Books. The omission has been noticed, but it cannot be satisfac-'torily accounted for. It could hardly be an oversight; for they 'who at the first revisal of Edward's Book, allotted proper first 'Lessons at least, to all the holidays that were before unprovided 'with them, could not easily overlook *Ash-Wednesday*: and they 'who at the last Review thought it expedient to appoint proper 'Psalms for this day, must one would think, have noticed its want 'of *proper Lessons*; and suitable proper Lessons might have been 'easily supplied. Yet till some better, or the true reason can be 'discovered, we must be content to attribute the omission, either to 'oversight in the Revisers, or to some other accident or mistake: 'for it is not to be presumed, that the want of proper Lessons was 'meant to be a distinguishing characteristic between *Ash-Wednes-'day* and every other holiday. In a note is added: So much of the 'Holy Scripture is quoted in the Office itself, as to make a selection 'of Lessons unnecessary.' (*p.* 97.)—*Eluc. of Book of Com. Prayer.* Vol. II.

527.—The Collect for the *First day of Lent* is the Collect for the *Season*, and was composed for the *first Liturgy* of Edward VI. (1549); while the Scripture for the Epistle, and the Gospel, are derived from the earlier Offices. This *Collect*,—according to the Rubric following it, which was introduced at the *last Review* in 1662,—is to be read throughout Lent '*after*' the Collect of the Day; a rule which may guide us in similar cases where the Collect of the *season* accompanies the Collect of the *day*. There are some Clergymen who incorrectly omit the *Collect of the Season* on the Sundays; from the supposition that, as they are Sundays *in* Lent and not *of* Lent, and rather *feast days* than *fast days*, such was the intention of the Compilers of the Liturgy. Others, again, erroneously exclude *Passion Week* from Lent, and consequently omit the *Collect of the Season* on the *Sunday before Easter*, and advance the title of this Sunday as given in the Liturgy—"*The Sunday next before Easter*" instead of "*the Sixth Sunday in Lent*"—in defence of their practice; but general custom derived from ancient usage decides it otherwise.

WHEATLY says with regard to the *Sundays in Lent*:—'Though 'the Church allows us to interrupt our fasts on the *Sundays in* '*Lent*, by reason of the eminence of those days; yet, lest the plea-'santness of those intervals should entice us to a discontinuance of 'our mortification and abstinence in the returning week-days, 'when we ought to renew it with the greater zeal, she takes care 'to remind us of the duties we have undertaken, and therefore in 'the *Epistles*, which were continued from the old Missals, sets 'before us the obligations we lie under of returning to our acts 'of self-denial and humiliation. But because all this without 'charity is nothing worth, the *Gospels*, which are of the same 'antiquity, are designed to excite us to the exercise of that great 'duty in all its branches, by proposing to us the example of our 'great Lord and Master, the blessed Jesus.' (*p.* 240.)—*Rat. Ill. of Book of Com. Prayer*

The Rev. S. Rowe observes upon the *Rubric*:—'Plain as this 'Rubric appears at first view, there is one point which still may be 'doubtful, and that is, whether *Lent* is to be considered as including '*Palm Sunday*, and consequently whether this Collect is to be read 'when the forty days, as some think, are completed, especially as it 'is called the *Sunday next before Easter*, and not *the sixth Sunday in* '*Lent*. The Collect for the day evidently also stamps the Paschal 'character which pervades all its Services, distinguishing it from 'the preceding Sundays in Lent; and thus seems to afford internal 'evidence that the Church designed the thoughts of her members to 'be exclusively occupied with the solemn events commemorated by 'the Services of Passion week and Easter.'—In a *note* is added:— 'Some exclude the *Sundays* from the calculation, being festivals and 'not fast days, and therefore hold that *Lent* extends to *Passion* '*week*; yet read the Lent Collect on the Sundays, which they 'exclude; but which the Rubric designates as *in* Lent.' (*p.* 155.)—*An Appeal to the Rubric.*

528.—The Commination Service* must on this day follow the *Litany*: and be said by the Minister either in the Pulpit, or in the Reading-Desk. (See *postea.*)

THE FIRST SUNDAY IN LENT.

Morning.	Evening.
First Lesson. *Gen.* xix. *to ver.* 29. *incl.*	*First* Lesson. *Gen.* xxii.

(For the *second* Lessons see the *date* in the Calendar.)

THE COLLECT.

(Followed by the *Collect of the Season.*)

The Epistle. II *Cor.* vi. 1—10. The Gospel. *St Matt.* iv. 1—11.

THE SECOND SUNDAY IN LENT.

Morn. *First* Lesson. *Gen.* xxvii. Even. *First* Lesson. *Gen.* xxxiv.

(For the *second* Lessons see the *date* in the Calendar.)

THE COLLECT.

(Followed by the *Collect of the Season.*)

The Epistle. I *Thess.* iv. 1—8. The Gospel. *St Matt.* xv. 21—28.

---

* In the American Liturgy the Collect for the *First day of Lent* is followed by three Prayers taken from our Commination Service which are to be used instead of that Office as this Rubric directs:—

'*At Morning Prayer, the Litany being ended, shall be said the* '*following Prayers immediately before the General Thanks*-'*giving.*'

THE THIRD SUNDAY IN LENT.

MORN. *First* Lesson. *Gen.* xxxix. EVEN. *First* Lesson. *Gen.* xlii.
(For the *second* Lessons see the *date* in the Calendar.)
THE COLLECT.
(Followed by the *Collect of the Season.*)
The EPISTLE. *Ephes.* v. 1—14. The GOSPEL. *St Luke* xi. 14—28.

THE FOURTH SUNDAY IN LENT.
(or Mid-lent Sunday.)

MORN. *First* Lesson. *Gen.* xliii. EVEN. *First* Lesson. *Gen.* xlv.
(For the *second* Lessons see the *date* in the Calendar.)
THE COLLECT.
(Followed by the *Collect of the Season.*)
The EPISTLE. *Gal.* iv. 21—31. The GOSPEL. *St John* vi. 1—14.

529.—This Sunday is generally considered *Mid-lent Sunday.* Some ancient divines have called it *Dominica Refectionis*, or *Refreshment Sunday;* either because the *first Lesson* in the Morning Prayer describes Joseph's entertainment to his brethren, or because of the Gospel narrating our Lord's miraculously feeding the five thousand. From one or other of these circumstances the custom has arisen in some parts of England of families meeting together on this Sunday, and giving to it the name of Mid-lenting, or *Mothering Sunday.* (WHEATLY.)

THE FIFTH SUNDAY IN LENT.

MORN. *First* Lesson. *Exod.* iii. EVEN. *First* Lesson. *Exod.* v.
(For the *second* Lessons see the *date* in the Calendar.)
THE COLLECT.
(Followed by the *Collect of the Season.*)
The EPISTLE. *Heb.* ix. 11—15. The GOSPEL. *St John* viii. 46—59.

THE SUNDAY NEXT BEFORE EASTER.

MORNING.	EVENING.
First Lesson, *Exod.* ix.	*First* Lesson. *Exod.* x.
Second Lesson. *Matt.* xxvi.	*Second* Lesson. *Heb.* v. *to ver.* 10. *incl.*

THE COLLECT.
(Followed by the *Collect of the Season.*)
The EPISTLE. *Phil.* ii. 5—11. The GOSPEL. *St Matt.* xxvii. 1—54.

530.—This day is generally known as *Palm Sunday*, or, as the Missals designate it, '*Dominica in ramis palmarum;*' a name intended to commemorate our blessed Lord's triumphal entry into Jerusalem, when the accompanying multitude strewed palm branches in His way; and which memento was retained till the era of the Reformation by the People carrying palm or other branches in procession to the Church, where they were placed on the Altar, and benedictory prayers pronounced over them. This Sunday is also called the first day of *Passion Week*, or the *Holy Week;* the *Great Week*, as Chrysostom terms it; by some styled the *Paschal Week.* On the Continent we find this day called *Olive Sunday*, in Russia, *Sallim Sunday;* in Germany, "dre stille Woche," or *Still Week;* and elsewhere *Yew Sunday*, or *Flower Sunday*, according to the floricultural taste displayed in the ornaments and processions. The whole of this week has ever been observed with greater strictness, abstinence, and devotion. The appointed Scriptures bring before us the history of Christ's passion, and the Services of these last days of Lent the Church has designedly arranged so as to involve especial meditation upon the mysterious sufferings of our Saviour.

WHEATLY remarks:—'The following week was by some looked 'upon as a distinct time of fasting from the foregoing Lent, and as 'instituted upon different accounts: *that* being observed in imitation 'of our Saviour's fasting, &c. as has been already observed; *this* in 'commemoration of His sufferings and passion; which were then 'completed. But by others it was only accounted a continuation 'of the same fast in a stricter degree: it being generally called the '*great week*, not because it had more hours or days in it than any 'other week, but because in this week was transacted an affair of 'the greatest importance to the happiness of man, and actions truly 'great were performed to secure his salvation: death was conquered, 'the devil's tyranny was abolished, the partition-wall betwixt Jew 'and Gentile was broken down; and God and man were reconciled. 'It was also called the *Holy-Week*, from those devout exercises 'which Christians employed themselves in upon this occasion. 'They applied themselves to prayer, both in public and private; 'to hearing and reading God's holy word; and exercising a most 'solemn repentance for those sins which crucified the Lord of life. 'They observed the whole week with great strictness of fasting and 'humiliation; some fasting three days together; some four; and 'others, who could bear it, the whole six; beginning on Monday 'morning, and not eating anything again till cock-crowing on the 'Sunday morning following. And several of the Christian Em-'perors, to shew what veneration they had for this holy season, 'caused all lawsuits to cease, and tribunal doors to be shut, and 'prisoners to be set free; thereby imitating their great Lord and 'Master, who by His death at this time delivered us from the prison 'and chains of sin.' (*p.* 242.)—*Rat. Ill. of Bks of Com. Prayer.*

SHEPHERD says:—'The days that Christians in general, in the 'first two centuries, particularly devoted to the commemoration of 'the death and passion of our Redeemer, were only the Friday and 'Saturday before Easter. On these days during this period, their 'worship more particularly consisted of mourning for their own sins, 'and of watching for two nights, accompanied with prayer, and 'entire abstinence from food for forty hours. The *Wednesday* and '*Thursdny* in this week were soon afterwards united with the fast; 'because on Wednesday the Chief Priests and Pharisees had effect-'ually conspired against the life of our Lord, and covenanted with 'Judas to betray him into the hands of the Gentiles: and it was not 'long before the Catholics judged it expedient to dedicate the *whole* '*week* to sacred solemnities. When the season, which we now call '*Lent*, came to be publickly established, and its duration extended 'to its present length, *this week* was always and every where con-'sidered as a principal part of Lent. It was observed with greater 'solemnity than any other portion of the season, and had peculiar 'Offices and Ceremonies of its own.' (*p.* 102.) — *Eluc. of Book of Com. Prayer.*

531.—The Collect for *this Sunday*, and *that of the Season*, are to be used every day until GOOD-FRIDAY. (See *par.* 486. *supra.*)

MONDAY BEFORE EASTER.

(For the *Lessons* see the *date* in the Calendar.)
The COLLECT OF THE SUNDAY.
(Followed by the *Collect of the Season.*)

For the EPISTLE. *Isa.* lxiii. 1—19. *incl.*
The GOSPEL. *St Mark.* xiv. 1—72. *incl.*

TUESDAY BEFORE EASTER.

(For the *Lessons* see the *date* in the Calendar.)
The COLLECT OF THE SUNDAY.
(Followed by the *Collect of the Season.*)

For the EPISTLE. *Isa.* l. 5—11. The GOSPEL. *St Mark* xv. 1—39.

WEDNESDAY BEFORE EASTER.

MORNING.
1*st* Lesson. *Hos.* xiii.
2*nd* Lesson. *St John* xi. *ver.* 45.

EVENING.
1*st* Lesson. *Hos.* xiv.
2*nd* Lesson. (see *date* in the Calendar.)

The COLLECT OF THE SUNDAY.
(Followed by the *Collect of the Season.*)

The EPISTLE. *Heb.* ix. 16—28. The GOSPEL. *St Luke* xxii. 1—71.

THURSDAY BEFORE EASTER.

(Popularly called *Maundy Thursday*.

MORNING.	EVENING.
1*st* Lesson. *Dan.* ix.	1*st* Lesson. *Jer.* xxxi.
2*nd* Lesson. *St John* xiii.	2*nd* Lesson. (see *date* in the Calendar.)

THE COLLECT OF THE SUNDAY.
(Followed by the *Collect of the Season.*)
The EPISTLE. I *Cor.* xi. 17—34. The GOSPEL. *St Luke* xxiii. 1—49.

532.—On this day, as we learn from the second Lesson of the Morning Service, our blessed Redeemer exhorted His disciples, through the symbolic action of *washing His Disciples feet*, to the practice of humility and charity; and also added a new commandment (*mandatum*), 'that they should love one another.' On this day also He instituted the LORD'S SUPPER, and gave commandment (*mandatum*) for its perpetual observation; hence this day has acquired the appellation of *Cœna Domini*, *Dies Mandati*, and popularly with us, *Maundy Thursday*. The washing of the feet of certain poor disciples, and giving them afterwards money and clothing by way of fulfilling our Saviour's injunction, was for some time a practice in the Church; and even Kings, as well as Bishops, imitated our Lord's example. *James* II. is said to have been the last English monarch who performed this duty, and a remnant of the custom now exists in the Maundy gifts of our present Sovereign, distributed annually on this day in the Chapel Royal, Whitehall, by the Lord High Almoner. The Divine Service on this occasion is as follows:—

'The *Exhortation*, *Confession*, *Absolution*, &c.
'41st Psalm (*The Grand Chant*)
'*First Lesson.* St Matt. xxv. 14—30.
'*First Anthem.*
[Distribution of money to *women* in lieu of clothing—to *men* of clothing.]
'*Second Anthem.*
[Distribution of woollen and linen cloth.]
'*Third Anthem.*
[Distribution of purses of money.]
'*Second Lesson.* Matt. xxv. 31 to end.
'*Fourth Anthem.*
'Two Prayers; a Prayer for the Queen;
&c. &c. &c.
(See STEPHEN'S Book of Com. Prayer. E. H. S. *p.* 891.)

GOOD FRIDAY.

PROPER PSALMS.

MORN. *Ps.* xxii. xl. liv. EVEN. *Ps.* lxix. lxxxviii.

MORNING.	EVENING.
First Lesson. *Gen.* xxii. *to ver.* 19. *incl.*	*First* Lesson. *Isa.* liii.
Second Lesson. *St John* xviii.	*Second* Lesson. I *Pet.* ii.

THE COLLECTS.

The EPISTLE. *Heb.* x. 1—25 The GOSPEL. *St John.* xix. 1—37.

533.—*Good Friday*, a name peculiar to the English Church, acquires its appellation from the great blessings of Redemption which flow to us through the crucifixion of our Lord accomplished on this day. By the Anglo-Saxons it was designated *Long Friday*, from the extent of its Services; but the more usual title was *Holy Friday*, or *The Friday in Holy Week;* and its observance as a day of rigid fasting and humiliation has continued from the very earliest ages of Christianity. The three COLLECTS are all derived from the ancient Offices, and express our prayers for the imitation of our Saviour's infinite and eternal love for the human race: the *first* Collect prays for the assembled Congregation; the *second*, for the general body of Christians; and the *third*, for the heathen, and the unbelievers, at large. The PSALMS, appointed to be used, were not selected till the *last Revision* in 1662.

EASTER EVEN.

MORNING.	EVENING.
First Lesson. *Zech.* ix.	*First* Lesson. *Exod.* xiii.
Sec. Lesson. *St Luke* xxiii. *to v.* 49. *incl.*	*Second* Lesson. *Heb.* iv.

THE COLLECT.

The EPISTLE.	The GOSPEL.
I *St Pet.* iii. 17—22.	*St Matt.* xxvii. 57—66.

534.—This Saturday of the 'Great Week' is called by Chrysostom the "*Great Sabbath*" (*Ep.* i. ad Invoc.); and was universally observed as a most solemn fast and vigil. Watchings, Services, Baptism of Catechumens, &c. in the midst of multitudes of torches were sustained till the dawn of Easter-day. This vigil has been considered as the origin of the other vigils assigned to Festivals. The *Collect* was introduced only at the *last Review* in 1662, and seems to be a condensation of that in the Scotch Liturgy of 1637. The preceding Liturgies had no proper Collect appointed for *Easter Even.*

EASTER DAY.

¶. '*At Morning Prayer instead of the Psalm,* O come, let us 'sing, &c. *these Anthems shall be sung or said.*'—Present Book of Com. Prayer.

PROPER PSALMS.

MORN. *Ps.* ii. lvii. cxi. EVEN. *Ps.* cxiii. cxiv. cxviii.

MORN. *First* Lesson. *Exod.* xii. EVEN. *First* Lesson. *Exod.* xiv.

„ *Second* Lesson. *Rom.* vi. „ *Second* Lesson. *Acts* ii. *ver.* 22.

(The *Athanasian Creed* to be used.)

THE COLLECT.

The EPISTLE. *Col.* iii. 1—7 The GOSPEL. *St John* xx. 1—10.

535.—From the very earliest times the *Festival of Easter* has been observed with the greatest solemnity and rejoicing; the long dispute respecting the exact day of its celebration, which was at last set at rest by a decree of the Council of Nice, A. D. 325. gives proof of its antiquity.—It was originally called '*the Pascha,*' or *Paschal Feast:* the word '*Easter*' comes to us from our Anglo-Saxon ancestors, who, Bede tells us, (de *Temp. Rat.* c. 13.) used to worship at this season of the year the goddess *Eostre*, or *Ostera;* possibly identical with the Syrian *Astarte* or *Ashtoreth;* hence '*Easter:*' but Wheatly supposes it to be derived from the Teutonic word *urstan*, to rise. (Ill. of Bk. of Com. Pr. p. 251.). It was always esteemed the Queen of Festivals, and in earlier ages comprised fifteen days, embracing the week preceding, and the week following; and terminating on the Sunday called the Octave of Easter.

536.—*The Anthems.*—The more ancient Offices commenced the Morning Prayer, or Matins, of Easter-day with a brief introductory Service, which was retained in the *first Liturgy* of Edward VI. (1549.) It began with this Rubric :—

'*In the morning afore Mattins, the People being assembled in 'the Church; these Anthems shall be first solemnly sung or 'said.*'—(KEELING. 105: CLAY. 76.)

Here followed the *Anthem* from *Rom.* vi. 9. which we now have, with "*Hallelujah, Hallelujah*" annexed; and then, the *Anthem*, from I *Cor.* xv. 20. with one "*Hallelujah*" annexed, after which there came

'*The Priest.* Shew forth to all nations the glory of God.
'*The Answer.* And among all people his wonderful works.

'Let us pray.

'O God, who for our Redemption didst give thine only 'begotten Son to the death of the Cross; and by His glorious 'Resurrection hast delivered us from the power of our enemy: 'Grant us so to die daily from sin, that we may evermore live 'with Him in the joy of His resurrection, through the same 'Christ our Lord. (Amen.'—KEELING. 107.)

We also find in the same Liturgy a Rubric before the '*Venite*' in Morning Prayer, and before the '*Magnificat*' in Evening Prayer, directing as follows :—

'Praise ye the Lord.
'*And from Easter to Trinity Sunday.*
'Hallelujah.'—(1549.)—KEELING. 11. 29.

There were also *Collects*, and *Epistles*, and *Gospels*, appointed for *two* Communions; the *first* of these Collects was used on Easter Monday; and the *second* on Easter Tuesday, and on the first Sunday after Easter.

At the *Revision* in 1552, the above *Anthems* and Collect as an introductory Service were dispensed with, and the *two Anthems* appointed to be sung or said instead of the '*Venite*' in Morning Prayer; and the Collect for the first Communion was then assigned to *Easter-day, Monday in Easter Week*, and the *first Sunday after Easter;* and the Collect for the second Communion left for *Tuesday in Easter Week.* At the *last Revision* in 1662, another Anthem was prefixed to the two before employed, and the Collect for *Easter-day* appointed for the entire week; the *second Collect* being transferred to the *First Sunday after Easter.*

[*Manner of singing and saying the Anthem.*]

537.—The *posture* and *manner* in which these Anthems are to be sung or said is not defined; but the *posture* for Minister and People should be that of *standing*, whether they be sung or said; and when '*said*' they are generally repeated *alternately* by Minister and People, as the Psalms are done.

MONDAY IN EASTER WEEK.

MORN. *First* Lesson. *Exod.* xvi. EVEN. *First* Lesson. *Exod.* xvii.
" *Second* Lesson. *St Matt.* xxviii. „ *Second* Lesson. *Acts* iii.

THE COLLECT.

(The same as on *Easter-day.*)

For the EPISTLE. *Acts* x. 34—43. The GOSPEL. *St Luke* xxiv. 13—35.

TUESDAY IN EASTER WEEK.

MORNING.	EVENING.
1*st* Lesson. *Exod.* xx.	1*st* Lesson. *Exod.* xxxii.
2*nd* Lesson. *St Luke* xxiv. *to v.* 12. *incl.*	2*nd* Lesson. I *Cor.* xv.

THE COLLECT.

(The same as on *Easter-day.*)

For the EPISTLE. *Acts* xiii. 26–41. The GOSPEL. *St Luke* xxiv. 36–48.

THE FIRST SUNDAY AFTER EASTER.

MORN. *First* Lesson. *Numb.* xvi. EVEN. *First* Lesson. *Numb.* xxii.
(For the *second* Lessons see the date in the Calendar.)

THE COLLECT.

The EPISTLE. I *St John.* v. 4—12. The GOSPEL. *St John* xx. 19—23.

538.—This Sunday used to conclude the Paschal Feast, and was formerly denominated the *Octave* of Easter-day. A few of the solemnities of that High Day were repeated on this day, but in a *lower* degree; whence this Sunday has acquired the name, says Wheatly, of '*Low Sunday.*' Neophytes, or the newly baptized, were accustomed to deposit their chrisomes, or white garments, in the Church at this time; hence the day was also called *New Sunday* from their new birth, and *Dominica in Albis* from their white garments.

DR. WATERLAND remarks:—'Why might not this day be called '*Lohe*, or *Low* (as we now spell it) Sunday, i. e. *Flame Sunday* or '*Light Sunday*, from the custom of offering lighted candles? (See '*Martene*. p. 142). But the name was anciently *Law-Sunday*, and 'the eve before *Lawson-even*. (*Gloss*. to Langtoft. 521). *Law* was 'anciently *Low*: but I suspect that the name ignorantly came from '*clausum*, as Shere-Thursday came from *cene*. The Greeks styled 'it '*The New Sunday*.' (See Bingham, xx. 5. §. 12.) The Latins 'anciently styled it *Clausum Pas-chæ*, as the Gallican Lectionary, 'and the *Missale Gothicum* of the viith and viiith (Vid. *Mabillon*, 'de Lit. Gall. p. 148:)—a name borrowed from the Jews, who called 'their Pentecost the *close of the Passover*. (See Lamy, p. 133.) '*Clausum Pas-chæ* is the name for this day also in Gregory of Tours, 'of the 6*th* century. (*Hist. Franc.* L. ix. *Sect.* 44. *Col.* 476.).'—WHEATLY'S *Ill. of Bk. of Com. Prayer*. p. 258.—Dr. Corrie's *Ed.*

THE SECOND SUNDAY AFTER EASTER.

MORNING. *First* Lesson. *Numb.* xxiii. xxiv. EVENING. *First* Lesson. *Numb.* xxv.

(For the *second* Lessons see the *date* in the Calendar.)

THE COLLECT.

The EPISTLE. I *St Peter* ii. 19—25. The GOSPEL. *St John* x. 11—16.

THE THIRD SUNDAY AFTER EASTER.

MORN. *First* Lesson. *Deut.* iv. EVEN. *First* Lesson. *Deut.* v.

(For the *second* Lessons see the *date* in the Calendar.)

THE COLLECT.

The EPISTLE. I *St Peter* ii. 11—17. The GOSPEL. *St John* xvi. 16—22.

THE FOURTH SUNDAY AFTER EASTER.

MORN. *First* Lesson. *Deut.* vi. EVEN. *First* Lesson. *Deut.* vii.

(For the *second* Lessons see the *date* in the Calendar.)

THE COLLECT.

The EPISTLE. *St Jas.* i. 17—21. The GOSPEL. *St John* xvi. 5—15.

THE FIFTH SUNDAY AFTER EASTER.

(or *Rogation* Sunday.)

MORN. *First* Lesson. *Deut.* viii. EVEN. *First* Lesson. *Deut.* ix.

(For the *second* Lessons see the *date* in the Calendar.)

THE COLLECT.

The EPISTLE. *St Jas.* i. 22—27. The GOSPEL. *St John* xvi. 23—33.

539.—This Sunday is commonly known as '*Rogation Sunday*,' from the three days next following being the ancient *Rogation-days*; a term derived from *rogare*, 'to supplicate,' and applied to them because of the fastings and prayers then exercised to prepare the mind for the due consideration of *Ascension-Day*, which immediately follows. There were formerly (A. D. 469.) *Processional Litanies* established on these days to deprecate God on occasions of national calamities; but these were done away with at the Reformation, and all that survives from this usage is the *Perambulation of Parishes*, which we have already fully described in *Vol.* **B.** *par.* 161., as well as these

ROGATION-DAYS.

540.—No Collect, Prayer, nor religious Service, is prescribed in the Liturgy for these days, although they are enumerated in the *Table of Fasts* following the Calendar; but there is a *Homily* in four parts appointed, "*For the days of Rogation Week;*" the *first* part for the *Monday;* the *second* for the *Tuesday;* the *third*, for the *Wednesday;* and the *fourth*, as its title imports, is "*An* EXHORTATION, *to be spoken to* "*such Parishes where they use their* Perambulation "in Rogation Week; *for the oversight of the Bounds* "*and Limits of their Town.*" This Perambulation is popularly called '*beating the bounds.*'—(See *Vol.* **B.**)

THE ASCENSION DAY.

[Popularly called *Holy-Thursday.*]
(Has an appointed *Eve* preceding it.)

PROPER PSALMS.

MORN. *Ps.* viii. xv. xxi. EVEN. *Ps.* xxiv. xlvii. cviii.

MORNING.	EVENING.
1st Lesson. *Deut.* x.	*1st* Lesson. II *Kings* ii.
2nd Lesson. *St Luke* xxiv. *v.* 44.	*2nd* Lesson. *Eph.* iv. *to v.* 16. *incl.*

(The *Athanasian Creed* to be used.)

THE COLLECT.

For the EPISTLE. *Acts* i. 1—11. The GOSPEL. *St Mark* xvi. 14—20.

541.—On this Festival, forty days after the Resurrection of our blessed Lord, the Church has from the earliest times of Christianity commemorated His ascension into heaven (*Augustin*. Ep. 54. *ad Jan.*).

Why this day was called "Holy *Thursday*" is not known, but the appellation has come to us from our Saxon ancestors. The Collect is derived from the Sacramentary of Gregory.

SUNDAY AFTER ASCENSION DAY.

MORN. *First* Lesson. *Deut.* xii. EVEN. *First* Lesson. *Deut.* xiii.

(For the *second* Lessons see the *date* in the Calendar.)

THE COLLECT.

The EPISTLE.	The GOSPEL.
I *St Pet.* iv. 7—11.	*St John* xv. 26. *and part of ch.* xvi. *to ver.* 4.

WHITSUNDAY.

(Has an appointed *Eve* preceding it.)

PROPER PSALMS. MORN. *Ps.* xlviii. lxviii. EVEN. *Ps.* civ. cxlv.

MORNING.	EVENING.
1*st* Lesson. *Deut.* xvi. *to v.* 17. *incl.*	1*st* Lesson. *Isa.* xi.
2*nd* Lesson. *Acts* x. *v.* 34.	2*nd* Less. *Acts* xix. *to v.* 20. *incl.*

(The *Athanasian Creed* to be used.)

(The first *Ember Collect* to be used.)

THE COLLECT.

For the EPISTLE. *Acts* ii. 1—11. The GOSPEL. *St John* xiv. 15—31.

542.—This Festival answers to the Jewish Feast of *Pentecost*, and is designed to commemorate the out-pouring of the holy Spirit upon the Apostles fifty days after our Saviour's Resurrection on Easter-Day. It is not accurately decided why this day acquired the name of *Whitsunday;* some imagine it is because of the *white garments* the newly baptized then assumed: others suppose it is from the great diffusion of wisdom (*Wit.*) and knowledge then shed upon the first Preachers of Christianity for the enlightenment of mankind; others, from the fact that anciently all persons were to pay their tythes of young before this day, or be liable to the *wite* i. e. *penalty*, or *mulct*, for omission. L'Estrange conjectures that it comes from the French word *huict*, eight, and then Whitsunday will be *Huict-Sonday*, i. e. the eighth Sunday, from Easter; and in confirmation of this opinion, he says that the Octave of any Feast is in the Latin called *utas*, which he derives from the French word *huictas:* (*Alliance* in loco.). Dr. Waterland, commenting upon this subject, quotes the following from an old work entitled "*Liber Festivalis*" printed A. D. 1500.—

"Good men and wymen: this daye is called *Whitsondaye*, be-"cause the Holy Ghoste brought *wytte* and wisdome into Christes "Disciples, and soo by their prechynge after in to all Cristendome." ......This, he adds, 'best answers to the ancient spelling and to those 'vast diffusions of light and wisdom (*Witt.* anciently, *wisdom*, know-'ledge, &c.) shed on that day.'......After citing other opinions, he 'concludes: — 'However, under such uncertainty, all is but con-'jecture.'—WHEATLY's *Ill. of Book of Com. Prayer.*' Dr. Corrie's *Ed.* 265. *note.*

The REV. F. PROCTOR in his History of the Book of Common Prayer (*p.* 269. *note*) quotes these verses in explanation of the etymology of the term *Whitsunday*:—

'This day *Witsonday* is cald
'For wisdom and *wit* seuene fald
'Was gouen to ye apostles as yis day.'
(*Camb. Univer. MSS.* Dd. I. i. *p.* 234.)

543.—Whitsun-week being one of the Ember-Weeks, only two days, Monday and Tuesday, are devoted to a continuance of the Feast; the three remaining days are the preparatory fasts for the due consideration of the *ordination* to take place on the Sunday following. On *Whitsunday*, therefore, the first of the Ember Collects should be used, as directed in the Rubric attached to them, and at the close of the week, the second Ember Collect is preferable. (See *par.* 458. *supra*). It was on *Whitsunday*, 1549 (*June* 9th) that the *reformed Liturgy* was first promulgated, and commanded by the Act of Uniformity of that year to be used in every Cathedral and Parish Church of the Realm.

MONDAY IN WHITSUN-WEEK.

MORNING.	EVENING.
1st Lesson. *Gen.* xi. *to v.* 9. *incl.*	*1st* Lesson. *Numb.* xi. *v.* 16. *to* 29. *incl.*
2nd Lesson. I *Cor.* xii.	*2nd* Lesson. I *Cor.* xiv. *to v.* 25. *incl.*

THE COLLECT.

(The same as for *Whit-Sunday.*)

For the EPISTLE. *Acts* x. 34—48. The GOSPEL. *St John* iii. 16—21.

TUESDAY IN WHITSUN-WEEK.

MORNING.	EVENING.
1st Less. I *Sam.* xix. *v.* 18.	*1st* Less. *Deut.* xxx.
2nd Less. I *Thess.* v. *v.* 12. *to* 23. *incl.*	*2nd* Less. I *John* iv. *to v.* 18. *incl.*

THE COLLECT.

(The same as for *Whit-Sunday.*)

For the EPISTLE. *Acts* viii. 14—17. The GOSPEL. *St John* x. 1—10

TRINITY SUNDAY.

MORN. *First* Lesson. *Gen.* i. EVEN. *First* Lesson. *Gen.* xviiii.

„ *Second* Lesson. *St Matt.* iii. „ *Second* Lesson. I *St John* v.

(The *Athanasian Creed* to be used.)

THE COLLECT.

For the EPISTLE. *Rev.* iv. 1—11. The GOSPEL. *St John* iii. 1—15.

544.—This Sunday was originally observed as the *Octave* of Whitsunday; it was not until about the 9th or 10th Century that we read of the Commemoration of the *Holy Trinity*. Durandus places this Festival as far back as Gregory IV. A. D. 834. (*Rational. lib.* VI. *c.* 14.) Gervase, the Chronicler of Canterbury, tells us that Thomas â Becket instituted this Feast in England about A. D. 1162; and Quesnel speaks of an Office '*pro festo Sanctissimæ Trinitatis* having been used by the Monks of Mount Cassia in A. D. 1086. So that the Festival is certainly 700 years old. It was kept in some Churches on the Sunday next before Advent, in others on this day; but, as an established Feast on the Octave of Whitsunday, as noted in the Calendar, it must be assigned to a later date than any mentioned above: some say this was accomplished by Pope Benedict XIII. A. D. 1305; others, by Pope John XXII. A. D. 1408: the latter is the date generally accepted.

545.—The *Collects*, *Epistles*, and *Gospels* for Trinity Sunday, and those which follow until Advent, are all derived from the Sarum Missal. No *proper Psalms* are appointed for *Trinity Sunday*, which is considered to have been an oversight of the Revisers of the Liturgy; still, the Officiating Minister is not at liberty to supply the omission, and must therefore use the Psalms prescribed for the day of the month. (See *par.* 87. *supra*).

THE FIRST SUNDAY AFTER TRINITY.

MORN. *First* Lesson. *Josh.* x. EVEN. *First* Lesson. *Josh.* xxiii.
(For the *second* Lessons see the *date* in the Calendar.)
THE COLLECT.
The EPISTLE. I *St John* iv. 7—21. The GOSPEL. *St Luke* xvi. 19—31.

THE SECOND SUNDAY AFTER TRINITY.

MORN. *First* Lesson. *Judg.* iv. EVEN. *First* Lesson. *Judg.* v.
(For the *second* Lessons see the *date* in the Calendar.)
THE COLLECT.
The EPISTLE. I *St John* iii. 18—24. The GOSPEL. *St Luke* xiv. 16—24.

THE THIRD SUNDAY AFTER TRINITY.

MORN. *First* Lesson. I Sam. ii. EVEN. *First* Lesson. I *Sam.* iii.
(For the *Second* Lessons see the date in the Calendar.
THE COLLECT.
The EPISTLE. I *St. Pet.* v. 5—11. The GOSPEL. *St Luke* xv. 1—10

THE FOURTH SUNDAY AFTER TRINITY.

MORN. *First* Lesson. I *Sam.* xii. EVEN. *First* Lesson. I *Sam.* xiii.
(For the *second* Lessons see the *date* in the Calendar.)
THE COLLECT.
The EPISTLE. *Rom.* viii. 18—23. The GOSPEL. *St Luke* vi. 36—42.

THE FIFTH SUNDAY AFTER TRINITY.

MORN. *First* Lesson. I *Sam.* xv. EVEN. *First* Lesson. I *Sam.* xvii.
(For the *second* Lessons see the *date* in the Calendar.)
THE COLLECT.
The EPISTLE. I *St Peter* iii. 8—15. The GOSPEL. *St Luke* v. 1—11.

THE SIXTH SUNDAY AFTER TRINITY.

MORN. *First* Lesson. II *Sam.* xii. EVEN. *First* Lesson. II *Sam.* xix.
(For the *second* Lessons see the *date* in the Calendar.)
THE COLLECT.
The EPISTLE. *Rom.* vi. 3—11. The GOSPEL. *St Matt.* v. 20—26.

THE SEVENTH SUNDAY AFTER TRINITY.

MORN. *First* Lesson. II *Sam.* xxi. EVEN. *First* Lesson. II *Sam.* xxiv.
(For the *second* Lessons see the *date* in the Calendar.)
THE COLLECT.
The EPISTLE. *Rom.* vi. 19—23. The GOSPEL. *St Mark* viii. 1—9.

THE EIGHTH SUNDAY AFTER TRINITY.

MORN. *First* Lesson. I *Kings* xiii. EVEN. *First* Lesson. I *Kings* xvii.
(For the *second* Lessons see the *date* in the Calendar.)

THE COLLECT.

The EPISTLE. *Rom.* viii. 12—17. The GOSPEL. *St Matt.* vii. 15—21.

THE NINTH SUNDAY AFTER TRINITY.

MORN. *First* Lesson. I *Kings* xviii. EVEN. *First* Lesson. I *Kings* xix.
(For the *second* Lessons see the *date* in the Calendar.)

THE COLLECT.

The EPISTLE. I *Cor.* x. 1—13. The GOSPEL. *St Luke* xvi. 1—9.

THE TENTH SUNDAY AFTER TRINITY.

MORN. *First* Lesson. I *Kings* xxi. EVEN. *First* Lesson. I *Kings* xxii.
(For the *second* Lessons see the *date* in the Calendar.)

THE COLLECT.

The EPISTLE. I *Cor.* xii. 1—11. The GOSPEL. *St Luke* xix. 41—47.

THE ELEVENTH SUNDAY AFTER TRINITY.

MORN. *First* Lesson. II *Kings* v. EVEN. *First* Lesson. II Kings ix.
(For the *second* Lessons see the *date* in the Calendar.)

THE COLLECT.

The EPISTLE. I *Cor.* xv. 1—11. The GOSPEL. *St Luke* xviii. 9—14.

THE TWELFTH SUNDAY AFTER TRINITY.

MORN. *First* Lesson. II Kings. x. EVEN. *First* Lesson. II *Kings* xviii.
(For the *second* Lessons see the *date* in the Calendar.)

THE COLLECT.

The EPISTLE. II *Cor.* iii. 4—9. The GOSPEL. *St Mark* vii. 31—37.

THE THIRTEENTH SUNDAY AFTER TRINITY.

MORN. 1*st* Lesson. II *Kings* xix. EVEN. 1*st* Lesson. II *Kings* xxiii.
(For the *second* Lessons see the *date* in the Calendar.)

THE COLLECT.

The EPISTLE. *Gal.* iii. 16—22. The GOSPEL. *St Luke* x. 23—37.

THE FOURTEENTH SUNDAY AFTER TRINITY.

MORN. *First* Lesson. *Jer.* v. EVEN. *First* Lesson. *Jer.* xxii.
(For the *second* Lessons see the *date* in the Calendar.)

THE COLLECT.

The EPISTLE. *Gal.* v. 16—24. The GOSPEL. *St Luke* xvii. 11—19.

THE FIFTEENTH SUNDAY AFTER TRINITY.

MORN. *First* Lesson. *Jer.* xxxv. EVEN. *First* Lesson. *Jer.* xxxvi.
(For the *second* Lessons see the *date* in the Calendar.)

THE COLLECT.

The EPISTLE. *Gal.* vi. 11—18. The GOSPEL. *St Matt.* vi. 24—34.

THE SIXTEENTH SUNDAY AFTER TRINITY.

MORN. *First* Lesson. *Ezek.* ii. EVEN. *First* Lesson. *Ezek.* xiii.
(For the *second* Lessons see the *date* in the Calendar.)

THE COLLECT.

The Epistle. *Eph.* iii. 13—21. The GOSPEL. *St Luke* vii. 11—17.

THE SEVENTEENTH SUNDAY AFTER TRINITY.

MORN. *First* Lesson. *Ezek.* xiv. EVEN. *First* Lesson. *Ezek.* xviii.
(For the *second* Lessons see the *date* in the Calendar.)

THE COLLECT.

The EPISTLE. *Eph.* iv. 1—6. The GOSPEL. *St Luke* xiv. 1—11.

THR EIGHTEENTH SUNDAY AFTER TRINITY.

MORN. *First* Lesson. *Ezek.* xx. EVEN. *First* Lesson. *Ezek.* xxiv.
(For the *second* Lessons see the *date* in the Calendar.)

THE COLLECT.

The EPISTLE. I *Cor.* i. 4—8. The GOSPEL. *St Matt.* xxii. 34—46.

THE NINETEENTH SUNDAY AFTER TRINITY.

MORN. *First* Lesson. *Dan.* iii. EVEN. *First* Lesson. *Dan.* vi.
(For the *second* Lessons see the *date* in the Calendar.)

THE COLLECT.

The EPISTLE. *Eph.* iv. 17—32. The GOSPEL. *St Matt.* ix. 1—8.

THE TWENTIETH SUNDAY AFTER TRINITY.

Morn. *First* Lesson. *Joel* ii. EVEN. *First* Lesson. *Micah* vi.
(For the *second* Lessons see the *date* in the Calendar.)

THE COLLECT.

The EPISTLE. *Eph.* v. 15—21. The GOSPEL. *St Matt.* xxii. 1—14.

THE ONE AND TWENTIETH SUNDAY AFTER TRINITY.

MORN. *First* Lesson. *Habak.* ii. EVEN. *First* Lesson. *Prov.* i.
(For the *second* Lessons see the *date* in the Calendar.)

THE COLLECT.

The EPISTLE. *Eph.* vi. 10—20. The GOSPEL. *St John.* iv. 46—54.

THE TWO AND TWENTIETH SUNDAY AFTER TRINITY.

MORN. *First* Lesson. *Prov.* ii. EVEN. *First* Lesson. *Prov.* iii
(For the *second* Lessons see the *date* in the Calendar.)

THE COLLECT.

The EPISTLE. *Phil.* i. 3—11. The GOSPEL. *St Matt.* xviii. 21—35.

THE THREE AND TWENTIETH SUNDAY AFTER TRINITY.

MORN. *First* Lesson. *Prov.* xi. EVEN. *First* Lesson. *Prov.* xii.
(For the *second* Lessons see the date in the Calendar.)

THE COLLECT.

The EPISTLE. *Phil.* iii. 17—21. The GOSPEL. *St Matt.* xxii. 15—22

THE FOUR AND TWENTIETH SUNDAY AFTER TRINITY.

MORN. *First* Lesson. *Prov.* xiii. EVEN. *First* Lesson. *Prov.* xiv.
(For the *second* Lessons see the *date* in the Calendar.)

THE COLLECT.

The EPISTLE. *Col.* i. 3—12. The GOSPEL. *St Matt.* ix. 18—26.

546.—If there are *more Sundays after Trinity* than the prescribed Collects, Epistles, and Gospels, can supply, a *Rubric* following the *Twenty-fifth Sunday after Trinity* directs that they shall be supplied here from the *Epiphany Sundays;* if there are *fewer Sundays*, then one or more of the preceding Services must be omitted: but in both cases the Collect, Epistle, and Gospel, designated for the *Twenty-fifth Sunday after Trinity*, must always immediately precede the Service for the *First Sunday in Advent*. (See *par.* 547. *postea*, where this *Rubric* is discussed.)

THE FIVE AND TWENTIETH (*or last*) SUNDAY AFTER TRINITY.

MORN. *First* Lesson. *Prov.* xv. EVEN. *First* Lesson. *Prov.* xvi.
(For the *second* Lessons see the *date* in the Calendar.)

THE COLLECT.

(If the Sunday *next before* Advent: if not, an *Epiphany* Collect must be used.)

For the EPISTLE. *Jer.* xxiii. 5—8. The GOSPEL. *St John* vi. 5—14.

(If the Sunday *next before* Advent; if not, then those of the *Epiphany* Collect used.)

¶. '*If there be any more Sundays before Advent Sunday, the 'Service of some of those Sundays that were omitted after the 'Epiphany shall be taken in to supply so many as are here 'wanting. And if there be fewer, the overplus may be omit-'ted. Provided that this last Collect, Epistle and Gospel 'shall always be used upon the Sunday next before Advent.*' Present Book of Com. Prayer.

547. The Collect, Epistle and Gospel, under the title of the "*Five and Twentieth Sunday after Trinity,*" must always be used on the Sunday immediately preceding the "*First Sunday in Advent.*" If the Sundays after Trinity are fewer than the number prescribed in the Liturgy the overplus must be omitted *before* the Twenty-fifth, so as to leave the Twenty-fifth Collect, &c. as the last: but if there are *more* Sundays than there are Services for them, then the supernumerary Services of the *Epiphany* Sundays are to be used. They must be introduced *between* the Twenty-fourth and Twenty-fifth Sundays after Trinity, so as to keep the prescribed Twenty-fifth Services for the Sunday next before Advent Sunday. If the Service for one Sunday is wanting take that for the *Sixth Sunday after the Epiphany;* if for two, then take those for the *Fifth*, and *Sixth;* if three, take those for the *Fourth*, *Fifth*, and *Sixth.* By so doing, not only will the early recurrence of those Services be avoided, but that of the *Sixth Sunday after Epiphany*, so relevant to the subject of the Advent, will come in its most appropriate place. The Lessons, however, are independent of the contingencies affecting the Collect, Epistle and Gospel, and are to be used as appointed, on the *Twenty-fifth Sunday after Trinity* whether it be near to *Advent Sunday*, or remote from it.

The *Rubric* we now have is an expansion of the Rubric which was introduced into the *second Liturgy* of Edward VI. in 1552; thus—

> '*If there be any more Sundays before Advent Sunday, to* '*supply the same shall be taken the Service of some of those* '*Sundays, that were omitted between the Epiphany and Sep-* '*tuagesima.*' (1552, 1559, 1604.)—KEELING. 144. 145.

The same Rubric was incorporated into the Scotch Liturgy of 1637, but considerably enlarged; thus—

> '*If there be any more Sundays before Advent Sunday, to* '*supply the same, shall be taken the Service of some of those* '*Sundays that were omitted between the Epiphany and Sep-* '*tuagesima. But the same shall follow the XXIV. Sunday* '*after Trinity. And if there be fewer Sundays than XXV.* '*before Advent, then shall the XXIII. or XXIV., or both be* '*omitted: so that the five and twentieth shall never either* '*alter, or be left out, but be always used immediately before* '*Advent-Sunday, to which the Epistle and Gospel of that do* *expressly relate.*'......(1637.)—KEELING. 144.

Thus it will be observed that the arrangement, which we have advocated above, is the most generally received, as will be seen from the quotations following—

DR. NICHOLLS' remarks:—'In the Order of *Sarum*, if there be 'more Sundays after *Trinity* than 25, it is appointed that the Service 'of the 24th Sunday shall be repeated over again, once, twice, or 'thrice, as the number of those Sundays may be. So that the '25th Sunday is always to be observed for the Sunday next before '*Advent*.'—*Add. Notes to Book of Com. Prayer*. p. 33.

WHEATLY says:—'In the Rubric following this Gospel, we see 'it is ordered, according to an old rule of Micrologus, an ancient 'Ritualist, that "*if there are either more or fewer Sundays between* '*Trinity-Sunday and Advent, the Services must be so ordered, that* '*this last Collect, Epistle, and Gospel be always used upon the Sunday* '*next before Advent;*" i. e. if there be fewer Sundays, the overplus 'is to be omitted: but if there be more, the Service of some of those 'Sundays that were omitted after the *Epiphany* are to be taken 'in to supply so many as are wanting; but which of those Services, 'the Rubric does not say. And for that reason there is generally 'a diversity in the practice; some reading, on those occasions, the 'Services next in course to what had been used at the Epiphany 'before; and others, at the same time, reading the last or two last, 'accordingly as one or both of them are wanting. The last of these 'practices I think to be preferable: partly upon the account that 'when there is an overplus of Sundays after Trinity one year, there 'is generally a pretty full number after Epiphany the next: so that 'if any of the Services for the early Sundays after Epiphany are 'taken in to supply those that are wanting after Trinity, the same 'Services will come in turn to be read again pretty soon: but the 'chief reason why I think the latter Services should be used, is 'because the Service that is appointed for the *last Sunday after* '*Epiphany*, is a more suitable preparation for the season that is 'approaching and makes way for the Service for the last Sunday 'after Trinity, as that does for the Services appointed for Advent.' (*p.* 275.)—*Rat. Ill. of Book of Com. Prayer*.

DR. MANT (late *Bishop of Down and Connor and Dromore*) observes:—'Of the Epiphany Sundays, the *latest* of the Services, 'which were omitted in their course, should be chosen to supply 'the want before Advent.' (*p.* 54.)—*Hor. Lit.*

The REV. S. ROWE states:—'With respect to the intercalary 'Sundays to be supplied from the *Epiphany*, much question has 'arisen, as well as consequent diversity of practice. Some have 'thought it right to recur to the Sundays of the Epiphany im- 'mediately following the last that had been read in the current 'year. Thus if Easter had been early, and Epiphany consequently 'shortened to three Sundays, they would supply the deficiency 'after Trinity by reading the Collect, &c., for the fourth Sunday 'after Epiphany. Others prefer taking the *sixth*, if one intercalary 'Service is wanted, or the *fifth*, and *sixth*, if two are required—a 'practice most in accordance with the spirit of our Ritual, since it 'brings into use Services which otherwise would rarely occur, and, 'besides this, has the weighty recommendation of introducing, in 'the Collect, Epistle, and Gospel for the sixth Sunday after 'Epiphany, subjects peculiarly adapted for the approaching Advent 'Season.' (*p.* 157.)—*An Appeal to the Rubric.*

MR. A. J. STEPHENS (*Barrister-at-law*) writes:—'The rule of 'the Roman Missal is the same in principle as ours, but more 'precise. The Roman Missal has Services for but 24 Sundays after 'Pentecost, i. e. 23 after Trinity. The Services for the last of these 'is always used as with us, on the *Sunday before Advent.* But if 'there be 25 Sundays after Pentecost, then the Mass for the 6*th* '*Sunday after Epiphany* is used: if 26, on the 24th that for the '5th Sunday after Epiphany; and on the 25th that for the 6th; 'if 27, on the 24th that for the 4th, on the 25th that for the 5th, 'and on the 26th that for the 6th; and if 28, on the 24th, that for 'the 3rd, on the 25th, that for the 4th, on the 26th, that for the 5th 'and on the 27th, that for the 6th.' (*p.* 1006.)—*Book of Com. Prayer.* E. H. S.

[THE TWENTY-SIXTH SUNDAY AFTER TRINITY.]

MORN. *First* Lesson. *Prov.* xvii. EVEN. *First* Lesson. *Prov.* xix.
(For the *second* Lessons see the *date* in the Calendar.)

The COLLECT, EPISTLE, and GOSPEL.

(If the Sunday *next before* Advent, those for the 25*th Sunday after Trinity;* if not then those for one of the *Sundays after the Epiphany.*)—(See *par.* 547.)

[THE TWENTY-SEVENTH SUNDAY AFTER TRINITY.]

(No Lessons appointed.)

The COLLECT, EPISTLE, and GOSPEL.

(If the Sunday *next before* Advent, those for the 25*th Sunday after Trinity;* if not, then those for one of the *Sundays after the Epiphany.*)—(See *par.* 547.)

548.—As there are no Lessons appointed for the *Twenty-Seventh Sunday after Trinity*, it is the more frequent usage to take those prescribed for the *Sixth Sunday after the Epiphany*, as preferable at this season to what may be found in the daily Calendar.—The *Collect*, *Epistle* and *Gospel*, will be those appointed for the twenty-fifth Sunday after Trinity, if the *twenty-seventh* be the last Sunday; if otherwise, then an *Epiphany* Service will be taken, as noted above. (*par.* 547.)

The Rev. F. Procter says:—'There is a difficulty in deciding 'what first lessons should be read on the 27*th Sunday after Trinity*. 'It is suggested, as the course most suitable to the occasion, the 'Sunday next before Advent, that the *First Lessons* appointed for 'the *sixth Sunday after Epiphany* should be read on this day; the 'corresponding Collect will have been used on the preceding Sun-'day with the Lessons for the 26th Sunday after Trinity; and the '*propria* of the sixth Sunday after Epiphany have been chosen with 'reference to their more frequent use, as preceding Advent, than as 'following Epiphany. Many reasons present themselves against 'the use of the *Lessons from the daily Calendar* on this extraor-'dinary Sunday.' (*p.* 276. *Note.*)—*Hist. of Book of Com. Prayer.*

The Rev. S. Rowe remarks upon the Lessons for the 26*th* '*Sunday after Trinity*, thus:—'The *Epiphany Lessons* also, which 'are all from the Prophet *Isaiah*, are highly appropriate, although 'it may be doubted whether it would be correct on the *twenty-sixth* '*Sunday after Trinity* (although an Epiphany Collect &c. must be 'used,) to read the accompanying Lessons, instead of those from the '*Proverbs* appointed for that day.' (*p.* 158.)—*An Appeal to the Rubric.*

Mr. A. J. Stephens' (*Barrister-at-law*) observes:—'It is to be 'remarked that *no Lessons* are appointed in the Calendar for the '27*th Sunday after Trinity;* and this has also led to a great 'diversity of practice; some Clergymen reading the *week-day Les-*'*sons* (contrary to all analogy, and the spirit of the Prayer Book), 'and others reading a lesson for one of the Sundays after the 'Epiphany. Though this be a *casus omissus*, still the strict con-'struction of the letter of the above Rubric supplies the remedy. 'It says that the service of some of those Sundays, &c., shall be 'taken in to supply so many as are wanting: and "the service" 'may undoubtedly be fairly construed to include the whole office 'for the day, including Morning and Evening Prayer.' (*p.* 1007.)—*Book of Com. Prayer.* E. H. S.

THE IMMOVEABLE HOLY-DAYS.

549.—The *Holy-Days* which follow, not being dependent on the fluctuations of Easter for the times of their observance, are termed the *Immoveable Festivals*, and are placed by themselves after the Sunday Collects, &c. so that they should not interfere with the order and arrangement of those Services. They will be found to be classed according to the date of their occurrence.

SAINT ANDREW'S DAY.

(Falls on *November* 30th; and has an appointed *Eve.*)

MORN. *First* Lesson. *Prov.* xx. EVEN. *First* Lesson. *Prov.* xxi.
„ *Second* Lesson. *Acts* i. „ *Second* Lesson. *Heb.* vi.

(The *Athanasian Creed* to be used.)

THE COLLECT.

The EPISTLE. *Rom.* x. 9—21. The GOSPEL. *St Matt.* iv. 18—22.

SAINT THOMAS THE APOSTLE.

(Falls on *December* 21st, and has an appointed *Eve.*)

MORN. *First* Lesson. *Prov.* xxiii. EVEN. *First.* Lesson. *Prov.* xxiv.
„ *Second* Lesson. *Acts* xxi. „ *Second* Lesson. I *St John* i.

THE COLLECT.

The EPISTLE. *Eph.* ii. 19—22. The GOSPEL. *St John* xx. 24—31.

THE CONVERSION OF ST PAUL.

(Falls on *January 25th.*)

MORNING.	EVENING.
First Lesson. *Wisd.* v.	*First* Lesson. *Wisd.* vi.
Second Lesson. *Acts* xxii. *to v.* 22. *incl.*	*Second* Lesson. *Acts* xxvi.

THE COLLECT.

The EPISTLE. *Acts* ix. 1—22. The GOSPEL. *St Matt.* xix. 27—30.

THE PRESENTATION OF CHRIST IN THE TEMPLE.

commonly called

THE PURIFICATION OF ST. MARY THE VIRGIN.

(Falls on *February* 2*nd*, and has an appointed *Eve.*)

MORN. *First* Lesson. *Wisd.* ix. EVEN. *First* Lesson. *Wisd.* xii.
„ *Second* Lesson. *St Mark* ii. „ *Second* Lesson. I *Cor.* xiv.

THE COLLECT.

For the EPISTLE. *Mal.* iii. 1—5. The GOSPEL. *St Luke* ii. 22—40.

550.—This Festival is popularly known as *Candlemas-Day*, an appellation derived from an ancient practice among Christians of using a multitude of *lighted candles* in their Churches and processions, commemorative of the declaration made this day by the aged Simeon, recorded in to-day's Gospel, that CHRIST was to be "*a light to lighten the Gentiles*," &c. The *custom* was prohibited in the second year of Edward VI. but the name of *Candlemas* is in certain localities still retained.

SAINT MATTHIAS'S DAY.

(Falls on *February* 24*th*, and has an appointed *Eve*.)
MORN. *First* Lesson. *Wisd.* xix. EVEN. *First* Lesson. *Ecclus.* i.
„ *Second* Lesson. *St Luke* vii. „ *Second* Lesson. *Ephes.* i.
(The *Athanasian Creed* to be used.)
THE COLLECT.
For the EPISTLE. *Acts* i. 15—26. The Gospel. *St Matt.* xi. 25—30

THE ANNUNCIATION OF THE BLESSED VIRGIN MARY.

Popularly called *Lady-Day*.
(Falls on *March* 25*th*, and has an appointed *Eve*.)
MORN. *First* Lesson. *Ecclus.* ii. EVEN. *First* Lesson. *Ecclus.* iii.
„ *Second* Lesson. *St John* xii. „ *Second* Lesson. II *Tim.* iii.
THE COLLECT.
For the EPISTLE. *Isa.* vii. 10—15. The GOSPEL. *St Luke* i. 26—38.

SAINT MARK'S DAY.

(Falls on *April* 25th.)
MORN. *First* Lesson. *Ecclus.* iv. EVEN. *First* Lesson. *Ecclus.* v.
„ *Second* Lesson. *Acts* xxii. „ *Second* Lesson. I *St John* i.
THE COLLECT.
The EPISTLE. *Eph.* iv. 7—16. The GOSPEL. *St John* xv. 1—11.

SAINT PHILIP, AND SAINT JAMES'S DAY.

(Falls on *May* 1*st*.)
MORN. *First* Lesson. *Ecclus.* vii. EVEN. *First* Lesson. *Ecclus.* ix.
„ *Second* Lesson. *St John* i. *v.* 42. „ *Second* Lesson. *St Jude.*
THE COLLECT.
The EPISTLE. *St James* i. 1—12. The GOSPEL. *St John* xiv. 1—14.

SAINT BARNABAS, THE APOSTLE.

(Falls on *June* 11*th*.)

MORNING.	EVENING.
First Lesson. *Ecclus.* x.	*First* Lesson. *Ecclus.* xii.
Second Lesson. *Acts* xiv.	*Second* Lesson. *Acts* xv. *to v.* 35. *incl.*

THE COLLECT.

For the EPISTLE. *Acts* xi. 22—30. The GOSPEL. *St John* xv. 12—16.

SAINT JOHN BAPTIST'S DAY.

(Falls on *June* 24*th*, and has an appointed *Eve*.)

MORNING.	EVENING.
First Lesson. *Mal.* iii.	*First* Lesson. *Mal.* iv.
Sec. Lesson. *St Matt.* iii.	*Sec.* Lesson. *St Matt.* xiv. *to v.* 12. *incl.*

(The *Athanasian Creed* to be used.)

THE COLLECT.

For the EPISTLE. *Isa.* xl. 1—11. The GOSPEL. *St Luke* i. 57—80.

SAINT PETER'S DAY.

(Falls on *June* 29*th*, and has an appointed *Eve*.)

MORN. *First* Lesson. *Ecclus.* xv.	EVEN. *First* Lesson. *Ecclus.* xix.
„ *Second* Lesson. *Acts* iii.	„ *Second* Lesson. *Acts* iv.

THE COLLECT.

For the EPISTLE. *Acts* xii. 1—11. The GOSPEL. *St Matt.* xvi. 13—19.

SAINT JAMES, THE APOSTLE.

(Falls on *July* 25*th*, and has an appointed *Eve*.)

MORN. *First* Lesson. *Ecclus.* xxi.	EVEN. *First.* Lesson. *Ecclus.* xxii.
„ *Second* Lesson. *St John* xiii.	„ *Second* Lesson. II. *Tim.* iv.

(The *Athanasian Creed* to be used.)

THE COLLECT.

The EPISTLE.	The GOSPEL.
Acts xi. 27. and *part of Chap.* xii. *to v.* 3.	*St Matt.* xx. 20—28.

SAINT BARTHOLOMEW, THE APOSTLE.

(Falls on *August* 24*th*, and has an appointed *Eve*.)

MORNING.	EVENING.
First Lesson. *Ecclus.* xxiv.	*First* Lesson. *Ecclus.* xxix.
Second Lesson. *Acts* xxii.	*Second* Lesson. I *St John.* i.

(The *Athanasian Creed* to be used.)

THE COLLECT.

For the EPISTLE. *Acts* v. 12—16. The GOSPEL. *St Luke* xxii. 24—30.

SAINT MATTHEW, THE APOSTLE.

(Falls on *September* 21*st*, and has an appointed *Eve.*)

MORNING. *First* Lesson. *Ecclus.* xxxv. *Second* Lesson. *St Matt.* xxii.

EVENING. *First* Lesson. *Ecclus.* xxxviii. *Second* Lesson. I *Cor.* vi.

(The *Athanasian Creed* to be used.)

THE COLLECT.

The EPISTLE. II *Cor.* iv. 1—6. The GOSPEL. *St Matt.* ix. 9—13

SAINT MICHAEL, AND ALL ANGELS.

(Falls on *September* 29*th.*)

MORNING. *First* Lesson. *Gen.* xxxii. *Sec.* Lesson. *Acts* xii. *to v.* 19. *incl.*

EVENING. *First* Lesson. *Dan.* x. *v.* 5. *Sec.* Lesson. *Jude v.* 6. *to* 15. *incl.*

THE COLLECT.

For the EPISTLE. *Rev.* xii. 7—12. The GOSPEL. *St Matt.* xviii. 1—10.

SAINT LUKE, THE EVANGELIST.

(Falls on *October* 18th.)

MORN. *First* Lesson. *Ecclus.* li. „ *Second* Lesson. *St Luke* iv.

EVEN. *First* Lesson. *Job* i. *Second* Lesson. *Gal.* iv.

THE COLLECT.

The EPISTLE. II *Tim.* iv. 5—15. The GOSPEL. *St Luke.* x. 1—7.

SAINT SIMON, AND SAINT JUDE, APOSTLES.

(Falls on *October* 28*th*, and has an appointed *Eve.*)

MORN. *First* Lesson. *Job* xxiv. xxv. „ *Sec.* Lesson. *St Luke* xiv.

EVEN. *First* Lesson. *Job* xlii. „ *Sec.* Lesson. *Philip.* ii.

(The *Athanasian Creed* to be used.)

THE COLLECT.

The EPISTLE. *St Jude* 1—8. The GOSPEL. *St John* xv. 17—27.

ALL SAINTS' DAY.

(Falls on *November* 1*st*, and has an appointed *Eve.*)

MORNING. 1*st* Lesson. *Wisd.* iii. *to v.* 9. *incl.* 2*nd* Lesson. *Heb.* xi. *v.* 33. *ch.* xii. *to v.* 6. *incl.*

EVENING. 1*st* Lesson. *Wisd.* v. *to v.* 16. *incl.* 2*nd* Lesson. *Rev.* xix. *to v.* 16. *incl.*

THE COLLECT.

For the EPISTLE. *Rev.* vii. 2—12. The GOSPEL. *St Matt.* v. 1—12.

THE ORDER OF THE

ADMINISTRATION OF THE LORD'S SUPPER,

OR

Holy Communion.

551.—We now arrive at what is termed in our Book of Common Prayer, "THE ADMINISTRATION OF THE LORD'S SUPPER, OR HOLY COMMUNION;" and it is with much diffidence, and no little difficulty, that we approach a subject, which of all others is the most solemn, and the most important and engaging, that can occupy the thoughts of man. The "*Lord's Supper*," the ordinance of our Lord's own institution, is the central point round which the whole scheme of Christianity revolves. Here faith acquires the influence of the Redeemer upon the heart—here she commemorates Christ's sacrifice once offered for the sins of the whole world—here she gathers strength for her daily conflict with the Evil one; and time after time, as she renews her communications with the Holy Spirit of Grace, she goes on her way rejoicing. God forbid that we should intrude ourselves irreverently on such holy mysteries, —our object is not to question or discuss any one point or feature of this high doctrine, nor indeed to intensify, or weaken in the least degree, what our admirable Church has declared on this head in her Articles, Homilies, Catechism, and Liturgy. All we aim at is the elucidation of the external and subordinate parts alone of the "*Administration*," as laid down in the Rubrics of the "COMMUNION OFFICE:" should we, therefore, in so doing, in the remotest degree trench on the doctrines involved, we beg our reader's kind consideration, and trust that he will look upon it as accidental and undesigned; for it would be madness to attempt in a work of this character to define the mysterious communion of the body and blood of Christ,—a '*communion*' which has baffled the endeavours of the profoundest of our theologians, and the best of our divines, to bring down to the level of our frail and feeble comprehension. We will, therefore, at once proceed with our task, and begin with the consideration of the *appellation* given to the Ordinance itself; following it up with an explanation of the *Title* applied to the Office in the Book of Common Prayer.

The name of the Sacrament.

552.—In the earlier ages of Christianity this holy Sacrament was distinguished by various appellations; viz. *The Lord's Supper*, (Δεῖπνον Κυριακὸν, Cœna Domini); *the Holy Communion*, (Κοινωνία); the *Mystery* (Μυστηριον); the *Eucharist*, or *Returning of Thanks* for the Blessed Saviour's merits (Εὐχαριστια, Εὐλογια); the *Meeting together* (Σύναξις); &c. Of these, the Church of England has retained the most ancient and the most scriptural, viz. The Lord's Supper, from the usage of St Paul in 1 *Cor*. xi. 20. (Κυριακὸν δεῖπνον); and the Holy Communion, from the adoption of the term by the same Apostle in 1 *Cor*. x. 16. (*Κοινωνία τοῦ αἵματος—κοινωνία τοῦ σώματος τοῦ* Χριστοῦ). Many give to this Sacrament the appellation of the Holy Eucharist, from St Paul's adoption of the word as expressive of public thanksgiving in 1 *Cor*. xiv. 16. (*ἐπὶ τῇ σῇ εὐχαριστίᾳ*); the term is employed in the 28th of the XXXIX Articles in the Latin copy, and is much used by the Fathers. It is deeply to be regretted, that these three words have been considered in modern times the *Shibboleth* of party, and mark in those who use them distinctively some peculiar views relative to the doctrine of this Sacrament, or to the mode of its celebration, like the terms '*Altar*,' and '*Table*.' It will generally be found, indeed, that '*The Lord's Supper*,' and '*The Table*,' are epithets that often go together: so, '*The Holy Communion*,' and '*The Lord's Table*: similarly, '*The Holy Eucharist*,' and, '*The Altar*.' We, however, are writing for no party, and, therefore, will endeavour to give an honest elucidation of these distinctive appellations, and also refer to various authorities. At the same time, we would urge the avoidance of any exclusive use of either of these terms that might tend to rouse, or perpetuate, party feeling.

553.—In the Latin of the XXXIX Articles we find the two phrases, "Cœna Domini," (*the Supper of the Lord*), and "Eucharistia" (*the Eucharist*), employed, thus:—

'Duo a Christo Domino nostro in Evangelio instituta sunt 'Sacramenta, scilicet, Baptismus et *Cœna Domini*, ("the Supper of 'the Lord. *Eng. Art.*).'—*Art.* xxv.

'*Cœna Domini* ("The Supper of the Lord." *Eng. Art.*) non est 'tantum signum," &c.......

'Panis et vini transubstantiatio in *Eucharistia* ("in the Supper 'of the Lord." *Eng Art.*) ex sacris literis probari non potest,' &c......

'*Sacramentum Eucharistiæ*, ("of the Lord's Supper." *Eng. Art.*) 'ex institutione Christi non servabatur,' &c.......—*Art.* xxviii.

554.—In the Book of Common Prayer we observe only these terms, '*The Lord's Supper*,' and '*the Holy Communion*.'

In the Homilies this Sacrament is designated, '*The Sacrament of the Body and Blood of Christ;*' '*The Lord's Supper*' or '*Supper of the Lord;*' '*The Lord's Commemoration;*' '*The Communion;*' &c. And in the Homily, 'Of the *Worthy Receiving of the Sacrament*,' Part II. there is this paragraph:—

'So then we must shew outward testimony, in following the 'signification of Christ's death; amongst the which this is not 'esteemed least, to render *thanks* to Almighty God for all his 'benefits, briefly comprised in the death, passion, and resurrection 'of his dearly beloved Son. The which thing, because we ought 'chiefly at this Table to solemnize, the godly Fathers named it '*Eucharistia*, that is, *thanksgiving*: as if they should have said, 'Now above all other times ye ought to laud and praise God. 'Now may you behold the matter, the cause, the beginning, and 'the end of all *thanksgiving*. Now if you slack you show your-

'selves most unthankful, and that no other benefit can ever stir 'you to thank God, who so little regard here so many, so wonderful, 'and so profitable benefits. Seeing then that the *name* and *thing* 'itself doth monish us of *thanks*, let us,' &c. See also the HOMILY "*Of Common Prayer and Sacraments.*"

555.—In the CANONS (of 1603-4) this Sacrament is generally called '*The Communion*,' and '*The Holy Communion:*' once (in *Canon* 57.) the phrase, '*The Lord's Supper*,' occurs.

The early Fathers make use of the terms, '*Eucharist*,' and '*The Lord's Supper*,' thus:—

JUSTIN MARTYR *ob.* cir. A. D. 165, writes:—'Η *τροφὴ αὕτη καλεῖται παρ' ἡμῖν εὐχαριστία.*—*Apol.* I. 66.

IRENÆUS *ob.* cir. 201. says:—'Nostra consonans est sententia '*Eucharistiæ*, et *Eucharistia* rursus confirmat sententiam nostram.' (l. 4. c. 18. 5.)

CYPRIAN (*ob.* 258.) writes:—'Cum tremore et honore *Eucha*-'*ristiam* accipiendam.'—*Ad Qurin.* l. 3. c. (94. p. 55.)

CYRIL (*ob.* 298.) says:—'Ο *ἄρτος καὶ ὁ οἶνος τῆς εὐχαριστίας.*—*Hieros. Catech.* (Mystag.). i. (4.)

BASIL (*ob.* cir. 378.) writes:—*Μητὲ τὸ κυριακὸν δεῖπνον ἐν οἰκίᾳ καθυβρίζειν.*—(*Reg. brevior. interrog.* 310. Vol. II.)

CHRYSOSTOM (*ob.* cir. 407.) observes:—*Εὐχαριστία καλεῖται, ὅτι πολλῶν ἐστιν εὐεργατημάτων ἀνάμνησις.*' [in Matt. hom. (25. Vol. II. p. 178. 35).].

Again:—*῞Οτι τὸ κυριακὸν δεῖπνον, τουτέστι τὸ δεσποτικὸν, ὀφείλει κοινὸν εἶναι.*—[in 1 *Cor.* Hom. 27. p. 419. 23. Vol. iii.]

AUGUSTIN (*ob.* 430.) states:—'Hanc ipsam acceptionem *Eucha*-'*ristiæ* Dominicam Cœnam vocans.'—(liv. 7.)

Again:—'Quapropter neminem cogimus *Dominica* illa *cœna* 'prandere, sed nulli etiam contradicere audemus.'—*ibid.* 9.

THEODORET (*ob.* 456.) says:—'*Dominicam cœnam* vocat Sacramentum Dominicum.'—[in 1 Cor. xi. (20. Vol. III.).]

556.—Of more modern writers, we may quote the following, beginning with those which speak of this Holy Sacrament as the *Lord's Supper*.

I. The LORD'S SUPPER:—

BISHOP COSINS (*ob.* 1672), writing on the *Lord's Supper* says: 'And so the Apostle *St Paul* calls the celebration of this Sacra-'ment, 1 *Cor.* xi. 20; and so, 1 *Cor.* x. 21, the *Lord's Supper, and* '*the Table of the Lord.* In the Acts of the Apostles, Cap. 2. 42. it 'is called *κοινωνια*, the *Communion*, *κλάσις τοῦ ἄρτου*, *the breaking* '*of Bread.* Which form of speaking the Ancients did imitate. 'For the Sacrament received its denomination from the first and 'more conspicuous action; by a figure not *new*, but commonly used. 'For to *break bread*, among the Hebrews, signified the same thing 'as to eat. For as on the other side the *Greeks*, from drinking, 'called the whole entertainment *συμπόσιον*; so the Hebrews, from 'the other more principal part, *viz.* eating, called it *breaking of* '*bread*. Besides, because our Saviour, when, in his last Supper, 'with his disciples, he instituted this Sacrament, ἐυλογησας και 'ἐυχαριστήσας, *having blessed and given thanks*, broke the Bread 'and distributed the Cup, and commanded the same thing to be 'done by us, from thence the Fathers and the Church have given 'it the name of the *Eucharist;* which word is made use of in the '*Syriack* Version, *Act* 2. 42. The Ancients likewise call it by other 'names; as that of λειτουργια, Σύναξις and Μυστήριον, which 'Compellations were likewise given to other Sacred Performances. 'It is not improperly called, *The Sacrament of the Altar ;* because 'it is performed or administered at the *Altar* or *Table ;* although 'it has not the same use, to which it doth allude.'—*Add. Notes to* NICHOLLS' *Com. Prayer.* p. 35.

NICHOLLS' remarks:—'As for the name *Lord's Supper* (which 'name the Papists cannot endure to have this Sacrament call'd by, 'because it destroys their notion of a propitiary Sacrifice for the 'living and the dead, and their use of private Mass,) we find this 'name given to it, as the proper one belonging to it in the Apostles' 'time, by *St Paul* himself: *When ye come together into one place* '*this is not to eat* THE LORD'S SUPPER, (1 *Cor.* xi. 20.). And 'besides, this name is frequently given it by Ancient Writers. By 'the Author *De Cœna Domini*, under St *Cyprian's* name; by 'St *Chrys.* Hom. XXVII. in 1 *Cor.* who makes the δεῖπνον κυριακὸν 'the δεσποτικὸν, which all are to partake of. And so does '*Theodoret* in 1 *Cor.* xi.'—*Com. Prayer* in loco.

BISHOP BEVERIDGE, in elucidating the 28th of our ARTICLES, 'tells us that this Sacrament is spoken to in the Article under the 'name of the *Supper of the Lord.* Which name, though the 'Papists are very angry at us for making use of it, yet we need 'not regard that, seeing the Scripture giveth us sufficient warrant 'for it, St Paul himself calling it the *Lord's Supper*, (1 *Cor.* xi. 20.) 'And therefore though the Fathers do often call it the *Eucharist*, 'yet do they frequently call it the *Lord's Supper* also. And there 'is good reason for the name too; for seeing it was instituted at 'eventide, yea, at supper-time, it may well be called a *supper;* 'and seeing it was instituted by the Lord himself, it may well be 'called the *Lord's Supper.*' (*p.* 243.)—*On the XXXIX Articles.* Vol. II.

ABP. WAKE says:—'It is called the *Lord's Supper*, because it 'was both instituted by our Lord at Supper, and was designed to 'succeed into the place of the Paschal Supper of 'the Jews.'— HOOK'S *Ch. Dict.* sub voce.

DR. HOOK writes:—'*The Lord's Supper.* An ancient name for 'the Sacrament of the *holy Eucharist.* The name occurs in 1 *Cor.* 'xi. 20.; but in that passage it is generally supposed by the most 'learned divines, that reference is made to the love feast, kept in 'imitation of our Lord's last Supper, which was previous to the 'original *Eucharist.* Thus much, however, says Dr. Waterland, 'is certain that in the Apostolical times the love feast and the '*Eucharist*, though distinct, went together, and were nearly allied 'to each other, and were both of them celebrated at one Meeting.'— *Church. Dict.* sub voce.

The REV. W. G. HUMPHRY states:—'The Sacrament is termed 'the *Lord's Supper*, from 1 *Cor.* xi. 20; 'When ye come together,' '&c.; although in this passage of St Paul the phrase probably 'includes the agape, or feast of charity, which was joined with the '*Eucharist*. See *Olshausen* on 1 Cor. xi. 20.' (*p.* 221.)—*Treatise on Bk. of Com. Prayer.*

The REV. J. E. RIDDLE writes:—'The term δεῖπνον κυριακόν, 'Sacra Cœna, Cœna Domini, *Lord's Supper*, has an historical 'reference to the institution of the rite by our blessed Lord on 'the night in which he was betrayed (*Matt.* xxvi. 20. 31; 1 *Cor.* 'xi. 20.); and so it intimates merely that the observance is to be 'regarded as a commemoration of our Saviour, and a repetition 'of his last intercourse with his disciples before his passion. Some 'critics maintain that this phrase, in 1 *Cor.* xi. the only passage 'of Scripture in which it occurs, is not to be regarded as signifying 'the *Lord's Supper*, strictly so called, or in its modern acceptation; 'but denotes rather the feast which accompanied the distribution 'and partaking of the consecrated elements. This position, how-'ever, has not been established; and it has been abundantly shewn 'that the early Christian writers applied this term as we do. See 'SUICERI *Observat. Sacr.* p. 91: CASAUB. *Exercit.* 16. *ad Baronii* 'annal. p. 450. seq: GERHARDI. *Soc. Theol.* t. x. p. 3.' (*p.* 543.)—*Christian Antiquities.*

II. The HOLY COMMUNION:—

NICHOLLS' speaking of '*the Communion*' says:—'This is plainly 'another Scriptural compellation of the same Holy Sacrament. "*The cup of blessing which we bless, is it not the* COMMUNION *of* "*the blood of Christ.*" (1 *Cor.* x. 16.). Which name is given to 'it partly because by this we testifie our *communion* with Christ 'our head. (*Damasc.* Orthodox. Fid. lib. IV.); partly because it 'unites us together with all our fellow Christians; and partly 'because all good Christians have a right to partake of it. (*Pachym.* 'in Areop. c. 3: *Chrysost.* Hom. xxvii. in 1 *Cor.*). Hence κοινωνεῖν 'is the common word to express the participation of this Sacra-'ment. St Chrysostom speaks of the ἀναξίως κοινωνούντων, of 'those that communicate unworthily. St Basil says, τεταρτον καθ' 'ἑβδομάδα κοινωνοῦμεν, we partake of the *Communion* four times a 'week. (*Ep.* 289.).'—*On Com. Prayer* in loco.

DR. HOOK writes on the word '*Communion*:'—'This is one of 'the names given to the Sacrament of the *Eucharist*, and was 'undoubtedly taken from St Paul's account of that Sacrament, 'where he teaches, as the learned Dr. Waterland observes, that 'the effect of this Service is the Communion of the body and blood 'of Christ (1 *Cor.* x. 16.). He does not, indeed, call the Sacrament 'by that *name*, as others have done since. He was signifying what 'the thing is, or what it does, rather than how it was then *called*.'—*Church Dict.* sub voce.

The REV. W. G. HUMPHRY observes:—'The term *Communion*, 'κοινωνία, as applied to the Lord's Supper was probably taken in 'the first instance from 1 *Cor.* x. 16, where we are said to have '*communion* (i. e. to be partakers) of the body and blood of Christ.

'Hence the Sacrament is called a *Communion*, because it unites us 'with Christ, and through him with each other......according to 'our present usage, to *communicate* is to partake of the *Communion*, 'and they who do so are said to be *Communicants*.' (*p.* 220.)—*Treatise on Bk. of Com. Prayer.*

The REV. J. E. RIDDLE states:—'The name by which this 'Sacrament has been most generally designated, is *The Communion* '(*κοινωνία*, communicatio, communio). This term has been in 'current use in all ages of the Church, and among all parties. It 'has been used both in a doctrinal or mystical sense, and in an 'historical and ecclesiastical signification. Doctrinally speaking, '*communion* denotes a Sacramental union and fellowship, which 'exists exclusively in and by the ordinance which it designates. 'It is so called say some, because it unites us with God; (quia 'nobis conjunctionem cum Deo conciliat, nosque regni ipsius con-'sortes ac participes reddit,—*Isidor. Pelus.* Ep. 228.). Others 'understand this *communion* especially of union and fellowship 'with the Saviour; and refer it either to the (supposed) connexion 'of his sacred body and blood with the elements of bread and wine; 'or to the union of the communicants with their head; or to their 'union among themselves in the bonds of holy love. In 1 *Cor.* x. 6, 'the expressions *κοινωνία τοῦ ἁίματος*, *communion of the blood*, and '*κοινωνια τοῦ σώματος τοῦ Χριστοῦ*, *communion of the body of Christ*, 'may be taken in either of these senses; and accordingly, inter-'preters differ in opinion as to whether the apostle speaks in this 'passage of a physical or of a moral union with Christ, and whether 'or not the expression *κοινωνία τοῦ υἱοῦ* is synonymous with it. 'In an historical and ecclesiastical sense, *communion* means a par-'taking in all the mysteries of the Christian religion, and so church 'fellowship, in its fullest sense, with all its accompanying rights 'and privileges. Hence the term *excommunication*. In a Liturgical 'sense, *communion* denotes sometimes the administration of the 'Sacrament, and sometimes the partaking of it.' (*p.* 544.)—*Christian Antiquities.*

III. The HOLY EUCHARIST:—

L'ESTRANGE writing upon the *Holy Communion* in the Apostolical age says that 'no spiritual, or temporal food, was received 'without some religious application to God, relative and directed 'to the ends for which those collations were prepared: which 'application, whether it concerned the creature destined for bodily, 'or for mystical refreshment, consisted of either two prayers dis-'tinct, or two distinct members of one prayer. The first was '*εὐχαριστια*, *Thanksgiving* to God for those benefits. The second '*εὐλογια Invocation*, of his blessing upon them. To speak appositly 'to the matter in hand, when this application related to the 'Elements separated for the Holy Communion, *Thanksgiving* was 'made to God the Father much to the same effect of this, that is, '*for the redemption of the world, by the death and passion of our 'Saviour Jesus Christ, &c.* And from this very use, the Com-'munion contracted the name of EUCHARIST, and not as hitherto 'hath been commonly supposed, from any words constituting Con-'secration. Consecration of the Elements was made indeed *with* 'Thanksgiving, not by it; *by blessing* it was performed, *by Blessing* 'joyned with *Thanksgiving* in one continued form of Prayer, or by '*Blessing* concomitant with *Thanksgiving* in two distinct forms.' (*p.* 201.)—*Alliance of Div. Offices.*

DEAN COMBER writes:—'Since the death of Christ hath reconciled God to mankind, and his intercession alone obtains all good 'things for us, we are enjoined to make all our prayers in his 'name; and, as a more powerful way of interceding, to commemorate his passion by celebrating the *holy Eucharist*, which 'in the purest ages was always joined to their publick and common 'prayer (*Acts* ii. 42.). And to evidence our Church wishes it were 'so still, she appoints a great part of this Office to be used on all 'Sundays and Holy-days, and orders the Priest to say it at the '*Altar*, the place where all prayers of the Church of old were 'wont to be made, because there was the proper place to commemorate Jesus our only Mediator, by whom all our prayers 'become accepted. And hence the Ancients call this Office "*the* '*Service of the Altar.*"' —Quoted in MANT's *Book of Com. Prayer* in loco.

WHEATLY appears to adopt the ideas of Dean Comber which we have just quoted. He says further 'that what we more compendiously express in that general conclusion of our prayers, 'through Jesus Christ our Lord, we more fully and forcibly 'represent in the celebration of the *holy Eucharist:* wherein we 'intercede on Earth, in conjunction with the great intercession of 'our High Priest in heaven, and plead in the virtue and merits 'of the same sacrifice here which He is continually urging for us 'there. And because of this near alliance between praying and 'communicating we find the *Eucharist* was always, in the purest 'ages of the Church, a daily part of the Common Prayer.' (*p.* 290.) —*Rat. Ill. of Book of Common Prayer.*

DR. WATERLAND says:—'*Sacramentum Eucharistiæ* is the name 'given to the Lord's Supper in our Latin Articles, signifying, 'properly, thanksgiving or blessing, and fitly denoting this holy 'Service as a Sacrifice of praise and thanksgiving. It occurs in 'Ignatius, Irenæus, Clemens of Alexandria, Origen, and others; 'and was adopted into the Latin language as may be seen from 'Tertullian and Cyprian in many places.'—Hook's *Church Dict.* Sub Voce.

The *late* REV. J. J. BLUNT (*Margaret Professor of Divinity* at the University of Cambridge), when elucidating points of Ritual, explains *Acts* ii. 42, thus:—"They continued stedfastly (1) in *the* "doctrine of the Apostles"—i. e. hearing and attending to the 'things spoken of them; and in *the* Communion (τῇ κοινωνίᾳ)— 'i. e. contributing to the Offertory......They continued stedfastly '(3) in *the* breaking of *the* bread—*i. e.* participating in the *Holy* '*Eucharist*, the very pivot of all primitive worship; and in *the* 'prayers—*i. e.* such prayers as appertained to the public worship 'of the Church, and were known.' (*p.* 284.)—*Duties of the Parish Priest.*

The REV. J. JEBB, speaking of the Communion Service, says:— 'This seeking for his (Christ's) special grace being in itself an act

'of praise and thanksgiving, and of most perfect commemoration,
'has therefore been from ancient times called the *Eucharist.*
(*p.* 454.)—*On Choral Service.*

The Rev. W. Palmer writes:—'We continually meet in the
'earliest writings of the Christian Fathers, the word *eucharistia,*
'or thanksgiving, applied both to the Service, and to the conse-
'crated elements, so great a portion of the liturgy in those days
'consisted of thanksgiving. The term was used in these senses
'by Ignatius in the apostolical age, by Justin Martyr, Irenæus,
'Clement of Alexandria, and Tertullian shortly afterwards, and
'thenceforward by numerous Christian writers. We have, how-
'ever, an earlier allusion to the liturgy under the title of *eucha-*
'*ristia,* or thanksgiving, in the first Epistle of St Paul to the
'Corinthians; where, in forbidding and reasoning against the
'practice of some persons, who used the miraculous gift of tongues
'in an improper manner, namely, by celebrating the liturgy in an
'unknown language, he says, "when thou shalt *bless* with the
"spirit, how shall he that occupieth the room of the unlearned
"say Amen at thy *giving of thanks,* seeing he understandeth not
"what thou sayest?" (1 *Cor.* xiv. 16.). The meaning of this
'passage is obvious: "If thou shalt bless the bread and wine in
"an unknown language which has been given to thee by the
"Holy Spirit, how shall the layman say Amen, 'so be it,' at the
"'end of thy thanksgiving or liturgy, seeing he understandeth not
"what thou sayest?" It is undeniable that St Paul in this place
'uses exactly the same expressions to describe the supposed action
'as he has employed a short time before in designating the sacra-
'ments of Christ's body and blood, and describing our Lord's
'consecration at the last supper. "The cup of *blessing* which we
"*bless,* is it not the communion of the blood of Christ?" (1 *Cor.*
'x. 16.). "The Lord Jesus, in the same night in which he was
"betrayed, took bread, and when he had *given thanks* he brake it."
'The language of St Paul also in the passage under consideration,
'as well as the action which he describes, is perfectly conformable
'to the description given by Justin Martyr of the celebration of the
eucharist.' (*p.* 113.)—*Origines Liturg.* Vol. II.

The Rev. J. E. Riddle says:—'The very ancient and general
'appellation εὐχαριστία, eucharistia, *The Eucharist,* does not itself
'occur in the New Testament; but it is founded upon the sacred
'phraseology. In the history of the institution, *Matt.* xxvi. 27.
'*Mark* xiv. 23, and *Luke* xxii. 19, the Evangelists use the expres-
'sion εὐχαριστήσας, which is repeated by St Paul, 1 *Cor.* xi. 24.
'And with evident allusion to this, the sacred ordinance is termed
'εὐχαριστία. in Justin Mart. *Apol.* i. 65. 66; Iren. *adv. Hæres.*
'iv. 34; Clem. Alex. *Pædagog.* ii. 2; because, according to the
'explanation of ancient writers, gratitude for the divine mercy
'and grace is the chief requisite in those who partake of the
'Lord's Supper.' (*p.* 545.)—*Christian Antiquities.*

THE TITLE OF THE OFFICE.

557.—With regard to the *Title* of this Office, we find that before the Office was incorporated into the Prayer Book it was simply styled "THE ORDER OF THE COMMUNION." (A. D. 1548); but when introduced into the *first Liturgy* of Edward vith (1549), it was designated "THE SUPPER OF THE LORD, AND THE HOLY COMMUNION, COMMONLY CALLED THE MASSE." Anciently, the form of administration of this Sacrament was known in the Eastern, or Greek, Church, as the "*Liturgy;*" or rather as, "*The Divine,*" or "*The Mystical, Liturgy,*" (λειτουργία, from λειτος, *public*, and ἔργον, *a work*; hence any public act or duty). And since no particular formulary was prescribed by our Lord, the early Churches, or their founders, used to frame for the Holy Communion a Service of their own, deriving the essentials from authentic sources, and differing only in the circumstantials of order and ceremonial. These *Liturgies* they distinguished by the names of their founders; hence the Liturgies of Jerusalem, Cæsarea, Constantinople, Alexandria, Rome, &c. have been styled the Liturgies of St. James, St. Basil, St. Chrysostom, St. Mark, St. Clement, &c. respectively. In the primitive Church, however, the word *Liturgy* was not limited to so restricted a sense, but was applied to *Divine Service* in general (*Suicer* ad voc); like as we read in the Septuagint, παρεστάναι ἔναντι τοῦ Κυρίου λειτουργεῖν, "*to stand before the Lord to minister to Him.*" (*Deut.* x. 8.); so in the *New Testament* λειτουργούντων δὲ αὐτῶν τῷ Κυρίῳ, "*as they ministered to the Lord*" &c. (*Acts* xiii. 2.): and this extended meaning has been adopted by the best Divines of the Church of England, who make the expression synonymous with '*Common Prayer,*' as may be seen in the Preface of our Prayer Book. The earlier Western Church employed occasionally the word '*Liturgy,*' to designate the administration of this sacrament; but the terms '*Communio,*' and, *Missa,*' were more generally used, and these words are found in the Title of the Office in Edward's first Prayer Book as shewn above, where they are translated the '*Communion,*" and the '*Mass.*' The origin of the term *Communion* has been already explained. (See *par.* 552.)

558.—The word "*Missa*," (anglicè, "*Mass*") is derived, Cardinal Bona informs us, from the Latin *a mittendo*, whence the expression "*Ite, Missa est*," (i. e. *Congregatio Ecclesia*) "Depart, the assembly is dismissed;" the usual form of dismissing the Congregation;—*first*, for the dismission of the Catechumens and others at the beginning of the administration; and, *secondly*, of the Faithful at the conclusion of the Service. (MASKELL *Anct. Liturgies*. p. 145: RIDDLE'S *Christian Antiq*. p. 548). Among the more ancient Ecclesiastical writers, '*Missa*' sometimes denoted the "*Liturgy*," or "Office of the Holy Communion," and sometimes the *dismission* from any Divine Office: at one time also, *Missa* was applied to that portion only of the Service at which Catechumens were present; at another time, to that portion at which only the Faithful were admitted. Occasionally, the word denoted certain *Collects*, or "*Prayers*," or "*Lections*," or the "*Hora Canonica;*" and in later times a *Feast-day;* as *Christ-mas, Michael-mas*, &c. Some writers, however, have endeavoured to trace the origin of '*Missa*' to the Hebrew '*Missah*,' an oblation, as Baronius has done: others refer it to the Greek μύησις; and some, of whom Albaspinæus is the chief authority, to the German '*Mess*' or '*Mes*:' (*ibid*. 83. 144.—*Du Cange*.—PALMER'S *Orig. Lit.* I.): but the interpretation given by Cardinal Bona is the one generally received.

BISHOP COSINS (*ob*. 1672) writes:—'The word *Missa* is used by 'the *Latin* Church in another sense, than that which does obtain at 'this day among the Papists: for the ancient *Latins* said, *Ite Missa* '*est*, (as the *Greeks* used the word ἄφεσις), meaning thereby '*Mission* or *Dismission;* as they used the word *Remissa* for '*Remissio*. From hence it came to pass, that from this only and 'last Act, they called the whole complication of actions in the 'Eucharist by the name of *Missa*. *Missa* is used for *dismission*, in 'the 84th Canon of the Fourth Council of *Carthage*, and in the '*First* Canon of the Council of *Valentia*, in which mention is made 'of the *Missa Catechumenorum*. For as heretofore the dismission 'was two-fold so the Service was likewise double, that which 'belonged to the Catechumens, and that which belonged to the 'Faithful. The Catechumens' *Missa* reached to the Offertory (who 'were obliged to depart before the offering was made), the *Missa* of 'the Faithful beginning with the Offertory. For each of these 'Offices followed immediately one after the other, but only that the

'*Dismission* of the Catechumens and the Penitents came between 'them......But the word *Missa*, as it is used at present among the 'Papists, for a true and proper *Sacrifice of Christ* offered in every 'Celebration for the Living and the Dead, is never used among the 'Ancients. And for this reason the name of *Missa* or *Mass* is 'rejected by the Church of England, which having exploded the 'opinion of the *Sacrifice of the Mass*, does disclaim the use of the 'word *Missa* in Modern, though not in the Ancient sense. Indeed 'in the *First Edition of the Common-Prayer-Book* under Edward the 'Sixth, the name of the *Mass* (as the Liturgy was then commonly 'called) was retained. But when men who were leavened with the 'doctrine of the Papists, detorted it to a wrong sense, it seemed 'good to the Bishops, that in the *Second Edition* of the Liturgy 'it should be omitted;—*Add. notes to* NICHOLLS' *Book of Com. 'Prayer*. p. 35.

DR. HOOK writes under the word *Mass*:—'In Latin *Missa*. 'This word at first imported nothing more than the dismissal of a 'Church assembly. By degrees it came to be used for an *Assembly* 'and for Church Service; and from signifying Church Service in 'general, it came at length to denote the *Communion Service* in par-'ticular, and so that most emphatically came to be called *Mass*. 'Since the Reformation, the word has been generally confined to 'express the form of celebrating the holy Communion in the 'Romish Church;—*Church Dict.*

The REV. F. PROCTER says:—'The traces of the form of 'worship used by the Christian converts, which we find in the New 'Testament, refer to the Eucharist, as being emphatically the 'Christian Service. Hence naturally arose the Ecclesiastical use of 'the word *Liturgy*, to designate the form employed by the Church 'in celebrating that office, which was called the *Mass* by the 'mediæval and the Latin Church, but which we now call the *Lord's 'Supper*, and the Holy Communion. From the scanty remains 'of very early Christian times we may gather so much concerning 'this form, as to allow that the various Churches, which were 'founded by the Apostles, had each a service for the Eucharist; 'and that these Liturgies, while differing it may be in some 'particulars all agreed in their main features (p. 281)......It is a 'general opinion that Liturgies were not committed to writing 'before the end of the second, or even of the third century; nor in-'deed can we confidently assert that we have a perfect example of 'so high antiquity.' (*p.* 283)......*Hist. of Book of Com. Prayer.*

559. The term *Mass*, as we have just seen, having passed from its simple and original meaning to a use and signification widely different, became very objectionable to the Reformers, and excited so considerable a controversy, that at the *Revision of the Liturgy* in 1552, the word was rejected and that, change made in the Title of the Office which has continued to the present time; thus:—

"The Order for the Administration of the Lord's Supper, or "Holy Communion."—(1552, 1559, 1604, 1662.)

560. The Statutes more immediately affecting the *Holy Communion*, to which we may have occasion to refer in treating on these Rubrics, are as follow:—

1 *Edw.* VI. *c.* 1.—On *Speaking against* the Sacrament, and the receiving thereof under both kinds.
2 & 3 *Edw.* VI. *c.* 1.—On *Uniformity*.
1. *Eliz. c.* 2.—On *Uniformity*.
7. *Jas.* I. *c.* 2.—Persons *naturalized*, and *restored in blood*, to receive the Sacrament &c.
9. *Geo.* IV. *c.* 17.
2. *Gul.* IV. *c.* 7. (Ireland) } *repeal* of the *Test. Acts*.

561.—The Canons affecting the *Holy Communion*, which may come under our notice, are these:—

Canon 20.—On the provision of the Bread and Wine.
Canon 21.—The Holy Communion to be received *thrice yearly*.
Canon 22.—*Warning* of Holy Communion to be given.
Canon 23.—*Undergraduates* to receive *four times* yearly.
Canons 24 & 25.—*Ornaments of the Minister* at the Communion.
Canons 26 & 109.—*Notorious offenders* to be repelled (26); and to be presented (109).
Canons 27 & 110.—*Schismatics* to be repelled (27); and to be presented (110).
Canon 28.—*Strangers* to be repelled.
Canons 56 & 57.—*Lecturers* and *unpreaching Ministers* to administer the Sacraments.
Canon 71.—Holy Communion not to be administered in *private* houses.
Canon 112.—*Non-Communicants at Easter* to be presented.

562.—The Articles (of the XXXIX) bearing on the *Lord's Supper* are:—

Article 25th.—Of the *Sacraments*.
Article 26th.—*Of the Unworthiness of Ministers*.
Article 28th.—Of the *Lord's Supper*.
Article 29th.—Of the *wicked which eat not the Body of Christ*.
Article 30th.—Of *Both Kinds*.

563.—The Homilies touching on the *Lord's Supper* are to be found in the *Second Book* of Homilies (see Art. xxxv. of the XXXIX Articles), and are entitled:—

Of Common Prayer and *Sacraments* in a known tongue.
Of the *worthy receiving of the Sacrament*.

[Church-Membership.]

564.—Before proceeding with the Rubrics, it may be remarked, that every person who has been *baptized* and *confirmed*, or '*who is ready and desirous to be confirmed*,' has a legal right to be admitted to the Holy Communion unless he be labouring under a disqualification which would require the Officiating Priest to repel him. The *legal disqualifications* sanctioning such a proceeding will be discussed presently. This right of Communion is enforced by the Statute, 1 *Edw.* VI. *c.* 1, which is still of binding authority, and will be found enjoined in the *7th Section* of the Act, directing the administration of the blessed Sacrament to the people under "both kinds," thus:—

......'The Minister *shall not* without a lawful cause *deny* the 'same to any person that will devoutly and humbly desire it.'— I *Edw.* VI. *c.* 1. §. 7.

565.—This admission to the Holy Communion at once establishes the recipient a *Member* of the United Church of England and Ireland, whether he be one who has been baptized and brought up from infancy in the Church, or one who has become in later years a convert to her doctrine and her discipline. In the latter case, whatever may have been his religious views and tenets before, he is to be considered now a *bonâ fide* Member so long as he holds to the doctrine, rites, and ceremonies of our Church embodied in her Articles, Canons, Homilies, and Liturgy.

Mr. A. J. Stephens (*Barrister-at-law*), says: — 'A person in 'order to have a *legal right* to be admitted to the Holy Communion, 'must either have been "*confirmed*," or be "*ready and desirous to* '*be confirmed;*" and the order of Confirmation only applies to 'those that are "baptized, and come to *years of discretion.*" It 'therefore seems that no person has a *legal right* to be admitted to 'the Holy Communion until the age of 14, which is the common 'standard at which both Males and Females, are, by our Law, 'presumed to have arrived at *years of discretion;* the law pre-'suming them at those years to be *doli capaces*, and capable of 'discerning between good and evil' (*p.* 1058.).........and *when* '*admitted* to the Holy Communion he becomes *eo instanti*, whatever 'his previous religious tenets may have been, a *Member* of the 'United Church of England and Ireland: and the right to be so 'admitted he can enforce by *mandamus*.' (*p.* 1061.)—*Book of Com. Prayer.* E. H. S.

566.—CHURCH-MEMBERSHIP, and *Membership in full Communion*, have been thus distinguished by our Colonial Bishops:—

AT A CONFERENCE OF THE METROPOLITAN AND SUFFRAGAN BISHOPS OF THE PROVINCE OF AUSTRALIA *held at Sydney* from Oct. 1st to Sep. 1st, A. D. 1850, it was decreed:—'We acknowledge 'as *Members of the Church of England* all persons who having been '*duly baptized* with water, in the name of the Father, Son, and 'Holy Ghost, are conformable to the doctrine, government, rites, 'and ceremonies contained in the Book of Common Prayer, it being 'understood that they are entitled to claim at the hands of its 'Ministers the rites and ceremonies of our Church, so long only as 'they shall continue conformable to the extent above required. By 'a *Member of the Church of England in full Communion*, we under-'stand every one who, being conformable as aforesaid, is a *partaker* '*of the Holy Communion*, as required by the rules of the Church.' —*Eccl. Gazette*, June 10, 1851.

Similarly, at *a Conference of the Bishops of our North American Colonies*, (viz. of the Bishops of Quebec, Toronto, Newfoundland, Fredericton, and Montreal,) it was thus decided:—'Doubts being 'entertained who are to be regarded as *Members of the Church of* '*England* in these Colonies, and, as such what are their special 'duties and rights, we are of opinion that *Church-Membership* 'requires (1) admission into the Christian covenant by *Holy* '*Baptism*, as our Lord commanded, "in the name of the Father, "and of the Son, and of the Holy Ghost;" (2) that all *Church* '*Members* are bound according to their knowledge and oppor-'tunities, to consent and conform to the Rules and Ordinances of 'the Church; and (3) according to their ability, and as God hath 'blessed them, to contribute to the support of the Church, and 'specially of those who minister to them in holy things. Upon 'the fulfilment of these duties, they may, as *Church Members*. 'claim at our hands, and at the hands of our Clergy generally, all 'customary services and administrations......We are further of 'opinion that *Church Members in full communion*, are those only 'who receive with their brethren the *Sacrament of the Lord's* '*Supper* at the hands of their lawful Ministers, as directed and 'enjoined by the Canons and the Rubrics of our Prayer Book.'—*Eccl. Gazette*, August 10th, 1852.

THE RUBRICS.

567.—We must now proceed with the consideration of the *Rubrics*, four of which immediately follow the Title of the Office. The first three apply to the Communicants, and their character of life; and the fourth, which is divided into two clauses, relates, first, to the preparation of the Lord's Table; and, secondly, to the Priest. In the "*Alterations*" recommended in the Liturgy in 1689, the following Rubrics were proposed to be inserted immediately after the Title:—

> '*When there is no Communion, there is not to be any Com-* '*munion Service.*'
> '*Q. The Minister that consecrates ought allwaies to be a** '*Archbp., Bishop, or Presbyter* [*N.B. "*Archbp.*" was inserted 'afterward leaving the Article *a* unaltered].'—*Alterations of Bk. of Com. Prayer: prepared by the Royal Commissioners,* &c. 1689.

These, however, were never accomplished; we will, therefore, pass to the directions of our Prayer Book.

COMMUNICANTS TO GIVE NOTICE THE DAY BEFORE.

(1) ¶. '*So many as intend to be partakers of the Holy Communion* '*shall signify their names to the Curate at least some* '*time the day before.*' (1662.)—Present Book of Common Prayer.

568.—This Rubric is one that affects the *Laity* rather than the Clergy; but from neglect, oversight, or indifference, it has completely grown into desuetude; and is now neither observed by the Laity, nor impressed upon them by the Clergy. In the *American Liturgy* it is omitted on this very account. The earlier of our Liturgies give this Rubric in the following words:—

> '*So many as intend to be partakers of the Holy Communion,* '*shall signify their names to the Curate over night; or else* '*in the Morning afore the beginning of Morning Prayer* (*Matins* 1549,) *or immediately after.*'—(1549, 1552, 1559, 1604.)

This variation affords us evidence that there was an interval between Morning Prayer and the Communion Office sufficient for the "Curate" to fulfil the intentions of the Rubric; and, consequently, that the Services of Morning Prayer, Litany, and Communion, were not so closely united into one Service as they now are, and have been since the *Revision* of the Prayer Book in 1662, as we have before shewn in *Vol.* B. There was an amendment proposed in the "*Alterations*" of the Royal Commissioners in 1689, viz. that the words, '*at least,*' in the Rubric should be struck out; and that '*the week before*' should be substituted for '*the day before:*' but these changes were not effected.

569.—It would materially strengthen and enhance the ministrations of our Church if the observation of this Rubric could in some measure be revived; and the "Curate" would do well to instruct and exhort his people now and then on the design of this injunction, so as to stimulate them to self-examination, and self-reproof; as well as to a stricter attendance at this holy ordinance. The object of the Rubric has been variously defined; some thinking its intention was to ascertain what (a) *number* was to be provided for; others, to inquire into the qualifications of the applicants as to fitness, (b) whether, that is to say, they had *come to years of discretion*, and had been *baptized* and *confirmed*, or, were '*ready and desirous to be confirmed;*' or whether they were labouring under any of the disqualifications objected to in the Canons, and in the two following Rubrics, such as being (c) *excommunicate*, (d) *idiotic* or *lunatic*, (e) *notorious offenders*, (f) *malicious*, (g) *schismatics*, (h) or *strangers;* all which we shall presently discuss with reference to the *legal* powers possessed by the "Curate" in these matters. There are some writers also who think conformity to this Rubric would be of great service to the "Curate" in enabling him thus to discover who *absent themselves*, and need his exhortations to a more regular attendance; but the numbers who communicate in these modern times would render the giving of this '*notice the day before*' inconvenient, if not impracticable. We will, however, quote a few authorities on the several points above enumerated:—

L'Estrange (*ob.* 1659—60), interpreting the Rubric as meaning immediately after the ending of Morning Prayer adds:—'And this 'I take it, is plainly inferrible from the very scope of this Rubrick, 'which was not as some may think, [to allot some space of time to '*make provision* according to the number of the Communicants] for 'the *interstitium* between the beginning of Morning Prayer, and the 'time of the Communion, is so slender a space for the *provision* of 'those Elements, as should there be a want, not half the Country 'Villages in this Kingdom can be timely supplied therewith: No, it 'is clearly otherways, and that the design was, that the Curate 'might have timely notice of the several persons offering themselves 'to the Communion, and consequently might persuade *notorious* '*Offenders*, or *malicious persons* to abstain, and if obstinate, abso-

'lutely *reject them* according to the purport of the two Rubricks 'following; for that those two Rubricks are of the same Syntax and 'coherence with this, the Relative Pronoun *those* infallibly implieth, 'for what, *those?* but they who were ordered before to *give in their* '*names over night, or else in the morning, before the beginning of* '*Morning Prayer, or immediately after.*' (*p.* 162.) — *Alliance of Divine Offices.*

NICHOLLS' (*ob.* 1712.) writes:—'The reason of this Injunction of 'the Rubrick is, That the Minister of the Parish may have time to 'inform himself of the parties who design to receive; so that, if 'there be any among them who are *not duly qualified* to partake of 'that Sacrament, he may persuade them to abstain for some time; 'or, in case of their refusal, *repel* them. Now in several cases 'persons may be unqualified to partake of this Sacrament, either by 'the *Prescript of God's Word* or by the *Canons* of the Church. '*First*, a want, or a contempt of the Rite of *Confirmation* un-'qualifies persons to receive; for the Rubrick of the Common 'Prayer, which is confirmed by the Act of Uniformity, says, "*No* "*one shall be admitted unto the Holy Communion, until such time* "*as he be Confirmed, or be ready and desirous to be Confirmed.*"...... 'The like is enjoined by our Provincial Constitutions; "*Nullus ad* '*Sacramentum*," &c. "*Let no one be admitted to the Sacrament of the* "*Body and Blood of our Lord, unless in the Article of Death, unless* "*he be Confirmed, or unless he have a reasonable Impediment for his* "*not receiving Confirmation,*" (Prov. Linw. *Cap. de Sacr. Unc.*) "And the *Gloss* says, that the only reasonable impediment is the 'want of a Bishop near the place. *Secondly*, persons *Excommunicate*, 'or who are *doing Penance* by Church-Censure, for any notorious 'fault, are unqualified to receive; for such persons are shut out 'from the *κοινωνία*, or Communion, and therefore are called by the 'ancients *ἀκοίνηζοι*, &c., *Excommunicati*. And to venture upon 'receiving the Communion under such censure was look'd upon, 'by Antiquity, as one of the greatest faults which any person could 'be guilty of......*Thirdly*, persons under *Frenzy*, or those who are 'possessed by an *Evil Spirit*, are unqualified to partake of the Holy 'Communion, (*Vid. Linw. Prov.* in the place before cited; *Dionys.* '*Areop. Cap.* 3.) Now persons who are under the foregoing un-'qualifications, may lawfully be *refused admission* to the Com-'munion by the Minister: for the Ecclesiastical Law imposes great '*penalties upon the Minister* who shall give them the Communion in 'such cases. *Fourthly*, a person may be unqualified by *notorious* '*wickedness*, or *flagitiousness of life.*' — *Book of Common Prayer* in loco.

WHEATLY (*ob.* 1742.) remarks:—'The design of which Rubric 'was partly that the Minister, by this means knowing the *number of* '*his Communicants*, might the better judge how *to provide* the 'Elements of Bread and Wine sufficient for the occasion; but chiefly, 'as appears from the following Rubrics, that he might have time to 'inform himself of the parties who intended to receive; that so if 'there were any among them not duly *qualified*, he might persuade 'them to abstain of their own accords; or, if they obstinately offered 'themselves, absolutely *reject* them.' (*p.* 292.)—*Rat. Ill. of Book of Common Prayer.*

SHEPHERD (*ob:* 1805) observes:—'The principal object of this 'injunction is, to afford the Clergyman the means of learning what 'persons intend to Communicate; that if any should appear to him 'not to be duly *qualified*, he may have an opportunity of conversing 'privately with them, and of dissuading them from approaching the 'Lord's Table. One disqualification is contempt, or wilful neglect, 'of *Confirmation*......Persons *excommunicate* or *insane*, *notorious* '*offenders*, and some others, must likewise be *refused* admission to 'the Communion; and the Clergyman who administers it to them, 'is, by our ecclesiastical laws, subjected to *very severe penalties*...... 'A secondary reason for requiring this notice to be given to the 'Minister, is to inform him which of his Parishioners *absent themselves* 'from the Communion, that he may admonish them of their neglect, 'and seize every favourable opportunity of exhorting them to 'a more regular attendance. A third reason is to enable the 'Minister to ascertain the *number* of Communicants, that he may 'judge what proportion of bread and wine it may be necessary for 'him to place upon the Table, and to consecrate.' (*p.* 150.)—*Eluc. of Book of Com. Prayer*. Vol. II.

At *a Conference of the Bishops of our North American Colonies* in 1852 it was decreed:—'We hold it to be of 'great importance that the Clergy should attend to the directions of 'the Rubric which precede the administration of the Holy Communion, 'respecting "*open and notorious evil livers*, and those who have *done* "*wrong* to their neighbours by word or deed, and those also betwixt "whom they perceived *malice* and *hatred* to reign;" and that the 'members of the church should signify to the Minister their 'intention to *present* themselves at the Holy Table, especially when 'they arrive in any place as *strangers*, or when, being residents in 'such place, they are purposing to communicate *for the first time*. 'We conceive that it would greatly promote the welfare of the 'Church, if all our members, who may be *travelling* from one place 'to another, were furnished with a *certificate of their membership* and 'their standing in the Church.' (Present—the Bishops of Quebec, Toronto, Newfoundland, Frederiton, and Montreal.)—*Eccl. Gazette.* August 10. 1852.

The REV. F. PROCTER says upon this '*giving of notice*:'—'The 'practice has fallen into disuse, and accordingly the Rubric is 'omitted in the American Prayer-Book; Ecclesiastical hinder-'ances to Communion are, *Contempt of Confirmation*, and *Excom-'munication*: personal hinderances are *frenzy*, and *notorious crime*.' (*p.* 316. *note*).—*History of Book of Com. Prayer.*

570. We may now briefly discuss the questions imported into this Rubric by the above authorities, and see how far they can be maintained in connection with it, or otherwise. We will adopt the arrangement we have employed in the preceding paragraph; and begin with

571. (*a*) The NUMBER *of Communicants, and the provision for them*—The Minister is not required to decide on this point till he

arrives at the prayer for the Church Militant, where there is a *Rubric* directing him to place on the Table so much Bread and Wine as he may think necessary:—what *quantity* may be necessary he has no other means of ascertaining than by observing how many of his usual Communicants are present during the reading of the Offertory Sentences. The Rubric, therefore, we are now considering has no relation to the *number*, or the *provision* for the Communicants. There is, however, a Rubric at the end of the Communion Service on the question of number, enjoining that '*there shall be no Communion except four* (*or three at* '*the least*) *communicate with the Priest.*' (See *postea*).

572. (*b*) Those Unconfirmed, or *not* '*ready and desirous to be confirmed*,' are to be excluded from the Holy Communion, as laid down in the *Rubric* at the end of the order for Confirmation (See *postea*); and, *à fortiori*, those *unbaptized*, and not *come to years of discretion*; this question, therefore, does not come under the Rubric before us.

573. (*c*) The Excommunicate are to be excluded from the Holy Communion. This was the ancient discipline; but this *disqualification* is now obsolete, the Church has practically no longer any power to exercise spiritual censures for the awakening of the consciences of transgressors; we find by the statute 53 *Geo.* III. *c.* 127. that *Excommunication* is commuted to *six months imprisonment:* the *second* and *third sections* enact

.........'That nothing in this Act contained shall prevent any 'Ecclesiastical court from pronouncing or declaring persons to be '*excommunicate* in definitive sentences, or in interlocutory decrees 'having the force and effect of definitive sentences, such sentences 'or decrees being pronounced as spiritual censures for offences 'of Ecclesiastical cognizance, in the same manner as such court 'might lawfully have pronounced or declared the same, had this act 'not been passed.'—*Sect.* 2.

'And be it further enacted, that *no person who shall be so* '*pronounced or declared excommunicate shall incur any civil penalty* '*or incapacity whatever* in consequence of such excommunication, 'save such *imprisonment, not exceeding six months*, as the court pro-'nouncing or declaring such person excommunicate shall direct.'—*Sect.* 3.—(5. *Geo.* III. *c.* 127.).

574. (*d*) The Idiot, and the Lunatic, must be excluded from the Holy Communion. This proceeding would be a matter of course; for not being in possession of their right mind, nor under the control of reason, not only would this holy Service be to them incomprehensible and a mockery, but their conduct would be attended with "*brawling*," and the "*disturbing of the Congregation*,"

which are in themselves offences against the statute law (See *Vol.* **B**), and would call for their immediate removal from the Church by the Churchwardens. The Idiot and the Lunatic therefore, may justly be repelled from the Holy Communion; but the question as affecting them is not involved in the present Rubric.

(*e*) NOTORIOUS EVIL-LIVERS, and (*f*) the MALICIOUS, TO BE REJECTED.

575.—Here we have two Rubrics, and two of the Canons (of 1603), elucidating this important point, as well as assisting us in connecting the first Rubric with these two which immediately follow it, as we may infer from the opening words, '*and if any of those,*' i.e. of those who 'intend to be partakers of the Holy Communion and have signified their names to the Curate sometime the day before.' This second Rubric thus reads:—

(2). ¶. '*And if any of those be an open and notorious 'evil liver, or have done any wrong to his neighbours by 'word or deed, so that the Congregation be thereby offended; 'the Curate, having knowledge thereof, shall call him, and advertise him, that in anywise he presume not to come to the Lord's Table, 'until he hath openly declared himself to have truly repented and 'amended his former naughty life, that the Congregation may 'thereby be satisfied, which before were offended; and that he hath 'recompensed the parties, to whom he hath done wrong; or at 'least declare himself to be in full purpose so to do, as soon as he 'conveniently may.*' (1662). Present Book of Common Prayer.

This Rubric has suffered little alteration since its first appearance in the original Liturgy of *Edw.* VI. A. D. 1549. It then read as follows, where we have introduced in Roman letters the changes which have been subsequently made:—

'*And if any of those be an open and notorious evil liver,* so 'that the Congregation ('Church' Lit.) by him is ('be thereby,' '1662) offended, *or have done any wrong to his neighbours 'by word or deed; the Curate* ('having knowledge thereof,' 1552, '1559, 1604. 1662) *shall call him and advertize him* ('That,' 1662) '*in any wise not to presume* ('he presume not to come,' 1662) '(not to presume to come;' *Sc. Lit.*) *to the Lord's Table, until he 'have* ('hath,' 1662) *openly declared himself to have truly 'repented, and amended his former naughty life, that the Con-*

'*gregation* ('Church,' Sc. Lit) *may thereby be satisfied, which* '*afore* ('before,' 1662) *were offended; and that he have* ('hath' '1662) *recompensed the parties whom he hath done wrong unto* '('to whom he hath done wrong,' 1662), *or at the least* ('at least,' '1662. 'declare himself to,' 1552, 1559, 1604, Sc. L.) *be in full pur-* '*pose so-to-do, as soon as he conveniently may.*'—(1549, 1552, '1559, 1604.) KEELING. p. 166, 167.—

It will be seen also that the clause '*So that the Congregation by him is*, (or *be thereby*, 1662) *offended*,' was transferred at the *last Review* in 1662 from the middle of the first clause to the end of it, so as to embrace likewise the *wrong-doing to his neighbour* in the offence to the Congregation.

576.—The *third* Rubric, respecting the repelling of those from the Holy Communion between whom *malice* and *hatred* are known to reign, being so closely allied to the Rubric preceding in object and effect, it will be necessary that they be considered together; we therefore introduce it here, as follows:—

(3). ¶. '*The same order shall the Curate use with those* '*betwixt whom he perceiveth malice and hatred to reign; not* '*suffering them to be partakers of the Lord's Table, until* '*he know them to be reconciled. And if one of the parties so* '*at variance be content to forgive from the bottom of his heart* '*all that the other hath trespassed against him, and to make* '*amends for that he himself hath offended; and the other party* '*will not be persuaded to a godly unity, but remain still in his* '*frowardness and malice: the Minister in that case ought to* '*admit the penitent person to the Holy Communion, and not him* '*that is obstinate. Provided that every Minister so repelling* '*any, as is specified in this, or the next precedent paragraph* '*of this Rubric, shall be obliged to give an account of the same* '*to the Ordinary within fourteen days after at the farthest.* '*And the Ordinary shall proceed against the offending person* '*according to the Canon.*' (1662)—Present Book of Com. Prayer.

This Rubric, as far as the word '*obstinate*,' was introduced into the *first Liturgy*, of Edward VI. A. D. 1549, and continued through the several *Revisions* of 1552, 1559, 1604, and 1662. At the last *Review* in 1662, the final clause beginning with the word '*Provided*,' and which refers the matter to the Ordinary, was annexed.*

* In the AMERICAN LITURGY the first of these *Rubrics* reads as follows, the Roman letters indicating the parts which differ from our Rubric, and the full points (......) where omissions occur:—

577.—The two CANONS (of 1603), which instruct the Minister on these points, and enforce the injunctions of the above Rubrics, are *Canon* 26, and *Canon* 109; the 26th CANON is entitled "*Notorious Offenders not to be admitted to the Communion,*" and thus reads:—

'*No Minister shall* in anywise *admit to the receiving of the 'Holy Communion*, any of his cure or flock, which be openly known 'to *live in sin notorious*, without repentance; nor any who have '*maliciously* and *openly contended* with their neighbours, until 'they shall be reconciled; *nor any Churchwardens* or *Sidemen*, who, 'having taken their *Oaths to present* to their Ordinaries all such 'public Offences as they are particularly charged to enquire of 'in their several parishes, shall (notwithstanding their said Oaths, 'and that their faithful discharging of them is the chief means 'whereby public Sins and Offences may be reformed and punished) 'wittingly and willingly, desperately and irreligiously, incur the 'horrible crime of *perjury*, either in *neglecting* or in *refusing to 'present* such of the said enormities and public offences, as they 'know themselves to be committed in their said Parishes, or are 'notoriously offensive to the Congregation there; although they be 'urged by some of their neighbours, or by their Minister, or 'by their Ordinary himself, to discharge their consciences *by 'presenting* of them and not to incur so desperately the said 'horrible sin of *perjury*.'—CANON. 26.

578.—The 109th CANON enumerates the *evil habits* which give offence to the Congregation, and call for *rejection from the Holy Communion.* It is entitled, "*Notorious Crimes and Scandals to be certified into Ecclesiastical Courts by Presentment;*" and thus reads:—

'If among those who come to be partakers of the Holy Com'munion, the Minister shall know any to *be an open or notorious 'evil liver*, or to *have done any wrong to his neighbours by word or 'deed, so that the Congregation be thereby offended*, (......) he shall '*advertize him, that* (......) *he presume not to come to the Lord's 'Table until he* have *openly declared himself to have truly 'repented and amended his former* evil *life, that the Congregation 'may thereby be satisfied;* (......) *and that he hath recompensed 'the parties to whom he hath done wrong; or at least declare him'self to be in full purpose so to do, as soon as he conveniently 'may.*'

The *other Rubric* varies but little in the AMERICAN LITURGY from that in our own Prayer Book, as we may thus perceive in Roman letters in the clauses annexed:—'*to make amends for that* wherein *he himself hath offended.*'—and in the first clause, '*repelling any, as is* herein *specified,......shall be obliged to give an 'account of the same to the Ordinary,......as soon as conveniently 'may be.*'

'If any offend their Brethren, either by *adultery, whoredom,* '*incest,* or *drunkenness,* or by *swearing, ribaldry, usury,* and 'any other uncleanness, and wickedness of life, the Churchwardens 'or Questmen, and Side-men, in their next *Presentments* to their 'Ordinaries, shall faithfully *present* all and every of the said 'Offenders, to the intent that they, and every of them, may be pun-'ished by the severity of the laws, according to their deserts; 'and *such notorious Offenders shall not be admitted to the Holy* '*Communion till they be reformed;*—CANON 109.

579.—It will be perceived that the first of these Rubrics (*Rubric* [2]) speaks of '*the open and notorious evil-liver,*' and '*the wrong-doer;*' and the second [3] of those between whom '*malice and hatred*' exist: the 26th CANON adverts to the same Offenders as the two Rubrics, but excludes from the Holy Communion likewise, the *Churchwardens* and *Sidemen,* who by wilfully neglecting to make '*Presentments*' of such Offenders to the Ordinary, are guilty of *perjury:* the 109th CANON strengthens the Rubrics by particularizing the Offences to which they refer, such as '*Adultery, whoredom, incest,* or *drunkenness,* or '*swearing, ribaldry, usury,* and any other *uncleanness,* 'and *wickedness of life.*' Now, there is very considerable difficulty involved in the interpretation to be assigned to the epithets '*open*' and '*notorious;*' and in defining, what may really be '*offensive to the Congregation;*' the Officiating Minister therefore must practice the greatest caution and delicacy and judgment in exercising the authority invested in him by these Rubrics, and Canons. One Rubric permits the 'Curate' to '*advertize,*' i.e. *admonish the offender to refrain* from the Holy Communion; the other directs him before repelling the Offender, should he reject his 'admonition,' *to take the advice of the Ordinary,* i.e. the *Bishop.* But we must observe, that *in law* no one comes under the designation of the Rubric,—'*a notorious evil-liver,*'—until declared so by the decision of a *Court of justice,* or by *confession;* so that publicly repelling any one from the Communion without these safe-guards might expose the 'Curate,' to an action for defamation. The CANONS may appear very precise and emphatic, but these are *not binding on the Laity* like as they are on the Clergy; and therefore the People at large are not amenable to their penalties; and whenever the Canons are contradicted by the Rubric, the Rubric must prevail. The usage also of making '*presentments*' of offences to the Ordinary is now obsolete, so that Churchwardens even are exempt from Ecclesiastical censures in this respect.*

580.—Hence the conclusion we arrive at is, that when necessity shall arise for questioning the propriety of a person presenting himself at the Holy Communion; and the "Curate," after enquiry, should think it expedient that he should be rejected; the individual should be first admonished to abstain: if he persist in the intention to present himself, and his misconduct has not been repented of, nor condoned, then the Churchwardens may be consulted, as to how far the evil has become an '*offence to the Congregation*,' and their opinion, if supporting that of the "Curate," might be put before the transgressor; who, if he *continue obstinate*, may then be warned not to present himself at the Holy Communion until the advice of the Bishop be taken therein. Still, it must be remembered that repelling a person from the Holy Communion, *without a legal justification*, is setting upon him such a mark of public infamy and disgrace, as will expose the Officiating Minister doing so, *ex suo motu*, or upon mere idle gossip, to an action in the Civil Courts for *defamation of character*. If, therefore, no *lawful* cause exists, which the Statute, 1 *Edw.* VI. *c.* 1. §. 7. requires, for denying the Holy Communion to a person, the Curate can be compelled by a mandamus at Common Law to administer it. Mr. Stephens indeed says, that 'the Curate has no power

---

* ARCHDEACON SHARP remarks on this part of *Canon.* 26:—'No doubt the design of this was very good, to represent to 'Churchwardens, in the strongest light, the guilt and bad con-'sequences of their not discharging this part of their duty faithfully 'and conscientiously. But I fear the injunction, considered as an 'act of discipline to be performed by the Minister, is almost 'impracticable.' (*p.* 101).—*On the Rubrics and Canons.*

'to try the question whether a person is, or is not, 'an *open* or *notorious evil liver*, or *offensive to the 'Congregation;* he cannot enforce the attendance of 'a witness; or impose an oath, if witnesses voluntarily 'tender themselves to be examined.' (STEPHENS' *Bk. of Com. Pr.* E. H. S. *p.* 1073.). In another work, this Author also remarks:—'It does not, however, 'seem that an action can be maintained against a 'Clergyman for refusing the Sacrament, unless such 'refusal be *malicious;* if, however, a Clergyman were 'improperly to refuse the Sacrament, the most ad-'visable course to adopt, would be to proceed against 'him under the Church Discipline Act, (3 & 4 *Vict. 'c.* 86.) for a breach of the Ecclesiastical law.' (*Laws Relating to the Clergy*, p. 630.). Mr. Stephens also discusses the judicial power of the Curate in this matter, in the *queries* following:—

'A * * * informs a Priest in Confession, that he is guilty of 'a crime; but at the same time declares himself impenitent, or 'rather glories in the crime; he is not suspected publicly of the 'crime; and therefore the Congregation is not scandalized. *Is 'the Minister, knowing this, but feeling bound not to divulge it, obliged 'nevertheless to admit to the Communion?* The answer is, that the 'Statute does not preclude such a person from partaking of the 'Holy Communion, because he is not a *notorious* evil liver: and 'the Canon Law is equally decisive upon this point.'

Again, 'B * * * confesses to a Priest that he is guilty of a 'crime, and manifests impenitence, but is popularly believed to be 'guilty; although acquitted in the Civil Courts. *Is the Minister, 'knowing him to be guilty, compelled to admit him to the Holy 'Communion?* The answer again is, the Minister is bound to 'admit him to the Holy Communion, because in the eye of the 'law the person is not only innocent, but "notoriously" innocent. 'To give a different construction to the Statute, would be to recog-'nize the Clergy as independent of the Statute Law, and of the 'Common Law.'

Again, in the case of *Maria Manning.*

'But if a Clergyman can doubt whether in such cases as those 'just stated, he is bound to administer the Sacrament, there can 'be no doubt entertained of its having been the legal duty of the 'Gaol-Chaplain to *refuse* to administer it to the criminal, *Maria 'Manning*, on the eve of her execution. The circumstances of her 'case rendered her as ***notorious*** an offender as she could well be 'in a legal sense: and if the Clergyman's own private knowledge 'could be allowed to avail, the Chaplain appears to have had 'ocular demonstration upon demonstration down to the last moment 'of this unfortunate woman's earthly existence, of the criminal's '*impenitence*, and the very reverse of her *amendment;* and yet, 'instead of his advertising her to "*presume not to come to the Lord's* '*Table*," and "repelling" her, he "did not deem it right to do more," 'to use his own words, "than to dissuade and solemnly to warn, by 'such means endeavouring to deter" her, and accordingly admitted 'her to the Holy Communion, and that too, in spite of his acknow-'ledged "fears" that her act in partaking of the Lord's Table 'would be "a desecration of the Holy Ordinance, and aggravation "of guilt and judgment to the Communicant herself." How such 'conduct can be reconciled with the Statute Law, or even with the 'commonest notions of clerical propriety is inconceivable. Had 'the criminal satisfied the Chaplain of her *penitence*, the case would 'have been very different. It would then have been his *duty* to 'admit her to the Holy Communion.'—*Book of Common Prayer.* E. H. S. *p.* 1073.

We will now cite a case or two; beginning with the judgment of *Bishop* WILSON, formerly Bishop of Sodor and Man, in the complaint of a *Mrs. Puller* v. *Archdeacon Horribin*:—

'The *Rev. Mr. Archdeacon Horribin* having, pursuant to the 'directions of the *Rubric*, given us an account, that he had repelled 'one *Mrs. Puller* from the Holy Sacrament, and the said *Mrs.* '*Puller* having likewise made complaint of the grievous injury done 'her by being so repelled, and praying that satisfaction may be 'made for so great an injury; ["The occasion," says the Bishop, 'in his letter to the *Earl of Derby*, March 12, 1721, "was this: "The *Archdeacon* having repulsed one *Mrs. Puller* from the Sacra-"ment, gave me notice thereof, in order to an hearing: amongst "other reasons he gave for so doing, one was, that *Madam Horne*, "the Governor's lady, had informed him, that she had seen *Sir* "*James Pool* and the said gentlewoman in so indecent a manner "together, as that he had thought it a sufficient reason for expel-"ing her from the Lord's Table, which he did, without any previous "admonition."]; upon hearing the whole matter, it appears, first, 'that the said *Mrs Puller* was repelled without any previous notice 'or admonition: secondly, that the causes of the said repulse alleged 'by *Mr. Archdeacon*, were not sufficient, being either personal 'injuries, of which he had no right to be the Judge, or a private 'information of a scandal of which she has since cleared herself to 'the satisfaction of the Court. We do therefore declare and adjudge, 'that the repelling of the said *Mrs Puller* as abovesaid, was irregu-'lar. And forasmuch as the said *Mr. Archdeacon*, in his defence, 'did insist upon repelling any person from the Holy Sacrament, 'whom he in his conscience thought unworthy, notwithstanding 'he was often told of the evil consequence and tyranny of such a 'procedure: We do hereby declare, that the said assertion is con-'trary to the rule of the Church in all ages: and, to the end that 'Christians may not be deprived of the means of grace through the 'private resentments of their Pastors, we do order and require, that 'neither the said *Mr. Archdeacon*, nor any other Minister, do for 'the future presume to repel any persons from the Holy Sacrament, '*whose crimes have not become notorious*, either *by their own con-'fession, by presentment, or adjudged to be so by some sentence of 'Law*. And that no private Christian may be discouraged from 'going to the Sacrament for fear of the like usage, we do require, 'that this our order be read at the next Lord's day, in the Parish 'Church of *Kirk Malew:* and that our Registrar do give the said '*Mr. Archdeacon* a copy thereof, and communicate the same, if 'need be, to the rest of our Clergy. Given under our hand, this '19th day of December, 1721.—THOMAS SODOR AND MAN.'—*Life of* BP. WILSON, *by Stowell*, 343—6.—quoted in STEPHENS' *Book of Common Prayer*. E. H. S. *p.* 1071.

Again,—'In *Clovell* v. *Cardinall*, an action upon 'the case was brought against a Minister for *refusing* the Sacrament 'to another, and the *Jury found for the Plaintiff*, and *gave damages:* 'and it was moved in arrest of judgment, among other things, that 'the party had not set forth in his declaration, that he gave notice 'according to the Statute, nor that he was *a Parishioner of that 'Parish*, without which the Minister might not admit him by the 'Laws of the Church. But these points appear not to have come 'under consideration, because another exception was of itself ad-'judged to be fatal, viz. that the Plaintiff declared for not adminis-'tering two Sundays, and had not set forth that in the second 'instance he desired the Minister to do it, and yet entire damages 'had been given for both.' (I *Sid.* 34. See *Davis* v. *Black* (Clerk). 1. 2. B. 910; Com. Dig. *Action upon the case upon Assumpsit.* (B. 19.)—quoted by STEPHENS', *Laws Relating to the Clergy*, p. 630.) See CRIPPS's remarks cited presently.

581.—It is necessary that we now proceed to give the opinions of such of our Ecclesiastical authorities who have spoken out on this very difficult question, and, to the "Curate," very dangerous responsibility.

BISHOP ANDREWES (*ob.* 1626), says:—'Our law in England, 'will not suffer the Minister to judge any man as a *notorious 'offender*, but him who is convicted by some *legal* sentence.'—*Add. Notes to* NICHOLLS' *Common Prayer*, p. 36.

L'ESTRANGE (*ob.* 1659—60), elucidating the word *notorious*, defines also the power of the Priest, thus:—'*Notorium* amongst the 'Civilians and Canonists, is threefold. *First*, there is *Notorium 'Presumptionis*, "a notoriousness of Presumption," where *Evidentia 'rei est evidenter à jure præsumta*, "The evidence of the thing is "taken for evident, by presumption of Law." As where it pre-

'sumeth one to be the Son of such a Man, because he was born in 'wedlock. *Secondly*, There is *Notorium Juris*, "a notoriousness of 'Law," when the Offence is proved either *per confessionem factam 'in Jure*, "by confession made in open Court;" or *per Sententiam 'Judicis*, "by the Sentence of the Judge." *Lastly*, There is *Noto- 'rium facti*, "a notoriousness of Fact," when *per evidentiam rei nulla 'potest tergiversatione celari*, "The Evidence is so clear, as the 'Accusation can by no shifts be avoided." Now to which of these 'three the term *notorious* in this Rubrick relateth, is a great ques- 'tion: The learned Prelate, Bishop Andrews restraineth it positively 'to the *second*: Our Law of England, saith he, will not suffer the 'Minister to judge any man a notorious Offender, but him who is so '*convinced by some legal sentence*: The Law of England will not 'suffer it, so that should the Ecclesiastical permit it, the Municipal 'Law would not, and if it comes to an Antimony, a pistle between 'the Canon Laws of our Church, and the Law of the Land, this it 'is must over-rulė. But doth our Canon Law give any such tolera- 'tion, Doth it impower any Minister to exclude his Parishioner, '(claiming his Christian priviledge in those blessed Mysteries) from 'the Sacrament, or to make his private discretion the supreme 'judge of the notoriousness here mentioned? Certainly no. As for 'the 26 and 27 *Canons*, which are produced to the contrary, they 'neither speak explicitly enough, nor do they sufficiently direct in 'this affair: The *Canon* wherein our Church declareth her mind 'more articulately, is the 109.' (here is quoted the *Canon* which we 'have given above).........where I note, *First*, the Crime must be '*scandalous*, an offence to the Brethren. *Secondly*, it must be '*presented to the Ordinary*. *Thirdly*, that such scandalous offenders, 'so presented to the Ordinary, are *not to be admitted to the Com- 'munion*. But some perhaps will say, this was one of the failings 'of an ill regulated State and Church, which justly called for a 'Reformation, and so indeed it was pretended by *Dr. Burgess*, and '*Mr. White* of Dorchester, at a Committee sitting in the Lord's 'House, in March, 1641. But, upon a full debate, it was determined 'at that Committee, to the very conviction of the opponents, that '*open and notorious evil livers, were none but such as the Laws had 'adjudged to be so*. Agreeable to this determination did the Par- 'liament afterwards ordain. (*Ordnance*, Oct. 20, 1645). "That *no " person be suspended from the Communion for any matter of scandal*, " but, either upon his *confession* before the Eldership to have com- " mitted such an offence, or upon the *testimony of two Witnesses* at " least, and those examined upon oath." So was it ordained by 'this Parliament, sufficiently Presbyterian, against the liking of an 'Assembly of Presbyters, which did *Enixius Dogmatis*, &c.; "vehe- "mently, though all to little purpose, (more than once) oppose "it with all the arguments they could," as *Mr. Selden* assures us: 'Having opened the mind of both our Church and State, as to this 'particular, it will not be amiss to represent the conformity it 'beareth with the Imperial Edict, and practice of the primitive 'Church. As for the Imperial Law, it speaks loud enough (*Novel.* '123. *c.* 11. *Collat.* 9. *tit.* 15. *c.* 11.) *Omnibus Episcopis*, &c. "We "prohibit all, both Bishops and Presbyters, *from shutting out any " one from the Communion, before just cause be shewn* that the holy " Canons warrant them so to proceed:" As for the primitive usage, '*St Augustine* fully, *Nos à Communione*, &c. "We *cannot repel any " man from the Communion*, unless he hath freely *confest* his offence.

"or hath been accused and *convicted in some secular Court, or Ecclesiastical Consistory:*" Indeed so was the Legislative pattern of 'our Saviour, in the first institution of his Supper: Never was 'there a more detestable crime, than *Judas* his Treason, never was 'delinquent convicted upon evidence so infallible, as his Master's 'Omniscience. But though he had already projected the Conspiracy, and our Saviour already knew it, yet did he not interdict 'him from participating with his elect Apostles, recommending 'thereby to his Church this Lesson, that *no outward Communion 'of the wicked with us*, in those sacred Ordinances, *can possibly 'render them ineffectual to his holy ones:* 'Tis true, I grant some 'learned men depart from this sense, and because S. John saith, 'that *Judas*, having received the sop, went immediately out, thence 'infer his absence at the time of Christ's instituting his last Supper. 'But our Church is positive in the contrary; nor can S. John be 'otherwise reconciled to the rest of the Evangelists: *To conclude*, 'the result of all the premises is, That *none are to be suspended 'from this Sacrament*, but the *notorious delinquents*, and that *none 'are notorious, but they whom the sentence of the Law*, or *their own 'confessions* have stated so to be.: All reason it should be so. My 'temporal Estate no private person can deprive me of, until it be 'legally evicted from me by course of Law, and shall it be in the 'power of any mortal man to divest me of my interest in that 'blessed Banquet, before I be adjudged to have forfeited it upon 'fair hearing? What were this, but to expose Christians to the 'Infirmities, Passions, and somewhat else, *quod dicere nolo*, of their 'spiritual Pastors?' (*p.* 163.)—*Alliance of Divine Offices.*

NICHOLLS' observes:—'In the primitive times, when discipline 'was kept up strict, all such persons, as soon as known, were put 'under Censure; but, if before Censure they offer'd themselves at 'the Communion, they were repelled. Τῆς ψυχῆς ἀποστήσομαι, 'κ. τ. λ. says *St Chrysostom*, "*I will sooner lay down my life than I "will deliver my Lord's Body unworthily, I will sooner pour out my "own blood, than deliver the tremendous Blood, to one who ought not "to receive it*," (Hom. 82. *in Matt.*) And we read in Church History, that *St Ambrose* refused the Communion to no less a person 'than the *Emperor Theodosius* himself, after his commission of a 'great crime; for there being a sedition among the people of *Thessalonica*, he ordered his Guards to fall upon them, who, in that 'heat, cut the throats of many thousands of poor people......This 'repulse the holy Emperor acquiesced in, and in tears repented him 'of the sad effects of his hasty anger, (Vid. *Theod. Hist. Eccl.* 'Lib. v.). And indeed such severe discipline might not be amiss, 'whilst it was grounded only upon piety and zeal for God's Honour, 'as it was in those devout times. But afterwards other, not so 'warrantable, passions mixed in the minds of some of those, who 'ministred in Holy things; and some persons *were debarred the 'Communion*, out of pique and resentment: Therefore there was an 'Imperial Injunction prohibiting *all both Bishops and Presbyters, 'from shutting out any one from the Communion, before just cause 'be shewn, that the holy Canons do give them power so to do*, (*Nov.* '123. *Can.* 11.) And the Canon-Law *did not allow a discretionary 'power to the Priest*, to thrust away every ill person from the 'Sacrament. Etiam criminosus, &c. "*A vitious person offering*

" *himself to receive the Communion, is not to be repelled, but is to be* " *carried privately aside, and to be exhorted not to receive the Com-* " *munion :* (Extr. de *Off. Ord.* Sacred.) Indeed the latter Canonists 'did interpret this only of *occult crimes*, and which were not 'generally known; (*Linw. Prov. de sacr. Unct.*) allowing only 'persons *notoriously guilty*, to be repelled: and of this opinion were 'the Compilers of our Rubrick in *Edward* VI., his times, by their 'wording the Rubrick, "*If any be an open and notorious evil liver,*" '&c. But, however, they limited this discretionary power of the 'Minister, obliging him, even in *notorious crimes*, to *admonish* such 'persons first to abstain, and only upon *obstinacy* to repel. But, 'nevertheless, this formerly gave occasion to several exceptions 'and disputes; and therefore in the *last Revision* of the Common 'Prayer, repulsion was not left to the absolute power of the 'Minister, but he was obliged to give notice thereof to the Dio- 'cesan, and to take his advice therein. And still it remains so 'uncertain what is *notoriety* both in *Presumption*, *Law*, and *Fact*, 'that a Minister is not out of danger of transgressing his Rule, if, '*before judicial conviction* of a crime, he goes farther than ad- 'monishing any person to abstain.'—*Book of Com. Prayer in loco.*

JOHNSON writes:—'Every Curate is, by the Rubric before the 'Communion Office, required *to call and advertise any notorious* '*Evil Liver, that he presume not to come to the Lord's Table;* and 'this is afterwards called *a repelling of him;* so that it is evident, 'the Minister in such a case, is not bound to admit the offender '(let him be never so great a man) to the Lord's Supper; but *the* '*Curate is, within* 14 *days, to give notice of it to the Ordinary;* that 'is, I suppose, if the Admonition or Repulse were publick; for if 'the Curate, laying aside his authority, do only in private advise 'him to refrain, then there is no necessity of giving an account of 'it to the Ordinary. But if the offender do, at the Curate's admo- 'nition, *openly declare himself to have truly repented, and amended* '*his naughty life*, then he is *not to be repelled;* and consequently 'no notice need be given to the Ordinary.' (*p.* 150.)—*Clergyman's Vade Mecum.* Vol. I.

WHEATLY remarks:—'Now here we must distinguish between '*absolutely repelling* and *shutting out* any one from the Communion, 'as by a *judicial act*, and only suspending him for a time, till the 'Minister has opportunity to send his case to the Ordinary. The 'first of these is what the Rubric cannot be understood to imply: 'for by the laws of the land, both Ecclesiastical and Civil, *none* '*are to be shut out from this Sacrament*, but such as are notorious 'delinquents, and none are *notorious* but such as the *sentence of the* '*law* hath, either upon their *own confession*, or *full conviction*, 'declared so to be. And this is conformable both to the Imperial 'Edict, and the practice of the Church as long ago as St Austin.' ......(After quoting the Imperial Edict, &c. he adds)......'But now 'all this plainly refers to the power of secluding from the Com- 'munion judicially and with authority; whereas the design of this 'Rubric is only to enable the Curate *to refuse to administer* to any 'of his Congregation (of whose ill life and behaviour he has received 'sudden notice) *till he can have opportunity of laying his case before* '*the Ordinary*.........But here I know it may be objected, that the 'persons, whom the Curate is by this Rubric empowered to repel 'are declared to be such as are *notorious evil livers*, and that I have 'already allowed that *none are notorious* but such *as the sentence of* '*the law has declared so to be*. But to this I answer, that *notoriety* 'in this place is taken in a lower degree; the Rubric using the 'words *open* and *notorious* for the same thing, and explaining those 'to be *notorious*, by whom the Congregation is offended. That it 'cannot mean those whom the *law* has declared to be notorious is 'plain, because such are supposed to be *already shut out from* '*the Communion*, and consequently the Curate must himself have 'received notice from his Ordinary not to admit them: whereas the 'persons whom the Rubric provides against, are such as the Ordi-'nary is supposed *not yet to have heard of*, whom therefore it 'requires the Curate to send him notice of, in order that he may 'proceed against them according to Law; and *whom, in the mean* '*while the Curate is empowered by this Rubric* (which is itself a law, 'being established by the Act of Uniformity) *to refuse the Com-* '*munion*, if, after due admonition to keep away, he obstinately offers 'himself to receive: insomuch that no damage from any prior law 'can accrue to him from a conscientious execution of the latter.' (*p.* 294.)—*Rat. Ill. of Book of Com. Prayer.*

ARCHDEACON SHARP (*ob.* 1792.) writes very fully on this difficult subject, he says with regard to this Rubric that:—It 'has no 'other difficulty in it, than what ariseth from the doubtful signifi-'cation of the term *notorious*, and from the uncertainty there is in 'judging of all those cases, when the Congregation may be said to 'be *offended*. For *notoriety in fact* is one thing; and *notoriety in* '*presumption* is another. And in either case it should be a *notoriety* '*in law* too, to indemnify the Minister for proceeding upon the 'Rubric, or to render him safe, in point of law, for *repelling* any 'person from the Communion. And then as to the Congregation 'taking offence, how to distinguish between what *doth offend* a 'Congregation, and what *ought* to give offence to it; whether we 'are to interpret it according to reason, or only according to fact, 'is another difficulty. Nay, whether this Rubric ought not to be 'extended to all crimes which are specified in the Canons as 'disqualifications for the Holy Communion, though they be not 'notorious or known to the Congregation provided they be suffi-'ciently discovered or made known to the Minister himself, is 'another question which will bear much to be said on either side 'of it. (*p.* 40.)......(After referring to *Canons* 26, and 109, he 'adds)......Might we venture to act upon that interpretation which 'it must be allowed these *Canons* fix upon the Rubric, our rule to 'proceed by would be much plainer than it is. But to prevent 'our claiming any benefit or authority from these Canons; the '*Statute Laws*, which supersede the Canons, interfere and lay us 'under certain restrictions. By a *Statute* in the first year of '*Edward* VI. it is enacted, "that the Minister *shall not, without a* "*lawful cause, deny the Sacrament* to any person that devoutly and "humbly desires it." But what is this lawful cause? Why, we 'are told that "the law of England will not suffer the Minister to "judge any man a notorious offender, but him who is *so convinced* "*by some legal sentence*." And it seems, according to the sense of 'the Civilians and Canonists, nothing amounts to *notorium juris*, or "notoriety in law," less than a *proof by confession in open court*, 'or *conviction by a sentence of the Judge*. By the Canons, all those 'offenders who ought to be *presented* to the Ordinary, ought also 'to be shut out from the Communion till they be reformed; and 'they whose duty it is to present them, neglecting so to do, are 'to be excluded likewise. And both these acts of discipline are 'intrusted with, and charged upon, the Minister alone. But so 'far are the canonical disqualifications for the Sacrament from 'being accounted, as such, lawful causes of exclusion, according 'to the Statute, that even persons lying under *ipso facto* Excom-'munications by the Canons may *not legally be withheld from the 'Communion*, till sentence of Excommunication hath formally 'passed, and is openly declared against them.' (*p.* 41.)......There 'are cases in which we are *bound to deny the Sacraments*, ante-'cedently to any obligations we are under to human constitutions; 'so that, whensoever we are obliged by virtue of our office, and 'in regard of the sacred trust committed to us, as stewards of the 'mysteries of God, to refuse the Communion, we must by no means 'be swayed by any secular motives, or intimidated by suspicions 'of dangerous temporal consequences, from doing what we ought, 'and discharging our great commission faithfully. And in this 'every Clergyman must be his own casuist, and will best judge for 'himself in such cases as shall come before him.' (*p.* 45.)...... 'Upon the whole, though this Rubric may "require some explana-'tion," as *Bishop Cosins* remarks, "for the avoiding of disputes "and doubts between the *Communicants* and *Curates*," &c. yet if 'it be taken in all its parts, viz. that no person, however notoriously 'wicked, shall be withheld from the Communion, till he be *admon-'ished* to withdraw himself; and that, when he is repelled upon his '*obstinacy*, it is only till such time as the *advice of the Ordinary* 'can be had therein, to whom the Curate is obliged to give early 'notice of such his act; it seems in this view *the best*, and, I think, 'the *only Ecclesiastical rule* we have to go by in such cases: nor 'doth it appear liable to exceptions, unless it be in that other 'particular I was to speak to, viz. how far we are safe in acting 'according to it. But as this is properly a *point of law*, it is not so 'fit for me to undertake any determination of it: it must be left to 'the gentlemen of that profession.' (*p.* 47.)—*On the Rubrics and Canons.*

The Rev. W. G. Humphry writes:—'Extreme cases, however, 'may, and sometimes do arise, in which a Minister is not only 'justified in withholding the Sacrament, but would be culpable if 'he omitted to do so.' (*p.* 224.)—*Treatise on Bk. of Com. Prayer.*

The Rev. F. Procter observes:—'These rules, implying an 'efficient system of corrective discipline, are wisely retained for 'self-reproof, and as a means of shewing what the Church requires 'in her Members, though in practice they have fallen into disuse 'from the uncertainty of their legal application. There is, how-'ever, no doubt as to the duty of admonition; and ordinarily 'conscience and public feeling will deter a notorious offender from 'Communion, if not from crime. In proceeding to repulsion it 'must be remembered that this is in fact excommunication, which 'requires the sentence of a competent judge; and that no private 'person may condemn a man upon common report as a notorious 'offender, unless he has been convicted by some legal sentence. 'The Ecclesiastical rule is, according to the third Rubric, to signify 'the case of one who will not be admonished, to the Bishop, and 'take his advice. The safety of such a step to the individual 'Clergyman consists in this that the Bishop is the party to institute 'legal proceedings, which he is bound to do, if the offender is to be '*repelled* from Communion.' (*p.* 317.) — *History of Book of Com. Prayer.*

Mr. H. W. Cripps, *Barrister at law*, after citing the above Rubrics and Canons, says: — 'All these causes are so general and 'appear to depend so completely upon the judgment and opinion 'of the Minister, that it has been doubted whether an action would 'not lie against him for the injury which would result to the 'character of one, whom he might refuse to receive as a Com-'municant. In Comyn's Digest (*Action on the Case.* B. 1.), it is 'said that an action on the case does not lie for refusing to ad-'minister the Sacrament: but the case referred to as an authority '(*Clovell* v. *Cardinal.* 1. Sid. 34.) is one which is also mentioned by 'Dr. Burn; and in which no express decision was given on the 'point, as the declaration was held bad: and the main question 'was therefore not decided. Probably the remarks which are to 'be found in a preceding Chapter (See *Lord Denman's* judgment 'in *Davis* v. *Black*) upon the subject of a Clergyman refusing to 'marry, may be as nearly as possible applicable to the present 'case.* The difficulty of drawing a good declaration would be 'considerable; the refusal must probably have been malicious; and 'even then the success of such an action would appear doubtful. 'There can, however, be no question but that the refusing to ad-'minister the Sacrament to any one without sufficient cause would 'be an offence of the highest order against the Ecclesiastical law, 'and one for which the Minister should now be punished by pro-'ceeding under the Church Discipline Act. And it is also declared 'by a Statute of the first year of Edward VI. that the Minister 'shall *not without a lawful* cause deny the Sacrament to any person 'that will devoutly and humbly desire it.' (*p.* 733.) — *The Laws Relating to the Church and the Clergy.*

Mr. A. J. Stephens, (*Barrister at law*) states: — 'If a Minister '*without a lawful cause* deny the Communion to any person, he can 'be compelled at Common law to administer it: for the Court of 'Queen's Bench can by Mandamus compel every person, lay or 'clerical, to obey the Statute law when no adequate or effectual 'relief can be obtained in the ordinary course by an action at law

---

* In the judgment referred to *Davis* v. *Black*, Lord Denman says he is not prepared to say "that such an action might not "be maintained upon the declaration raising a proper complaint "of a public Officer neglecting his public duty, to the temporal, "and, it might be, the very great damage of an individual. Such a "neglect of the duty of a Clergyman may be actionable, if it be "malicious and without probable cause." (*p.* 699.) — *The Laws Relating to the Church and the Clergy.*

'or a suit in equity (*Rex.* v. *England* (*Bank of*). 2 B. & A. 622.) '......The language of the Rubric under consideration is not, however, per se, very clear as to what will constitute a "notorious evil 'liver," or a "wrong" whereby "the Congregation be offended:" 'but it must be a notoriety, or scandal, *in law*, to indemnify the 'Minister for repelling any person from the Communion. This 'Rubric (2) must be construed by the principles of the Common 'law, and must be construed strictly, because it is penal. (*p.* 1065.) '......Under this Rubric, until the fact has been established by the '*sentence of a temporal or Ecclesiastical Court of Justice*, or by the '*presentment* of the party, or by his *public confession*, that a person 'is a notorious evil liver or offensive to the Congregation, the law 'will presume him to be innocent, and the Minister has *no legal* '*right to refuse* the Communion. The temporal Courts cannot 'impose *spiritual* punishments, and therefore the Rubric provides, 'that, if a convicted person offer himself to receive the Communion, 'and the Curate find him impenitent, the Curate shall then repel 'him from it, and refer the case to the Ordinary. (*p.* 1070)....... 'If a person unconvicted in a temporal Court, were leading a life 'of such "evil," or had done his neighbour such wrong, as is within 'the cognizance of the Ecclesiastical Court, proceedings might be 'instituted against him before such tribunal, and a sentence against 'him in that Court would render him an "open and notorious evil 'liver," or an "offender" against "the Congregation," within the 'penal language of the Rubric. (*p.* 1071.)......It is clear, that if a 'person were to present himself to receive the Communion when in 'a state of *intoxication* or *with an irreverence of manner*, it would 'be the imperative duty of the Churchwardens to remove such a 'disturber from the Church. And at Common law a person disturbing Divine Service can be removed by any person there present, 'upon the same principle which allows a man to abate a nuisance.* '*Glever* v. *Hynde*. 1 Mod. 168.'—*Book of Common Prayer*. E. H. S. *p*. 1080.

582.—The following opinions bear more especially upon the *third* Rubric, the "*malice and hatred*," and confirm the views we have already advanced as to the extreme care that is necessary in fulfilling the intentions of the Rubric, and how desirable in the "Curate" to avail himself of the guidance and support of the Ordinary in the measures he may adopt for repelling unworthy Members from communicating in this holy Sacrament.

Bishop Andrewes (*ob.* 1626.) says:—'It seems, he may rather 'make open protestation of his *obstinacy*, than repel him with safety 'at the Common-law.'—*Add. Notes to* Nicholls' *Com. Pr.* p. 36.

Archdeacon Sharp writes on this Rubric that: 'The Minister 'seems to have power given him, to *deny the Sacrament* upon his

---

* See also the recent Statute on cases of '*Brawling*.' 23 & 24 *Vict. c.* 32.

'own personal knowledge of the party's unfitness to receive it. 'There is only one instance indeed of this unfitness there men- 'tioned, viz. in cases where "*he perceiveth malice and hatred to* '*reign*," in which cases "*he is to use the same order as before*," of 'admonishing, and, upon obstinacy, of excluding from the Com- 'munion. And this too without regard to the notoriety of the 'malice, or the offence given thereby to the Congregation. And, 'by parity of reason, what he is allowed to do upon his own know- 'ledge in one case, he may be presumed to have the liberty of 'doing in any other that is parallel, that is, where he himself is 'equally convinced that he has a just and sufficient cause, accord- 'ing to the Canons, to refuse the Sacrament, though at the same 'time he cannot produce any legal testimony of the crime for which 'he debars the party from communicating. Hence then arises 'another question different from the former; viz. whether a Minister 'ought at any time, by denying the Sacrament, to pass a public 'and open censure upon secret crimes, to which none are privy but 'the parties and himself, and that perhaps by accident, as may be, 'and sometimes hath been declared to be the case? To this it hath 'been said, and I think justly, that every Minister in the public 'execution of his office represents the Church, and is therefore to 'exclude none from the Sacraments, but such only as by the Laws 'of the Church he is expressly required to exclude. That when he 'is secretly, and in his private capacity, apprised of any just im- 'pediment in any person, though he ought most solemnly to ad- 'monish him to refrain, nay, and ought to withhold from him a 'private Communion, (because in that case he is allowed himself 'to judge of any just impediment,) yet, when he celebrates in 'public, *he is bound to admit such offending person offering himself*, 'at *his own peril*; forasmuch as the Church is yet ignorant of any 'crime or default for which, according to her rules, the Communion 'is to be withheld. That he doth by his previous admonition '*liberare animam suam*; and if the delinquent will still venture 'to obtrude himself, after such warning given, his blood will be 'upon his own head, that is, he only, like other hypocrites who 'receive unworthily, will be condemned for his presumption; while 'the Minister shall be held guiltless, having done all that was 'incumbent upon him, and indeed all that he could warrant, to 'prevent such profanation of the Holy Mysteries. (*p.* 48.)......But 'it doth not follow that they are therefore bound in all cases to 'administer it, saving those in which they are prohibited expressly. 'No doubt there is an use of their discretion left them, and some 'cases may arise so circumstantiated, that it will go directly against 'a Clergyman's conscience to administer the Sacrament; in which 'cases, as I before observed, he lies under an obligation to discharge 'his duty, superior to that which he owes to the Rubric, or Acts 'of Parliament; and though he cannot perhaps discharge it with 'safety *if the Statutes be interpreted rigorously;* yet it is better to 'fall into the hands of men, and patiently suffer temporal incon- 'veniences, than fall with a sin of presumption into the hands of 'God. The *conclusion* here then is the same as in the former point; 'viz. that *every Minister must be his own judge and guide in ex-* '*traordinary occurrences which come not within the letter or supposed* '*meaning of the rules* that are set him by authority for his direction, 'Only it will greatly concern him to act *with the utmost care, fidelity* '*and circumspection*, that he do not either deprive any persons of 'the privilege of Christian Communion, or set upon them such a 'public mark of infamy and disgrace as a repulse from the Sacra-'ment is commonly held to be, without a real necessity to justify 'his conduct herein.' (*p.* 52.)—*On the Rubric and Canons.*

Mr. A. J. Stephens (*Barrister at law*) says:—'This paragraph 'of the Rubric apparently refers to the "*malicious contention*" 'contemplated by *Canon* 26: but it is clear, that in order to justify 'the repulsion from the Holy Communion, each of the parties must 'bear "*malice and hatred*" towards the other; "malice and hatred" 'upon one side only will not be sufficient. This construction is 'borne out by the subsequent part of the paragraph, which con-'templates forgiveness by one of the parties and obstinacy in the 'other. It would seem that the Curate must experience greater 'difficulty in exercising such power as he may have under this 'paragraph of the Rubric, than he can feel in acting under the 'former paragraph; for he must bear in mind that under the 'proviso, with which this paragraph concludes, *he will have to give* '*an account of the case to the Ordinary*, and be bound to *establish the* '*existence* of the "malice and hatred," an offence most difficult 'legally to define: and that he should also bear in mind, that if he 'do not satisfy the Ordinary of that fact, he will have laid himself 'open to an action by the "repelled" person in a Court of Common 'Law for damages. (*p.* 1082.)......The Curate is also punishable 'under the Church Discipline Act for an *improper refusal*, as a 'breach of the Laws Ecclesiastical; and so is he, it may not be 'unimportant to observe, for *the admission of an improper person to* '*the Holy Communion, if he* "*perceive*" *the person's unfitness*, or the 'unfitness be "notorious." (*p.* 1083.)—*Bk. of Com. Pr.* E. H. S.

(*g*) Schismatics to be rejected.

583.—Schismatics (from the Greek, *σχιζω, to divide* or *separate*) are those who separate from our Church on account of holding different opinions on certain matters of faith or discipline. The *Rubric* gives us no directions with respect to them, but the 27th Canon (of 1603), enjoins that they are to be excluded from the Holy Communion; while the 110th Canon orders that Churchwardens are duly to make presentments of such Schismatics to the Ordinary at their Visitations. Our business is more with the '27th *Canon*' entitled, "*Schismatics not to be admitted to the Communion*," which is as follows:—

'No Minister, when he celebrateth the Communion, shall wit-'tingly administer the same......under pain of suspension......to any 'that refuse to be present at Public Prayers according to the orders 'of the Church of England; nor to any that are common and 'notorious depravers of the Book of Common Prayer and Adminis-'tration of the Sacraments, and of the Orders, Rites, and Ceremonies 'therein prescribed, or of any thing that is contained in any of the 'Articles agreed upon in the Convocation, 1562, or of any thing 'contained in the Book of ordering the Priests and Bishops; or to 'any that have spoken against and depraved his Majesty's sovereign 'authority in Causes Ecclesiastical; except every such person shall 'first acknowledge to the Minister, before the Churchwardens, his 'repentance for the same, and promise by word (*if he cannot write*) 'that he will do so no more; and except (*if he can write*) he shall 'first do the same under his hand-writing, to be delivered to the 'Minister, and by him sent to the Bishop of the Diocese, or Ordi-'nary of the place. Provided that every Minister so repelling 'any......shall upon complaint, or being required by the Ordinary, 'signify the cause thereof unto him, and therein obey his order 'and direction.—CANON 27.

584.—Here it will be perceived, that Ministers, under pain of suspension, are to refuse the Communion to all *Schismatics* unless they acknowledge their repentance, in the presence of the Churchwarden, and declare in writing, or verbally, if they cannot write, that they will not offend in the like again; and it is also enjoined that this declaration, and the facts of the case, are to be forwarded to the Bishop, or Ordinary. There is some difficulty involved in the interpretation to be given to the expression, '*common and notorious depravers*,' found in this Canon, and likewise in the discretionary power assigned to the Minister in determining this question. It seems that the best usage would be to follow the practice recommended in carrying out the injunctions of the Rubrics we have just been discussing, i. e. to take the opinion of the Bishop (see *par.* 579.); for unless Ecclesiastical censure comes with authority, difficulties may arise which will frustrate the Church's intention laid down in this Canon. We are referring more particularly to doubtful and questionable cases of Schism, and which now are purely religious, the repeal of the 'Test Acts' having removed much of the difficulty attending politico-religious cases. As to the 'open and notorious' Schismatics, Dissenters, and others, they are not in these times likely to trouble us on this point, as they did when this Canon was called for; and therefore the necessity of enforcing the Canon with regard to them will now rarely present itself.

WHEATLY, but briefly refers to this *Canon*, observing: 'There 'are other persons by the laws of our Church disabled from com- 'municating; such as are of course all *Shismatics*, to whom no '*Minister, when he celebrateth the Communion, shall wittingly ad- 'minister the same under pain of suspension.* (Can. 27.) But of 'these too, unless they have been *legally* convicted, *the Minister 'who repels them should upon complaint, or being required by the 'Ordinary, signify the cause thereof unto him, and therein obey his 'order and direction.*'—ibid. (*p.* 298.)—*Rat. Ill. of Book of Com. Prayer.*

ARCHDEACON SHARP says that:—'Though the 27th *Canon*, 'entitled, *Schismatics not to be admitted to the Communion*, is express 'for their exclusion; yet both the Common Lawyers and Civilians 'have given it as their opinion, that Schismatics not lying under 'any Ecclesiastical censure, and humbly and devoutly desiring the 'Sacrament, are not to be withheld from it, notwithstanding the 'direction of the Canon.' (*p.* 43.)......Again he remarks, By this *Canon*, 'the Sacrament is to be withheld from "Schismatics and "depravers of the Common Prayer, the Articles of Religion, and "the King's ecclesiastical supremacy." These offences are not 'mentioned in the Rubric, yet so great a stress is laid upon them 'here, that nothing less than *suspension* is threatened to the Minis- 'ter who complies not with this direction. That there were good 'reasons for this strictness, when the Canons were drawn up, we 'will make no dispute. But whether there be any now, or how 'we stand bound by this Constitution at this present day, deserves 'our inquiry. In the first place, the *Test Act* hath superseded the 'obligation of this Canon in all cases where the Sacrament is re- 'ceived for a qualification: so that even an avowed Schismatic, 'offering himself under shelter of this Act is sufficiently screened 'from the censure of the Canon. And, secondly, the *Act of Tolera- 'tion*, allowing to all Schismatics the use of the Sacraments in their 'own way, not only leaves them under no temptation of occasional 'conformity, (save in cases of qualifications,) but exempts them 'from all trouble and prosecution in the Ecclesiastical Courts, to 'which their repulsion from the Communion is in effect or by 'consequence a leading step. And, thirdly, what is still more 'material, it doth not yet appear whether the Canon directeth any 'to be excluded as Schismatics, but such as are *declared so by some 'lawful and judicial sentence.* For, though by the Canons under 'the first title, Schismatics be Excommunicated *ipso facto*, yet as 'this Excommunication has no effect at Common Law, without 'a declaratory sentence pronounced by an Ecclesiastical Judge, so 'say the Civilians, the censure of the Canon in excluding them 'from the Communion is not to have effect till they be *after legal 'process Excommunicated.* Which opinion was given upon a very 'extraordinary occasion, viz. in the case of the famous *Richard 'Baxter* in the last century; than whom scarce any Nonconformist 'in the Kingdom was more obnoxious upon the footing of the *ipso 'facto* Excommunications; and yet *he often Communicated with the 'Church of England*, and was permitted so to do, upon this single 'distinction, that, "not being legally declared Excommunicate, he "could not Canonically be repelled from the Sacrament." The 'same distinction, as I take it, holds equally good with respect to 'the "*Impugners of the Thirty-nine Articles*, and the King's sove-

'reign authority in causes Ecclesiastical." They are laid under this 'censure here as being Excommunicated *ipso facto* in the Canons 'under the first title; but, *till a sentence hath passed upon them*, this 'discipline of repelling will not reach them.' (*p.* 103.)—*On the Rubrics and Canons.*

(*h*) Strangers to be rejected.

585.—It was formerly the usage when the intercourse of communities was rare, and travelling less frequent, to exclude *Strangers* from admission to the Holy-Communion, lest any should present themselves, who, in their own parishes, were labouring under the censure of these two Rubrics, either as '*notorious evil-livers*,' or as indulging '*malice and hatred*' against a neighbour. This condition of mind would of course render such persons unfit recipients of so holy a Sacrament, and their state of unrepentance would not be known to the Minister officiating in this great service in another Parish. Now, however, that 'many run to and fro, and knowledge is increased,' the strictness of the Canon is relaxed; if not, indeed, practically obsolete. The Clergy, nevertheless, are not released from its authority, and, occasionally, instances will arise which may call for the application of the Canon; particularly when any ill-conditioned member of a Congregation takes unreasonable offence at some proceeding of his Minister, and with angry feelings withdraws from the Communion of his own Church to seek the satisfaction to be derived from another's ministrations: desiring possibly by this step to publish abroad his resentment, and excite popular sympathy; and at the same time to wound the sensibilities of God's minister whose constant anxiety and prayers are for the comfort and well-being and eternal happiness of each and every member of the flock committed by the providence of God to his spiritual charge. We will here quote the Canon, which is entitled—"*Strangers not to be admitted to the Communion*," and is as follows:—

'The Churchwardens or Quest-men, and their assistants, shall 'mark, as well as the Minister, whether all and every of the

'Parishioners come so often every year to the holy Communion, 'as the Laws and our Constitutions do require; and whether any '*Strangers come often* and commonly from other parishes to their 'Church; and shall show their Minister of them, lest perhaps they 'be admitted to the Lord's Table amongst others, *which they shall 'forbid; and remit such home to their own parish Churches and 'Ministers*, there to receive the Communion with the rest of their 'own neighbours.'—CANON 28.

So far back as the time of ARCHDEACON SHARP (*ob.* 1792.) however, this Canon had grown into desuetude, for we find him saying:—

'It (*Canon* 28.) seemeth now to have no longer any force in it, 'from the constant and universal custom of mixed Communions: 'where none by the practice of our Church, and allowance of our 'governors, are so much as questioned, if there be no notorious or 'apparent reason to refuse their communion with us.'.........In a 'word, let it be remembered of all these kinds of persons, which are 'forbid the Communion, by the three *Canons* (CANONS 26, 27, 28.) 'that I have been now speaking to, that as none of them are now 'inquired after, or *presented as delinquents;* that as we have no 'instance of suspension, or even of admonition, of Ministers by 'their superiors for admitting them; that there yet remains great 'doubt in some of these cases what shall be judged acting in 'conformity to the Canon, and what not; that the cognisance 'of some of these offences ought not to be left wholly to the 'private judgment of the Officiating Minister; and that he can 'hardly be safe and secure in what he doth, if he be bound to 'make proof of them in a Court of Judicature; I say, for these 'reasons it hath been thought proper *to let these* CANONS *lie 'dormant*, till some just occasion shall arise to move our governors 'to revive them, and reinforce the execution of them. And, there'fore, in the mean time we plead a general tacit dispensation for 'our not acting according to the letter of them.' (*p.* 105.)—*On the Rubrics and Canons.*

586.—The strictness of this *Canon* may also in some measure be relaxed in the case of *Travellers*, should they present themselves at the Communion-Table; and likewise when instances of emergency or necessity in sickness, &c. may arise. There is a Constitution of *Abp. Peccham* applicable to these several cases, enjoining that "none shall give the Communion "to the Parishioner of another Priest without his "manifest Licence: which ordinance nevertheless shall "not extend to *Travellers*, nor *to persons in danger*, nor "to *cases of necessity.*"—*Lyndwood* thus gives it:—

'Nullus etiam sacram Communionem præbeat Parochiano 'alterius Sacerdotis sine ipsius licentia manifesta. Quam Ordina'tionem non intendimus ad *peregrinantes* extendere, vel *perecli-*

'*tantes*, nec necessitatis casui derogare.' The Gloss thus explains:—'*Peregrinantes* i. e. Viatores namque cujuslibet Ecclesiæ Parochiani 'existent. *Periclitantes*, i. e. In periculo mortis constitutos.'—*Prov. Const.* l. iii. *t.* 23. *p.* 233.

587.—It would be well when Members of one Church are sojourning in a strange neighbourhood, to take with them 'letters of commendation' from the Clergyman of their own Parish to the Officiating Minister of the other, as it would tend in many ways to the comfort and convenience of such Visitor. And this is particularly desirable in a permanent change of abode; especially in the case of Governesses, Apprentices, Servants, &c. At a Conference of the Bishops of the Church in British North America a similar recommendation occurs in these words:—

'We hold it to be of great importance that the Members of the 'Church should signify to the Minister their intention to present 'themselves at the Holy Table, especially when they arrive in any 'place as *Strangers*, or when, being residents in such place they are 'purposing to communicate for the *first time*. We conceive that 'it would greatly promote the welfare of the Church, if all our 'Members, who may be travelling from one place to another, were 'furnished with a *Certificate of their Membership* and their standing 'in the Church.'—*Eccl. Gazette*, August, 1852.

We would recommend the Clergy, therefore, to impress these views upon their people whenever an opportunity may present itself; and we will now pass to the consideration of the next Rubric.

The Communion Table.

(4 *a*) ¶. '*The* Table *at the Communion-time*,' &c.

588.—This Rubric was introduced at the Revision of the Liturgy in 1552, and has continued with but trifling alteration down to the present time. The especial question for consideration here is the designation of the structure as a "*Table*," in contradistinction to that of "*Altar*." We have already enlarged upon this subject in *Vol.* C. to which we may refer those of our readers who are desirous of a full knowledge of the subject; yet we may be expected to introduce here a few remarks derived from more recent decisions in our Courts of Law. It must be borne in mind, that both *Altar* and *Table* are employed by the Apostle Paul when speaking of the Holy Communion. He says — 'ye cannot be 'partakers of the Lord's *Table* (τραπέζης) and of the 'Table of Devils.'—(1 *Cor.* x. 21.). Again, 'We 'have an *Altar* (θυσιαστήριον), whereof they have no 'right to eat which serve the Tabernacle.' — (*Heb.* xiii. 10.). Besides which we find the ancient Fathers, generally speaking, as Ignatius, Irenæus, Tertullian, Cyprian, and others giving the preference to the word '*Altar;*' while their more immediate followers used *Altar* and *Table* indifferently. The distinction that has been assigned to these terms in modern times seems to be that '*Altar*' has especial reference to the oblations of the Eucharist, and to the offering of praise and thanksgiving, and the dedication of ourselves to God's Service; and that the word '*Table*' refers rather to the participation, or 'Communion.' At all events for the first three hundred years it appears, says *Wheatly*, that the term '*Table*' had been employed to distinguish God's board more than once. (*Rat. Ill. of Book of Com. Prayer*, p. 258.). The Rubric we now quote determines what is the designation to-day: we will however add here an opinion or two, which will shew more clearly what is the present usage; citing first of all the *Canon* of 1603–4, bearing on the subject.

'Whereas we have no doubt but that in all Churches within 'the Realm of England, *convenient and decent Tables* are provided 'and placed for the celebration of the Holy Communion, we appoint 'that the same *Tables* shall from time to time be kept and repaired 'in sufficient and seemly manner......to be done *at the charge of the* '*Parish.*'—CANON 82.

CLUTTERBUCK in his "*Vindication and Explanation of the Liturgy,*" observes upon the distinction between "*Altar*" and "*Table:*"—'It is called an "*Altar.*" 1. Because the Holy Eucha-'rist being considered as a *sacrifice*, we offer up the commemoration 'of that sacrifice which was offered upon the cross. 2. We offer 'with the action prayers to God for all good things, and we need 'not fear to call the whole action by the name of a *sacrifice*, seeing 'part of it is an oblation to God of hearty prayers, and it is not 'unusual for that to be said of the whole, which is exactly true but 'of one part; and as the word "*sacrifice*" may be used without 'danger, so also the ancient Church did understand it. And it 'is called a "*Table*," the Eucharist being considered as a *Sacra-'ment;* which is nothing else, but a distribution and application 'of the sacrifice to the receivers, and the proper use of a *Table* is 'to set food upon, and to entertain guests, both which are applicable 'to this.'—(quoted in MANT's *Book of Com. Prayer*, p. 280.).

The Rev. W. G. HUMPHRY says: —'In the first Prayer Book of 'Edward VI. the words *altar*, *table*, and *God's board*, were all used; 'but in the later revisions *table* alone was retained. In common 'language, however, the *table* is frequently spoken of as the *altar;* 'and that term is vindicated by some of our best divines. It was 'also sanctioned by the convocation of 1640, in the following *canon:* "We declare that this situation of the holy table doth not imply "that it is, or ought to be, esteemed a proper *altar*, whereon Christ "is again really sacrificed; but it is and may be called an *altar* by "us, in that sense in which the primitive Church called it an altar, "and in no other." The sense here referred to is a figurative one, 'corresponding to that in which the Eucharist was called a *sacrifice* '(θυσία). (*p.* 225.)—*Hist. of Book of Com. Prayer.*

The *Judgment of the Judicial Committee of Privy Council* in the Knightsbridge cases, *Westerton & Beal* v. *Liddell*, (March 21st, 1857.) was, on this head, as follows:—'The Appellants, in their pleadings, 'term these tables *altars* or *communion-tables;* and in the argument 'they have referred to two recent statutes in which the word '"*altar*" is used to signify the *communion-table*. When the same 'thing is signified it may not be of much importance by what 'name it is called; but the distinction between an *altar* and a '*communion-table* is in itself essential and deeply founded, in the 'most important difference in matters of faith between Protestants 'and Romanists—viz., in the different notions of the nature of the 'Lord's Supper which prevailed in the Roman Catholic Church at 'the time of the Reformation, and those which were introduced by 'the Reformers. By the former it was considered as a *sacrifice* of 'the Body and Blood of the Saviour. The *altar* was the place 'on which the sacrifice was to be made; the elements were to be 'consecrated, and being so consecrated, were treated as the actual 'Body and Blood of the victim. The Reformers, on the other hand, 'considered the *Holy Communion* not as a sacrifice, but as a *feast*, 'to be celebrated at the *Lord's Table;* though as to the consecration 'of the elements, and the effect of this consecration, and several 'other points, they differed greatly amongst themselves. This dis-'tinction is well pointed out in CUDWORTH's *Discourse concerning* '*the True Nature of the Lord's Supper*, (c. 5. *p.* 27.):—"We see how "the theological controversy which hath cost so many disputes, "whether the Lord's Supper be a sacrifice, is already decided; for "it is not *sacrificium*, but *epulum de sacrificio;* not a sacrifice, but "a feast upon sacrifice; or else, in other words, not *oblatio sacrificii*, "but, as Tertullian excellently speaks, *participatio sacrificii;* not "the offering of something up to God upon an *altar*, but the eating "of something which comes from God's altar and is set upon our "*tables*. Neither was it ever known amongst the Jews or heathens "that those tables upon which they did eat their sacrifices should "be called by the name of *altars;* therefore he (*St Paul*) must "needs call the *communion-table* by the name of the *Lord's table*—"*i. e.*, the *table* upon which God's meat is eaten, not His *altar* upon "which it is offered." That the Roman Catholic *altars* are con-'structed with a view to this doctrine of sacrifice admits of no 'doubt.'......The JUDGMENT then goes on to speak of the difference between the two Books of Edward VI., as to *Altars* and *Communion Tables*—of the distinction between the *Supper of the Lord*, and the *Sacrifice of the Mass*, and that the latter was abolished by 5 & 6 *Edw.* VI. and the 39 *Articles.* And after citing the *Injunctions of Bishop Ridley*, with Bishop Burnet's remarks upon them, and the *Injunctions* likewise of *Elizabeth*, the JUDGMENT thus proceeds:—'These *Injunctions* plainly show that the communion of the Lord's 'Supper was to be held at a *table* as distinguished from an *altar*—a '*table* in the ordinary meaning of that term; that as by the Rubric 'the bread used was to be "the ordinary bread eaten at table with "other meats," so the *table* was to be of the character of those 'employed on such occasions; that it was not only to be moveable, 'but was from time to time to be moved.........The 82*nd Canon* of '1604, that which is now in force, introduces no material alterations. 'It assumes the existence in all churches of convenient and decent '*tables* for the celebration of the Holy Communion, and provides 'that they shall be kept in repair, &c.........Since this period no 'alteration has been made by the law with respect to the nature of 'the *table* to be used. The Rubric of the present Prayer-book pro-'vides only that at the Communion time the *Table*, having a fair 'white linen cloth upon it, &c......The term "*altar*" is never used 'to describe it, and there is an express declaration at the close of 'the Service against the doctrine of transubstantiation, with which 'the ideas of an *altar* and *sacrifice* are closely connected.'

The '*Guardian*' Newspaper, condenses the above decree in these words:—'With respect to the material of the *Altar* or *Communion-'Table*, it is decided that this structure must be of wood and 'moveable, and *the whole must be capable of being covered* with the 'linen cloth to be used on the celebration of the Sacrament. "Their "Lordships are satisfied that the decision upon this point (of Sir "H. J. Fust) in "Faulkner *v.* Lichfield," is well founded," and they 'affirm the decree of the Court below as to the removal of the stone 'structure at 'St Barnabas,' and the Cross upon it, and the substi-'tution of a *Communion-Table* of wood.' The *Editor* then proceeds to make the following comment:—'The second part of the Judg-'ment, however, relating to the *form* and *material* of the *altar*, 'seems to us, as we have said, open to considerable criticism. A 'Canon of the time of the Reformation prescribes, as is well known, 'that the *altar* or *communion-table* shall be "moveable;" and on 'that ground Sir H. Fust in the noted "stone altar case," prohibited 'the erection in the Round Church of St Sepulchre at Cambridge 'of a fixed table of stone, as part of the structure of the Church...... 'The Privy Council refer to that Judgment, and adopt it, and on 'that ground decide, in the present instance, that a fixed altar 'already erected shall be pulled down......The *table*, it is said, must 'be "moveable." Why? Because a Canon says so, passed at a 'time when the altar was held to be *really*—and not, as now 'only *technically*—a table, and not an altar; and was, in that view 'of the case, actually moved out into the body of the church, and 'was there used as a table, the Communicants sitting round it. 'This is the Puritan and Presbyterian view of the Sacrament; and 'it was once, and for a very short time, the view of a dominant 'party in the Church of England. Is it, or is it not, the view of 'the Church of England now? Mr. Pemberton Leigh knows as 'well as we do, that it is not. Everybody knows now that the 'altar or table, call it which you will, is now, as a matter of fact, '*never moved.* Everybody knows that Communicants do not now 'sit round it, but kneel at it. Everybody also knows the reason 'why. Everybody knows that some years after that "moveable" 'Canon, certain other regulations, wholly ignored by Mr. P. Leigh, 'were made by competent authority, by virtue of which all altars that 'had been then made tables of, and had been moved for that purpose 'out into the church, were ordered to be placed back again *altar-'wise*, at the east end of the church, and to be surrounded with a 'rail, at which all Communicants were not to sit, but to kneel; and 'that this was directed in order that the altars might never be 'made into tables again. Everybody knows that all the altars '"moved" have been centuries ago moved back again, and have 'ever since been used accordingly, not table-wise, as in Scotland, 'but altar-wise, as in the Catholic Church. Everybody, too, knows 'the reason of this also. Everybody knows that the ritual, and 'rubric, and Prayer-book of the Church of England are wholly 'inconsistent with any other course. And yet, in the face of all 'this, we have really grave and learned men, in the middle of the 'nineteenth century, actually causing a fixed altar to be destroyed, 'and to be replaced by a moveable one, to be called a moveable 'table; they knowing all the while, as well as we do, that, in point 'of fact, it never will be moved,—that it never will be used as 'a table at all, in the sense of the Canon, *i. e.*, in the sense of the 'Communicants sitting round it, but will at all times and invariably, 'and for all intents and purposes, be used as an altar, after it is '"moveable," just as much as it is now that it is fixed. The dis-'tinction, indeed, will not be seen. A wooden altar of precisely the 'same dimensions, and covered in precisely the same way, will 'replace the stone one. But then it will be "moveable." True, 'But how, and in what point, will it be the less practically an altar? 'In no one single respect. And, if all the altars in England are to-'morrow made of wood and moveable, ***but on the distinct understand-'ing nevertheless that they are never to be moved*** (!), it certainly is 'not very easy to see in what way any question of doctrine can be 'in the slightest degree affected, or how any practical change will be 'made in the matter at all.'—(*No.* 590.—Pub. *March* 25th, 1857.)

We will now proceed with the Rubric.

THE COVERING OF THE TABLE.

(4 *b*) ¶. '*The Table, at the Communion time, having a fair 'white linen cloth upon it*,' &c.

589.—Precise as the direction of the Rubric may appear to be on the point of the covering of the Communion Table; yet the character of the *fair white linen cloth* has been a matter of considerable controversy. The *Canon* is of like import to the Rubric, and gives force to its injunctions, although it involves in its directions the style of the covering to be used on the Table at *other* seasons than at Communion time. Thus:—

'We appoint that the same *Tables* shall......be covered in time 'of Divine Service, with a *carpet of silk or other decent stuff*, thought 'meet by the Ordinary of the place, if any question be made of it; 'and with a *fair Linen Cloth* at the time of the ministration, as 'becometh that Table......All these to be done at the charge of the 'Parish.'—CANON 82.

The *white linen* covering at Communion-time in many Churches lately departed from the simplicity prescribed in the Rubric and Canon, and, undesignedly, we believe, gave great offence to the scruples of many among their Congregations; so likewise had the use of *coloured Cloths*, during the other times of Divine Service; and which were varied according to the season of the Church's year. Indeed, so much bitterness and animosity did these practices engender in the parishes of St Paul, and St Barnabas, in London, that an inhibition was prayed for in the Ecclesiastical Courts; and the long acrimony and heart-burning have been scarcely composed by the decision of the Judicial Committee of Privy Council, whose decree is given below, and which decided that the *fair white linen Cloth* to be used at Communion-time was to be *free from lace and embroidery;* yet that *more Coverings than one* might be used at the other times of Divine Service. We have already discussed this Subject in *Vol.* C., to which, therefore, we would refer our Readers for other information than he will find annexed. We may remark that the *fair white Linen Cloth* should be put on the Table, and over "the Carpet," before the commencement of Divine Service.

BP. COSINS remarks:—'It is enjoined, that the *Table* or *Altar* 'should be spread over with a *clean Linnen-Cloth*, or other decent 'covering: upon which the Holy Bible, the Common Prayer-Book, 'the Paten and Chalice, are to be placed: two Wax Candles are to 'be set on; and the Person who celebrates, is to be arrayed with a 'solemn Ecclesiastical Habit; that is, a *Surplice* and a *Hood.* Now 'by this Solemnity we declare, that it is not an ordinary action 'which we are then upon, but a sacred and mystical one; to the 'end that the minds of all persons may be intent upon it: and that 'they may be put in mind of the dignity of so great a mystery.'—*Add. Notes to* NICHOLLS' *Com. Prayer, p.* 34.

GOAR says:—'In the primitive ages, the *white linen Cloth* and 'the *Vessels* for the Sacrament were not placed on the Table until 'the time when the catechumens had been dismissed, and when the 'offerings of the faithful were to be received. In the Church of 'Constantinople this practice continues to the present day, when 'the linen cloth, or εἰλητὸν, is laid by the Priest, after the cate-'chumens are dismissed.'—(*Liturg. Chrysost.* p. 70.)

The REV. M. PLUMMER writes:—'The *white cloth* is merely to 'cover the top of the Table, not to hang down on the ground. It 'should not hang over the sides of the Table more than six or 'eight inches.' (*p.* 99.)—*Observations on Bk. of Com. Prayer.*

The REV. J. PURCHAS says:—'The *fair white linen cloth* should 'cover the top of the Altar, and hang down at the ends thereof, 'but not over the front, more than an inch or two to show a border 'of lace or embroidery. It should never cover the Antependium. '(In a *Note.*) It is well to have one fair white linen cloth with a 'border worked in colours for Festivals. No *cushion* should be 'allowed upon the Altar, and only one book (for the Celebrant,) 'with a small brass desk to support it.' (*p.* 25.)—*Directorium Anglicanum.* (The *lace* and *embroidery* additions here recommended are *illegal.* W. H. P. (See *below.*)

590.—We will now give the opinions of *Dr. Lushington,* and *Sir J. Dodson,* and the final decision of the *Judicial Committee of Privy Council* in the Appeal case of "Westerton and Beal *v.* Liddell," in the matter of St Paul's Church, *Knightsbridge,* and St Barnabas Church, *Pimlico.*

In the Case of Westerton *v.* Liddell, heard in the *Consistory Court* (Dec. 1855), DR. LUSHINGTON thus decides on the question of *Communion-Cloths*:—'I must now dispose of the question which 'has been raised with respect to the *coverings* on the Communion-'table, used in both churches. The facts are as follows:—With 'respect to St Paul's, it is alleged that the Communion-table at 'the time of the administration of the Holy Communion, is covered 'with a *covering of worked* and *embroidered* white linen, *ornamented* 'and *enriched* and *bordered at the ends with elaborately worked lace.* 'This is denied, and I will assume the denial to correspond with 'the truth; but it is admitted that the Communion-table is *covered* 'and *decorated* by *five differently coloured coverings*, each of which 'is *embroidered* and *adorned*, and which are *varied at different* '*periods of the year*, as follows, to wit:—A *white* one from the 'evening of Christmas Eve to the octave of Epiphany inclusive, '(except on the feasts of St Stephen and the Holy Innocents); 'from the evening of Easter Eve to the vigil of Pentecost, on 'Trinity Sunday, Purification, Conversion of St Paul, Annun-'ciation, St John Baptist, St Michael, St Luke, All Saints. A '*red* one on the vigil of Pentecost to the next Saturday, Holy 'Innocents (if on a Sunday), and all other feasts. A *violet* one 'on Ash-Wednesday to Easter Eve, Advent to Christmas Eve, 'Ember Week in September, Holy Innocents, unless on Sunday. 'A *darker violet* one on Good Friday and funerals. A *green* one 'on all other days. The law appears to me to lie within a very 'narrow compass—the notice in the Book of Common Prayer, 'the *Rubric* before the Communion Service, and the 82*nd Canon*. 'There are specific directions given, and in the Book of Common 'Prayer, in these words:—"*The table at the Communion Service,* "*having a fair white linen cloth upon it,*" &c. The covering is to 'be a *fair white linen cloth;* and any addition to it of any kind 'would not fall within the description, but necessarily be forbidden, 'and would not be consistent with it. This brings me to the 82*nd* '*Canon*, which is in the following words:—"The Communion-table "is to be covered, in time of Divine Service, with a Carpet of silk or "other decent stuff," &c. This *canon* is in entire conformity with 'the *Rubric.* It is therefore valid, and must be considered the *law* '*of the Church on the subject.* It must be observed, however, 'that this *Canon* applies only to the time of Divine Service, and 'that it does not leave an absolute discretion to the Ordinary, but 'only, *if the carpets be not of silk, the Ordinary shall determine what* '*is the other decent stuff.* Confining myself at present to the *cloths* 'used at the time of Divine Service, the first question is, by what 'authority is the use of *divers cloths*, ornamented or not, at fixed 'periods of the year, sanctioned; or is not their introduction into 'our Parish Churches an entire novelty? Certainly this *Canon* 'could not be said to support the practice, for not a word is there-'in to be found of *divers cloths* to be used at different periods, 'or of any *ornaments* at all. The *Canon* says, the "Table shall be "covered with a carpet of silk or other decent stuff." I admit that 'these words do not necessarily exclude carpets; that the expression 'in the singular, '*a carpet,*' does not *vi termini*, exclude the plural, 'though it gives no authority for it. But the question is not 'whether there might not be several cloths, but several cloths of '*different colours*, placed on the Communion-table at stated periods. 'For such a practice the *Canon* affords no sanction whatever. The 'fact is that *embroidered* and *ornamented cloths of different colours* 'are used to cover the Communion-table, in precise accordance 'with the usages of the Roman Catholic Church, the colours being 'emblematic of particular periods. What warrant is there for 'engrafting into our Churches this ceremonial of Rome? I have 'heard none. Then the plain truth is, that, without authority, 'without reason, this practice of the Roman Catholic Church has 'been introduced into a place of Protestant worship. What is this 'but a servile imitation of the Church of Rome? And what is a 'servile imitation of that Church but a direct violation of all the 'principles and all the rules established for the regulation of the 'ceremonies and ornaments of the Church of England? A decorous 'simplicity is the characteristic of the Church of England. What 'is *lace* and *embroidery* but a meretricious display of fantastic and 'unnecessary ornament? But look at its accompaniment—more 'especially with respect to St Barnabas—a *metal cross ornamented 'with jewels*, a *rood screen*, and *brazen gates*. I am of opinion that, 'if I am to decide this as a question of law, *this practice is not 'justified by the statute, the Rubric, or the Canon*. If it be a question 'to be governed by the discretion of the Court, I entertain no doubt 'whatever that it is *my duty to prohibit* the use of these cloths in 'the manner in which it is admitted they have been used. If it 'be objected to this my judgment that the Court would leave the 'House of God barren and desolate, I answer, that no such 'consequences would ensue. Chastity and simplicity are not at 'variance with grandeur and beauty; but they are not reconcile-'able with *jewels, lace, variegated cloths*, and *embroidery*, which are 'better fitted for the gorgeous pageantry of the Church of Rome, 'than the pure and severe dignity of the Church of England...... 'For these reasons MY DECREE will be to the following effect...... 'To *take away all the cloths* at present used in the Church for 'covering the structure used as a Communion-table during Divine 'Service, and *to substitute only one covering* for such purpose, *of silk* 'or *other decent stuff*; and further, *to remove any cover used at the 'time of the ministration of the Sacrament, worked*, or *embroidered 'with lace or otherwise ornamented, and to substitute a fair white 'linen cloth, without lace or embroidery or other ornament*, to cover 'the Communion-table at the time of the ministration of the Sacra-'ment.'—*The Guardian*, (*Supplement*) Dec. 12th, 1855.

591.—This decision was appealed against, and the case carried into the Superior Court, the *Court of Arches*, (*Dec.* 10th, 1856), where SIR JOHN DODSON confirmed the Judgment of the inferior Court, remarking as follows:—'The consideration of the *Coverings* of the 'Communion Table in the time of Divine Service, and at the 'celebration of the Holy Communion. He would consider the latter 'point first. The law upon the point, he apprehended, was to be 'found in the *Rubric* prefixed to the Communion Service in the 'Book of Common Prayer. It was in these words—"*The table at "the Communion Service, having a fair white linen cloth upon it*," '&c. The directions of the 82*nd Canon* were to the very same 'effect—"The table is to be covered with a *fair linen cloth* at the "time of ministration." Those directions seemed to be sufficiently 'plain and explicit. It was to be a *fair linen cloth*, and nothing 'whatever was ordered, or even suggested, as to the additions of '*lace, embroidery*, or *any other ornament;* nor had he been able to 'discover any authority for such addition, or that any such usage 'had prevailed in the Church of England since the Reformation. 'He did not mean to assert positively that no such instance had 'ever occurred, but merely that it never came within his cogni-'zance. He did not wish it to be understood that he considered 'this to be of very grave importance in this case, but, supposing 'the law as cited to have left the matter unsettled, and that it was 'diversely taken by the parties, resort must be had to the *Ordinary* 'as directed by the instructions prefixed to the Prayer-book, and 'that was the course which had been pursued—for the decision of 'the learned Judge sitting in the Consistorial Court of the Ordinary 'had been obtained, and he saw no reason for departing from it. 'A similar observation applied to the use of the *various coloured* '*cloths* on the Communion-table at the time of divine Service, and 'the results must be similar......The conclusion of the Court, there- 'fore, was that the *judgment of the Court below* must be *affirmed* 'in all respects.'—*Supplement to the "Guardian."* Dec. 24th, 1856.

592.—This judgment was also objected to, and the case carried to the final Court of Appeal, the *Judicial Committee of the Privy Council*, (March 21, 1857,) who thus set the matter at rest, decreeing as follows:— 'As to the *embroidered Cloths*, it is said that the Canon orders a '*covering of silk*, or of some other proper material, but that it does 'not mention, and therefore, by implication, excludes more than 'one covering. Their Lordships are unable to adopt this construc- 'tion. An order that a table shall always be covered with a cloth 'surely *does not imply that it shall always be covered with the same* '*cloth, or with a cloth of the same colour or texture.* The object of 'this Canon seems to be to secure a cloth of a sufficiently handsome 'description, not to guard against too much splendour. In practice 'as was justly observed at the bar, *black cloths* are in many Churches 'used *during Lent*, and on the *death of the Sovereign*, and *some other* '*occasions*, and there seems nothing objectionable in the practice. 'Whether the cloths so used are suitable or not is a matter to be 'left to the discretion of the Ordinary. In this case their lordships 'do not see any sufficient reason for interference; and they must 'therefore *advise the reversal of the sentence as to the cloths used for* '*the covering of the Lord's table during the time of Divine Service*, 'both with respect to St Paul's and to St Barnabas. The last 'question is with respect to the *embroidered linen* and *lace used on* '*the Communion-table at the time of the ministration of the Holy* '*Communion.* The Rubric and the Canon prescribe the use of a '*fair white linen cloth*, and both the learned Judges in the Court 'below have been of opinion that *embroidery* and *lace* are not con- 'sistent with the meaning of that expression, having regard to the 'nature of the table upon which the cloth is to be used. Although 'their lordships are not disposed in any case to restrict within 'narrower limits than the law has imposed the discretion which, 'within those limits, is justly allowed to Congregations by the 'rules both of the Ecclesiastical and the Common Law Courts, the 'directions of the Rubric must be complied with; and, upon the 'whole, *their lordships do not dissent from the construction of the* '*Rubric adopted by the present decree upon this point, and they must* '*therefore advise her Majesty to affirm it*......In the present case 'it is satisfactory to their lordships to be able to state that both the '*Archbishop of Canterbury*, (Sumner,) and the *Bishop of London*

'(Tait) concur in the judgment which has just been delivered.'—*Supplement to the "Guardian."* March 25th, 1857.

THE POSITION OF THE TABLE.

4 c) ¶. '*The Table, at the Communion-time having a fair 'white linen cloth upon it shall stand in the body of 'the Church, or in the Chancel, where Morning and 'Evening Prayer are appointed to be said.*' (1662.)—Present Book of Common Prayer.

593.—The *position* of the Communion Table is not accurately defined in this Rubric, nor do we derive much light from a perusal of the *Canon* on this head, which thus reads :—

'We appoint that the same *Tables* shall......so stand, saving 'when the said Holy Communion is to be administered: *at which 'time* the same shall be placed in so good sort within the Church or 'Chancel as thereby the Minister may be more conveniently heard 'of the Communicants in his Prayer and Ministration, and the 'Communicants also more conveniently, and in more number, may 'communicate with the said Minister.'—CANON 82.

When *moveable Tables* were first introduced, they were placed at Communion-time in Cathedrals, and College Chapels, *in the Chancel;* and in Parish Churches, very frequently, *in the body of the Church,* at the discretion of the Minister, in accordance with the above injunctions; but the later usage has been to retain the Communion Table in its usual place and position, i. e. *altar-wise,* at the east end of the Chancel: and this usage now universally prevails. A fuller elucidation of this question will be found in *Vol.* **C**. We may remark, however, that there has been but little variation in this Rubric since its

---

* In the SCOTCH LITURGY, (1637,) we have a very full Rubric on this matter:—

'*The holy Table having at the Communion-time a carpet, and 'a fair white linen cloth upon it, with other decent furniture, meet 'for the high mysteries there to be celebrated, shall stand at the 'uppermost part of the Chancel or Church, where the Presbyter 'standing at the North-side or end thereof, shall say the Lord's 'Prayer, with this Collect following for due preparation.*'—KEELING. (66.)

introduction into the Second Liturgy of Edw. VI., 1552; and this variation is merely verbal, such as—'*The Table, having at Communion-time*,' &c. (1552. 1559. 1604.) altered in the last Revision to, '*The Table, at the Communion-time, having*,' &c. (1662.) So again, in the earlier Liturgies we read :—'*or in the Chancel where Morning Prayer and Evening Prayer be appointed*, &c. (1552. 1559. 1604.)—but in the last Review, the words run, '*or in the Chancel where Morning and Evening Prayer are appointed*,' &c. (1662). The latter part of this last clause is omitted altogether from the American Liturgy. We will now add an opinion or two by way of corroboration of what we have advanced.

BISHOP COSINS says:—'There was much ado about the posture 'of the Table, and the Priests standing at it in King *Edward's* time; 'for in the second year, the Altar stood still in the usual place, and 'the Priest was appointed to stand before the midst of the Altar 'with his face towards it, and this was confirmed by Act of Parlia'ment. Notwithstanding which Act, there were so many excep'tions taken, and oppositions made against that Order, some 'standing at the West-side of the Altar, with their faces turned 'towards the People, others at the East, others at the South, and 'others at the North; that at last they agreed to set forth this rule 'in the fifth of King *Edward*, instead of the former, set forth in the 'second year,' &c.—*Add. Notes to* NICHOLLS' *Com. Prayer*, p. 36.

L'ESTRANGE writes:—'This Rubrick being not explicit enough 'as to the proper station of the Holy Table, is illustrated by com'paring the 82 Canon with Queen *Elizabeth* her first *Injunctions*, 'and succeeding *Orders*. In the Canon the Order is, that the Table 'shall stand where it is placed, *viz.* at the East end of the Chancel, "*saving when the holy Communion is to be administred: at which* "*time the same shall be placed in so good a sort, as thereby the* "*Minister may be more conveniently heard of the Communicants, and* "*the Communicants also may more conveniently, and in more number* "*communicate with the Minister.*" Which words are almost *verbatim* 'transcribed out of the Queen's Injunctions, these only superadding. "*And after the Communion done from time to time the same holy* "*Table to be placed where it stood before.*" Nothing can be more 'express and demonstrative, that the Table placed where the Altar 'stood, was best seposed, set out of the way, during only the time 'of Non-Communication; and that at the time of the Communion, 'it was to be removed, as the word *Saving*, mentioned both in the '*Canon* and in the *Injunctions*, and the cited member of the *Injunc*'*tions* infallibly implieth: if these instances afford not satiety to 'quiet all scruples, the Order of that Queen speak shrill enough. "*And if in any Church the steps be transposed, that they be not* "*erected again, but that the place be decently paved, where the Com*"*munion-Table shall stand, out of the time of receiving of the holy*

"*Communion*." (Order, Oct. 10. 8 *Eliz.*). So that *out of Com-*
'*munion time* the Table is to stand *Altar-wise*, as we, and only
'we do phrase it; for *Altar-wise* is an idiom peculiar to us English,
'not known abroad in foreign parts; and they who can find Popery
'in that position, have better eyes than ordinary. *Altars* with
'them do not observe one regular position; some are placed in the
'middle of the Choir; some at the upper part, end-ways North and
'South; and if eye-witnesses may be trusted, the chief Altar in
'*S. Peter's* Church at *Rome* stands in the midst of the Chancel.
'*As for the Priest standing at the North-side of the Table, this*
'*seemeth to avoid the fashion of the Priest's standing with his face*
'*towards the East, as is the Popish practice.* So the MS. Collections.'
(*p.* 166.)—*Alliance.*

The REV. J. JEBB, after citing *Canon* 82, says:—'This license 'has been rarely if ever acted upon. Happily for the Church of 'England, our Ordinaries have deemed fit to let the Holy Table 'remain in its ancient place, hallowed by the precedent of ages, 'and by the universal practice of the Church.' (*p.* 465.)—*Choral Service.*

THE OFFICIATING MINISTER MUST BE A PRIEST.

(4 *d*) ¶. '*And the Priest standing at the North Side of the 'Table shall say the Lord's Prayer, and the Collect 'following, the People Kneeling.** — Present Book of Common Prayer.

THE OFFICIATING MINISTER.

594.—This Rubric was introduced at the *Revision* of the Liturgy in 1552, and continued through the Revisions of 1559, 1604, and 1662, to the present time; except that the clause, "*the People kneeling*," was not added till the *last Review* in 1662. In the first Prayer Book of Edward VI., the Rubric ran thus:—

'*Upon the day, and at the time appointed for the Minis- 'tration of the Holy Communion, the Priest that shall execute 'the ministry, shall put upon him,*' &c.—KEELING. 167.

---

* In the AMERICAN LITURGY this Rubric reads:

'*And the Minister standing at the right side of the Table, 'or where Morning and Evening Prayer are appointed to be said, 'shall say the Lord's Prayer and the Collect following, the People 'Kneeling; but the Lord's Prayer may be omitted if Morning 'Prayer hath been said immediately before.*'

and in the '*Alterations*,' suggested in 1689 by the Royal Commissioners, it was proposed that the Rubric should be as follows :—

'*And the Minister shall at the North Side of the Table 'say the Lord's Prayer with the Collect following, All Kneeling.*'

From these Rubrics, and the rejected '*Alterations*' of 1689, it may indisputably be concluded, that the Minister who performs the Office of the Holy Communion must be one in Priest's Orders. But, as the whole Office is not used when there is to be *no celebration* of the Sacrament, the portion employed on such occasions, and designated the "*Ante-Communion Service*" or "*Second Service*," extending to the conclusion of the Sermon, has been often delegated to a *Deacon*. This relaxation of the Rubric, however, is only excusable in the event of no Officiating Priest being present; or when pressing necessity may require it; but the absence of a Priest cannot be permitted when an '*administration*' is to take place. In the *first* Liturgy of Edward VI. (1549.) the *Rubric* at the end of the Communion Office, directing the curtailment of the Service when there were '*none to communicate*,' orders that:—

'*The Priest shall......say all things at the* Altar (*appointed 'to be said at the celebration of the Lord's Supper) until after the 'Offertory. And then shall add one or two of the Collects afore-'written as occasion shall serve by his discretion. And then turn-'ing him to the People shall let them depart with the accustomed* 'Blessing.' (1549.)—KEELING. 229.

Here we find a *Priest* is expressly appointed to the Ante-Communion Service; and '*the Blessing*,' moreover, to be pronounced, which is limited by Rubric to the *Priest*. In the Liturgies of 1552, 1559, and 1604, the term '*Priest*' is omitted from this Rubric; which commences:—'*Upon the Holy-days* (*if there be 'no Communion*) *shall be said all that is appointed*,' &c.: the pronouncing of '*the Blessing*' is also not enjoined; hence, we may conclude that, latitude was given for a *Deacon* to officiate in this Service. In the *last Review*, however, in 1662, though the term *Priest* was not restored to this Rubric, yet '*the blessing*' was directed to be used; in these words:—

'*concluding with the blessing.*' Since, therefore, this '*blessing*' can only be pronounced by a *Priest*, we may suppose that the altered Rubric intended to enforce the employment of a Priest in the *Ante-Communion Service.*

595.—As a General Rule, therefore, the chief person of the Church (*persona ecclesiæ*), the *Incumbent*, should be the chief Minister in the Communion Office; as well in the *Ante-Communion Service*, as in the '*Administration.*'

596.—We may also add, that it is sometimes the practice for the '*Preacher*,' if a stranger, or another person than the Minister officiating in the Reading Desk, to occupy the north side of the Table, and undertake the reading of this earlier portion of the Communion Office. And it has been said that, if the *Preacher* should be a stranger, this function *ought to be* assigned to him 'by way of compliment;' but surely this is neither the time, place, nor occasion, for the passing of compliments; therefore the wholesome, time-worn, custom of devolving the duty upon the *Incumbent* should not, we think, be departed from. Exceptional cases will, of course, arise; such as instances of indisposition, infirmity, or being overtasked, when the Incumbent would satisfy the requirements of the Liturgy by taking simply the *Epistle*, should he be present: we shall also find that where a Church is provided with a staff of Clergy, and a division of duty apportioned, the Ante-Communion Service is sometimes allotted to the second officiating Minister in Priests' Orders, while the Gospel and Epistle are delegated to certain appointed Readers, termed at one time the *Gospeller* and *Epistoler;* or, it may be, the *Epistle alone* is appropriated to a distinct Reader; this, however, is not often the case: still, the *general rule* above given should be departed from as seldom as possible. Should a *Deacon* be the only Officiating Minister, a circumstance that may occasionally and unavoidably happen, custom allows him to take the *Ante-Communion Service.*—(See *postea.*)

Bp. Cosins remarks:—'This term or title of *Priest*, is here used 'throughout this whole Communion Service, unless it be in such 'parts of it which may be read upon Sundays and Holidays *when 'there is no Communion*, for then *any other Minister may perform 'the Office*. But the Sacrament of the Eucharist is reserved for the '*Priest*, no other Minister of an inferior Order having any com-'mission or power given him, to meddle either in *consecrating the 'Elements*, or *absolving the penitents* that come to receive them.'—*Add. Notes to* Nicholls' *Book of Com. Prayer*. p. 88.

The Rev. J. Jebb writes:—'It never could have been intended 'to construe the *Rubrics* of the Communion Service so rigidly, as 'to contradict the universal practice in all ages, which has ever 'sanctioned the ministration of *three Clergymen* at the Communion. 'The distribution of the service between them has, in fact, been 'very exactly defined, at least as to certain portions of the Office, '*e. g.*, the *Epistle* and *Gospel*. In some cases, indeed, the law of 'the Church enjoins it; thus, the *24th* Canon has these words: "'The principal Minister' (at the Communion) 'using a decent "cope,' and being assisted with the *Gospeller* and *Epistler* agreeably, "according to the Advertisements published *anno* 7 *Eliz.*" In the "Form and Manner of making of Deacons," &c......this is made still 'more definite in the charge which follows: "Take thou authority "to read the Gospel in the Church of God;" and that the Gospel 'in the Communion Service is here meant is proved by the fact 'that immediately after one of the *Deacons* is appointed to enter 'upon his office by reading the *Gospel*. And it can be proved that 'in this instance the Church of England but confirms the custom 'of the Church universal. It may be observed that the license 'given in the above charge, implies that the Officiating Priest is 'not of necessity the *Preacher*, since *Deacons* may preach; but they 'cannot perform the full Communion Service.........But looking 'merely at the letter of the Prayer Book, *the* Priest may fairly 'be construed to mean *that* Priest, to whom that particular part 'of the Service to which the Rubric refers has been by authority 'or custom assigned. He must of necessity be a *Priest*, when but 'one Clergyman is present. The delegation to a lawful Minister 'of a part of the Office surely satisfies the intention of the Rubric. 'The *Priest*, that is, the principal Minister present, in Collegiate 'and Parish Churches, is responsible; but he may call in the 'assistance of another, according to the universal custom of the 'Church.'—(Stephens's *Book of Common Prayer*, E. H. S. *p.* 1123.)—In another Work this Author says:—'The universal custom 'of the Church assigns, in Collegiate Foundations, the Office of the 'Communion to the *Senior Member* present, that is, to the *Bishop* 'or the *Dean;* and next to them, to the first in rank either by 'temporary office, as *Vice-dean* in the Cathedrals of new founda-'tion, or by permanent place in the Chapter, as in those of old...... 'This Collegiate rule, however, would seem to be the proper one 'to adopt in *Parish Churches*. As it is, the *Rectors* or *Vicars* in 'those places, by a very general, if not universal custom, yield to 'their Bishops alone in the administration of the Holy Communion, 'taking upon themselves the performance of that part of the Service 'which follows the Sermon. To the *Preacher*, however, whether 'a *Stranger* or a *Curate*, is, by an anomalous courtesy, assigned the 'principal part at the *Ante-Communion*. To this arrangement there 'are two objections. The first is, the impropriety of making the 'Sermon the standard by which the distribution of the sacred Offices 'among the ministers is to be regulated: the second is, the effect 'it has in breaking the unity of the Service. The Minister who 'performs the principal Office of the day, that is, the *Consecration* '*of the Elements*, ought to begin the Communion Service at its 'proper place. Besides, the *Incumbent* of the Parish ought always 'to take this principal part as the *Persona Ecclesiæ*, and it is not 'seemly that he should compliment away this station, assigned to 'him by his Bishop. The impropriety of suffering a *Deacon* to read 'the *Ante-Communion Service* in the presence of a Priest, is too 'obvious to require comment.' (*p.* 472.)—*Choral Service.*

[*The Ornaments of the Priest at Communion Time.*]

597.—The Rubric of the First Prayer Book of Edw. VI., (1549), which we have just *partly* quoted, refers particularly to the *Ornaments of the Minister* to be used at the time of the Administration of the Holy Communion, as follows:—

'*Upon the day, and at the time appointed for the ministra-* '*tion of the* HOLY COMMUNION, *the Priest that shall execute the* '*holy ministry, shall put upon him the Vesture appointed for* '*that ministration, that is to say, a* white Albe plain, *with a* 'Vestment *or* Cope. *And where there be many Priests, or* '*Deacons, there so many shall be ready to help the Priest in the* '*ministration, as shall be requisite. And shall have upon them* '*likewise the Vestures appointed for their ministry, that is to* '*say,* Albes *with* Tunicles'......(1549.)—KEELING. p. 167.

Here we perceive that the Chief Minister used to wear an *Albe* with a *Vestment* or *Cope;* and the Assistant Ministers to wear *Albes* with *Tunicles.*

598.—At the ANTE-COMMUNION SERVICE, and when there is *no administration*, the Officiating Minister was directed by another Rubric at the end of the Communion Office in this early Liturgy of 1549, to wear an *Albe*, or *Surplice*, with a *Cope:* it thus reads.—

'*Upon* Wednesdays *and* Fridays *the English* Litany '*shall be said or sung, &c.........And though there be none to* '*communicate with the Priest, yet these days (after the* Litany '*ended) the Priest shall put upon him a plain* Albe *or* Sur- 'plice *with a* Cope, *and say all things at the Altar, &c.*

'*And the same order shall be used all other days &c......* '*and none disposed to communicate with the Priest.*' (1549.)—KEELING. 229. 231.

599.—These *Rubrics*, as we have already fully shown in *Vol.* D. to which we must refer our Readers for every detail connected with the *Ornaments of the Minister*, are now obsolete; and both CANON (58), and USAGE, prescribe that in performing the Communion

Office no change shall be made from the Vestments employed at *Morning* and *Evening Prayer*. We have cited these Rubrics of 1549, lest it should be supposed we had designedly, or accidentally, passed them over. We will now proceed to discuss briefly

The Place of the Priest.

600.—The *Rubric* at the beginning of the Communion Office, which we have already quoted (4 *d*), directs that the Priest shall stand at the *north side* of the Communion Table; that is to say, '*at the left hand side, as one approaches the Table from the Nave.*' This gloss is necessary, because in some Churches the Chancel does not stand at the *east end* of the Church. In London there are several instances to be met with where the Churches have not been built in the usual direction, on account of the difficulty of procuring sites extending lengthways from east to west.

The Rubric at its first introduction in 1549, ran thus :—

> '*The Priest standing humbly afore the midst of the Altar, 'shall say the Lord's Prayer, with this Collect.*' (1549.)—KEELING. 169.

and did not, as we can well imagine, contemplate that frequent omission of the celebration of the Eucharist which till lately had become almost an universal custom; yet provision was made for the event of there being 'none to communicate with the Priest' by a Rubric at the end of the Communion Office, of the same Liturgy, and continued with a little variation in all the subsequent *Revisions*, directing that, on such occasions only, the earlier portion of the Office should be used—that which we now call the '*Ante-Communion Service.*' At first, this Service was read by some at the *north side* of the Altar; by others, from their *Stall* in the Chancel, or from the *Reading Pew;* and thus did the usage vary, until the time of Archbishop Laud; who is charged with enforcing a strict adherence to the Rubric, and commanding that the Office of the Holy Communion, wholly, or in part, should at all times be read from the *north side* of the Altar, whether there was to be an actual Celebration, or not. Among the '*Exceptions* against the Book of Common Prayer' taken at the Savoy Conference (*May* 4th, 1661.) by the Presbyterian Divines at the last Revision, was this :—

'That the Minister be not required to rehearse any part of the 'Liturgy *at the Communion Table*, save only those parts which 'properly belong to the Lord's Supper; and that *at such times* '*only* when the said holy Supper is administered.' (*p.* 307.)—CARDWELL'S *Conf.*

To this the Bishops reply:—'That the Minister should not read 'the Communion Service at the Communion Table, is not reason-'able to demand, since all the primitive Church used it, &c......The 'Priest standing at the Communion Table seemeth to give us an 'invitation to the Holy Sacrament, and minds us of our duty, viz. 'to receive the Holy Communion, some at least every Sunday; and 'though we neglect our duty, it is fit the Church should keep her 'standing.'—(*ib.* 342.)

601.—The *present usage* is certainly to read the 'Ante-Communion Service,' whether there be a celebration or not, from the *north end* of the Communion Table facing the south, and turning occasionally to the Congregation (see *postea*): the *exception* as to *place* prevails only in a few *rural* Churches, where they read this Service on *no-communion days* from the Desk; the *exception*, however, as to *position*, prevails only in extreme ritualistic Churches where the Priest stands at the *north-end* of the *west side* of the Communion Table, and faces the east. To enter into the dispute which so long existed as to what is implied in the Rubric by the expression '*the north side of the Communion Table*'—whether, that is to say, it means the *north-end* of the Table, the Priest to face the south, or the *north-end of the west side* of the Table, the Priest to face the east, would neither be interesting, nor profitable; (see LATHBURY'S *Hist. of Book of Com. Prayer*, pp. 323. 397. 425.); we may, therefore, close the consideration of this Rubric with a few authorities.

L'ESTRANGE (A. D. 1659—60) remarks:—'As for the Priest 'standing at the *North-side* of the Table, this seemeth to avoid the 'fashion of the Priests standing with his face towards the East, 'as is the Popish practice. So the MS. Collections of a learned 'man.' (*p.* 166.)—*Alliance.*

Bishop Cosins (A. D. 1672) quotes on this head the following:— 'Quando stamus ad orationem. (B. *Cypr.* de Orat. Dominic.) Stantes 'oramus, quod est signum Resurrectionis, tempore Paschali, unde 'etiam omnibus diebus Dominicis ad Altare id observatur. (S. Aug. 'Epist. 119.) "The *Jews* prayed standing, (*Matth.* 6. 5.) but only "in the time of Mourning; for then they prayed prostrate, or upon "their knees." Formerly the Priest stood in the middle of the 'Sacred Altar. (*Dionys. Eccl. Hier. Cap.* 3. *Tertull. de Orat. Cap.* '14.) *Si ad aram Dei steteris.* "And the Writings of the Ancients 'abound with testimonies of the same thing." Again this Writer says with respect to *standing at the Table*:—'which was the custom 'of the ancients, that all things which pertained to the Celebration 'of the Lord's-Supper should be said *at the Altar.* Now in this 'Celebration, there is hardly any difference between us and the 'Protestants in *Germany*, but *that* among us the Prayers are said 'by the Bishop or Minister *at the Altar*, but among them *in the 'Desk*: In which they do not agree with the Ancients.'—*Add. Notes to* Nicholls' *Book of Com. Prayer.* (*p.* 38.)

Bp. Sparrow says:—'The place for this Service is *the Altar*, 'or *Communion-Table*; *Rubric* before the Communion. And so it 'was always in primitive times, which is a thing so plain, as that it 'needs no proof.' (*p.* 158.)—*Rationale.*

Dr. Bennett (A. D. 1708) says:—'If it be ask'd, whether those 'parts of the Communion Office which are allow'd to be read when 'there is *no Communion*, may be read without going to the Com-'munion Table; I answer, they certainly may. And for this I need 'offer no further reason, besides its being an allow'd practice, which 'our Governors do never blame, or endeavour to alter. There are 'some expressions in the Rubric, I confess, which intimate the con-'trary. But certainly an allow'd custom is sufficient to satisfie any 'man's conscience in this case.' (*p.* 155. *Note.*)—*Paraphrase on the Book of Common Prayer.*

Dr. Bisse says;—'Now in many Parish Churches, instead of 'this Anthem, is commonly sung a Psalm: which is very proper, 'though the Minister should *not go up to the Communion-Table*; 'and rather the more so when he does: because this interposal of a 'Psalm makes a separation and distinction between the two Ser-'vices, which ought to be thus made by distance of time, when 'it *cannot be done by difference of place.* Not but in all Parish 'Churches, as well as in Quires, where it can be done with con-'venience to the Congregation, this Service *ought regularly to be said 'at the Lord's Table*: a thing which Bishop Beveridge, that great 'saint and ornament of our Church, and great admirer and pro-'moter of our Liturgy, much desires and insists upon, as useful to 'remind people, that there ought at least to be a Sacrament, though 'there be not, on every Sunday and Holy-day.'—(Quoted in Mant's *Book of Common Prayer.* p. 281.)

'WHEATLY says:—'Wherever it (the *Table*) be placed, the 'Priest is obliged to ***stand at the north side***, (or ***end*** thereof, as 'the Scotch Liturgy expresses it; which also orders, that it shall 'stand at the uppermost part of the Chancel or Church), the design 'of which is, that the Priest may be the better seen and heard; 'which, as our Altars are now placed, he cannot be but at the 'north or south side. And therefore the ***north side***, being the ***right*** '***hand*** or ***upper side*** of the Altar, is certainly the most proper for 'the Officiating Priest, that so the assisting Minister, if there be 'one, may not be obliged to stand above him. And Bishop Beveridge 'has shewn that wherever, in the ancient Liturgies, the Minister is 'directed *to stand before the Altar*, the ***north side*** of it is always 'meant.' (*p.* 303.)—*Rat. Ill. of Book of Common Prayer.*

ARCHDEACON SHARP writes:—'For since the customary placing 'of Altars in Chancels it becomes sometimes impossible in large 'Churches, and where the Chancels are almost equal in length to 'the Churches themselves, to perform that part of the Commuuion 'Service which is to be read always on Sundays and Holy-days, 'at the Lord's Table, without quite defeating the intention of its 'being read at all, viz. "that it should be heard of all the people." 'But then, pray let us observe further, that where this necessity 'for breaking through the Rubric cannot be pleaded by us; that is, 'where this Service "may be conveniently enough performed at the "Table itself," situated in the Chancel; there will be ***no excuse for us*** '***for reading it in the Desk;*** as is but too commonly practised in our 'Churches, contrary to the letter and plain meaning of the Rubric. (*p.* 53.)......Where this Rubric cannot be observed, as I before said, 'an absolute necessity must overrule the order; but no prescription 'of nonobservauce or customary neglect can avail to the setting it 'aside. It is true, the Ordinary may connive at this customary 'neglect, but he cannot warrant nor even excuse the Minister in it, 'because he is bound, by prior obligations of conformity, to obey 'the Church in what she commands in her Rubrics.' (*p.* 55.)...... In a *Note* is added;—'Should it be insinuated that this Rubric, by 'expressly directing what should be done "in Communion time," 'may mean that the Priest should then only stand at the ***north side*** 'of the Table; the answer is, that there he is ordered to stand '***whensoever he begins the Office;*** and there he is commanded "to "say the Lord's Prayer, with the Collect following," &c. (*p.* 55.)—*On Rubrics and Canons.*

The REV. J. J. BLUNT, (late *Margaret Professor of Divinity at Cambridge,*) observes:—'Here the Rubric is express against a 'practice, not uncommon, that of reading this Service, when there 'is no Communion, ***from the Desk.*** This, I say, is a clear ***infraction*** '***of the Rubric***, which directs that "the Priest is to stand at the "north side of the Table, and say," &c. (*p.* 325.)—***Duties of the Parish Priest.***

The REV. J. JEBB states:—'Whatever license may be given to 'the Ordinary to change the place of the Holy Table, during the 'Administration of the Communion, no license whatever is given 'to the Minister by the letter, and I will add, by the spirit of the 'Prayer Book, to say any of the prayers of that Service, even on 'non-Communion days, in any other place than ***at the Holy Table*** '*itself*. All the Rubrics imply and suppose the use of the Table. 'And I cannot see why there is not as strong a ground for violating 'the Rubric directing the weekly use of the Ante-Communion 'Service, as for transgressing these. It may be said, indeed, that 'the *Canon* sanctions the removal of the Table at the Communion 'time only, and therefore that it is not only physically impossible 'in many places for the Minister to read the Ante-Communion in 'the Chancel, but that he has no option to do otherwise than *read* '*it in the Desk*, if he is to be heard. To this it may be answered; 'it is far from clear whether the Church contemplates the non-'administration of the Holy Communion on Sundays, except as an 'unhappy accident. (*p.* 468.)......Our best Ritualists have held 'that the theory of the Church is to give an opportunity at least 'to all, every Sunday: and the Communion Service is to be read 'to as far as a certain place, to terminate there, should no persons 'have signified their intention of communicating......As to the plea 'often urged, that in long Chancels the Minister is *not seen*, this 'can apply to a part of the Congregation only: and in large 'Churches, there is no position whatever where he can be visible 'to all: besides, the Church has laid a stress upon his being *heard*, 'not upon his being *seen*. But whatever necessity may in some few 'instances exist, for reading the Ante-Communion *from the Desk*, it 'is in all instances to be deeply deplored. There is, perhaps, no one 'external practice, next to irreverence or apathy, which is more 'repugnant to all Christian precedent, and which has more injured 'the real edification of the people, as keeping out of remembrance 'the Table of the Lord, the recollection of His death, and the special 'obligations of the Sunday Communion, in which the devotion of 'the faithful ought mainly to consist. A thousand times more is 'lost to the cause of edification by the non-observance of this signi-'ficant ceremony, than is gained by the more audible recitation of 'the Ante-Communion prayers. (*p.* 469.)......No pains should be 'spared to obviate a custom so essentially uncatholic... ..But even 'at times when the Communion is administered, every pains seem 'to be taken in many places, to dissociate the former division from 'the latter, by performing the part preceding the Sermon in the 'Desk. (*p.* 470.)......Doubts have arisen with regard to the mean-'ing of the term "*north side*," into which the Author must avow 'his incapacity to enter. It seems a very plain matter, that the 'Church intended merely that which universal custom exhibits; 'not an angle, but *an end*, or shorter side, of the Table, placed as it 'is now, altarwise. So the Church has interpreted it by the uniform 'position both of the Table itself, and of her Ministers, at least ever 'since the last Review.' (*p.* 471.)—*On the Choral Service.*

The REV. J. PURCHAS writes:—'*The north side* (as distinguished 'from the *north end*, the Altar being a parallelogram) is the tech-'nical phrase for *the north part of the west side*, called also the 'Gospel or left corner. It occurs in the Syriac Liturgy of S. James: '—"*Venitque* (i. e. *sacerdos*) *a latere septentrionali ad australe.*" (Renandotii *Lit. Or. Coll.*, tom. ii. p. 24.)—(*p.* 33. *note.*)—*Directorium Anglicanum.*

The REV. J. C. ROBERTSON says:—'In favour of the usage' (of reading from the Altar) 'may be pleaded those Rubrics which speak 'of the Lord's Table in connexion with *parts* of the Communion-

'office which are read in the Second Service; and there is certainly 'no ground for finding fault with the observance of it, unless, as 'may happen in some Churches, it render the Service *inaudible.* It 'is not, however, as appears to me, the only allowable practice. In 'the *Rubric* at the end of the Office, by which it is directed that 'certain parts of the Service "shall be said if there be no Com-"munion," there is no order as to the *place* where they shall be 'said; whereas, in the Liturgy of 1549, it was expressly enjoined 'that the Priest should say them "*at the Altar.*" (KEELING. 229.) 'This circumstance would lead us to presume that the later Books 'intend to allow the custom of reading elsewhere. The Rubric 'which directs that the "Priest shall say the opening prayers stand-'ing at the *north side* of the Table," is interpreted by Laud to mean, 'that whenever he reads these prayers, he must stand there, 'although there be no Communion. (*Three Speeches*, 375.) This 'Rubric, however, plainly refers in strictness to times when the 'Table is prepared for a *Celebration*, and the change which has just 'been mentioned appears to shew that it and the other Rubrics 'which suppose the Priest to be at the *Altar* are not necessarily to 'be extended to all times when a *part* of the Office is used;—an 'inference which is strengthened by the fact, that this Rubric and 'the omission of a special direction for the *place of Second Service* 'date alike from the Liturgy of 1552. From the order in the 82*nd* '*Canon* of 1604, that the Table shall stand in the east, "saving "when the Holy Communion is to be administered; at which time "the same shall be placed in so good sort within the Church or "Chancel, as thereby *the Minister may be more conveniently heard of* "*the Communicants in his prayer and ministrations*," it is evident 'that the framers of the *Canons* did not contemplate the Minister's 'officiating at the Table except on occasions of actual Communion; 'and, as we have already had reason to know, the practice of that 'age, until Laud attempted to introduce a change, was that the '*Second Service should be read from the Desk* (*p.* 169.)......My own 'feelings are strongly in favour of going to the *Altar* at all times; 'but I have thought it well to call attention to the true state of 'the case, as one among many proofs how little ground there really 'is for the assumptions of some persons who talk very confidently 'as if all authority were unquestionably with them.'' (*p.* 172.)—*How shall we Conform to the Lit.*

MR. A. J. STEPHENS (*Barrister-at-Law*) writes):—'Where a 'Statute will bear two interpretations, one contrary to plain sense, 'the other agreeable to it, the latter shall prevail. Doubts have 'arisen with regard to the meaning of "*north side of the Table.*" It 'is clear that the Table must be moveable and that the Ordinary 'can order it to be placed, during the Communion Service, to satisfy 'the language of the Rubrics. But then a question suggests itself, 'whether there is any language to satisfy upon which a doubt can 'arise. It is contended that if an oblong table be used, then, as the '*sides* are different in length from the *ends*, or "head" and "foot," 'standing either at the head or foot of an oblong table is not stand-'ing at either of its sides; and therefore, that, to satisfy the language 'of the Rubric, if an oblong table be used, the "head" and "foot" 'of the Table should be *east* and *west* and then a *north side* will be 'acquired. But this is in fact forgetting that no form of table has 'been prescribed by the Statute, and therefore that it may be square 'or of any other rectilinear figure, or even circular, where of course 'you cannot have *any* side, in the sense which it is contended "*side*" 'here bears. The meaning of "*at the north side*" therefore seems 'really to be simply "*to the north*" of the Table.' (*p.* 1125.)—*Book of Common Prayer*. E. H. S.

The *Kalendar of the English Church Union* says:—' "The *north* '*side*" does not mean the north *end*. Ancient usage (independent 'of the balance of Historical evidence as to all the Reformed Prayer 'Books) seems to prove that the *correct* Position of "the Priest," at 'the commencement of the Service, is "*standing*" in *front of the* '*Altar, near the North-Corner*. If another Priest or Deacon is 'present, he should stand at the *South* (or Epistle) *side of the Altar*, 'but on a lower step or level than the Celebrant. If two other 'Priests or Deacons are present, the second should occupy a similar 'position on the *North*-side. If a Priest and Deacon are present, 'the Deacon should stand on the *Gospel* side, the Priest on the '*Epistle* side.' (*p.* 79.)*—*For* 1863. (Pub. by Masters)

In a *Note* we find:—'No *chairs* or *seats* should be placed at 'either end of the Altar facing the people; but, when the Bishop is 'present, a *Throne* or *Chair* should be provided for him and placed 'stall-wise on the *North-side* of the Sanctuary and *westward* of the 'Altar. The Celebrant (when not the Bishop) should, it seems, *sit* '*in the middle of the Sedilia;* the Deacon or Gospeller being on his 'right hand, and the Epistoler on his left.' (*p.* 74)—*ibid.*

THE LORD'S PRAYER.

(4 *d*) '*The Priest.........shall say the Lord's Prayer,*' &c.

602.—The Rubric directs that the Priest shall begin the Service of the Holy Communion by saying the *Lord's Prayer*. Palmer tells us that this 'prayer of the faithful' was introduced into this Office in the earlier English 'Uses,' about the eighth or ninth century. (*Orig. Lit.* ii. 24.). There are, however, no especial instructions for the People to say it with the Priest, as we find laid down in the Morning and Evening Services, and in the after part of this Office; because it is looked upon here rather as a prayer of consecration, than of supplication, whence the *Doxology* is omitted; which, however, the Royal Commissioners of 1689, proposed should be introduced. In consequence of this silence with respect to the duty of the people as regards the utterance of this prayer, there is a diversity of usage. The question turns on the extent of the interpretation to be given to the expression '*Divine Service*,' employed in the Rubric following the 'Absolution' in Morning Prayer where it is enjoined:—

> '*Then the Minister shall kneel and say the Lord's Prayer* '*with an audible voice; the People also kneeling and repeating it* '*with him, both here, and wheresoever else it is used in Divine* '*Service*.'—Present Book of Common Prayer.

603.—It must necessarily therefore be inquired, whether the COMMUNION OFFICE is a part of the '*Divine Service*' here referred to? We may answer, that subsequent Rubrics in this Office would lead us to the inference that it was considered, when this Rubric was introduced, as a part of Divine Service. In a Rubric before the Offertory Sentences, it is directed, that '*Nothing shall be proclaimed or published in the* '*Church during the time of Divine Service, but by* '*the Minister*,' &c.; and, again, at the end of the Communion Office, there is a Rubric beginning '*After* '*Divine Service ended, the money given at the* '*Offertory*,' &c. So in the 'MARRIAGE OFFICE,' the first Rubric enjoins that the '*Banns*' are to be published '*in the time of Divine Service immediately* '*before the Sentences for the Offertory*.' The *Reviewers* of 1662, when introducing these Rubrics in that, the *last Revision* of the Prayer Book, must have considered the Communion Office a part of 'Divine Service,' or these words could not have been employed in the Rubrics, where we find them; and this may easily be accounted for, from the fact of the three Offices of *Morning Prayer*, the *Litany*, and *Communion Service*, being then combined into one long Service: a custom which prevailed some time before that Revision, and which has continued since to the present day, as we have already shewn in *Vol.* **B.** It may, therefore, be laid down as the *Rule*, that when the *Communion Office* is appended to MORNING PRAYER, it forms a part of the Morning Service, or, what the Rubric designates, '*Divine Service*;' and in such case, the *Lord's Prayer here is to be repeated by the People with the Minister*. But when the *Communion Office* is used as a separate and distinct

Service, the Lord's Prayer should be said *by the Priest alone*, as the whole Office then acquires a different character, from what may be conveyed to People's minds when merely the Ante-Communion Service without a celebration of the Eucharist is employed. (See a further discussion of this question, *pars.* 49—54. *Vol.* **E.**) It may be remarked likewise, that when the Communion Office is used as a separate and distinct Service, and for 'a Celebration,' it should *begin with the Lord's Prayer*, and not with the Offertory Sentences, as is sometimes done. In confirmation of these opinions, we will add a few authorities in addition to those cited in the preceding Volume. (*Vol.* **E.**)

In the previous citations in *Vol.* **E**, it will be found that *Yardley*, *Bisse*, *Shepherd*, *Bp. Mant*, *Jebb*, and *Robertson*, advocate the repetition of the Lord's Prayer by the People with the Priest.

The Rev. J. J. Blunt (late *Margaret Professor of Divinity at Cambridge University*) observes:—'Are the People *to repeat* 'the prayer, on this occasion, after him? The custom is *not* to 'do so, in spite of the general injunction contained in the Rubric, 'prefixed to the Lord's Prayer, where it first occurs, that they are 'to repeat it after the Priest "*wheresoever it is used in Divine* '*Service.*" I think the custom of *abstaining* from doing so in this 'particular instance, may be right, the theory being this (I propose 'it merely for your consideration): In primitive times the Lord's 'Prayer seems, probably, to have been regarded as a portion of the 'prayer of consecration of the Elements; and, for this reason, in 'the early Liturgies, always has a position *before* the Communion; '"Give us this day our *daily bread*," considered to have a reference 'to the Eucharist, about to be celebrated. Accordingly, under that 'view of it, it was the business of the Priest, and not of the People, 'to say the prayer; the People having no share in the act of con-'secration. And this would account for the usage which *Mr.* '*Robertson* tells us now obtains in Westminster Abbey, that not 'only the Priest alone says the prayer, but that the people do not 'even accompany him in the *Amen*. On the other hand, the Rubric 'before the Lord's Prayer, where that prayer *follows* the Com-'munion, runs, "then shall the Priest say the Lord's Prayer, *the* '*People repeating after him every petition*;" because here that 'prayer has no longer the character of a prayer of consecration, 'but of general petition, to be joined in by all. And the same 'consideration, perhaps, would be the key to having the prayer, 'in the first position, without the Doxology; in the second, with it, 'as it stands in our Service.' (*p.* 326.)—*Duties of the Parish Priest.*

Dr. Corrie, *Master of Jesus College, Cambridge*, states:— 'Contrary to the direction added at the review of the Liturgy in '1662, that whenever the Lord's Prayer is used, the whole Con-

'gregation shall join with the Minister in an audible voice, the 'custom universally is for the Priest, in this case, to say the Lord's 'Prayer alone. Such was, also, the usage in England before the 'Reformation. In the Greek and Gallic Churches the custom, in 'the celebration of Mass, was for all the Congregation to join in 'the recital of the Lord's Prayer. See Mabill. Liturg. Gallic. *p.* 49.' *Note* in WHEATLY'S *Illus. of Book of Common Prayer*, p. 304.

The REV. J. C. ROBERTSON, speaking of the custom of the Priest saying here the Lord's Prayer *alone*, remarks—'that the practice 'has continued in this place, may perhaps be ascribed to the force 'of tradition, prevailing over the new order......I am informed that 'at Westminster Abbey the custom is that the Priest alone should 'say the Prayer without being accompanied even in the *Amen.* 'This practice, as well as that of joint repetition throughout, would 'satisfy the rule by which the 'Amen' is printed in upright letters. 'It appears to me, however, that it is a tradition of the time before 'the last Revision, not an exemplification of our present Rubric.' (*p.* 211.)—*How shall we Conform*, &c.

The "*Amen*" is to be uttered here by those only who say the Lord's Prayer.

POSTURE OF PRIEST, AND PEOPLE.

(*Priest standing, People kneeling.*)

604.—The Rubric directs that the '*Lord's Prayer*,' and *Collect*, following, are to be said by the Priest '*standing*,' the People, the while, '*kneeling*.' This attitude of standing the Priest assumes from exercising here the function, rather of administration; and the People kneel to express their sense of supplication. The omission of the celebration of the Eucharist was not contemplated when this Office was compiled, therefore the characteristic of the Lord's Prayer we have noted above and which is conveyed in the petition, "*Give us this day our daily bread*," loses the beauty of its application when there is no Communion. While saying the *Lord's Prayer*, and the *Collect* following, the Priest turns towards the *south*, as addressing God.

BP. MANT, says:—'He is at first to turn to the Lord's Table; 'and after the Lord's Prayer, and following Collect, to turn to the 'People.' (*p.* 53.)—*Hor. Lit.*

The REV. H. R. MOODY writes:—'Read the Lord's Prayer and 'Collect, *standing*, with your face towards the Table. Then *turn to* '*the Congregation*, to rehearse the Commandments; after which, 'read the Collect for the Queen, and that of the day, "*standing as* '*before*," i.e. *with your face towards the Table*. Then turn again '*towards the people*, to read the Epistle and Gospel.' (*p.* 33.)—*Hints to young Clergymen*.

The Collect for Purity of Heart.

(To be *said by the Priest alone*—the Priest *standing*, and turning towards the Table; the People *kneeling*.)

605.—This Collect for purity of heart is of very early date, having been found in the Sacramentary of Alcuin at the end of the 8th century, and in that of Leofric, bp. of Exeter, in the 9th century. It occurs in the prayer for the preparation of the Mass in the Salisbury Missal, and was introduced, with the Lord's Prayer, into the *first Liturgy* of Edward VI. 1549. It is to be uttered by the Priest alone standing and looking to the Table, the People kneeling and silently following in their thoughts, but repeating aloud at the close the "*Amen*," as the difference of type will indicate. In the "*Alterations*" suggested by the Royal Commissioners in 1689, we find the word 'operation,' proposed in the place of 'inspiration.'

In the *first Liturgy* of Edward VI. 1549, there followed here these Rubrics, &c. in the place of the Ten Commandments and Responses we now have.

'*Then shall he say a Psalm appointed for the* Introit: *which* '*Psalm ended, the Priest shall say, or else the Clerks shall sing*.'

'iij. Lord have mercy upon us.

'iij. Christ have mercy upon us.

'iij. Lord have mercy upon us.

Then the Priest standing at God's board shall begin.

'Glory be to God on high.

'*The Clerks*. And in earth peace, &c.' (to the end of the Gloria in Excelsis.)

'*Then the Priest shall turn him to the People and say*.

'The Lord be with you.

'*The Answer*. And with thy Spirit.

'*The Priest*. Let us pray.'

THE TEN COMMANDMENTS.

(5) ¶. '*Then shall the Priest, turning to the People, rehearse* '*distinctly all the* TEN COMMANDMENTS; *and the People* '*still Kneeling shall after every Commandment ask God* '*mercy for their transgression thereof for the time past,* '*and grace to keep the same for the time to come, as* '*followeth.*' (1662.)—Present Book of Com. Prayer.

(The Priest *standing* and *turning to the People*—the People still *kneeling*.)

606.—It was formerly the usage in the Church of England, to read before the Epistle and Gospel a portion of the "Law," and at the *Revision* of the Liturgy in 1552, it was thought desirable to introduce here that portion of the 20th Chapter of Exodus, comprising the Commandments, so as to form a permanent and invariable Lesson from the Old Testament, and the one most suited to the circumstances of the reign, and the occasion of the service. It was divided into ten short verses or *capitula*, each provided with a *Response*, whence they acquired the appellation of the "TEN COMMANDMENTS." They formed no part of any ancient Liturgy, and the idea, probably, was suggested to our Reformers by the Strasburg Liturgy of *Valerandus Pollanus*, (LAURENCE's *Bampton Lectures*, p. 210.). This foreign Liturgy was used by those strangers who had fled from Strasburg on account of the '*Interim*,' and taken up their abode at Glastonbury.

The Rubric at its first appearance in the Prayer Book of 1552, did not much differ from our present Rubric; it ran thus:—

'*Then shall the Priest rehearse distinctly all the* X *Command-* '*ments, and the People Kneeling shall after every Commandment,* '*ask God's* (*God.* 1604) *mercy for their transgression of the same* '*after this sort.*' (1552. 1559. 1604.)—KEELING. 170, 171.

607.—In the '*Alterations*' suggested by the Royal Commissioners in 1689, it was proposed to read the first clause of the Rubric we now have, thus:—'*Then* '*shall the* Minister standing with his face towards '*the People* shall *rehearse distinctly all the* TEN

'COMMANDMENTS ('as in Exodus,' *in the Margin*); '*and*,' &c.: (the Roman letters indicate the changes). It was also proposed to strike out this Rubric and the whole text of the Commandments, and put in their place these words:—"*Refer to the Litany.*" It was also advised to insert a Rubric permitting the reading of the *Eight Beatitudes* in the stead of the "Ten Commandments," adding to each a suitable *Response*: thus—

'*Or the* 8 BEATITUDES, *the People still kneeling, and after* 'every Beatitude, *praying as is hereafter directed.*

'*Minister.* Our Lord Christ spake these words and said, Blessed 'are the poor in spirit, for theirs is the Kingdom of Heaven.

'*People.* Lord have mercy upon us, and make us partakers of 'this blessing.

&c. &c. &c.

The last *Response* was in these words:

'*People.* Lord have mercy upon us and indue us with all 'these Graces, and make us partakers of the blessedness promised 'to Them we humbly beseech Thee.'

There was also a rough draft of the above Beatitudes with Responses very much enlarged, inserted in the Book on paper, with this *Note*:—'*This is* '*to be used after or instead* [*of*] *the* X *Commandments up-* '*on the great Festivals.*' (Copy of '*Alterations*' printed by Order of the *House of Commons*, 1854. *p.* 44—46.)

It was likewise suggested to add to the 'Fourth Commandment' a *marginal Note* at the word "*Sabbath*" as follows:—'*which is now the Lord's Day.*' But none of these changes were accomplished.

In the *Scotch Liturgy* of 1637, the reading of this Rubric is important; thus—

'*Then shall the Presbyter, turning to the People, rehearse* '*distinctly all the* TEN COMMANDMENTS: *the People all the while* '*Kneeling, and asking God mercy for the transgression of every* '*duty therein; either according to the letter, or to the mystical* '*importance of the said Commandment.*'*—(KEELING p. 170.)

---

* In the AMERICAN LITURGY the only deviations from our present Rubric are—'Minister' for '*Priest*'—omitting '*all*' after '*distinctly*'—omitting '*thereof*' after '*transgression*'—Keep the 'law' instead of '*Keep the same.*' And there is appended at the close of the Commandments our Lord's summary of the Law found in *Matt.* xxii. 37—40.

Hence we see the origin of the insertion of these Commandments, and what care should be taken to read them aloud clearly, and distinctly. The opinions following will defend their introduction into the Office of the Holy Communion.

Bp. Cosins (*ob.* 1672), commenting on the word '*distinctly*' says, 'i. e. with pauses between every one,' and then adds:— 'I do not 'find in any Liturgy, old or new, before this, of the fifth of '*Edward* VI. (here continued) that the *Jews*' Decalogue was used 'in the Service of the Christian Church: but it seems, that the 'rehearsal of it in the beginning of the Communion, was appointed 'with the People's Answers, and craving pardon and grace to 'observe them, instead of Confession of Sins, always set in this 'place. It serves to actuate our repentance, by calling to mind 'our Offences by retail.'—*Add. Notes to* Nicholls' *Book of Com. Prayer*. p. 38.

Dean Comber writes:—'We vowed to keep them' (these divine 'precepts) 'in our Baptism, and we renew that vow at every 'Communion, and therefore it is very fit we should hear them 'often, and have them repeated *now*, when we are going to make 'a fresh engagement to observe them......And where could the 'Law be placed in our Service more conveniently, than immediately 'before the Gospel, to make that more welcome to us, when the 'Law hath humbled us by its terrors? And since we are to confess 'all our sins before we come to this blessed Sacrament of pardon, 'the Church holds out this glass unto us by which we may discover 'all our offences.'......When we hear these holy *Commandments* 'read in the Church, we must receive them with equal reverence 'and humility as if God Himself spake them from Mount Sinai: 'and, because we have offended against them all, we must kneel 'down as criminals ought to do, and diligently consider, as the 'Priest reads them, what sins we have done against each Com-'mandment; and when we have found out the particular trans-'gressions, we must at the close of every command, most earnestly 'beg pardon for them, saying, "*Lord have mercy upon us*," and 'forgive us for these great offences.' (*p.* 282, 283.)—Mant's *Book of Common Prayer*.

Dr. Bennet remarks;— 'Here let me intreat the People to 'consider well the seriousness of this part of the Office. The Words 'of God Himself are read unto them by God's Ambassador; and 'they are to be received with the utmost reverence, and a mind 'sincerely resolved to obey them. Now the Congregation must not 'even mentally repeat them together with the Minister; much less 'must they mutter them over aloud, and thereby disturb those who 'are placed near them: but attend to them as spoken by the 'Minister with an awful silence; and at the end of each Command-'ment fervently say, '*Lord, have mercy upon us*,' &c.' (p. 157.)—*Paraphrase of Book of Common Prayer*.

The Responses.

608.—The *Responses*, which are only another form of the *Kyrie eleison*, are derived, it is supposed, from a passage in *Deuteronomy:* 'O that there were such 'an heart in them that they would fear me and keep 'all my Commandments always,' (*ch.* v. 29.) combined with the following clause from *Jeremiah* xxxi. 33.—'*I will put my law in their inward parts, and write it 'in their hearts.*' (See also I *Kings* viii. 57, 58.) As the Responses are supplications it is the general opinion that they should be '*said*' rather than '*chanted;*' although *chanting* them with proper tone and suitable effect would not be in violence of the Rubric, which simply directs the People to '*ask God*' for 'mercy' and 'grace' to keep them. Where the Service is conducted *chorally*, or *chanting* them is the usage, of course, this practise would be continued.

Bp. Mant writes:—The common tone of prayer is proper for 'the succeeding prayers "for mercy and grace." They ought *not 'to be chanted*, unless in connection with the Choral Service, (*p.* 53.)—*Hor. Lit.*

The Rev. J. Jebb remarks:—'They are not expressly enjoined 'to be *sung* by the Rubric: nothing, however, forbids the practice: 'and the whole analogy of the Choral Service requires that every 'part allotted to the Choir or Congregation should be *chanted* or '*sung*. Still, there is more direct rubrical sanction for the singing 'of the Creed than of the Kyrie; and therefore those Choirs who 'merely say the former and sing the latter, reverse the proper 'alternative, if indeed any is necessary. The regular Choral usage 'prescribes the *singing* of both......They are not Chants but rather '*short anthems*......being set to a varied melody. It is altogether 'irregular to sing them to Chants, and quite inconsistent with their 'intrinsic character. In some Parish Churches, only the last is 'sung, a practice which interrupts the unity of this part of the 'Service.' (*p.* 476.)—*Choral Service.*

Posture.

609.—The Rubric directs the Priest to continue *standing* at the north side of the Table, and to turn towards the Congregation; the People to continue *kneeling*. The Priest is not to advance from the Table to the Altar-Rails, as is frequently done.

Bishop Andrewes' (*ob.* 1626) writes:—'The Priest after the 'Collect, descends to the door of the *Septum*, makes a low adoration 'towards the Altar: then turns to the people, and standing in the 'door, readeth the *Ten Commandments* (as from God), whilst they 'lie prostrate to the end, as to God speaking.' (*p.* 38.)—*Add. Notes to* Nicholls' *Book of Com. Prayer*.

Dr. Bennet observes:—'Whilst the Commandments are read- 'ing, the People are justly order'd to *kneel*, because of the frequent 'use of that excellent petition, '*Lord have mercy upon us*,' &c. which 'ought to be repeated in a praying posture. For the so frequent 'and sudden change of the posture, from standing to kneeling, and 'again from kneeling to standing, which must otherwise be made, 'would cause disturbance and confusion.' (*p.* 157.)—*Paraphrase of Book of Com. Prayer*.

Dr. Bisse remarks:—'The Priest, in rehearsing the Command- 'ments, speaks as from God; and therefore is ordered to "*turn* '*himself to the people*:" whilst they receive them "*kneeling*;" the 'posture of reverence and submission to what God commands, and 'of humiliation for the breach thereof.' (*p.* 382.)—Mant's *Book of Com. Prayer*.

Archdeacon Yardley writes:—'Hitherto the Minister, who 'officiates, is enjoined to "*stand*" and the people to "*kneel*:" because 'the posture of *standing* is in him very becoming in eucharistical or 'thanksgiving offices; and it is especially proper, when he delivers 'the Commandments from God, as Moses from Mount Sinai, that 'he should do it in a gesture intimating his authority, and that he 'is the messenger of the Lord of hosts. And *kneeling* is as proper 'for the Congregation, whilst they humbly implore grace and par- 'don of God, and beg a blessing for those, whom He hath set over 'them. And this is the rather taken notice of, because several, for 'want of observing the directions of the Rubrick, though they kneel 'during the other parts of the Service, are, whilst the Communion 'Office is reading, *wanting* in the decent and humble posture here 'required of them. Whereas the very nature of this solemn Office 'demands of us as much penitential humility and lowly reverence 'in our gestures, as any other part of the Liturgy.'—(*Quoted in* Mant's *Book of Com. Prayer*. p. 287.)

Wheatly merely gives the substance of Dean Comber's remarks, annexing the Rubric of the Scotch Liturgy.

The *late* Rev. Professor Blunt observes:—'Before rehearsing 'the Ten Commandments, the Priest is directed to "*turn to the* '*People*," i. e. still to stand at the north side of the Table, but with 'his face to the Congregation, and no longer to the south.' (*p.* 327.) —*Parish Priest*.

The Rev. J. Purchas says:—'These are said by the Celebrant, 'still standing at the north side of the Altar, but with his face 'towards the Faithful.' (*p.* 33.)—*Directorium Anglicanum*.

Mr. A. J. Stephens (*Barrister-at-law*) states:—'Under this 'Rubric the Priest is to turn his face from the south to the west, 'by which he "*turns to the People*." Under the preceding Rubric 'the Priest was not turning to the People, but standing at the north 'side of the Table, with his face to the south; if he were not so 'situated, the language of this Rubric would be, "still turning to 'the People." (*p.* 1128.)—*Book of Common Prayer*. E. H. S.

The Collects for the Queen.

(6) ¶. '*Then shall follow one of these two Collects for the 'Queen, the Priest standing as before, and saying.'*—Present Book of Com. Prayer.

'Let us Pray.'

(The Priest *standing* and *turning to the Table*—the People still *kneeling*.)

610.—Although Prayer for the reigning monarch has already been offered up in the MORNING PRAYER, or in the LITANY, in accordance with the Apostolic rule, I *Tim.* ii. 1, 2; still it is directed here also, from the fact of the HOLY COMMUNION having been originally a distinct Service, and performed at a different hour. These two *Collects* are somewhat similar; yet the former is the fuller of the two, inasmuch as it embraces the Church, Queen, and People; while the latter confines its petitions exclusively to the Queen, and was derived from a Synod of the Church of Scotland, A. D. 1225. They are placed immediately after the Commandments from the ancient consideration that the Sovereign was the *Custos utriusque tabulæ*, the guardian of both Tables of the Law, of religion, and of morals. The expressions, "*in* thee, and *for* thee," have been explained by an old writer, whose elucidation we will quote; to which we will add also one of more modern date.

DR. BENNET (A. D. 1701) writes:—'St Paul says, "Children 'obey your parents *in* the Lord," (*Eph.* vi. 1); *i.e.* in all such 'particulars, as are agreeable to, and consistent with, the laws of 'the Lord. In this sense we pray, that we may obey the King '"*in* the Lord," *viz.* as far as we can with a safe conscience: and 'we also pray that we may obey him "*for* the Lord," *i. e.* for his 'sake, out of a principle of duty, as he has God's authority, and is 'his Vicegerent.' (*p.* 161.)—*Paraphrase upon the Bk. of Com. Pr.*

The REV. W. G. HUMPHRY remarks on these phrases thus:—"*In thee,*" i. e. in all things agreeable to the will of God; as St Paul 'says, *Eph.* vi. 1.—"*for thee,*" i. e. for thy sake, from the desire to 'fulfil thy word and ordinance which has commanded that Kings 'should be obeyed and honoured.' (*p.* 236.)—*Treatise on the Book of Com. Prayer.*

611.—In the Rubric of the *first* Liturgy of Edward VI. (A. D. 1549,) the Collect for the Day was ordered to precede that for the King, thus:—

'*Then shall follow the Collect of the Day with one of these two 'Collects following for the King.** (1549.)

In the *second* Liturgy of this same King (A. D. 1552), there was added the clause—'*the Priest standing up and saying;*' which continued in the succeeding Liturgies of 1559, and 1604. In the *Scotch Liturgy* of 1637, we first find the Collects for the King placed before that for the Day, and the Rubric in accordance with this change. In 1662, however, the directions respecting the Collect of the Day were transferred to the beginning of the next Rubric; and the Rubric under consideration assumed the form we now have, and which will be found at the head of this Section.

POSTURE OF PRIEST AND PEOPLE.

612.—The instructions for the Priest, involved in the expression '*standing as before,*' imply that he shall stand in the same posture as when saying the Lord's Prayer and the Collect for purity of Heart at the commencement of the Service, and '*before*' he turned to the People to read the "Ten Commandments:" that is to say, the Priest is now *to turn to the Table,* and thus, as addressing God, repeat one of the Collects for the Queen, and follow it with the Collect (or Collects) for the Day. The *People,* the while, are

---

* In the AMERICAN LITURGY these two Collects are, of course, omitted, and their place is supplied by the *Second* Collect at the end of the Communion Office, beginning with, "O Almighty Lord, and everlasting God, vouchsafe," &c.

to continue *kneeling*. In the "Alterations" proposed by the Royal Commissioners in 1689, we find this *Note* attached to the Rubric—"The Collects for the "King and the Day are to be omitted when the "Communinon Service is not alone used." But this Note was struck out, and the following superscribed;— "To be put at the end of the Litany."

BISHOP MANT remarks:—'It is sometimes made matter of 'question, in what direction the Minister is to turn, when he reads 'the prayer for the King in the Communion Service. To me the 'Rubric seems to give a very plain instruction in saying, that he is 'to be "*standing as before;*" namely, "*standing at the north side,*" 'as he stood "before" he was directed to "turn to the people," in 'order to "rehearse the Ten Commandments:" in fact, this is not 'only the plain signification of the words, but is agreeable likewise 'to the reason of the thing, as well as to other directions in the 'Communion Service whereby the Priest is told to "turn himself to 'the people," when he addresses himself to them; and to "*turn to* '*the Table,*" when he addresses himself to God.'—*Clergyman's Obligations Considered.* 145.

COLLIS writes:—'Not *standing*, as he rehearsed the Command- 'ments: for, if that were designed, nothing would have been said 'here. But "*standing as before,*" namely, as he stood *at the north* '*side of the Table*, "before" he was ordered to "*turn to the people.*" 'When the Commandments are read by him, he directs himself to 'the people: when he comes to the Collect, he directs himself to 'the Almighty by prayer.' (Quoted in MANT's *Book of Common Prayer* in loco.)

The *late* REV. J. J. BLUNT, (*Margaret Professor of Divinity at Cambridge*) observes:—'The Commandments delivered, the Rubric 'says, "then shall follow one of these two Collects for the King, "*the Priest standing as before.*" The question, therefore, is, whether 'by the expression "*the Priest standing as before,*" is meant his 'continuing in his last position of all,—his face to the Congregation, '—or his reverting to his penultimate position, his face to the south. 'There is little doubt but that the latter was intended. He was to 'stand as he was "standing before," when he was uttering prayers 'to God, which he was about to do again; the rehearsing the 'Commandments having for the time, interrupted his posture of 'devotion, and turned him from the Altar to the people. In this 'position, then, to which he has reverted, namely, *standing on the* '*north side of the holy Table, and looking to the south*, he reads the 'Collect for the King and the Collect for the day.' (*p.* 327.)— *Duties of the Parish Priest.*

The REV. J. JEBB states:—'The words "*standing as before*" 'refer of course to the position of the Priest during the Lord's 'Prayer and Collect; that is, not turning to the people, but *to the* '*North side of the Table.* Were it meant that he should still 'remain as when he read the Commandments, the wording would 'be, "still turning to the people." The word "*standing*" obviously 'recalls us to the Rubric just preceding the Service, where it had 'occurred. The reason of the matter must show us, that a different 'position is required for a lecture and for a prayer, as in all the 'other Services and Offices, and so the general usage of the Clergy 'has interpreted it.' (*p.* 478.)—*On Choral Service.*

The Rev. H. R. Moody says:—'Read the Collect for the Queen, 'and that of the day, "*standing as before,*" i. e. with your *face* '*towards the Table.* Then turn again towards the people, to read 'the Epistle and Gospel.' (In a *Note* is added). 'In rehearsing the 'Commandments, he is to turn towards the people. In the Collects, 'he is to *turn towards the Table,* as more immediately addressing 'God. Having finished these, it seems but consistent to turn again 'towards the people, when he is to read the Epistle and Gospel 'to them.' Such accordingly is the usual practice.' (*p.* 33.)—*Hints to Young Clergymen.*

The Rev. J. Purchas writes:—'"*Standing as before,*" viz. in 'the position the Priest was in before rehearsing the Commandments '—at the *north side of the Altar, with the face eastwards.*' (In a *Note* is added.) 'The corresponding Rubric in the Nonjurors Office 'explains their *north side* to mean the *north end*; and thereby 'shows by implication that the then practice of the Church of 'England *did not.*' (*p.* 33.)—*Directorium Anglicanum.*

'Let us pray.'

613.—As we have before observed, it was the ancient custom for the Deacon to direct the People to pray, and by some such proclamation as this; whence our expression '*Let us Pray:*' and the Deacon often instructed them as to what to pray for—'ad altare populum exhortantis orare.'—(See *supra,* pars. 229, 230; and Nicholls' *Add. Notes to Book of Com. Prayer.* Palmer's *Orig. Lit.* Vol. II. *p.* 37.)

The Collect, *or* Collects, of the Day.

(7 *a*) ¶. '*Then shall be said the Collect of the Day.*'—Present Book of Common Prayer.

The Priest still *standing*—the People still *kneeling.*

614.—After the Collect for the Queen, and for the outward prosperity of the Church, follows the *Collect of the Day* for inward grace: if there be two, or more, appointed, as during the seasons of Advent, and

Lent, they must all be said in this place. These Collects especially appertain to the Communion Service, and the same that are required here, are to be used in Morning and Evening Prayer, and in the Litany. In the Communion Office, particularly, there must be no announcement of the Collect.

The Epistle, and Gospel.

(7 c) ¶. '*And immediately after the Collect, the Priest shall read* '*the Epistle, saying,* The Epistle [*or,* The portion of 'Scripture appointed for the Epistle] is written in the '——Chapter of——beginning at the——Verse. '*And the Epistle ended, he shall say,* Here endeth the 'Epistle. *Then shall be read the Gospel,* (*the People all* '*standing up*) *saying,* The holy Gospel is written in the '——Chapter of——beginning at the——Verse, '&c.'—Present Book of Common Prayer.

615.—This Rubric having been already fully discussed, (see *pars.* 493 — 505), we, therefore, shall merely enumerate the duties enjoined in it:—

The Epistle.

616.—The Epistle is to be *announced* and *concluded* in the express words of the Rubric. (See *pars.* 493. 495.)

The Reader of the Epistle may be a *Priest,* or *Deacon.* (See *pars.* 503, 504.)

Posture.—The Reader of the Epistle is to *stand;* and immemorial usage has found him, the while, *facing the People,* i. e. to *westward;* yet on this point no directions are given in the Rubric. Similarly, custom has sanctioned the People *sitting* during the reading of the Epistle.

Place.—The Reader, if the only Officiating Minister, usually remains on the *north side* of the Table; if he be an assistant Minister, he occupies the *south side* of the Table, and there reads the Epistle. (See *pars.* 505, 506.) If there is a staff of

Clergy, and the Services are chorally and ritualistically conducted, we find the following usage prevails:—

'The Priest shall read the Epistle—If no one is present to assist 'the Celebrant, he should go to the Epistle (or South) side of the 'foot pace or step on which he is standing.' (*p.* 80.)—*Kalendar of the English Church Union.* 1863.

The Gospel.

617.—The Gospel is to be ***announced*** in the express words of the Rubric (see *pars.* 496, 497.); immediately upon which, it is *usual* to say or chant the *Doxology*, "Glory be to Thee O Lord." For the *conclusion of the Gospel* no instructions are given: it is customary, however, to say, or sing, the *Thanksgiving*, "Thanks be to Thee, O Lord."—(See *pars.* 498—501.).

The Reader of the *Gospel* may be a ***Priest***, or *Deacon*. (See *pars.* 503, 504.)

Posture.—The Reader of the Gospel *stands;* and from immemorial usage, like in the reading of the Epistle, he turns towards the People. The People also are here to *stand.* (See *par.* 502.)

Place.—The Reader of the Gospel occupies the ***north side*** of the Table. (See *pars.* 505, 506.). As to the distinction between ***north side***, and ***north end of the west side*** of the Table, see ***supra. par.*** 601.

The late Rev. J. J. Blunt, (*Margaret Professor of Divinity at Cambridge*), says:—'I am disposed, to think, that here, as in some 'other instances, no explicit directions are given, because it was 'taken for granted that *immemorial usage* would supply the want 'of them; and not that it was intended that the *Epistle* and *Gospel* 'should be read in the same position as the previous Collects, i. e. 'the Minister looking to the south; but that here—as elsewhere, 'when the people are addressed—the Minister was to turn to the 'people; as, in like manner, when *God* was addressed, he was to 'turn to the Altar, though, in the Reformed Church, from the north 'side of it. For, certainly, in the *old* Service of England, the Epistle 'and Gospel were read after the aforesaid manner. "Subdiaconus "per *medium chori*, ad legendam *Epistolam*, in *pulpitum accedat*," is 'the use of Salisbury. "Deinde legatur *Epistola*, super lectrinum "a subdiacono ad *gradum chori*," is the use of Hereford. The 'directions for reading the *Gospel* are similar; the "pulpitum" 'and "gradus chori" sufficiently marking that the Epistle and 'Gospel were addressed to the *people*, whose convenience was 'consulted in the position of the Reader. And accordingly, this 'tradition has come down to our own times, it being the almost 'universal practice now, though no Rubric directs it, for the '*Minister to turn to the people* when reading these portions of the 'Service.' (*p.* 327.)—*Duties of the Parish Priest.*

The extreme ritualists adopt the following usage:—

'Then' (after the Epistle) shall be read the Gospel.—'Before 'giving it out, he should return to his place at the *North side of the 'Altar*. If only one Assistant is present, he should read the Epistle 'from the *Epistoler's place*, and then *cross over to the Gospeller's 'place* to read the Gospel, unless it is read by the Celebrant. If 'two Assistants are present, they should read the Epistle and Gospel 'from their respective places. If the number of Communicants 'requires four Clergy to administer, the fourth should stand in the 'middle, between the Epistoler and Gospeller. Before the Gospel 'is read, should be said or sung "*Glory be to Thee, O Lord;*" and 'afterwards, "*Thanks be to Thee, O God.*" (*p.* 81.)—*Kalendar of the Church Union.* 1868.

[Bowing at the name of Jesus in the Epistle and Gospel.]

618.—*Bowing at the name of Jesus* whenever it occurs in Divine Service, is prescribed in the 18*th Canon;* the usage is found more frequently observed in the *Creeds*, and in the *Gospels*, from the People being then in the attitude of standing; a posture rendering the gesture more easy of accomplishment. The Officiating Minister will by his example prompt the Congregation to conformity. (See the question fully discussed *supra* Vol. B. and Vol. E.).

The Nicene Creed.

(7 c) ¶. '*And the Gospel ended, shall be sung or said the Creed 'following, the People still standing as before.*'—Present Book of Common Prayer.

619.—The *Nicene Creed*, so called from having been for the most part drawn up at the Council of *Nicæa* in Bithynia, A. D. 325, in condemnation of the heresy of *Arius*, a priest of Alexandria in Egypt, who maintained that Christ was not a Divine person, yet a creature superior to human nature, but not partaker of the supreme Godhead. This Creed was perfected, however, at the Great Council of Constantinople, (A. D. 381,), when the heresy of *Macedonius*, opposing the divinity and procession of the Holy Ghost, was condemned; whence it is also distinguished as the *Constantinopolitan Creed.* In the "*Alterations*" proposed in 1689, which, as we have repeatedly observed, were never carried out, an *asterisk* is placed at the clause of the Nicene Creed, '*Who proceedeth from the Father and the Son,*' referring to the following *Note:* —'It 'is humbly submitted to the Convocation whether a 'Note ought not here to be added with relation to 'the Greek Church, in order to our maintaining 'Catholic Communion.' The substance of this Creed was employed in the Communion Service so early as A. D. 339, but the Creed itself was not introduced into England before the 9*th* century; and fitly follows the reading of the Epistle and Gospel, from being founded on the doctrine and teaching of Christ and his Apostles; and as preparing the heart for the reception of the holy mysteries of the Eucharist by a right and true confession of belief in all the Articles of the Christian faith.

'*Shall be Sung or Said.*'

620.—In the Rubrics of the previous Liturgies, we do not find the permission allowed of *singing*, or *saying*, this Creed. In the Liturgy of 1549, the Rubric is:—

'*After the Gospel ended, the Priest shall begin.*' (1549.)—KEELING. 177.

In the Liturgies of 1552, 1559, and 1604, we have this Rubric:—

'*And the Epistle and Gospel being ended shall be said the 'Creed.*'*—KEELING. 176, 177.

---

* In the SCOTCH LITURGY of 1637, the Rubric reads:—

'*And the Epistle and Gospel being ended, shall be said or sung 'this Creed, all still reverently standing up.*'—KEELING. 177.

The *Rubric* of 1662, our present Prayer Book, allows this Creed to be '*sung* or *said*.' The *singing* of this Creed was derived, probably, from the decree of the Third Council of Toledo, A. D. 589, which directed it to be *sung* by the People aloud before the Lord's Prayer; thence it passed to the Gallican Church, and afterwards was introduced into the Roman Liturgy, A. D. 1014. The *Nicene Creed* we have is a translation of that in the Sarum Missal.

In Parish Churches, generally, the Nicene Creed is '*said*;' where, however, the Services are conducted chorally, it is sometimes repeated in *monotone*, and sometimes *chanted*. A discretionary power is invested by the Rubric in the Officiating Minister.*

DR. BISSE writes:—'What so proper a subject of *song* and joy, 'as triumph and victory, and that over the world? What is the 'victory that overcometh so great an enemy? It is even our faith, 'which is proclaimed before the Altar in the rehearsal of our '*Creeds*.' Besides, this recounts the grand Articles of our Faith, 'of the ever blessed Trinity, particularly of the Incarnation, the 'Nativity, the Crucifixion, the Resurrection, the Ascension of our 'Lord; all which are the subjects of the greater Festivals of our 'Church. And since the celebration of each of these is attended 'with an anniversary feast-day, the public rehearsal of them, though 'made every day, may justly be accompanied and expressed with 'the *concurrent joy* of the Congregation.' (*p.* 258.)—*On Cathedral Worship.*

The REV. J. JEBB says:—'In order to establish the propriety of '*singing* this Eucharistic Creed, it would be sufficient to refer, *to* '*the Rubric*, which sanctions, that is, enjoins in Choirs, the custom,

---

* In the AMERICAN LITURGY there is this Rubric:—

'*Then shall be read the Apostles', or Nicene Creed; unless one of* '*them hath been read immediately before in the Morning Service.*'

Upon this, the REV. J. JEBB remarks:—'The *American Prayer* '*Book*, among its many lamentable alterations, has given the 'Minister the option of using either the *Apostles'* or the *Nicene* '*Creed* here. The improved state of Church feeling in America 'would not now suffer such alterations, made at a time when the 'spirit of the Liturgy was imperfectly understood there; and it is 'well known that several of the most eminent members of that 'branch of the Anglo-Catholic Communion, are desirous to repair 'these innovations. May they succeed in this, and every other 'good object to which their godly zeal is now so energetically 'directed!' (*p.* 485. *Note.*)—*On Choral Service.*

'and, *to the usage* of most Choirs from the time of the Reformation: 'an usage kept up throughout the Western Church, according to 'Mr. Palmer, since the year 1012. But upon the highest religious 'grounds, I feel that there is no one incident of the Choral Service 'which more requires strenuous defence, or which should be more 'solicitously guarded against the novel objections of modern times, 'that have occasioned in some Choirs, the laying aside of this godly 'and significant practice.' (*p.* 483.).........Elsewhere, this writer remarks:—'The Nicene Creed is often left *unsung*, because men's 'apprehensions, enfeebled by the apathetie training of later times, 'have been unable to understand how the confession of God's Name, 'attributes, and acts, is a song of praise, a Te Deum, a Gloria Patri, 'in another form, and how its peculiar position in the Communion 'Service exalts it to a character more specially eucharistic, as the 'Western Church for above eight hundred years had practically 'held.' (*p.* 456.)—*On the Choral Service.*

621.—In reciting this Creed care should be taken to pause before the expression, '*By whom all things were made,*' because it refers especially to the 'Son.' So, likewise, in the last section, a slight pause should be made after the word 'Lord' in the expression, '*The Lord, and Giver of life,*' as in the Greek original :—*τὸ Κύριον, τὸ ζωοποιὸν.* The several clauses also should not be uttered too hurriedly, or the Congregation will be unable to repeat them with sufficient solemnity. We will now pass to the

Posture of the Priest and People.

(*The Priest* standing *with his face from the People, the People also* standing.)

622.—The Rubric merely prescribes that the People shall be '*still standing as before*'—a direction, as regards *them*, plain and decisive. With respect to the Officiating Minister, however, the silence of the Rubric has led to a difference of usage. The prevailing custom is for him *to continue standing*, but with his *face eastward*, or *towards the Table.* Herein custom rules, '*mos pro lege.*'

Bishop Beveridge writes:—'We *stand* at the Creeds; for they 'being confessions of our faith in God, as such they come under 'the proper notion of hymns or songs of praise to Him.' (*p.* 28.)—*Sermon on the Excellency and Usefulness of Common Prayer.* Vol. II. (Horne.)

BISHOP MANT says:—'At the reading of the Gospel it is ordered, 'that "*the people shall be all standing up.*"......During the recitation 'of the Nicene Creed, the Minister's proper direction is *towards the 'Lord's Table.*' (*p.* 54.)—*Hor. Lit.*

The *late* REV. J. J. BLUNT (*Margaret Professor of Divinity at Cambridge*) says: — 'The absence of Rubric with respect to the 'position in which the *Nicene Creed* is to be read, is no less remark-'able; and here again, I apprehend, *custom* was thought to be rule 'enough—"mos pro lege." In the use of Hereford, the following 'Rubric occurs immediately after the Creed: "Quo finito, vertat se "sacerdos *ad populum* et dicat;" which shows that, when reciting 'the Creed, his face was *not towards the people.* The same time-'hallowed usage obtains, also, with respect to the Apostles' Creed; 'for in the recital of that again, no authority is found in the Rubric 'for *turning to the east.*' (*p.* 328.)—*On the Duties of the Parish Priest.*

The REV. J. PURCHAS writes: —'The Celebrant now proceeds 'to the *midst of the Altar* immediately before the cross, and, ex-'tending his hands, intones the first sentence of the Creed.' (*p.* 37.) —*Directorium Anglicanum.**

The *Kalendar of the English Church Union* prescribes:—'"And "the Gospel ended, shall be sung or said the Creed."—Here the 'Priest should *go to the middle of the Altar, and turn to the East;* 'his Assistants (if any) remaining in their respective places, but 'also *turning Eastward.* It is convenient at the Creed to remove 'the *Service Book* nearer the middle of the Altar, placing it at an 'angle towards the South, so that the Celebrant may easily read 'from it.' (*p.* 81.)—*For* 1868.

[TURNING TO THE EAST AT THE CREED.]

623.—The *turning to the East* at the repetition of the Creeds is not directed in any Rubric or Canon, but is a usage defended by immemorial custom; and has a very imposing effect when practised by a whole Congregation. Those in the body of the Church are usually facing eastward, but the Clergy, and such as occupy the Chancel and the side aisles, have to alter their position to conform to this usage. Where the

---

* This elucidation seems to be derived from the Rubric in the *Hereford Missal*, which reads:—'Et sacerdos stando in medio altaris 'manibus junctis aliquantulum levatis dicat vel cantis,' &c.

MASKELL adds in a Note:—'On *bowing at the name of Jesus*, and 'at the Gloria Patri, see among others, two Constitutions in *Wilkin's* 'Concilia. tom. iii. *p.* 20.'—(*Ancient Lit. of Ch. of England*, *p.* 51.)

practise has become obsolete, care must be taken in attempting its revival. (See the question fully discussed in *Vol.* **B.** and *Vol.* **E.**).

[BOWING AT THE NAME OF JESUS IN THE CREED.]

624.—The *bowing at the name of Jesus* when it occurs in the course of Divine Service, as we have before observed, (*par.* 618.), and particularly in the Creeds, is enjoined in the 18th CANON of 1603; and is a practise, therefore, binding on the Clergy. The obedience of the Laity, however, to these Canons cannot be enforced, yet much may be done by the example of the Clergy in winning them over to a conformity to this reverent, and time-honoured, usage. (See the matter more fully considered in *Vol.* **B.** and *Vol.* **E.**)

ANNOUNCING THE HOLY-DAYS, &c.

(8 *a*) ¶. '*Then the Curate shall declare unto the People what* '*Holy-Days, or Fasting-Days are in the Week* '*following to be observed.*' (1662.)—Present Book of Common Prayer.

The Minister, and People, still standing.

625.—Prior to the last *Revision* in 1662, the three preceding Liturgies of 1552, 1559, and 1604, gave priority to the second part of this Rubric which directed that the *Sermon*, or *Homily*, should be delivered *first* after the Creed, and then that the Curate should announce the Holy-Days, &c.; thus:—

'*After such Sermon, Homily, or Exhortation, the Curate shall* '*declare unto the People whether there be any Holy-Days, or* '*Fasting-Days, the Week following, and earnestly exhort them to* '*remember the Poor, saying one, or more,*' &c. (1552, 1559, 1604.) —KEELING. 180, 181.

626.—In the *first Liturgy* of Edward VI., that of 1549, there is no Rubric of this kind; nor is there at the present day any reason existing like to that which called for the introduction of this Rubric; for with us there is rather a deficiency in the keeping of Holy-Days, than any superstitious or excessive observance of them, as formerly prevailed. Still, it is important that a specific place be appointed for proclaiming the times when the Holy-Days we now have are about to be observed, and here for some centuries has been the customary place for making such announcements; the object having originally been, doubtlessly, to suggest to the Preacher a topic for exhortation. And even now, our Congregations require to be reminded that the Holy-Days, &c. connected with our Blessed Lord's life and ministry demand especial consideration.

627.—The 13th & 14th CANONS direct, as their titles express, the "Due Celebration of Sundays and Holy-Days," and "the Prescript Form of Divine Service to be used on Sundays and Holy-Days:" And the 64th CANON also strictly enjoins the Minister's attention to this especial Rubric. It is entitled, "*Ministers solemnly to bid Holy-Days*," and thus reads:—

'Every Parson, Vicar, or Curate, shall in his several Charge 'declare to the People, every Sunday at the time appointed in the 'Communion-book, whether there be any *Holy-days* or *Fasting-'days* the week following. And if any do hereafter wittingly offend 'herein, and being once admonished thereof by his Ordinary, shall 'again omit that duty, let him be censured according to law, until 'he submit himself to the due performance of it.'—CANON 64.

628.—It must also be remarked that no Minister can *suo motu* appoint any other Public Festival, or Fast to be kept in his Church than what is enjoined in the Liturgy, or imposed by the legislature. The 72nd *Canon*, bears on this very point: it is entitled:—'*Ministers not to appoint Public or Private Fasts*,' &c.

'No Minister or Ministers shall, without the licence and direction 'of the Bishop of the diocese first obtained and had under his hand 'and seal, appoint or keep any solemn Fasts, either publicly or in 'any private houses, other than such as by law are, or by public 'authority shall be, appointed, nor shall be wittingly present at any 'of them under pain of suspension for the first fault, of excommu-'nication for the second, and of deposition from the Ministry for the 'third. Neither,' &c.—CANON 72.

ARCHDEACON SHARP, commenting on this *Canon*, says:—'Now 'the Canon is evidently levelled against the private presumption of 'Ministers, who took upon them, without order from their Superiors 'to enjoin *public fastings*, and not against their holding private fasts 'themselves at their own discretion, nor against their enjoining or 'recommending them in a private manner to others within their 'own cures, as they should see occasion.' (*p*. 267.)........'Every 'appointment, of this kind, where numbers were concerned, and con-'sequently the public peace and communion more or less interested, 'is justly forbidden, unless it proceeded from, or at least had the 'approbation and express license of, the *Bishop of the diocese*, with-'out whose privity and concurrence, no such deviations from estab-'lished rule and order ought to be suffered.' (*p*. 268.)—*On Rubrics and Canons*.

629.—The necessity for this Rubric now may be gathered from the opinions annexed.

Wheatly says:—'The first reason of which (direction) was 'lest the people should observe any such days as had been formerly 'kept, but were laid aside at the Reformation; and therefore the 'Bishops inquired in their Visitations, *whether any of their Curates 'bid any other days than were appointed by the new Calendar*. This 'danger is now pretty well over; there being no great fear of the 'people's observing superstitious Holy-days. But there is still as 'much reason for keeping up the Rubric, since now they are run 'into a contrary extreme, and, instead of observing too many Holy-'days, regard none; which makes it fit that the Curate should dis-'charge his duty, by telling them beforehand what Holy-days will 'happen, and then leaving it upon his people to answer for the 'neglect if they are passed over without due regard.' (*p*. 310.)—*Ill. of Book of Com. Prayer*. Dr. Corrie's Ed.

Dr. Waterland writes:—'But perhaps the order of the Rubric 'might be altered, because of the custom of many Churches of 'concluding with the *Sermon*, and not adding the Prayer for the 'Church Militant. For the people would be apt to run out, and 'would not stay (at least not quietly) to hear the Briefs, Banns, '&c.'—*ibid*. Note.

Shepherd observes:—'This part of the Rubric was first inserted 'to prevent the people's observing such Holidays as had been intro-'duced by Popery, and were abrogated by the Reformation. And 'since the time that things have taken a different turn, it has been 'wisely retained, to remind those of their duty, who are disposed to 'observe *no Holidays* or *Fasting-days at all*.' (*p*. 180.)—*Elucid. of Book of Com. Prayer*. Vol. ii.

Bp. Mant remarks:—'The Order for the Curate's declaration of 'the *Holy-days* and *Fasting-days* to be observed in the week follow-'ing is imperative, and is therefore good to be obeyed; it is good 'also as a permanent testimony to the people of the Church's care 'for their edification. Where the people cannot be persuaded to 'observe the other Holy days, efforts should nevertheless be made 'for the observance of those which have special reference to our 'blessed Redeemer; such as, not *Christmas day* only and *Good 'Friday*, but the *Circumcision*, the *Epiphany*, the *Presentation in 'the Temple*, the *Annunciation*, and, particularly and most of all, 'the *Ascension*. If the Morning Service be impracticable, the day 'might be fitly marked by an Evening Service.' (*p*. 55.)—*Hor. Lit.*

The REV. J. JEBB says:—'The notice of *Holidays* is always 'given in Choirs; but that of the *Fasting days*, as of the Vigils of 'certain Festivals, is commonly neglected. Whether there be Ser-'vice in the Church or not on ordinary Holidays, it would seem 'that the people ought always to be reminded of the Church's fasts 'and feasts: and it may be for want of these warnings that they are 'so generally neglected.' (*p.* 488.)—*On Choral Service.*

630.—The word '*Curate*' in this Rubric implies the *Officiating Minister;* although in some Churches it is confined to the Minister who has 'the Cure of Souls;' so we find laid down in the *Kalendar of the English Church Union*, where the term '*Curate*' in this place is explained as 'the person having the 'ordinary Cure of Souls, if present, whether or not 'acting as Celebrant.' (*p.* 81.). In the "*Alterations*" of 1689, it was suggested to change '*Curate*' to '*Minister;*' and this we find has been carried out in the American Liturgy.

631.—The FORMULARY generally employed in announcing the Holy-days, &c. is "DEARLY BELOVED! "(Wednesday) *next being————there will be Divine* "*Service in this Church in the Morning, and in the* "*Evening, at* (the usual hours.)"

The REV. J. PURCHAS states:—'The proper way of giving Notice 'of Days to be observed during the week is thus: "Thursday in "this week is the Feast of S. ————; Wednesday is the Vigil of "that Festival." "Monday and Tuesday in this week, being within "the Octave of Easter, (or Whitsun-day), have special Services "appointed for them." (*p.* 38.)—*Directorium Anglicanum.*

Give Notice of the Communion.

(8 *b*) ¶. ………'*And then also* (*if occasion be*) *shall Notice be* '*given of the Communion.*'……(1662.)—Present Book of Common Prayer.

632.—There is a difficulty in reconciling the injunction of this Rubric with the directions given in a later Rubric following the 'Prayer for the Church Militant.' In this, the earlier Rubric, '*Notice of the Communion*' is to be given *before* the Sermon or Homily; in the later Rubric, the '*warning*' is to be given *after* the Sermon or Homily. The later Rubric is as follows:—

¶. '*When the Minister giveth warning for the celebration* '*of the Holy Communion, (which he shall always do upon the* '*Sunday, or some Holy-day, immediately preceding). After* '*the Sermon or Homily ended he shall read this Exhortation* '*following.*'—(1662.) KEELING. 188.

633.—It seems that some time antecedent to the *last Revision* in 1662, the Celebration of the Holy Communion was the *rule*, and the neglect of it the *exception*; and the *exception* had at that time become so general as to render it necessary that public notice should be given in the Church when the Holy Sacrament would be administered. Hence the Rubrical directions above quoted were then introduced, and a change made in the commencing clauses of the Exhortations. We infer this also from the Rubric following, which we transcribe from the Liturgy of 1549, and which provides for the omission of the not uncommon practice of exhorting the people from the Pulpit to a worthy attendance at the Holy Eucharist; thus:—

'*After the Crede ended, shall folowe the Sermon or Homily,* '......*wherein if the People bee not exhorted, to the worthy* '*receyving of the Holy Sacrament,*......*then shall the Curate* '*geve this Exhortation to those that he minded to receyve the* '*same.*' (1549.)—CLAY. 112.

634.—The *Exhortation* here referred to is the *third* of those in our present Book of Common Prayer, beginning "Dearly Beloved in the Lord," &c.: After which in this same Liturgy came two other Rubrics, and the *first* of the Exhortations in our present Prayer Book, (which we shall have occasion to speak of by and by): whence it may be concluded that the Rubrics enjoin that *before* the Sermon a simple *notice* was to be given of the celebration of the Holy Communion; and, if no mention was made of the subject in the Sermon, then that *warning* should be given of the Administration of this holy Sacrament, *after* the Sermon ended, in the words of either of the Exhortations annexed to the later Rubric: this usage, however, is rarely practised at the present day.

635.—The RULE now is to combine the directions of the two Rubrics, and instead of giving the '*notice*' of the Holy Communion after the Creed, and the '*warning*' after the Sermon, to give both *notice and warning* after the Creed and before the Sermon, employing part, or whole, of one of the two earlier Exhortations. In some few Churches, *notice of the Communion* is given *here* 'in any suitable form, as no form is prescribed;' and the advocates of this usage add, 'this is not the place to read either of the first two Exhortations, "Dearly beloved, on——— day next I purpose," &c.; or, "Dearly beloved brethren, on ——— I intend," &c. When we arrive at the Rubric preceding these Exhortations, we may possibly make a few additional remarks; in the mean time, we may quote a few authorities, who have attempted to reconcile the discrepancy we have been discussing.

WHEATLY says:—"*And then also (if occasion be) shall notice be* "*given of the Communion:*" though by another Rubric, just before 'the first Exhortation, this is supposed to be done *after* Sermon. 'For there it is ordered, that "*when the Minister giveth warning,*" '&c. The occasion of this difference was the placing of this Rubric 'of directions, at the last Review, before the Rubric concerning the 'Sermon or Homily. For by all the old Common Prayer Books, 'immediately after the Nicene Creed, the Sermon was ordered: and 'then after that "*the Curate was to declare unto the people whether* "*there were any holy-days or fasting-days in the week following, and* "*earnestly to exhort them to remember the poor, by reading one or* "*more of the Sentences, as he thought most convenient by his discre-* "*tion.*" This was the whole of that Rubric then. All the remaining 'part was added at the Restoration, as was also the Rubric above 'cited just before the Exhortation. Now it is plain by that Rubric, 'that the warning to the Communion was intended to be given *after* '*the Sermon;* and therefore I should have imagined that there was 'no design to have changed the places of the two Rubrics here, but 'only to have added some other directions concerning the proclaim-'ing or publishing things in the Church: and that consequently 'the placing of them in the order they now stand, might have been 'owing *to the printer's*, or some other *mistake;* but that I observe 'in the next Rubric the Priest is ordered to "*return to the Lord's* '*Table,*" which supposes that he has been in the Pulpit since he was 'at the Table before; and therefore inclines me to believe that the 'Rubrics were transposed with design; and that the intent of the 'Revisers was, that when there was nothing in the Sermon itself 'preparatory to the Communion, *both this* and the *other Rubric* 'should be complied with, viz. by giving *warning* in this place, that 'there will be a Communion on such a day, and then *reading the* '*Exhortation after* Sermon is ended.' (*p.* 311.)—*Rat. Ill. of Book of Com. Prayer.*

SHEPHERD writes:—'Each of these Rubrics, *separately taken* is 'clear and explicit enough; but between the two, there is a plain 'contradiction, which it is impossible to reconcile. The contradic'tion I think, can only be accounted for, by ascribing the insertion 'of the words "*after the Sermon or Homily ended*" to accidental 'inadvertency.' (*p.* 180.)......'MR. WHEATLY supposes, that the '*intent of the Revisers* was, that the Rubric after the Creed; and 'the Rubric before the Exhortation should both be complied with; 'that notice of the Communion should be given after the Creed; 'and that when there was nothing in the Sermon preparatory to 'the Communion, the Exhortation should be read after the Sermon 'was ended. But the words of the Revisers indicate no such intent. 'Again, according to WHEATLY's own plan, the two Rubrics cannot 'always be complied with; for if the Sermon be preparatory to the 'Communion, then the Exhortation is not to be read; and what 'becomes, in this case, of conformity to the latter Rubric? The 'truth is, that to endeavour to comply with both the Rubrics is an 'idle attempt to conform to an undoubted oversight. The primary 'object of the Rubric before the Exhortation was to order, that, in 'compliance with the request of the Presbyterians, notice of the 'Commnnion should be given prior to the day of its celebration.' (*p.* 183.)—*Eluc. of Book of Com. Prayer.* Vol. ii.

ARCHDEACON SHARP, after saying that Wheatly 'proposes that 'both Rubrics should be complied with; that is, that the *warning* 'should be given immediately after the Nicene Creed, and the '*Exhortation* read immediately after Sermon; adds—'Whereby he 'shews how both Rubrics may be observed. But nevertheless this 'is only a *conformity to a mistake;* and for that reason I suppose 'not much attended to, or regarded by the Clergy.' (*p.* 63.)—*On Rubrics and Canons.*

The *late* REV. J. J. BLUNT (formerly *Lady Margaret Professor of Divinity at Cambridge*) observes:—'It has been objected, that 'whilst one Rubric directs the notice of the Communion to be given 'immediately after the Creed, another directs it to be given im'mediately after the Sermon......the inconsistency is here *seeming*, 'rather than *real.* It may be reconciled thus; a mere *notice* was 'to be given after the Creed, just as a notice of a holy-day to be 'kept would be then given; but, after the Sermon, the *Exhortation* 'was to be read, as consequent upon this notice. And to such a 'conclusion we are led by the Rubric, after the Creed, in the Prayer'Book of 1549, which directs that the Sermon or Homily shall 'follow, "wherein, if the people be not exhorted to the *worthy* "*receiving of the Holy Sacrament......then* shall the Curate give "this Exhortation,"—not otherwise. WHEATLY solves the difficulty 'in the same way as I do, though without developing the cause of 'it. The confusion, it may be added, seems to have been increased 'by the modern printing of the Rubric before the Exhortation, 'where the word "After" stands with a small (a) instead of a 'capital (A), as in the true copy, marking that word to be the 'beginning of a sentence, not to be in the middle of it; as thus; "When the Minister giveth warning for the celebration of the Holy "Communion; After the Sermon he shall read this Exhortation;" 'and not thus: "When the Minister giveth warning for the celebra"tion of the Holy Communion; after the Sermon, he shall read," '&c. I have entered into this question, rather with a view to 'relieve the present Rubrics of inconsistency, than to suggest any 'practical change in the present custom—except that of not mutila-'ting the Exhortation by reading only a few of the first sentences 'instead of the whole, which seems to be doubly objectionable 'where the Sermon itself is not on the subject of the Holy Com-'munion.' (*p.* 329.)—*On the Duties of the Parish Priest.*

Bp. Mant remarks:—'After the Nicene Creed it is directed 'that "*then shall Notice be given of the Communion.*" But after the 'Prayer for the Church Militant it is directed, that "*when the* "*Minister giveth warning for the celebration of the Holy Communion,* "......*after the Sermon or Homily ended he shall read this Exhorta-*"*tion following.*" It is an opinion of ritualists and commentators, 'which cannot be fully set forth here, that, by an oversight, these 'directions do not correctly convey the Church's intentions, which 'are best fulfilled by the *giving of the Notice and the reading of* '*the Exhortation together*, after the Nicene Creed, and before the 'Sermon.' (*p.* 56.)—*Hor. Lit.*

The Rev. J. Jebb observes:—'Some have supposed that a 'contradiction exists between this Rubric and that preceding the 'long Exhortation, the use of which is prescribed after the Sermon 'or Homily is ended. But both may be reconciled, if *Notice* in a 'few words be given before the Sermon, and the *long Exhortation* 'be read after it. In University Colleges, in which the Act of 'Uniformity permits the omission of the Sermon, the Exhortation 'of course comes in here.' (*p.* 488.)—*On the Choral Service.*

The Rev. F. Procter, speaking of the Notice of the Communion, writes:—'This should be given *after the Creed*, and may be *in any* '*terms;* and if the Sermon has not exhorted the people to come to 'the Communion, one of the Exhortations should be read after the 'prayer for the Church militant; the general practice, however, is 'to read a portion, or the whole, of one of the *Exhortations after the* '*Creed.*' (*p.* 322. *Note.*)—*Hist. of Book of Com. Prayer.*

The Rev. J. Purchas, referring to the giving Notice of Holy-days, adds:—'At the same time, the celebration of the Holy 'Sacrament, during the week and on the following Sunday, should 'be announced. The Exhortations which come after the Prayer 'for the Church need only be used when it is wished to give some 'special "warning" to the people, either of their coming too little, 'or too carelessly, as it may be. When *Notice* of Communion is 'given the Priest may use *any short form that is convenient.* When 'he giveth *warning* the whole Exhortation is read, in which case it 'is read after the Sermon, and from the Pulpit, as a kind of Homily, 'rather than a notice.'......In a *Note* he says:—It is customary to 'use the first paragraph of the first Exhortation, down to the word '"Christ" inclusive, for this purpose.' (*p.* 38.)—*Directorium Anglicanum.*

Mr. A. J. Stephens (*Barrister-at-law*) states:—'It has been 'considered by *Mr. Shepherd*, *Mr. Wheatly*, and by other writers 'that there is a plain contradiction between this Rubric and the 'Rubric immediately preceding the first Exhortation, which it is 'impossible to reconcile. It seems however to the Editor, that the 'present Rubric only requires *notice* to be given upon the Sunday of 'the Communion when it is to be celebrated upon some day during 'the week following; or where it is discretionary with the Priest to 'administer it or not.' (*p.* 1150.)......'Some Clergymen, however, 'adopt the practice of giving notice of the Communion *after the* '*Creed*, in these words; "*You are desired to take notice that on* '——*day next, the Holy Communion will be here administered*," and '*after the Sermon* to read the Exhortation at length.' (*p.* 1151.)—*Book of Com. Prayer.* E. H. S.

The *Kalendar of the English Church Union*, with respect to the Notice of the Communion, says:—'The Notice may be given in any 'suitable form as no form is prescribed. This is not the place to 'read either of the first two Exhortations, "Dearly beloved, on '———day next I purpose," &c.; or, "Dearly beloved brethren, on '———I intend," &c.' (*p.* 81.)—*Pub. by Masters.* 1863.

[(8 c) ¶. ......'*The Banns of Matrimony published*'......]

636.—In subservience to a misinterpretation of the Marriage Acts, 26 *Geo.* II. *c.* 33. *s.* 1, and 4 *Geo.* IV. *c.* 76. *s.* 2, which directed that 'all *Banns of Marriage* shall be 'published......according to the form of words *prescribed by the* '*Rubric prefixed to the Office of Matrimony in the* Book of 'Common Prayer, upon *three Sundays* preceding the Solemni-'zation of the Marriage, during the time of Morning Service, 'or of Evening Service, (if there be *no Morning Service* in 'such Church or Chapel upon the Sunday upon which such 'Banns shall be so published,) *immediately after the Second* '*Lesson*,'—this clause of the Rubric, bearing upon the publication of the Banns of Marriage, has been improperly omitted from the Prayer Book by the Printers to prevent the continuance of what they thought an obsolete or improper usage. The object of the Statute was to provide for the '*publication of Banns*' in the Evening Service in those remote Churches where there was no *Morning Service;* and consequently, in those lax times, no Communion Office read, and, therefore, no legally appointed place where the "*Banns*" should be published. To conform to Rubric, and Statute, both, the 'Banns' should be published, where Morning Service is performed, *after the Nicene Creed* as here directed; and where only Evening Service is performed, then *after the Second Lesson* as enjoined in the Act of Parliament. But it is now the universal custom to publish the Banns of Marriage *after the Second Lesson* of Morning Service, and where there is no Morning Service then *after the Second Lesson* of Evening Service. The Subject, however, has been fully handled in *pars.* 170—173. *Vol.* **I.**, to which we would refer our readers for additional information.

The Rev. Thos. Lathbury writes:—'In the Books previous to '1662, *Banns* were to be published in the time of Service, "the 'people being present." The object was publicity, and one Service 'only is specified. Had there been a division of the Morning 'Service, the Rubric in the old Books would have mentioned the 'portion at which the publication should take place. In 1753, the '*New Marriage Act* provided that banns should be published *after* '*the Second Lesson*, and not after the Nicene Creed, as was appointed 'in 1662; but the change was made because in some Churches the 'publication could be better heard in the *Desk*, where the Lessons 'were read, than at the Communion Table, at which the Nicene 'Creed was recited.' (*p.* 85.)—*Hist. of Book of Com. Prayer.*

The Rev. J. Purchas remarks:—'In the "sealed books," after 'the word Communion, is this clause, "*and the Banns of Matrimony* '*published:*" these words have been omitted in later editions of 'the Prayer Book,—the Queen's printer, the delegates at Oxford, 'and the syndics at Cambridge, having not only committed a breach 'of the Act of Uniformity, but having assumed to themselves the 'province of Convocation. The Marriage Act, 26 *Geo.* II., *c.* 33, 'on which this unauthorized omission is based by a wrong inter'pretation thereof, would seem to provide for the publication of 'Banns of Matrimony after the Second Lesson at Evening Prayer 'in Churches where *there is no Morning Service;* and after the 'Second Lesson at Morning Prayer *as well as after the Nicene* '*Creed* when the Services are divided; *but when they are combined,* '*not after the Second Lesson*, but after the Creed, as the unmutilated 'Rubric directs. For the words of the Act are not, during Morning 'Prayer or Matins, but "*during the time of Morning Service*," i. e. 'such divine offices as take place before noon. Such is the course 'for those who regard Parliament as having authority to alter or 'interpolate Rubrics.........The Rubrical direction of the "sealed "books," the only authorized standard of our present Prayer Book, 'must be observed, and such observance is moreover in accordance 'with the right interpretation of the Marriage Act.' (*p.* 38.)—*Directorium Anglicanum.*

The *Kalendar of the English Church Union* for 1863, observes:—'This is still the Legal place to publish "Banns of Matrimony," if a 'larger Congregation is usually present at this Service than at the 'Morning Prayer. Subsequent to the *Statute*, 26 *Geo.* II., *c.* 33, 'A. D. 1753, "An Act for the better preventing of Clandestine "Marriages," the Crown and University Printers have without any 'authority, omitted this part of the Rubric of the Sealed Book. The 'object, however, of the Statute was not to *abolish* the *Rubrical* 'time of Publication, but only to *legalize* another time, when the 'presence of more of the Parishioners would probably be a greater 'security against fraud.' (*p.* 81.)—*Pub. by Masters.*

Public Notices.

(8 *d*) ¶. ......'*And Briefs, Citations, and Excommunica*'*tions read. And nothing shall be proclaimed or* '*published in the Church, during the time of Divine* '*Service, but by the Minister: nor by him any thing,* '*but what is prescribed in the Rules of this Book, or* '*enjoined by the King or by the Ordinary of the place.*' (1662).—Present Book of Common Prayer.

637.—Whatever *Public Notices* are to be proclaimed or published in the course of Divine Service, *this*, the above Rubric directs to be *the place*, and the *Minister* alone to be the person to proclaim them.

Formerly it was the custom to publish *here* aloud Ecclesiastical *Briefs*, *Citations*, and other *proceedings* of the Ecclesiastical Courts; and likewise *Sentences of Excommunication*. This was done as far back as the 9th century, as we find the practice enjoined by Hincman, Abp. of Rheims of that date. 'At this time 'also,' says Palmer, 'in many Churches, those who 'had performed public penance were absolved and 'reconciled.' (*Orig. Lit.* ii. 60.). In later times, the *holdings* of *Courts-leet*, *Courts-baron*, and *Customary Courts*, were published here; and *Proclamations of Outlawry*, *Notices of Vestry Meetings*, and matters affecting *Poor-Rates*, and *Highway-Rates*, were also here proclaimed: but all these, and such like NOTICES, were forbidden to be made in the Church by a recent Statute, 7 *Will.* IV. and 1 *Vict.* c. 45. *ss.* 1, 4. To avoid repetition, we must refer our Readers to *pars.* 262, 263. *Vol.* **B.** where he will find the enactments of the Act fully quoted.

638.—The NOTICES which the Rubric allows the Minister to give out, are '*What Holy-days and Fasting-days are in the Week following*'—'*Notice of the Communion*'—'*Banns of Matrimony published;*' *and what is prescribed in the Rules of this Book* (of Common Prayer), *or enjoined by the Queen, or by the Ordinary of the place.*' To the last word of this Rubric is suggested to be added in the '*Alterations and Amendments*' of 1689, the clause:—'*and is agreeable to the Laws of the Land.*' We may also infer that Notices of the *celebration*, and *hour* of the Services, and of *Sermons*, for especial occasions, and of public *Fast* and *Thanksgiving Days*, are sanctioned by this Rubric, and by the Act we have just referred to. The latter indeed provides:—

'That nothing in this Act shall extend, or be construed to 'extend, to the publication of *Banns*, nor to notice of the *celebration* '*of Divine Service*, or of *Sermons*, nor to restrain the Curate, in 'pursuance of the Rules in the Book of Common Prayer, from 'declaring unto the People what *Holy-Days* or *Fasting-Days* are 'in the week following to be observed, nor to restrain the Minister 'from proclaiming or publishing *what is prescribed* by the Rules of 'the Book of Common Prayer, or enjoined by the Queen, or by 'the Ordinary of the place.' 7 *Will.* IV. and 1 *Vict. c.* 45. *s.* 5. A. D. 1837.

639.—What power the *Ordinary* possesses to direct other *Notices* to be given in the Church under this Rubric, has been much disputed. We may gather some information on this head from the '*Counsel's opinion*' annexed, procured by *Mr. Henry Seymour, M. P.* on the occasion of the *Bishop of* Oxford, (*Dr. Wilberforce*) issuing an injunction to his Clergy to make a '*short pause*' for private prayer in certain parts of Divine Service, for supplicating Almighty God, "that He will promote peace among our brethren in America." The 'injunction' and 'opinion,' as far as they affect this Rubric, are as follow, as we find reported in the "Times," *August* 20th, 1862:—

"Cuddesdon Palace, July 30, 1862.

"My dear Mr. Archdeacon,—May I request you to communicate "to the clergy of your archdeaconry the following injunction from "me as ordinary?—

"That, on the Sunday after the receipt of it, they give notice "to their congregations, at the conclusion of the Nicene Creed, "in these terms:—

"'You are earnestly desired to make your humble supplications "to Almighty God, who is the author of peace and lover of concord, "that He will promote peace among our brethren in America, and "inspire their hearts with Christian unity and fellowship.

"'To allow of which prayer a short pause will for the present "be made after the suffrage in the Litany, "That it may please "Thee to give to all nations unity, peace, and concord;" and also "in the prayer "For all Sorts and Conditions of men," after the "words, "we commend to Thy fatherly goodness all those who are "in any ways afflicted or distressed in mind, body, or estate."'

"I am, my dear Mr. Archdeacon,
Your faithful friend and brother,
"S. OXON."

The '*Case*' for the joint '*Opinion*' of Mr. A. J. Stephens, L.L.D., Q. C., and Mr. Richard Jebb, was

'1st. Whether the Bishop of Oxford has a legal right to enjoin 'the Clergy of his diocese to make the *two pauses* specified in the 'above communication.

'2d. Whether the Clergy of the diocese of Oxford could be 'punished by the laws ecclesiastical for *disobeying* such injunction.

'The answers to the questions submitted to us must depend 'upon the construction of the *Act of Uniformity* (13 and 14 '*Charles* II., *cap.* 4), and of the *Canons* of 1603.' After citing the *second Section* of the Act, (which we have given in *par.* 61. *Vol.* **B.**), and the 14th *Canon* (see *par.* 48. *Vol.* **B.**), and the case of *Newberry* v. *Goodwin*, (see *par.* 227. *Vol.* **B.**), and the opinion of Dr. Kaye late *Bishop of Lincoln*, (which we have already cited at *par.* 83. *Vol.* **B.**), the Counsel thus proceed—'We assume that the Bishop of Oxford issued the injunction 'in question under the *Rubric* which immediately follows the '*Nicene Creed.* That Rubric is as follows:—"*Then the curate* '*shall declare unto the people,*" &c., &c. This *Rubric* does not 'qualify the express language of the 2nd and 17th *sections* of 'the *Statute of Uniformity*, nor of the 14*th Canon;* it does not 'enable the Ordinary to alter, add to, or diminish the "*order*" or '"*form*" of Public Prayer. The object of the Rubric is twofold:—'1, To enable a Curate to declare, give notice of, publish, and read 'certain matters specifically mentioned; 2, To restrain the Minister 'from "*proclaiming or publishing*" anything but what is prescribed 'in the Prayer Book, or enjoined by the Queen, or by the Ordinary. 'This latter restrictive clause does not confer on the Ordinary an 'indefinite power of altering the Statute of Uniformity by enjoining '*pauses* to be made in the prescribed Public Prayers in order that 'the Congregation may interpolate *private prayers.* There is but 'one place in our formularies where any such pause for the purpose 'of interposing *private prayer* is enjoined,—viz., in the "*Ordering* '*of Priests*," where the congregation are "*desired, secretly in their* '*prayers to make their humble supplications to God for all these* '*things; for the which prayers there shall be silence kept for a* '*space.*" The very fact of such a *pause* being made the subject of 'express and positive Rubrical provision here militates against an 'implied right in the Minister to make, or in the Ordinary to direct, 'a similar pause elsewhere in the Public Services. The direction 'in the above *Rubric* is exceptional, inasmuch as the language and 'spirit of the Act of Uniformity, and of the Canons of 1603, con-'template Public Prayer, and not a mixture of Public and Private 'prayer. The power attributed to the Ordinary of enjoining the 'Minister to "*proclaim*," or "*publish*," must be construed with 'reference to the preceding objects of publication expressly enu-'merated—viz., the observance of *Holy Days* or *Fast Days*, cele-'bration of the *Communion*, *Banns of Matrimony; briefs, citations*, 'and *excommunications;* and applies to those objects, or to other 'matters *ejusdem generis*. The necessity for giving this power in 'the indefinite terms used, results partly from the omission in other 'parts of the Prayer Book of specific directions to the Minister to 'give Notices of a similar nature, and partly from the requirements 'of several of the Canons. Thus in the Prayer Book there is no 'specific direction to give notice of an intended *Confirmation*, or of 'a *change in the hour* of Divine Service. And though the Rubric 'directs the Curate to read *excommunications*, the 65*th Canon* 'requires that the Ordinary shall first "*give order*" to that effect. 'Again, under the 72*nd Canon*, Ministers are prohibited from ap'pointing *Fasts*, without the direction of the Bishop.*......In all the 'Statutes of Uniformity of Edward VI., Elizabeth, and Charles II. 'the same paramount object is apparent—namely, to provide "one 'uniform order of common service and prayer," and to prevent 'every diversity in divine service, so that "all the whole realm 'shall have but 'one' use." (*Preface*, to the PRAYER BOOK, *Con'cerning the Service of the Church.*) If the Bishop of Oxford's '*Injunction* be legal, that principle would be violated; and in the '40 dioceses of England and Ireland, every possible diversity might 'be introduced, in case the several Bishops should think proper to 'direct similar *pauses*, but with different objects, to be introduced 'in different parts of the Public Services. The Bishop of Oxford's '*Injunction* has reference to the *civil war* pending in America. If 'his Lordship's *Injunction* be legal, it would be equally legal for the 'Bishop of A**** to direct a *pause* to enable his Congregations to 'pray mentally for the success of the Northern States as the sup'posed champions of anti-slavery; and for the Bishop of B**** to 'direct a prayer to be offered for the success of the Southern States, 'as needful for the supply of cotton to England. It cannot be 'reasonably contended, if this diversity prevailed, that there would 'be one uniform Order or Form of Prayer in accordance with the 'Act of Uniformity. The Common Prayer of the Church cannot 'be made up of special Diocesan intercessions suggested by the 'Ordinaries of the respective dioceses, as expressive of their indi'vidual sentiments.

'In some Churches a practice is pursued of making a *pause* in 'the Litany after the petition on behalf of *Sick Persons;* but such 'a *pause* has *no legal warrant*. And in the special remembrances, 'in the "*Prayer for All Conditions of Men*," as well as in the '"*General Thanksgiving*," the remembrances are not made silently, 'and by the private prayer of the Congregation, but audibly by the 'Minister in a prescribed form.

---

* The 65th CANON enjoins, that 'all Ordinaries shall in their 'several jurisdictions carefully see, and give order that all *Recusants* 'and *Excommunicates*, shall be every six months ensuing, as well 'in the Parish Church, as in the Cathedral Church of the Diocese 'in which they remain, by the Minister openly in time of Divine 'Service upon some Sunday, *denounced* and *declared Excommunicate*, 'that others may be thereby both admonished to refrain their 'company and society, and excited the rather to procure out a writ '*de excommunicato capiendo*, thereby to bring and reduce them into 'due order and obedience,' &c.

The 72nd CANON orders '*Ministers not to appoint Public or 'Private Fasts, or Prophecies, or to Exercise, but by Authority.*' So runs the title.

'For the foregoing reasons we are of *opinion*,—

1. 'That the *Bishop of* OXFORD has *not a legal right* to enjoin 'the Clergy of his Diocess to make the two *pauses* specified in his 'communication to his Archdeacons; and,

2. 'That the Clergy of the Diocess of Oxford could not be 'punished by the laws Ecclesiastical, for *disobeying* such injunction.

'A. J. STEPHENS.
'RICHARD JEBB.

'61, *Chancery-lane*, Aug. 16th, 1862.'

We will now annex a few Ecclesiastical opinions :—

BP. MANT writes:—'Every Clergyman is forbidden to allow 'any thing to be proclaimed or published in the Church during 'Divine Service, *except by himself*; and any thing which is not 'prescribed by the Book of Common Prayer, or by Royal or Epis'copal authority.' (*p.* 55.)—*Hor. Lit.*

The REV. M. PLUMMER states:—'Were this Rubric strictly 'adhered to, we should get rid of many absurd notices uttered by '*Parish Clerks*, to the annoyance of our Congregations. It may 'be as well to observe that a Lecturer is not *the* Minister; and 'that this is the only time appointed for giving out Notices during 'Divine Service.' (*p.* 106.)—*Observations on the Book of Common Prayer.*

MR. H. W. CRIPPS, (*Barrister-at-law*), after citing the 5th *Section* of the Act, 7 *Will.* IV. and 1 *Vict.* c. 45. adds:—'A great 'part of which proviso, it will be seen, is merely an affirmance of 'the directions of the Rubric, and a declaration that they are to 'be obeyed, and that they are not interfered with by this Act.' (*p.* 629.)—*The Law relating to the Church and the Clergy.* 3rd Edition,

MR. A. J. STEPHENS, (*Barrister-at-law*) says:—'Under this 'Rubric the Minister is bound, during Divine Service, to proclaim 'or publish every *Notice* himself, and cannot direct the Clerk to 'perform that duty.' (*p.* 1154.)—*Book of Com. Prayer.* E. H. S.

640.—The practice adopted in Ireland, in some of the Protestant Churches, of collecting '*alms*' for the Poor immediately after the Nicene Creed has no Rubrical sanction; much less the proclamation necessarily made here by the Officiating Minister where such usage prevails:—"*Pray remember the Poor.*" This custom we do not find observed in England. The proper time for such collection is during the reading of the Offertory Sentences.

BP. MANT writes:—'An interruption in the Service after the 'Nicene Creed, for inviting and collecting Alms for the Poor, is not 'agreeable to the provisions of the Church, who directs such Col- 'lection to be made at another time, when she connects the act of 'charity with an act of devotion.' (*p.* 56.)—*Hor. Lit.*

[Psalmody.—Retiring to the Vestry.]

641.—It is the general custom to introduce in this place just before the Sermon, a *Psalm* or *Hymn*; and after it has been announced by the Officiating Minister, for him to retire to the *Vestry* to exchange his Surplice for the *Black Gown*, and thence to proceed to the Pulpit for the *Sermon*. With others it is the practice to pass at once to the *Pulpit* after the Nicene Creed, without the interruption of Psalmody, or the change of Vestments; this usage is more in accordance with rubrical authority; but the preceding custom is generally adopted. The Rubrics of the *first Prayer Book* of Edward VI. A. D. 1549, enjoining a *change of Costume*, are now considered obsolete (see *Vol.* **D.**); had it been otherwise, the change could not have been made here, but before the Communion Office was begun.

Psalmody.

Bp. Mant says on this point:—'*Singing* after the Nicene Creed 'is out of place, and disturbs the appointed order of the Service. 'The Church's direction, '*Then shall follow the Sermon*,' is a plain 'indication of her mind and will.' (*p.* 57.).—*Hor. Lit.*

Mr. A. J. Stephens (*Barrister-at-law*): —'It is very usual in 'Parish Churches, and even in some Cathedrals, to introduce a '*Psalm* or *Anthem* before the Sermon. Not only is there *no* '*authority* for this, but it disturbs the order of the Service, and it 'is in the eye of the Law, *brawling*. It must be remarked that the 'Communion Service is the place of all others in which such an 'offence should not be perpetrated. The Apostolic Scriptures are 'followed by the words of our Lord Himself, the teaching of Holy 'Writ is succeeded by the teaching of the Church in the Creed, and 'this by the instruction of the Ministers of the Church. Besides, it 'is preposterous to leave a prescribed *hymn* of the Church (the '*Creed*) unsung, and to sing immediately after its simple recitation 'a hymn that is unauthorized. The *Anthem* is omitted in its proper 'place, and is inserted in the very part of the Service where it 'is most inappropriate. The effect of the practice is to exalt 'unduly the importance of the *Sermon*, which is thus ushered in, 'as it were, with an *Introit*.' (*p.* 1155.)—*Book of Common Prayer.* E. H. S.

Retiring to the Vestry.

On this subject we may quote the following :—

Bp. Mant observes:—'Neither at this, nor at any other, time 'of the Service should the Minister *separate and absent himself from 'his Congregation.* If his withdrawal were necessary, for the pur- 'pose of *changing his dress*, having changed it, he ought to return 'instantly. But the Church imposes on him no such necessity. 'She neither injoins, nor sanctions, nor permits, nor recognizes, a '*change of dress;* but sends him straight, not to the Vestry, but to 'the *pulpit.* Nor does she know any thing of a *black gown* for her 'Officiating Minister. To some minds indeed any change of dress 'is an innovation, savouring of Rome; the particular change, of 'Geneva. At all events, neither the one, nor the other, is acknow- 'ledged by the Anglican Church. Her prescript dress is the same 'for all their ministrations.' (p. 57.)—*Hor. Lit.*

Prayer before the Sermon.

(9) ¶. '*Then shall follow the Sermon, or one of the Homilies,*' &c.

642.—By the *Act of Uniformity*, 13 & 14 *Car.* II. *c.* 4. we are bound "to use the Service in such *order* "*and form* as is mentioned in the Book of Common "Prayer," and the above Rubric of the Prayer Book requires the *Sermon* to be proceeded with at once after the Nicene Creed, *without any antecedent prayer.* The 55th Canon (of 1603–4), however, enjoins :—

'Before *all* Sermons, Lectures, and Homilies, the Preachers and 'Ministers shall move the People to join with them in prayer, *in 'this form*, or *to this effect*, as briefly as conveniently they may:— "*Ye shall pray for Christ's holy Catholic Church*, &c. &c......always 'concluding with the Lord's Prayer.'—Canon 55.

And we find also, *temp.* George I., a Royal Letter calling on the Bishops to enforce this *Canon* throughout their several Dioceses. It ran in these words :—

'Whereas also we are credibly informed that it is the manner of 'some in every Diocese, before their *Sermon*, either to use a *Collect* 'and the *Lord's Prayer*, or the *Lord's Prayer* only (which the 55th 'Canon prescribes as the conclusion of the Prayer, and not the 'whole Prayer), or, at least, to leave out our titles, by the said 'Canon required to be declared, and recognized, we do further 'direct that you require your Clergy, in their prayer *before Sermon*, 'that they do keep strictly to the form in the said Canon contained 'or to the full effect thereof.'—*His Majesty's Directions*, 1714, *for 'preserving Unity in the Church.*' (Cardwell's *Doc. Ann.* ii. 360.)

643.—Now we know that the prescribed formula had a *political* object, which was to secure the loyalty of the Preacher, and maintain the supremacy of the Crown 'in all causes ecclesiastical and temporal,' which was a vital point against the pretensions of the Papacy, and the claims of the Pretender; but *Bp. Taylor* says, "a law made for particular reason, "when the reason wholly ceases, does no longer oblige "the conscience." (*Works*, Vol. XIV. 242.); hence the injunction of the 55th *Canon* has long been obsolete in Parish Churches; and it is only in the University Pulpits, College Chapels, Cathedrals, and on certain public occasions in ordinary Churches, that we find the prescribed formula, termed improperly the "*Bidding Prayer*," brought into requisition.

644.—This "*Bidding Prayer*" is, correctly speaking, a '*bidding*,' or invitation, to prayer; and not in itself a Prayer, as the *title* of the 55th CANON would lead one to suppose; and, therefore, while being read by the Preacher, he and the Congregation should *stand;* and when arriving at the *Lord's Prayer*, the acknowledged summary of the petitions set forth in the 'bidding' to prayer, then, the Congregation should *kneel*, and repeat aloud the Lord's Prayer with the Preacher. Formerly, as we learn from COXE's "*Forms of Bidding Prayer*," the People would sometimes *stand*, and sometimes *kneel*.

WHEATLY complains of the growing disuse of the prescribed formulary laid down in the *55th Canon*, and published a Treatise on the subject, saying:—'For the sake of those who may be 'desirous to look into the question, I have inserted the *title* at the 'bottom of the page, not without hopes that my sincere endeavours 'may contribute a little to put a stop to the custom of *praying in the 'Pulpit;* which, the Reader will there see, has once been attended 'with fatal consequences, and which has been discountenanced and 'prohibited almost in every reign, since the Reformation, by our 'Governors and Superiors both in Church and State.' In a *Note*, the *Title* of this 'Treatise' is thus given:—"*Bidding of Prayers* before "Sermon, no mark of disaffection to the present Government: or, "an *Historical Vindication of the fifty-fifth Canon.* Shewing that "the form of Bidding Prayers has been prescribed and enjoined "ever since the Reformation, and constantly practised by the "greatest Divines of our Church; and that it has been lately "enforced both by his present Majesty [George I.], and our Right

"Reverend Diocesan [D. J. Robinson] the Lord Bishop of London." 'By *Charles Wheatly*, M.A. Lecturer of Saint Mildred's in the 'Poultry, London,' &c., &c. To this, *Dr. Corrie* adds:—'It is, how- 'ever, by no means the fact that this form of Bidding Prayers 'prescribed in the fifty-fifth Canon has been "constantly practised 'by the greatest Divines of our Church." (See Coxe, *Forms of 'Bidding Prayers*, Oxf. 1840.')—*Rat. Ill. of Book of Com. Prayer.* Corrie's Ed. *p.* 314.

Secker says:—'Great stress was laid on the use of this Prayer 'for some time after the Reformation; because when that took 'place, an acknowledgment of the *Kings's supremacy*, which the 'Papists denied, was very prudently, as things then stood, inserted 'into it. And hence it hath continued to our days, though it is 'frequently shortened into a *Collect* and the *Lord's Prayer*, the 'reason for enlarging being now become less. The original manner 'of performing this part of the Preacher's Office was by "*bidding*," 'that is, inviting and exhorting, the people to pray for the several 'particulars, mentioned by him: which they were understood to do, 'either *silently* in their minds, as they went along with him, or by '*comprehending them all* in the Lord's Prayer at last.' (*p.* 295.)—*Quoted in* Mant's *Book of Com. Prayer.*

Archdeacon Sharp devotes a whole 'Charge' to the consideration of the 55th Canon, and tells us, that 'they who adhere 'to the very letter of the Canon are no doubt *Canonum observantis- 'simi;*' and that 'they who condense the whole into a prayer with 'suitable enlargements of their own, provided they keep to the 'order and effect of the Canonical form, and do it likewise as the '*Canon admonishes, i. e.* "briefly as conveniently they may," are not 'to be charged with wilfully contravening the Canons.' He then speaks of those Preachers 'who adopt a middle way, and instead of 'abiding by the monitory form of the Canon closely and *verbatim*, 'or, on the other hand, using a prayer of intercession, which is 'against the tenor of the Canon; contrive to disguise a real exhor- 'tation by introducing it with an *oremus*, "Let us pray;" the 'common invitatory sentence in all Liturgic Offices, and the most 'apposite expression that can be used for moving the people to 'prayer as the Canon directs.' This seems to be the way of accommodation he himself adopted. He, however, strongly censures those who can content themselves at all times with the bare use of a Collect before Sermon. — (On Rubrics and Canons. Visitation Charge. A. D. 1745. *pp.* 169—195.).

The *late* Rev. J. J. Blunt (formerly *Margaret Professor of Divinity at Cambridge*) writes:—'I apprehend, that they are mis- 'taken who consider this "bidding" to prayer as a prayer in itself, 'and who assume the posture of prayer, accordingly, during the 'reading of it. So long they are *listeners* merely, and not suppliants '—listeners to an invitation to pray, and to the nature of the prayer 'in which it is proposed to them to join—not *worshippers*, till the 'prayer itself (which is the Lord's Prayer) begins, and in which 'they are to join.' (*p.* 331.)—*Duties of the Parish Priest.*

The Rev. J. Jebb remarks:—'The *Bidding of Prayers* is read 'in most Cathedrals. The words of the Canon enjoin its use before 'all Sermons and Homilies: and therefore it does not appear on 'what ground the substitution of a *Collect*, or the omission of the 'substance of this form (which, however, is not a prayer, but the '*bidding* of prayers) is justifiable. The *Canon* expressly permits 'the abbreviation of the form it sets forth, so that its length cannot 'be pleaded as an excuse. To the alleged objection, that it is 'much the same in substance as the *prayer for the Church Militant*, 'it must be replied, that if the Church has thought proper to enjoin 'repetitions, her individual Members have no authority to curtail 'them.' (*p.* 494.)—*On the Choral Service.*

The Rev. W. Palmer observes:—'How long the present form 'of prayer, directed by the *Canons* of 1603, may have been used 'in the English Church, would be difficult to determine. We have 'memorials of these prayers as used in England in the fourteenth 'century. Ivo Carnotensis, who flourished about A. D. 1080, cites 'a Canon of a Council of Orleans, which evidently alludes to a form 'of prayer like that of the Church of England. The characteristics 'of both are that the Preacher admonishes the people what they 'are *to pray for;* and the people being supposed to offer up a silent 'petition for each object that is mentioned, the Preacher at the 'conclusion sums up their devotions in *Collects*, or the *Lord's* '*Prayer*.' (*p.* 61.)—*Orig. Lit.* Vol. ii.

The Rev. J. Purchas says:—'It should be remembered that 'the Preacher has no legal right to deliver an *introductory prayer* '*in the Pulpit* before the *Sermon;* because there has been none 'provided by the Rubric. In the *Canons* of 1604, a bidding of 'prayer is ordered, and which was to terminate with the *Lord's* '*Prayer;* but no Rubric commanding such observance is in the 'present Prayer Book, 1662. In fact no prayers should be used 'publicly, but those that are prescribed, lest through ignorance 'or carelessness anything be uttered before God contrary to the 'Catholic Faith. The Preacher should *never kneel in the Pulpit;* 'as to his *prayer* before preaching he had better say it in his 'chamber, or in the Sacristy, or in his place in the Sanctuary, or 'in his Stall in the Chancel.' In a *Note* is added:—'The *Canon* '(LV.) probably referred to *Lectures* apart from the Holy Com-'munion. Then the *Bidding Prayer* is in place and might precede 'the Litany.' (*p.* 41.)—*Directorium Anglicanum.*

The Rev. J. C. Robertson writes:—'All the authorities that 'have fallen in my way are for the Ministers saying *something*, and 'concluding with the *Lord's Prayer*, which the Canon requires. '(*p.* 174.)......The use of *privately composed prayers* is objectionable 'on many grounds; and the practice of some, who spoil a Collect 'by alterations of their own, changing the tone of the prayer, and 'the character and flow of its language, although not so dangerous, 'is perhaps at least as offensive. I do not, however, see anything 'inadmissible in the use of a *Collect* as we find it. The objections 'made by the Bishops in Charles the Second's time against *ex-'temporal* and *privately-composed* prayers, do not hold against the 'employment in this place of words which have been provided by 'the Church for use in some part of her Service. Where such a 'practice has hitherto obtained, it appears to me that the Clergy 'may continue to follow it with a safe conscience, unless, their

'Bishops should think fit to revive the Canon by a special Order.' (*p.* 182.)......'In England before the Reformation, the custom was, 'either that both Priest and people should pray in silence, after the '*bidding;* or that the Priest should say the Prayer as far as the 'word "*temptation*," and the people should add the rest as a re-'sponse. (See *Burnet*, H. R. ii. 30; *Martene*, i. 137; iii. 24.) In 'after times, the latter of these practices was observed at Sermons, 'as most commonly in the other parts of Public Worship. (See '*Coxe*, p. 69.) Hence, therefore, we have analogy, as well as the 'plainest meaning of the words, for extending to the *Lord's Prayer* 'in this place, the general Rubric, which orders that the *people say* '*it with the Minister*, "wheresoever it is used in Divine Service." (*p.* 185.)—*How shall we conform to the Lit.*

645.—The prevailing custom at the present day, is for the Preacher to employ before the Sermon one of the *Collects*, followed by the *Lord's Prayer;* but as an outcry has been raised of late against the frequent repetition of the Lord's Prayer in Divine Service, many Preachers omit it. *Others*, again, proceed at once to deliver their text without any preliminary prayer; while a *third party* preface the Sermon with the words, "*In the Name of the Father and of the Son, and of the Holy Ghost, Amen.*" *Extemporaneous* prayer is certainly inadmissible, having the sanction neither of *Canon*, *Custom*, nor of *Rubric*.

Bisse writes:—'This prayer of the Minister before the Sermon, 'be it of what sort or size it will is not only contrary to the inten-'tion of the Church, but also to the law of the land.........Since 'it must be in itself, wholly superfluous, and far inferior to the 'Common Prayer; and since in its consequences it tends directly 'to the derogation and despising, if not depraving of it.'—*On the Common Prayer*. p. 186—188.

Bp. Mant remarks:—'*Extemporaneous prayer* in publick wor-'ship is altogether repudiated by the Church, and she allows no 'prayers but those of her own Liturgy. If therefore any prayer 'be used before the *Sermon*, it should be taken from the Book of 'Common Prayer. But I can find no authority for any prayer 'there, and it is my belief that not any is intended by the Church. 'Her silence indeed seems to be conclusive. The 55*th Canon* 'in the English Code, which is the nearest approach to an authority, 'contains a *form*, which is however not precatory, but injunctive 'or monitory; "*Ye shall pray for Christ's Holy Catholick Church*, '&c.:" so that this form, whatever may have been, and may 'be, its authority for the purpose to which it was directed, is 'in fact no authority for a prayer. If however the popular 'prepossession should be in favour of a prayer before the *Ser-'mon*, and the Minister should think it desirable to indulge such 'a prepossession, he might perhaps, I will not say justify, but 'excuse his indulgence on the plea of *long-continued usage*, in a 'case which he may deem not clearly defined, and where the 'negative is not secured by an express prohibition. Still I cannot 'but retain my opinion that the silence of the Church is very 'expressive: (for surely, had she intended any prayer to be here 'introduced, she would have declared her intention, not merely by 'a general order, but would have moreover ordered what the prayer 'should be: and that therefore *for the Sermon to follow immediately*, '*without the intervention of a prayer*, is the course agreeable to her 'mind and rule. For the EVENING, if a *Sermon* be needed, the same 'course might be taken as in the MORNING: the Sermon being 'followed by the *Blessing*.' (*p.* 57.)—*Hor. Lit.*

The BISHOP OF EXETER (*Dr. Phillpotts*), in a Pastoral Letter to his Clergy dated *Bishopstowe*, Nov. 19th, 1844, writes on this head:— 'I direct (and I do so with the express sanction of his Grace the 'Archbishop), that, where there is a *Sermon* in the Evening, it 'be delivered after EVENING PRAYER, in the accustomed manner; 'that is, preceded by a *Collect*, (unless the *Bidding Prayer* be used), 'and the *Lord's Prayer*, and followed by the *Blessing*. I hope it is 'unnecessary for me to add, that there must be *no prayer of your* '*own composing* either before or after the Sermon.'— Cited in STEPHENS' *Ecclesiastical Statutes*. Vol. II. *p.* 2064.

The REV. J. PURCHAS says:—'The Preacher may precede the 'Sermon with the words:—"*In the Name of the Father, and of the* '*Son, and of the Holy Ghost. Amen.*" "The Lord be with you," is 'also an ancient form of Salutation that has been used before the 'Sermon; to which the People reply, "And with thy Spirit." It is 'much preferable to the use of a prayer in this place.' (*p.* 40.)— *Directorium Anglicanum.*

MR. A. J. STEPHENS (*Barrister-at-law*) states:—'The priest 'has no legal right to deliver an introductory prayer in the pulpit 'before the *Sermon*, because there has been none provided by the 'rubric. In the *Canons* of 1604. a "*bidding prayer*" was ordered, 'and which was to terminate with the *Lord's Prayer;* but no 'Rubric commanding such observance is in the Book of Common 'Prayer of 1662; and saying a prayer not expressly authorized by 'stat. 13 & 14 *Car.* II. *c.* 4. is introducing a different rite, form, or 'ceremony from that which has been directed by the Statute of 'Uniformity: in fact, as BISHOP SPARROW (*Rationale* 164.) says, "no prayers should be used publicly, but those that are prescribed; "lest through ignorance or carelessness, any thing contrary to the "faith should be uttered before God." (*p.* 1157.)—*Book of Common Prayer.* E. H. S.

THE SERMON.

646.—Anciently, the *Sermon* seems to have followed the Gospel, of which it was an exposition, and it acquired the name of '*Postil*' on this account; a term abbreviated from *post illa Evangelia.* Sermons had originally various appellations, such as *Homilies*, ομιλιας; *Sermons*, λογος, Sermo; *Tractates* or *Tracts*, tractatus, i. e. handled; and *Disputations*, disputatio. With us, the more familiar names, besides that of *Sermon*, are *Discourse*, and *Lecture*. At the Reformation we find it to have been a general practice to exhort the people in the Sermon to a worthy reception of the Holy Communion, as we may infer from the Rubric following the Nicene Creed in the *first Liturgy* of Edw. VI. A. D. 1549, which thus reads:—

'*After the Creed ended, shall follow the* SERMON *or* HOMILY '*or some portion of one of the* HOMILIES, *as they shall be hereafter* '*divided: wherein if the people be not exhorted, to the worthy* '*receiving of the holy Sacrament of the body and blood of our* '*Saviour Christ, then shall the Curate give this Exhortation*,' &c. [Here follows the *third* of the Exhortations in our present Book of Com. Prayer beginning, "DEARLY Beloved in the Lord, ye that mind to come," &c.]

647.—In primitive times, the Bishops usually delivered the Sermon or Exhortation, and when he was not present, Presbyters were allowed to preach to the people. Sometimes there was a succession of preachers who delivered each a discourse to the same assemblage; in these instances the superior functionary closed the instruction. In the Roman Church there was formerly very little preaching. *Leo*, the Romish bishop in the 5th century, was the only Bishop who then preached, and for five hundred years after none imitated his example; then *Pius 5th* restored the ancient usage. Now, however, since the revival of learning, and the great advance that has been made in knowledge and education, preaching is the rule, and not preaching the exception: and herein lies the danger of the present age; lest the worship of God be held second to the worship of man—not that we would disparage the power and product of preaching, but give the right pre-eminence to prayer, and praise, and thanksgiving.

648.—The *Sermon*, as the position of this Rubric shews, being a part of the Communion Service, it should always occupy its appointed place; when, however, this Service is not used, as at EVENING

PRAYER, then it is usual for the *Sermon* to be preached at the close of the Service. In some Churches it occurs immediately after the *third Collect*, and before the Anthem there appointed to be sung. This system is adopted more especially where the Services are conducted chorally, because it became a very frequent practice for persons to come to EVENING PRAYER merely to hear the Anthem, and when this was concluded to leave the Church, and, consequently, not only lose the instruction of the Sermon, but disturb very seriously the minds of the more devout worshippers who remained. This usage is, however, rare.

A few opinions now may not be here unacceptable.

L'ESTRANGE writes:—'In the primitive Service, no Creed interposing, the *Sermon* immediately followed the *Gospel*, and was an usual explication upon it, whence I conceive the name *Postil* is derived, *quasi post illa Evangelia*, '*Postil*' being nothing but a discourse upon, and subsequent to the Gospel. These popular discourses had in antiquity various appellations, in the earliest times παρακλησις, was the most usual, so λογος παρακλησέως, '*a word of exhortation*,' *Acts* xiii. 14.........then they call them ὁμιλίαι, *Homilies*, then λόγοι, *Sermons*. Among the Latines, St CYPRIAN especially, *Tractatus*, a tract, is most familiar; in AUGUSTINE and AMBROSE, *disputatio*, a disputation frequently occurreth, because therein they usually undertook the confutation of either Heathens, Jews or hereticks. Lastly *Sermo*, a Sermon, was then also in use.' (*p.* 170.)—*Alliance of Div. Offices.*

SPARROW observes:—'After the Epistle and Gospel, and the Confession of that Faith which is taught in holy Writ, follows the *Sermon*; (*Amb.* Epist. 83. ad *Marcel*; *Leo* I. *Ser.* 2. *de Pascha*); which usually was an Exposition of some part of the Epistle or Gospel, or proper Lesson for the Day......And the Preacher was in his Exposition appointed to observe the Catholick Interpretation of the old Doctors of the Church; as we may see in the 19th Canon of the 6th Council of *Constantinople*, held in *Trullo*......To this agrees the *Canon* made in Queen Elizabeth's time, A. D. 1571. ......The *Sermon* was not above an hour long. *Cyril. Catech.* 18.'—*Rationale.* p. 162.

DEAN COMBER says:—'For more effectually explaining the mysteries of the *Creed*, and for more vigorously pressing the duties of the *Gospel*, the ancient Church appointed a *Sermon* or *Homily* in this place, which is useful every Sunday, and more especially when there is a Communion: because by a pious and practical discourse, suited to the Holy Communion, the minds of the receivers are put into a devout frame, and made fitter for the succeeding mysteries.'—(quoted in MANT's *Book of Com. Prayer* in loco.)

Dr. Bisse writes:—'As to the frequency or plenty of the word 'preached which continually flows from these fountains, this pro-'vision of our Church, which appoints a *Sermon* once on the Lord's 'Day, must appear sufficient, yea, abundant: if we look back to the 'scarcity of it in the days of the Reformation, when the provision 'of a Sermon was but *quarterly*, as made in *Edward VI.* time, 1547; 'and for many years after but *monthly*, according to an injunction 'of *Queen Elizabeth*, 1559. Wherefore this present provision of our 'Church, in appointing one Sermon on the Sundays, ought to be 'received with all thankfulness. And in truth a greater plenty 'than this may turn perhaps not to our nourishment, but only 'create in us a waste and wantonness. That appetite in many 'after a *multitude of Sermons* is no other than that of the Israelites, 'when, not content with the regular provision of their daily manna, "they required meat for their lusts." Far be it from me that I 'should discourage or straiten the ordinance of *preaching*: but 'God forbid, that the enlarging of that should ever straiten the 'Ordinances of divine worship, or be esteemed before them! God 'forbid that ever in the Church of England the Sermon, how excel-'lent soever, should be valued before the Service, which is incom-'parable! For to what end do we come to the House of Prayer? 'Is it to adore God, or to admire men? Is it to praise Him for the 'excellency of His greatness, or them for the excellency of their 'talents? Should this plenteous provision of preaching be ever 'again exalted and abused to the neglecting, despising, and dis-'paraging of our publick worship, as it was before the Great 'Rebellion, it will well provoke God to take it again from us: and 'instead thereof to feed our lusts with preaching as He did the 'Israelites with quails, till it "came out of their nostrils, and 'became loathsome unto them," (*Numb.* xi. 20.) It was a remark-'able saying, so founded on the judgments of God, that a preaching 'Church cannot stand: and it is also founded on the judgments of 'God, that a Church which plans its religion in preaching shall 'never stand.'—Quoted in Mant's *Book of Com. Prayer* in loco.

Wheatly remarks:—'Sermons have been appointed from the 'beginning of Christianity, to be used upon all Sundays and Holy-'days, but especially when the Lord's Supper was to be admin-'istered. For by a pious and practical discourse suited to 'the Holy Communion, the minds of the hearers are put into a 'devout frame, and made much fitter for the succeeding mysteries. '......The reason of its being ordered here, is because the first 'design of them was to explain some part of the foregoing Epistle 'and Gospel, in imitation of that practice of the Jews mentioned 'in *Nehemiah* xiii. 8. For which reason they were formerly called '*Postillis*, (quasi post illa, sc. Evangelia,) because they followed 'the Gospel.' (*p.* 312.)—*Rat. Ill. of Book of Com. Prayer.*

The Rev. J. Jebb observes:—'The duty of preaching at the 'Communion Service is expressly enjoined by the Rubric: nor can 'conformity to the Liturgy be justly pleaded, when, on any Com-'munion day, whether Sunday or Holiday, this duty is neglected. 'It has been urged, indeed, that the meaning of the Rubric is, "here 'is the place for a Sermon, if it be expedient or customary to preach 'one." But surely the same mode of interpretation may just as 'fairly be claimed for the Psalms, Collects, or Scripture; and then 'what becomes of the Prayer Book? No command is more explicit. '......It may be that the omission of the Morning Sermon, customary 'in many Country Parishes, is sought to be justified by the practice 'of the Universities. But the Universities are specially excepted 'from the operation of the Rubric by the Act of Uniformity, which 'sanctioned an ancient and immemorial custom. If it is done in 'deference to the corrupt and slothful habits of society both high 'and low, who prefer the *afternoon* for their devotions, a worse 'reason cannot be found. But it is sometimes justified on Sacra-'ment Sundays at least, on the ground of the extreme length of the 'Service, or of the great labour that is then thrown, in a populous 'Parish upon a single Clergyman. As to the length; the Psalmody, 'often so immoderately long, and introduced too in improper places, 'might be well shortened; and the Sermon need not occupy, on 'these occasions, many minutes.' (*p.* 491.)—*Choral Service.*

The REV. J. C. ROBERTSON says:—'We may conclude *that*, the 'Prayer-Book was never understood to prescribe for Churches and 'Chapels of all kinds an uniform order of Sermon in the morning 'of Sundays and Holy-days, and peremptorily to forbid preaching 'at any other time; *that* Sermons and Lectures on the afternoons 'of such days, and at other times, are *tolerable*, though not com-'manded; and if they treat on catechetical subjects, or be simple 'expositions of Scripture, without any mischief in the matter of 'them, Sermons in the afternoon of Sundays have been held com-'mendable by our best Divines; *that* Weddings and Funerals may 'give an occasion for a Sermon on any day; and *that* the Bishop's 'authority has always been held sufficient to regulate the practice, 'so as to sanction what the Prayer-Book does not prescribe.' (*p.* 253.)—*How shall we Conform*, &c.

MR. A. J. STEPHENS (*Barrister-at-law*) writes:—'Under the '*Statute of Uniformity* the Priest has no right upon any occasion 'to abridge the Service of the Holy Communion by omitting the '*Sermon* or one of the Homilies, and if the Congregation be suffi-'ciently numerous, and willing to receive the Holy Sacrament, he 'is bound to administer it. And whenever he begins the Com-'munion Service, he must proceed with it so far as to *preach a* '*Sermon*, or *read an Homily*, for it is not until after he has done 'so, that he can ascertain whether there is a Congregation suffi-'ciently numerous, the time for commencing the strictly Sacra-'mental Service not arriving until *after* the Offertory. (*p.* 1157.)—*Book of Com. Prayer.* E. H. S.

649.—The *number* of Sermons to be preached in the course of the Sunday, the Statute law enjoins shall be *two*, and in some instances *three*; and the Bishop is invested with authority to enforce them: thus—

'It shall be lawful for the Bishop in his discretion, to order that 'there shall be two *full Services*, each of such Services, if the 'Bishop shall so direct, to *include a Sermon* or *Lecture* on every 'Sunday throughout the year,' &c. 1 & 2 *Vict. c.* 106. *s.* 80. (See more fully, *par.* 98. *Vol.* **B.**)

For a *third Sermon*, another Statute thus enacts:—

'In any Parish or extra-Parochial place in which it shall appear 'to the Bishop of the Diocese that the *Churches* or *Chapels* now 'existing, or which may be built or provided under any of the 'provisions of this Act, do not or will not *afford sufficient accommo-'dation* for the Parishioners or inhabitants thereof to attend Divine 'Service......and in which such Bishop shall be of opinion that it is 'expedient that additional accommodation should be provided for 'such purpose, and that such purpose would be answered by the 'celebration on Sundays, and on the great Festivals of a *third* or '*additional Divine Service*, being either the Morning or Evening 'Service......as shall be directed by the Bishop of the Diocese, *with* '*a Sermon*, in the Churches or Chapels existing at the time of 'passing this Act, or by the celebration of a *third* or *additional* '*Service* as aforesaid, *with a third Sermon*, in any Church or Chapel 'which may be built or provided under any of the provisions of this 'Act, it shall be lawful for such Bishop *to require the Incumbent* of 'every such Parish, District Parish, or Extra-Parochial place, *to* '*nominate* to him a proper person to be licensed to serve as a 'CURATE in the existing Church or Chapels for the performance 'of such *additional* or *third Service* with a *Sermon*, or in any Church 'or Chapel which may be built or provided as aforesaid, for the 'performance of such *additional* or *third* Service with a *third* '*Sermon;* and such *Incumbent* shall, *within six months* after such 'requisition, nominate such CURATE to the Bishop to be licensed; 'and *in default* of such nomination, such *Bishop* is hereby em-'powered *to nominate* and license a proper CURATE for the purpose 'aforesaid; and the said Bishop is hereby empowered to require 'the *Churchwardens* of every such Church or Chapel *to let* for the 'said additional Service such proportion of *the Pews* of such Church 'or Chapel, *not* being a *Pew held by faculty* or *prescription*, and at 'such rates, as in the opinion of such Bishop shall be sufficient to 'afford a competent *salary to such Curate*,' &c. 58 *Geo.* III. *c.* 45. *s.* 65. (See more fully *par.* 99. *Vol.* **B.**)

[STRANGERS PREACHING.]

650.—In virtue of the 50th *Canon*, entitled, '*Strangers not admitted to Preach without shewing their Licence*,' some Bishops do not approve of Preachers from another Diocese delivering a discourse in the Pulpit, within their jurisdiction, without permission. Canonical obedience, therefore, will require the Clergy to conform to this injunction should occasion call for its exercise. Another *Canon*, the 52nd, also directs, as its title imports, '*The Names of Strange Preachers to be entered in a Book*.' This would be desirable; and the perusal of the Book in after times would be interesting and satisfactory. As this question is treated more at large in *Vol.* **C.**, under the head "BOOKS," we would refer our Readers to that Volume for any additional information.

The PLACE, and POSTURE *of the Preacher.*

651.—The PLACE of the Preacher is the ***Pulpit***, which the 83rd *Canon* requires shall be set in a convenient spot in every Church at the charge of the Parishioners; the usual position is on the north-side of the Nave, near the Chancel Arch; but there are many exceptions, which arise, for the most part, from the architectural structure of the Churches interfering with this usage. (See 'PULPIT.' *Vol.* **D.**). In *Cathedrals*, it will be found, that the Choir is the locality generally assigned to the Pulpit; though in some few instances, the Nave is the appointed place, as at Ely, Exeter, Bristol, &c.: this involves a change of situation on the part of the Congregation, which is attended with much inconvenience. When the Bishop of the Diocese is present in the *Cathedral*, and *preaches*, or delivers a *Charge;* this is sometimes done from his Throne, or from his Seat at the Altar. When in *Parish Churches*, the Bishop more frequently speaks from his Seat at the Altar, or from the Altar Steps.

652.—The Officiating Minister, and Assistant Clergy, other than the Preacher, occupy during the Sermon the Sedilia, or other seats provided for them on the south side of the Chancel; the chief Minister having his Assistants on either side of him. If there are no Sedilia, nor other seats provided on the south, or north, side of the Chancel, then it is customary for the chief Minister to occupy the Chair on the north side, and his Assistant, if any, that on the south side. At EVENING PRAYER, it is not unusual for the Officiating Minister, when not the Preacher, to remain in his stall in the Chancel, or in the Reading Desk.

The REV. J. JEBB writes:—'The *place of* Preaching is usually 'the *Choir*. And that this usage is not modern is evident from the 'existence of ancient pulpits in the Choirs of Winchester and 'Worcester. In some places, as Exeter, Bristol, and Ely, the *Pulpit* 'is outside the Choir, in the *Nave*, or in the intersection of the 'Nave and Transepts. At Ely the *Sermon* is preached there still. 'At Canterbury it used formerly to be preached in the Chapter 'House. The inconvenience and indecency of leaving the Choir, 'for the Sermon, must be felt by those who have witnessed the 'effect at Ely......If Sermons in the Nave be expedient, they ought 'to be preached in the Afternoon, before the Evening Service, as 'we have reason to believe was the custom in ancient times.' (*p.* 493.)—*On Choral Service.*

The REV. W. PALMER observes:—'In the primitive ages, the 'Bishop generally delivered his Sermon or Exhortation from the 'steps of the Altar; Presbyters preached from the *Pulpit*, or *Ambon*. 'But these Rules were not strictly adhered to, and the Preacher 'generally took his seat in the place where he could be best heard 'by the people.' (*p.* 66.)—*Orig. Lit.* Vol. ii.

The REV. J. PURCHAS says:—'After the Creed is finished the 'Celebrant and Ministers take their seats in the sedilia, each in his 'own place, and the Preacher ascends the pulpit.' (*p.* 39.)—*Directorium Anglicanum.*

The *Kalendar of the English Church Union* prescribes:—'During 'the *Sermon* the Celebrant (when not the Preacher) and his Assist-'ants (if any) should occupy the *Sedilia*, or *other seats* provided for 'them.' (*p.* 81.)

In a *Note* at p. 74, we read:—'The Celebrant (when not the 'Bishop) should, it seems, sit in the middle of the *Sedilia;* the 'Deacon *or* Gospeller being on his right hand, and the Epistoler on 'his left.'—*Pub. by Masters.* 1863.

653.—The POSTURE of the Preacher is that of *standing;* the Congregation, during the Sermon, *sitting*. The ancient custom was the reverse of this, being derived from the usage of the Jewish Synagogue. Our Saviour, as we learn from the Gospels, *sat* while teaching, whether he discoursed in the Temple, the Synagogue, on a mountain, or out of a ship.' (*Matt.* xxiii. 2; xxvi. 55; *Luke* iv. 20; v. 3.)

BINGHAM writes:—'The Preacher very generally *sat* during the 'Sermon, while the hearers *stood*.' *Christian Antiquities*, b. xiv.

THE DOXOLOGY.

[The People *standing*.]

654.—The *Ascription of praise* to the Holy Trinity generally given at the termination of the Sermon is derived from the two closing verses of the Epistle of St Jude, and is usually expressed thus:—

"*And now, to God the Father, God the Son, and God*
"*the Holy Ghost, be ascribed, as is most justly due, all*
"*honour, power, might, majesty, and dominion, hence-*
"*forth, and for ever.*"

At the repetition of these words, the Congregation ought to *stand*, as at all other services of praise. In some few Churches, the Choir here sing the *Gloria Patri*.

The Homilies.

(9 *b*) ¶. '*Or one of the Homilies already set forth, or hereafter* '*to be set forth by* ('*common*' 1552. 1559. 1604.) *authority.*' (1552. 1559. 1604. 1662.)—Present Bk. of Com. Prayer.

655.—This clause of the Rubric in the *first Liturgy* of Edward VI. (1549) read thus: '*Or Homily, or* '*some portion of one of the Homilies, as they shall be* '*hereafter divided.*' (Keeling. 177.) In the Preface to the Second Book of Homilies, we also find a similar direction:—"Where the Homily may appear too long "for one reading to divide the same, to be read part "in the forenoon, and part in the afternoon." However, notwithstanding these instructions of the Rubric, and the recommendations of the 35th of the *XXXIX Articles*, which says:—

> 'The *Second Book of Homilies*, the several titles whereof we 'have joined unto this Article, doth contain a godly and whole-'some doctrine, and necessary for these times, as doth the *former* '*Book of Homilies*, which were set forth in the time of Edward VI; 'and therefore we judge them to be read in Churches by the 'Ministers, diligently and distinctly that they may be under-'standed of the people.'—*Article* 35.

—as well as the injunctions of the *Canons* (of 1603) following:—

> 'Every Beneficed man, not allowed to be a preacher, shall 'procure sermons to be preached in his Cure once in every 'month at the least, by *Preachers* lawfully licensed, if his Living, 'in the judgment of the Ordinary, will be able to bear it. And 'upon every Sunday, when there shall *not be a Sermon* preached 'in his Cure, he or his Curate shall *read some one of the Homilies* 'prescribed or to be prescribed by authority, to the intents afore-'said.'—*Canon* 46.

'No person whatsoever, not examined and approved by the 'Bishop of the Diocese, or not licensed, as is aforesaid, for a 'sufficient or convenient Preacher, shall take upon him to ex- 'pound in his own Cure, or elsewhere, any Scripture or matter 'of doctrine; but shall only study *to read* plainly and aptly '(without glossing or adding) the *Homilies* already set forth, or 'hereafter to be published by lawful authority, for the confirma- 'tion of the true faith, and for the good instruction and edifica- 'tion of the people.' *Canon* 49.

—the custom of reading the Homilies in our Churches has grown quite obsolete; which may be accounted for, in the first place from the established loyalty of the Clergy; and in the second place from their superior learning, and intellectual capabilities. But an old Canon reads:—'If the Parish Priest 'be sick, or cannot preach, let the Homilies of the 'holy Fathers be read by the Deacon.' (*Conc. Vasc.* Can. 4.). (See this subject further discussed in *Vol.* C. under the head "BOOKS.)

656.—As to the authorship of these Homilies, the *first Book* is thought to be the composition of Cranmer, Ridley, Latimer, Hopkins, and Becon. With regard to the *second Book*, Burnet attributes it to Bp. Jewel. But Abp. Parker says (A. D. 1563) these Homilies "were revised and finished, with a second "part by him, and the other Bishops." (STRYPE's *Parker*. i. 253.). To Cranmer is attributed the Homilies on Salvation, Faith, and Good Works; and that on Adultery to Becon. The *first Book* is considered the more valuable of the two, and appeared in 1547: the *second Book* was published in 1563. Nothing more need be said on this subject in a work of this character, and therefore we will conclude with a few explanatory opinions.

BP. OVERALL remarks:—'It seems the Author of the Homilies 'wrote them in haste, and the Church did wisely to reserve this 'authority of correcting them and setting forth others. For they 'have many scapes in them in special, though they contain in 'general many wholesome lessons for the people; in which sense 'our Ministers do subscribe unto them, and no other.'—*Quoted in* MANT's *Book of Com. Prayer* in loco.

BP. TOMLINE writes:—'At the time of the Reformation in 'England, many of the Clergy were exceedingly illiterate, and it 'was also suspected that some of them still favoured the tenets 'of the Church of Rome. Therefore to supply the defects of some, 'and to oblige the rest to teach according to the form of sound 'doctrine there were *two Books of Homilies* prepared: the first was 'published in *King Edward the Sixth's* time, 1547, supposed to be 'written chiefly by *Abp. Cranmer;* the second was not finished 'till about the time of Edward's death, so it was not published 'before *Queen Elizabeth's time*, 1560, having been probably written 'by *Bp. Jewel.* The design of them was to mix speculative points 'with practical matters; some explain the doctrine, and others 'enforce the rules of life and manners. These are plain and short 'discourses, chiefly calculated to possess the nation with a sense of 'the purity of the Gospel, in opposition to the corruptions of Popery, 'and to reform it from those crying sins, which had been so much 'connived at under Popery, while men knew the price of them, how 'to compensate for them, and to redeem themselves from the guilt 'of them by Masses and Sacraments, by Indulgences and Absolutions. 'These *two books of Homilies*, upon their first publication, were dis'tributed throughout the kingdom; and the parochial Clergy were 'commanded to *read them in their Churches.* When compared with 'the age in which they were written, they may be considered as 'very extraordinary compositions, though perhaps every argument 'and expression in them is not to be approved: but whoever will 'peruse them with candour and attention, will be convinced that 'they contain, as the *35th Article* expresses it, "a godly and whole'some doctrine." The Compilers of the Articles thought them '"necessary for the times" in which they lived: and directed them '"to be read in Churches by the Ministers, diligently and distinctly, 'that they may be understanded of the people." The English 'language has changed so much since those *Homilies* were written, 'that they would scarcely now be understood by a common con'gregation: and therefore the reading of them publicly, as it would 'no longer answer any good purpose, has *fallen into general disuse*, 'with the tacit consent of the governing part of the Church. The 'Clergy, however, may still study them with advantage to them'selves; and may, with advantage to others, transfer parts of them 'into their Sermons, with such alterations as the change of circum'stances may render expedient.' (*p.* 294.)—*Quoted in* MANT's *Book of Com. Prayer* in loco.

ABP. WHATELY observes:—'The *Homilies* were provided to meet 'the deficiency of persons qualified to preach. It is well known 'that it was found necessary to fill many Parishes with Clergy who 'were not licensed Preachers. But those who did appear qualified 'did obtain a license to preach; and not only this, but those who 'were not Preachers, and were accordingly left to the use of the '*Homilies*, were enjoined to procure a licensed Preacher to deliver 'a Sermon to their Congregations at least once a month; so mani'festly did our Reformers regard the Homilies merely as a substitute, 'and an imperfect substitute, adopted for the existing emergency, 'for Sermons from the Ministers.'—(Quoted in PLUMMER's *Observations on Book of Com. Prayer.*

WHEATLY says:—'The *Homilies*, mentioned in the Rubric, are 'two books of plain Sermons, (for so the word signifies,) set out by 'public authority, one whereof is to be read upon any *Sunday* or

'*Holy-day*, where there is no Sermon. The ***first volume*** of them was 'set out in the beginning of King Edward VI.'s reign, having been 'composed (as it is thought) by Archbishop Cranmer, Bishop Ridley, 'and Latimer, at the beginning of the Reformation, when a com- 'petent number of Ministers, of sufficient abilities to preach in a 'public congregation, was not to be found. The ***second volume*** 'was set out in Queen Elizabeth's time, by order of Convocation, 'A. D. 1563.' (*p.* 313.)—*Rat. Illus. of Book of Com. Prayer.*

[THE CANONS.]

657.—The CANONS (of 1603,) bearing upon *Preachers*, and *Preaching*, are the following, with their titles:—

CANON 45. '*Beneficed Preachers being resident upon their 'Livings to preach every Sunday.*'

CANON 46. '*Beneficed Men, not Preachers, to procure monthly 'Sermons.*'

CANON 47. '*Absence of Beneficed Men to be supplied by Curates 'that are allowed Preachers.*'

CANON 49. '*Ministers not allowed Preachers, may not expound.*'

CANON 50. '*Strangers not admitted to preach without shewing 'their Licence.*'

CANON 51. '*Strangers not admitted to preach in Cathedral 'Churches without sufficient authority.*'

CANON 52. '*The names of strange Preachers to be noted in a 'Book.*'

CANON 53. '*No public opposition between Preachers.*'

CANON 54. '*The Licences of Preachers refusing Conformity to 'be void.*'

CANON 56. '*Preachers and Lecturers to read Divine Service 'and administer the Sacraments twice a year at 'least.*'

CANON 71. '*Ministers not to preach or administer the Com- 'munion in private houses.*'

CONCLUSION OF THE SERVICE.

[If there be no Communion.]

¶. '*Upon the Sundays and other Holy-Days* (*if there be no 'Communion*) *shall be said all that is appointed at the 'Communion, until the end of the General Prayer,* [For 'the whole state of Christ's Church Militant here in Earth,] '*together with one or more of these Collects last before 'rehearsed, concluding with the Blessing.*' (1662.) — Rubric at the end of the Communion Office—Present Book of Common Prayer.

658.—We now arrive at the termination of Divine Service when there is '*no Communion*' immediately following; and herein we find *Custom* and *Rubric* completely at variance. We will take them in order.

659.—CUSTOM, which seems to be very general, particularly in Rural Parishes, sanctions the Clergyman remaining in the Pulpit after the Sermon, and there offering up a prayer, chosen from among those at the end of the Communion Office, and dismissing the Congregation with 'the Blessing,' to be found there also. A *Deacon* will use the 'Benediction,' from 2 *Cor.* xiii. instead of 'The Blessing.' If there be *no Sermon*, which is often the case when the Holy Communion is to be administered immediately upon Morning Prayer and the Litany, this way of dismissing the Congregation likewise prevails, when adherence to Rubric is not a consideration. Strictly, however, these practices are *illegal*, and can only be defended under the plea of '*mos est lex.*' But now to Rubric.

660.—The RUBRIC requires immediately *after the Sermon*, and before uttering from the Pulpit a prayer and 'the Blessing,'—

(10) ¶. '*Then shall the Priest return to the Lord's Table and 'begin the Offertory, saying one or more of these 'Sentences following, as he thinketh most convenient in 'his discretion.*' (1662.)—Present Bk. of Com. Prayer.

This injunction deviates but little from the Rubrics of the previous Liturgies, which ran thus:—

'*After such Sermon, Homily, Exhortation, the Curate shall 'declare unto the People whether there be any Holy-days, or 'Fasting days the Week following, and earnestly exhort them 'to remember the Poor, saying one, or more, of these Sentences 'following, as he thinketh most convenient by his discretion.*' (1552. 1559. 1604.)—KEELING. 180, 181.

During the reading of the Offertory Sentences, other Rubrics tell us that here are to be collected '*the alms 'for the Poor and other devotions of the People in a 'decent bason;*' and this is reverently to be brought '*to the Priest who shall humbly present and place it 'upon the holy Table.*'.........'*After which done, the 'Priest shall say,*' 'Let us pray for the whole state 'of Christ's Church Militant here in Earth.' This prayer ended, then, in accordance with the Rubric at the head of this subject, will follow *one* or *more* of the *Collects* to be found at the end of the Communion Office, '*concluding with the Blessing*,' placed at the beginning of those Post-Communion Collects. These Rubrical directions are very clear and decisive. There is, however, a difficulty in carrying out these rules where there is but one Officiating Minister, and who has exchanged the Surplice for the Gown to preach the Sermon. He must not return to the Communion Table and officiate in the Black Gown; and to retire to the Vestry to assume once more the Surplice for the few minutes necessary to conclude the Service would not satisfy the Congregation. Where, however, the '*Weekly Offertory*' has been established this may be done; or, which might be preferred under such circumstances as a matter of convenience rather than as an expression of party feeling, the *Sermon might be preached in the Surplice*, which is usually the case where this practice prevails. When there is no Offertory, the Officiating Minister having returned to the north side of the Table, has a discretion committed to him of reading *one*, or *more*, of 'the Sentences,'—the first and last are commonly used 'on these occasions;' following them with the 'Prayer for the Church Militant;' and then under a like allowed discretion saying *one*, or *more*, of the Post-communion Collects, and dismissing the People with the 'Blessing.' This is the *authorized* RULE. And *this* RULE has existed from the earliest times of the Reformation, as we may gather from the Rubrics of previous Liturgies. In the *first Liturgy* of Edward VI. A. D. 1549, the Rubric cited at the head of this subject read thus:—

'*Upon Wednesdays and Fridays the English Litany shall be 'said.........and though there be none to communicate with the 'Priest, yet these days* (*after the Litany ended*) *the Priest shall 'put upon him a plain Albe or Surplice, with a Cope, and say 'all things at the Altar,* (*appointed to be said at the celebration 'of the Lord's Supper until after the Offertory. And then 'shall add one or two of the Collects aforewritten, as occasion 'shall serve by his discretion. And then turning him to the 'People shall let them depart with the accustomed blessing.*' (1549.)—KEELING. 230.

In the subsequent Liturgies this Rubric was as follows:—

'*Upon the* (Sundays and other, 1662) *Holy-days, (if there be* '*no Communion) shall be said all that is appointed at the Com*'*munion, until the end of the* (General Prayer, 1662) *Homily,* '*concluding with the General Prayer,* For the whole estate '(state, 1662) of Christ's Church militant here in Earth, *and* '(together with, 1662) *one or more of these Collects,* (last, 1662) '*before rehearsed,* (concluding with the Blessing, 1662) *as occa*'*sion shall serve.*' (1552. 1559. 1604.)—KEELING. 228, 229.

At the *last Revision* in 1662, we find the word *Sundays* introduced at the beginning of the Rubric, and, with the few verbal alterations, as seen above, this final clause, "*concluding with the Blessing.*"* It must be remembered that the Prayer for the Church Militant is not included under the term 'Offertory;' and further, this Prayer for the Church was in the *first* Liturgy (1549) appointed to be used only on Communion-days. (See *Rubric* 38. *postea.*)

661.—When there *is* a Communion, and the CUSTOM prevails of concluding with a Prayer and the Blessing, or the Benediction, in the Pulpit, the *Non-communicants* here retire. Where RUBRICAL adherence exists, the *Non-communicants* retire after the Prayer for 'the Church Militant,' and before the Exhortation. It is incorrect to introduce in this latter case after the Church Militant Prayer a Post-communion Collect, and the Blessing; or the Benediction.

We may now quote a few opinions on these points.

BP. MANT writes:—'*After the Sermon,* "then shall the Priest "return to the Lord's Table, and begin the *Offertory,* saying one or

---

* In the AMERICAN LITURGY this Rubric reads:—

'Upon the Sundays and other Holy-days (if there be no Sermon 'or Communion) shall be said all that is appointed at the Com'munion, unto the end of the Gospel, concluding with the Blessing.'

The other Rubric (10. above) is as follows:—

'Then shall follow the Sermon. After which, the Minister 'when there is a Communion, shall return to the Lord's Table, and 'begin the Offertory, saying one or more of these Sentences follow'ing as he thinketh most convenient.'

"more of the Sentences following;" during which, "the *alms* for "the poor and other devotions of the people" are to be "collected "in a decent bason, and reverently brought to the Priest, who "shall humbly present and place it upon the Holy Table." And, "if there be no Communion, shall be said all that is appointed at "the Communion, until the end of the General Prayer, "*For the* "*whole state of Christ's Church militant here in earth*, together with "one or more of these Collects last rehearsed," those, namely, in 'the post-communion, "concluding with the *Blessing*." These 'instructions of the Church are as imperative, as they are unam- 'biguous and easy to be understood. In two respects they leave 'the Minister to his discretion: namely, the "saying of *one* or *more* 'sentences" at the Offertory, the duration of which will of course 'be regulated thereby; and the "saying of *one* or *more*" of the post- 'communion Collects. But no discretion is allowed for the Minister's 'use or omission of the Prayer for the Church Militant; nor is there 'any sanction for his *remaining after the Sermon in the Pulpit*, and 'thence delivering a *prayer* and the *Blessing*. The sanction which 'appears to be given, by the delivering of the Blessing from the 'Pulpit, for the *departure of the general congregation* after the 'Sermon, is a strong argument against that practice, besides others 'which the following Rubricks supply.' (*p.* 59.)—*Hor. Lit.*

The *late* Rev. J. J. Blunt (*Margaret Professor of Divinity at the University of Cambridge*) says:—'*After the Sermon*, the Priest, 'if he strictly complies with the Rubric, "returns to the Lord's 'Table," says "one or more of the Sentences of the Offertory;" and 'certainly the Prayer for the Church Militant; and then, if there 'be *no Communion*, dismisses the People with a Collect and the 'Blessing.' (*p.* 331.)—*Duties of the Parish Priest.*

The Rev. J. Jebb remarks upon the Rubric at the end of the Communion Office beginning "*Upon the Sundays and other Holy-* "*days, (if there be no Communion) shall be said*," &c.:—'This Rubric 'has never become what is called obsolete in the Church. The 'neglect of it cannot be excused by the plea of universal desuetude; 'since, not only in most Cathedrals and Colleges, but in many 'Parish Churches, it has been uninterruptedly obeyed......But no 'prescription can overrule a Rubric; and after all, the prescription 'alleged for this and similar neglects cannot be proved to be more 'ancient than the last century, a time of all others the most lax 'and apathetic. But the authority of some of our Bishops has of 'late enforced the renewed observance of this Rubric, which it is 'to be hoped may before long be universal. And this implies a 'restoration of the *weekly collection of Alms;* a primitive, nay 'Apostolic custom, the neglect of which has had a deadly effect 'upon the people; so that the obligation of almsgiving has well 'nigh ceased to be considered as one of the most stringent duties 'of Christian men.' (*p.* 515.)—*On Choral Service.*

Mr. A. J. Stephens (*Barrister-at-law*) states:—'After the 'Sermon the Priest has no legal right to remain in the Pulpit, 'and thence deliver a *prayer* and the *Blessing*—he is legally bound, 'immediately upon the conclusion of the Sermon, "to return to the 'Lord's Table, and begin the Offertory," by saying one or more of 'the Sentences that are prescribed for this particular part of the

'Service in the Book of Common Prayer.' (*p.* 1164.).........But 'notwithstanding the express language of the Rubric in question, the celebration of the Lord's Supper in most of our Parish 'Churches does not occur oftener than *once a month*. On other 'Sundays and Holy-days it is usual to conclude the portion of the 'Communion Service which is then read, with the *Nicene Creed*, 'and then to terminate the Sermon with a *Collect* and the *Blessing*:—a practice which is *illegal*.' (*p.* 1230.)—*Book of Common Prayer*. E. H. S.

With regard to the *dismissal* of the NON-COMMUNICANTS, when there *is* an Administration, this occurs generally, as we have just observed, at the close of the Sermon, when the Clergyman retires to the Vestry to exchange the Gown for the Surplice. In other instances, merely a pause takes place for this object between the Prayer for the Church Militant and the Exhortation. On these points we may quote the following:—

WHEATLY says:—'In our own Congregations, when there is a 'Communion, those who do not communicate never depart till the 'end of the *Nicene Creed*.' (*p.* 370.)—Rat. Ill. of Bk. of Com. Pr.

BP. MANT writes:—'If there be a Communion, the Minister is 'to return from the Pulpit to the Lord's Table, and there continue 'for the discharge of his Office. He has *no business in the Vestry*, 'and he ought to be on his post, waiting on his Congregation, lest, 'by departing from the Church, he encourage the departure of the 'people. For the avoiding of confusion by the *withdrawal of non-communicants*, and for the "convenient placing of the Communicants," a brief *pause* in the Service is necessary; the best place for 'which in my judgment is the interval between the Prayer for the 'Church militant, and the Exhortation to the Communicants "at "the time of the celebration of the Communion." (*p.* 60.)—*Hor. Lit.*

662.—We now pass to the Rubrics appertaining more especially to the Administration of the Lord's Supper, and in treating of these, bearing as they do upon so solemn and important a matter, we shall refrain from the quotation of opinions; as it would involve a considerable, and by no means profitable, enlargement of the Volume: but at the same time we shall take care to give the Laws and Usages which regulate the course of proceeding to be pursued.

When the PRIEST is to *Kneel*, and *Stand*.

663.—We may premise that the Officiating Priest *kneels* but *three times* during the entire Administration, viz.—

(*a*) At the *General Confession*, beginning, "Almighty God, Father of our Lord Jesus Christ," &c.
(*b*) At the *lowly Address*, beginning, "We do not presume," &c.
(*c*) At his *own reception* of the Communion.

In every other case he is to *stand;* and whenever he addresses the People he turns to them; and when addressing God he looks towards the Table; extreme Ritualists, in the latter case, will be found to face the East.

The Offertory.

(10) ¶. '*Then shall the Priest return to the Lord's Table, and 'begin the Offertory, saying one or more of these Sen- 'tences following, as he thinketh most convenient in his 'discretion.*'

The Priest *standing*—the People also *standing*.

664.—As a general rule, the *Non-communicants* have here retired, and the Priest now takes the place he occupied before he proceeded to the Pulpit: usually at the *north side* of the Table; but in those Churches which adhere doctrinally, to the term Altar, he will go to the middle of the Altar, where he continues throughout the Service. And as he is here, in either case, *addressing the People* he turns towards them. The *Communicants* in some Churches at this time also assemble in the Chancel.

665.—'*One or more of the Sentences*' will be repeated according to the time that may be required for the collecting of the Alms: a sufficient pause should be made between the Sentences, in order to avoid the repeating of them, if possible. When there is an *assistant Clergyman* they are sometimes uttered *antiphonally:* but where the Service is *chorally* conducted, the Priest enunciates a Sentence and the *Choir* immediately take it up; but the Rubric does not in this place sanction 'singing.'

666.—Of the *twenty Sentences* here introduced, the 6th, 7th, 8th, and 10th, which refer to Offerings formerly made for the use of the *Clergy*, and for the *Service of God*, are omitted when the collection is solely for the *Poor*. Of the remaining Sentences, the 1st. 2nd. 3rd. 4th. 9th. 12th. 13th. 14th. and 18th. enforce the duty and the blessing of giving. The 5th. 17th. 19th. and 20th. exhort to *charity to the Poor* in general, while the 11th. 14th. and 16th. advocate the cause of the '*household of faith.*'

Collecting the Alms.

(11) ¶. '*Whilst these Sentences are in reading, the Deacons, 'Churchwardens, or other fit person appointed for 'that purpose, shall receive the Alms for the Poor, and 'other Devotions of the People, in a decent Bason, to 'be provided by the Parish for that purpose, and reve-'rently to bring it to the Priest, who shall humbly present 'and place it upon the holy Table.*'

667.—'*The Deacons, Churchwardens, or other fit 'person.*'—The *Deacon*, in accordance with the institution of his office, (*Acts* vi.) is the fittest person for this duty; and should not a Deacon be present, then one or both of the *Churchwardens* ought to collect the Alms, &c.; this is now the usual custom. It is only in the absence of a Deacon, and Churchwarden, that the *Clerk*, or *Sexton*, should be permitted to exercise this function. In Cathedrals, and Collegiate Churches, the two junior Clergymen, Vicars Choral, or Minor Canons, perform this Office.

668.—'*Receive the Alms*,' *and* '*other Devotions.*'—The word '*receive*' implies that the Communicants on entering the Chancel dropped their 'Alms' into the 'basin' held there by the proper functionary. It is, however, now the custom to *collect* the 'Alms' from the People as they are stationed in the Chancel, or from their seats, and pews. The '*Alms*' are for the Poor; the '*other Devotions of the People*' are offerings for the Priest, the maintenance of the

Church, and for 'pious and charitable uses not necessarily confined to the Poor:' (*Bp. of Exeter*, Dr. Phillpotts). The second expression originally included also the *Bread and Wine.* (*Prof. Blunt.*)

669.—'*In a decent Basin.*' The employment of any thing but a "decent basin" is not sanctioned by the Rubric. *Wooden boxes*, and *leathern bags*, are unauthorized, and can only be excused when the Congregations are very large. These, when used, should properly be emptied into the "decent basin" before presenting them to the Officiating Priest. Collections at the '*Doors*,' after the use of the Communion Office, and the Congregation have been dismissed by the Preacher, are far from Rubrical; as these 'devotions of the people' cannot then be placed on the Holy Table. *Evening Collections* were never contemplated, and therefore fall not under Rubrical direction.

670.—'*Reverently to bring it to the Priest, who 'shall humbly present it.*'—This usage is derived from the practice of the ancient Jews. The term '*reverently*' has been thought by extreme Ritualists to mean *kneeling*, or in a *bending posture;* but, certainly the Rubric does not imply this attitude: similarly, the word '*humbly*' is supposed to mean '*standing, in a bowing posture.*' The act also of '*presenting*' it to God, it is suggested, should be accomplished by a 'slight elevation of the Alms-dish,' accompanied by an inward prayer; and then placed on the holy Table; after which, it is to 'be removed to the Credence Table, or elsewhere.' The ordinary usage, however, is to present the Alms according to the common acceptation of the word 'reverently.'

The Placing of the Elements.

(12) ¶. '*And when there is a* Communion, *the Priest shall then 'place upon the Table so much* Bread *and* Wine, *as 'he shall think sufficient. After which done the Priest 'shall say.*'

671.—'*Then place upon the Table.*'—Here, immediately after the depositing of the Alms, is the proper time to introduce the *Bread* and *Wine*. The Priest takes them from the Credence or Side-Table, where such is provided; and solemnly places them on the Table; but where there is no convenience of this kind, the usage varies. In some Churches the Priest brings the Elements from the Vestry, whither he has proceeded after the Sermon to exchange the Gown for the Surplice; and then, *before commencing the Offertory Sentences*, places them on the Table. In other Churches, the custom prevails of placing the Elements on the Table *before the beginning of Morning Prayer*, by the hands of the *Parish Clerk*, or *Sexton*, 'which,' says Wheatly, 'is a profane and shameful 'breach of the Rubric,' (*Rat. Ill.* p. 320.); 'and illegal,' adds Mr. A. J. Stephens. (*Bk. of. Com. Pr.* E. H. S. *p.* 1172). Certainly, the Alms for the poor should not be placed upon the Lord's Table with greater reverence than the symbols of the Christian Passover. The Priest, however, may receive the Bread and Wine from the hands of a Deacon, the Churchwardens, or the Parish Clerk; but he himself must put them on the Table, first the Bread, next the Wine; and, as the word '*then*' implies, to be rubrically correct, this must be done immediately after the placing of the Alms. The Elements are not ordered to be *covered* till after consecration.

The Prayer for the Church Militant.

(13) ¶. '*After which done, the Priest shall say.*'

The Priest *standing*—the People *kneeling*.

672.—Here follows the Prayer for the *Church Militant*. The previous Rubric (12) was introduced at the *last Revision* of the Liturgy in 1662, and at the same time the word '*oblations*' was inserted in the marginal Rubric of this Prayer. This evidently proclaims that the term refers to the offerings of Bread and Wine, so that, whenever there is a Communion, the word '*oblations*' must not be omitted.

In the *Liturgy of* 1549, this prayer contained *intercession for the dead*, and when this was struck out at the *Revision* in 1552, the words '*militant here in earth*' were annexed to the Rubric.

THE EXHORTATIONS.

(14) ¶. '*When the Minister giveth warning for the celebration of the Holy Communion (which he shall always do upon the Sunday, or some Holy-day, immediately preceding): After the Sermon or Homily ended he shall read this Exhortation following.*'

'DEARLY BELOVED on———next I purpose, 'through God's assistance,' &c.

(15) ¶. '*Or in case he shall see the People negligent to come to the Holy Communion, instead of the former, he shall use this Exhortation.*

'DEARLY BELOVED BRETHREN, on———I intend, by God's grace,' &c.

The Priest and People *standing*.

673.—The former of these *Exhortations* has more the object of urging the people to a due preparation; the latter, of combating the excuses too often made for negligence in participating in these great mysteries. The choice of them is left to the discretion of the Officiating Priest; and while uttering either Exhortation he turns towards the People. The custom of repeating only the first portion of the former Exhortation, though very general, yet is not an authorized abbreviation, and this Exhortation should properly be read, as the latter always is, *in extenso;* and, it should also be borne in mind that, these Exhortations are the only authorized formularies we have for instructing the people in the nature of this great Sacrament, and the manner of preparing for it: and to be strictly correct, they should neither of them be read before the Sermon, as is the usual custom, but *after* it.

(16) ¶. '*At the time of the Celebration of the Communion 'the Communicants being conveniently placed for 'the receiving of the holy Sacrament, the Priest shall 'say this Exhortation.*'

'Dearly Beloved in the Lord, ye that mind to 'come, &c.

The Priest, and People *standing.*

674.—In this Exhortation the worthy are encouraged, and the unworthy warned. "The former Exhortations," says *Dean Comber*, "were to increase the number of the Communicants, this to rectify their dispositions." At this part of the Service, it was the custom for the *Communicants* to enter the Chancel, or Choir; and, if numerous, to take up their position kneeling in rows; the men on the one side, and the women on the other, as a Rubric in the Liturgy of 1549 directs: if few, they knelt, or stood, at the Altar Rails. The *non-Communicants* also used now to withdraw; but there is no law to compel them to do so. In some Churches, the words of the Rubric, '*at the time of the Celebration*,' are interpreted to mean *not at every time;* and, therefore, with them this Exhortation is occasionally, but not rightly, omitted. It may be read by the assistant Minister. The '*Amen*' is to be said by the People.

The Invitation, or Invitatory.

(17) ¶. '*Then shall the Priest say to them that come to re'ceive the Holy Communion.*'

The Priest, and People, still *standing.*

675.—This should be said by the Priest, though often delegated to the assistant Minister; and he should, the while, face the People. The three preceding Exhortations might be addressed to the whole Congregation: but this invitation applies only to the Communicants. 'Draw near with faith,' is thought not to refer to any bodily approach to the Table, but, as having rather a spiritual meaning.

The Confession.

(18) ¶. '*Then shall this general Confession be made, in the 'name of all those that are minded to receive the Holy 'Communion, by one of the Ministers; both he and all 'the People kneeling humbly upon their knees, and 'saying.*'

The Priest, and People, *kneeling*.

676.—This *Confession*, like as in the Daily Service, is to be said by the People *after*, not *with*, the Minister; and the leading off may be apportioned to the Assistant Minister, who turns to the Table, as addressing God.

The Absolution.

(19) ¶. '*Then shall the Priest (or the Bishop being present), 'stand up, and turning himself to the People, pro-'nounce this Absolution.*

The Priest *standing*—the People still *kneeling*.

677.—The *Absolution* should be pronounced by the Bishop, if present; if not, by the Officiating Priest, not by a Deacon; because to the Priest is given at ordination this *ministerial* function: he should, the while, be *standing*, and facing the People, because acting as Christ's *messenger* or ambassador. The '*Amen*' is to be said by the People.

The Comfortable Words.

(20) ¶. '*Then shall the Priest say.*'

The Priest, and People, *standing*.

678.—These passages of Scripture are designed to impart comfort and confidence in the 'Absolution' preceding; and are to be repeated by the Priest facing the People.

The Sursum Corda.

(21) ¶. '*After which the Priest shall proceed, saying.*'

The Priest and People still *standing.*

679.—We now arrive at the thanksgiving portion of the Communion Office, which is considered the most ancient, universal, and sublime portion of the Service, and the commencement of that Eucharistic element, which gives name to the whole Celebration. (*Acts* ii. 46.). Here we are exhorted to 'lift up our hearts,' lately pressed down with guilt and fear (*Lam.* iii. 40, 41.); and to fix our thoughts on the mystery of love we are entering upon, and not on the things of the world. These Versicles were anciently known by the Latin words for '*lift up your hearts,*' viz. "*Sursum Corda.*" Where the Services are conducted chorally here the chanting is resumed; if otherwise, the Sentences are antiphonally read by Priest and People. The Priest turning towards the Congregation.

The General Preface.

(22) ¶. '*Then shall the Priest turn to the Lord's Table, and say.*'

The Priest and People still *standing.*

680.—The General Preface begins with the words '*It is very meet,*' &c., and terminates with '*evermore praising thee and saying;*' thus far is to be said by the Priest alone. Then, conjointly, by Priest and People, is to be said, or sung, the *Trisagium*, or Seraphic Hymn, commencing with '*Holy, Holy, Holy.*' It is a common, but incorrect, practice for the People to join in with the Priest at the words, '*Therefore with Angels and Archangels,*' &c. (See *Rubric* 24 *postea.*); but this should be set right. It must not be forgotten that the words '*Holy Father,*' in this Preface, must, as the Rubric directs, be omitted on Trinity Sunday.

Proper Prefaces.

(23) ¶. '*Here shall follow the Proper Preface, according to* '*the time, if there be any specially appointed; or else* '*immediately shall follow,*' (the Trisagium).

To be said by the Priest alone, all *standing.*

681.—The five greater Festivals of *Christmas-Day*, *Easter-Day*, *Ascension-Day*, *Whitsunday*, and *Trinity Sunday*, have especial *Prefaces*, illustrative of the great blessings they commemorate, superadded to the General Preface. Those of the first three festivals are to be repeated eight successive days, in order that opportunity may be offered to every one in the Parish to communicate on one of the days appointed; and thus be enabled to praise God for those unspeakable mercies they severally refer to. Whitsuntide occupies but seven days; because the eighth is itself the festival of the Holy Trinity. From the introduction of these Prefaces into the Liturgy, we may certainly conclude that our Church intended that the Holy Communion should be celebrated on these days especially.

The Trisagium.

(24) ¶. '*After each of which Prefaces shall immediately be* '*sung or said.*'

The Priest and People still *standing.*

682.—Under the sublime impression of faith in the presence of *Angels* during the performance of divine mysteries, (I *Cor.* xi. 10; I *Pet.* i. 12.), this Hymn is appointed to be sung here; and is on this account called the *Seraphic Hymn* (*Isa.* vi. 3.) Because of the emphatic use of 'Holy' in this Hymn, it has been named '*The Sanctus;*' and from the term being *thrice* repeated, as declaratory of the doctrine of the *Trinity*, it has also been distinguished as the τρισαγιον, *Trisagium*, and *Tersanctus*. The People should remain silent until the words '*Holy*, *Holy*,

Holy,' &c. occur, when they immediately unite their voices with that of the Priest in one great chorus of praise and adoration.

THE LOWLY ADDRESS.

(25) ¶. *'Then shall the Priest, kneeling down at the Lord's 'Table, say in the name of all them that shall receive 'the Communion, this prayer following.'*

The Priest and People all *kneeling.*

683.—This Address is to be delivered with great reverence and humility by the Priest alone; the People repeating aloud only the *'Amen.'*

THE PRAYER OF CONSECRATION.

(26) ¶. *'When the Priest, standing before the Table, hath so 'ordered the Bread and Wine, that he may with the 'more readiness and decency break the Bread before 'the People, and take the Cup into his hands, he shall 'say the Prayer of Consecration, as followeth.'*

The Priest *standing*—the People *kneeling.*

684.—*'Standing before the Altar.'* This Rubric is variously interpreted; but the more generally received sense is, that the Priest is to *stand,* because about doing an act of authority; but to stand *in front of the Table with his back to the Congregation* for the purpose only of *ordering,* i. e. *placing, and preparing* the Elements, and reverently uncovering them, so that he may with the greater readiness and facility perform the Rite of Consecration. He remains between the Table and the People, only so long as the merely *mechanical* arrangement has been completed: the Church not intending that the meaner part of the Service should be a spectacle. This done, he returns to the north side, and at the appointed time breaks the Bread, and takes the Cup *'before the People,'* i. e. in their sight; in order that the manner of consecration may not be made a mystery after the fashion of the Romish priesthood. They mistake this Rubric altogether, and violate both its letter and its spirit, who remain the *whole of the time* occupied in the Prayer, and act of Consecration of the Elements, with their back towards the People, after the manner of the Church of Rome. Such is the opinion of the late *Prof. Blunt* on this important and impressive act. (See 'Duties of the Parish Priest.' *p.* 334.).

685.—This Prayer may be divided into three parts; 1st. the *Introduction*, or *Commemoration*, beginning with "Almighty God," down to "coming again;" 2ndly. the *Invocation*, or *Prayer*, from "Hear us, O Lord," down to "Body and Blood;" 3rdly. the *Consecration*, beginning with "Who in the same night," down to the end. The '*Amen*' only is to be repeated by the People.*

686.—The MARGINAL RUBRICS are sufficiently explicit: but should any further information with respect to the *Bread*, and *Wine*, or the sacred Vessels, &c. be needed, it will be found in *Vol.* **C.**

THE ADMINISTRATION OF THE COMMUNION.

(27) ¶. '*Then shall the Minister first receive the Communion 'in both kinds himself, and then proceed to deliver the 'same to the Bishops, Priests, and Deacons in like 'manner (if any be present) and after that to the People 'also in order into their hands, all meekly kneeling.*

The Communion of the Priest himself.

The Priest *kneeling.*

687.—'*Then shall the Minister first receive.*'—The Officiating Priest first receives the Communion him-

---

* In the AMERICAN LITURGY, the *Prayer of Consecration* is mutilated by the omission of the central portion, called the Invocation, and is followed by a *Prayer of Oblation* taken from the first *Liturgy* of Edward VI. (1549), beginning with 'Wherefore O Lord and Heavenly Father,' &c. (see *Keeling*. 211.), and containing the Invocation above mentioned, and the first of our eucharistical Prayers in the Post Communion, and this is succeeded by a *Hymn.* After which, the Priest receives the Communion himself, and proceeds as in our Liturgy.

self in both kinds; and, by the 21st *Canon*, this is to be done 'as oft as he administereth,' whether it be twice, or more, in one day: but this is a controverted point. A *formula* for the Priest himself, however, is not prescribed in the Liturgy; he is, therefore, left to his own inward devotional thoughts; although it cannot be considered reprehensible for him to adapt the words of administration enjoined for the People, by changing 'thee' to '*me*,' and 'thy' to '*my*.'

The Communion of the Clergy.

The Recipients *kneeling*.

688.—'*Then to deliver the same to the Bishops,* '*Priests, and Deacons:*' — The Clergy in their order take precedence of the Laity so as to be ready to assist the Officiating Priest—'*that they may help the* '*chief Minister,*' says the Rubric of 1552; and they communicate within the rails of the Altar. If any are among the Congregation, they should present themselves early at the Lord's Table, in order that they may be distinguished; and when a Clergyman is known to be such he can claim the privilege; but not within the Septum unless officiating.

The Communion of the People.

The People *kneeling*.

689.—'*And after that to the People also in order* '*into their hands.*'—It is the custom generally for the People to kneel at the Communion Rails in sections, and there receive the Communion in both kinds. Some receive the *Bread* in the hollow of the right hand, according to ancient usage; others, take it with their fingers, which is the more usual method. The *Gloves* should, of course, be removed from the hands before touching the consecrated Bread; and all should receive the holy Sacrament '*meekly kneeling*.' There are frequently instances where *the whole body of Communicants* kneel in Rows in the Choir, or Chancel, and the Officiating Ministers pass successively from row to row: this usage prevents noise and confusion, and is particularly solemn and impressive. (see *infra.*)

THE WORDS OF ADMINISTRATION.

(28) ¶. *'And when he delivereth the Bread to any one, he 'shall say:'*

(29) ¶. *'And the Minister that delivereth the Cup to any one 'shall say:'*

The People *kneeling.*

690.—The injunction of the 21st *Canon* (of 1603), which thus concludes:—'Likewise the Minister shall 'deliver both the Bread, and the Wine to every Com- 'municant *severally;*' and the addition of the words '*to any one*' made in the two Rubrics above at the *last Revision* of the Liturgy in 1662, clearly direct that the Words of Administration are to be repeated *severally* to each individual. 'And,' says Mr. A. J. Stephens, 'any other line of conduct is a positive 'breach of the laws ecclesiastical.' (*Book of Com. Pr. E. H. S. p.* 1213.) The practice, therefore, originating with Calvin, of delivering the elements to more than one person at a time, and repeating the formularies once only to a whole rail-full is an illegal alteration of the form of Public Worship. We find it, indeed, strongly opposed by the late PROF. BLUNT in "*The Duties of the Parish Priest,*" pp. 334—9. Still, where the Communicants are very numerous, and but one, or, perhaps, two Clergymen officiating, it might be necessary to depart a little from the strictness of the *Canon,* and repeat the 'form of words' to *two Communicants* at a time. In very populous places, under the pressure of exigency, custom has adopted the more irregular usage of saying the Words of Administration to a rail-full of Communicants at once; but this should be avoided, if possible. (See Crosthwaite's *Communio Fidelium.*)

MR. A. J. STEPHENS, (*Barrister-at-law*), inveighing against the laxer practise says:—'Some of our Bishops, and a large majority of 'the Clergy, do not obey the Rubric; and, in order to save them-

'selves trouble, which is the most charitable construction, do not 'repeat the words, "The Body," &c....." The Blood," &c.....severally 'to each Communicant, but only to large batches, or, as it is tech-'nically called, to "a table." This conduct cannot be too severely 'reprehended: it is not only positively illegal, and for which the '"Bishops" and "Priests" could be punished at law, but it is 'discreditable to those who practise it, as trifling with the holiest 'mysteries of our Christian Religion.' (*p.* 1217.)—*Book of Com. Prayer*. E. H. S.

691.—If there is more than one Clergyman officiating, the chief Minister, i. e. he who consecrates, proceeds first to administer the Bread; and the Assistant Minister follows with the cup; a usage very necessary in these populous days, although not directed in the present Prayer Book. It was sanctioned by a Rubric in Edward's *first Liturgy*, A. D. 1549, thus:—

'*If there be a Deacon, or other Priest, then shall he follow 'with the Chalice: and as the Priest ministereth the Sacrament 'of the Body, so shall he (for more expedition) minister the 'Sacrament of the Blood, in form before written.*' (1549.)—KEELING. 219.

The Assistant Minister should keep to an interval of four persons between the administration of the Bread and following with the Cup; and the Words of Administration should be pronounced by both Ministers in a very low tone, to prevent confusion in the Sentences and the intermingling of voices. A *Deacon*, by the ancient Canons of the Church, must not administer the *Bread*. When each person has communicated, he returns to his seat for private prayer, and meditation, and to make room for others to receive.

SECOND CONSECRATION.

(30) ¶. '*If the consecrated Bread or wine be all spent before 'all have communicated; the Priest is to consecrate 'more according to the form before prescribed: Begin-'ning at*—" Our Saviour Christ in the same night" &c.—'*for the blessing of the Bread; and at*—" Likewise 'after Supper," &c.—*for the blessing of the Cup.*'*

---

* In the AMERICAN LITURGY, when making an additional Consecration, the entire *Prayer of Consecration* is repeated; as well as a great portion of the *Prayer of Oblation* following it.

692.—During this additional Consecration, the People continue *kneeling;* and, at the close, are to repeat aloud the '*Amen.*'

[*Singing.*]

693.—In some Churches it is the custom derived from the *first Liturgy* of Edward VI. (1549), to *sing* the '*Agnus Dei,*'* or *Psalm* xxxiv., during the Administration of the Elements. In others, for the organ to give out a soft and solemn symphony, as is now done in Durham Cathedral: but either practise is not common.

Replacing the Elements.

(31) ¶. '*When all have communicated, the Minister shall return to the Lord's Table, and reverently place upon it 'what remaineth of the consecrated Elements, 'covering the same with a fair linen cloth.*'

694.—The 'fair linen cloth' for covering the Elements is called sometimes the *Napkin*, the *Chalice Veil*, the *Corporal*, or the *Pall;* and it is to be reverently placed over the Bread, and the Cup, to screen them from the gaze of the Congregation. *Covering the Elements* when first placed on the Table is not prescribed, because our Church considers them then common bread and common wine; still, oblations to God. The custom, however, exists in the Greek Church. (*Prof. Blunt's* 'Duties of the Parish Priest,' *p.* 339.). A full description of this Cloth, and its various appellations, will be found in *Vol.* C.

THE POST-COMMUNION.

The Lord's Prayer.

(32) ¶. '*Then shall the Priest say the Lord's Prayer, the 'People repeating after him every Petition.*'

The Priest *standing*, the People *kneeling* and *repeating it* after him.

---

* The "*Agnus Dei*" is:—'O Lamb of God that takest away the sins 'of the World: have mercy upon us.'
'O Lamb of God that takest away the sins 'of the World: grant us thy peace.'

695.—In the *Liturgy of* 1549, the Clerks are directed to sing the Post-Communion, which then began with a sentence of Holy Scripture; but in the next, and subsequent revisions, the *Lord's Prayer* was ordered to be used in the place of those sentences. The Doxology is appended to it, and the People are to repeat every petition *after*, not *with*, the Minister, as is prescribed in the Rubric at its first occurrence in Morning Prayer.

The two Eucharistic Prayers.

(33) ¶. '*After shall be said as followeth.*'
(34) ¶. '*Or this.*'

The Priest *standing.*—the People still *kneeling.*

696.—The first of these Prayers was, in the *Liturgy* of Edward VI. (1549), placed *before* the delivery of the Sacrament, immediately after the prayer of Consecration; like as it now is in the American Liturgy (see Note, *p.* 1799. *supra.*) There was then some additional matter in it which made it an admirable prayer of Oblation. Now, however, it is simply designed to offer in behalf of the People, their sacrifice of praise and thanksgiving, and the dedication of their souls and bodies, a living sacrifice, holy and acceptable to God, which is their reasonable service. The earlier Prayer consists chiefly of vows and resolutions; the second Prayer abounds more in praises and acknowledgments.

The Gloria in Excelsis.

(35) ¶. '*Then shall be said or sung.*'

The Priest and People *standing.*

697.—This *Hymn of Glory* is here appointed to be said or sung, *all standing;* and its use is derived from the practice of Our Lord Himself (*Matt.* xxvi. 30.). In the *first Liturgy* this 'Angelic Hymn' stood at the beginning of the Office after the Prayer for Purity; but our present allocation of it at the close seems the more suitable and desirable. It has been employed in the Communion Office above a thousand years, and the language of the earlier part is borrowed from the Angel's hymn at the Nativity. (*Luke* ii. 14.) In some Churches a metrical Psalm, or Hymn, is here sung, like as is permitted in the American Liturgy; but this usage is with us out of rubrical order. The Ministers and People should all *stand* at the singing or recitation of this glorious Hymn; a practise, however, on the part of the Congregation much neglected.'

The final blessing.

(36) ¶. '*Then the Priest* (*or Bishop if he be present*) *shall let 'them depart with this Blessing.*'

The Priest *standing*, and turning to the People.
The People all *kneeling*.

698.—This Benediction at the dismissal of the People is not to be uttered by a *Deacon;* nor is it to be inwardly repeated by the People. If a Bishop be present, *he* pronounces the Blessing (*Heb.* vii. 7.); and the Priests, and other Ministers, then *kneel down* like the rest of the People. Otherwise, the Priest, who pronounces it, *stands;* and all the rest kneel. It seems to be derived partly from *Phil.* iv. 6, and partly from *Numb.* vi. 22—25. The '*Amen*' must be said aloud by the Congregation.

The Additional Collects.

(37) ¶. '*Collects to be said after the Offertory, when there 'is no Communion, every such day one, or more; and 'the same may be said also, as often as occasion shall 'serve after the Collects either of* Morning *or* Evening 'Prayer, Communion, *or* Litany, *by the discretion of 'the Minister.*'

699.—To provide against any thing being left unasked for in Divine Service; the six Collects following are added; and any one or more of them may be used in the previous Offices as directed in this Rubric. In Moring Prayer, after the 'Collect for Peace;' and in Evening Prayer, or Litany, before the 'Prayer of St Chrysostom.' When introduced into the Communion Service on occasions of *no Communion*, they may follow the Offertory Sentences. The following Rubric (*Rubric* 38. *infra.*), hoewver, admits their use after the Prayer for the Church Militant. This discrepancy is to be explained by the fact, that in the *First Liturgy* of Edward VI. (1549) the *Church Militant* Prayer was only to be used on Communion days; and when the Communion Office was subsequently recast, and the above Prayer appointed to be used on non-Communion days, this Rubric remained by an oversight unaltered. The Collects, therefore, if employed according to the following Rubric (38), will still fulfil the injunctions of the present order in coming *after the Offertory*, though not immediately. Their use, however, is open to the discretion of the Minister. The words, '*after the Offertory*,' were suggested to be struck out in the "*Alterations*" of 1689.

These six *Collects* are designed as follows:—

(1) 'Assist us mercifully, O Lord,'—is a prayer for help in all the changes and chances of life.

(2) 'O Almighty Lord, and Everlasting God,'—is for the preservation of our bodies and souls.

(3) 'Grant, we beseech Thee, Almighty God,'—is for a blessing on the preaching and hearing of the Word.

(4) 'Prevent us, O Lord,'—is for help and guidance in all our undertakings.

(5) 'Almighty God, the Fountain of all wisdom,'—is for pardon for the deficiencies and imperfections in our prayers and supplications.

(6) 'Almighty God, who has promised to hear,'—is for the acceptance of our petitions.

The Concluding Rubrics.

The Communion Office on Non Communion days.

(38) ¶. '*Upon the Sundays and other Holy days* (*if there be* '*no Communion*) *shall be said all that is appointed* '*at the Communion until the end of the general Prayer*, '[For the whole state of Christ's Church Militant here in 'Earth], *together with one or more of these Collects* '*last before rehearsed, concluding with the Blessing.*'*

---

* In the American Liturgy this Rubric reads:—

'*Upon the Sundays and other Holy Days* (*if there be no Sermon* '*or Communion*) *shall be said all that is appointed at the Com-* '*munion, unto the end of the Gospel, concluding with the Blessing.*'

None of the subsequent Rubrics (39 to 47) at the end of our Communion Office, except the latter part of *Rubric* 43, are to be found in the American Liturgy.

700.—The reading of the Ante-Communion portion of the Office is intended to shew the readiness of the Minister to celebrate the holy Sacrament, if there be sufficient People desirous and prepared to participate in this high privilege. The requisite number is defined in the *next three Rubrics*. If there are not sufficient to communicate, then this Rubric directs what portion of the Office is to be employed. (See *par*. 571. *supra* where the matter is more fully explained.) In the "*Alterations*" of 1689, instead of the word '*Sundays*,' it is proposed to use '*Lord's days*.'

MUST BE THREE COMMUNICANTS AT THE LEAST.

(39) ¶. '*And there shall be no Celebration of the Lord's 'Supper, except there be a convenient number to 'communicate with the Priest, according to his dis'cretion*.'

(40) ¶. '*And if there be not above twenty persons in the 'Parish of discretion to receive the Communion; yet 'there shall be no Communion, except four or three 'at the least communicate with the Priest*.'

701.—The design of these Rubrics was to prevent the solitary masses practised by the Priests of the Romish Church, and to forbid the consecration of the Elements unless there be a Congregation of *three at the least* to communicate with the Priest. This number is derived from our Lord's promised presence when two or three are gathered together in His name. (*Matt*. xviii. 20.). In the "*Alterations*" of 1689, the word '*Priest, according to his discretion*,' is to be supplanted by '*Minister, three, at the least;*' and the second Rubric (40) was struck out altogether.

IN CATHEDRALS, &c. COMMUNION MUST BE EVERY SUNDAY.

(41) ¶. '*And in Cathedral, and Collegiate Churches, and 'Colleges, where there are many Priests and Deacons, 'they shall all receive the Communion with the Priest 'every Sunday at the least, except they have a rea'sonable cause to the contrary*.'

702.—This Rubric enforces *weekly Communion* in Cathedrals, Collegiate Churches, and Colleges, though there be no Laymen to communicate. These exemplars, as such Institutions are designed to be, of the piety and Churchism of the nation, are sadly deficient in conformity; and, we might add, in religious zeal. Our forefathers, judging from the *first Liturgy* of Edw. VI., communicated *daily*, after the manner of the primitive Church; then, subsequently, as piety grew colder, only on Sundays and Holy-days; but the Christianity of these days is diluted down in the generality of our Churches to a *monthly* Communion; and in some, alas! to but *three* or *four* times in a year. In the "*Alterations*" suggested by the Royal Commissioners in 1689, '*Sunday at the least*' was struck out for '*Lord's day*;' and it was proposed also to insert here the following Rubric, compelling in towns and cities at all events a *monthly* Communion:—

'*In every great Town or Parish there shall be a Communion* '*once a month; and in every Parish at least four times a year,* '*that is, on* Christmas-day, Easter-day, Whit-Sunday, *and some* 'Lord's day *soon after Harvest, at the Minister's discretion. And* '*all Ministers shall exhort their People to communicate frequently.* '*And every Parishioner shall communicate at least three* '*times in the year, of which* Easter *shall be one.*'

The Quality of the Bread and Wine:

(42) ¶. '*And to take away all occasion of dissension, and* '*superstition, which any person hath or might have* '*concerning the Bread and Wine, it shall suffice that* '*the Bread be such as is usual to be eaten; but the* '*best and purest Wheat Bread that conveniently may* '*be gotten.*'

703.—The object of this Rubric is doubtlessly, to prevent the use of *Wafers;* which came into fashion in the 11th century. The Bread must be leavened, and made of the best *wheaten flour;* the employment of any other would subject the Clergyman using it to an action in the Ecclesiastical Courts at the instance of any of his Parishioners. This question has been fully discussed in *Vol.* C.; to which, therefore, for the sake of avoiding repetition, we would refer our Readers. The *Bread* should be '*prepared*' by one of the Officiating Clergymen, and not by the Churchwarden, or Parish-Clerk. The *Wine* may be red or white, Tent, or Claret, or Port, are usually preferred; but whether it may be mixed with *Water* is a controverted subject. This we have also handled in *Vol.* C., and need not, therefore, enlarge upon the question here.

The Surplus Bread and Wine.

(43) ¶. *'And if any of the* BREAD *and* WINE *remain unconsecrated, the Curate shall have it to his own use: but if any remain of that which was consecrated, it shall not be carried out of the Church, but the Priest, and such other of the Communicants as he shall then call unto him, shall, immediately after the Blessing, reverently eat and drink the same.'*

704.—The *unconsecrated* BREAD and WINE brought into the Church, which remains over and above what is required, '*the Curate shall have to his own use:*' because the Bread and Wine are no longer common Bread and Wine, having been dedicated to God; and are looked upon in the light of a portion of the Offerings, which in primitive times the Clergy were entitled to a share of. It is the common practice to appropriate, what surplus there may be, to the poor sick Parishioners. The term '*Curate*' here is he that has the 'cure of souls.'

705.—But the *consecrated* BREAD and WINE, which remains, should be divided amongst the Officiating Clergymen, and the Communicants who may be near the Altar, and desire it. The term '*reverently*' is thought to imply '*kneeling*,' as at the time of communicating; but this is not always practised. The reason of the injunction that it shall '*not be carried out of the Church*' is, that formerly, and in the Romish Church at the present day, the consecrated Elements would be applied to superstitious uses. The Laity would frequently take away privately a portion of the Bread, and keep it as a 'charm,' or preservative, against troubles and misfortunes. The 'Bread' used also to be reserved for the sick and infirm; and sometimes despatched to absent friends as memorials of love, and agreement in the unity of the same faith; but these practises led to so much abuse that they were prohibited by the Council of Laodicea. These questions are also treated on in *Vol.* C.*

The Bread and Wine to be provided by the Parish.

(44) ¶. '*The* Bread *and* Wine *for the Communion shall be 'provided by the Curate and the Church-wardens at the 'Charges of the Parish.*'

706.—It was anciently the custom for every house in the Parish, to provide in turn the *holy loaf;* this being attended with inconvenience, the *first Liturgy* of Edward VI. (1549) transferred the duty to the Clergymen; requiring, however, the Parishioners to make a *money offering* in the place thereof at the Offertory: this arrangement not answering the purpose so satisfactorily as was anticipated, the present system was adopted, and enforced by the above Rubric introduced into the *Revision* of the Liturgy in 1552; and is continued in our own Book of Common Prayer.

707.—It is a very common practise now for the Clergyman to provide the Bread, and the Church-wardens to supply the Wine. It is not unusual for the Incumbent to find both the Bread and Wine. This question has also been handled in *Vol.* C.

Parishioners to Communicate three times in the Year.

(45) ¶. '*And note, that every Parishioner shall communicate 'at the least three times in the Year, of which Easter 'shall be one.*'

---

* In the American Liturgy this Rubric is limited to the concluding part, thus:—

'*And if any of the consecrated Bread and Wine remain 'after the Communion, it shall not be carried out of the Church; 'but the Minister and other Communicants shall immediately 'after the Blessing, reverently eat and drink the same.*'

This, and a version of *Rubric* 38, are the only Rubrics of the nine annexed to the Communion Office, adopted in the American Liturgy.

708.—This Rubric does not refer to the Clergy, nor to Cathedral, or Collegiate Churches, or Colleges; but to the Laity; and is enforced by the 21*st Canon* (of 1603–4), which enjoins:—

'That in every Parish Church and Chapel, the *Holy Communion* 'shall be ministered.........so often, and at such times, as *every* '*Parishioner* may communicate, at the least, *thrice* in the year, 'whereof the Feast of Easter to be one.'—*Canon* 21.

The 23rd *Canon* requires, indeed, that all *Students in Colleges* receive the Communion *four* times in the year at least; and the 24th *Canon* imposes the same on all members of *Cathedral* foundations; but this does not negative the more recent injunction set forth in the Rubric (*see* (41) above), requiring the Holy Communion to be administered in Cathedrals, and Collegiate Churches, and Colleges, *every* Sunday. This Rubric (45) was struck out in the "*Alterations*" of 1689.

Easter Offerings.

(46) ¶. '*And yearly at Easter every Parishioner shall reckon 'with the Parson, Vicar, or Curate; or his or their 'Deputy, or Deputies, and pay to them or him all Eccle-'siastical Duties, accustomably due, then and at that 'time to be paid.*'

709.—This Rubric was introduced into the *Liturgy* of 1552, and enjoins in accordance with the Statute, 2 & 3 *Edw.* VI. *c.* 13. the payment to the Incumbent at Easter, annually, of the Offerings '*accustomably due.*' These payments originated probably in the voluntary liberality of the faithful, and were continued in after ages by the emulous generosity of their posterity. They are not due of common right, but *by custom* (*Rex* v. *Reeves*, 2 E. & Y. 55.); and for payment to be enforced, the custom must be established. Some authorities consider the Easter Offerings a composition for personal tithes; and some again maintain their obligation by a common law right, and that they are due at the rate of *twopence a head for every person of sixteen years of age and upwards*. (*Laurence* v. *Jones*. Bunb. 173: *Egerton* v. *Still*. ib. 173—198. *Carthew* v. *Edwards*. Trin. 1749. Exchap.). In London, it is said, 'a *groat* a house' is due annually for the Easter Offering. (*Leifield*, D.D. v. *Tysdale*. Hob. 11.) Still, a special custom may be proved for the payment of a less or larger sum per head; or of a composition for the household.

When the custom is undisputed, the claim may be enforced in the Ecclesiastical Court; but this Court cannot enter into the validity, or otherwise, of the custom; for this is a matter for the Common Law Courts to decide.

When they amount to under £10., they may be summarily recovered by complaint before two Justices by 7 & 8 *Will.* III. c. 6; and 53 *Geo.* III. c. 127; like as small tithes. 5 & 6 *Will.* IV. c. 74, 4 & 5 *Vict.* c. 36.

Easter Offerings, *Oblations*, *Surplice Fees*, and *Mortuaries*, may be commuted for a certain sum by a parochial agreement any time before the confirmation of the apportionment, when there has been a compulsory award for commutation of tithes; and this sum is payable and recoverable, when, and as, the Tithe Rent Charge is.

THE OFFERTORY MONEY.

(47) ¶. '*After the* DIVINE SERVICE *ended, the money given 'at the* OFFERTORY *shall be disposed of to such pious 'and charitable uses, as the Minister and Church-'wardens shall think fit. Wherein if they disagree, 'it shall be disposed of as the Ordinary shall ap-'point.*'

710.—This Rubric appears to be derived from that on this subject in the Scotch Liturgy of 1637; the perusal of which will tend, from its explanatory character, far to elucidate our own: it follows '*the Blessing*' in that Liturgy, and thus reads:—

'*After the Divine Service ended, that which was offered shall be 'divided in the presence of the Presbyter, and the Churchwardens, 'whereof one half shall be to the use of the Presbyter, to provide 'him Books of holy divinity: the other half shall be faithfully 'kept and employed on some pious or charitable use, for the 'decent furnishing of that Church or the public relief of their 'Poor, at the discretion of the Presbyter and Churchwardens.*' (KEELING. 226.)

It will be seen that the Scotch Rubric bears epecially upon the Offertory Sentences also which speak of payments to the Clergy, while the Rubric of the English Liturgy appropriates the money collected at the Offertory only to 'pious and charitable uses.'

711.—It is now the general custom to apply these '*Alms*' to the benefit of the Poor; and if any other religious appropriation of a sum that may be given by any Donor is desired, its destination must be distinguished by a written paper explanatory of its use enveloping the offering. It is better, however, in exceptional cases of this kind, for the Contributor either to put his oblation, particularized as above, in the Plate at a collection at the Church Door; or to reserve it for especial calls of this nature; or to forward it directly to the Incumbent with instructions as to his wishes.

712.—It is not usual to distribute the offerings *immediately on the conclusion of* the Service; for such a method would be likely to tempt the needy and unworthy to become Communicants, for the sake merely of these temporal benefits. Nor would it be wise to save up the 'gatherings' *till Christmas*, to divide them *then* among the poor Communicants; for this would be equally liable to foster corruption and hypocrisy. It has been found better to reserve the money for the sick and the needy; bestowing it, here and there, during the intervals of the Offertory collections, on such cases as may be worthy of assistance, or imperatively call for help. The *amount* of every Collection should be *registered*, and the *names* and necessities of every *recipient* duly entered in a book provided for the purpose. This will be not only a check against imposition; but it will furnish at any moment a detailed account of the distribution of the fund; and provide satisfactory evidence of the faithful discharge of so grave a responsibility. In the "*Alterations*" of 1689, it is proposed to introduce after the words "*Divine Service ended,*" this clause:—'*or at some other convenient time.*'

713.—In *large Towns* and *Cities*, where the Offerings are great and valuable, the Churchwardens should be taken into counsel with regard to their distribution. They can, indeed, as a perusal of the Rubric will shew, *demand* this to be done. And if the Incumbent objects to their participation in the manner of disposing of the Alms; the Churchwardens can require a *moiety* of the amount collected to be handed to them for distribution. But should this claim be rejected by the Clergyman, then the *Bishop*, as directed by the Rubric, is to determine the appropriation of the alms-money.

714.—In *District Churches*, or *Consolidated Chapelries*, the Offertory money there collected is to be disposed of by the Minister and Churchwardens of such Churches and Chapelries, as laid down in 8 & 9 *Vict. c.* 70. *s.* 6. But the collections made at the Offertory in *Chapels-of-ease* are to be handed over to the Incumbent and Churchwardens of the mother-Church.

INDEX

TO THE LAWS AND USAGES

Affecting

PUBLIC WORSHIP,—(EVENING PRAYER, LITANY, AND HOLY COMMUNION.)

[Nos. XXXI. to XXXVIII. *inclusive;* p. 1421 *to* 1814.]

Paragraph

ABSOLUTION, The, in Evening Prayer . . . 292
not said by Deacons 292
posture at 293
in the *Communion Service* . . 677
Address, The, in the Communion Service 683
Administration of the Bread 691
" *Cup* 692
the Words of 690
Adult Baptism 338
Advent, 1st Sunday in 507
2nd and 3rd ditto 509
4th ditto 510
All Conditions of Men, Collect for . . . . 467—470
All Saints' Day, Collect for 550
Alleluia Versicles 299
Alms Bags 669
" Basin 669
" Boxes 669
" Collecting 667
" " in Ireland 640
" disposal of . . . . 710—714
" presenting the 670
Altar, The 588
" Chairs, use of 279
" Covering . . . . 589—592
Andrew's St Day 549
Announcing Holy Days, &c. . . . . . 625—631
Ante-Communion Service . . . . . . 594—595
" " when used 601
Anthem, the 375
Apostles' Creed, the 345

6 A

Articles, the XXXIX, on Holy Communion . . . 562
Ascension Day 541
Ascription of Praise before Sermon 645
" after " 654
Ash-Wednesday 522
Assistant Clergy 388
ATHANASIAN CREED 390
called "Quicunque Vult" . . 392
damnatory clauses in . . . 394
how uttered 396
objections to 393, 395
posture at 397
when used 391, 395

BANNS OF MARRIAGE after Nicene Creed . . 636
" " Second Lesson . 319
" publication of . 318, 636
" ditto from Banns Book . 320
BAPTISM after Second Lesson 325
" at Font 334
" *Adult* 338
" discretionary in Minister 332
" manner and posture at 333
" of one's own Children 335
" on week days 328
" origin of the Service of 329
" receiving in Congregation after . . . 337
" removing the Water after 336
" returning from, to the Desk . . . 339
" rubrical directions 326
" Seasons for 330
Barnabas's Day, St 550
Bartholomew's Day, St 550
Benedictory Prayer, the (2 *Cor*. xiii.) . . . 384, 418
Bidding Prayer, The 643, 644
Bishop's power in publication of Notices . . 639
Blessing, the final 698
Bowing at the name of Jesus 618, 624
" on entering Church 277
" to the Altar 277
BREAD AND WINE, provided by Incumbent . . . 707
" " Parish . . . 706
" quality of 703
" surplus 704
" " if consecrated . . . 705

CANDLEMAS-DAY 550
Canons on Holy Communion 561
" Preachers 657
Cantate Domino 312
" omitted 313
Canticles, the 310, 312, 340, 343
Caput Jejunii 524

Catechizing after 2nd Lesson 321
" before Evening Service 282
" in place of Sermon 323
" place for 324
CHRIST, circumcision of . . . . . . 514—516
" Presentation of 549
Christening, term explained 327
Christmas-day Collect 510
" " repeated 513
" 1st Sunday after 514
" 2nd ditto 516
Chrysostom, St Prayer of 383, 417
Church Militant Prayer 672
Church Membership . . . . . . 564—566
CHURCHING OF WOMEN 280
" before General Thanksgiving 471—472
Circumcision, Eve of the 363
" of Christ . . . . . . 514—516
Clergy, Assistant 388
Clergy and People, Prayer for 382
COLLECT, announcing 371, 490
for aid against Perils 374
" Ember Weeks 458
" Holy-days 370, 486
" Peace 373
" Purity of Heart 605
" Saturday Eve 368
" rules for . . . 370, 486
" the Queen 610, 611
posture at 612
" Vigils or Eves 360, 370
" Week day Evenings 359, 369
of Sunday 370, 486
posture at 372, 491
of the Day 358, 486, 614
the term explained 482
COLLECTS, *Post-Communion* 699
Tables of the 483
throughout the Year 477
(Collects) to serve the Week 487
when two or more used 488, 489
COMMINATION SERVICE, the 528
Litany at 438
COMMUNICANTS, number to provide for . . . 571, 701
their qualification 569, 570
to give notice 568, 569
power to repel Offenders . . . 578—582
Schismatics . . . 583—584
Strangers . . . 585
Travellers . . . 586
unconfirmed . . . 572
repelling, Curate's Duty in . . . 580
Communicate, to, how often 708
Students 708
COMMUNION, THE HOLY . . . . . . 551—556
Administration of . 662, 687—689

COMMUNION, THE HOLY, Appellations of . . 552
Articles on (XXXIX) . 553, 562
Canons on . . 555, 561
Giving notice of . . 632—635
Homilies on . . 554, 563
in Cathedrals, &c. how often 702
of Clergy 688
of People 689
of Priest 687
part of Divine Service . 603
Statutes on . . . 560
who officiates at . . 594—596
" place of . 600, 601
" ornaments of 597—599
——— OFFICE, its Title 557
" *Rubrics* of the . . . 567
" the *Comfortable Words* in . . 678
——— TABLE 588
Covering of . . . . 589—592
position of the 593
Conclusion of the Service . . . . . 658—661
Confession, The 289
in Communion Office 676
Confirmed, not, denied Communion . . . 572
Consecration of Elements, prayer of . . . 684—686
the *second* 692
Covering of the Communion Table . . . 589—592
CREED, the Apostles' 345
of *St Athanasius* 390
Curate, the term explained 630

DEPRECATIONS, the, in the Litany 403
" Occasional Prayer . . 446
Deus misereatur, The 343
manner and posture at . . . 344
Doxology, the 298
at the Gospel . . . . . . 499—501
in the Litany 413
obeisance at 298

EAST turning to at the Creeds 623
EASTER-DAY 535
Anthem for 536, 537
Even 534
Offerings 709
the Days before 531, 532
the Sunday *before* 530, 531
" Sundays *after* 538
the 5th 539
Week, the days in 537
Elements, the, placing on the Table 671
replacing after Communion . . . 694
Ember-days, the 455, 456

Ember-weeks, prayer in . . . 454, 457, 458, 510, 543
Epiphany Sundays 517
sixth Sunday after 518, 519
Epistle, the announcing 493, 494, 616
concluding 495
posture at 502, 616
reader of 503, 596
place of the 505, 616
Epistles and *Gospels* 484, 485
announcing and concluding . 493
rubrics of the 492
to serve the week . . . 487
Eucharist, the Holy 551, 556
Eucharistic prayer 696
EVENING PRAYER, the 274
commencement of . . . 283
time of 366
Eves and Vigils 360
not to Sundays 367
origin of 365
Excommunicate, refused Communion 573
Exhortation, the 288
at Communion 673, 674

FAIR WEATHER, Prayer for 450
thanksgiving for 476
Famine, prayer in time of 451
Fast-days, announcing 638

GENERAL THANKSGIVING, the . . . 382, 474
names mentioned in 475
Gloria Patri, the 298
Gloria in Excelsis 697
GOOD-FRIDAY 533
Gospels and Epistles 484, 485
announcing 496, 497, 617
concluding 498, 500, 501
doxology at 499
posture at 502, 617
reader of 503, 596
place of the . . . 505, 617
thanksgiving at 500, 501

HOLY DAYS, the, announcing . . . 625, 631, 638
immoveable 549
with Eves or Vigils 360
without ditto 361
Homilies, the 655
on the Holy Communion 563

IDIOT refused Communion 574
Incumbent's duty at Communion 596

Infant Baptism 325
Innocent's Day 513
Intercessions, the, in the Litany 408
in the Occasional Prayers . . 446
Introits . . . . 478—481
Invitatory at Communion 675
Invocations in the Litany 401

JAMES, St (Apostle) Day 550
John Baptists (St) Day 550
Eve of 365
John, St Evangelist's Day 513

KYRIE ELEISON 402, 410

LENT, 1st day of . . . . . . 522—527
Psalms and Lessons for . . 525, 526
Sundays in 528
4th Sunday in 529
Lessons, the 303
announcement of 308
at coincidence of Holy-days . . . 304
first 303
posture at 307
reader of 306
second 314
reader of 316
"Let us Pray" 613
Litania major 399
LITANY, The 398, 399
as distinct Service . . . . . 428—431
by whom said 443
Deprecations of 403
Divisions of 400
end of 444
in Cathedrals 439
Intercessions of the 408
Invocations of the 401
manner of saying 435, 436
Obsecrations of 406
on Wednesdays and Fridays . . . 421—423
„ Sundays 424
place where said 438
posture at . . . . . . 440—442
Prayers 415
Sick announced in 437
Suffrages of 411
Sung or said . . . . . . 432—434
Supplications of 411
Time and place when said . . . 425—427
Versicles and Doxology 413
when used . . . . . . 419—421

Litany, the Lesser 351, 410
LORD'S PRAYER, the 295
said by the People 296
the second 353
„ doxology omitted . . 354
—————— in Communion Office, 1st time . 602
posture at . . 604
2nd time 695
LORD'S SUPPER, the 552, 556
Low Sunday 538
Luke's (St) Day 550
Lunatics refused Communion 574

MAGNIFICAT, the 310
chanted 311
Malicious, the, refused Communion . . . 576—582
Canons on 577
Manning Maria, at Holy Communion . . . 580
Mark's (St) Day 550
MARRIAGE, *Banns of*, publishing . . . 318, 636
in Service time 276
Mary, St the Virgin, annunciation of 550
purification of 550
'Mas' an affix 511
Mass, the 558, 559
Matthew's St Day 550
Matthias's St Day 550
Maundy Thursday 532
Membership of Church of England . . 564, 565, 587
Michael's St and All Angels' Day 550
Mid-Lent Sunday 529
Missa 558

NEW YEAR'S EVE 363
NICENE CREED 619
bowing at Name of Jesus in . . 624
posture at 622
sung or said 620
turning to East at 623
Non-Communicants, dismissing 661
Notices, publishing. . . . . . . 637—640
Notorious Evil-livers refused Communion . . 575—582
Canons respecting . . . 577
cases 580
Nunc Dimittis 340
posture at 342

OBSECRATIONS in the Litany 406
Occasional Prayers 382, 416, 446
Offertory, the 664
Money . . . . 710—714
Sentences 665
Organ Symphony 279
Ornaments of Minister at Communion . . . 597—599

PALM SUNDAY 530
Parliament, the Prayer for . . . . . 462—464
when used 465
Paul St Conversion of 549
Peace, Collect for 373
and Deliverance from Enemies, thanksgiving for 476
Peter's St Day 550
Philip St and St James' Day 550
Plague and Sickness, Prayer in time of 453
Thanksgiving from . . . 476
Plenty, thanksgiving for 476
Post-Communion, the 695
PRAYER, before Sermon . . . . . . 642—645
Benedictory, the 384, 418
for All Conditions of Men . . 382, 467—470
„ Clergy and People 381
„ Ember Weeks 454
„ Fair Weather 450
„ Parliament 462
„ „ when used 465
„ the Queen 379
„ Royal Family 380
„ Rain 449
in the Pulpit 387
„ time of Famine 451
„ „ Plague and Sickness . . . 453
„ „ War and Tumult 452
(Prayer) of Congregation desired 468
„ St Chrysostom 383, 417
PRAYERS, The *Occasional* 382, 416
and *Thanksgiving* 446, 447
in the Litany 415
Preacher, Canons respecting 657
„ place 651
at Communion 596
if Strangers 650
posture of 653
Precedence in Processions 279
Preces, the 349
Prefaces, the, in Communion Service 680, 681
Presentation of Christ in the Temple 549
Priest to officiate at Communion 594
place of . . 600, 601
posture during . . 663
Procession in Church 279
Psalmody, at the Litany 445
Evening Service 386
before Sermon 641
given out by Officiating Minister . . . 386
PSALMS, the 300
announcing 300
doxology at 300
posture at 300
Public Notices, giving out . . . . . 637—640
Pulpit for Epistle and Gospel 506
prayer in 387

Punctuality 276
Purification of St Mary the Virgin 550
Eve of 364

QUEEN, the Collects for 610
Prayer for 379
Quincunque Vult, the 392
Quinquagesima Sunday 521

RAIN, Prayer for 449
Thanksgiving for 476
Reader of the Lessons 306
2nd Lesson 316
Receiving the Baptized into the Congregation . . 337
Restoring Public Peace, thanksgiving for 476
Rogation Sunday 539
Days 540
Royal Family, Prayer for 380
Rubrics of the Communion Office 567

SALUTATION, the 349
posture at 350
Sanctus, the 481, 682
Saturday Evening Collect 368
Schismatics, refused Communion 583, 584
Sedilia, when used 279
Sentences at beginning of Evening Prayer . . . 284
choice of 287
manner of utterance of 286
posture at 285
Septuagesima Sunday 520
Sermon, the . . . . 646—648
after the 3rd Collect 376
in Cathedrals 377
at close of Evening Prayer 389
doxology after 654
number of 649
Sexagesima Sunday 520
Sick, the, announcing to pray for . . . 437, 469, 470
Prayers for 468
Simon St and St Jude's Day 550
Singing at Communion 693
Song of Simeon 340
Statutes on the Holy Communion 560
Stephen's St Day 512
Stranger's preaching 650
rejected from Communion . . . . 585—587
Suffrages in the Litany 411, 414
Sunday no Eve 367
Collect when used 370
Supplications, the 356
in the Litany 411
Sursum Corda 679

TEN COMMANDMENTS, the 606, 607
posture at . . . 609
responses at . . . 608
Tersanctus, the 481, 682
Thanksgiving 446, 473
at Gospel 500, 501
for Deliverance from Plague and Sickness 476
" Fair Weather 476
" Peace and Deliverance . . . 476
" Plenty 476
" Rain 476
" Restoring Public Peace 476
the *General* 382, 474
Thanksgiving Days, Announcing 638
Third Collect, the 374
Trinity Sunday 544, 545
Sundays after 545
24th Sunday after 546
25th and 26th " 547
27th " 548
Trisagium, the 682

VERSICLES the 297
in the Litany 412, 413
Vestments, the 278
changing before Sermon . . . 641
Vestry, retiring to before Sermon 641
Vigils . . . . 360—362
Virgin Mary, annunciation of 550
purification of 550
Voluntary, the 302

WAR AND TUMULT, *Prayer in* time of . . . 452
Whitsunday 542
Whitsun-week 543

—o—

CPSIA information can be obtained
at www.ICGtesting.com
Printed in the USA
LVHW110805120522
718525LV00003B/39

9 783375 002312